Emma Blair Devon. She is including *Sca* both of which Novelist of th

Praise for Emma Blair

'An author who so easily gets to grips with everyday life'
Torquay Herald Express

'From start to finish readers will be in the safe hands of an experienced writer of romantic fiction. The characters are beautifully portrayed with a real understanding of their lives'
Historical Novels Review

'[Her] characters . . . are endearing and portray an innocence that befits the period'
Publishing News

'Fascinating characters'
Devon Life

EMMA BLAIR OMNIBUS

Moonlit Eyes

Little White Lies

sphere

SPHERE

This omnibus edition first published in Great Britain by
Sphere in 2009
Emma Blair Omnibus copyright © Emma Blair 2009

Previously published separately:
Moonlit Eyes first published in Great Britain by
Little, Brown in 2002
Published by Time Warner Paperbacks in 2002
Copyright © Emma Blair 2002

Little White Lies first published in Great Britain by
Time Warner Paperbacks in 2005
Reprinted by Sphere in 2007
Copyright © Emma Blair 2005

A CIP catalogue record for this book is available from the British Library.

ISBN 978-0-7515-4145-8

Printed and bound in Great Britain by
Clays Ltd, St Ives plc

Sphere
An imprint of
Little, Brown Book Group
100 Victoria Embankment
London EC4Y 0DY

An Hachette UK Company
www.hachette.co.uk

www.littlebrown.co.uk

The door opened and someone she didn't recognise emerged, a woman roughly her own age. The woman didn't even give Jess a glance as she hurried on her way.

Jess took a deep breath, tempted. And then she remembered the time. She should be home cooking Paul and Ellie their dinner. Both would be back soon, Ellie from work, Paul from school, expecting to be fed.

That was it then. Another day perhaps. Yes, another day.

'I do believe we're the only people in the street to have a phone,' Beulah declared proudly, the telephone having been installed out of necessity for Julius's work.

'The pub has a phone,' Julius commented drily. 'I saw it when I was there.'

'Well then, apart from the pub.'

'I suppose so,' Julius agreed, having already used it several times to ring the Embassy on business. It had been put in earlier that day.

Beulah glanced at him out the corner of her eye. 'When you seein' that Marybeth again? She sure is one nice young lady.'

Julius couldn't help but smile. Beulah and Marybeth got on like a house on fire. 'Oh soon. Sometime soon,' he replied off-handedly.

Beulah's expression became one of concern. 'You ain't losin' interest I hope?'

'Mom,' he scolded softly. 'You shouldn't interfere. Even if you do like Marybeth.'

'Interfere, I ain't interferin'!' Beulah protested. 'And

even if I was that's a mother's duty. Her job. As your pop would say, damn right if it ain't!'

Julius decided to humour her. 'Probably this Saturday night. There, that satisfy you?'

'Sure does, hon. I was only askin', that's all. I weren't doin' no interferin'.'

That was a lie, Julius thought. And well she knew it. No matter, it wasn't important. And neither was Marybeth, if he was honest. They got on well, she could be fun. But that special something simply wasn't there. Possibly for her it was, but not him.

He changed the subject.

Jess ran into Beulah in Chapel Market, a large, mainly fruit and vegetable, street trading venue situated only minutes away from Florence Street. There were also a few stalls selling household goods and other sundry items.

'Something wrong, Beulah?' Jess inquired, having noted the black woman's exasperated expression.

'I just can't get no chilli peppers. No one seems to have them.'

'Chilli peppers?' Jess queried with a frown. 'I've never heard of those.'

Beulah sighed. 'Neither has anyone else round here it appears.' The exasperated expression vanished and she regarded Jess keenly. 'Now, has you finished your shoppin'?'

'Yes, I have actually.'

'Good, so has I. Why don't you come back to my place

and we'll have some coffee and fresh brownies I baked earlier.'

Jess had never heard of brownies either. 'I don't know,' she prevaricated.

'Why, you got something else on?'

Jess shook her head. There was a pile of ironing to be dealt with but that could easily be done later.

'Then I insist. Pee Wee's gone out so we'll have the house to ourselves and can have a good old gossip. Though Lord knows what I'll gossip about as I knows no one round here yet except you and your family.'

Jess instantly took pity on Beulah, and agreed. As they made their way through the milling people Beulah did her best to explain what chilli peppers were.

They were on their third cup of coffee, Beulah chattering away nineteen to the dozen about life in New York City, when Jess's face suddenly contorted and she bent over.

Beulah stared at her in consternation for a moment, then came to her feet and went to take Jess by the shoulders. 'What's wrong, hon?'

'Pain. Terrible pain in my stomach,' Jess gasped.

'What can I do?'

Jess gulped in a deep breath and then sobbed as the pain intensified. It felt as though her insides were being dragged out of her.

'You'd better lie down, Jess. You can use the chesterfield in the other room.' That was an American type of sofa or couch, she explained.

Jess tried to struggle upright but couldn't manage it. She collapsed again onto the chair.

'Oh my God!' she whispered in horror as a bright red stain spread rapidly across the front of her skirt.

Chapter 4

Beulah had been hovering by her front window for the past two hours, but now she saw Albert hurriedly striding down the street. She immediately went to her front door and opened it.

'Albert, come in. It was me who telephoned the fire station,' she called out as he drew close.

His face clearly mirrored his anxiety. 'What's wrong, Beulah? Your message said it was urgent and that I had to come home right away. Something to do with Jess.'

She shut the door behind him and ushered him through. 'Jess has had a miscarriage and been taken to hospital,' she explained.

He stared blankly at her. 'What?'

'Jess has had a miscarriage and been taken to hospital,' she repeated.

He stared uncomprehendingly at the fat woman. 'That's impossible,' he said eventually. 'She wasn't expecting.'

'She was, Albert. And lost the baby right there in my kitchen. I saw it with my own eyes.'

Albert staggered where he stood, reaching out to a piece of furniture to help steady himself. This was incredible.

Jess pregnant! She'd never said. Unless . . . could it be Jess hadn't known? He'd heard such things were possible.

'How is she?' he croaked.

'As you'd expect. There's no danger though. They've taken her in as a precaution.'

He swallowed hard. 'The kitchen?'

'We were havin' coffee when it happened. One moment she was fine, the next . . . It was all over very quickly. I telephoned the emergency services and then your station. The man I spoke with there said you were on a call-out but would be informed the moment you returned.'

'Christ!' Albert muttered, still finding it difficult to take this in. It was such a bolt from the blue. Jess pregnant! But she'd told him those days were over. Now this.

Beulah had already laid out a bottle of whisky and a glass. She poured Albert a large one and handed it to him. 'Get that down you. It'll help.'

'I must go to her, Beulah. Right away.'

Beulah wished Julius had been there for he'd have taken Albert in his car. But Julius was at work.

'Drink the scotch first.'

'Which hospital?' he demanded after he'd demolished the whisky in one swallow.

'One of the guys with the ambulance said the Whittington.'

Albert nodded. He knew it. He was mildly surprised it wasn't the Royal Free which was closer. 'I'm on my way then,' he declared, setting the now-empty glass aside.

'Aren't you goin' to get changed first?' For he was still in his working gear.

'No time for that.'

Beulah had a sudden thought. 'You might be a while, Albert, so what about Paul and Ellie?'

Albert frowned, he'd forgotten all about them. 'Ellie has a key but Paul will be back from school long before she gets home.'

Beulah placed a hand on his arm. 'Don't worry, I'll see to them. Now, what shall I say?'

He was fidgeting to get going. 'The truth, I suppose. To Ellie anyway. Just tell Paul his mother's been taken ill.'

'I understand. Leave it all to me.'

He hesitated. 'Thanks for this, Beulah. You've been a friend and good neighbour.'

The sincerity of his words touched her. 'We all gotta help one another in this world, Albert. It's the only way.'

He smiled at her, then hurried out of the house and up the road to the nearest bus stop. It never entered his head to take a taxi, he'd never flagged one down in his entire life. Men of his class simply didn't.

'What time are you leaving, Pa?' Ellie asked anxiously. Albert had been to the hospital where he'd learned that Jess had had an operation, or, to be more precise, was actually undergoing some internal repairs while he was there. He'd waited till she was out of theatre and been assured everything was all right before heeding the doctor's advice and returning home. He'd be allowed in to see Jess later when she'd come round from the anaesthetic.

Albert glanced at the clock on the mantelpiece. 'I'll leave shortly.'

Ellie was about to say something when there was a knock on the outside door. 'I'll get it,' she declared, and left Albert staring disconsolately into empty space. He was racked with worry, sick with it.

Ellie returned with Julius. 'I was so sorry to hear the news,' Julius immediately said to Albert.

Albert nodded. 'She's going to be all right. That's what they've told me.'

Julius could see the state Albert was in. Poor guy, he thought. His own pop would have been just the same if it had been Beulah. 'I understand you're going back to the hospital?'

Albert nodded again. 'They've promised to let me see her when I do.'

'Then I'll drive you.'

Albert didn't know quite what to say to that. 'Are you sure?'

'Of course I'm sure. I'm not doing anything else anyway so it's hardly putting me out.'

'That's very kind of you,' Ellie acknowledged.

'Don't mention it.'

She turned to her father. 'I'm coming with you.'

'They said only I could see Jess,' he protested.

'I don't care. I'm still coming with you and that's final.'

Albert had to smile. 'You're as stubborn as your mother. When she digs her heels in that's it. But what about Paul? We can't leave him round with the Postons any longer. That really would be imposing.'

'He's absolutely fine where he is,' Julius said. 'He and

Mom are having a heck of a time. Believe me.'

'All right then, Ellie,' Albert capitulated.

They waited another fifteen minutes, Ellie offering to make tea which both Albert and Julius declined. Then they left the house, Albert locking up, and got into Julius's car, Ellie in the back seat as before.

Julius didn't know where the Whittington was so Albert directed him.

'Well, girl, this is a right to-do,' Albert said, standing staring down at a pale-faced Jess.

'Isn't it just,' she replied weakly.

He fought back the tears that threatened to flood his eyes. Bending over he kissed her tenderly on the mouth, then sat on the bedside chair. 'How are you?'

'How do I look?'

'Terrible.'

She smiled. 'That's exactly how I feel.'

They enjoyed that little joke for a few silent seconds. Then, hesitantly, he inquired, 'Are you sore?'

'Just a bit,' she lied.

'That's natural I suppose.'

'I suppose.'

Another few silent seconds ticked by, then Jess suddenly said, a choke in her voice, 'Oh, Albert, hold me. Please hold me.'

A sort of peace descended on Jess as his arms went round her, and the nightmare began to recede. She'd have had him climb into bed alongside her if that had been possible.

After a while she started to talk, telling Albert all about it.

While this was going on Ellie and Julius were sitting on a wooden bench outside in the corridor. 'I'm glad Mum's in a single room and not a ward. At least for now,' Ellie commented.

Julius had been thinking how unimpressed he was by the English hospital, the first time he'd ever been in one, so unlike the American hospitals he was used to. It seemed so . . . well, primitive was the word that came to mind. He could only wonder if they were all like this.

'Yes,' he agreed softly.

'I had no idea, you know. None whatever.'

He frowned. 'About what?'

'Mum expecting. She never said anything.'

A nurse bustled past carrying a kidney dish. He did approve of the English nurses' uniforms though, Julius reflected. They were most attractive. Quite sexy really.

'I'm sure she had her reasons,' he replied.

Ellie worried a nail. 'I wish I could go in and see her. Even a minute would be enough.'

Julius regarded her thoughtfully. 'You're very close to your mother, aren't you?'

'We're very close as a family. It might not look that way sometimes, but we are.'

Julius smiled. 'Same with us. That's why I was so pleased when Mom and Pop came over here. She says I missed her cookin', which is true enough. But there's more to it than that. A lot more.'

'It must be awful belonging to a family that don't get on,' Ellie mused. 'Especially if the mother and father are always fighting. I have a couple of friends whose parents are like that. Forever at it like cat and dog. The atmosphere in the house must be terrible.'

Julius's attention had been caught by an elderly doctor who'd appeared at the far end of the corridor, surrounded by a gaggle of younger doctors hanging on his every word. 'I wonder who that old guy is?' he said quietly to Ellie.

She glanced down the corridor. 'That'll be the specialist probably.'

'Specialist? The main guy?'

She smiled at his phraseology. 'You could put it like that.'

'The main guy,' Julius repeated, and came to his feet. 'You stay here. I won't be long.'

She couldn't imagine what he was up to as he sauntered along the corridor. She watched as he broke into the conversation and then drew the specialist to one side.

Julius returned a couple of minutes later, clearly pleased with himself. 'You've got five minutes with your mom after your pop comes out,' he announced, sitting again beside Ellie.

She stared at him in astonishment. 'How did you manage that? The Sister we spoke to earlier was adamant only my father could go in.'

Julius winked. 'It's amazin' what an American accent and State Department, not to mention Embassy, accreditation can do. It impresses most folk.'

'Oh, Julius,' Ellie breathed in delight. Impulsively she

kissed him on the cheek. 'Thank you.'

She suddenly blushed, realising what she'd done, turning away so he couldn't see her face. Which of course he already had.

'My pleasure, Ellie,' he smiled.

When she turned round again she was quite composed, though her eyes sparkled with gratitude. Before either could speak further Albert emerged from Jess's room.

'Ellie, you go on in and get Paul. I'm going for a pint. I certainly need one.'

'Will you be long?'

'Half an hour, no more. I just need a drink after all that.'

Ellie could well understand, she'd never seen her father so rattled. 'I'll get Paul ready for bed and tonight I think you should take him up yourself. To reassure him like.'

'I'll do that, Ellie. Good idea.'

Julius came to stand beside them having locked the car. 'I'll say goodnight then.'

'I was hoping you'd come in with me,' Albert stated earnestly to him. 'A drink is the least I can do to say thank you.'

Julius could see how eager Albert was for him to agree. 'OK, Mr Sykes. That would be great.'

'Good chap.'

Harry, the publican, was behind the bar when Albert and Julius went into The Florence. There were only a handful of others present, all playing darts.

'Evening, Albert,' Harry greeted him. 'What'll it be?'

'A pint of best and a large whisky.'

Harry raised an eyebrow. 'That's unlike you during the week. I've never known you touch spirits then.'

'It's been a bad day.' Albert turned to Julius. 'What's yours?'

'A pint of the same.'

'Scotch or brandy?'

Julius held up a hand in refusal. 'I'll pass on that if you don't mind, take a rain check. I've got a lot on tomorrow morning.'

'By the way, Harry, have you met Julius Poston, my new neighbour? He's a Yank.'

Harry beamed. 'Pleased to meet you, Julius. I've seen you in here but we've never been introduced.'

The two men shook hands, then Harry went over to the gantry. 'The wife told me there was an ambulance outside your house earlier,' he remarked casually over his shoulder.

'Jess has been taken in,' Albert informed him. 'I've just been to visit her. Julius here very kindly drove Ellie and me there in his car.'

'Nothing serious, I hope?' Harry queried in concern.

Albert decided to be evasive, not wanting the entire street knowing their business. It was too private for that. 'She'll only be in for a short while,' he prevaricated. 'She'll be right as rain after that.'

Harry took the hint. 'Well, give her our regards, will you?'

'Of course.'

Albert lapsed into silence until their drinks had been set before them and Harry had moved off down the bar to watch the darts players, the nucleus of the pub team having a practice.

'Have you ever played darts?' Albert asked.

The question took Julius by surprise. 'No, I haven't,' he confessed. 'Looks fun though.'

'If you like I'll teach you the rudiments of the game one night.'

Julius acknowledged the offer with a nod. 'Thank you. Yeah, that would be great.'

Albert picked up his scotch. 'Cheers!'

'Cheers, Mr Sykes.'

They both drank. 'And I think it's high time we did away with this mister nonsense. The name's Albert. But never Bert. Jess hates that.'

'Albert it is then.'

Julius gazed about him. 'I sure adore English pubs. We've nothin' similar back home. We have so-called taverns, but they're not the same. They lack the ambience and friendliness.'

'Well, you'll be all right in here from now on, that's why I made a point of introducing you. You'll be regarded as a local and regular, one of the lads so to speak. Word will soon get round that you're a friend of mine.' He paused, then added softly, 'And Jess's.'

Julius could see the strain etched deeply into Albert's face and felt sorry for the man. What had happened must have been an awful shock. 'If there's anythin' I can do while Mrs Sykes is in the hospital you just have to say.'

Albert smiled his gratitude. 'Thanks, son. I appreciate that.'

'And I mean anythin'. It's amazing what I can swing with my contacts at the Embassy. So don't be shy in speakin' up.'

Albert nodded that he understood. 'Your ma and pa seem to be settling in all right.'

'They're findin' it strange, but that's only to be expected. So many things are different here. But they're copin', and Pop's sure enjoying playin' with the band. He says it wails, which is jazz talk meaning swingin', or good.'

'Wail,' Albert repeated, and shook his head in amazement. 'How extraordinary.'

'Now can I ask you somethin', Albert?'

'Fire away.'

'Are people roundabout happy to have black folks livin' here?'

Albert considered that. 'It's something of a novelty I must admit. You come across black people down at the docks, but they're mainly Indians, Laskars they're called, which isn't the same thing. Other than that they're something of a rarity. I will say this, the English, generally speaking, are very fairminded. As long as you try to fit in you'll be accepted, in my opinion.'

'Good,' Julius murmured.

'There's one thing been puzzling me though.'

Julius frowned. 'What's that?'

'Why Islington? I would have thought you'd have arranged accommodation in a better area. You working with your Embassy, I mean.'

'Oh that's easy,' Julius smiled. 'Mom and Pop have always lived in what you would call workin'-class neighbourhoods. Pop might be a great musician but he's never made a lot of money out of playin'. So when they asked me to find them a place I looked for somewhere they'd feel right at home, and Islington was what I came up with.'

Well, that was that mystery solved, Albert thought. 'You must be used to better though?'

'I had an apartment in Kensington before coming here, a real luxury one too paid for by the Embassy. Mom and Pop would have hated it though, not their sort of neighbourhood at all. Far too classy, and I mean no disrespect by that. And there was no way I was going to live apart with Mom and Pop in town. Mom would have thought that downright unnatural, and I guess so would I.'

Albert approved of that. He was rapidly warming to Julius Poston, and even getting used to him being black. It seemed to Albert, now he'd come to know some, that black people weren't all that different to white. He certainly couldn't have asked for better neighbours.

'Good for you, son,' he smiled.

They ended up staying far longer than the half hour Albert had told Ellie he'd be.

Ellie wondered what had woken her, normally she hardly stirred until the alarm went off. And then she heard it, the sound of muffled crying.

Instantly she was out of bed and shrugging into her dressing gown. Barefoot she padded from her bedroom.

The crying stopped when she tapped the door. 'Paul?' she queried quietly.

There was no reply.

'Paul?'

Again no reply.

She opened the door and went inside, moonlight shining through the open curtains. Paul had his bedclothes pulled up over his head.

She sat beside him, squirming a little to make room for herself. 'Come on now, I know you're awake. I heard you,' she gently cajoled.

He appeared from under the bedclothes, his face tear-streaked. He gave a quiet sob.

'There there,' she murmured comfortingly, stroking his forehead. 'Is it Mum?'

'Yes,' he choked.

'Well, there's no need to cry. She's going to be fine.'

'I dreamt she died, Ellie. I dreamt she never came back again from the hospital.'

'It was only a dream,' she crooned. 'That won't happen. I promise you.'

'Pa won't tell me what's wrong with her. He just said she's been taken ill and that's all.'

'It's a woman's problem,' Ellie explained. 'Pa was probably too embarrassed to say.'

The boy's brow furrowed. 'What's a woman's problem?'

She sighed. This was difficult. 'Well you know how men and women are physically different?'

Paul nodded.

'Well, it's to do with the difference.'

He sort of understood. 'Are you sure she won't die?'

Ellie made several quick motions over her chest. 'Cross my heart. She'll be home before you know it and things will be back to normal.'

He took a deep breath. 'It was a horrible dream, Ellie. It frightened me awfully.'

'Dreams that do that are called nightmares. That's what you had. A nasty nightmare. We all get them from time to time.'

'Even you?'

She groped in her dressing-gown pocket for the hanky she knew to be there. Using it she wiped his cheeks and then held it under his nose. 'Blow.'

When he'd done that she put the hanky away again. 'Do you want me to stay with you for a while?'

'Will you, Ellie?' he demanded eagerly, what had been a tear-stained face now shining.

'I've just said I will.'

'Thanks, Ellie. You're not a bad sister really.'

'I'm pleased to hear it,' she joked, tucking him in. 'Now you close your eyes and think nice thoughts.'

'Like sweeties and ice cream?'

That made her smile. 'Like sweeties and ice cream,' she agreed.

Within minutes Paul was fast asleep, nor did he wake again till called in the morning.

Jess lay staring up at the ward ceiling. She had been moved to a general ward four days previously. She'd been told that morning, all going well, she'd be out of hospital the day after next, the doctors being pleased with her progress.

Glancing down the ward Jess saw the night nurse busy writing at her desk, a single shaded lamp illuminating her work. Jess had nothing but praise for all the Whittington staff; without exception they'd been kindness itself. She couldn't have asked for better treatment.

Despite being tired her mind was churning with thoughts about the baby she'd lost. The feeling of emptiness that had engulfed her afterwards had taken her by surprise. A terrible emptiness.

Despair welled within her, despair as black as a bottomless pit. Her sense of grief was profound.

A boy or girl? She kept speculating about that. She had asked but no one was able to tell her. The foetus had been taken away by the ambulance crew and disposed of, whatever that meant. Now she would never know what she'd been carrying.

Not that it really mattered. The baby, her baby, was dead and gone. Her baby, and Albert's. Now there truly would never be another child for them, not even an accidental one, her operation had seen to that.

Albert had been a brick about the whole thing. Shocked by what had happened of course, but then that was only to be expected when she'd miscarried a baby he'd known nothing about.

One day she'd ask him would he have been pleased had the baby been born, or not? During his daily visits to the hospital he'd given nothing away in that respect. Nothing at all. Not even the slightest hint.

Jess wondered what time it was? It seemed hours ago

that the lights had been turned out. There again, perhaps that was only her imagination. Lying here with nothing to do gave full rein to the imagination, as she was only too well aware.

One thing was certain. She'd never be the same again. Not even if she lived to be a hundred. Losing the baby had done that to her. From here on in there would always be a part of her that was missing. A wound that would never heal over, but fester on and on. She was in no doubt about that.

Stop being so self-pitying, she scolded herself harshly. You're not the first woman to lose a baby and will hardly be the last. But the truth of that did nothing whatever to ease the pain. This particular loss was hers and hers alone to bear. A loss she'd carry to the grave.

One of the other patients began to snore, a strangely comforting sound that reminded her of Albert.

And still the night wore endlessly on.

'We're here, missus, let's be having you,' the ambulance-man announced jovially, taking her by the arm. 'Can you manage?'

She was stiff and sore, but able to walk, if somewhat awkwardly. 'I'm all right.'

'I'll give you a hand just the same.'

Jess was surprised when their door opened and Albert appeared – she'd expected Beulah or one of the other neighbours.

Albert's hand replaced the ambulanceman's, whom they both thanked. Then Albert helped Jess inside.

'Have you taken the day off work?' she queried.

He raised an eyebrow. 'You're not complaining, are you?'

'No, no, just . . . well it's so unlike you. I would have coped.'

He kissed her on the cheek. 'It's good to have you back. We've all missed you.'

'It's good to be back,' she replied, feeling as though she'd been away for at least a year.

'Now you're not to worry about anything. Ellie has kept the house just as you'd want, and Beulah has popped in on occasions to see what she could do. But first things first, we must get you up to bed.'

She was more tired than she would have thought. The short journey had sapped what strength she had.

Another surprise awaited her in the bedroom. On her bedside table was her favourite vase filled with fresh flowers. 'How lovely!' she exclaimed. 'Who are those from?'

'Me.'

She stared at Albert in astonishment. 'You! You've never bought me flowers in your entire life.'

He coloured slightly. 'Well, there's always a first time. Like them?'

She crossed over and smelt the blooms. 'They're gorgeous.'

'Bought them in the market earlier on. I would have brought some to the hospital but I'd have felt a right berk going on a bus with them.'

Jess couldn't have been more touched. 'Oh, Albert,' she whispered. 'Thank you.'

'Now you get into bed and I'll make you a nice cup of tea. How's that?'

She was too choked to reply.

He made to leave, then hesitated. Putting his arms round her he drew her close and kissed her on the mouth. 'I love you, girl, never forget that,' he declared in a cracked voice.

'And I love you, Albert.'

He gave her another kiss, a quick peck this time, after which he left.

Sitting on the bed Jess began silently to cry tears of happiness.

Chapter 5

Julius was frowning deeply as he laid down the latest report to reach his desk. He stared at it for a few seconds.

'Want some coffee?'

He glanced over at Shelby Robbins, who held the same grade as himself, and whom he shared the office with. 'Not for me.'

Shelby went out into the corridor, returning with a paper cup from the vending machine situated there. Sitting again he lit up.

'It's gettin' worse over in Germany,' Julius said slowly. 'They've now confiscated all Jewish property. That's really puttin' the screws on the poor bastards.'

'Thank God I don't live there,' Shelby exhaled in a worried tone.

Julius guessed what he was referring to. 'You mean Phyllis?' Phyllis was Shelby's Jewish wife.

'Yup.'

'If these Nazis keep on as they are, well . . .' He trailed off, and shrugged.

They both thought about that. 'It won't be our concern,' Shelby said at last. 'Roosevelt would never get us involved in another European war. The country wouldn't stand for it. Once was enough.'

Julius also believed that. There again, nothing was ever set in stone. Things could change.

'We know what the Ambassador thinks,' Shelby went on. 'He's said often enough that the British wouldn't stand a chance against the Germans.'

Julius smiled. 'He never has exactly been pro-British though, has he?'

'You can say that again. Deep down I believe he hates them. Hardly surprising as he's of Irish descent. The Irish have no great reason to love the British.'

'True,' Julius agreed.

'One thing's for certain though,' Shelby said.

'What's that?'

'If there is a war it's going to be helluva exciting round here.'

Could there be another war? Julius wondered. He fervently hoped not. But suppose there was and the Ambassador was right, then Britain would be an occupied country which was a horrifying prospect and one that would shift the entire balance of global power. Would Roosevelt really allow that to happen? Faced with the actual threat of the invasion of mainland Britain Roosevelt might feel forced to intervene.

'What do you think of this guy Hitler anyway?' Shelby asked.

'A crazy, pure and simple. But a damned dangerous one. Like one of those mad characters out of the comic books intent on conquerin' the world.'

74

Shelby laughed. 'That about sums him up I guess. Only we're not living in a comic strip which is what makes it, and him, scary.'

'Real scary,' Julius agreed.

'Changing the subject, are you taking Marybeth to the Ambassador's Ball New Year's Eve? She sure is some piece of ass that lady. Yes sir, I envy you there.'

Julius had to smile. 'Not jealous are you?'

Shelby pretended innocence. 'Not me, buddy. I'm a happily married man with eyes for no other.' He paused, then added impishly, 'Well maybe eyes, but no more than that. A guy can look and imagine, can't he? Hell, there's no harm in that.'

'I haven't asked her yet,' Julius confessed, somewhat amused by this.

'Well, I'd hurry up if I were you before someone else gets in first.'

Julius thought of Marybeth whom he was seeing later. He'd take the opportunity of asking her then. There was certainly no one else he wanted to take and his presence at the Ball, having been invited, was obligatory.

Shelby winked conspiratorially, dropping his voice when he spoke next. 'Tell me, are you and she . . . ?' He trailed off expectantly.

Now it was Julius's turn to pretend innocence. 'What?'

'You know, don't play the dumbass with me.'

Julius regarded his colleague thoughtfully, knowing if he told Shelby anything in so-called confidence it would be round the entire Embassy before he knew it. There wasn't a bigger gossip, and that included the women, in the building.

'The English have a sayin' I rather like,' Julius stated, straight-faced.

'Which is?'

'That's for me to know and you to wonder about.'

Shelby's disappointment clearly showed and he let out an exasperated sigh. 'Going to be that way about it, eh?'

''Fraid so. I could be, there again maybe not. I take the Fifth.'

'I bet you are,' Shelby prompted, trying again.

'Bet all you want. You'll never know whether you've won or lost.'

At that point their conversation was interrupted by Shelby's phone ringing. Julius took the opportunity to escape the office and any further grilling.

Ellie answered the door to find Julius standing there holding an enormous parcel. 'Come in,' she said quickly, for it was bucketing outside.

'I hope I'm not intrudin'?'

'Not at all. How have you been? I haven't seen you in ages.'

He shrugged. 'I've been tied up at work a great deal. Gettin' home late, leavin' early, that sort of thing. Anyway, is your mom home?'

'In the kitchen. So's Pa.'

Julius found Jess up to her elbows in flour, baking for the holidays. 'Hi, Mrs Sykes, how're you keepin'?'

She gave him a large smile. 'Just fine, Julius. In the pink.'

'Hello, son,' Albert greeted Julius from his chair. 'To what do we owe the honour?'

Julius placed the parcel on the table. 'I hope you don't take offence at this. I ordered a turkey through the Embassy for our Christmas dinner and instead of one I've been given two. I thought you might care to have the second.'

Jess's eyes gleamed. 'A turkey! We've never had one of those.'

Julius groped in a pocket to produce a jar. 'This is cranberry sauce which we Americans traditionally serve with it.'

Albert was now on his feet. 'How extraordinarily kind of you, Julius.' He eyed the parcel. 'Just look at the size! Are you sure there isn't an ostrich in there?'

Everyone laughed. 'It's a turkey all right. Shall I take it out?'

Jess began wiping the flour from her hands and lower arms. 'I suppose you cook it just like a chicken, only longer, which is what we normally have?'

'That's right.'

Jess gasped when the bird was revealed. It was massive. 'My God in Heaven!'

'Mom would have offered to keep it in her fridge for you but the fridge is full to burstin' as it is. Anyway, Christmas Eve is only the day after tomorrow. Just put it somewhere cool, that'll do.'

Albert spread his hands wide. 'I wish I could offer you a little something but I've nothing in. I'm picking up the Christmas drink tomorrow night.'

'That's OK, Albert, don't you worry about that. Now, I'd better be on my way.'

'I'll see you out,' Ellie volunteered.

They were leaving the kitchen when Julius suddenly stopped and turned. 'Oh, I nearly forgot. Mom says if you've got a chance why don't you drop by for coffee in the morning,' he related to Jess.

Jess forced a smile onto her face. 'I'm rather busy then, but I will if I can.'

That was a lie, for she had no intention whatsoever of going for coffee with Beulah. Or even entering the Postons' house ever again. Not if she could possibly help it anyway.

Albert rejoined Jess, Ellie and George in the pub, having nipped across the street. It was New Year's Eve and The Florence was jam-packed. They'd been lucky to get a table.

'There's no one home,' he declared. 'I rang and rang but no answer.'

Jess shrugged. 'Beulah has probably gone to the club with Pee Wee and Julius is out elsewhere. Pity, it would have been nice to have had them here to join in.'

'Take it easy,' Ellie whispered to George. 'That's your third pint and we've only been here an hour.'

'I'm all right,' George replied earnestly. 'I won't embarrass you. But it is New Year's Eve don't forget.'

'I appreciate that, but nonetheless.'

'Just like an old married couple,' Albert teased and laughed while Ellie blushed.

'Dad!'

'Well, you are.'

Jess spotted old Ma Jenkins sitting at the far side with some of her cronies and gave her a wave, Ma returning the gesture. Jess idly wondered if Ma had been there all along for she hadn't seen her come in.

A group of men burst into loud, raucous laughter, one of them going quite puce and shaking his head, while another slapped the bar with a hand.

'They're a merry bunch,' Albert commented, guessing someone had told a really filthy joke to get that reaction. Still, it was all harmless fun.

'Are you having a good time?' George asked Ellie. 'It's still not too late to go to the Roxy if you'd prefer that?'

'I am having a good time. And no, I don't want to go to the Roxy, I'm fed up with the place.'

He shrugged. 'Only asking. Being polite like.'

Taffy Roberts, the Welshman, belching as he went, lurched past their table. 'He's had a few,' Albert observed drily to Jess, remembering how Taffy had called Pee Wee a nigger. Obnoxious man.

The pianist, who'd been taking a break during the past ten or so minutes, struck up again, 'I'm Looking Over A Four-Leaf Clover . . .'

Customers began singing, all of them loving and appreciating the old favourites. 'Auld Lang Syne' would be played on the stroke of midnight when all bedlam would break loose.

Behind the bar Harry and Hazel were working flat out. As was their daughter Marje, drafted in especially for the evening. The floor beneath their feet was already awash with spilt beer.

Jess had been happy enough up until then, but suddenly her mood changed and she began to feel depressed and morose. The jollity had for some reason started to irritate her.

'Who's for another?' Albert queried, finishing his pint.

'It's my shout, Mr Sykes,' George quickly replied.

'On you go then. Get them in.'

Jess was the only one who declined a replacement, saying she'd had enough for the moment. Albert didn't take any heed of that, or urge her to the contrary, knowing Jess wasn't a great drinker at the best of times.

It was about half an hour later, the pub now positively heaving, when Jess turned to Albert. 'I'm going to go home, if you don't mind.'

He stared at her in surprise. 'What's wrong?'

'I've developed a thundering headache. The noise in here is just deafening.'

He was obviously disappointed, it was a special occasion after all. A once-a-year event. 'I'll come with you then,' he reluctantly replied.

'No, Albert, I won't hear of it. You stay, I insist. I'll take a couple of aspirin and if the headache clears then I'll come back.' That was a lie, she had absolutely no intention of returning.

'Are you sure, girl?' he frowned.

'Yes, now don't you worry. Stay and enjoy yourself.'

'Will you be all right?' Ellie asked anxiously, as concerned as her father, having overheard the conversation.

'I'll be fine. I just need a bit of quiet, that's all.'

Outside Jess sucked in a deep lungful of chilly air, then hurried across the road. Once in the house she went straight up to their bedroom and, without putting the light on, sat down on the bed.

For a few moments she remained perfectly still, then placed both hands on her stomach. It was the baby of course, that's what was really bothering her. She had suddenly been plunged back into the great, black bottomless pit of agony and despair. The baby she'd lost and who'd forever haunt her.

She began to cry, racking sobs that shook her entire body.

'How do I look?'

Julius had called for Marybeth at her apartment to take her to the Ambassador's Ball. Neither had been that keen to attend so they had agreed to arrive later rather than sooner.

Marybeth was wearing a formal evening gown of crisp rayon taffeta that was shadow-patterned in a brocade effect with a lovely flower design. The bodice was shirred to give a flattering fullness above a pointed set-in girdle which pulled in her waist. Taffeta pleats emphasised the heart-shaped neckline while the sleeves were full puffed. The colour of the gown was blood red which contrasted dramatically with Marybeth's black skin.

Julius swallowed hard. He was impressed, very much so. 'Absolutely stunnin',' he managed to get out at last.

Her face broke into a beaming smile. 'I'm rather pleased

with it if I say so myself. I bought it in Bond Street from a very high-class and exclusive store.'

'You're a knockout, kid. A real knockout. Good enough to eat.'

She laughed, then said tantalisingly, 'Perhaps later, if we're in the mood.'

Her meaning wasn't lost on Julius.

'I'll just get my wrap,' she added.

The wrap, a black velvet cape, completed the ensemble.

Ellie was coming out of the toilet when she ran headlong into Taffy Roberts enroute to the gents a little further down the corridor. There was almost a collision which he staved off by catching hold of her shoulders.

'Why, hello, Ellie fach,' he slurred.

She wrenched herself free. 'If you'll just let me past.' The man was obviously horribly drunk.

'Don't you look pretty as a picture. I swear to God you do.'

Compliments from Taffy Roberts were the last thing she wanted, or needed. She tried to edge past him but he blocked her way.

'I tell you what, Ellie,' he said, groping in a pocket. 'I have some mistletoe here, so why don't you give me a kiss? There's a beautiful girl then.'

The thought of kissing Taffy disgusted her. She backed off as he held the mistletoe above his head and leered, his lips bright and shiny with spit.

'I'll do no such thing,' she retorted hotly, though beginning to be scared. 'Now let me by.'

'But it's New Year's Eve! Surely that merits a nice kiss, eh?'

She backed off even more. 'Don't come near me or I'll scream.'

'Oh no you won't!' he replied, and rushed her, swiftly pinioning her with his arms.

Now she really was scared. His hot, foetid breath washed over her, making her stomach heave.

'Just one little kiss,' he cajoled. 'That's all I ask.'

She twisted her head to one side. 'Go away.'

He laughed. 'Oh, I likes it when they struggle. More exciting that way.'

'What in hell's going on here!'

Ellie instantly recognised the voice as George's.

'Fuck off!' Taffy snarled over his shoulder.

'Let her go, Roberts, or so help me I'll deck you.'

Taffy released Ellie, who fell away with a sob, and slowly turned on George. 'Oh you will, will you?'

'That's what I said,' George stated quietly and defiantly, meaning every word.

Taffy opened his mouth to say something further, but instead suddenly gagged. Clapping a hand over his mouth he wheeled round and ran for the gents where he barged inside.

Ellie sagged with relief. 'Oh George,' she whispered, never having been more pleased to see anyone in her entire life. From the gents came the sound of Taffy being violently sick.

'We'd better get back,' George said, taking her by the hand.

She looked into his eyes and smiled gratefully. 'You'd really have fought that brute for me?'

'Damn right. The Welshman doesn't scare me.'

'Well, he did me. I was almost wetting myself.'

George gave a low laugh. 'You're all right, Ellie, that's all that matters.'

Ellie shuddered. 'He's vile. Really vile. He was slobbering all over me. And his breath stank. You wouldn't believe how awful it was.'

'Well, it's over now. Come on.'

She hesitated. 'What were you doing out here anyway?'

'I decided I also needed to go to the khazi. But that can wait now. I'll go later.'

At the door leading into the saloon Ellie stopped. 'Don't say anything about this to Dad. I don't want to spoil his evening.'

'Mum's the word.'

'No, she's gone home.'

It was a silly joke, but they both laughed nonetheless, a release of tension.

'And George?'

'What?'

'Thank you.'

She kissed him, French style, her tongue wriggling frantically against his. In the middle of this the pianist struck up 'Auld Lang Syne'.

'Happy New Year,' George said when the kiss was finally over. 'I hope 1939 is going to be a good one for the pair of us.'

'I'm sure it will be,' she enthused. 'Happy 1939.'

* * *

Heart pounding, chest heaving, Julius flopped onto his back to gulp in air. He'd never known Marybeth so wild and frenzied, so incredibly passionate.

'You're supposed to hold me afterwards,' she purred.

'Will in a moment. Let me catch my breath first.'

She came onto an elbow to stare at him, her body now soft and relaxed where only moments before it had been taut with expectation. 'How was it for you, hon?'

'Do you have to ask?'

She gave a throaty chuckle. 'Not really. I just wanted to hear you say.'

He swivelled his head sideways to look at her, noting with satisfaction the sweat running down between her magnificent breasts. His gaze then swept over the curve of one hip. Reaching out he gently touched it. 'I swear the earth really did move. God damn if it didn't.'

Her lips twisted upwards. 'That good, eh?'

'That good,' he assured her. 'The best yet. A man could die happy after that.'

'Well, don't die on me just yet, sugar,' she teased. 'I've got other plans for you.'

'Oh?'

'Yeah.'

'Such as?'

'You'll find out.'

'Why not tell me now?'

'Because,' she leant closer and brushed her lips over his, 'I don't want to.'

He placed a hand on her firm bottom and squeezed,

knowing she loved that. He was rewarded with a groan of pleasure. 'I could sure use a drink,' he said.

'Could you now?'

'Bourbon.'

'With ice. The way you like it. You see, I know all the things you like.'

He raised an eyebrow. 'Do you now?'

'Oh yeah. You bet your sweet butt I do. I've made it my business to find out. And you know why?'

He shook his head.

'I want to please you, that's why.' She stared intently at him, her eyes boring into his, then rolled off the bed onto her feet. Gathering up a flimsy see-through negligée she threw it round herself. 'You sure am some stud, hon.'

'Am I?'

'Oh yeah, you'd better believe it. You're a dream come true. At least for me anyway.'

'You're not so bad yourself,' he replied drily, delighted by the compliment. Well, what man wouldn't be?

'Thank you, kind sir.'

His gaze lingered on her figure. Stripped, she truly was stunning. She could easily have been a movie star, if Hollywood had allowed black leading ladies that is. 'So come on, give?' he persisted, still wanting to know what her plans were.

'I thought I just had.'

It took a moment for the penny to drop, and then he laughed. 'I wasn't talking about that.'

'Bourbon, wasn't it?'

'Marybeth!'

Smiling, she sashayed, there was no other word for it, from the room.

'Ma, have you seen my pistol?' Paul asked, having searched, as far as he was concerned, everywhere for it.

'That drawer over there,' she replied, pointing.

He went to the drawer and there, sure enough, it was. 'Thanks, Ma.'

'What is it today, cowboys and indians?'

He nodded. He and the rest of his pals were still on their school holidays.

'Well, make sure you wrap up warm, it's cold out there.'

'I will, Ma.'

'Let me see you before you go then.'

She watched him hurry from the kitchen, her heart swelling within her. How emotional she'd become of late, especially where children were concerned, her own in particular. Losing the baby had heightened her awareness of how precious they were.

He returned wearing a belted raincoat that was long past its best, and an equally old Arsenal football team scarf.

'Where are your gloves?' she queried.

His face dropped. 'I don't like wearing them, Ma. They're itchy. Besides, cowboys don't wear gloves.'

That made her smile. 'Why don't you put them in your pocket just the same.'

'I'll do that on the way out.'

'Make sure you do.'

'Can I go now?'

'Yes, of course, and don't be late for your dinner. I don't want it to spoil.'

'All right, Ma, I won't forget.'

The face of a cherub, she thought. Innocence personified. 'Come here first,' she husked.

Frowning, he did.

Jess put her arms round him and hugged him tight.

'Oh, Ma!' he protested, mortified, considering himself far too old for such nonsense. Thankfully no one else was there to see.

'There,' she sniffed, releasing him. 'Be off with you then.'

He fled, intentionally leaving his gloves behind. Amongst the lads it was considered sissy to wear them, especially woollen ones.

Jess used the bottom of her pinny to wipe her nose. Stupid, sentimental cow, she chided herself. But she just hadn't been able to resist.

'He would have fought for you!' Connie Fox breathed. 'How romantic.'

Ellie and Connie had just left the office and Ellie had recounted the story of New Year's Eve, the first chance she'd had of telling Connie.

Yes, it had been romantic, Ellie realised. Why hadn't she thought of that?

'The other chap sounds awful,' Connie went on, eyes wide.

'He was, believe me.'

'Would your George have won, do you think?'

Ellie considered that. 'I heard my da say once that it isn't the size of the man that counts but what's in his head. That's where fights are lost and won. So yes, I believe he might have done.'

They came to the street corner that was the parting of the ways for them. 'He must really love you, Ellie. I'm quite green.'

Her hero, Ellie thought. George was her hero. She didn't say it out loud though, it would have sounded far too soppy. 'I was very proud of him,' she declared instead.

'And so you should. I certainly would have been. Lucky old you, gel, lucky old you.'

'I know that now. I've had my doubts about George in the past, but not any more.'

'He's definitely the one then?'

Ellie nodded.

'Just make sure I get an invite to the wedding, that's all,' Connie laughed.

'You'll be there. That's a promise.'

'I'll keep you to that. Now I'm off, it's freezing out here.'

She *was* lucky, Ellie told herself as she hurried home. And it had been romantic.

Exciting too, in retrospect.

Chapter 6

Albert rose and switched off the wireless. He and Jess had been listening to the very sobering news on the Home Service.

Jess looked at Albert as he sank back into his chair, his expression one of troubled foreboding. 'It's bad, isn't it?' she said quietly.

Albert nodded. 'I don't quite understand why we have to pledge ourselves to defend Poland, but apparently Chamberlain thinks otherwise.' Chamberlain was the Prime Minister.

'And we're to be allied with France in this.'

'According to Arthur Greenwood.' He was the Deputy PM. Albert shook his head in despair. 'It's all brewing up, just like the last time, sheer bloody nonsense.'

'It's not our fault,' Jess reminded him. 'It's the Germans who want to cause trouble. This man Hitler should be taken out and shot.'

Albert couldn't have agreed more.

'At least you won't have to serve, being in a reserved occupation,' Jess pointed out. 'And Paul is only ten. Any war will surely be over and done with before he's of an age for the Forces.'

'Hopefully,' Albert murmured.

Panic gripped Jess. 'Do you mean there is a chance he might have to?'

Albert's eyes clouded in memory. 'At the end of the last war the Jerries were conscripting boys as young as twelve. That's a fact.'

Jess had read that somewhere years ago but had forgotten about it. She glanced up at the ceiling, fearful for Paul upstairs in his bed. 'Dear God,' she whispered.

'He's already gone into Prague,' Albert stated, referring to Hitler. 'So why not Poland?'

'Because we've now said we'll stop him. Us and the French.'

Albert shrugged. 'Hitler might think it's a bluff on our part. It seems to me he's entirely capable of being that stupid.'

'And we're not?'

'No, I wouldn't say so. For all his faults Chamberlain isn't one to bluff. Not at these kind of stakes anyway. Trouble is, and I'm not the only person to think this, the lads down at the station all agree with me, he's not a war leader. Clever politician yes, but no war leader. He's far too soft for that.'

War, the word reverberated through Jess's head making her go cold all over and break out in gooseflesh. Could anything possibly be more awful? If so, she couldn't imagine what. She shuddered. 'It doesn't bear thinking about.'

'No, it doesn't,' Albert agreed softly.

They both lapsed into silence for a few moments, each lost in their own thoughts.

'Still, look on the bright side,' Albert said eventually. 'It may never happen.'

'Please God.'

'But if it does my money's on Winnie to take over as PM. He's got real fire in his belly.'

Jess had been a Conservative all her life but had never liked Churchill. She didn't know why, there was no sound reason, she simply didn't. 'What about Lord Halifax?'

Albert pondered that. 'He's a possibility, and would certainly be better than Chamberlain in my opinion. But Winnie is the chap for me. He's the one would get my vote.'

Jess sighed and got to her feet. All this talk about possible war was so depressing. Not to mention alarming. 'I'll put the kettle on,' she declared.

'Is there any of that cake left?'

She smiled. 'I put a bit by for you before Paul scoffed the lot. He's got the very devil of an appetite that lad!'

'You can say that again. He costs us an absolute fortune in grub.'

Jess frowned. 'You don't begrudge him though, do you? He is a growing lad after all.'

'That's what you always say.' Albert's face softened. 'But no, I don't really begrudge him. You know that.'

All conversation about the war stopped when they heard Ellie arrive home, after an evening out with George.

George, who was just the right age to be called up, Albert reflected grimly as Ellie breezed into the kitchen.

'What are you staring at?'

Julius snapped out of his reverie to find it was Ellie

who'd spoken, the pair of them meeting by chance in Upper Street, the closest main thoroughfare to Florence Street.

He indicated a dray from Whitbread's Brewery that was stationary outside a pub where a delivery was taking place. 'That,' he replied. 'It sure is one beautiful sight.'

Ellie regarded the dray thoughtfully thinking, yes it was rather lovely. They were a common enough sight thereabouts, common enough to be simply taken for granted. 'Don't you have anything like them in America?' she asked.

'Sure. But nothin' so fancy or ornate. I mean, look at those absolutely huge horses for a start. See how groomed and handsome they are. And just look at the size of those hooves! Son of a bitch, they're enormous.'

Ellie blushed.

'Sorry, Ellie,' he instantly apologised. 'My big mouth ran away with me there.'

'That's all right.'

His gaze went back to the dray and he smiled in admiration. The horses had leather halters round their necks while their manes were plaited and knotted with different coloured ribbons. Big leather straps also hung around their necks covered with gleaming brass ornamental emblems. The wagon itself was brightly coloured and positively screamed of not only being lovingly looked after, but also deeply cherished.

'There are certain things you English do better than anyone else,' Julius commented. 'From your Royalty right down to somethin' like that. No wonder we Yanks can sometimes be in awe of you. You got class as a race, real class, which is what we respect and envy more than anythin' else. Yessir.'

Ellie felt proud to hear him speak of England in such a way. 'Why aren't you in your car?' she queried, changing the subject.

He regarded her with amusement. 'I don't always drive, you know. I do have legs and enjoy using them from time to time.'

That flustered her. 'I didn't mean to be rude.'

'You weren't, Ellie. I was just teasin'. Havin' you on.'

'It's just . . . I mean . . .' She broke off and smiled. 'I don't know what I meant. That I usually see you in your car, that's all.'

'Well not today, at least till later.' He glanced again admiringly at the dray and the two leather-aproned draymen unloading more barrels to be rolled, via a ramp, into the pub cellar. 'What are you doin' out here anyway. Shoppin'?'

'No. I'm meeting George actually. My boyfriend.'

'Oh yeah, he and I haven't met yet. No doubt we will sometime. I'd enjoy that.'

Julius turned up the collar of his coat, for it was nippy. 'Now if you'll excuse me.'

'Nice talking to you, Julius.'

He flashed her a set of perfect white teeth. 'And you, Ellie.'

He strode off a few yards, then suddenly turned. 'Look, Ellie, I'm walkin'!' And having said that he laughed.

Ellie blushed, feeling as if she'd made a right fool of

herself. Of course Americans walked, daft of her to have commented otherwise.

'Where have you been? You're late.'

George gulped in a deep lungful of air, out of breath from running. 'Sorry, I had something else to do which took longer than I expected.' He pecked her on the cheek. 'Anyway, I'm here now.'

Her feet were frozen but she decided not to mention the fact. He'd said sorry and explained, that was enough. 'So where are we off to?'

'The pub.'

She stared at him in astonishment. 'At this time of day?'

'I want to have a quiet word and where better than there?' He pointed at the pub still taking its delivery. 'We'll try that one.'

Again she was astonished, The Florence being only a few minutes away. This was unusual, George normally such a creature of habit. Something she both liked and disliked about him.

He took her hand and hooked the arm round the inside of his. 'Shall we?'

'There you are, a shandy,' he declared, setting the drink in front of her. His was a pint.

The pub wasn't a particularly popular one which was why George had chosen it. The table they'd decided on was in a corner well out of the way where their conversation wouldn't be overheard.

'So what's this all about?' she frowned. 'I must say you're being rather mysterious.'

'Not really. I just wanted us to be alone, that's all.' He sipped his pint.

'Well?' she queried.

'As you know, I've finished my apprenticeship and am now taking home a full wage packet every week.'

She nodded. They'd celebrated that the week before last.

He looked into his glass, suddenly unsure of himself. It was a tremendous step after all. One of the biggest of his entire life. And what if she refused?

'Go on, George,' Ellie urged softly.

'I thought . . .' He cleared his throat. 'I thought we might get engaged?' That last came out in a rush.

Ellie caught her breath. She'd known this would happen but hadn't imagined it would come so soon. It had completely caught her off guard.

His expression was both pleading and defiant. 'What do you say?'

This was it, she mused. If she committed herself it was wedding bells. Then she remembered the night in The Florence. New Year's Eve, when George had stood up to that dreadful Taffy Roberts on her behalf, ready to fight for her.

'When do you think we'd get married?' she prevaricated, her heart seemingly fluttering in her chest.

'A year at least. Probably more. We'd have to save up first so we can do it all properly.'

She nodded, but didn't reply.

'I've already been to the bank and drawn out my savings,' he went on. 'If you say yes we can go straight from here to the jeweller's and buy a ring. I can't afford a really expensive one, Ellie, but I have enough to get something decent.'

'I see,' she murmured, wondering why she was putting him through this when she already knew what her answer was going to be.

'I love you, Ellie,' he whispered and, reaching across the table, placed a hand over hers.

There it was. She couldn't resist any longer. 'And I love you, George. Of course my answer's yes.'

His face radiated delight. 'Oh, Ellie! I just know we'll be happy together. I just know it. You're everything I've ever wanted in a woman. Truly you are. I realised that not long after we started going out together.'

His confession touched her to the very depths of her being. 'We're engaged then,' she smiled. 'As from right now, this moment, we're engaged.'

'I'll make you a good husband, I swear. You'll never have any worries about me.'

'And I'll do my best to make you a good wife, George.'

He glanced around to ensure no one was watching. Satisfied they weren't he leant across and kissed Ellie on the lips. 'That seals it then.'

'I'll tell you something, George.'

'What's that?'

'This was well worth being kept waiting for.'

They both laughed.

* * *

There were tears in Jess's eyes when she finally released George. 'This is the most wonderful news!' she husked. 'I couldn't be more pleased.'

'Thank you, Mrs Sykes. I take it you approve.'

Jess laughed. 'Of course I approve, you silly bugger. And so does Albert. I can't wait to tell him when he gets home from work. He'll be straight over The Florence I'm sure.'

George put an arm round Ellie's waist and drew her to him.

'Now let's see that ring again,' Jess went on.

Ellie held out her left hand. Jess took it and moved it first one way then another so that the stones sparkled. 'It's a beauty,' she declared. 'Very tasteful too.'

'It was Ellie's choice,' George explained, somewhat unnecessarily. For who else's would it have been?

Jess released Ellie's hand and took a deep breath. 'I'll have to sit down for a minute, my legs have gone all wobbly.'

'Shall I put the kettle on, Ma?'

'You do that, Ellie, and make sure you brew a good strong cuppa. I need that.'

'We're not staying long, Mrs Sykes. We want to go and tell my parents after this.'

'Of course, of course,' Jess nodded. 'And so you should. I'm just pleased you came and told me first.'

Her Ellie engaged, she was thrilled to bits. And George such a nice and steady chap too. Ellie couldn't have done better. Albert was going to be so excited.

'Now, what are your plans?' Jess queried, settling back

in her usual chair. Like Ellie, she'd been fully expecting this, but also, like Ellie, not quite so soon.

Not that it mattered. Not in the least.

Albert switched off the light and lay back in bed. As Jess had predicted he'd gone over to The Florence for a few after being told of Ellie and George's engagement.

'Happy?' Jess asked in the darkness.

'About Ellie? Very much so. I approve of that young man. He'll do Ellie proud. You mark my words.'

Ellie a married woman before too long! Jess smiled. It seemed like only yesterday she was changing the girl's nappies. How time flies.

'Did George mention where they might live? Around here I hope. Possibly even in the street if there's something going.'

'I don't think they've thought that far ahead yet,' Jess replied. 'It could be George will want to be near his parents in Highbury.'

Albert grunted, hoping that wouldn't be the case. But if it was, well Highbury wasn't that far away. Just up the road really. No distance at all.

'It's going to cost us,' Jess said. 'Ellie will expect the full works, church wedding, reception after. Won't be cheap.'

'I won't let her down,' Albert replied. 'We'll have morning suits for the men and Paul can be a pageboy.'

Jess laughed. 'He might not like that. You know Paul.'

'He'll do as he's told,' Albert declared darkly. 'Or he'll have me to contend with.'

'Do you think we'll be able to go up West for the dress?' Jess queried. 'Anything bought locally wouldn't be half so good.'

Albert considered that, turning the pros and cons over in his mind.

'There again, we could have it made. That might be an idea. It would certainly be a lot cheaper than Oxford Street and the like.'

Albert started making mental calculations. They did have some money put by, but not a lot. It was difficult to save on what he earned, which was sufficient for the upkeep of the family but not much else. But he'd manage. It would just mean a bit of belt tightening for a while, that's all. Perhaps he could even get a part-time job to earn extra, though with his hours that would be difficult.

'Goodnight, love,' Jess whispered when she didn't get a reply.

Albert shifted and turned on his side to face her. Reaching out he slipped a hand up her nightdress, stopping when he felt Jess tense.

'I'm sorry, Albert,' she whispered. 'I'm just not in the mood.'

With a sigh he withdrew his hand. 'That's all right. I understand.'

'I really am sorry. I know this is hard for you, but it's just the way things are at the moment.'

He rolled onto his back. She didn't always refuse him since coming home from the hospital, but did more often than not. And when she did comply he guessed she was simply going through the motions for his sake. He could only wonder if that side of their life, which had always been so good, was more or less gone for ever. He didn't know how he'd cope if it had.

Albert didn't consider himself particularly highly sexed, but he was normal, and still at an age where he had regular urges. 'Is there anything I can do?' he asked quietly.

'Be patient. That's all I ask. All I can ask.'

'I'll try, Jess.' He had to, he told himself. There was nothing else for it. He certainly wasn't going to force himself on her as some men might have done. That was definitely out of the question as it would have gone completely against his nature.

'I still love you, Albert. Never doubt that. It would break my heart if you did.'

'It's just a temporary thing, Jess, it'll pass in time.' He wished he believed that, but it was hope more than anything.

'There is something, Albert.'

'What's that?'

'Will you cuddle me? That would be lovely. Just a cuddle, that's all.'

He took her into his arms and held her close. Like babes in the wood, he thought, remembering the children's story. Like babes in the wood.

They were still entwined when they fell asleep.

Connie Fox was the first to notice Ellie's ring when they turned up for work on the Monday morning. They were coming out of the ladies, which doubled as a cloakroom, when she spotted it. Connie squealed and grabbed Ellie's hand.

'An engagement ring! You've gone and got engaged, you lucky sod.'

Ellie grinned as the other girls in their department came crowding round. 'Let's have a look! Let's have a look!' several cried in unison.

The ring had a small central stone surrounded by chips. It hadn't been the cheapest in the shop but not far off. Despite that Ellie was as pleased as punch with it. Besides, it was on a par with the sort of ring any of the other girls would have expected to receive.

'It's a smasher!' Connie declared, bright-eyed with delight for her friend. Delight and, she'd have been the first to admit it, more than a tinge of jealousy.

'When did it happen?' Agnes Short queried. 'Let's have all the details.'

'Saturday afternoon. George proposed in a pub.'

'Did he go down on a bended knee?' another girl asked, and giggled.

'Don't be daft. Of course he didn't. It wasn't like that at all. It was romantic though, if I say so myself.' The latter wasn't exactly true, but why should she tell the others that.

'He's such a handsome bugger too,' Connie beamed. 'You are jammy. Knowing me I'll probably end up with the hunchback of Notre Dame.'

Everyone, including Ellie, laughed when Connie said that. 'Who'll also have a squint,' Connie added for good measure.

'It is lovely,' Elaine McIntosh, the senior typist, commented. 'Good for you, Ellie.'

'What's the cause of this commotion!'

They all froze when Miss Oates' voice cut through their banter. It was Connie who answered. 'Miss Sykes has just got engaged, Miss Oates, and we're admiring the ring.'

For a fraction of a second Miss Oates' stern expression softened, then hardened again. 'Be that as it may, it's no excuse for all this noise and general kerfuffle. You can admire Miss Sykes' ring later I'm sure.' Adding meaningfully, 'Out of work time. Now get about your duties. All of you.'

'Yes, Miss Oates,' was chorused in reply.

'Rotten old bat,' Connie whispered to Ellie as they turned away.

'Did you say something, Miss Fox?'

Connie was innocence personified, looking as though butter wouldn't melt in her mouth. 'I said it was so cold this morning I wished I'd worn a hat,' she lied.

Miss Oates sniffed, clearly not believing a word of that. 'Get on with it then.'

To Ellie's utter amazement Miss Oates later stopped by her desk. 'Congratulations, Miss Sykes,' Miss Oates said in a low voice, and briefly smiled before sweeping regally on her way.

Ellie was left dumbstruck.

Shelby Robbins hung up his coat and hat and greeted Julius who was already in the office and hard at work. 'Guess what Phyllis and I did last night?' he said.

Julius was concentrating, the report he was drafting proving a tricky one.

'Not the obvious I hope,' he replied drily.

Shelby laughed. 'Well we did actually, but that was later. No, we went and saw your old man. He sure is a great player. We just adored the band.'

Julius glanced up with a frown. 'I didn't know you liked jazz?'

'Hell, yeah. I got stacks of records at home that I brought over from the States. Muggsy Spannier, Art Tatum, Lester Young, Teagarden, all those famous guys. But last night was the first time I'd ever heard your old man. I sure was impressed.'

'What did you make of the club?'

'The Chicory House? It was OK. Nothing special, but OK. Good atmosphere. And hey, those English audiences sure appreciate their jazz. That surprised me. They're usually so buttoned up about everything.'

Julius smiled. 'That's what Pop says. They can be fantastic accordin' to him.'

Shelby pointed a finger at Julius. 'You take my word for it, boy, halfway through the evening . . .' He trailed off when he saw the sudden look in Julius's eyes. They were shooting daggers at him. 'What's wrong?'

Julius counted to ten before replying. 'Do me a favour, Shelby, never call me boy again. I find it insultin'.'

'Oh shit,' Shelby apologised. 'I didn't mean nothing by it. It's an expression, that's all.'

'It's more than an expression if you're a negro. As I said, it's insultin'. And I do mean it when I told you never to call me that again.'

Julius didn't need to elaborate on the threat, Shelby

had got the message loud and clear. 'Sorry, truly I am. I'll remember.'

'Do that.' Julius's tone was as cold as ice.

He returned to his report while Shelby beat a hasty, and wise, retreat to the vending machine in the corridor outside.

Julius's eyes flickered upwards as Shelby left the room. There was one thing he would never allow himself to be called, and that was boy. The connotations, and history behind it, made his blood boil.

Jess put the last dish away and threw down the tea towel. Ellie had already gone out as she was meeting George, and Paul was spending the night at a pal's whose father was taking them fishing early in the morning.

'Finished?' Albert queried from his chair.

Jess nodded. 'All done.'

Albert glanced at the clock on the mantelpiece. 'Then get your things, I'm taking you to the pictures. A Ronald Colman film, I believe.'

For a moment Jess thought she'd misheard. 'The pictures?'

'That's right. Just you and I, the pair of us. And when we come out we'll have fish and chips just like we used to in our courting days.'

Somewhat in a daze Jess took off her pinny. Albert suggesting the pictures, it was unheard of! Usually it took a great deal of persuading on her part for him to go along. Now here he was actually suggesting it.

'Some sort of mushy nonsense according to Ellie,' he

went on. 'You're bound to enjoy yourself.'

Jess laughed, this was incredible. 'You'll be proposing we sit in the back row next?'

'And why not!' he retorted, pretending indignation. 'We may be older but we're not decrepit. There's nothing wrong with a couple canoodling, even at our age.'

What a wonderful man he was, she thought, guessing correctly why he was doing this.

'And you can have a box of chocolates before we go in,' he further added. 'As long as you don't scoff the lot and I get one or two.'

Chocolates, pictures, fish and chips! 'What about the pub?' she queried. 'You usually go there on a Friday night when you're not on duty.'

'I can miss the pub for once. And who knows, we might even get back in time for last knockings providing there isn't too long a queue at the fish and chip shop.'

She dropped her gaze for a moment, a great warmth for Albert bubbling inside her. Then she looked up again, straight into his eyes. 'Thanks, darling. A night out is just the ticket.'

'Then you'd best get ready.'

A little make-up, she thought, and a change of dress. Suddenly she felt like a young girl again. And a courting one at that.

She pecked Albert on the cheek before hurrying upstairs, leaving him with the broadest of smiles on his face.

Chapter 7

It was baking hot in the scullery where Jess was doing her weekly wash. A scullery that always smelt, at least so Ellie claimed, of Sunlight soap and boiled beetroot.

Jess removed the lid from the copper where the wash was coming along nicely and took out the dolly blue. When the wash was finally done it would come out of the boiler, whose fire now blazed underneath, and be put, piece by piece, through the large manually operated mangle situated to one side.

Jess was thinking about Beulah who'd yet again asked her in for coffee, and whom she'd yet again refused with a made-up excuse. This time it had been different though, the hurt of rejection clearly showing in Beulah's soulful eyes.

This couldn't go on, Jess told herself. The Postons had been kindness itself to her and her family and her response was continually to snub them when invited in.

Jess wiped away wisps of damp hair that had fallen across her face, tucking them neatly behind one ear.

She was being unfair by not explaining to Beulah; surely that was the least she could do. Better still, explain and force herself to go into that kitchen of terrible memories.

Except, she couldn't bring herself to do either, for that would mean talking about what had happened, going through the whole damn thing all over again, which would be torment.

Stupid woman, she thought. That's what she was, a stupid woman. What had happened had happened, she'd come to terms with that fact, even found herself living more easily with it, as Albert could testify thanks to their intimate life getting back more or less to normal. She simply hadn't been able to shut Albert out in that way for ever, her love for him being too strong to keep denying him.

Of course the wound would never properly heal, it went far too deep for that. And the great black hole remained and always would. She'd known that right from the start. But she was coping with it better now, not falling into it nearly as much.

'Buggeration,' she swore. She just wasn't being fair where Beulah was concerned. Not fair at all. And that wasn't like her. It went completely against her principles.

Jess glanced out the small, open scullery window to check the weather. Earlier she'd feared it might rain but that threat had cleared away which meant she'd be able to peg out as she'd intended.

God, her hands, she thought. They always looked so awful on wash day, all red and horrible, as if they'd been boiled along with the wash. And she was fresh out of hand cream too! She'd meant to buy some earlier but had forgotten after being in a conversation with old Ma Jenkins whom she'd bumped into.

She brought her mind back to Beulah, knowing she had to do something.

Beulah opened the door to find Jess standing there. 'Why, hi!' she exclaimed in surprise.

Jess was holding a box from the bakery which she now indicated. 'I've got six French Fancies here which I imagine will go well with that wonderful coffee you make. Can I come in?'

'Of course, hon. Of course.'

Jess took a deep breath and forced herself to step forward. Her heart was hammering nineteen to the dozen as she moved into the Postons' hallway.

'I can't remember the last time you were here,' Beulah said affably.

Ouch! Jess thought. She could, only too damn well. The occasion was burnt into her soul. 'I know. That's why I've called by. To explain to you. Can we . . . can we . . .' Jess steeled herself. 'Go into the kitchen?'

'Sure. Or we could use the other room.'

'No, the *kitchen*,' Jess declared emphatically. 'I have a reason for that.'

'Oh?'

Jess followed Beulah, the larger woman leading the way. In other circumstances Jess might have been amused by the ancient, heavily embroidered and garish slippers Beulah was wearing. But she didn't even notice them.

She started to tremble as they approached the kitchen, the trembling increasing as they went through the door.

The first thing she saw was the chair she'd been sitting in when she'd miscarried.

'Oh my God!' she croaked, and dropped the bakery box.

Beulah had listened in sympathetic silence as Jess had recounted why she'd been avoiding the house, and kitchen in particular, berating herself for not realising what the problem had been. Now it made perfect sense.

'So that's it,' Jess concluded quietly. 'And I do apologise if I caused you any upset.'

'Oh, honey,' Beulah breathed. 'I been so bone-headed. It just never crossed my mind you'd feel that way.'

Jess picked up her cup and sipped her coffee which had started to go cold during the time she'd been speaking. 'I simply had to get a grip of myself, face the situation. That's why I made myself come. That and because I was so ashamed of appearing to slight you.'

'You ain't never done that, honey. I just couldn't figure why you always turned down my invitations. And yet when I stopped by your place you were always welcomin'. Plain as the nose on your face of course, except I didn't see it.' Beulah studied Jess. 'You OK now?'

Jess glanced around. 'I think so.'

'Still want to stay here, there's always the other room?'

'I'd prefer to stay here.' Jess hesitated. 'There's a question I want to ask you.'

'Shoot.'

'Did you . . .' She paused to draw in a breath. 'Did you happen to notice if it was a boy or girl?'

110

Beulah shook her head. 'I didn't. It was all happenin' so fast, and I was so worried.'

'I understand.' Jess swallowed back her disappointment. Now she'd never know. But maybe it was better that way.

'Besides, hon, it was . . .' Beulah decided referring to it as an 'it' wasn't exactly tactful. 'The child was too little, hardly formed at all. Even if I'd looked I don't know if I could have seen what the child was. That's the honest truth.'

Jess placed her cup back in its saucer. 'Am I forgiven, Beulah?'

'Of course you is, Jess. There's nothin' to forgive anyway. You was havin' a real bad dose of the blues, understandably so. That's all. Now . . .' She clapped her meaty hands together. 'How about those French Fancy jobs you brought, why don't we try them out?'

Jess reached for the box. 'I hope they're not too bashed.'

'Don't matter if they are. Won't spoil the taste. And I could sure do with somethin' sweet right now. Though Pee Wee always tells me I'm sweet enough. Lyin' hound dog that he is.'

They both laughed.

A little later as Jess was saying goodbye, Beulah queried quietly, 'Will you be back?'

'Any time I'm asked, Beulah. Any time.'

'That's good. That's real good. I'm pleased. And hey, I won't be mentionin' this to anyone, includin' that husband of mine. It's strictly between you and me. OK?'

'OK,' Jess agreed.

She felt buoyant, and definitely freer, as she turned towards her own house.

That particular demon had been vanquished.

'Where have you been?' Jess demanded as Ellie entered the kitchen. 'We were getting all set to start without you. I thought maybe you'd been offered overtime and taken it.'

'I'm starving,' Paul complained.

'You're always starving,' Jess retorted without even bothering to look at him.

'I've been over in The Florence,' Ellie explained.

Albert frowned. 'Drinking at this time of the evening?'

'No, Dad, I wanted a word with the Cliffords before they got busy.' The Cliffords were Harry, the landlord, and his wife Hazel. 'I had the idea at work that a part-time job would be useful to help George and me save up for the wedding. I'll be doing Friday and Saturday nights to start with. Possibly more if I get on well.'

'Can you all sit down and I'll dish out,' Jess requested. 'It's stew and dumplings with boiled tats.'

Albert wasn't at all sure what he made of Ellie's news. His initial reaction wasn't to be all that keen on the prospect.

'Well, Dad?'

'The extra money would certainly help, I'll give you that. But . . . well, all those men?'

'I'll be safe enough, Dad. It's our local, for goodness sake. I know almost everyone who goes in there, and they me. Besides, neither Harry nor Hazel would let me come to any harm. Or any of the regulars come to that. I'll be safe as houses.'

That was a point, Albert reflected. 'What do you think, Jess?'

Jess shrugged. 'As you say, the money would certainly come in handy for Ellie. We can't dispute that.'

Paul's eyes gleamed as Jess filled his plate. Three dumplings! He usually only got two. He immediately fell to eating.

'Can't you wait?' Ellie reprimanded him sharply.

'And don't reply with your mouth full,' Jess warned when she saw that's what he was about to do. Honestly, you'd think the boy had never been taught manners.

'I'll enjoy it,' Ellie said to her parents. 'It should be fun. A good laugh.'

'Have you discussed this with George?' Jess queried.

'I told you, Ma, I only had the idea earlier. There hasn't been a chance yet.'

'Well, I think you should have done that before applying at The Florence. George might be dead against it.'

'If he is I'll talk him round,' Ellie replied confidently.

'Hmmh!' Jess snorted, indicating they could now start on the meal.

'Do you begin this Friday?' Albert asked.

'To be there prompt at opening time.'

'What about your tea?' Jess queried in alarm. 'You can't not eat first.'

'I've to have something there. It's part of the arrangement.'

'Well, that's all right then,' Jess reluctantly conceded.

She preferred to feed her own family, knowing they'd have good wholesome food and not the muck some folks ate.

'I'll go and see George straight after this,' Ellie declared. 'He should be home.'

Paul speared another potato with his fork and wondered if there was any more stew in the pot when he finished what was on his plate.

George was appalled. 'A *barmaid*?'

Ellie had walked up to Highbury and his parents' house to find that they'd gone out leaving George alone. 'That's right. Think of the help the money will be.'

His face clouded over. He didn't like this one little bit. 'I don't know,' he said grudgingly.

'What's to know? I'm doing it for us, George, to make things easier. What's wrong with that?'

'How much will you get per shift?' he asked.

She told him. 'And that'll soon add up if I put it by every week, believe me.'

He certainly couldn't disagree, it would make quite a difference to their savings. Make things a lot easier as she'd said. He broke away, his brow furrowed in thought.

'George?'

'I can't pretend I like it, Ellie. God knows what you'll have to contend with. When men have been drinking they can come out with all sorts. Be downright crude. You've heard it yourself.'

She sighed. 'I'm grown up, George. There's not a lot will bother me.'

'You hate swearing for a start,' he reminded her.

'Then I'll just have to develop a thicker skin, that's all. Let it wash over my head. Anyway, there isn't much swearing when Hazel or Harry are about, they don't appreciate it either.'

'Well, what about our Friday and Saturday nights together? What happens to those?'

Ellie had already thought of an answer to that. 'We'll go out more during the week instead. It won't be a problem.'

'But Fridays and Saturdays are *the* nights to go out. It won't be the same during the week.'

She went to him and curled an arm round his neck. 'We'll be together. Surely that's what's important?'

'Just the same.'

'I want to do this, George. Please don't be angry?'

'I'm not angry. I . . . just disapprove, I suppose.'

Pulling his head down she blew gently into his ear, knowing how much he adored that. 'Please don't. It'll mean we can get married sooner than we otherwise might have done. Live together under the one roof, spend our nights together in the same bed and all that entails.'

He closed his eyes for a brief second, imagining himself and Ellie in bed. How desperately he wanted that.

She kissed him on the side of the mouth. 'So you agree then?'

He tentatively lifted a hand and brushed it over the swell of her breast which sent what felt like an electric shock coursing through him. 'Oh, Ellie,' he whispered.

'It'll work out, George. You'll see.'

He was about to kiss her full on the lips when, from

out in the hallway, came the banging shut of the door announcing that his folks had returned.

'Damn,' said George, smiling ruefully.

Neither of them mentioned the pub job to George's parents, thinking it wisest that way.

Julius ran a hand over his forehead. It had been a long, tiring day and he was thoroughly bushed. He wished he hadn't arranged to meet Marybeth later in town. He could have done without that now.

'What's new?' Pee Wee asked, having been playing music inside his head, working out various variations for a jam session scheduled for that evening.

Julius flopped wearily onto a chair.

'Hi, son!' Beulah greeted him from the stove where she was cooking chicken jambalaya.

'I've got to go away for a few weeks,' he informed them.

Beulah stopped what she was doing to stare at him. 'Where to?'

'Paris. Probably two weeks, no more than three.'

'You mean Paris, *France*?'

He smiled at her excited expression. 'Uh-huh!'

'Hey, that's great.'

'For the Embassy I take it?' Pee Wee queried.

'Yeah. And don't ask what it's about. I can't say. Except that it's routine, nothin' more.'

'Must be important "routine" to send you all that way?' Pee Wee commented shrewdly.

Actually it was very important. He was taking over a number of high-level documents plus a letter from his own Ambassador to the Ambassador in France. There was also a message to be delivered orally.

'Now, Pop, don't try and pry. You know it won't get you anywhere,' Julius teased.

'When are you leavin'?'

'Day after tomorrow.'

'I'll pack your bag, son.'

'I can do that, Mom,' he protested.

Her expression became defiant. 'When you is in this house that's my job, and don't you forget it. So if there's anythin' special you want to take then make sure you tell me beforehand.'

He sighed in defeat. 'OK, Mom, you win.'

'Darned tootin' I do. Just like always. That so, Pee Wee?'

'Just like always,' he smiled in agreement.

Julius closed his eyes, thinking about the forthcoming trip. When he'd mentioned it to Marybeth she'd asked if she could come with him. All she needed, she'd said, were the dates and name of the hotel he'd be staying at. She'd make her own arrangements and join him there. As she'd said, she had some vacation due and had never been to France. And he wouldn't be working all the time, now would he?

It should be an interesting trip, Julius thought to himself. Between one thing and another.

As luck would have it, Ellie's first customer was Taffy Roberts. Her heart sank when she saw him come through the door.

He stared at her in surprise. 'What are you doing there?' he demanded.

'Growing tomatoes, what does it look like?'

He laughed. 'Lippy cow, eh? Mine's a large rum and black and a pint of mild. I take it you can pull a pint?'

'Oh, I think I can just about manage,' she replied offhandedly, having had some instruction on arrival from Harry who'd also taken her through the prices.

Taffy pulled out a filthy hanky and hawked into it. He then used the hanky to wipe his nose. 'When did you start?'

'Tonight.'

He grinned, thinking there might be some sport here. 'You won't last. I'd bet on it.'

She placed his rum before him and stared him straight in the eye. 'I'll last just as long as I want to. You'd better believe that.'

Harry reappeared after having popped out the back for a few moments. 'All right, Ellie?'

'Fine, thank you.'

She was aware of Taffy watching her closely as she drew his pint. Thankfully she didn't make a hash of it. Now she had the till to contend with, but that was easy.

Without uttering another word she put the Welshman's change in front of him, then moved on to another customer who'd wandered in meanwhile.

Soon the bar was busy.

'How was it?' Jess demanded eagerly.

'Exhausting. My feet are killing me. I shan't wear heels

118

tomorrow night, that was an obvious mistake.'

Jess nodded her sympathy as Ellie slipped off her shoes. 'Would you like a cup of tea?'

'Just the ticket. I'm parched.'

'Any trouble?' Albert asked casually.

She shook her head. 'Taffy Roberts was a bit mouthy to begin with, but he didn't stay long. Ignorant man. That laugh of his is absolutely horrendous. I swear he sounds like a braying donkey.'

'You didn't mind me popping in?'

'Not in the least, Dad. You usually do on a Friday night and there's no reason to stop that just because I'm there.'

Ellie reached down and massaged her feet. They really were sore. Still, she'd probably get used to it.

'I sat with George who wasn't too happy about you being behind the bar,' Albert remarked.

'I gave him a piece of my mind when he walked me home. Honestly, he sat there glaring at me the entire time. I can't put up with that.'

'He's only concerned, Ellie. Give him a while to get used to the idea.'

She'd actually felt quite sorry for George who'd looked like a fish out of water without her being with him. In a way it was complimentary though, if irritating. Afterwards she'd told him straight she wasn't going to put up with him glaring at her night after night. It was off-putting to say the least.

'What did you get to eat?' Jess asked anxiously.

'Shepherd's pie and veg, Ma. Same as the Cliffords had. It was very nice.'

'I was worried you'd get fobbed off with a Scotch egg or something. No real goodness in that at all.'

How caring her mother was, Ellie reflected. As was her father. She was very fortunate to have parents like them, a fact she appreciated.

'And did you enjoy yourself?' Albert queried.

'Thoroughly. Once the pub got busy the hours just whizzed by. Some of the regulars can be very funny when you're serving them. They sort of flirt with you, but you know they don't really mean it. It's just a game where they're concerned.'

'And you're back there again tomorrow night,' Albert stated, already knowing that to be so.

'At opening time sharp. I'm looking forward to it.' Far better, and more exciting, than the Poxy Roxy, she thought to herself. Just as she'd expected, it had been a right good laugh.

'What do you notice about the people?' Julius asked Marybeth, as they sat at a table outside a rather chic café. Marybeth had arrived that morning while Julius was at the Embassy.

Marybeth shook her head. 'Nothin' in particular. They seem perfectly normal to me.'

'Their faces,' Julius said slowly and thoughtfully. 'Everyone looks strained, worried sick. No one is laughin' or jokin', they're all so grave.'

Marybeth could now see that was so. 'You're right.'

'And you know why?'

'Do you mean the Germans?'

Julius nodded. 'I don't blame them. I'd be worried too. France could well be next on the list for Hitler to invade.'

Despite the July heat Marybeth shivered, wondering if it had been such a good idea after all to come over and join Julius. There again, she might never get another chance to visit Paris.

'Another thing,' Julius went on. 'It's rare to come across a black person in London, but here they're not uncommon. I like that.'

He glanced over at Marybeth who was wearing a pretty summer dress which showed off her superb figure to the full. Made of rayon jersey, the dress was sleek, smooth-fitting and boasted a floral print on a cream background. It had a cross-over bodice with a modified peg-top skirt that had curved, set-in pockets. Round her waist was a self belt.

Marybeth sipped her Pernod, wrinkling her nose as she did.

'What's wrong?'

'This stuff is crap. It tastes like swamp water.'

Julius laughed. 'It's a typical French aperitif.'

'I don't care if it's typical or not. It's still crap. Can I have somethin' else?'

'Sure.'

'Scotch on the rocks.'

Julius was still laughing as he beckoned the waiter over.

'My God, that was the best yet,' Marybeth sighed, giving Julius a satisfied, feline smile. 'You sure are some lover, honey. You ring my ting-a-ling every time.'

When they'd returned to the Georges Cinq where they were staying in individual rooms for propriety's sake, they'd gone to hers and popped the bottle of champagne Julius had brought along. Within minutes they'd both stripped off and tumbled into bed, Marybeth, never shy to say the least, immediately taking the lead.

'I'm glad you came,' Julius smiled in return.

'I sure did. The full bazooka!'

His eyes twinkled. 'I didn't mean that. I meant come to Paris.'

'You're joshin' me now,' she pretended to scold, wagging a finger at him.

'More champagne?'

'Please.'

She watched the wine bubble and froth into her glass. 'I wish this could go on for ever,' she purred.

'Do you?'

'Oh yeah. And in a way it could.'

'How's that?' He sat back on the bed, supporting himself with pillows.

'You know.'

He shook his head. 'No, I don't actually.'

'Well, let me put it this way, lover, you and I could have beautiful babies together.'

There it was, the plans she had for him. Marriage and a family. He should have guessed.

'What do you think?'

He could see she was being light-hearted, but underneath deadly serious about this. Marybeth wasn't joking.

'Children, beautiful or not, don't figure on my agenda,

Marybeth. At least not in the foreseeable future.'

She didn't reply to that, instead dropped her gaze to stare at the bed. 'OK, so kids are out for now,' she eventually whispered.

Christ, Julius thought. That still left marriage.

'Why don't we talk about this another time?' he suggested. 'The way things are who knows what could happen. Everythin's so uncertain right now.'

Instinct told her not to push the matter, even if she desperately wanted to do so.

Marybeth swung herself off the bed. 'I'm goin' to have a hot tub. Won't be long.'

Despite the smile on her face he could hear the hurt in her voice. And that hurt him too.

Chapter 8

Julius arrived home to find Beulah and Pee Wee had gone out. Thirsty after his journey he decided to nip across the road and have a drink of English beer which, despite being warm and not at all what he'd been used to back in the States, he was becoming increasingly fond of. He pulled up in astonishment when he saw Ellie behind the bar.

'Hi! When did this happen?' he asked when it was his turn to be served.

'A few weeks ago. I'm only part-time, Friday and Saturday nights.'

'Well, good for you, kid.'

It irritated her to be called that, but she didn't comment. 'What'll it be?'

'A pint of your best.'

'How was France?' she queried as she was pouring it.

'How did you know I was there?'

'Your ma told my ma who mentioned it. Whereabouts were you?'

'Paris.'

Her eyes widened. 'I hear it's a marvellous place and that the women are really elegant.'

'They're certainly that.' What he didn't say was that they made their English counterparts look absolutely dowdy by comparison. It wasn't only the way they dressed; they had an indefinable something that set them apart, made even the oldest of them look truly glamorous. Marybeth had been so taken with the clothes and fashions she'd bought a whole bunch of stuff to bring back with her.

'I envy you,' Ellie admitted. 'I'd give my eye teeth to go there.'

'Maybe someday,' he smiled.

'Fat chance of that. There's no more likelihood of my going to France than there is of me flying to the moon.' She placed his pint in front of him. 'You must tell me all about it sometime when you get the chance.'

'Sure. I'd be pleased to.'

She glanced round the bar to see she wasn't needed elsewhere. 'I've heard the food's awful though. Is it true they actually eat horses and snails?'

He nodded. 'It's true.'

She pulled a face. 'Uck! How disgusting.'

Julius was trying not to laugh. 'And they use lots of garlic. Do you know what that is?'

'I read about it in a book once. It makes your breath stink.' Her expression was one of total revulsion. 'How can they eat something that makes your breath stink? It doesn't make sense.'

'Tastes nice though,' he teased.

'You mean you actually ate it?' She was incredulous.

'Sure thing. We use garlic in the US as well. Apart

from givin' the food flavour it's supposed to be good for you.'

'Flavour!' she exclaimed in derision. 'If food is fresh it doesn't need any fancy flavouring added. That sort of thing is to disguise poor-quality meat and the like. Everyone knows that.'

'Except obviously in France,' he commented drily, still teasing.

'Are you serving, Ellie?'

'Excuse me,' she apologised and hurried away to attend to the customer who'd called.

Julius took out a pack of cigarettes and lit up. Ellie had rather a neat little figure, he noted absent-mindedly. Curiously he'd never been aware of it before. Nothing to compare with Marybeth's of course. Marybeth's figure was a completely different ball game.

Marybeth, he reflected. Their time together had been a success, the sex mind-blowing. Well, it certainly had been for him and she'd assured him it had been the same for her.

She'd never mentioned babies or marriage again, which had been a relief, though on several occasions he'd thought she was about to.

He could do a lot worse than have Marybeth for a wife, he mused, she was certainly a class act. Rich too, or at least her folks were. Or so he'd been led to believe, though what her father's occupation was he had no idea.

Lots of guys would have jumped at the chance of Marybeth plus money, so what was stopping him? He simply wasn't ready for marriage, he guessed. The thought of being tied down, coming home to the same woman night after night didn't appeal at all.

On the positive side, she'd be a definite asset in his career. The Department favoured married guys, believing it made them more stable. And Marybeth being an ex-member of the Department – he presumed she'd give up work if they tied the knot – could only be helpful too. All in all a very attractive package.

One thing was certain, he needed to give this a lot of careful thinking before reaching a final decision. It would be stupid not to. Damn stupid. And whatever else he considered himself to be it wasn't that. No sirree.

'I didn't know you smoked?'

He snapped out of his reverie to find Ellie had returned and was starting to wash glasses in the sink situated directly beneath where he was standing.

'Only occasionally, and usually cigars,' he replied. 'My preference is Havanas. They're the best.'

'Cigars, oh my!' She was impressed. 'Winston Churchill smokes those. I've seen him on Pathé News at the cinema. Huge ones.' She studied Julius speculatively for a moment. 'Do you know who Winston Churchill is?'

He thought the naïveté of that endearing. 'Sure do. I met him a while back at a reception we had at the Embassy.'

Ellie was stunned. 'You've actually *met* him? What's he like?'

Julius considered that. 'I thought him very funny to tell the truth. Extremely humorous. Though obviously, goes without sayin', there's a far deeper side to him.'

'How long did you speak to him for?' She was agog.

Julius tried to remember. 'A couple of minutes I guess. And yes, he was smokin' a cigar at the time. A large one, as you said.'

'What did you talk about?'

'This and that, nothin' of consequence. I'm not high enough up the totem pole to be doing that.'

If she'd been impressed to learn Julius smoked cigars, this had impressed her a hundred times more. He'd actually met and spoken to Winston Churchill! It was incredible.

Nice skin, Julius noted. But then most English girls had. Not so American women, their skins paled by comparison. Especially in the mid- and far west where the sun could, and invariably did, do a lot of damage.

Ellie had finished the washing up and now began drying the glasses and putting them away.

Any further conversation was halted when the door swung open and a half-dozen or so men came crowding in, quickly followed by another group.

When Ellie found time to look at where Julius had been she discovered he'd gone. Smiling ruefully she got on with the job, thinking how much she'd enjoyed their chat. She couldn't get over the fact he'd not only met Winston Churchill but actually spoken to the great man.

'I want to talk to the pair of you,' Julius stated, stirring sugar into his coffee.

'What about, son?' Beulah asked. She and Pee Wee

had just returned from the West End where they'd had a splendid lunch in a little Bohemian Soho restaurant Pee Wee had discovered.

'I think the pair of you should consider goin' back to New York. Preferably quite soon.'

Pee Wee glanced up at Julius. 'Why's that?'

'You must have read the recent newspapers. The situation in Europe has deteriorated dramatically during the past few weeks. If, and so far it's only that, Hitler invades France, then England could be next. The last thing I want is for you two to be caught up in a war.'

'We'll be safe enough,' Pee Wee replied slowly. 'We're American citizens, the Germans wouldn't dare lay a finger on us. Uncle Sam would have somethin' to say if they tried.'

Beulah's eyes were flicking from one man to the other. This was serious.

'What if the Nazis were to bomb London? A droppin' bomb can't distinguish between an Englishman and an American,' Julius pointed out.

'Do you really think he will invade England?' Beulah queried in a frightened voice.

A large part of the reason Julius had been sent to Paris was to hear first-hand reports from agents coming out of the rest of Europe. He'd personally interrogated, and debriefed, several of them. Of course he couldn't tell his parents that. 'It's a distinct possibility in my opinion.'

'What does our Ambassador say?' Pee Wee frowned.

Julius made a pyramid with his hands. 'How shall I put this? The Ambassador doesn't have great faith in

England, or its Empire. He believes the German war machine would simply roll right over this country.'

'Holy shit,' Pee Wee muttered.

'Do you agree with him?' Beulah queried.

'To be honest, Mom, I just don't know. What I do know is I'd be a lot happier if you two were on a boat steamin' Stateside. Then I wouldn't have to worry about you.'

'I see,' Pee Wee murmured.

'Would you come with us?' Beulah asked.

Julius shook his head. 'Can't do that, Mom. London is where I'm posted and here I stay until either the Department, or Ambassador, say otherwise. That's how it is.'

'I wonder what the other guys in the band will do?' Pee Wee mused. 'One thing's certain, they're goin' to be awfully disappointed if we do leave, the band that is. We're all havin' a ball here. The English audiences sure do love our music. They're some of the most appreciative cornflakes I've ever come across.' The latter was a jazz term referring to the general public. 'And ain't that the truth.'

'I can fix up passage for you anytime you like,' Julius went on. 'All you have to do is say and I'll get you on an American liner sailin' out of Southampton.'

'Well, I ain't makin' no decision right here and now,' Pee Wee declared. 'I got to think this through.'

Beulah gazed around her, reflecting on how fond she'd become of this house, and Islington. She'd miss both dreadfully if they were to go.

'You think on it then,' Julius said to Pee Wee. 'But it would be better, and perhaps safer, if you reached that decision sooner rather than later.'

'I got you, son.'

Julius rose from his chair. 'Won't be a second. I brought you both somethin' from Paris.'

The 'something' transpired to be perfume for Beulah and a fancy vest, waistcoat that is, for Pee Wee which he'd known he would love.

He wasn't wrong – his parents were delighted with their gifts.

When Pee Wee got home in the early hours Beulah was in bed, but wide awake. 'I been waitin' for you,' she explained.

He kissed her on the forehead. 'Is it what Julius said?'

'Yeah.'

'Thought it might be.'

He quickly undressed and slipped in alongside her. 'So what do you reckon?'

'I ain't leavin', Pee Wee. I'm stayin' right here.'

'What about the Germans?'

'Screw them. All I know is that Julius has to stay so I is too. I ain't skedaddlin' off leavin' my only son in danger. Shit no. I stays put and that's an end of it.'

He slid an arm round her considerable bulk, enjoying the warm, musky smell of her body. A feeling of sublime contentment swept through him as it sometimes did when he and Beulah were in bed, snuggled up together. 'Then that's how we'll play it,' he agreed.

'You sure, Pee Wee?'

'Well, I ain't gettin' on no boat without you. What kind of man do you take me for?'

She smiled. 'The lovin' kind.'

'Same with you, hon. Same with you. Now put that light out and let's get some shuteye.'

When the light was out she gathered his head into the fullness of her ample bosom.

'Julius ain't goin' to take kindly to this,' Pee Wee murmured.

'You just leave him to me. I'll sort that out.'

She would too, Pee Wee thought dreamily. His Beulah could sort anything out.

God bless her.

A grim-faced Albert switched off the wireless to turn and stare at Jess whose expression was one of shock. 'So there we are,' he said. 'We're at war.'

Jess couldn't think of a suitable reply, so instead just shook her head.

They'd been listening to the Prime Minister, Mr Chamberlain, making the dreaded announcement. The formal declaration of war had been issued at 11 a.m. when Britain's ultimatum to Germany had expired. The Germans had not suspended hostilities in Poland and so Britain was at war with Hitler's Reich.

Albert felt sick inside. How many young men were going to be killed as a result of this madness? Legions of them, just like the last time when the flower of the nation's youth had been decimated.

'I need a drink,' Albert declared. 'Badly.'

Jess was thinking of Paul who was playing out in the street somewhere, and shuddered. Tears rolled down her cheeks.

'I'd hoped . . . I'd prayed . . .' She trailed off, overcome with emotion.

'There there, girl, we'll be all right. You'll see.' He wished he felt as confident as he was trying to sound.

'Oh, Albert!' she husked, and went to him. He wrapped his arms round her. 'When do you think it'll start?'

'I've no idea. That depends on all sorts of things I should imagine.'

They stood like that in silence for a little while, then Jess broke away to dab at her nose with the end of her pinny. 'I'll put the kettle on.'

'Not for me, pet. I'm going over to the pub. Want to come?'

'No, tea's fine. On you go then. Just don't be late for dinner. It's chicken.'

'I won't be late,' he assured her. 'Are you certain you don't mind me going out?'

Jess shook her head.

'You'll be all right?'

'Of course I will. Now stop fussing. And if you see Paul tell him I want him.'

Hazel, behind the bar, took one look at Albert's face. 'You've heard the news then?'

'On the wireless.'

He glanced around. People were sitting in small groups,

huddled together, as if for protection, and talking quietly. The atmosphere was funereal.

'So what are you having?'

'A large scotch and a pint of the usual.'

'It's terrible, don't you think?'

'Oh yes,' he agreed softly.

As Hazel moved off to get his order, Albert ran a hand over his face. Although he'd had a lie-in that morning, it being his weekend off, he felt bone weary. The PM's statement on the wireless had sapped the strength right out of him.

'Those are on the house,' Hazel declared, setting down his drinks. 'All the regulars get a free one this morning. Two in your case. Harry said it was the least we could do in the circumstances.'

'Thanks.'

Hazel lit a cigarette. 'I suppose we all knew it was coming. Nonetheless it was a shock when it actually did.'

Albert knew exactly what she meant.

'You'll be all right though,' she went on. 'Being a fireman I mean. You'll be exempt.

'We've got a couple of nephews, lovely lads, living in Coventry. Just the right age to join, or be called up,' she added. 'My sister will be beside herself. Poor mare. I feel so sorry for her.'

Albert smiled his sympathy, thinking of Paul whom he hadn't come across on his way over.

Harry appeared from out back. 'Some to-do, eh, Albert?'

'To be honest, it hasn't fully sunk in yet. But I suppose

it will soon enough. Thanks for the drinks by the way.'

'You're welcome.'

Harry sighed. 'Bloody Germans. I hate those bastards, I truly do. I hope they all fry in hell.' He shook his head. 'I feel I should be doing something, except I don't know what. I'm all at sixes and sevens.'

Albert was about to reply to that when an air-raid siren suddenly began wailing, causing everyone to look up in alarm.

'Oh my God!' Hazel exclaimed. 'They're bombing us already.'

As if by common consent the entire pub, including Harry and Hazel, made a beeline for the door. Once outside they all, some of the regulars still holding their pints, stared up at the sky. Residents from the houses round about were emerging to do the same.

'See anything?' someone asked.

Dozens of pairs of eyes were scanning the heavens, but there wasn't a single plane, German or otherwise, to be seen.

'Must be a false alarm,' a woman declared hopefully.

After about five minutes, during which nothing happened, people started drifting back to where they'd come from.

'That was scary,' Hazel said when she was again behind the bar.

Whereas the pub had been quiet before, now it was buzzing with excited conversation, everyone talking animatedly.

Albert saw off his scotch and ordered another, wishing

he could shake off the feeling of terrible dread and fore-boding that had taken hold of him.

Julius had simply never known a Sunday at the Embassy like it. The place, from top to bottom, was a veritable madhouse, every phone in the building seemingly ringing non-stop.

Being a Sunday, most of the staff had been off duty. Without being told they'd all returned to work knowing their presence would be required. The Ambassador was closeted in a meeting with his closest advisors.

'Want a coffee?' Shelby Robbins asked Julius, looking as harassed as Julius felt.

'Not at the moment.'

'OK.'

Shelby hurried from the office to the vending machine in the corridor where he found a queue.

Marybeth came into the room. 'How're you doin'?'

'Same as everyone else. Up to my ass in it.'

She laughed. 'Me too. Ever since I got here I been runnin' around like a headless chicken.'

'So what can I do for you?'

'I was thinkin', why don't you come by tonight? I'll fix us a little somethin' to eat and you can stay over if you want.'

Julius considered that. 'I'm tempted, Marybeth. But I really should get back to my folks. It's not every day a war's declared after all. Mom especially will want me there.'

Marybeth shrugged. 'I understand. It was only a thought.'

'Maybe tomorrow night, huh?'

'Yeah, sure.'

She smiled weakly at him, then abruptly left, hurrying, as everyone in the building appeared to be doing, on her way.

He could always return home first and then go on to Marybeth's, Julius reflected. That would be OK. As long as he saw and spent some time with his mom and pop.

In the event it was after ten when he finally arrived at Florence Street, which ruled that right out of the question.

Ellie didn't know whether to laugh or cry at what George had just told her. 'But what about our engagement?' she protested.

'We'll still be engaged. That won't change.'

'But you . . . you won't be here for most of the time. You'll be at sea. And why the Merchant Navy anyway?'

'Listen,' Jess interjected, who was in the kitchen with them. 'I'll leave the pair of you to it. I've got things to do upstairs.'

George turned pleading eyes to her. '*You* understand, Mrs Sykes, don't you?'

She sighed. 'I suppose so, George, if that's any consolation. There are going to be an awful lot of young men go off before long. That's as inevitable as day following night. It's war for you.'

'So, why the Merchant Navy?' Ellie demanded again when her mother had gone, her thoughts in turmoil. This had come like a bolt from the blue. And a most unwelcome bolt at that.

'If I wait to be conscripted it'll be the Army, Ellie, and I don't want that. If I have to do something, and I will, then my preference is the Merchant Navy. I'm an engineer by trade after all, they'll be crying out for chaps like me. And the way I see it, life with them will be a lot easier than with the Royal Navy. I'd hate all that rigid discipline, it goes totally against the grain.'

Despite herself, Ellie could see the sense in that. It was just so soon after war being declared. It could have been months yet if he'd waited for conscription.

George took her into his arms. 'I'm going to miss you like buggery, Ellie.'

'I'll miss you too,' she husked in reply.

'It won't be so bad. You'll see.'

She wished she could believe that, but couldn't. 'When do you leave?' she asked.

'I don't know. As soon as I've signed the necessary papers I presume. Certainly not long afterwards.'

Her mind, which had been in turmoil, had now gone numb. Within the space of a few short minutes her world had been turned on its head.

'I'll write whenever I get the chance,' he promised.

'Me too.' She took a deep breath. 'Have you spoken to your parents about this?'

'Not yet. I wanted you to be the first to know.'

She appreciated that. For some reason it meant an awful lot to her.

'Can you stay for a bit? Have a cup of tea?'

'Of course. But not too long. The parents, I want to get that over and done with.'

'Right then.'

There were tears in her eyes as she filled the kettle.

'This is a right pain in the ass,' Beulah complained to Jess who'd come round to help her put up the black-out curtains which every house had now been ordered to have at every window.

Jess slipped another hook into place. The curtains were crude affairs hastily run up from cheap, but heavy, material currently being sold in a number of the local shops. 'We may be thankful for them before long,' she replied.

Beulah paused to stare fearfully at Jess, knowing that she meant should bombing start, as everyone believed it soon would. 'Did I tell you that Julius wanted Pee Wee and myself to go back to the States?' she said.

Jess glanced at her friend. 'Seems good advice to me. This isn't your war after all.'

Beulah's expression became one of defiance. 'I ain't leavin' my baby behind. No sirree! I ain't doin' that. He says he has to stay, and as I's here with him then I stays too.'

Jess nodded that she understood, thinking of Ellie and Paul. If she'd been in Beulah's position she'd have done the same. Black or white, she further reflected, colour didn't matter when it came to your family. The same bond was there irregardless.

'I wonder how long it will be before they introduce rationing?' she mused.

139

'They likely to do so?'

'It's almost certain. Don't forget we're an island, Beulah. A great deal of what we use has to be imported by sea. That's bound to be disrupted which will lead to inevitable rationing.'

'I never thought of that,' Beulah frowned. 'I'm used to the States where we grow, or manufacture, everythin' we want or need.'

'Well, we're not so lucky I'm afraid. And if rationing does come in then it's going to make life a lot more difficult. Belts will have to be tightened all round.'

Beulah completed her section of curtain and heaved herself down off the chair she'd been standing on. 'I doubt it'll affect us too much, Julius will see to that. They ain't goin' to be sinkin' no American ships comin' in, that's for sure. We'll get what we need through the Embassy.'

'Lucky you,' Jess muttered, though not unkindly.

A huge smile lit up Beulah's face. 'Don't you fret none, Jess, I'll make sure some of what we gets comes to you. That's what friends are for, ain't it?'

Jess smiled her gratitude. 'You're very kind, Beulah. But if you take my advice don't tell anyone else about you getting supplies from the Embassy. It could easily lead to a lot of bad feeling. And you don't want that.'

'I hears you, lady. I hears you loud and clear.'

Jess hoped she had. And wouldn't forget.

Chapter 9

Connie Fox hastily lit a cigarette and took a deep drag. 'Christ! I needed that,' she exhaled. 'Miss Oates, the bitch, has been getting at me all bloody morning. If I thought I'd get away with it I'd strangle her.' Then, as an afterthought, 'Very slowly so I could watch her eyes pop.'

'You don't really mean that,' admonished Agnes Short, who was with Connie and Ellie in the toilet having their tea break, that being where they had to have it.

'I damn well do,' Connie hissed. 'The woman's a menace. And to pick on me today of all days too.'

Ellie frowned. 'What's different about today?'

Connie had another puff on her cigarette, her expression showing she was thoroughly relishing it. 'My chap told me last night he'd had his conscription papers. He's to report in next Monday.'

'Oh, Connie,' Ellie sympathised.

Agnes Short sniffed. She was a plain girl who'd never had a single boyfriend in her entire nineteen years. She couldn't help but be jealous of Connie, even if Connie's lad was off to the war.

'It's a sod, isn't it?' Connie said.

Ellie thought of George who'd been gone a fortnight now. True to his word he'd written, twice. And then the letters had stopped as he'd gone to sea. 'Don't I know it.'

'Of course!' Connie exclaimed softly. 'Your George. I'd forgotten. You've been through the same thing.'

'Excuse me,' muttered Agnes, and vanished into a cubicle.

Connie finished her tea and rinsed her cup at the sink. 'We're going to be like a couple of old maids, you and I,' she commented.

Agnes, on hearing that, felt terrible. She was convinced that was to be her fate in life. An old maid like Miss Oates.

'Can I try one of your fags?'

Connie stared at Ellie in surprise. 'But you don't smoke?'

'And I've never tried. I'd like to now though.'

Connie produced a packet of Players and offered it to Ellie. 'What's brought this on?'

Ellie thought about that. 'I suppose I'm so fed up with everything. At least trying a cigarette is different and exciting.'

Ellie put the cigarette between her lips, then bent towards the match Connie had struck. Next moment she was furiously coughing.

Connie laughed. 'That happened to me first time too. You just have to persevere. You soon get used to it.'

'Dear God,' Ellie gasped when she at last managed to catch her breath. 'You actually enjoy that? It's terrible.'

'As I said, you have to persevere. Then you get to like it.'

Ellie took a second, tentative draw, and this time she didn't cough or choke.

'It rather suits you,' Connie pronounced.

'What, smoking?'

'Having a cigarette in your hand. Makes you look very sophisticated.'

Sophisticated? Ellie hardly thought of herself as that. She began to warm to the idea of being a smoker.

A toilet flushed and Agnes emerged from the cubicle. 'That's a mug's game,' she commented, nodding at Ellie's cigarette.

'Sez you,' a sarcastic Connie replied.

'You wouldn't get me spending my hard-earned money on fags,' Agnes declared, starting to wash her hands.

'I don't suppose you drink either,' Connie retorted cuttingly.

'Occasionally. But not often.'

'And I'll bet you it's sherry too.'

An amused Ellie watched this exchange, thinking it served Agnes right for being so judgemental.

Agnes blushed, for the sherry jibe was true. 'Excuse me, it's time to get back to work.' With that she brushed past Connie and Ellie and out of the toilet.

'Can't bear her, the sanctimonious cow,' Connie declared disapprovingly. 'If she'd been a Catholic she'd have ended up a nun. You know? None of this, and none of that. And none of the other either.'

Both girls laughed, Ellie thinking that very funny. None of the other! As if any of them did that.

'She's right about the time though,' Connie went on.

'Have another drag then nip it for later.'

Ellie had the drag, this one leaving her slightly light-headed which wasn't an entirely unpleasant sensation.

'Here, I'll do it for you,' Connie said and, taking the cigarette from Ellie, nipped the end off into the sink where she flicked it down the plughole.

'Put that in your pocket,' she instructed, handing back the remainder.

Miss Oates was watching the clock when they returned to their desks, but couldn't say anything as they were dead on time, having had their allotted fifteen minutes almost to the second.

Albert arrived home in a particularly good humour for it had been one of those rare shifts when there hadn't been a single call-out. His good humour vanished the moment he saw Jess's anguished expression. 'What's wrong?' he demanded.

Without replying she came over and handed him a letter, Paul standing by the sideboard watching this inter-play.

Albert began to read the letter which was from the school and it soon became apparent why Jess was in such a state. The school was closing and the pupils were being evacuated into the country.

'I'm not going,' Paul declared stubbornly, having already been through this a number of times with his mother. 'I'm staying here. I'm just not going.'

'Albert?' Jess's eyes were wide and staring.

'It would be for his own good, Jess. Who knows what

it'll be like round here when the bombing starts, as it's bound to sooner or later.'

Jess stumbled to her chair and sank into it. 'I couldn't bear being parted from him, Albert. Please say he can't go.'

Christ, Albert thought. This was difficult. He didn't want Paul to be evacuated either.

'We must think of the boy, Jess. It's his welfare that's at stake. If something happened we'd never forgive ourselves for keeping him behind.'

Jess sobbed and dropped her face into her hands, her chest and shoulders heaving.

'You can't make me go,' a thoroughly frightened Paul declared in a quavering voice.

'I'm your father and you'll do as I say,' Albert told him sternly.

Paul ran to Jess and threw his arms round her. By now he too was crying.

Albert crossed to the mantelpiece and leant against it. This, although it hadn't been mentioned between them, wasn't entirely unexpected. Children were being evacuated from all over London. Now it appeared to be St Margaret's turn, Paul's school.

Jess wrapped Paul against her bosom, hugging him for dear life. The thought of him being sent off somewhere to live amongst strangers was total anathema to her. Unthinkable.

Albert could only watch helplessly, feeling utterly wretched. What on earth was he to do?

* * *

Jess shrugged into her dark green candlewick dressing gown and sat on the end of their bed. It had taken her hours to get an almost hysterical Paul off to sleep.

'Am I wrong about this?'

Albert stopped undressing to stare at her, noting yet again her red-rimmed eyes. He sighed. 'Yes, I think you are. I'm not saying it's an easy decision to take, far from it, but one, in my opinion, that has to be. As I said earlier, it's for his own good, Jess. We have to put the lad's safety first and foremost.'

That was the last thing she wanted to hear. Yet, in her heart of hearts, she knew Albert to be right.

'We both love him, Jess,' Albert went on softly. 'And that's why he has to go. Not easy for any of us, I admit. In fact downright bloody difficult. But there we are.'

Jess stayed silent, trying to get her mind to think straight through all the emotion that was churning inside her.

'Why don't I speak to him tomorrow night? Try and make him see sense. Just he and I, the pair of us. A man to man so to speak. How about that, eh?'

'He'd be with strangers, Albert. What if they're not very nice?'

'I'm sure whoever he gets boarded with will be. And, after a few weeks for him to settle in, you can go and visit to make certain everything's all right.'

Jess brightened at the prospect of that, realising she was coming to accept the situation. 'What will you say to him?'

'Explain the good points, that it isn't the end of the world. That in actual fact it's probably going to be a huge adventure which he'll thoroughly enjoy.' Albert laughed. 'And let's hope it's not too enjoyable an adventure or he might not want to come home again when the time comes.'

He went to Jess and took a hand in his, squeezing it reassuringly. 'Leave it to me. Agreed?'

She looked up into his face, loving every inch of him, appreciative of how good a man he was and how lucky she was to have him. 'Agreed.'

'I thought you only worked here Friday and Saturday nights?' Julius queried of Ellie who was behind the bar at The Florence.

'Hazel's down with the flu and Harry asked me to do some extra shifts to help out,' Ellie explained.

'There's a lot of flu about,' Julius replied. Shelby Robbins at the Embassy was one of the number off with it.

'So what can I get you?'

'A pint of best.'

'Coming right up.'

It was funny, she reflected as she pulled the pump. She was beginning not to even notice that Julius was black. Well, of course he was, that was obvious. But now she was beginning to see him as just a man and not a black man.

'Quiet tonight,' Julius commented, making conversation.

'I prefer it busy. Time passes more quickly that way.

'There you are,' she declared, putting his pint in front of him. 'That's ten pence ha' penny.'

He slid a shilling across the bar. 'You know, even after all this while I still have trouble with English money. It's so complicated! Give me good old dollars and cents any day.'

She rang the ten pence ha' penny up on the till. 'I suppose it must be difficult for a foreigner. I hadn't really thought of that.'

'Threepennies, sixpennies, florins, half-crowns, farthings, ha' pennies . . .' He trailed off and shook his head. 'It just goes on and on. You almost need a college degree to understand it all.'

That amused her. 'Did you go to college?'

'Sure. University of Wisconsin, that's in the mid-west. Milwaukee is the town. Famous for making beer and steel. Schlitz! The beer that made Milwaukee famous, as their ads go. Then there's Pabst, Blatz, Miller, all good beers.' He corrected himself. 'Or I should say, lagers. That's what you call that type of beer over here.'

Ellie was fascinated. 'Why didn't you go to college in New York?'

A cynical smile twitched his lips upwards. 'How shall I put this? A lot of colleges in the east, the good ones anyway, don't accommodate coloured folk – unless you're an outstandin' football or basketball player that is. Then they make exceptions. But I wasn't particularly talented at either, so I went where they'd have me.'

Ellie thought that awful. 'Did you have to pay for college?'

'Sure did. Doesn't come free. At nights I worked in a big food store called A&P. Sometimes I stacked shelves, other times I packed sacks at the check-outs.'

'What's a sack and a check-out?' Ellie frowned.

'A sack is what you'd call a paper bag, the sort you put your groceries into. And a check-out is where you take your cart – you'd call it a trolley – to pay.'

Ellie couldn't imagine a trolley in a food shop. How bizarre! It was all beyond her. Sounded fascinating though. There again, she reminded herself, if she went to America wouldn't she find it just as bewildering as an American coming to England.

'That paid for my college, my keep and to run my car,' he further explained.

'You had a car even as a student?' She was astounded.

'Needed it to get around. Nothin' fancy, mind you, an old jalop Chevy. But it did me.'

Jalop and Chevy? He'd lost her again. It was a different language. 'Does everyone there have a car?'

Julius shook his head. 'Nearly everyone, except the very poor. And before you ask, yes we do have poor in the States same as everywhere else. It isn't quite the land of milk and honey that you English think. Though it's still God's own country, and ain't that the truth.'

'You must miss it?'

He smiled at her, showing off his perfect white teeth. 'Like crazy sometimes. But that's just how the cookie crumbles. I chose my job and have no regrets.'

He produced a packet of cigarettes and lit up.

'Can I have one of those?'

That surprised him. 'I've never seen you smoke?'

'I only started recently. And those look fun.' She took

the unfamiliar, soft pack which he'd placed on the bar, looking at one side, then the other. 'These are American I presume?'

'As apple pie, babe. Help yourself.'

The taste was different to English cigarettes. A sort of toasted flavour, she decided.

'What do you think?' he asked.

'They're nice. I think I prefer them to the English variety.'

That pleased him. 'Tell you what, why don't I get you a carton?'

'A carton?' What was that?

'Yeah, ten packs. Two hundred.'

Ellie gulped. 'I couldn't possibly afford so many. But it's kind of you to offer.'

He waved a dismissive hand. 'I wasn't meanin' for you to pay. A gift, from me to you.'

'I couldn't possibly, Julius. It would be far too expensive.'

'I get them through the Embassy, Ellie. Believe me, the cost is peanuts. So what do you say?'

What else could she say? 'Thank you very much.'

'It's a deal then. I'll pick them up tomorrow and drop them by your house.' He had a thought. 'Are you in the pub again tomorrow night?'

She nodded.

'Then I'll bring them here. A good excuse to have another beer, eh?'

What a lovely smile he had, she reflected. Quite a bobby dazzler. 'It's a deal, to use your words.'

Julius hadn't meant to stop long, but in fact stayed well over an hour chatting to Ellie, The Florence remaining quiet.

Ellie was on her way home for dinner when she halted, her attention caught by a poster. It was an appeal on behalf of the London Auxiliary Ambulance Service who wanted new members, full training given.

The germ of an idea was born in her mind, something she'd have to give a lot of thought to. Ambulances and crew were going to be desperately needed once the bombing started, which had to be a far more exciting, and worthwhile, job than she now had.

She rather fancied the idea of whizzing round the streets in an ambulance with its bell clanging. Now that would be exhilarating! Doing her bit, as people were now calling service to their country in any form of war effort.

As she walked away she wondered what the uniform was like.

'So what do your pals at school think about this evacuation?' Albert queried off-handedly. Jess had left them only minutes before, saying she was popping round to see Beulah. He knew she wouldn't be back for at least an hour.

A sullen-faced Paul shrugged.

'It must have been mentioned?' Albert tried again.

Paul muttered something inaudible.

'It's terrible getting old,' Albert joked. 'I'm going deaf.'

Paul shot his father a withering look, having realised

during the meal that something was up. Now he knew what. Albert was going to have one of his 'little talks'. 'None of them want to go.'

'None at all?'

Paul shrugged again.

This was going to be tough going, Albert thought. But then he'd expected as much. 'I find that odd.'

'Well, speccy Watson is keen, but he's strange.'

Albert hid his smile. 'How is he strange?'

'He swots.'

'Oh!' Well, that explained it then. A lad, in Paul's book anyway, who swotted had to be strange. If not from another planet altogether.

'Pity, the others are going to miss all the fun.'

Paul showed a flicker of interest. 'What fun?'

'Bound to be lots of that. A bunch of pals away from their parents, out in the country where things are so different. I have to say, if I'd still been at school I'd have jumped at the chance to live in the country for a while.'

Paul frowned. 'Why?'

'All the animals for a start. You don't see many cows, sheep and saddle horses in Islington, do you now?'

'Saddle horses,' he repeated slowly. 'You mean like cowboys and indians have. That sort?'

'Oh yes. Folk in the country ride, as well you know. They dress up in red coats and go chasing foxes all over the place. It's called a hunt.'

Paul tried to imagine that. 'Many people?'

'Dozens and dozens, I believe. Riding over fields, jumping hedges, wading streams. That's what they do sometimes.'

Paul's attention had now been well and truly caught. 'What happens to the foxes when they get them?'

'The dogs kill the fox. Hounds they're known as. A great pack of them, and when they finally catch the poor beast they rip it to shreds with their teeth. Then the head hunts-man cuts off its tail.'

'Cuts off its tail?'

'As a trophy. So I read anyway. They say the chase, all those horses, people and hounds in full flight, is a sight to behold.'

Doubt entered Paul's mind; it seemed too good to be true. 'Are you telling fibs, Dad?'

Albert made a sign across his chest. 'Cross my heart and hope to die, every word is the gospel.'

Paul imagined himself, wielding a large knife, cutting off a fox's tail. That appealed.

Albert could see he was getting through to the lad. 'Then there are the trees and woods where you can go exploring. You could play Robin Hood there.'

'We've got trees in Islington,' Paul replied stoutly.

'So we have, but not many. I'm talking about an entire wood full. Hundreds and hundreds of them, all sorts, shapes and sizes. Trees where you could tie a rope and make a swing for example. And no one to tell you off either. Nobody else in sight at all, just you and your pals getting up to whatever.'

Albert paused, thinking he was beginning to enjoy this. Paul was certainly starting to show enthusiasm. 'Then there are the streams and ponds where you can go swim-ming,' he went on. 'When the weather's good of course.

Just strip off and in you go. Just like Tarzan, only there won't be any crocodiles to worry about.'

'Could we fish there?' Paul asked eagerly.

'Probably. I don't see why not. Unless it's private and then you'd need permission.' He suddenly had a brain-wave, recalling an old fishing rod in a local pawnbroker's. The damn thing had to be dirt cheap as it had been in the window for years.

'And I know where I can lay my hands on a rod too,' he declared enticingly.

'You do?'

'Not that you'll need one as you aren't going. But if you were I could always get it for you. That would make you popular with the other lads. Make them jealous too.'

Paul had really enjoyed the time he'd gone fishing with a pal and his dad. A country stream or pond would be far better than the dirty old canal any day. His mouth almost watered at the prospect.

Albert decided to play his trump card. 'The food in the country is absolutely wonderful. Home-made butter and jam, milk straight from the cow. Enormous break-fasts, huge joints at the weekend. Stacks and stacks of grub, as much as any grown man can eat at any meal. Those people in the country certainly know how to live. Why, if you want a fresh egg you simply go out and pick one up, probably newly laid only moments before. The taste of those is unbelievable.'

Although he'd just had tea, Paul's stomach rumbled. What his dad was describing was sheer heaven.

'While country folk are gorging themselves at every

opportunity we townies are going to be having it hard. It's only a matter of time, weeks possibly, before rationing is declared. We're all going to have to pull our belts in then all right.'

He glanced sideways at Paul hanging on his every word. 'Naturally rationing won't apply in the country. Well, stands to reason when you think about it, they grow and produce the stuff right there. It's all on their doorstep so to speak.'

He shook his head. 'No, they won't be going short, lucky sods.'

Paul's stomach rumbled again, louder than before.

Albert knew then he had him. In fishing terms, hook, line and sinker.

'Another couple of waffles, Pee Wee? Plenty of batter left.'

'I's full, Beulah, and that's the truth. I couldn't manage another mouthful.' He leant back in his chair and stared at her. 'Three of the guys in the band announced last night that they're goin' home. Say they don't want no part of no war.'

'Who are they?'

Pee Wee told her.

'So what happens now?'

'We spoke to Lord Fitzaran who naturally was disappointed, but wants to continue on with the three of us remainin'. If we agree, that is.'

'And did you?'

Pee Wee nodded. 'It won't be the same without those guys, all we'll have left is a trio. But we'll be OK.'

Beulah dropped her gaze, knowing Pee Wee was only staying because of her. No doubt the other two who'd also agreed to stay had their reasons.

'Thanks, honey,' she said softly.

Pee Wee took a deep breath. 'Now how about another cup of coffee? I could sure use me one.'

Beulah came to her feet and hurried over to the pot.

'Let's have a look at you,' Jess said. She and Paul were in Paddington Station where they'd joined the others from St Margaret's waiting to be evacuated. There were hundreds of children and parents milling about, from a number of schools, all for the same reason.

She straightened his tie, which didn't need straightening, fighting back the tears that threatened to engulf her. With his best raincoat, schoolclothes and cap, he looked very smart indeed, she thought. Well turned out. His small suitcase was by his side.

'Hello, Eddy!' Paul called out, and waved. Eddy was in his class.

'Now you'll remember to write as soon as you can,' she reminded him. 'Everything you need for that, including stamps, are in your case.'

'I won't forget, Ma,' he replied wearily, wishing she'd stop making such a fuss. Honestly, you'd think he was still a baby!

Jess grabbed the sleeve of one of the teachers walking by. 'Do you know where they're going yet, Mr Bailey?' she queried.

He shook his head. 'Nothing definite. Only that it's

supposedly in the West Country. That's all I can tell you.'

Jess's face clearly reflected her disappointment. It was bad enough that Paul was going off, but to not even know where!

'They're starting to board now,' Mr Bailey declared. 'You'd better get Paul in line.'

She wouldn't cry, she told herself. She mustn't. Not until he'd gone.

Paul could see her distress. 'I'll be all right, Ma. You mustn't worry.'

'I'll try not to, son,' she promised, knowing full well she would, like buggery.

He protested when she suddenly hugged him to her. 'Watch my fishing rod, Ma. You might break it!' He held the rod he was clutching, his pride and joy, slightly away from her. He was also mortified at being publicly hugged. How embarrassing!

Jess released him. 'Let's get you into line then.'

It was another twenty minutes before Paul was safely aboard, and the last door banged shut. The platform was crowded with parents, mainly women. A sort of collective groan went up as the guard blew his whistle and waved his green flag. Jess could just make Paul out at the far end of the carriage he was in.

The train creaked and clanked, then began to move, a long brown serpent snaking its way out of the station.

'Oh Paul!' Jess sobbed, voice clogged with emotion.

Finally, at long last, she allowed the tears to come.

157

Chapter 10

'God, I hate this black-out!' Ellie complained. 'It doesn't half make life difficult.' She glanced at Connie Fox walking alongside, the pair of them having just completed their day's work and now on their way home. Connie didn't reply or comment.

Ellie frowned. 'What's wrong with you today? You've hardly said a word and you've been going round like you'd lost a pound and found sixpence.'

'I've got a lot on my mind.'

'Oh?'

Connie came up short to stare at her friend. 'Can you keep a secret?'

'Of course.'

'No, I really mean it. If I say what's bothering me then you must swear not to tell another soul.'

Ellie was intrigued. 'I promise, Connie. I swear.'

Connie took a deep breath. 'I think I'm in the pudding club.'

Ellie's hand flew to her mouth. This was terrible! Worse, a catastrophe. 'How?'

Connie gave a cynical laugh. 'How the hell do you think? The usual way. I let Barry do it the night before he had to report to the Army.' Barry was the name of her chap.

'Oh Connie,' Ellie sympathised.

'Just my bloody luck to be caught out. The only time I've ever gone all the way too. My parents are going to kill me.'

Ellie had no doubts about that. The shame this would bring on the family. The humiliation! Not to mention the stain on Connie's character. 'Didn't you use a . . . well, froggy?'

Connie nodded. 'That's the joke. I insisted, wouldn't have done it otherwise. But the damn thing came off. We didn't realise until it was over and then I found it by fishing around inside.'

How horrible, Ellie thought. And disgusting too. She hoped Connie hadn't done that in front of this Barry. But she didn't ask.

'Talk about a pantomime,' Connie went on bitterly. 'Farce more like. Barry kept saying afterwards everything would be all right, that the chances of anything happening were one in a million. Well, he was wrong. Couldn't have been more so.'

Ellie shivered, for it was a freezing December evening. 'Let's walk on,' she said.

They continued for a little way in silence. 'How . . . how far gone are you?'

'Only the month.'

'Then perhaps your period is just late?'

Connie shook her head. 'If it is it's the first time ever. I'm regular as clockwork. Always have been. So there's very little likelihood I'm late or skipped a month. I'm up the duff, have to be.'

Ellie wished she could think of something constructive to say, but couldn't. 'So what are you going to do?'

'Write to Barry I suppose. Maybe he'll get compassionate leave and we can get married. If he does the right thing by me, that is.'

Ellie doubted the Army would let him away so soon, no matter what the reason. In peacetime yes, but not with a war on. There again, if there hadn't been a war on he wouldn't have been conscripted in the first place, and this wouldn't have happened.

'Failing that,' Connie continued, 'there is a woman I've heard of over the Caledonian Road way who helps girls like me. Gets them out of their spot of bother.'

Ellie abruptly halted, utterly appalled. 'Surely you wouldn't do that, go to an abortionist? That's . . .' She swallowed hard. 'That's murder. And downright dangerous as far as you're concerned.'

Connie sighed. 'I wish I could think straight. One moment I'm thinking this, the next that. I'm so confused.'

Ellie took Connie's hand in hers. 'Just promise me you won't go to an abortionist, please?'

Connie stared her friend straight in the eyes. 'It isn't you who's pregnant, so you can't ask that.'

'I'm only thinking of you.'

'So am I,' Connie replied softly. 'So am I.'

What a mess, Ellie thought. Thank God she hadn't been tempted before George went off. If she had she might have ended up in the same predicament.

They arrived at the spot where they always parted. 'I'll keep your secret, Connie. It's safe with me.'

'Thanks. I know that.'

Ellie hesitated. 'There is something . . .' She trailed off.

'What?'

'I've . . .' Thankfully it was dark, she thought, for her face was flaming. 'I've always wondered. What was it like?'

Connie laughed. 'A disappointment really.'

Ellie frowned. 'In what way?'

'It was all over so quickly. Hardly any time at all. I thought it was supposed to last a while, but not in our case. We'd hardly started before it was finished. I was disappointed all right.'

'Did you . . . did it feel good?'

'What there was of it. Quite pleasant actually. But not the huge experience I always thought it would be. I felt terribly let down afterwards. If that's all there is to it then it's awfully overrated in my opinion.'

Ellie was fascinated, but didn't feel she could continue the conversation any further. Perhaps another time. She wanted to learn more about the great mystery.

'Write to Barry tonight,' she advised. 'That's what I would do. The sooner he knows about this the sooner he can maybe do something about it.'

'I'll do that,' Connie nodded. 'And listen, thanks for being a pal.'

'Anything I can do, you only have to ask.'

Connie appreciated that, fear flickering again inside her that if the worst came to the worst she might have to tell her parents without having Barry to stand by her. She offered up a silent prayer he would.

It was when she was walking down Florence Street that it dawned on Ellie that the word love had never been mentioned. Not once.

She found that incredibly sad.

Mrs Selly laid down a cup of tea on Paul's bedside table, then lit the candle standing there. 'Paul! Paul!' she said, shaking him by the shoulder.

'Don't want to get up,' he moaned. 'Still tired.'

'It's four thirty, Paul. Time to be up and doing. There's jobs to be done before school.'

He came groggily awake to gaze up at the middle-aged woman hovering over him. In the few short weeks he'd been there he'd come to hate life in High Barton. 'It's freezing,' he complained.

'Don't be so soft, lad. Get thae clothes on and come downstairs for first breakfast. There's a good lad.' And with that Mrs Selly left the room.

Four thirty in the morning! he thought in despair. He'd never been up at that time in his life before arriving at the farm. Now it was every morning, seven days a week.

He couldn't say the Sellys were cruel, they merely expected him to fit in with things. To help with the chores as their own son would have done, if they'd had one. To them, what he was expected to do was quite normal.

Cows first, milk those along with Mr Selly. Then feed the pigs, hens after that. On and on till it was time for second breakfast after which he had to trudge the two miles to school.

On arriving back again he'd have to work till supper. Even when that was over there would be no respite. There was always something to do, some job to be done.

How he wished he'd never left Florence Street. His dad had been right about the food, there was plenty of that, lashings of it. But so far that was the only thing his dad had been right about.

·'Are you up, lad?' Mrs Selly called from downstairs.

Gritting his teeth, Paul swung out of bed and literally threw on his clothes, as fast as he possibly could. Thankfully the wood stove would be burning in the kitchen, he'd soon get warm in front of that.

A warmth that wouldn't last long, only until he had to leave the house.

'Son of a bitch!' Julius yelped. 'That's painful.'

Marybeth treated him to one of her catlike smiles. 'It's meant to be.'

He put a hand to his back which came away streaked with red. 'You've drawn blood.'

She pretended innocence. 'Have I?'

'You goddamn well have. As you intended.'

Marybeth laughed and lay back on the bed from where she studied him. 'I thought you might enjoy it,' she purred.

'Well, I didn't.' His face screwed up in a grimace; what she'd done had really hurt. And still did.

Marybeth's nostrils dilated and her breath started

coming in short, sharp pants. Slowly, provocatively, she opened her legs. 'I'm ready for you now, hon. Real ready.'

Julius stared at Marybeth, aware of blood running down his back. This was a side of her he'd never seen before, and not one he was certain he liked.

He decided a few words were in order.

Ellie stopped beside Connie's desk. 'Heard anything yet?' she asked in a whisper, not wanting to be overheard.

Connie shook her head.

'And are you still . . . ?' She trailed off, not completing the sentence.

Connie nodded.

Ellie made a sympathetic face, and continued on to her own desk. It was early days, she reminded herself. Barry's reply was probably even now in the post.

She hadn't failed to notice how haunted and fearful Connie's eyes were.

'I very nearly fell asleep in class,' Eddy Ackworth, Paul's schoolchum, confided in him. Like Paul, Eddy had been billeted on a farm, the only difference being that his farm was closer to the village of Talyton, where the school was located, than Paul's, which meant he didn't have to walk so far there and back again.

The St Margaret's pupils were being taught in the village hall, the tiny Talyton school just not being large enough to accommodate the evacuees, so they were separated from the village children, none of whom impressed the Islingtonians one little bit.

Paul yawned. 'Me too. I'll never get used to being here. Never.'

Eddy morosely stuck his hands into his trousers' pockets. 'If I knew how I'd do a bunk home.'

Paul had also thought of that. 'It's too far, Eddy. We'd have to get to Clyst Binkleigh first to catch a train, and that's over ten miles away. And if we did get there what would we use for the train fare? I don't have any money. Have you?'

'Not a sausage.'

'Well then. We're stuck here and there's nothing we can do about it.'

Eddy's shoulders slumped. 'They say this war could last for years. Years and years.'

'I know,' Paul replied, wishing with all his heart he'd never been talked into coming here.

'I'm not sure I can stand that. It's not only the work, it's the smell. Everything round the farm stinks.'

Paul nodded his agreement. Animal muck everywhere it seemed to him, and no way of getting away from it. If he'd known the word he'd have said it hung over the Sellys' farm like a miasma.

'And I never get out to play any more,' Eddy went on miserably. 'Even if I did there's no one to play with.'

Paul reflected it was exactly the same with him. He couldn't remember the last time he had any fun.

'Have you been able to use that fishing rod of yours yet?' Eddy queried. He'd thought it smashing when he'd first seen it and had made Paul promise to let him have a go of it sometime. Fat chance of that now.

Paul shook his head. 'And I don't think I ever will. It was a waste of time bringing it with me.'

Their conversation was cut short by the handbell being rung for their return to class.

Both boys slouched hang-doggedly back into the hall.

'Something's wrong, I just know it,' Jess declared to Albert who'd just arrived in off the night shift. She brandished the latest letter from Paul. 'He's not saying there is, but I know better. Call it a mother's intuition if you like.'

Albert sighed. It had been a long, hard night centred round a major call-out in a local mattress manufacturers. Beside anything else, he had a splitting headache thanks to some smoke inhalation.

Albert sat at the table. 'Let me see it.'

Jess handed him the letter then busied herself with his breakfast, fried egg with bread and dripping.

Albert had to screw up his eyes, thanks to the headache, in order to focus. It certainly wasn't a long letter, no more than a dozen lines. He read it through, shaking his head as he laid it aside. 'He seems fine to me.'

'It's what he's not saying that's worrying. As if he's holding something back. I know Paul, I should do, I'm his mother after all. The boy's not happy.'

'He's just taking a while to settle in, that's all,' Albert argued. 'It can't be easy.'

Jess snorted. 'There's more to it than that.'

Could she be right? he wondered. He had a lot of respect for his wife's judgement, it didn't often let her down. But in this particular instance he suspected she was simply being over-protective.

Ellie gazed about the pub, thinking how quiet it was for Christmas Eve. The previous year it had been positively heaving by this time.

'Are you thinking what I'm thinking?'

She turned to find Hazel beside her. 'How quiet it is?'

Hazel nodded. 'There again, it is the first Christmas of the war, people might not be feeling like celebrating. And don't forget, an awful lot of young men are away who were here last year. Including your George. How is he by the way?'

'Fine. I had a letter from Canada, a place called Halifax. He's enjoying himself apparently, though keen to get home again.'

'Any news of that?'

'No. Nothing. He had no idea.'

'But he's safe, that's the main thing,' Hazel pointed out.

Ellie rubbed her hand. She'd developed a rash around her fingers which could itch terribly. She'd been to the doctor who'd given her some cream for it.

'We might get busy later,' Hazel said hopefully. 'Are your parents coming in?'

Ellie shook her head. 'Dad's working. But he will have New Year off. They'll definitely be in then.'

Hazel glanced over at the decorations – paper rings and paper bells, the latter hanging from the lights. The tree had all sorts of sparkly bits on it while little balls of cotton wool represented snow. Even the decorations seemed lacklustre this year, she thought. As if they too were aware there was a war on.

'Give me a shout if we get a sudden rush,' she declared, and left Ellie to it.

What a miserable Christmas Eve, Ellie reflected as she got ready for bed. Business had been steady later on, but no more than that. There certainly hadn't been any fizz about the occasion. Harry had pronounced the evening a flop when they'd been having their staff drink afterwards.

Ellie picked up and examined the small bottle of scent that Harry and Hazel had given her as a present. How kind that had been of them, she thought, as she unscrewed the top. It smelt gorgeous, reminding her of a garden in summer. She dabbed a little behind her ears and then on a few other pulse points.

She'd half expected Julius to have popped in. If only for a quickie, but he hadn't appeared. He must have gone to a party or function, she decided. Oh well, he may drop by next day. As could Beulah and Pee Wee, the pair of them having been to his club in Soho that night.

Dad would be at work Christmas Day, but she might suggest to Jess that she come on over with the Postons. That might cheer her up a bit. Jess had been somewhat down since Paul went off. She herself would be behind the bar.

A few moments later she froze in horror on realising that her engagement ring was missing from her finger.

'Stupid mare!' she berated herself, knowing full well what had happened. Because of the rash she'd taken it off later in the session while washing up, and clearly forgotten to put it back on again.

A quick glance at her bedside clock confirmed that it was too late to return to the pub. Harry and Hazel would be in bed by now. Anyway, even if they weren't they were hardly likely to answer a knock at this time of the morning on the presumption it was some drunk wanting another drink.

Ellie took a deep breath and told herself not to panic. The ring was bound to be where she'd left it, and would still be there at opening time. She'd get it back then.

The last thing she did before getting into bed was to put some more cream on her hands to soothe the irritating itching.

'It was there, right there,' Ellie declared, pointing to a corner of the draining board. Only it wasn't any more.

'Well, I never picked it up,' Hazel replied. 'But perhaps Harry did, though he never mentioned it which I'm sure he would have done. I'll go and fetch him.'

Ellie kept hunting while Hazel was out back. Where was the damn thing? It couldn't be far away. She went all round the draining board and then beyond, first to the left and then the right. There was no sign of her ring.

Harry appeared with Hazel in tow, both wearing concerned expressions. 'Have you found it yet?' he demanded.

She shook her head, aware that she was close to tears.

How could she have been so stupid and forgetful!

'Are you certain that's where you left it?'

'Absolutely, Harry. I quite clearly remember laying it down.'

'Then let's have these glasses off this bottom shelf and see if it's somehow dropped down there.'

'I'll do that with Ellie while you open up,' Hazel instructed.

They had ten minutes before the first customer appeared during which they scoured the entire bar area, to no avail.

'I've already put out last night's empties,' Harry said as Hazel served. 'It might be amongst that lot, though how it could have got in the bin is beyond me.'

'What about the sink itself?' Ellie suggested. 'What if it's fallen down the plughole?'

That was another possibility, Harry mused. And a good one at that. Luckily there was a trap at the bottom of the waste pipe before it ran off.

'Give me a couple of minutes,' he said, and hurried away to find a pair of suitable pliers.

Ellie served and watched anxiously as Harry got to work on the trap when he returned. Thankfully it was still quiet just like the previous evening.

With a grunt Harry freed and removed the trap, water spilling onto the floor when he did. A quick examination found it to be empty apart from a silver threepenny bit and a kirby grip.

'Sorry, Ellie,' he apologised. 'No joy.'

Ellie was frantic, what was she going to say to George

if it didn't turn up? It was her engagement ring after all, something far more precious than what it had actually cost. And that was enough, considering they were work-ing-class people.

'I'll start on the empties,' Harry declared, coming to his feet, the trap securely back in place. 'Give me a shout though if I'm needed here.'

'We'll find it,' Hazel assured Ellie, patting her arm. 'It has to be around somewhere. It certainly couldn't have been stolen, not from behind the bar.'

True, Ellie thought. Except, where was the bloody thing!

'What am I going to do, Mum?' Ellie asked Jess in despair when they'd returned home. As Ellie had suggested, Jess had come over to the pub with the Postons where Ellie had quickly informed her that the ring wasn't to be found. Jess had returned at closing time to help when they'd all looked for the ring again. And again, to no avail. It had simply vanished.

Jess shook her head. 'I honestly don't know, love. I suppose all you can do is hope that it will eventually turn up.'

Ellie couldn't believe this had happened. All her own fault too, there was no one to blame but herself. 'And what if it doesn't?'

Jess thought about that. 'You could go back to the shop and buy a replacement, one exactly the same. That way George need never know.'

Ellie rubbed her temples. A splitting headache had come

on halfway through the session and was still there even though she'd taken a couple of aspirins. She had no doubt that the headache had been brought on by anxiety.

'Was the ring expensive?' Jess queried.

'More than I can lay my hands on right now. I'd have to save up. Money that was supposed to be for the wedding.'

Jess sighed. Life could be so cruel at times. She didn't blame Ellie for removing her ring, it was quite natural in the circumstances. She might have put it somewhere safer though.

Ellie slumped into a chair. What a mess to get herself into. And at Christmas too! Christmas was ruined as far as she was concerned. Well and truly.

'Buck up,' Jess smiled. 'I'll put the kettle on. Dad will be awake and down for his dinner soon. There's that to look forward to.'

Jess checked the chicken she'd left in the oven – it was coming on a treat. The potatoes and vegetables were all prepared and just needed putting on which she'd do as soon as she heard movement upstairs announcing Albert was out of bed.

She wondered what sort of Christmas Paul was having, and wished with all her heart he was with them. Christmas wouldn't be the same without him.

When Albert appeared he was told the bad news that the ring was missing and he couldn't have been more sympathetic, for a man that is. But that didn't console Ellie any.

* * *

'Christ, Marybeth! How did you get yourself into such a state?' They'd been to a departmental drinks party at the Embassy and were now on their way to Florence Street for a late Christmas lunch.

Marybeth giggled. 'Too many martinis, honey. I should've counted.'

Julius was furious for two reasons. One, he hated drunk women, it was so unfeminine and undignified. Secondly, how could he take her to his parents like this?

Marybeth suddenly croaked, 'Stop the car! Stop the car!'

Julius immediately drew alongside the pavement and hastily opened her door moments before she was violently ill.

That was it, he thought grimly. He was taking her home and leaving her there. Goddamn her!

When it was over Marybeth fell back into her seat where she used the back of her hand to wipe her mouth. 'Sorry, hon,' she slurred.

Julius almost gagged at the stench wafting in. It was stomach-turningly horrendous.

Marybeth closed her eyes and was almost instantly asleep.

Paul had never known such an awful Christmas. If he'd imagined he was going to get a break from working then he'd been wrong. The animals don't take the day off, Mr Selly had explained. They still had to be looked after no matter what day it was. He'd been roused as usual at four thirty.

The food had been good, Paul couldn't deny that. And lots of it. But that was about all he could say. There had been no fun, or presents. Nothing at all. Not even a cracker. After the meal it had been back to work again.

He should write and tell his parents how unhappy he was, Paul thought. How desperately unhappy. Maybe they'd be able to do something if he did.

The truth was, what if they couldn't? Then they'd be as unhappy as he. Which he didn't want. And there wasn't anything really to complain about, except the work and the fact the Sellys were such a miserable, joyless pair. Their intentions were good, he knew that. What it all boiled down to, he supposed, was the fact he missed his pals. Seeing them at school wasn't enough, not the same. They were in class most of the time. He missed his pals and Islington.

But most of all he missed his mum. Heart-breakingly so. It was terrible feeling so utterly alone.

Chapter 11

'What's wrong with you, you look dreadful?' Ellie asked Connie Fox as they went into the toilet for their morning tea break. She'd been worried about her friend ever since arriving at work, but this was the first chance she'd had to have a word.

'I've finally had a reply from Barry,' Connie replied, voice brittle and crackling at the edges.

'And?'

Before Connie could explain, Agnes Short and Elaine McIntosh joined them which halted that line of conversation.

Connie shook her head. 'I'll tell you when we leave at dinner-time,' she said quietly.

Ellie pulled out a packet of cigarettes. 'Here, have one of these.'

'More Yankee ones?' Connie commented.

'I told you, it's my next-door neighbour. He gets them for me. Refuses to take payment either.'

'Lucky you,' Connie said, lighting up.

'Isn't he the black chap?' Agnes smirked her disapproval.

'So what?'

'Nothing, nothing at all. I just don't think I'd like black people staying so close. My father says they lower the tone.'

That angered Ellie, who thought Agnes a right bitch. 'He's obviously never met any then. The whole family's lovely.' Then, cuttingly, 'I must say I'd rather have them next door than some I could name.'

Agnes bridled, knowing Ellie meant her. 'Just what do you mean by that?'

Ellie's eyes hardened; she was in no mood to take any nonsense from Agnes. Casually, she too lit a cigarette, then proceeded to blow smoke in Agnes's direction. 'Probably what you think it means.'

If Connie hadn't been so distraught she'd have laughed. 'I'd shut up if I were you,' she told Agnes.

Elaine McIntosh moved away and sipped her tea. She wanted none of this. She'd never said, being a quiet girl, but she too didn't have much time for Agnes.

'Don't talk to me like that!' Agnes snapped back.

'I'll talk to you any fucking way I choose, you nasty little snot.'

Agnes gasped in indignation, her face going bright red.

That was telling her, Ellie smiled inwardly, though she was shocked to hear Connie use *that* word. She certainly didn't approve, thinking it even worse to have been uttered by a woman. It just showed how upset Connie was.

Ellie couldn't wait for dinner-time when she returned to her desk, dying to know what Barry had said in his letter. From the looks of things it wasn't promising for Connie.

* * *

Ellie was outraged. 'He said *what*!'

'How could he be sure that he was the only one and the child was his,' Connie repeated, tears glinting in her eyes.

'The rotten sod,' Ellie hissed. No wonder Connie had been so distressed all morning. What an accusation. It was beyond belief.

'He won't be applying for compassionate leave or coming home. He more or less told me to sling my hook.'

Even though they were in the street Ellie took Connie into her arms and hugged her tight. 'I'm so sorry.'

Connie sobbed, overcome with emotion. How she'd managed to get into work that morning she didn't know. It had taken every ounce of her willpower.

'If that's his attitude then you're well rid of him,' Ellie declared.

'Maybe so,' Connie choked. 'But there's still the baby. What am I to do about that?'

'There is only one thing to do,' Ellie stated quietly. 'Tell your parents and have it.'

Connie closed her eyes, thinking of the explosion that was going to cause. Not only fury but terrible hurt. Her parents would be beside themselves with shame and humiliation. Their lives ruined, or so they would claim.

As for her, no one would ever marry her now. Not with an illegitimate child in tow. A bastard.

When they finally parted Connie didn't go home as usual, instead she went into a pub. She needed time by herself to think. To try to come to terms with the situation.

In her heart of hearts she'd been certain Barry would stand by her, do the right thing.

How wrong could you be.

Albert came into the kitchen to find Jess poring over a map. 'What are you doing?' he queried in surprise.

'It's Devon and Cornwall,' she explained. 'I got it from the garage.'

'Are you trying to find Talyton?'

Jess nodded, not sure what his reaction was going to be.

'I see,' he murmured. 'Any luck?'

'Not so far, Albert. It must be terribly small, or else I'm just missing it.'

He joined her at the table. 'Here, let me have a shufti.'

He knew it was somewhere near Exeter, but had no idea if it was north, south, east or west of there. Using a finger he began to trace an ever-widening circle.

It was five minutes before he found it. 'There we are!' he declared triumphantly.

Jess peered at the indicated spot on the map. 'It is small,' she observed.

And seemingly right in the middle of nowhere, Albert thought. He studied the map again to locate the nearest railway station, all of which were marked.

He soon found that as well. 'Clyst Binkleigh,' he pointed out to her. 'Some sort of branch line ending in Exeter itself. So, it can't be reached direct. You have to go to Exeter first, and then change. All in all quite a journey by my reckoning.'

'How far between this Clyst place and Talyton?' she queried.

Albert made a face. 'Maps aren't exactly my strong suit, but a fair old distance I'd say.'

'Then there must be a bus?'

Albert was only too well aware of what this was leading up to, nor was he all that surprised. Jess had never come to terms with Paul's evacuation and had convinced herself something was wrong with the lad. Which he doubted very much.

'Probably,' he replied slowly. 'Though how often they run is something else. It's not like here, you know, one along every few minutes or so. Country buses may only run once or twice a day. Especially in such remote areas.'

'What about taxis?'

He almost laughed out loud at the ludicrousness of that. 'It's hardly likely judging by the size of the place. You could maybe hire a horse and cart if you're lucky.'

Jess bit back her disappointment.

'Why don't you put the kettle on? I could use a cuppa,' he said, hoping to change the conversation.

Jess hesitated. 'Albert?'

Here it was. 'Uh-huh?'

'We did agree I could go and visit Paul sometime. I thought, well, maybe next week?'

He had agreed, dammit. It might even have been his own suggestion, he couldn't remember. 'I don't see how you can actually get there, Jess. It seems downright impossible to me.'

She glanced again at the map, realising the difficulties

of reaching Talyton. Why, oh why, did it have to be so out of the way!

'Besides,' Albert went on. 'Paul still hasn't settled in, we know that from his letters. If you turn up don't you think it's only going to make matters worse?'

'It's more than unsettled, Albert. I'm convinced of that.'

He regarded her steadily. 'You believe that because it's what you want to believe, girl. Paul's fine. A little home-sick perhaps, but fine nonetheless. He just needs a while longer to find his feet and get into the swing of things. You'll see.'

Jess remained unconvinced, every fibre of her being urging her to go to her son.

'He has his pals around him,' Albert continued. 'So he's hardly lonely. It's not as if he's been sent somewhere he didn't know anyone. You're worrying unnecessarily, Jess, take my word for it.'

He began filling the kettle at the sink. 'Now let's drop this. All right?'

There was no reply. And when he turned round again it was to discover he was the only one in the room. Jess had gone.

Connie sat brooding, staring at her parents. Her father was engrossed in the daily crossword puzzle, which he did every night, while her mother was knitting. It was a scene of perfect domestic tranquillity.

How could she tell them? she asked herself for the umpteenth time. How could she possibly?

'Things are getting hard to come by in the shops,' Minnie Fox commented quietly.

'Oh?' Her husband Dick didn't bother to look up.

'Mainly food. I had terrible trouble getting those chops we had for supper. In fact I had quite an argument with the butcher before he'd sell them to me.'

Dick sighed. 'I suppose it'll only get worse before it gets better.'

'At least rationing hasn't come in yet. Though that could happen any time according to what you hear.'

Connie's eyes flicked from one to the other. She loved her parents in a deeply satisfying way. As parents went they were comfortable to be with, easy-going really. Understanding, patient, most of the time. But if she dropped her bombshell . . .! She could well imagine the shock, tears, and everything else that would go with those. It would quite simply be the end of their world as they'd known it and she the culprit, the perpetrator of the terrible deed . . . It made her feel sick to the very pit of her stomach.

'Whatever happens, we'll be all right for coal. I'll see to that,' Dick replied, writing in an answer. He was a clerk in a local coalyard.

'Well, that's something at least,' Minnie nodded, her knitting needles clacking nineteen to the dozen.

Dick closed his eyes. 'Now what's a six-letter word for . . .'

Connie decided to go to bed. She couldn't tell them, she just couldn't.

Not yet anyway.

* * *

Marybeth caught up with Julius in the corridor leading to Acquisitions. 'Hi, stranger!'

His heart sank on hearing her voice, for he'd been avoiding her since Christmas Day. 'Hi!' he smiled back.

'Where have you been?'

He shrugged. 'Busy, I guess. You know how it is.'

Using an index finger she stroked his cheek. 'Am I forgiven yet?'

'Sure.'

'Truly, hon?'

'Well, it was a tad inconvenient. And I had to lie, I don't like doing that to my folks. I said you'd developed a migraine.'

She smiled, her expression one of enticement and promise. 'I'm missin' you.'

'As I said, I've been busy. There's a war on, remember? That makes things kinda hectic to say the least.'

'You can't be workin' all the time, hon. A little R'n'R is required as well.' That meant rest and recreation.

'If you don't mind, I'll take a rain check for now, Marybeth. I'll call when I can. That's a promise.'

She could see he wasn't going to commit himself. 'I'll hold you to that now.'

'I'll call.'

For a moment he thought she was going to kiss him, then she was walking away, her hips swaying provocatively.

He *was* missing her, he realised. But only where bed was concerned. He'd never known anyone like her between the sheets. She was pure dynamite.

As for Marybeth herself? That was something else. He didn't appreciate women who got drunk, far less drunk to the point of vomiting.

That really put him off.

Connie had found the street without difficulty having looked it up first in the *A to Z*. The house whose number she'd been given was exactly the same as all the rest. It had seen better days.

She took a deep breath, steeling herself to go through with this, which wasn't easy. The thought of what lay beyond the door she was now staring at made her flesh creep.

This was only to find out what was what, she reminded herself. She wasn't committing herself to anything. There was no need for that yet. And if she wasn't happy she could just walk away and never return. Nobody was going to pounce on her the moment she walked through that door.

She was horribly aware she was covered in goose bumps and her teeth were chattering. The latter because it was such a cold night, she tried to reassure herself, knowing it to be nonsense. She was plain scared through and through, to the point where she wouldn't have been surprised if she'd wet herself.

Slowly she mounted the steps to the door and, taking another deep breath, rang the electric bell.

She forced a smile onto her face when the door opened.

'Get your back stuck into it, boy, we got a lot to shift before supper,' Mr Selly urged Paul, as they forked hay down from the upper level of the barn. The next job was shovelling out muck from the pig pen, a task which Paul absolutely loathed.

Mr Selly shook his head in despair. 'You're willing, boy, I'll give 'ee that, but you townies just don't know how to graft. You're soft now, but I'll soon harden you up. Make a man of you.'

Paul didn't reply to that, knowing better. Mr Selly didn't like being answered back. Giving cheek, as he called it.

Paul strained to do better.

Jess came breezing into the kitchen. 'Someone here to see you, Ellie.'

It was Connie. 'I hope you don't mind me barging in?'

'Not at all,' Ellie replied quickly, wondering what this was all about. 'Mum, this is Connie Fox who works with me.'

'Pleased to meet you, Connie,' Jess beamed and shook Connie's hand.

That was the only introduction necessary as Albert was out, Ellie didn't know where.

'Can I have a word?' Connie asked, trying not to let her anxiety show.

'Of course. Go ahead.'

Connie looked faintly embarrassed. 'In private I meant.'

Ellie knew that Jess was about to get on with a pile of ironing that she'd been putting off. 'Let's go to my room,' she suggested.

'Shall I bring up a cup of tea?' Jess offered.

'No, no, but thanks all the same,' Connie answered. 'I won't be here long.'

Ellie led the way upstairs, closing her bedroom door behind the pair of them. Connie glanced about, noting that the bedroom was bigger than hers. Quite a bit bigger actually. She envied Ellie the space.

'So what is it?' Ellie queried.

Connie sat on the edge of the bed. 'You're not going to like this. I know you'll disapprove. But I've decided to go to the woman just off the Cally Road. In fact I've already seen her and made an appointment.'

Ellie was aghast. 'Oh Connie, how could you?'

Connie dropped her gaze. 'There's no other way, honestly. And I'm not just being selfish either. If I tell my folks it'll ruin their lives, and I don't want to do that to them. Can't, Ellie.'

Ellie could understand that, though she was certain, after all Connie was only human, that the excuse about not being selfish wasn't entirely true. Connie was thinking of herself as well.

'I see,' Ellie murmured. 'When's the appointment for?'

'Next Monday night at eight. It's to cost a tenner.'

A lot of money, Ellie thought. 'Have you got that much?'

Connie nodded. 'I can scrape it up.' She looked beseechingly at Ellie. 'Can I have one of your fags? I've run out.'

Ellie produced a packet and they both lit up. 'So why are you here to tell me this?' she queried.

'I don't want to go on my own, Ellie. I need a friend to be with me.'

Ellie swallowed hard. The friend was obviously her.

'Will you do it?' Connie pleaded. 'Please?'

Ellie didn't see how she could refuse. A friend in need, as the saying went. 'I'll go with you,' she agreed. 'Though on the strict understanding I don't approve.'

Connie relaxed slightly. 'Thanks. You're a pal.'

Ellie was curious. 'This woman, what's she like?'

Connie considered that. 'Pretty ordinary really. You'd certainly never give her a second look in the street. Like someone's nan I suppose. Elderly, grey-haired, with a nice, kindly manner about her. Her name's Mrs Smith.'

Ellie laughed. 'I'll bet!'

'No, that's what it is. At least that was the name on the door.'

'Did she say . . .' Ellie hesitated. 'How . . .?'

'She didn't and I never asked,' Connie interjected swiftly. 'I didn't want to know.'

Ellie couldn't blame her. In similar circumstances she didn't think she'd want to know either. It simply didn't bear thinking about. 'Are you sure about this?' she asked.

'Absolutely. Get it over and done with, that's the best thing. Put it behind me so to speak.' She paused, then went on, 'You know what really hurts?'

'What?'

'Barry's letter and his saying how could he be sure he's been the only one. I hope now the bastard gets shot.'

'Connie!' Ellie exclaimed in horror. 'You don't mean that.'

'Yes I do, I bloody well do. Serve him right, the rotten, insinuating swine.'

She was very upset, that was all, Ellie thought. She couldn't believe Connie would have wished such a thing otherwise. And Connie had a right to be deeply upset after such an insulting letter. But not to the extent of wishing this Barry dead.

They agreed where and when they'd meet up on the Monday night. Ellie was dreading it. But undoubtedly nowhere near as much as Connie.

She must be terrified out of her head.

'When are you going to see that nice Marybeth again, Julius?' Beulah asked.

Julius inwardly groaned. Here we go again, he thought. 'No idea, Mom,' he replied offhandedly.

'Thin's OK between the pair of you, I take it?'

'Sure.'

'You don't sound too convincin'.'

He didn't reply to that.

'Julius?'

He produced a cigar and trimmed the end. He didn't answer until he'd puffed it alight. 'Mom, why don't you stop meddlin'?'

That flustered Beulah. 'I ain't meddlin'. No sirree! I ain't no meddler. I's just askin', that's all. Bein' polite. Besides, she sure is one pretty gal.'

'So you keep sayin',' he replied sarcastically.

Beulah gave him a baleful look. 'I take it you's tellin' me to mind my own business?'

'That's right, Mom.'

'Huh!'

He could see how peeved she was, and wished he hadn't been quite so abrupt. But it had been a long hard day at the Embassy and he was bone tired. 'Marybeth is very busy at the moment,' he explained, which was true enough. 'Like me. There isn't much time left for socialisin'.'

'Then why didn't you just say that in the first place,' Beulah replied waspishly. 'Instead of accusin' me of being a meddler.'

'Well you are,' he smiled. 'Being a typical mom I suppose. It's simply that you've got to remember I'm grown up now. I make my own decisions.'

'I knows you grown up. Like I said, I was just bein' polite. Showin' interest, that's all.'

'OK then.'

'OK.'

They stared at one another. Then, simultaneously, both burst out laughing.

But the point had been made. Beulah had got the message.

'Goin' home?'

Shelby Robbins shrugged. 'If it was up to me I'd stay. But there's Phyllis and the kids to consider. Even if they have political immunity I don't want them here when the Krauts arrive.'

'*When?*' Julius repeated. 'You seem certain about that.'

'That's what the Ambassador thinks, it's only a matter of time. Shit, Julius, you know that.'

Julius sat on the edge of his desk and smiled thinly.

'The Ambassador could be wrong. The English might fight off the Germans. And, in my opinion, they probably will. They're tough cookies, Shelby. Real hard-asses.'

'We ship out next week,' Shelby replied. 'We've got till then to get everything packed and ready.'

'Anyone else chickenin' out?'

Shelby winced. 'That's not fair, Julius. You don't have kids so it's easy for you to sit in judgement. Hell, man, I've got responsibilities.'

'So why not just send the family Stateside and you remain here?'

Shelby turned away so Julius couldn't see his face. The truth was, he was as anxious to leave as his wife, not wanting to end up in the middle of a shooting war. The English might get beaten but they wouldn't give up easily. Julius was right, they were tough cookies. Stubborn too.

'Well, Shell?'

Shelby sighed. 'Phyllis has forced my hand on the matter. Won't hear of me staying when the offer's there to get out.'

True, but not the full truth, Julius thought. He knew Shelby Robbins to be a coward of the first water; the family was simply an excuse to get his butt out the firing line.

'I hope you have a good trip,' Julius said. 'And don't get sunk enroute.'

'Sunk!' Shelby exclaimed in alarm.

'It's just come in from our people in Berlin. U-boat commanders have been ordered to attack all neutral shipping as well as Allied vessels.'

'Jesus,' Shelby breathed. He hadn't counted on that. 'You sure?'

'Uh-huh. The signal arrived about an hour ago.'

Shelby swallowed, then swallowed again. 'I've gotta get some coffee,' he said and hurried off to the vending machine.

That had been nasty of him, Julius reflected. But he had enjoyed it. He'd never liked Shelby anyway. And the news was true.

Sitting at his desk he got on with work. Shelby did not reappear in the office for the rest of that day.

It was a real pea-souper with visibility reduced to only a couple of yards. That, combined with the black-out, was making it extremely difficult for Ellie and Connie to find their way in what was relatively unfamiliar territory, this part of Islington not being particularly well known to either of them. They were walking arm in arm for support, with mainly Ellie supporting Connie.

'How do you feel?' Ellie asked.

'Terrible.'

Ellie wasn't at all surprised.

'I hope we're not going to be late,' Connie said.

Ellie glanced at her friend's face in the dark. Even through the fog she could see Connie was as white as a sheet.

'Here we are,' Connie announced a little later and they turned into the street where Mrs Smith lived.

On arriving outside the door Connie stopped and gulped. This was it, she thought. This was bloody it.

'All right?'

Connie nodded.

'Up we go then.'

They climbed the steps and halted in front of the door, Connie closer to the electric bell. Ellie waited for her to push it.

Instead Connie closed her eyes. Then gave a sudden whimper.

'Connie?'

Clickety clack, clickety clack. In her mind's eye Connie was watching her mother knitting, the needles going nineteen to the dozen. What if it was a knitting needle Mrs Smith used? She'd heard tales, blood-curdling tales. The thought of one of those inside her, probing, prodding, made her almost scream out loud.

'I can't, Ellie. I can't,' she whimpered, the vision of her mother's knitting needles still clearly before her. She shuddered from head to foot.

Ellie let out a huge sigh of relief. 'Let's go to my local and have a drink,' she suggested.

Connie needed no additional prompting. Both girls turned away and stumbled back into the fog and blackout.

Chapter 12

Ellie's jaw dropped in surprise when she opened the door to find George smiling at her.

'Hello, angel!'

'George!' She flew into his arms and the pair of them, not caring what the neighbours might say or think, kissed deeply.

'What are you doing here?' she gasped when the kiss was finally over.

'We docked in the Pool a few hours ago and I've got three whole days before we're off again.' The Pool referred to was the Pool of London.

This was marvellous. 'You might have written and warned me,' she chided.

'I didn't know our destination till we were at sea. Then, of course, it was too late.'

'Well, you're here, that's the main thing. Now come inside, I can't have you standing on the doorstep.'

He laughed as she pulled him into the hall. 'It's so good to see you again, Ellie. I can't tell you how good.'

'And for me to see you.'

Albert and Jess were also delighted at George's unexpected appearance and made much of him, Albert producing a bottle of whisky, or what was left of it anyway, that he had put by. George was only too happy to accept the offered scotch.

'I thought we might go to The Florence,' George suggested to Ellie. For there they could find a quiet corner and be more or less alone which was impossible with Albert and Jess at home.

'I'll only take a tick to get ready,' Ellie beamed and hurried off upstairs to her bedroom.

'So how has it been?' Albert asked, watching George closely. To date a lot of merchant shipping had been sunk, lost mainly to German U-boats.

George shrugged. 'It's difficult to explain, Albert. Monotonous most of the time, incredibly exciting at others.'

'Do you mean the U-boats?'

'Partly. It certainly makes you think when you know they're in the area. But so far, thank God, we've been lucky.'

'Let's hope you stay that way,' Jess commented.

'And the other exciting things?' Albert prompted.

'Some of the places I've been ashore. New York was the best. We had a terrific time there. New York followed by Maracaibo. Now that was exotic to say the least.'

'Maracaibo,' Albert repeated, eyes gleaming. He'd always wanted to travel but never had. 'You certainly have been getting around.'

George was thinner than the last time she'd seen him, Jess noted. And somehow older too, which showed in his face and the set of his mouth. There was a new-found confidence about him.

Ellie surpassed herself and was back down again in just over ten minutes, George frowning ever so slightly when he saw her.

'That was quick,' he acknowledged.

'Shall we go then?'

'Enjoy yourselves,' Jess told them as she and Albert watched them leave.

As George had hoped The Florence was quiet and they managed to find a suitable corner. He went up to the bar while Ellie settled herself at the table.

It was Hazel who was serving and she made a big fuss of him, declaring that the first round was on the house in celebration of his safe homecoming. They had a bit of a chat before George picked up the drinks and rejoined Ellie.

'This is new,' he observed as he sat.

'What is?'

'You smoking.'

She sensed, rather than heard, the disapproval in his voice. 'Do you mind?'

He shrugged. 'Not really. It's your choice if you enjoy it.'

'I'm told it makes me more sophisticated,' she declared earnestly.

He laughed. 'I don't know about that.' He glanced at the packet she'd laid on the table. 'Aren't those American?'

She explained about Julius and his getting them for her and not charging. 'Isn't that kind of him?'

George wasn't sure what to make of that. What he wasn't going to say to Ellie was that he didn't like women smoking, thinking it made them look tarty.

'I suppose,' he said slowly, and took a deep drink of his beer. Good old English draught, so much better than the bottled stuff they got on board or the foreign muck you found abroad.

'They really are good neighbours,' Ellie bubbled on, still not over the shock of George turning up out of the blue.

'You've changed your hair,' he stated quietly.

'Had it cut short. It's all the rage at the moment. Everyone is having it done.'

'It's very nice,' he lied. He preferred it long, especially when, occasionally, she had done it up in a French pleat. Now that had been attractive.

'I'm glad you like it.'

She was also wearing more make-up than she'd used to, he thought. That didn't do her any favours either in his opinion. Like smoking, he considered it tarty.

George glanced about him. 'At least this place hasn't changed. It's just as I remember it.'

Ellie didn't catch the inference. 'Now tell me everything that's happened to you,' she urged.

Well, there were certainly some things he couldn't relate, he thought. The girl in New York most definitely being one. He was about to begin recounting what he could when he suddenly noticed Ellie wasn't wearing his engagement ring.

Ellie went bright red when he mentioned the fact, hastily telling him what had happened and ending the explanation with a profuse apology.

'I'm going to replace it when I get the money,' she declared. 'One exactly the same if the jeweller can match it.'

Her losing the ring had made him angry and saddened him too. This wasn't turning out at all as he'd expected and hoped. It was all a bit of an anti-climax. Ellie had changed so much and, he hated to admit it, was actually irritating him. The evening, as far as he was concerned, was proving something of a disaster. Where was the girl he'd left behind? She certainly wasn't sitting opposite.

'Well?' she demanded.

'Accidents happen.' He couldn't help but feel that her losing the ring was somehow an omen.

'I know, but it was my own stupid fault. I should have put it somewhere safer.'

He had a swallow of beer to save himself from having to reply to that, and, changing the subject, started telling her about Maracaibo instead.

'Now, what about here, the Home Front?' he asked when he'd finished.

'You'd hardly know there was a war on,' Ellie answered. 'Rationing has been brought in at long last, but that's about it so far.'

'No bombing?'

'We were expecting a lot of that, except it just hasn't happened. According to the *Evening News* the occasional German plane has flown over London, but only the occasional one. Nothing to worry about.'

George nodded as he digested that. It more or less tied in with what he'd already heard. 'Then you're lucky.'

'That's what we think. Some people are beginning to believe we might escape bombing altogether, though that's doubtful according to Dad. He says it's only a matter of time. In the meanwhile we're all thankful for the respite.'

George was about to comment further when someone came bursting into the pub immediately capturing Ellie's attention. 'It's Connie!' she exclaimed. 'A pal who works with me.'

Connie waved and hurried straight over. 'Your mum said you were here,' she explained. Then, to George, 'I'm sorry to burst in like this, but I must have a word with Ellie.'

Not bad, George thought. A bit of a cracker. He rose to his feet and shook Connie's hand as Ellie introduced them.

Ellie was furious. What on earth could be so important for Connie to break in on them as she'd done? George's first night home too.

'Let me get you a drink while you have that word,' he smiled to Connie.

'Are you sure? I've got money.'

'I wouldn't hear of it,' George replied gallantly, not at all fazed by this intrusion. In fact he rather welcomed it. 'Now, what'll it be?'

'Gin and orange please.'

'Large?'

'If you can stretch that far.'

He laughed. 'I can.' And with that he left them, crossing to the bar.

'What's this all about?' Ellie demanded.

'I had to tell you. Just had to. Guess what?'

Ellie shook her head.

'I came on when I got back from work this evening.'

It took a moment for that to sink in. 'You mean . . .?'

Connie nodded vigorously, her eyes ablaze with excitement. 'I wasn't pregnant after all. Don't ask me how I missed a couple of periods when I've never missed a single one before, or even been late.'

'Oh Connie,' Ellie breathed, delighted for her friend. 'What a relief.'

'You can say that again. You can understand now why I just had to rush here and tell you. I'm over the moon. Ecstatic!'

Ellie suddenly frowned. 'Didn't Mrs Smith examine you when you went to see her?'

'She did, and confirmed I was up the duff. All I can think is the rotten old cow was going to pretend to do the business and then charge me as if she had.'

Ellie thought that appalling. Truly despicable. 'Anyway, it doesn't matter now. You're in the clear.'

Connie shook her head. 'Thank God I've been putting off telling my parents. Now they need never know anything about my scare.'

'And Barry was shown up in his true light. You're well rid of the swine, believe me.'

'Can I have one of those?' Connie requested, pointing at Ellie's cigarettes.

'Of course.'

Both girls lit up. 'I'm so pleased for you,' Ellie declared.

'You can imagine how *I* feel. It's as if I was due up for

execution and then given a reprieve at the last moment. Hallelujah!'

George reappeared at the table. 'Finished with whatever, or shall I go away again?'

'Quite finished,' Ellie stated.

George glanced from face to face. 'Good news I take it?'

'The best,' Connie replied. 'But don't ask what. I can't say.'

'Girlie stuff,' Ellie explained.

'Oh!'

'I must go and leave you two to it,' Connie declared a little later when her glass was empty.

George was disappointed; he'd thought her fun. 'No need to leave on our account.' Ellie shot him a look which he chose to ignore. 'Now how about another all round?'

Ellie wasn't best pleased, wanting George to herself. But what could she say?

Nothing.

'Would you like to come in for a cuppa?' Ellie asked when they finally left the pub, having arranged with Hazel to have the next two nights, a Friday and Saturday, off. 'Dad's on early so he and Mum are bound to have gone to bed by now.'

George didn't find that proposition attractive in the least. He was amazed at how much he'd cooled on Ellie in such a short space of time. It was as if she'd become a different person entirely during his absence. There again, maybe he was the one who'd changed.

'I won't, Ellie. I've been on the go for over eighteen hours now and I'm about collapsing,' he lied. 'Do you mind?'

She forced a smile onto her face. 'No, of course not. It would just have been nice, that's all.'

'I'll pick you up tomorrow evening, say about half past seven. Or would eight be better?'

'Seven thirty's fine, George.'

He kissed her, but not the passionate kiss she'd been expecting. 'See you then, Ellie.'

'I'll be ready and waiting.'

She watched him disappear into the black-out, disappointment heavy within her. She'd been hoping for a nice bit of canoodling to round things off. To sort of cement their being back together again.

Oh well, she thought philosophically. There was always tomorrow night.

Paul lay in his bed listening to the wind howl and roar and rattle at his window. How he'd come to hate High Barton, particularly the smells and hard work that went with it.

If only there was someone else his own age around, if not to play with at least to talk to. But there wasn't. There were times, like now, when the loneliness made him want to cry. And sometimes did.

He wished with all his heart he'd never let his father talk him into being evacuated. That had been a terrible mistake on his part.

He pulled the bedclothes up until they were just under

his chin, thankful at least that the bed was warm and cosy. After a storm like this there was bound to be a lot of clearing up to do in the morning, a morning that would start at half past four as usual. He groaned inwardly at the thought.

Closing his eyes he waited to get back to sleep, hoping the wind wouldn't wake him again.

His window continued to rattle furiously.

'You're a sly one. He's gorgeous,' Connie whispered to Ellie, Miss Oates not in evidence for the moment.

Ellie smiled. 'You mean George?'

'Who else! He's a real dreamboat. Lucky you.'

Ellie had never considered George to be a dreamboat, far less gorgeous. But who was she to argue with her friend's opinion. 'How are you feeling today?'

'You can imagine. Simply wonderful. What a load that was lifted from my shoulders.' She hesitated. 'I'm sorry again for barging in on you like I did. I really shouldn't have.'

'It's all right,' Ellie reassured her. 'Forget it.'

'Are you seeing him again tonight?'

Ellie nodded.

'Where are you going?'

'No idea. The flicks maybe. Or perhaps up West. It all depends on what George wants to do.'

'Well whatever, I'm sure you'll have a smashing time.'

Ellie failed to detect the jealousy reflected in Connie's eyes and tone of voice. Connie had been serious when she'd declared George a dreamboat. She'd have cut off her arm for a bloke like him.

'I'm sure we will.'

Connie leant even closer. 'Just don't make the same mistake I did with Barry. I don't want to be escorting *you* round to Mrs Smith's.'

'There's no likelihood of that,' Ellie stated firmly. 'The wedding night and not before. War or not.'

Connie found herself wondering what George would be like with his clothes off?

The picture she conjured up made her smile.

Julius killed his car engine and sat back to stare up at Marybeth's apartment. Because of the black-out he couldn't tell whether or not she was at home.

He sighed. It was months now since the incident at Christmas during which he hadn't taken her out again or visited her. She'd come to accept the situation, even if she had done so with bad grace.

Truth was, he missed her. No he didn't, he corrected himself. It was their lovemaking he missed. Sometimes thinking about it, remembering, brought him out in a sweat and made him jumpy as hell.

Should he go up or not? There was part of him desperately wanted to, the ultimate male part that is. It wanted to very much indeed.

'Damn!' he muttered and reached for the ignition key. This wasn't doing him any favours. He should get out of there. Go home. Have a drink, relax. Take a hot tub. Put Marybeth right out of his mind.

Except, he couldn't. His urges were too strong for that. They were tearing him apart.

If only she hadn't been so good in bed, had such an incredible body. Hadn't . . .

Julius took a deep breath. 'Son of a bitch!' he exclaimed softly. Just thinking about her had made him excited.

He removed the key from the ignition and reached for the door handle. Maybe she wasn't at home in which case it was that drink and hot tub.

As it transpired, she was.

The number came to an end and they both applauded. 'Fancy a breather?' George queried.

Ellie nodded, but didn't reply. Of all places to bring her to, the bloody Poxy Roxy!

It had been George's suggestion, he saying how much he'd thought about the dancehall while he'd been away, and how he'd love to go there that evening. She'd felt there was nothing else she could do but fall in with the idea, even though it was the last place she wanted to be.

'The band's great,' George enthused as they left the floor.

Ellie didn't think them great at all, indifferent more like. And that was being kind.

'I adore the name. Doctor Crock And His Crackpots! That's funny.'

Their name was far better than their music, Ellie reflected. Then mentally chided herself for being such a misery guts. She was with George, that was all that mattered. And he was enjoying himself, so the least she could do was give the impression she was too.

'Why, hello again, I thought I saw you up.'

It was Connie who'd materialised beside them, smiling hesitantly. 'Hello, Connie,' George enthused. 'Where did you spring from?'

'Are you with someone?' Ellie inquired.

Connie shook her head. 'I came by my lonesome to eye up the talent. Well, there's precious little of that around. I suppose most of the chaps who'd normally be here are in the Forces.' She pulled a face. 'Just my luck.'

'No matter, you've found us to talk to now,' George replied, pleased to see the blonde whose company he'd enjoyed the previous evening.

She could have done without this, Ellie thought in despair. Would she never get George to herself? It seemed not.

'Great band, eh?' George smiled to Connie.

'Terrific. Especially when they do their novelty numbers. Those are a right laugh.'

George eyed Connie up and down. 'Lovely dress.' The dress in question was a young whirl-skirt frock in fine rayon crêpe romaine. The elongated bodice and lowered waistline gave it a chic, longer look. Its figure-moulding drapery was released from shoulder shirring to be caught up into a solid shirred triangle at the waist. The colour was cadet blue.

'This old thing!' Connie laughed dismissively. 'I've had it for ages. Trouble is, it's so difficult to buy anything new nowadays with a war on. Almost impossible. Isn't that right, Ellie?'

Ellie, feeling quite drab by comparison, nodded. She thought Connie looked stunning, especially with her long hair brushed into a Veronica Lake peekaboo.

'Have you danced yet?' George asked Connie.

'Not so far.'

He turned to Ellie. 'Do you mind? Can't have your pal being a wallflower after all.'

Ellie forced a smile onto her face, wishing Connie far away. 'No, we can't have that. Go ahead, give her a twirl. I'll be here when you get back.'

'Are you sure?' Connie frowned at Ellie.

'Course I am, be my guest. Just watch his feet, that's all. He's got two left ones.'

'That's not true!' George protested.

Ellie smiled sweetly, a smile that hid the fact she was seething.

It was.

'Ellie!'

She glanced round in surprise as George came hurrying across the street. It was Saturday afternoon and she'd just left work.

'This is nice,' she declared as he came up beside her. Taking him by the arm she continued on her way, hoping that Connie, who hadn't yet emerged, wouldn't try to catch up with them. She'd had quite enough of Connie sticking her nose in the previous evening.

George's expression was one of concern. 'It's bad news, I'm afraid.'

'Oh?'

'There's been a change of plan and I have to report back to the ship right away. We're sailing in a few hours.

'I'm sorry,' he added when he saw her stricken face.

'Why's that?' she managed at last to ask.

He shrugged. 'No idea, angel. I'm not exactly privy to the whys and wherefores. I had a telegram earlier on saying we sail at six and to be on board as soon as possible.'

His whole leave had been a disaster right from the word go, she thought miserably. Now this. 'Do you know when you'll be home again?'

He shook his head. 'Who's to say! I really am sorry, Ellie. Truly I am.'

'Isn't there even time for a coffee or something?'

'I've hung on long enough waiting for you to get out of work as it is. I really must make tracks. There's a lot to do before we leave.'

'So that's it for now then,' she stated leadenly.

'I'm afraid so.'

'You will take care?'

'I'll certainly be doing my best.' He suddenly pointed. 'Look, there's my bus. I'll write. That's a promise.'

'But, George . . .' Her protestations were cut short by a hurried kiss. Then he was gone, sprinting back across the street. He turned and waved before jumping on board.

Easy as pie, George congratulated himself, settling into a seat. What he'd told her was a load of nonsense: he wasn't due back to the ship till the following late afternoon. He glanced back to see Ellie walking dejectedly along the pavement. How he'd been looking forward to coming home and being with her again, only the reality hadn't been at all as he'd anticipated.

Maybe the fault was his, perhaps visiting foreign

countries had widened and altered his outlook. He just didn't know. What he did know was that Ellie wasn't for him any more. She somehow irritated him, made him want to be elsewhere, preferably with another woman. Whatever spark, chemistry, had been between them had disappeared. Gone, puff! In a cloud of smoke.

He certainly didn't feel proud about lying to her, far from it. But he simply couldn't face another night in her company, which he found really sad.

He already knew how he'd spend that evening, his last ashore, which should have been with her. It would be the dockside pubs with any of his mates who were around. A right good piss-up and laugh, that's what he'd have. And there were bound to be gash females about, there always were in dockside pubs, the sort you certainly wouldn't take home to Mother.

He thought of the girl in New York City. What a cracker, a real bobby dazzler. He'd be looking her up again if he ever returned that way. No doubt about it.

Lily was her name, Lily Gomez. A dark-haired beauty with flashing eyes and a figure to die for. The two of them had got on like a house on fire. Her Limey, she'd called him. Her London Limey. He smiled in recollection.

He would write to Ellie, he'd keep that promise. But it wouldn't be the sort of letter she'd be hoping for. One last letter, and that would be it.

The losing of her engagement ring *had* been an omen, he thought. Very much so.

He put Ellie out of his mind.

* * *

Paul arrived at school having braved torrential rain to get there. He went straight inside, although the bell was not due to be rung for another five minutes yet, to look for Eddy.

'Have you seen Eddy Ackworth?' he asked Sylvia Hebden who sat next to Eddy.

Her eyes widened. 'Haven't you heard?'

'Heard what?'

'About last night?'

She was being annoying, he thought. 'How could I? I've just got here, dope.'

'There's no need to be rude,' she snapped.

'All right, go on. What's happened?'

He felt sick after she'd told him.

Chapter 13

'You can't go out like that, Julius, your shirt's all wrinkled,' Beulah chided.

He quickly glanced down his front. 'It's OK, Mom. It'll do.'

Beulah snorted in indignation. 'No son of mine's going out in a shirt like that. Whatever will folks think?'

'I can't change it, Mom. It's the only one of this colour in my closet.'

'Then get it off and I'll do it here and now.' She held up a meaty palm. 'No arguments either. You ain't steppin' over no door of mine unless you's right and proper. Now get it off. Pressin' it will only take a few minutes.'

Julius sighed, knowing further argument was useless. Beulah would have her way come what may.

Shrugging out of the shirt he handed it over. 'There you are.'

Her eyebrows shot up as he moved away. 'How did you do that, son?'

Frowning, he turned to her. 'What are you talkin' about?'

'Your back's all scratched.'

Shit, Julius thought. He'd been with Marybeth the previous night, clearly the scratches were her doing. He inwardly cursed her, and himself for not realising at the time that she was marking him. 'Is it?' he replied, pretending surprise.

Beulah was no fool, it didn't take a genius to put two and two together. 'How's that Marybeth by the way?'

He couldn't look his mother in the eye. This was embarrassing in the extreme. He felt like a little boy who'd been caught in a naughty act. He grunted something unintelligible.

Beulah gave a low, throaty laugh. 'She must be a wild thing all right. Hot diggety!'

'Mom!' he cringed.

'So you two's together again. You never said. But then you never tell your poor old momma nothin'. I swears you don't.'

'Mom, leave it be, eh?'

'If she does that then I just wonders what else she does to you,' Beulah teased, thoroughly enjoying his discomfiture. 'But I suppose I can imagine.'

Thoroughly flustered, Julius fled the room, Beulah's knowing laugh echoing in his ears.

Albert frowned when he entered the kitchen, for Jess was sitting staring distractedly into space, and there was no sign of breakfast. 'What's wrong?' he demanded.

Jess held up a letter. 'This came in the morning post. It's from Paul. It says . . .' She broke off and took a deep breath. When she spoke again there was a choke in her voice. 'His friend Eddy Ackworth is seriously ill in hospital after being bitten by rats.'

'Rats!' Albert exclaimed, knowing full well what a rat bite could lead to.

'It seems the boy was forking hay in a barn when the attack took place. Paul says he's got menilitis as a result.'

Menilitis? 'You mean meningitis?'

Jess shrugged. 'Paul's handwriting. Spelling or whatever.'

The lad could easily die, Albert thought grimly. He knew the father, but only to nod to.

'If he can get bitten then so can Paul,' Jess stated, staring directly at Albert. 'According to this he too forks hay in a barn.'

Albert sighed and leant against the mantelpiece, aware of what was coming next.

'We sent Paul away because we thought there would be bombing,' Jess went on. 'Well, that hasn't happened.'

Albert nodded. 'But it will eventually. Take my word for it.'

'You've been saying that for months, Albert, and still no bombs. What if you're wrong?'

He was certain he wasn't, but how was he going to convince Jess of that. 'Paul's safe where he is.'

'Not when his pal gets bitten by rats he isn't!' Jess retorted, hysteria creeping into her voice. She shuddered. 'Rats are filthy animals who carry all sorts of horrible diseases. You told me that yourself once when one of your mates at work got bitten.'

Albert remembered the incident clearly. Rats in a frenzy running from a burning warehouse. Sandy Bass had been unlucky to have got in the way of a whole demented stream of them. Sandy had nearly lost his leg as a result.

'I'm sure Paul's having a whale of a time,' Albert said doggedly.

'Then how come he never mentions that? Not once in all his letters has he ever said he's enjoying himself. You've read them, you know that to be true.'

Albert didn't reply.

'Well?'

'So what do you propose we do?' he asked softly.

'Bring him home of course. What if it was Paul who was in hospital, what then? You'd be the one blaming yourself because you'd sent him away.'

'We can't,' he said, equally softly.

'Why the hell not?'

He turned to face her, hurting at the anguish he saw deeply etched into her face. 'We looked at the map together, Jess, where Paul is staying is completely out of the way. I'm not even sure, with the best will in the world, we could get there.'

Her shoulders slumped, for what Albert said was true enough. 'I only know I want him home,' she sobbed.

'There there, girl.' He swiftly went to her and took her into his arms. 'Don't go on so.'

Ellie, who'd come downstairs, was standing in the doorway staring at them, wondering what on earth this was all about. Something had clearly upset her parents.

'Oh Albert,' Jess further sobbed. 'I just want my son home again. It's not right that he's living with strangers, it's tearing me apart.'

Albert racked his brains. How to actually get to Talyton,

212

that was the problem. 'Let me think about this,' he crooned.

Eyes glistening with tears looked beseechingly into his. 'Does that mean you agree?'

'If it's what you really want, Jess.'

'Oh I do. More than anything.'

Albert was still convinced the country was the safest place for Paul, and yet this rat business had sown doubts in his mind. And who was to say, perhaps he *was* wrong about the bombing? It was seven months now since war had been declared and everything remained, rationing and shortages apart, more or less exactly as it had been before.

Maybe he was being too cautious, his job taught him to be that way. Caution above all else. It saved lives.

'I'll come up with something,' he promised.

Ellie came into the room and put the kettle on. Her mother was going to need a cup of tea when she calmed down. By now she'd gathered something of what the upset was about.

They might fight like cat and dog at times, but she too was missing her brother. He was a decent soul really.

'What's wrong with you?' Albert asked Ellie later that evening. They were alone, Jess upstairs resting.

Ellie shook her head.

Albert laid his paper aside having been catching up on the latest regarding the war. The news wasn't good, Hitler had invaded Norway, Denmark already overrun after showing little resistance. The outlook was bleak for Britain.

'Come on, what is it?' he prompted, feeling incredibly weary. It had been a hard day with five call-outs, one of them major. Not to mention the business with Jess that morning.

'It's George and me,' Ellie replied in a quiet voice.

'What about the pair of you?'

She glanced over at her father, and smiled. What a comfort he was, always solid as a rock. A great surge of affection for him welled through her.

'Something's not right between us, I can tell.'

Albert remained silent, waiting for her to go on.

Ellie lit a cigarette, inhaling the smoke deep into her lungs. 'I think he might have lost interest.'

'Did he say that?'

'No, but then it's what he didn't say that's the problem. It was as though . . .' She groped for the right words. 'He was uneasy with me. As if he almost didn't want to be in my company.'

Albert wasn't sure what to reply to that. 'Are you certain?'

'Oh yes. He didn't really like it when we were alone and only brightened up when someone else joined us.'

Albert studied his daughter. The girl was no fool, far from it; if she thought something was amiss then it probably was. 'You mustn't forget George has been away, in daily danger. That must affect a man.'

Ellie could understand that. 'But that wouldn't necessarily mean he'd go off me, would it?'

Albert had to agree. 'No,' he admitted.

'It just wasn't the same, Dad. I realised that the first

214

night he was home. He'd changed towards me, become distant.'

'And you? How did you feel about him?'

'The same as before he went off. I hadn't changed, but he had. Noticeably so.'

Bending over, Albert picked up the poker and attended to the fire. He'd give it a little longer before putting on more coal, that being another thing that was becoming in short supply. 'Any idea when he's back again?'

Ellie ran a hand over her face. She had the beginnings of a headache, whether or not it was brought on by her worries she didn't know. She only hoped it didn't worsen. 'No. None at all.'

'Well, I suppose all you can do is wait and see. I can't offer any better advice than that I'm afraid. Lame advice though it might be.'

Her father was right, she thought. That's all she could do. 'Thanks, Dad.'

'Why don't you pop over to the pub and have a drink? That might cheer you up.'

She considered that, and decided against it. She didn't want to be surrounded by people, preferring the peace and quiet of where she was. 'I'd rather not.'

'Short of a bob?'

'I have money. I just don't want to go.'

They both lapsed into silence, Ellie thinking about George, Albert about Paul and wondering how they could get to Talyton.

A silence disturbed only by the steady ticking of the clock on the mantelpiece.

'I was hopin' to find you in,' Beulah said. 'I got you somethin' here. Somethin' real nice.'

Beulah laid a cardboard box on the table while a puzzled Jess looked on. 'If you's like most women I know then you loves candy,' Beulah declared.

'Candy? Do you mean candyfloss?'

Beulah laughed. 'Naw, that's our word for . . .' She hesitated, searching her memory. 'I believe you folks call them sweeties.' She laughed again, pleased with herself and her new-found knowledge of colloquial English.

'I certainly do. Particularly chocolate.'

'Ah!' Beulah's face lit up. 'I'm glad about that, Jess, because that's what I got here. All kinds of chocolate bars.'

Beulah delved into the box and produced several dozen gaily wrapped bars, all obviously American. 'It's my Julius, he brought me back a whole mess of these. And I thought, I's sure Jess would like some. And so here you are. From me to you.'

'How kind,' Jess murmured, quite touched. 'This is enough to last us for months, particularly with Paul not about to guzzle them.'

'And how is that little son-of-a-gun?'

Jess's face immediately crumpled. 'Oh, Beulah!'

Pee Wee stared out of their back window, watching the council workers erecting an Anderson shelter. The shelter was comprised of two curved sections of corrugated steel bolted together at the top and sunk three feet into the ground, with an entrance protected by a steel shield and earth embankment. The recommendation was that the householder should cover the roof with at least eighteen inches of soil, the assurance then being that the shelter would survive anything other than a direct hit. All Pee Wee could think was how uncomfortable an overnight stay would be in there.

'How those guys comin' along?' Beulah queried.

'Nearly finished I reckon.'

Beulah joined him in staring out the window. 'Spooky, eh?'

'Yup,' he agreed. 'We'll be like a couple of jack rabbits down a hole in there.'

Beulah laughed at that idea. 'Sure enough. All snuggled up, comfortable as can be. My ass! I tell you, Pee Wee, just goin' in that thing will play merry hell with my rheumatism.'

He put an arm round her. 'That ain't bad at the moment, is it? You ain't said nothin'.'

'Not at the moment, but this English climate sure don't help none.'

'It's the goddamn' damp,' Pee Wee sympathised. ''Tain't cold like we's used to back in New York, but it sure is damp. Gets into your bones too. Why, even I's beginnin' to creak a bit.'

As if to emphasise the point, it started to rain. And it quickly turned into a downpour.

'I'll fix some coffee for those poor guys out there,' Beulah said, the workmen showing no sign of stopping or taking cover.

When the coffee was ready she called the two workmen

to the back door and gave it to them. They were extremely grateful but declined her offer to come inside until the rain stopped. They had a quota to fulfil, they explained, and the rain could continue on for God knows how long.

Returning to the kitchen Beulah discovered Julius was home from the Embassy, busy complaining about having got wet while dashing from his car to the house.

'I want to talk to you, Julius,' she declared sombrely.

He stared at Beulah, having noted her tone. 'Sounds serious, Mom?'

She nodded. It was.

'Are you quite sure?' a very much taken-aback Jess queried. This was the last thing she'd expected.

'Yeah, the weekend after next. I suggest we leave early on the Saturday morning which should give us plenty of time to reach Talyton.'

Jess could have kissed Julius; here was the answer to their problem. She really didn't know what to say.

'What about petrol?' the ever-practical Albert asked, he too most appreciative of this kind offer.

'There's no shortage of gas at the Embassy,' Julius replied with a broad smile that showed off his perfect white teeth. 'I'll simply fill up on the Friday night and put a couple of full jerry cans in the trunk. That should be more than enough.'

'We're in your debt,' Ellie smiled at him.

Julius made a dismissive gesture. 'It's my pleasure to help you folks. I'm sure you'd do the same for us if it was the other way round.'

Albert nodded. Yes, he would have done. 'We seem to be taking all the time from your family and giving nothing in return,' he commented with a frown.

'Baloney! You're good neighbours, made us feel right at home the moment we moved in. That goes a long way as far as I'm concerned. Anyway, I haven't seen anythin' of England outside London. It'll be like a short vacation for me. I'll enjoy it.'

'I'm working that weekend,' Albert mused. 'It might be difficult for me to get a switch of duty.'

'You don't need to come along,' Jess told him. 'I'll be fine on my own with Julius. Isn't that right, Julius?'

'Hope so, ma'am.'

Jess crossed over and sank into a chair. 'I can't tell you what a relief this is. I've been worried sick since that letter arrived.'

'And before,' Albert quietly reminded her.

'It's a date then,' Julius declared. 'Saturday after next. We'll finalise arrangements closer to the time.'

'It's a date,' Jess agreed, enjoying saying the strange expression.

Albert saw Julius out, thanking him profusely at the door, explaining unnecessarily, for Beulah had already done so, how important this was to Jess.

'I'm just pleased I can be of help,' Julius replied and then hurried to his car, for he was meeting Marybeth and was already late.

Ellie laid her letter aside. Like Paul's to Jess, hers had also come in the morning post. Her face had gone deathly white and drawn while reading it.

'From George?' Jess asked casually, having already recognised the handwriting when she'd brought the letter through.

Ellie nodded, but didn't reply.

'How is he then?'

Ellie picked up her cup of tea, and sipped it. Very carefully she replaced the cup on its saucer. 'He doesn't say.'

'Oh?'

'He's in Liverpool it seems. Or was when he posted this. He expected to sail at any moment.'

Jess sat at the table and took Ellie's hand in hers. 'What is it, poppet?'

Ellie looked her mother straight in the eye. 'He's broken off our engagement.'

Jess had feared the worst on seeing Ellie's reaction to the letter. 'Does he say why?'

'According to him he's realised he made a mistake and that it just wouldn't work out between us.'

'I see,' Jess murmured.

Ellie took a deep breath. 'I knew this was coming. I told Dad he'd lost interest and I was right.'

Jess squeezed Ellie's hand in sympathy. 'How do you feel?'

'How do you think?'

Jess smiled thinly. 'Stupid question, I suppose. Awful, I should imagine.'

She wouldn't cry, Ellie told herself. She was damned if she would, even if her whole world had just collapsed around her. 'I really fell for him that night in the pub when he was willing to fight Taffy Roberts in my defence,' she said quietly. 'Up until then I wasn't sure. But that night made my mind up for me. Now this.'

Jess's heart went out to her daughter; what a dreadful thing to have happened. How painful it must be for Ellie. She wished she had a magic spell to take at least some of the pain away.

'Look at it this way,' Jess said. 'Better this to have happened now than after the wedding. That really would be a tragedy.'

Ellie frowned. 'How do you mean?'

Jess told herself she must try and put this delicately. 'Better to fall out of love before marriage than afterwards. This way no lasting harm has been done. And you must remember, no matter what you're feeling right now, there are always plenty more fish in the sea.'

'I suppose so,' Ellie murmured.

'Now can I make a suggestion?'

'What?'

'Why not take the day off from the office. Do something different, go for a walk or whatever. That's what I would do.'

Ellie could see the sense in that. She certainly wasn't in the mood for putting up with Miss Oates. 'All right, Mum, I will.'

'Good girl. Now, is there anything I can get you?'

Ellie shook her head.

'If there is later on just say.'

Ellie smiled her appreciation, a smile that came out all lopsided and crooked.

After a few minutes she picked up the letter again and slowly tore it into tiny pieces.

Ellie returned from her long walk along the canal to find her father waiting for her when he should have been upstairs in bed, since he was on the night shift.

'Your mum told me,' he stated quietly. 'I'm so sorry.'

Ellie shrugged. 'It's happened, and that's all there is to it.'

'You're being very brave.'

She almost laughed to hear that. She didn't feel brave, far from it. What she did feel was a terrible humiliation, and loss. For she had loved George, even if it wasn't the grand passion you sometimes read about in novels. She would have made him a good and loyal wife, and hopefully a good mother to their children.

Again, for the umpteenth time, she fought back tears. 'If you don't mind, Dad, I'd rather not talk about it any more.'

He nodded his understanding. 'If that's what you want.'

She went to him and kissed him on the cheek. 'Thanks for waiting up, I appreciate it. Now you'd better get off to bed where you belong at this time.'

He started to turn away, then stopped. 'Life's full of knocks, Ellie, for everyone. We just have to learn to put up, and deal, with them, no matter how hard they are.'

'I know that,' she whispered.

Albert left her to it, he'd done what he could for now. He'd be there for her if she needed him. As she was well aware.

* * *

'I must say I'm impressed with the countryside round here. It really is quite beautiful,' Julius commented to Jess. They'd been on the road for a long time but were now nearing their destination.

Jess gazed out over the rolling, lush fields, some dotted with cows, others sheep. She couldn't think of a bigger contrast to Islington than this. The air was wine compared to the soot-laden atmosphere she was used to.

'It is lovely,' she agreed, thinking she must be wrong about Paul. Surely he was happy in these idyllic surroundings?

'I hope Paul's around when we get there,' Julius said, navigating a nasty bend in the lane they were travelling along.

'As it's Saturday he might be out playing football with his pals,' Jess replied. 'But don't worry, we'll find him.'

'After all this way I certainly hope we do,' Julius commented drily. A joke on his part.

They'd stopped once to have a picnic, Jess having brought along sandwiches and a flask each of tea and coffee. There was more than enough left for the return journey.

Julius stopped the car a little further on, and pointed up at a road sign. 'High Barton, that's the place isn't it?'

'That's it,' Jess confirmed, excitement bubbling up in her at the thought of seeing Paul again.

Ten minutes later they entered a yard in front of a typical thatched Devon farmhouse that Julius thought to be rather run-down.

'Here we are,' he declared.

Several chickens ran away squawking, as Jess got out of the car. She thought that was delightful.

Julius strode towards the main door with the intention of knocking on it when he spotted a man and boy busy in some sort of pen. He gestured towards the pen and he and Jess made their way over.

Paul's face was a picture when he saw her, his mouth dropping open in amazement. 'Mum!' he yelled and, quickly scaling one side of the pen, flew at her.

She held out her arms. 'Oh, my darling!'

Mr Selly was standing gawping at Julius as though Julius was the very Devil incarnate. This was the first black person he'd ever seen. Without realising what he was doing, and albeit he was Church of England, he crossed himself.

'Take me home, Mum, take me home,' Paul sobbed when he was in Jess's embrace. 'I hate it here.'

She couldn't believe the smell of him, he stank to high heaven! He was covered in what she didn't know to be pig muck, having been mucking out the pig pens.

A tear-stained face peered up into hers. 'Will you take me home, Mum, please? Please?'

Jess was rattled to say the least. She hadn't known what to expect, but it wasn't this. Something was clearly wrong.

Mrs Selly appeared to also gawp at Julius, her expression one of fright. She went swiftly to her husband and muttered, 'Don't ask 'em in, for pity's sake.'

Mr Selly had no intention of doing that. All he wanted was this black fella off his land as soon as possible.

Jess knelt in front of Paul and, using a hanky she'd had in her pocket, wiped his face and nose. 'Now what's this all about, Paul?'

It all came tumbling out. The time he had to get up every morning, the hard work he had to do on the farm, a lot of it back-breaking, the loneliness, only seeing other children when at school. So on and so forth.

It didn't take Jess long to ascertain the full story. As Paul had admitted, the Sellys hadn't been cruel, merely expected him to work all hours when not at school.

'Pack your things, son,' she said at last, he immediately scampering off to the house.

The Sellys backed away when she and Julius approached. 'Get him to stay where he is!' Mr Selly said in a quavering voice.

Smiling, Julius hung back.

Jess spoke to the Sellys for almost quarter of an hour, establishing the truth of what Paul had told her. They were clearly puzzled that Paul should have objected to their treatment of him, seeing nothing unusual in it.

Jess thanked them for looking after Paul, but it was obvious he just wasn't suited to country life.

Paul was waiting for her, suitcase by his side, when she and Julius returned to the car. She and Paul got into the rear where Paul immediately cuddled up to her.

As they drove off Julius rolled down his window wishing Paul had had time for a bath before they'd left.

It had been a long drive down. It was going to seem an even longer one back.

Chapter 14

Albert and the rest of his shift sat grouped round the station's wireless set listening to Churchill delivering a pep talk to the nation, Churchill having now been Prime Minister since the previous May when Neville Chamberlain had resigned. What Churchill called the Battle of Britain was now at its height, raging in the skies over southern England.

'Never in the field of human conflict,' he declared, 'was so much owed by so many to so few . . .'

Albert listened in rapt admiration as the great man's words boomed out. Thank God Churchill was now Prime Minister, he thought. What confidence Churchill exuded, what inspiration. He was certainly the leader the country needed in this terrible time of crisis.

When the speech was finally over Danny McGiver switched off the set, each man in the shift looking from one to the other.

'That voice,' Henry Leway said, shaking his head in admiration. 'It's just amazing.'

Albert couldn't have agreed more.

'At least London isn't affected so far,' Percy Noble commented, raising a laugh when he held out a hand and crossed two fingers.

Any further discussion was interrupted by the alarm bell ringing for a call-out.

The entire shift immediately erupted into action.

Julius was the first into the pub when Ellie opened the door for the evening session. 'You must be thirsty,' she joked as he headed for the bar.

'Not so much thirsty as angry. I want to cool off a bit before going into the house.'

'The usual?'

'Uh-huh.'

She went to the pump and began pulling his pint. 'Want to talk about it?'

He smiled and shook his head. 'Can't.'

'You mean won't?' she teased.

'That's right. It's to do with the Embassy.'

He took out a packet of cigarettes and lit up, laying the packet on the bar. 'Help yourself.'

'Thank you. I will.'

He studied her through a haze of smoke. 'How are you off for tabs?'

She now knew what he was referring to having heard him use the expression before. 'I'm a bit low, to tell the truth.'

'Then I'll get you another couple of cartons.'

'Please let me pay this time?' she pleaded as she set his pint in front of him.

'Now, Ellie, don't start that again. It's my little gift, OK? Besides, I enjoy givin' them to you.'

'Well if you insist,' she replied reluctantly.

'I do. Now that's an end of it.'

She touched his hand. 'You're a real sweetie, Julius. Thank you.' And with that she moved away to serve another customer who'd just come in.

How different English girls were to their American counterparts, Julius reflected. They were so much easier and relaxing to be with, not having the aggressiveness, and abrasiveness, of American women. Even their accents, once you got used and attuned to them, were far more pleasant, less harsh, on the ear.

He'd heard about George breaking off their engagement, but had never mentioned the fact thinking it best, and less embarrassing for her, that way. Personally, he thought George a fool. Ellie was a right good-looking gal, a fact he was noticing more and more. Bright too, with a lovely personality.

'How's Paul?' he asked when Ellie returned to his part of the bar.

'Fine. Still thrilled to be home again. For the first week he hardly left Mum's side, it was as though they were attached to one another. But that's stopped now, which I'm sure Mum is delighted about. It must have been wearing for her with him shadowing her everywhere except into the toilet.'

Julius laughed at that.

'Much to his annoyance he's started school again. Quite a few of the St Margaret's lot have also come back, their complaints the same as Paul's, so the school has re-opened to accommodate them. The authorities aren't best pleased after the trouble they went to in the first place, but there we are. Once Paul had gone I believe there was almost a revolt with the others demanding to return home. Only a few have stayed on I understand.'

'Can I have a large scotch as well?' Julius asked, admiring Ellie's bottom when she turned to the gantry. Larger than Marybeth's, and a different shape. What the English called pear. But delicious all the same.

Ellie quickly delved under the bar when she saw him reach for his cigarette packet. 'Here, have one of my fags this time.'

Julius couldn't help but laugh again. The English usage of that word never ceased to amuse him.

'What's so funny?'

His eyes twinkled. 'Don't ask.'

'Is it me?' She glanced down her front. 'Is there something wrong?' She checked her slip to make sure that wasn't showing.

'It isn't you,' he assured her.

'Then what? It must be something for you to laugh like that.'

He was about to reply when two more customers came in claiming Ellie's attention. He waited patiently, smiling all the while, for her to return.

'Well?' she queried a few minutes later. The fact he was still smiling annoyed her. She'd already peered in the mirror behind the bar to make sure there wasn't something wrong with her face, like a bogey hanging from her nose.

'In my country fag has a different meanin' altogether.'

She raised an eyebrow, waiting for the explanation.

'You certain you want to hear this, Ellie, you might think it rude?'

'I want to hear,' she stated emphatically, flushing furiously when he told her.

'Well, I never,' she managed to say at last, not daring to match his gaze.

'Now you understand why I laughed. It always tickles me pink when I hear you English refer to a cigarette as that.'

'I can well imagine.'

Clearing her throat she began energetically wiping down the bar, even though it didn't need wiping down.

Julius stayed a little longer, then left, Ellie having avoided him during this time.

Beulah roared when he recounted that part of their conversation.

Julius arrived in his office to find a new guy installed behind what had been Shelby's desk.

'Hi! You must be Julius Poston,' the man said, rising and extending a hand. 'I'm Walter Zwicke. I've taken over from Robbins.'

Zwicke was short and slim with a foxy face topped by thinning red hair brushed straight back. Julius took an instant dislike to him.

'Pleased to meet you,' Julius declared as they shook. 'Just got to England?'

'Yeah, from Toronto. I've been there the past five years. Great place Toronto, if you know your way around.'

Julius wondered what he meant by that. 'You must

know Marybeth Emerson then? She was stationed in Toronto before bein' posted here.'

The foxy look became even foxier. 'Sure do. One helluva gal! I'll look forward to seeing her again.' He paused, then made a funny little movement with his head. 'Hot damn! Pretty girl that Marybeth. A real snake.'

Julius wasn't at all sure he liked Marybeth being called a snake. He'd always considered that a derogatory expression. 'You fixed up with an apartment yet?'

'Yeah, I've already moved in. Nice number, if not as classy as the one I had in Toronto. That was just off Yonge Street.'

'Sorry, Walter, I don't know Toronto.'

Zwicke shrugged. 'No matter. Now, if you'll excuse me, I'll get on and try to clear up some of this mess Robbins left behind.'

That astonished Julius who simply couldn't imagine Shelby leaving a mess behind, Shelby having been the most diligent of people. 'That so?'

'Yeah. But I'll soon fix it. No sweat.'

Now Julius was certain he didn't like Walter Zwicke. The guy was a creep.

'So why are you so smug today?' Agnes Short demanded during the morning tea break. 'You've been staring into space and mooning ever since you arrived.'

'Have I?' Connie replied innocently.

'I'm only surprised Miss Oates didn't come down on you like a ton of bricks for wasting company time.'

'I noticed her staring into space as well,' Elaine McIntosh piped up.

Ellie, who was also present, hadn't. But then she'd spent most of the morning downstairs in the basement filing.

Connie had a sip of tea. 'I'm sure I don't know what you're talking about,' she prevaricated, wishing they'd change the subject. This could be embarrassing.

Agnes suddenly smiled. 'Do you have a new beau? Is that it? Is there a new man in your life?'

Damn! Connie thought.

'Is there?' Ellie queried, wanting to know all about him if there was.

''Fraid not.'

Agnes wagged a finger at her. 'I think you're telling porkies, Connie Fox.'

'This is ridiculous,' Connie blustered. 'I wasn't even aware of staring into space far less anything else. What a load of nonsense. Utter rubbish.'

Ellie was intrigued; why was Connie over-reacting like this? For she most certainly was, she knew Connie only too well.

Connie resolved her immediate dilemma by laying down her cup and saying, 'Excuse me.'

And with that she vanished into a cubicle and didn't come out again until it was time to resume work.

'*Have* you met someone?' Ellie asked as they hurried home for dinner.

Connie sighed. 'Now don't *you* start. Agnes is just

trying to mix it, that's all. Cause trouble. You know what that bitch is like?'

Ellie dropped it, but kept on wondering why Connie had over-reacted as she had.

A married chap perhaps? She wouldn't put it past Connie to do that sort of thing.

He'd never get used to this bloody black-out, Albert thought as he stepped out of The Florence into the pitch dark. Well not quite pitch, for the moon was up.

He halted abruptly when he saw the fight taking place on the opposite pavement. He could just make out three figures laying into a fourth who was down on the ground.

'Fucking nigger!' one of the assailants yelled.

'Black cunt!' shouted another.

Their Geordie accents gave them away as the three squaddies who'd also been in the pub, nasty pieces of work. Loud, boisterous and clearly looking for trouble. Harry, the landlord, had had to speak to them several times and come within an inch of throwing them out.

The person on the pavement had to be either Pee Wee or Julius, Albert grimly deduced, they being the only black blokes living thereabouts.

He was across the street like a flash to grab the nearest squaddie by the shoulders and spin him round. He might be an older man but he was strong and, thanks to his job, tremendously fit. His first punch, which connected squarely with the squaddie's chin, knocked the man senseless.

Julius, for it was he on the ground, grabbed another squaddie's foot, but the squaddie kicked himself free and

233

took to his heels. Albert was about to pounce on the remaining one when he also ran off. Quickly Albert knelt beside Julius. 'Are you all right, son?'

Julius groaned. 'They took me completely by surprise. There was no reason. They just jumped me.'

'Can you get up?'

'Ahhhh!' Julius grunted when he tried.

Albert glanced at the squaddie he'd knocked out who showed no signs of moving. 'Wait here,' he said tersely, and hurried to the Postons' front door.

Beulah's eyes flew open when he told her what had happened. Brushing past him, not caring about the black-out, she rushed to Julius.

As luck would have it Jess was visiting. 'Call the police on their telephone,' Albert instructed her when she appeared. 'Tell them there's been an attack and we have one of those involved. We also need an ambulance.'

Without uttering another word Albert hastily returned to Julius and Beulah who was cradling him and crying uncontrollably.

Oh Christ! Albert suddenly thought when he saw the squaddie still hadn't stirred. Had he killed the sod? A feel of the neck pulse reassured him that wasn't so.

'How are you now?' he asked Julius anxiously.

'Pain in my chest, bad pain. I think some ribs might be broken.'

Beulah's crying became an hysterical wail.

Another customer emerged from The Florence. 'Who's that?' Albert called over.

'Mike Pratt.'

'Mike, can you get a couple of the lads out here? We've had a bit of trouble.'

'Okey-dokey, Albert.' Mike vanished back into the pub, re-emerging shortly with two others plus Harry, the landlord.

The squaddie on the ground was beginning to come round, Albert watching as he pulled himself into a sitting position.

Quickly Albert explained to Mike, Harry and the others what had happened. 'I knew they were no good,' Harry declared, shaking his head.

Jess appeared at Albert's side. 'The police and an ambulance are on their way.'

The squaddie stared up at those surrounding him, realising he wouldn't get very far if he tried to make a bolt for it. 'You hit me,' he accused Albert.

Albert laughed, thinking that funny. 'Of course I hit you. You and your mates were knocking ten bells out of Julius there.'

'Let me go?' the squaddie pleaded. 'He isn't worth anything. He's only a coon. The scum of the earth.'

Albert fought back his anger. 'That man happens to be a good friend of mine. And it's you who's the scum of the earth, certainly not him.'

'Arsehole,' the squaddie muttered venomously.

Albert was sorely tempted to haul the squaddie to his feet and give him another smack.

'All right, lads, what's to do?'

The speaker, whom nobody had heard approach, was PC McKechnie, the local bobby. McKechnie was a giant of a man who came from the Highlands of Scotland. This had been his beat for years.

Again Albert explained what had happened. He and McKechnie knew each other well, the latter often being present at fires Albert and his crew were attending.

'I see,' McKechnie said when Albert had finished. 'I'll just escort this wee chappie back to the station where we'll telephone the Military Police. They'll soon find out who his mates were, and take the matter from there.'

He pointed his truncheon at the squaddie. 'Get up and put your hands behind you.'

The squaddie, who looked a midget alongside the giant Highlander, yelped as the handcuffs were clicked shut.

'That hurt?' McKechnie queried.

'Yes.'

McKechnie smiled. 'Good.'

An ambulance, its lights reduced by tape to mere pinpricks, rounded the corner to halt beside them. Jess was kneeling alongside Beulah, trying to console her, Beulah's wailing having given way to deep sobs.

McKechnie had a word with the ambulance people and Julius was soon put on a stretcher and lifted into the vehicle.

'I'll keep Beulah company,' Albert said quietly to Jess. 'She can't go on her own.'

'No you won't,' Jess replied firmly. 'You're on early tomorrow and need your sleep. Besides, what Beulah needs is another woman along. You see to things here and I'll be back when I can.'

'All right.' That was a relief. Concerned as he was,

Albert didn't really fancy a hospital visit.

Beulah was helped aboard the ambulance where Jess joined her. The doors were closed and moments later they were on their way.

'Now,' said McKechnie, prodding the squaddie with his truncheon. 'Let's be having you.'

McKechnie and the squaddie disappeared up the street leaving Albert and the others standing outside the pub.

'Want another drink?' Harry asked Albert. 'On the house.'

Albert decided he would. 'I'll just lock up and then I'll be back over,' he replied.

'Right.'

Albert hoped Julius was going to be all right, the lad had taken quite a beating before he'd intervened. A kicking could lead to all manner of internal injuries.

'Bastards,' he muttered, referring to the squaddies. They deserved all they got at the far from tender mercies of the MPs.

'I'll fix us some coffee,' Beulah declared, she and Jess having just returned from the Royal Free Hospital where Julius had been taken. Julius had been correct in thinking he had broken ribs, but apart from that, plus a pretty bruised and cut face, he'd escaped further injury. He was being kept in overnight with the promise of being allowed home the next day.

Jess sat and watched Beulah fill the kettle, feeling terribly sorry for the fat woman. Tonight must have been such a shock, not to mention worry.

'I'm sorry about all this,' Jess stated quietly. 'And ashamed that it happened here.'

Beulah glanced over at her. 'Yo's no need to feel ashamed, hon, 'tain't your fault in any way.' Beulah's eyes flicked to the clock. 'Pee Wee will be home soon. He's going to be real upset when he hears. Lord knows he will. He'll take it bad.' Beulah sighed. 'I wondered what it would be like for black folk in England. Now I know. Just the same as everywhere else, I guess.'

Jess had no answer to that.

'Hungry, hon?'

Jess shook her head.

'I got chocolate cake. That not tempt you?'

'No, Beulah, but thanks anyway.'

'It don't tempt me neither,' Beulah admitted. 'Now that's a thing. Dear God if it ain't. I swear it's almost unheard of.'

Despite herself, Jess had to smile.

Beulah sat, her ample buttocks overflowing the wooden chair. 'I got such a fright tonight, Jess. I can't tell you.'

'I can well imagine.'

'No, you can't, hon. It always scares me when whites turn on us black folks. My pappy's pappy came from the south you know, Georgia that is. Some Klan members got hold of him one time, tortured the poor son-of-a-bitch and then strung him up. No reason for that either, he just happened to be a black man in the wrong place at the wrong time. It was after that the family packed its bags and headed north.'

'Klan?' Jess frowned.

'Ku Klux Klan, honey. They's real mean white folk. Mean as hell. Why, in the old days they killed a black just for sport, like they did my grandpappy. 'Twasn't nothin' to them. We ain't human in their eyes, see?' Then vehemently, 'But we *is*! As human as anyone else, no matter what colour they are. And that's a fact.'

Jess thought the story of Beulah's grandfather a truly appalling one.

'As for womenfolk,' Beulah went on. 'If you was pretty and caught some white man's eye it was common to be raped. And no one would ever do anythin' about it afterwards, no sirree. The woman was just meat to be used.'

'How awful,' Jess murmured, horrified.

''Twas no use goin' to the sheriff, he'd just laugh in your face and tell you to get your black ass out of there.'

Beulah fell silent, only rousing herself again when the kettle started to boil. 'Ain't life wonderful,' she commented caustically, heaving her huge frame aloft.

Ellie paused when she heard voices coming from Julius's bedroom. Beulah hadn't mentioned that he already had a visitor.

'Come in!' Julius called out when she knocked.

The other visitor was Marybeth, sitting on the edge of Julius's bed and holding his hand. Marybeth frowned when she saw the new arrival.

'I'm sorry,' Ellie apologised. 'I'll come back another time.'

'Not at all, join us,' Julius insisted, removing his hand from Marybeth's.

What a truly beautiful woman, Ellie reflected, wishing

she had a figure as stunning. 'I'm only here for a minute,' she said. 'I just wanted to see how you were.'

'Pretty sore I guess.' He indicated his chest. 'I'm all trussed up like a chicken here. Now, you haven't met Marybeth yet.' He proceeded to introduce the two.

'Your poor face,' Ellie sympathised when that was over. It was indeed a sight, all puffed and swollen with nasty-looking abrasions in places, while a section of his left cheek had been stitched.

'Looks worse than it is,' Julius assured her. 'Though the stitches do smart a tad.'

'I think he's bein' terribly brave,' Marybeth purred in a silky voice, eyes boring into Ellie's to the point it made Ellie feel decidedly uncomfortable.

'Bullshit, I'm being nothin' of the sort,' Julius protested.

'Oh but you are,' Marybeth insisted. 'At least I think so.'

Ellie wished now she hadn't come, but how had she been to know Marybeth would be here.

'I'll be round to thank your dad when I'm on my feet again,' Julius declared. 'I could have ended up really hurt if he hadn't shown up. I owe that guy.'

'It's just lucky he left the pub when he did,' Ellie replied.

'It certainly was for me.'

'I'm on my way over there now,' Ellie smiled. 'I'm working tonight.'

'Of course, it's Friday,' Julius nodded.

'A *barmaid*, how sweet,' Marybeth declared with just a hint of condescension in her voice, knowing that to be the English equivalent of what she would normally have called a cocktail waitress.

240

The hint was enough for Ellie to pick it up, colouring slightly. 'It's only part-time. I have a proper job during the day.'

'And what's that, honey?'

Ellie told the American woman.

'Interesting,' Marybeth murmured, giving Ellie the impression she found it quite the opposite. A position of little consequence.

'Ellie, go over to that drawer and open it will you?' Julius requested, pointing.

She crossed to a chest of drawers and indicated. 'This one?'

'That's it.'

She found two cartons of cigarettes inside which she took out.

'I've been meanin' to drop them by for days but never found the time,' Julius explained.

Ellie glanced at Marybeth whose expression had become inscrutable, with the exception of the eyes which had hardened. Oh God! she thought. Why oh why did Julius have to give her these now?

'Thank you,' she smiled at him.

'My pleasure, as always.'

Ellie's feeling of being uncomfortable had deepened even further. For the life of her she couldn't think why Marybeth was being so antagonistic, she hadn't done or said anything untoward after all. 'I suppose I'd better get along,' she murmured.

Julius was genuinely sorry to see her go and would have asked her to hang on if Marybeth hadn't been there.

'Give my thanks to Harry and the others who came out last night.'

She nodded. 'I will. They'll want to know how you are.'

She hesitated at the door. 'Goodbye, Marybeth. Nice to meet you.'

'And you, Annie.'

'It's *Ellie*,' Julius quickly corrected her.

'Oh, sorry. My fault.'

The misnaming had been quite intentional, Ellie was certain of that. She gave a last smile, and then was gone.

'Sweet child,' Marybeth said, picking up Julius's hand again. 'Seems fond of you.'

Marybeth's bitchiness hadn't been lost on Julius who wondered why on earth she'd behaved as she had. Then it dawned; she was jealous!

He found that highly amusing. Amusing, and surprising.

Chapter 15

'I wonder if I could have a word in private, Miss Oates?' Agnes Short requested.

Miss Oates halted, having been hurrying past. 'Can't it be said here, girl? I am rather busy.'

'I'd prefer in private if you don't mind.'

Miss Oates sighed, what now? 'All right, come with me.'

Agnes rose from her desk and dutifully followed the older woman to another part of the building where they could be alone.

Ellie glanced over at Connie who pulled a face and shook her head, indicating she had no idea what that was all about. Ellie then shook hers, indicating the same.

How mysterious, Ellie thought.

Ellie was first in the toilet at morning tea break, immediately lighting up which she'd been looking forward to for the past hour. Connie was next, also lighting up immediately.

Agnes was last to appear, the others speculating amongst themselves as to why she'd wanted to speak to Miss Oates.

'Come on, Agnes, give,' Connie demanded the moment the door was shut behind the girl.

'You mean Miss Oates?'

'Of course.'

Agnes smiled, but didn't instantly reply, enjoying being the centre of attention for once. 'I'm leaving,' she finally announced.

'Leaving!' exclaimed Elaine McIntosh. She hadn't thought of that possibility.

'Why?' Ellie frowned.

'I'm joining the WRNS.'

The others were completely taken aback. 'Bloody Nora!' Connie murmured. This was a complete surprise.

'Everybody is talking about doing their bit nowadays,' Agnes explained. 'So I thought I should too. Anyway, it has to be better than working here which bores the backside off me.'

'The WRNS?' Ellie mused. The female branch of the Navy. Pretty uniform too. She'd seen it.

'When do you go?' Elaine inquired.

'I'm not sure, but soon. I've had the interviews and been accepted. Next thing will be a letter in the post telling me where, and when, to report. It could be any time.'

Agnes was right, Ellie reflected. 'Doing your bit' was a favourite topic of conversation of late. Agnes's action in joining up gave her pause for thought.

'How did Miss Oates take the news?' Connie queried.

'There wasn't much she could say or object to. There is a war on, after all. What she did do was wish me all the very best, and to say pop in any time in future when I was passing.'

'Well,' murmured Elaine. Who would have thought the old bat would have suggested that.

Connie was tempted to remark that Agnes might land herself a boyfriend at long last, but didn't. That would have been too catty, given the circumstances.

'Tell us about the interviews?' Ellie prompted.

Agnes's news was the sole topic of conversation during the entire tea break.

'I tell you, Churchill isn't the man for the job,' Percy Noble declared with the air of someone who's convinced he's right.

So far it had been a quiet day at the fire station, the only call-out having been earlier to a chip pan that had caught alight. Albert had often said if he had a pound for every chip-pan fire he'd attended he'd be a million-aire. An exaggeration of course.

'So who would you have as PM?' Danny McGiver queried.

'Halifax. He's the obvious one.'

Albert, being a great fan of Churchill's, was fuming. 'Nonsense,' he retorted.

'Look at Churchill's history,' Percy persisted. 'One balls-up after another. India for instance, and what about Gallipoli? An awful lot of people lost their lives because of Gallipoli. It was a complete cock-up right from the word go, and all Churchill's doing. It was his idea to send the troops in there.'

Albert's expression became grim, knowing that to be

245

true. 'Everyone makes mistakes,' he replied rather lamely.

'Not on that scale they don't.'

'I don't like or trust any politician,' Henry Leway stated. 'As far as I'm concerned they're all a bunch of shysters. Grumbles every last one.'

'Isn't that a bit harsh?' Danny smiled, knowing his Cockney slang.

'I don't think so.'

'Churchill was lucky about Dunkirk,' Percy Noble said. 'I doubt he would have survived as PM if that miracle hadn't taken place. And believe me, a miracle it was. The Germans made a blunder and let our boys off the hook. Thank God.'

They all paused for a few moments to reflect on that. No one knew for certain what would have happened next if the entire BEF, British Expeditionary Force, had been killed or captured; it certainly would have been a blow of staggering enormity and consequence.

'Yes, Churchill would have been kicked out of office and we'd have sued for peace,' Percy went on.

The others stared at him in disbelief. 'Sued for peace?' Danny choked.

Percy shrugged. 'What else could we have done, you tell me? It would have been the only logical thing to do.'

'Bugger logic,' Albert hissed. 'We'd never have surrendered, never!'

'I didn't say surrender, I said sue for peace. There's a difference.'

'Like hell there is,' Albert riposted sharply. 'It's simply playing with words.'

'Well, that's what I think would have happened,' Percy insisted doggedly.

Danny decided this had gone far enough. The last thing they needed was a falling-out amongst themselves. Apart from anything else, that could be dangerous when out on the job.

'Let's not allow this to get out of hand,' he said in a placatory tone. 'I suggest we stop this argument and listen to the wireless instead. Agreed?'

Even Albert could see the sense in that, though he remained utterly convinced Percy and Henry were wrong about Churchill. There were various mutterings of agreement, including his.

The wireless set was already tuned to the Home Service on which the announcer was relaying the war news.

It made depressing listening.

It was Julius's first day back at the Embassy and pleased he was to be there having become extremely restless languishing at home. He was still trussed up, and sore, but his ribs were well on the mend according to the doctor whose instructions were to take it easy and not exert himself in any way.

He was about to turn into his office when he spotted Walter Zwicke and Marybeth further down the corridor, the pair of them laughing together.

Sharing reminiscences no doubt, he thought, and went inside.

* * *

'Yuck!' exclaimed Paul, screwing up his face. 'This tastes terrible, Mum.'

Albert gave his wife a sympathetic look. 'He's right, Jess. It's not very nice.'

Ellie sat in silence, not making a comment.

'It's powdered egg,' Jess explained. 'And before you say anything further that's all I could get. There isn't a fresh egg to be had in any of the shops.'

'Powdered egg,' Albert mused. 'Whatever next?'

'Spam.'

He stared at her in amazement. 'Never heard of it.'

'It's something new. Don't ask me what's in it, a sort of mishmash I believe. But that's what the butcher's selling now in place of what we're used to.'

'Sounds revolting,' Albert muttered.

'I don't know, but we'll soon find out if that's all that becomes available.'

Paul thought fondly of the wonderful meals he'd enjoyed at High Barton, his mouth watering at the memory. Not only wonderful but as much as you could eat at every sitting. Then he scowled, that was the only good memory he had of the place. Nothing, not even the temptations to be found in such abundance, would have got him back there. He'd loathed High Barton and his life there.

'Can I say something?' Ellie asked quietly.

Jess glanced at her, expecting another complaint about the powdered egg which she too found horrid. 'Of course.'

Ellie cleared her throat, not quite sure how her parents were going to take this. Well, she hoped.

'I've decided to join the ambulance service.'

'Ambulance service?' Albert queried with a frown. 'What's brought this on?'

'One of the girls at the office has joined the Wrens to do her bit for the war effort. And that set me thinking I should do something as well. I considered the Wrens and the WRAC, but realised that would mean me being away from home which I didn't want. Then I remembered a poster I saw a while back about the ambulance service and decided that was ideal.'

She stopped and stared from her mother to her father and back again. 'What do you think?'

Jess smiled. 'It's a tremendous idea, Ellie. I'm proud of you.'

'Have you applied yet?' Albert queried.

'No, I wanted to speak to you both first. I didn't want you thinking I'd gone behind your backs.'

Albert nodded his approval. 'I agree with your mum, it is a tremendous idea. You'll certainly be contributing a lot more than you do in that office of yours.'

A warm glow spread through Ellie, who was excited at the prospect of what lay ahead. And the best bit was, no more Miss Oates! 'It's settled then. I'll go along this evening and make inquiries.'

She hesitated, then said, 'One more thing.'

'What's that?' Jess queried.

'This powdered egg, it really does taste disgusting.'

They all laughed, Ellie hugely relieved that her parents were in favour of her plan.

* * *

'Good God, look at what just walked in,' Hazel whispered to Ellie, the pair of them behind the bar.

Taffy Roberts, resplendent in a brand-new army uniform, swaggered over. 'A pint of best,' he declared.

'Joined up I see,' Hazel observed.

'That's right, me beauty. They didn't have to conscript me neither. In I went and put me monicker on the dotted line. King and Country, eh?'

'I wondered why we hadn't seen you for a while,' Hazel remarked.

'Training on Salisbury Plain. Putting me and a lot of others through our paces. Now I'm a fully fledged fighting man.' He puffed out his chest. 'Bring on those German boyos. I'll show them what a Welshman can do. Oh yes indeed.'

Ellie was trying her best not to laugh. For some inexplicable reason the uniform made Taffy look ridiculous. Well, it didn't fit properly for a start, being at least one size too large. But it was more than that, though for the life of her she couldn't say what. It simply made him look ridiculous, that was all.

'That one's free for joining up,' Hazel declared, placing a pint in front of him. 'Everyone who does that gets one on the house.'

Taffy beamed. 'Why thank you, missus. I appreciate that.'

Picking up his drink he swaggered away. What he'd told Hazel and Ellie was a lie. He hadn't joined up at all, he *had* been conscripted, and it had taken a visit from PC McKechnie, plus the threat of jail, to get him to comply.

* * *

Deputy Section Officer D'Arcy was a woman in her mid-fifties with a no-nonsense look about her. She ran an experienced gaze over the six latest recruits for training. At first glance anyway, they seemed a likely bunch.

Ellie had reported at eight o'clock sharp to Lawn Road, Hampstead, not quite knowing what to expect. She was both excited and nervous, desperately hoping she'd fit in all right. There hadn't been much time to get acquainted with the other trainees, but they appeared to be friendly enough.

'You'll be here for two weeks,' D'Arcy informed them, having first introduced herself. 'And I have two words of advice. The first is, pay attention at all times, the second, if you don't understand something don't be frightened to say so. Is that clear?'

There was a chorus of yeses and nods.

'Does anyone know anything about first aid?'

No one did.

Pity, D'Arcy mused. It would have made things a bit easier. 'Can any of you drive?'

Again the answer was no all round.

This was the fifth lot of trainees and not a driver amongst them, D'Arcy thought in dismay, the service being chronically short of drivers.

Ellie had applied to join the London Ambulance Service, but instead had been assigned to the auxiliaries, known as the London Auxiliary Ambulance Service, an adjunct of the regular service.

'Well, we're going to have to do something about that,'

D'Arcy went on. 'So on top of the usual training you'll also be taught to drive a vehicle. Any objections?

'Good,' D'Arcy smiled when there weren't any. 'Now if you'll follow me into the building we'll make a start.'

Pee Wee arrived home to find Beulah sitting staring morosely into the fire. 'Hello, hon.'

She glanced over at him and smiled. 'You're even later than usual.'

'Had trouble findin' a cab. Waited ages before I could get hold of one.'

'You want somethin' to eat?'

Pee Wee shook his head. 'Just a drink, that's all. How about you?'

'I'm fine.'

He went to where the liquor was kept and poured himself a large bourbon. 'We were full again tonight. Lot of military people present.'

'Uh-huh.'

'We played good. Better than usual with a lot of jammin'. Lord Fitzaran was there with a Lady Hermione somethin' or other. You should have heard her talk, all fancy lah-di-dah. But pleasant enough.'

Beulah nodded, continuing to stare into the fire.

Pee Wee crossed over and sat opposite. 'You OK, hon?'

'Yeah, sure. I just . . .' She trailed off and bit her lip.

'You just what?' he prompted softly.

'It don't make sense. It's crazy. But I got this feelin' that's real peculiar.'

He was suddenly alarmed. 'You ain't sick, are you?'

'Not that kind of feelin', Pee Wee. Not the sick sort.' She snorted. 'I guess it's just my imagination, that's all.'

'Come on, Beulah, spill it.'

She glanced over at him. 'I believe it's called a premonition.'

He had a deep swallow of bourbon. 'Yeah? What sort of premonition?'

'That somethin' real bad is about to happen. And I mean *real* bad. The worst kind of bad. The kind that makes your skin go all creepy.'

Pee Wee wasn't sure what to reply to that. He'd never before known Beulah to have a premonition, if indeed that's what it was. 'Is it just a general thing, hon, or anythin' specific?'

'General, I guess. I ain't seein' no visions if that's what you mean.'

They sat in silence for a few seconds. 'Well, we gotta remember there's a war on here,' he said eventually. 'It could be to do with that.'

'Could be,' she agreed.

Pee Wee didn't like this, not at all. It made him distinctly uneasy. Spooked even.

'I just hope and pray it don't involve Julius,' Beulah muttered. Please God, not him. Her only son.

Pee Wee gulped down the remainder of his bourbon and shuddered. That had also crossed his mind, though he hadn't said. 'I'm sure it don't,' he declared, trying to reassure her. 'Hell!' he laughed. 'You been starin' into that fire for too long. It flickerin' and dancin'. It's got you hypnotised, that's what. Hypnotised into seein' things that ain't there.'

She forced a smile onto her face, well aware of what he was trying to do. 'You's probably right, Pee Wee. And you know somethin'?'

'What?'

'I think I will have a drink after all.'

'That's my girl!' he enthused, coming to his feet. 'Now don't you go worryin' no more, hear?'

'I hear, lover boy.'

He kissed her tenderly on the cheek. 'Three fingers or two?' Those were colloquial American measures of spirits.

Her reply made him roar.

Corporal Mann of the Transport Corps grimaced as Ellie ground the gears of the Vauxhall Cadet VX she was attempting to drive.

'Sorry,' Ellie apologised.

Patience, Corporal Mann told himself. Patience. Remember she's a woman and don't swear or yell her out.

'It's the clutch,' Ellie went on. 'That's what's giving me trouble.'

That and everything else, Corporal Mann thought. Christ, but she was clueless. 'Down into third now,' he instructed, wincing as she ground the gears yet again.

This was impossible.

'How long you been seeing Marybeth for?' Walter Zwicke casually asked Julius. 'I only found out the other day that you two were romancing one another.'

That surprised Julius. 'Hasn't Marybeth mentioned it?'

Zwicke stuck the end of a pencil into his mouth and shook his head.

'I'd thought she would have done.'

'We don't bump into one another very often. I suppose it's just never crossed her mind.' Zwicke's eyes glittered mischievously as he watched Julius.

'Oh I don't know. A good while I guess,' Julius returned to Walter's original question.

'Is it serious?'

Julius was careful how he answered that. For all he knew Zwicke and Marybeth might have been, and still were, good friends. 'You know how these things are? We rub along OK I suppose.'

Julius's evasiveness wasn't lost on Zwicke. 'Just wondered, that's all.'

Taking the pencil from his mouth he resumed work.

Julius thought about Marybeth and Zwicke. He had mentioned Zwicke to her shortly after he'd taken over Shelby's desk, her reply being, yeah, she remembered Zwicke, and that had been about it. Neither enthusiastic or unenthusiastic, non-committal rather, which surely meant they hadn't been good friends, simply colleagues.

Zwicke was simply being polite, showing interest, nothing more, he decided.

His first impression of the man hadn't changed. He still didn't like the guy.

Julius slammed his car door shut and locked it.

'Hello, Julius.'

The moon was up and there were many stars out so

he was able to recognise her standing on the pavement at the other side of his car. 'Hi!'

'Just back from the Embassy?'

'You got it.'

He walked round and joined her. 'How's the ambulance service doing?'

'Oh, it's doing fine, but I'm not. Far from it.'

He frowned. 'What's the problem?'

She pointed at the car. 'These things. Try as I might I just can't seem to get the hang of driving. The army corporal trying to teach me, although he hasn't said, is at his wits' end I think.'

'I'm sorry to hear that, Ellie. It's a bitch,' he sympathised.

'Having been given the opportunity I do want to drive, and drive well. But I don't think it's going to be. Part of the trouble is I've only got a fortnight to learn, and there's only so much time in a day when there's all sorts of other things to learn as well.'

Julius could see her point, it must be difficult. Then he had an idea. 'What are you doing after you've eaten?'

She failed to see the relevance of that. 'Nothing. Why?'

'I could take you out in my car if you want?' He glanced about. 'The black-out doesn't make the best of conditions, but if we go around the back streets we shouldn't run into much traffic. If any at all. What do you say?'

Ellie was thrilled. 'That would be wonderful!'

'OK, you got yourself a date. Knock on our door when you're ready.'

What a lovely man, she thought, not for the first time.

This was exceptionally kind of him. 'I'll do that.'

He smiled, his white teeth gleaming in the darkness. 'See you then.'

As Ellie went inside she was already mapping out in her mind what route they'd take, one that should be the quietest.

'Easy on that clutch, baby, easy. Don't stab with your foot, be more fluid,' Julius advised softly.

They were crawling along, but then that was the only safe way to drive under these conditions. The limited light from his taped-up headlights gave only a minimum of illumination.

Ellie for her part felt far more relaxed than she did with Corporal Mann. When Julius spoke to her there was no criticism, or exasperation, in his voice, which boosted her confidence.

'That's it,' he crooned. 'It's just a case of gettin' the right rhythm.'

'Like music?' she smiled.

'Yeah, like music. Think of the clutch and gears as instruments that you're playin'. Get to have a feel for them like they were an extension of yourself. Understand?'

'I think so.'

'You're doin' good, Ellie. Honestly. No BS.'

That puzzled her. 'What's BS?'

Julius laughed. 'Bullshit. An American expression. It means I'm not joshin' you.'

'Lying to me?'

'Exactly.'

Ellie was at a loss to see how bullshit equated with lying, but there you are. The American usage of English could be quite bizarre; at times it almost seemed a different language altogether.

'Now change down to turn this corner,' Julius instructed.

Ellie managed to do so without grinding the gears, which pleased her enormously. When she moved back up it again went smoothly.

'See, you can do it. Easy as pie,' Julius grinned.

Ellie's stomach contracted when his leg accidentally brushed against hers. She found she was holding her breath.

Julius had also been aware of the touch, enjoying it as well. Sitting this close to Ellie he could smell her, a smell he liked a lot. It certainly appealed.

They drove in silence for a little bit, so far having been lucky in not having encountered any other traffic. There again, no one in their right mind drove in the black-out unless they had to.

'You can start headin' for home now I reckon,' Julius said. 'I think that's enough for one night.'

'All right.'

'I thought I might have a beer at The Florence after this,' he declared casually. 'Care to join me?'

Ellie didn't have to be asked twice. 'I'd love to. Learning to drive is thirsty work.'

He laughed, a deep rumbling sound. 'If you say so, kid.'

'Ellie please. I don't like being called kid.'

That amused him. 'OK, *Ellie.*'

'That's better.'

He was enjoying this, her company, he truly was. 'We can have another lesson tomorrow night if you wish?'

'Are you sure, Julius? I don't want to take up too much of your time. That wouldn't be fair.'

'I'm free, so it's up to you.'

'Then it's a date, as you would put it.'

'A date,' he agreed.

'Well, I don't know how you've managed it but you pass,' Corporal Mann declared.

Ellie beamed. 'Thank you.'

'You've certainly improved over the past few days. Quite incredible really.'

All down to Julius, Ellie thought. He was a terrific teacher, and great fun to be with. Not to mention a handsome sod who was charming with it.

Later that day, Ellie's fortnight completed, Deputy Section Officer D'Arcy posted her to the station in Pentonville Road, the closest to Florence Street.

Chapter 16

'You sure are one vocal lady,' a sweat-slicked Julius commented, staring in admiration at Marybeth's naked body. It was as slicked as his own.

She took that as a compliment. 'Surely some of your past lovers have been just as noisy?' she teased, probing at the same time.

He cocked an eyebrow. 'What sort of question is that?'

'A fairly straightforward one, I should think.'

'Oh really?'

'Yes really.'

He gently stroked a silky thigh, appreciating the length and shape of her legs. 'I was brought up never to discuss bedroom matters other than with the person involved. I was taught that was manners.'

'Oh really?'

He laughed. 'Yes really.'

'You're probably right,' she admitted. 'I was just curious, that's all. I mean, I don't know how other women behave, never havin' been to bed with one.'

'I should hope not.'

Marybeth was lying; she had once years previously while at college. Enjoyable it had been too, but not really for her. She preferred the real thing. The hardness of a man's body, the male penetration. The differences between the genders.

'You want a drink?'

He shook his head.

Marybeth considered having one herself, then decided against it. 'What are you thinkin' about?'

He hadn't been thinking anything. 'You,' he lied, knowing that was the answer expected.

'Nice thoughts I hope?'

'How could they be otherwise with you involved?' She adored flattery and he was quite capable of laying it on thick when he felt like it. But not too often, that would have spoilt her.

'You are sweet, baby.'

There was a look in her eyes which told him their lovemaking wasn't finished, that this was merely a breathcatcher between bouts. His eyes flickered to the top of her legs. 'Not as sweet as some things I could name.'

Marybeth sighed, feeling that urgent urge returning. Not yet though, she told herself. Give him time to recover. She moved her bottom sensuously against the sheet beneath her, as Julius had so recently been.

Julius smiled as he watched. 'You certainly know how to get to a guy, don't you?'

'If you say so,' she purred huskily.

He turned away. 'Mind if I have a butt?'

That annoyed her slightly, as he'd hoped it would. 'Do you have to?'

He came to his feet and reached for his cigarettes. She

wasn't the only one who could play games. 'I'll have to go.soon,' he replied, lighting up.

He enjoyed the uncertainty and irritation that flashed across her face. 'I thought you were stayin' the night?'

He shrugged. 'I got a bunch of work in the car that needs doin'.'

'Then do it here,' she urged.

Of course there wasn't any work, he was just playing. 'That wouldn't happen, Marybeth. You're far too great a temptation,' he answered, changing tack, flattering her again.

She preened. 'I'll promise to leave you alone for a while till you're finished.'

'Is that a real promise?'

'Sure is, honey. On my life.'

Yeah, he thought. And he was the President of the United States.

Marybeth also came to her feet and shrugged herself into a rose-coloured cotton wrap that she'd bought in France. A favourite of Julius's. Going to him she kissed him on the cheek. 'Can't I make you change your mind?'

He simply smiled.

'Can't I?'

'I don't know,' he prevaricated, pretending to consider the matter. Of course he was going to stay, as he'd intended all along. But why let her have things all her own way?

She ran a hand across his chest, her breathing becoming shallower to the level he recognised only too well. Slowly she sank to her knees in front of him.

A moment later, before anything further could happen,

an air-raid siren close by began to wail.

Christ! he thought, tensing as he always did whenever a siren went off.

'It's only another false alarm,' Marybeth said, looking up at him. 'That's the third this week.'

He was about to reply when from off in the distance came the sound of what could only be bombs exploding. 'Holy shit!' he exclaimed; this wasn't a false alarm at all, but an actual raid.

'Put out the lights,' he instructed her, and hurried to the nearest window. When she'd done that he threw back the drapes and opened the window.

The explosions were louder now, although he couldn't see where they were impacting. He became aware of Marybeth holding tightly onto his arm.

'It's finally happened,' he said. 'The Krauts are hittin' London.'

Marybeth shivered, which had nothing whatsoever to do with the cold. Somewhere out there people were being killed and maimed. God alone knew how many. Standing there listening to that excited her in a way she'd never been excited before.

Suddenly there was a massive explosion, far louder than any of the others, which caused the glass to rattle in its panes.

Julius quickly shut the window again and pulled the drapes back into place. There could be no doubt about it, London itself was under attack. And a very heavy attack at that.

'Is there a shelter here?' Julius asked.

'We've been told to use the basement.'

'Then get dressed and we'll go down there.'

She clutched even more tightly onto his arm. 'Not yet, Julius. Not yet.'

'We could get killed standin' here, for Christ's sake!'

Her entire body was alive, throbbing with need. To her ears it seemed the mass bombing was getting closer.

'Come to bed,' she husked, voice choking with desire.

'Marybeth . . .'

His protest was stifled when her lips fastened onto his, her tongue a red-hot snake stabbing into his mouth, her hands everywhere, pleading with him to do as she wanted.

'Julius, please? Please?'

He groaned when a hand fastened onto him and began urgently to move. He was only flesh and blood after all.

Within minutes Marybeth was screaming like some animal being slaughtered in an abattoir. If Julius had thought her loud before then that was nothing compared to this.

And all the while there was the sound of exploding bombs and the rattle of ack-ack fire.

'I have to go back on duty, Mum, I might be needed,' Ellie declared to Jess, the pair of them trying to come to terms with what was happening, that at last the long-expected bombing was now actually taking place.

'You can't go out in that!' Jess exclaimed in horror.

A white-faced Paul watched them in mute terror, having come downstairs from his bedroom after the noise woke him.

'I have to, Mum. It's my duty.'

'But . . . but . . .' Jess trailed off impotently, every fibre of her being wanting her to protect her children, keep them safe from harm.

'I'll be all right. You'll see.'

Tears welled in Jess's eyes. This was terrible. She wished with all her heart Albert was here and not at work. 'You will take care?'

'Of course I will. Now you and Paul get out to that shelter. Tuck yourselves up in there.'

Jess followed Ellie into the hall where Ellie quickly slipped on her coat. It wasn't a long walk to Pentonville Road, she'd be there in ten or so minutes.

Ellie pecked Jess's cheek, and then was gone, the door slamming shut behind her.

Jess bowed her head, her lips moving in a muttered prayer.

'There must be hundreds of the bastards,' Percy Noble observed in awe, every member of the station outside staring up at the sky.

Albert could make out the shadowy outlines of the German planes, the occasional one being picked up by searchlights. Long lines of tracers seared heavenwards reminding him of a firework display he'd once seen in Highbury Fields.

Suddenly there was the sight of a plane being hit, its entire tail section disintegrating to leave fire streaming from where that had been.

A cheer went up as the stricken plane spiralled towards

the ground to vanish somewhere in Clerkenwell.

'I hope they roasted all the way down,' Danny McGiver declared vehemently, meaning every word of that. He truly did.

Albert turned to face the fiery inferno that lit up the horizon. It might have been the very gate to hell itself, he thought grimly. There was no doubt where the Jerries were targeting, the Docks, obviously their main attack point.

'I wouldn't like to be in the middle of that,' Henry Leway commented, joining Albert to stare at the orange and crimson conflagration lighting up the night sky.

'No,' Albert agreed softly.

The ack-ack gunners hit another plane, this one knocked sideways and then dropping like a stone. 'That's going to land in our manor,' Danny McGiver judged.

The section trooped back into the station waiting for the call-out which duly came ten minutes later.

An exhausted and still frightened Pee Wee arrived home about six in the morning. He called out Beulah's name, then Julius's. When he didn't get a reply to either he went out to the shelter in the back from which came the sound of Beulah snoring.

That made him smile as he poked his head into the entrance. 'Beulah, wake up, hon. Wake up.'

She did so with a grunt. 'That you, Pee Wee?'

'Sure is.'

'What's the time?'

He glanced at his wristwatch and told her. 'You OK?'

'Yeah yeah,' she replied dismissively. 'Is Julius with you?'

'He ain't in the house so he must have hung on wherever he was when the raid started. He'll probably call or be along soon.'

Beulah crawled out of the shelter, Pee Wee helping her to her feet. 'Oohhh!' she groaned.

'What's wrong?'

'My rheumatism. It's damp in there.' She made to move, and stumbled, Pee Wee quickly catching her.

'I's stiff all over and my back aches like hell,' she complained. 'What I need is a good hot tub.'

'I'll fix one for you,' he offered.

Beulah stared up at the sky. 'That sure was one son-of-a-bitchin' clambake last night,' she declared. 'I was so scared I nearly peed my pants.'

Pee Wee ran a hand over his face; he was dog tired. 'I had to walk back,' he said. 'Couldn't get a cab no way.'

'You must be bushed?'

'I am. Bushed as can be.'

Beulah glanced over at their house, and then next door to where the Sykeses lived. There was no apparent damage to either that she could make out. In the confusion of the night before, and shut up in the shelter, it had been difficult to know where the bombs were landing.

'Let's get some coffee,' she said.

'There's nothin' shamin' in changin' your mind you know,' Pee Wee declared over their second cup.

Beulah stared blankly at him. 'What you talkin' about?'

'Stayin' on here. In London that is. It wouldn't be no sweat for Julius to arrange a boat for us. We could be back in the good ole US of A before the month is out.'

She regarded him steadily. 'That what you want, Pee Wee?'

'Want? I told you before, hon, it ain't what I want. It's what you want that matters.'

Beulah would never have admitted it, but during the height of the raid she actually had considered returning. 'I'm stayin' put,' she declared stubbornly. 'As long as Julius is here then I stays with him.'

Pee Wee sighed, he'd thought that's what she'd say. 'That's OK by me then.'

'You sure? I won't take offence if—'

'I said it's OK by me, Beulah,' he interjected. 'And I means it. Sheet! We been married too long for me to go off leavin' you now. What kinda man you take me for?'

She gave him a broad, loving smile. 'The best kind, Pee Wee. But then I've always known that. The very best kind.'

Reaching across he took hold of her hand and squeezed it. 'You too, hon. A lady of the first water.'

At which point their conversation was interrupted by a call from Julius to tell them he was safe, and how were they?

'I'll fix you that tub,' Pee Wee said to Beulah when, much relieved, she came off the telephone. 'Then I gotta hit the sack before I falls over.'

'You want me to come with you? I could use some more sleep. It sure was uncomfortable in that shelter, and that's a fact.'

'I couldn't think of anythin' nicer.'

'Hell no,' she agreed, and they both laughed.

What they'd just experienced was the first night of what was to become known as the Blitz.

'That was only the start you know,' Albert said wearily, sinking into a chair, having just come off shift.

'Was it bad for you?'

He shook his head. 'But it must have been for the poor buggers who do the Docks area. They took a real pounding. The figures are unofficial, but I'm told there are hundreds dead. Between three and four by all accounts. And that's only the dead, not the injured.'

A great feeling of sadness settled over Jess. All those lives! 'Would you like some breakfast?'

'What have you got?'

'Powdered egg.'

He groaned. 'Better than nothing I suppose.'

'I'll put the kettle on.'

Jess was in the middle of cooking, wishing she had some bacon to go with the egg but that wasn't to be had for love nor money, when Ellie arrived in. 'I could use some of that tea, Mum. I'm dry as a bone.'

Jess set out a fresh cup and saucer. 'How did your night go?'

'Not too bad, considering. A stray stick of bombs fell over the Cally Road way, but luckily landed mostly on waste ground. There were only a few casualties, and none of them serious.'

Albert glanced around. 'Paul gone to school?'

'He went and hasn't come back, so it must be open,' Jess replied.

'How's he?'

'Very frightened at the start of the raid, then we went into the shelter and he thought that was a great adventure. Said it was just like camping.'

Albert laughed. 'Trust him.'

'Egg for you, Ellie?'

'It's powdered,' Albert informed his daughter, screwing up his face.

'I'm not really that hungry, Mum. Toast will do. Is there any jam?'

Jess shook her head. 'It's finished and we won't get our next allocation till Friday. So you'll have to do without I'm afraid.'

Ellie shrugged; they were getting used to having to do without thanks to the severe rationing in place. 'The last lot wasn't all that nice anyway. Tasted funny.'

Jess had heard the rumour going round that jam was now being made out of turnips and swede instead of fruit, but decided not to mention that. They griped enough about powdered egg and the ubiquitous Spam.

Albert glanced at the mantelpiece clock. 'Let's hear the news and what they have to say about last night. Ellie, you're closest.'

Ellie switched on the wireless set, the news predictably dominated by the air raid.

It had been a frantic morning for Julius, his phone ringing seemingly non-stop. He absent-mindedly stroked his chin where he'd nicked it when using Marybeth's unfamiliar razor.

After their lovemaking they'd gone down to the basement where they'd spent the duration of the raid with other inhabitants of the apartment block. At one point, when there had been something of a lull in the bombing, he'd nipped back upstairs for bedding which he and Marybeth had wrapped round themselves before finally going to sleep sitting propped up against a wall.

Julius smiled to himself. On arriving at the Embassy the word had been that the Ambassador had decamped for safety reasons to a house in Windsor. The majority of staff had thought that funny, if cynically so. Wasn't it just like Joe Kennedy to hightail it at the first sign of danger with scant regard for those he'd left behind in the hot seat?

Julius sat back in his chair and closed his eyes. Christ, but he was tired. Between Marybeth and the raid he hadn't gotten much sleep, a couple of hours at most, if that.

Walter Zwicke frowned as Julius lit a cigarette. 'Do you have to do that in here?' he asked waspishly.

That surprised Julius, for Zwicke had never previously complained about his smoking. 'You got a problem with it, Walter?'

'I've never mentioned, but I do suffer from asthma. Not badly, but I'm a sufferer nonetheless.'

Anyone else and Julius would have immediately put out his cigarette, but not with Zwicke. His aversion to the man grew with almost every passing day. The guy was a slimeball. A real jerkoff.

'You married, Walter?' he queried, evading the subject of smoking.

Zwicke blinked. 'As a matter of fact I'm not.'

'It's just, that's something else you've never mentioned. I reckoned you probably weren't.'

'I guess the right little lady has never happened along. Leastways, not so far,' Zwicke smiled.

Zwicke was lying about being asthmatic, Julius just knew that to be so. He probably simply didn't like being round smokers, that's all. Well, tough shit.

'So why London during a war?' Julius probed. 'Were you posted here?'

Zwicke shook his head. 'It was volunteers only. I reckoned it would be a great help to being promoted. Hell, it must look good on your record, don't you think?'

Julius had to agree with that. 'And you're ambitious?'

'You got it. I want to go straight to the top. Be a main man. How about you?'

Julius considered that. 'Yes and no I suppose. If it happens, fine. If not, well I can live with that. I'm not the pushy sort if that's what you mean.'

Zwicke frowned, being pushy was second nature to him. Julius made it sound as if it was wrong. A fault of some kind.

Julius took a deep drag on his cigarette, then slowly exhaled, enjoying Zwicke's look of irritation.

'How's Marybeth?' Zwicke suddenly inquired.

'Jim Dandy.'

'As I said before, she sure is some good-looking dame. You're to be envied.'

Julius couldn't stop himself, Zwicke was beginning to show an overkeen interest in Marybeth. 'By you?'

Zwicke laughed. 'By any red-blooded guy I'd imagine.'

Neatly dodged, Julius thought. A politician's answer. 'Yeah, I guess you're right.'

'Wonderful ass.'

That jolted Julius, finding it insulting. It was Zwicke's tone of voice, a combination of licentiousness and sleaze that made the so-called compliment sound dirty.

Julius didn't reply.

Zwicke glanced at his wristwatch. 'Hey, look at the time! I got a meeting. Catch you again later.'

Julius watched Zwicke hurry from the office, wondering about the man.

Wondering.

It was bedlam in the Casualty Department, wounded people sitting and lying absolutely everywhere. The atmosphere was one of pain coupled with despair.

'Set her down,' Ellie instructed Josie Farnham who was partnering her in the makeshift ambulance she'd been given to drive. Gingerly they laid the stretcher they were carrying, and the patient on it, on the floor.

A Nursing Sister walked briskly over. 'How many have you got?' she demanded brusquely.

'Four, including this one,' Ellie replied. 'The other three can walk but need help to get in here.'

Sister nodded and glanced down at the young woman on the stretcher who was unconscious and groaning piteously. Both legs had been blown away at the knee, the wounds temporarily bandaged by Ellie herself.

Sister squatted and made a hasty examination. She knew from experience, and because all the available doctors were already working flat out, that the woman hadn't a hope of surviving.

Standing, she glanced around. 'Find a space somewhere and put her there,' she instructed. 'Then bring in the others.'

For a brief moment a look of terrible hopelessness crossed Sister's face, then it was gone, her professional, no-nonsense expression back in place.

'Right,' she said, and left them.

'You heard her,' Ellie nodded to Josie. Picking up the stretcher again they carried it to the first available space where they made the young woman as comfortable as they could.

Ellie stared at the still groaning young girl, wishing there was more she could do. But there wasn't. At least the woman was unconscious, which was something of a blessing.

When the three walking wounded had been brought in and deposited Ellie whispered to Josie that she had to go to the bathroom. She'd be out in a minute or two.

On entering the bathroom she locked herself in a cubicle and, leaning over the bowl, threw up.

Somewhere someone was shrieking in agony.

Hazel was taken aback as Ellie came into the pub next morning when they'd only been open ten minutes.

'I need a drink,' Ellie declared, slumping onto a bar stool. 'Large gin and orange please.'

'At this time?'

Ellie nodded. 'I've just come off duty. My first night at the sharp end.' She shuddered, then said in a whisper, 'It was terrible. Ghastly. You've no idea.'

Hazel poured the drink and placed it in front of Ellie who immediately had a swallow. 'Do you know Mackenzie Road?'

'Of course.'

'Well, it isn't there any more. The whole street was flattened. We think the Jerries must have been after the power station there. Well, they got it.'

Ellie took another swig. 'There were bodies everywhere, Hazel. And bits of bodies, arms, legs.' She halted for a second, then croaked, 'I saw a decapitated head. It was just lying on the pavement, eyes open, the expression one of surprise. He'd been an old man with white hair.'

Ellie finished her drink and fumbled for her cigarettes. Her hands were shaking as she lit up.

'Another?'

'Please.'

Hazel was doing that when she remembered. 'I found something of yours,' she said.

'Oh?'

Hazel gave Ellie her drink, then went to a drawer. 'Your engagement ring,' she declared, laying it beside Ellie's glass.

Ellie had forgotten all about the lost ring. 'Where was it?'

'On one of the shelves. God knows how it got there or wasn't found when we were searching. But you've got it back now.'

Ellie stared at the ring, remembering, thinking of George.

'It's a keepsake if nothing else,' Hazel sympathised. 'And worth a bob or two if you want to sell it.'

'Yes,' Ellie agreed dully. It was both of these things.

'Do you want to talk some more about last night?'

Ellie shook her head.

'Be alone?'

'Not really. But I'd better get back, Mum will be worried.'

Hazel patted Ellie on the hand and then turned away to get on with things.

Outside again, Ellie took the ring from her coat pocket and crossed to the nearest drain. The diamonds twinkled briefly in the harsh morning light before vanishing into the depths below.

Chapter 17

Try as he might Julius just couldn't get comfortable, the platform at Victoria tube station unyielding beneath his backside. He reckoned he was one of several hundred spending the night on that particular platform.

The air was hot, and smelly, some of the latter from the tube itself, but mainly arising from the heavy concentration of bodies.

Earlier in the day he'd been sent to Windsor with several highly classified documents for the Ambassador. Having delivered them safely he'd started back, only to break down close to the station after nightfall.

He knew what was wrong with his car and could easily have fixed it himself, but when he'd opened the hood, and switched on his flashlight, an irate ARP Warden had materialised seemingly out of nowhere screaming, 'Put that light out!'

Explanation, even argument and showing his diplomatic credentials, had been useless. The Warden had insisted the flashlight stay off, and if he disregarded that the police would be summoned.

Not wishing to be involved in a police incident, which would be embarrassing, Julius had been left with two choices. Either try to walk home, which would have been a total nightmare in the black-out, or else spend the night in the tube and fix his car come daylight. He'd decided on the tube as the sensible thing.

He spotted a young girl staring at him, and guessed it was because he was black, the girl quickly turning away when he smiled.

Marybeth was going to be wondering what had happened when he didn't show, having arranged to take her out. Wondering? She'd probably be livid thinking he'd deliberately stood her up. Marybeth could be very unreasonable at times and had a ferocious temper.

He thought about the documents he'd delivered to the Ambassador skulking out at Windsor away from the dangers of the Blitz. He didn't know why, but he'd gotten the distinct impression something was wrong, and that the documents were closely related to whatever it was. The atmosphere in the Ambassador's residence had been unusual to say the least.

How incredibly resilient these people were, Julius reflected, gazing about him. None of them seemed in the least way put out at having to spend their night like this. He knew from the newspapers that this was a common occurrence for many of them, and not a one-off as it was for him. You simply had to admire their fortitude and ability to just get on with things no matter what. He couldn't imagine Americans being the same way. But then the English prided themselves in being called the bulldog breed, he could see now how apt that nickname was.

And then he spotted them, his jaw almost dropping

278

open in amazement. A young couple, covered by a blanket so that only their heads remained visible, were, and there was no doubt about it, actually having sex, their bodies moving slowly and rhythmically together.

'Holy shit!' he swore softly, unable to believe his eyes. How could they, surrounded as they were by so many other people, in full view of all, actually do that, the act of utmost intimacy. It was mind-boggling.

Julius shook his head in bewilderment. Where was the famous English reserve he'd heard so much about before leaving the States? Another casualty of war perhaps, if it had indeed ever existed at all.

He tore his eyes away to look elsewhere, that being the least he could do, the decent thing.

'Holy shit,' he repeated, stunned.

He couldn't wait to tell Marybeth. She'd scream with laughter.

And she did.

Jess groped for the candle she'd extinguished several hours previously and the box of matches beside it. Moments later the candle flickered into life lighting up the inside of the shelter. An eerie interior where shadows danced with every movement she made.

She couldn't sleep; try as she might she just hadn't been able to drop off. Not helped by the far-off crump of exploding bombs and the rattle of incessant ack-ack fire.

Paul, tucked up warmly, was gently snoring. His innocent face might have been that of a cherub fallen to earth.

Reaching across she gently ran a hand over his hair,

smiling to think of how much she loved this darling son of hers. How like his father in looks he was fast becoming. The spit, a chip off the old block. She must mention that to Albert when he got home off shift.

Her own face clouded over to think of Albert and Ellie out there in the middle of what was going on. What a worry it was, a sick pain that gnawed at her insides and stretched her nerves almost to breaking point.

She'd developed the art of not showing too much concern when they arrived back from work; they'd had enough to deal with without her adding to the problem. But they both knew what she went through, of course they did. Especially Albert.

She glanced at the wind-up bedside clock she always brought into the shelter with her. Twenty past three, hours to go yet before the nightly ordeal would be over and they could return to the house.

She shivered for, despite having several cardigans on, she was still cold. This wouldn't have been so bad in summertime, but it was mid November and the weather that went with that. Perhaps she could lay her hands on a small paraffin stove somewhere. Though getting the paraffin would be difficult. It, like everything else, was scarce. And undoubtedly horrendously expensive if she did find some.

There was always the black market of course, but Albert wouldn't allow her to buy from that, he being dead against it. Every spiv dealing in the black market should be taken out and shot, he'd declared more than once. There again, he wasn't the one having to endure this damn shelter night after night. God bless him.

Outside the bombs continued to fall and the ack-ack rattle.

Albert had never seen anything like it. From where he was standing it seemed as if all of London was ablaze. The sweat was running off him in rivers.

The Islington Fire Service had been called in to help the City of London Fire Service. His understanding was that Moorgate, Aldgate, Cannon Street and Old Street were taking the full brunt of what was the heaviest attack yet. Building after building, whole streets of them, had already been devastated. And still the conflagrations raged despite the Herculean efforts being made to bring them under control.

In front of Albert and the others was a wall of flame, a great beast intent on devouring all in its path. More fires, none of them small, burned fiercely all around.

'Parachute mines!' someone shouted. And there they were, serenely floating downwards, all with a lethal load of explosives attached.

From overhead came the drone of the German planes, their pilots being guided from afar by the extent and ferocity of the blaze.

Danny McGiver cursed volubly as the hose he was holding and directing at the fire suddenly ran dry, the water source having been used up.

'Look out!' Henry Leway screamed at Albert as a nearby office block buckled and began to crash earthwards, great chunks of masonry flying and bouncing in all directions.

Percy Noble was running to help Danny when the

ground opened up beneath his feet and, with a yell, he disappeared from sight. A sheet of flame roared up from the hole into which Percy had fallen.

Jess was a bag of nerves, Albert and Ellie should have been home hours ago and still there wasn't any sign of them. She worried a nail, a habit she'd recently got into.

She started a little later at the sound of the front door opening, then closing again. It was Ellie who entered the kitchen.

'You're late,' Jess declared unnecessarily.

Ellie sank into a chair where she ran a hand over her soot-blackened face.

'And where's your dad? That's what I want to know,' Jess went on, a tremble in her voice.

'He's probably still down at Moorgate,' Ellie replied. 'I saw him there earlier.'

Jess frowned. 'Moorgate?'

Ellie explained what had happened, words failing her when she tried to describe the sheer immensity of the fires that had been raging there and elsewhere.

'Dear God,' Jess whispered, horror-struck.

'I've been to-ing and fro-ing to the hospitals all night long,' Ellie said. 'The casualties were never-ending.'

'Many killed?'

Ellie nodded. 'Hundreds from what I could gather. And I presume those are just the ones we know about.'

Jess took a few moments to digest that. 'But your father's safe?'

'He was when I saw him. I don't think he noticed me

282

though. He was too busy at the time.'

Jess's expression became sympathetic. 'You look dead beat.'

Ellie yawned. 'I am. All I want to do is crawl into bed and sleep for a week at least.'

Jess could understand that. 'Would you like something to eat?'

Ellie shook her head. 'The mobile canteens were out in force with cups of tea and sandwiches for whoever wanted them. I had a bite before my last run to a hospital. That'll do for now.'

'Then up you go to bed. And wash your face first. It's filthy.'

'I'm not surprised,' Ellie muttered, thinking she didn't give a toss what she looked like. All she craved was sleep, and hoped she didn't have nightmares about what she'd just been through and witnessed, knowing some of the scenes from the previous night would stay vividly etched in her mind till her own dying day.

Ellie had been in bed for nearly an hour before Albert arrived home to slump into the same chair she had.

'Ellie told me about it,' Jess said. 'She saw you earlier.'

Albert glanced up at her, his face strained and haggard. 'We lost Percy Noble. Poor bastard.'

Jess had met Percy on several occasions but couldn't say she knew him well. 'He was married, wasn't he?'

Albert slowly nodded. 'Wife and four kids. The youngest only a nipper.'

'Would you like a cup of tea?' she asked grimly.

'Please. That would be lovely.'

She filled the kettle and put it on. 'I take it you're not hurt in any way?'

'No. Danny McGiver got a bit burnt though. Nothing serious.'

That was a relief. 'Do you want to go to bed right away, or stay up for a while?'

He sighed, a sigh that seemed to come from the very depths of his being. 'No bed for me. I'm due back in two hours, so I'll just have a doze in this chair.'

'Two hours! But you've only just come off,' she protested.

He was only too well aware of that. 'Fires are still burning, Jess. We have to return and assist those still at the scene.'

What could she say? Nothing. It was his job and he had to do what had to be done. 'Was it really as awful as Ellie described?' she asked softly.

Albert's eyes momentarily clouded over in memory. 'It was . . . it was . . .' He broke off and shook his head. 'Monumental,' he said at last. 'An ocean of flame stretching as far as the eye could see. I honestly don't think London can take another night like it.'

Jess went to him and kissed him on the forehead. 'I'm sorry about Percy. He seemed a decent man to me.'

'He was. I trusted him with my life, and have done on occasion. He'll be sorely missed at the station.'

Jess busied herself with the tea things. 'How about some breakfast?' she asked over her shoulder as the tea was mashing.

There was no reply.

Turning she found Albert was already fast asleep, his head lolling to one side.

She was tempted not to, but knew he'd be furious if she didn't, so she woke him when it was time to go back to the station.

Josie Farnham glanced at her watch, and frowned. Twenty past ten and no bombing yet, what was going on? 'Do you think it's possible they're not coming tonight?' she queried hopefully of Ellie.

There were eight of them present, four playing rummy, two others immersed in books.

Ellie shrugged. 'Search me. I don't know.'

'It's beginning to look like it.'

Ellie thought about that. 'Maybe it's bad weather over the Channel?'

'Could be.'

'There again, perhaps they're on their way even now. Changing tactics by coming later than usual.'

Ellie hesitated, then said slowly, 'I wonder . . .'

'What?'

'According to the papers and news broadcasts our boys have been giving them a right pasting when they reach the coast. Maybe they've halted for a while to regroup, or assemble new planes to replace the many they've lost.'

'If that's true,' Josie mused. 'Who knows what's true any more? If the figures put out are right then we've already shot down the entire Luftwaffe twice over.'

Ellie laughed. 'Maybe somebody can't count?'

Josie also laughed. 'Maybe that's so.'

Josie settled into a chair and picked up her knitting. She was making a pullover for her brother in the Army, though since the Blitz had started she'd hardly made any progress with it.

When midnight came and went the general agreement was it was going to be a raid-free night. For which they were all profoundly grateful.

'I'm not going!' Paul declared, his face screwed up in defiance. 'You can't make me. I'll run away if you do.'

'Enough of your cheek,' Albert growled. 'I won't have you speaking to us like that. We're your parents, don't forget.'

Paul sobbed and, running to Jess, buried his face in her skirt.

The cause of all this was the letter they'd received from Paul's school. Many of the children originally evacuated had returned home and now the authorities wanted to re-evacuate them. This time, which they hadn't been informed before, the children's destination was to be Lincolnshire.

'There there, don't get yourself into such a state,' Jess crooned, stroking Paul's hair. She didn't want him to go either. That was the last thing she wanted after his experience with the Sellys.

'Albert?'

He was at a loss what to do for the best. It was over a week now since the bombing had stopped, and life had more or less returned to normal. Well, normal for wartime that is. For the time being at least, London was relatively safe again.

Albert could plainly see how distressed Paul was at the thought of going away again, and he could hardly blame him after the Sellys. That had been awful for the lad and it had made him extremely angry when Jess had told him about it. The boy had been treated virtually like slave labour. On the other hand, as Jess had pointed out, that was the way of things for youngsters in the country.

'I don't know,' he said at last.

'Please, Dad?' Paul whimpered, his face now tear-streaked.

'What do you think, Jess?'

She felt Paul's grip tightening on her skirt. 'It's so difficult, Albert.'

He couldn't have agreed more. The trouble was, he firmly believed this was only a temporary lull in the bombing and that it would soon start again. But he might be wrong.

'It was horrible in Devon,' an anguished Paul choked. 'And I missed you both so much. I was promised cowboys and indians, and all sorts, but it was only hard work.'

Albert listened to that with a sinking feeling in the pit of his stomach. He remembered only too well the rosy picture of life in Devon that he'd painted for Paul to persuade him to go. A rosy picture that couldn't have been more untrue. Who was to say things would be any different in Lincolnshire, another rural community.

Albert took a deep breath. All his instincts told him

Paul should leave the city, but what effect would that have on the boy, not to mention Jess, after what had gone on before? 'I just don't know what to do,' he confessed.

'Then let him stay,' Jess said quietly.

Paul sobbed again, this time in relief.

'Are you sure, Jess?'

She looked down at her son, then again at Albert. 'It'll break my heart if he goes. Truly it will.'

Moments ticked by while Albert and Jess stared at one another. He knew she meant what she said, literally. He couldn't do that to Jess, not in a million years.

'All right,' he agreed.

Jess quickly knelt and gathered Paul into her arms. And now it was she who cried.

Albert prayed they weren't making a mistake.

Marybeth came into Julius's office and closed the door behind her. 'Where's Zwicke?' she queried, Julius being alone.

'Gone to a meeting with one of the Russian attachés. Why?'

She crossed over and sat on the edge of his desk. 'Heard the latest scuttlebutt?'

'Which is?'

'Kennedy is bein' recalled to Washington.'

'Aaahhh!' Julius exhaled, and laid down his pen. Now this was news. 'Are you sure?'

She shrugged. 'I said scuttlebutt, nothing's official yet. But I'm told it came from an impeccable source in the British Government.'

Who would be well pleased, Julius thought, Kennedy being no friend of theirs. He couldn't help but wonder if Churchill himself was behind Kennedy being recalled, *if* it was true. 'Any idea who the new guy might be?'

Marybeth shook her head. 'Nothin' on that so far. Though the appointment must have been made by now.'

Julius couldn't say he was sorry to see the back of Kennedy, who hadn't been popular with many of the staff, especially those, and he was one of them, who liked England and the English.

Julius then remembered the documents he'd taken out to Windsor and the unusual atmosphere he'd encountered. Could it be one of them was the actual document informing Kennedy he was being recalled? It was certainly a possibility.

'I wonder who it will be?' Marybeth mused. 'The new guy I mean.'

Julius had no answer to that. Any name he might come up with would be sheer speculation. He only hoped whoever it was would be better-suited to the post, by which he meant more sympathetic to the English, than Kennedy had been. However, they were getting beyond themselves here. They didn't know for certain Kennedy was going. So far it was only rumour.

'I was thinkin' about you earlier,' Marybeth smiled at Julius. 'Which is the real reason I'm here.'

'Oh?'

'Why don't we go away for a weekend together? Get out of London and into the countryside. I thought we could book into one of those quaint old English taverns with a thatched roof and crazy beams everywhere. What do you say?'

Julius sat back in his chair and studied Marybeth. She was becoming even more clinging of late, even more demanding of his time. Nonetheless, the idea appealed. 'Anywhere specific in mind?'

'Not really. I'll leave that up to you. You're the guy after all. You make the arrangements. Just one thing though, we register as Mr and Mrs Poston. I'm not havin' any of that shit with separate bedrooms, the English bein' so prudish and all.'

'You'll have to wear a weddin' ring to pull that off,' he pointed out.

'Don't worry, hon. That'll be my department. When we leave I'll be wearin' a gold band. Bet your sweet butt I will.'

He continued to study her, noting the amused glint in her eyes. Why, oh why, did he feel there was some secret agenda here?

Imagination, he decided, shrugging off the notion. And he certainly could use the break. 'Any weekend?' he queried.

She nodded. 'Just say the word and off we toddle.'

'I'll get onto it then.'

Bending over she kissed him on the lips. 'You do that.'

After she'd gone he made a note in his diary before resuming the work she'd interrupted.

'Gosh!' Paul exclaimed, eyes popping. 'Are you sure they're real?'

Eddy Ackworth, long since having recovered from his meningitis, and also returned to Islington, nodded vigorously. 'Cannon shells from a Jerry fighter.' He pointed. 'Look, you can see the Jerry writing.'

A well-impressed Paul could indeed see the strange, Gothic lettering. 'Where did you get them?'

'Found them of course. They were lying in the road close to a bombed-out house. I searched all around but couldn't find any more.'

Paul gazed at the shells in awe.

'Mickey Silver has a parachute from a mine that was dropped that never went off. The soldiers who defused the mine left it behind.'

Paul was green with envy, desperately wanting a souvenir for himself.

Eddy put the shells away in his pocket. 'What do you want to play at?'

Paul shrugged.

'Shall we get the tyres out?'

Paul thought that was a good idea. 'All right.'

The tyres in question were old ones from cars which they played with by propelling them along the road using the palm of a hand. Sometimes they used a stick instead of their hand. It just depended.

'Let's go then.'

The tyres were kept in a shed at the rear of Eddy's house which was four streets away. All the way there, and for the rest of that morning, Paul couldn't help thinking enviously of the shells and parachute.

* * *

A laughing Marybeth collapsed onto the large antique bed that dominated their bedroom. An amused Julius came and sat beside her. 'What's brought this on?'

'I don't know. I'm just enjoyin' myself, I guess. Today's been fun.'

'For me too,' he smiled.

'Those English lanes are wonderful to walk along and the olde worlde decor of this place just blows my mind.' Then, seductively, 'But most of all I'm enjoyin' just bein' with you.'

'And I with you,' he further smiled, standing up. 'Let me put some more logs on the fire and then we'll turn in. OK?'

'Oh yes,' she breathed, a voice filled with sexual promise.

'You use the bathroom first then. Sorry it's along the corridor, but that's how it is.'

Marybeth collected what she needed and left him attending to the fire.

She'd do what she intended when it was his turn in the bathroom.

Marybeth was already in bed when he returned, her smile catlike and full of anticipation. She'd turned off all the lights except the bedside one. The fire, with the guard securely in place, crackled merrily.

She watched him undress, admiring the lean and taut body that she knew so well. She squeezed her thighs together, eager for what was coming next.

'Shit,' Julius exclaimed softly a few moments later, rummaging through his bag.

'What's wrong, hon?'

'I can't find the rubbers. I'm sure I packed them.'

Of course he wouldn't find them, she gloated. She'd already removed them and hidden them in her own bag. 'If you packed them they must be there,' she declared disingenuously.

He kept on rummaging, to no avail. 'Son of a bitch,' he swore.

'No luck?'

Making a face, he looked at her and shook his head. 'I'm certain I packed them. I can remember doing it.'

'Well, you're obviously mistaken.'

'Sorry, hon,' he said, going to the bed and getting in.

'That's all right. It doesn't matter.'

'Honest?'

'Honest,' she lied.

She switched off the bedside light and snuggled up close. 'Why don't you kiss me?'

As their lips met she ran a finger down the crack of his buttocks, delighted at the reaction it had when she felt a nudge on her leg. He'd always been quick like that.

'No, hon, sorry,' Julius apologised, drawing slightly apart. 'I hate disappointin' you but I can't without a rubber.'

'Of course you can,' she husked, fondling him.

He was tempted, sweet Jesus he was. But common sense managed to override that. 'What if somethin' should happen?'

'It won't,' she replied glibly.

'But it could.'

Her hands were now moving everywhere, urging, caressing, stroking, everything she could think of to make him throw caution to the wind, her own need growing with every passing second.

Julius groaned; if only he could have bought some more rubbers, but that was impossible this time of night, especially in the deepest countryside. And tomorrow was Sunday, everything would be shut.

'We can't stop now, hon. We can't,' she pleaded.

It took every ounce of his willpower, but he managed it. With a muffled exclamation he rolled out of bed and onto his feet. 'I said no, Marybeth, and I mean it. Now you cool down a bit and I'll do the same. We just can't take the risk and that's all there is to it.'

She knew there was no persuading him, the moment having come and gone.

She was absolutely livid. Her plan had failed.

Chapter 18

'We've had terrible rows about it,' Beulah declared. 'But I'm just not sleepin' in that damn shelter any more. It wasn't built for someone my size anyway.'

Jess nodded her sympathy, having dropped by for a chat as she hadn't seen Beulah for several days.

'It's also playin' murder with my rheumatism being out there where it's hellish damp. So I told Pee Wee, that's it. My fat ass stays in here at night-time and if I get blown to kingdom come, then so be it, goddamn it.'

Jess had to smile at Beulah's colourful language, even if she didn't approve of it. But that was Beulah for you and her friend was American so you had to make allowances for the cultural differences.

'What about you, Jess, doesn't it bother you?'

'Our shelter isn't that damp,' Jess replied truthfully. 'Not that you'd really notice it. And I can't say I have all that much trouble getting in and out.'

Beulah sighed. 'That's because you're a stick compared to me, honey. You don't know how much I envy you that. There was a time you know, yeah, there was a time. But Pee Wee swears he likes me as I am, so who am I to argue?'

'It is a lot safer out there, don't forget,' Jess tentatively pointed out.

'That's what Pee Wee says. But then I remind him he don't have no rheumatism. Fit as a fiddle that man. Yes sir. And another thing I remind him, his ass ain't as humongous as mine. Why, when I'm in there I feel that if I stood up I'd take the whole goddamn shelter with me. And what if I get stuck with no Pee Wee to help, what then?'

'He does come home every morning, he'd find you,' Jess smiled.

'I don't want him to find me stuck like that. It would be humiliatin', that's what. Humiliatin'.'

Jess had a sudden thought. 'What about Julius? Where does he sleep then?'

'He keeps real weird hours. Ain't home most of the time. And if he is home night-time he sleeps in his own bed because he knows there really ain't room in the shelter for the pair of us.'

Jess could understand that. Without being cruel, Beulah was an extremely large lady, more than built for comfort. 'How about Pee Wee's band, are they still getting good audiences?' Jess asked, changing the subject.

'Sure am. Even durin' all that bombin' the band played on and the audiences stayed right in their seats. There again, there ain't been no bombs fallen on Soho yet, so probably that's a factor.'

'And he's still enjoying it?'

'Loves every moment. Loves English audiences. Thinks they're wonderful.'

'That's good,' Jess nodded.

'Don't even get homesick, which surprises the hell out of me. I know I do. Sometimes real bad. Nothin' to do with you English or England, it's simply there ain't no place like home as the sayin' goes.'

Jess could well understand that. She couldn't imagine living abroad, in someone else's country. Nor would she want to live in another part of the country. She was a Londoner through and through and an Islingtonian first and foremost.

'Hey, you want a cup of chocolate? I got that,' Beulah asked.

Jess's face lit up. 'Oh Beulah, have you really?'

'Sure have.'

'There hasn't been drinking chocolate in the shops for months. Plus lots of other things.'

Beulah winked. 'That Julius of mine comes in real handy at times. I don't think there's nothin' he can't get out the Embassy. Which reminds me.'

She went to a cupboard and opened it. 'For you, hon.'

Jess gasped as a large tin of ham was placed in front of her. It was her entire family meat ration for two months at least. Maybe longer. 'I can't take that, Beulah!'

'You sure can, sweetie pie. You don't want to upset me none, do you?'

Jess shook her head.

'Then you take it.' She returned to the cupboard to produce more tinned foodstuffs. 'And these.'

There were apricots, raspberries, carrots, potatoes, all sorts. 'Oh Beulah!'

Beulah filled the kettle and put it on. 'And I know Julius is gettin' some more cigarettes for Ellie, so you can tell her that.'

'How can I thank you. How can *we* thank you?'

'Don't need no thanks. We're friends, Jess, that's all that matters.'

Jess watched Beulah spoon two large measures of chocolate into cups, her mouth watering at the prospect of this unexpected treat. 'There's something I've been meaning to ask you for a while, it's been puzzling me.'

'Shoot.'

'Pee Wee means small, is that right?'

Beulah nodded.

'But he isn't. I mean, he's not exactly tall, but he's not small either.'

An amused glint came into Beulah's eyes. 'It's a joke, hon, given him by members of a band he belonged to years ago.'

Jess was still mystified. 'Oh?'

'You see, it's just the opposite. He ain't small, but real big. And I mean *real* big. Where it counts.'

It took a moment for the penny to drop, then Jess's face flamed scarlet.

Beulah burst into cackling laughter.

'Hi, stranger!'

Ellie, standing at the bar of The Florence, found a smiling Julius beside her. 'Why hello. I haven't seen you in ages.'

'Been busy. You know how it is?'

She did indeed.

'Can I buy you a drink?'

'It's me who should buy you one, Julius, as a thank you for those cigarettes you dropped off at the house.'

'Another time, Ellie, the drinks are on me tonight. I'm celebratin'.'

He gestured Harry over and ordered a repeat screwdriver for Ellie, large he insisted, and a double scotch for himself plus a pint of best.

'Can I ask what you're celebrating?'

His expression immediately became coy. 'It's Embassy stuff, Ellie.'

She nodded. 'I see. So you can't tell me.'

He considered that. 'Maybe I can. It's going to be in the newspapers tomorrow anyhow. A new Ambassador has taken over from the old one who leaves tonight for the States. The new guy's called Winant. John G. Winant.'

She regarded him keenly. 'Do I take it you didn't like the old one then?'

Julius took out a cigar case, extracted one and then clipped it. 'It wasn't that exactly. I just didn't think him the right man for this particular job. Hopefully Winant will be better.'

Their drinks arrived which he paid for. 'Want to sit down?'

She had no objections to that, pleased Julius had turned up. She always enjoyed his company, he was so easy and relaxing to be with.

'Talkin' of jobs, how's the ambulance business?' he queried.

Ellie lit a cigarette. 'Not too busy at the moment, I'm happy to say. Nothing like when the bombing was going on. That was horrendous.'

'Yeah, I guess.' She looked older, he reflected. Somehow more mature. And there was a new depth in her eyes that hadn't been there before, the result of her recent experiences he presumed. He felt himself in the presence of a woman as opposed to a young lady.

'And the drivin'?'

She laughed. 'Oh that's come on by leaps and bounds. I'm quite the expert nowadays.'

'And modest with it,' he teased drily.

'Of course.'

A neighbour came into the pub and waved to Ellie. She waved back. 'I'm driving an American vehicle at the moment,' she informed Julius.

That interested him. 'Really?'

'A Buick eight that's been converted into what's referred to as a regulation multi-purpose box van mode. The only trouble is it's a left-hand drive, but I've learned to cope with that. God alone knows where the car came from in the first place, but I've been landed with it.'

'Good cars Buicks,' Julius commented. He'd driven one himself for a while in the States.

'How about you?' she asked. 'Is it this change over of Ambassador that's making you so busy?'

'Partly.'

She could see he didn't want to elaborate on that. 'How's the girlfriend?'

'You mean Marybeth? Fine, I guess.' He frowned,

thinking of the weekend they'd had away together. What a disaster that had been. All day Sunday she'd been cold as ice to him.

'Why the furrowed brow? Is it to do with Marybeth?'

He took his time in replying. 'Yeah, she and I don't see eye to eye on certain things.'

'Oh?'

He wasn't sure he wanted to explain this to Ellie, then decided he would confide in her. 'It's simple really. She wants to get married and have kids. I don't.'

Ellie had a sip of her drink, followed by a puff on her cigarette. 'Is that because you don't want to get married in general,' she asked slowly. 'Or because of Marybeth herself?'

Julius glanced at Ellie, then away again. 'The truth is, I don't know,' he replied honestly.

'Do you love her?'

This was beginning to make him feel uncomfortable. Did he love her? Marybeth loved him, but did he love her? He'd said he did on several occasions, but had he meant it?

'Well?' Ellie prompted.

'Again, I don't know.'

'Then you don't.'

That harsh judgement startled him. 'Why do you say that?'

'Because if you did you'd know it. According to my mum anyway, she says love's unmistakable. Anything else just isn't the real thing.'

He smiled. 'Surely that's a bit black and white?'

Ellie couldn't resist the joke. 'Like you and me?'

He laughed, and so too did she. 'Sorry, I hope that wasn't offensive? It wasn't meant to be.'

'Not in the least,' he assured her. 'Yeah, like you and me.'

'So you don't love her.'

'I never said so.'

'Then you do?'

'I never said that either,' he protested.

It amused Ellie that he was floundering. 'In this country we call it sitting on the fence. Neither one thing nor the other.'

'Do you indeed?'

'Yes we do.'

Julius took a deep breath. 'I certainly don't want kids. Not for now anyway. I want to be a bit older before I commit to those.'

Ellie didn't reply to that.

'The trouble is . . .' He hesitated.

'Go on.'

'Marybeth keeps tryin' to push me into marriage. Why, only recently she tried to trick me into, hopefully on her part, gettin' her pregnant.'

That shocked Ellie a little. Not everyone had her morals, she reminded herself. Connie Fox for one, Julius, it would seem, for another. 'You're sleeping with her then?'

Julius nodded. 'Have been for a long time.' He studied her face. 'You don't approve, do you?'

Ellie shrugged. 'It's none of my business.'

'But you don't approve?'

302

Ellie dropped her gaze to stare into her drink. 'I believe that act should be kept for the wedding night, or at least the honeymoon,' she stated quietly. 'It's how I was brought up.'

'So you didn't with George, even though you were engaged?'

She shook her head. 'There were times when he wanted to, but I wouldn't allow it. Just as well too, considering what happened. If I had I'd have felt ever so cheap when he broke it off. Cheap and degraded having squandered something that rightfully belongs to the man I presume I will marry one day.'

Julius was impressed. What a difference between Ellie and Marybeth, a difference that had absolutely nothing whatsoever to do with colour. 'Maybe you're right,' he declared.

'I am for me anyway,' she replied.

They sat for a little while in silence, each smoking and drinking, Julius contemplating his relationship with Marybeth. He and she got on well enough, most of the time anyway. And she was fabulous in bed, not to mention stunningly good-looking. But was that enough? Perhaps he was in love with her and too stubborn to admit it to himself? On the other hand, perhaps not.

'Just one thing,' Ellie said at last.

'What's that?'

'Whatever you do, don't make a mistake. You could regret it for the rest of your life.'

True, he thought. Very true. 'Another drink?' Ellie had now finished hers.

'No, I'd better be getting along. But thank you all the same.'

'My pleasure, Ellie. Any time.'

She rose from her seat. 'I'll be seeing you.'

He rose also, out of manners. 'Thanks for listenin' to me. You've been a friend.'

She smiled. 'Goodnight, Julius.'

'Goodnight, Ellie.'

He watched her walk from the pub, uneasy, and thoughtful, after their conversation. She was right of course. Did he or did he not love Marybeth?

That was the question. But one he couldn't answer.

Julius discovered it to be snowing when he left the Embassy. Shivering, he turned up the collar of his coat. Ambassador Winant had thrown a party to introduce himself to the staff, personally going round and shaking every single individual by the hand and having a few words. Julius had taken to the man right away, which he never had with Kennedy.

What had further impressed him was that Winant had refused to go and live in Windsor, setting up in an apartment adjoining the Embassy instead where his wife, still Stateside, would shortly be joining him. No bolt hole for Winant.

Julius glanced at his watch to note it was still relatively early. The arrangement was he'd go to Marybeth's place where they'd meet up later, she being detained at the Embassy with some unfinished work to do before calling it a day.

On a whim Julius decided to stop in at a little local pub that the Embassy staff used. The canapés he'd had at the party had left him with a thirst to which beer seemed the more enjoyable answer than water.

The King's Head was small and somewhat dingy, but the atmosphere was friendly enough. It also had the reputation for selling a wonderful pint of Bass which Julius had recently developed a fondness for.

Once inside he ordered and then lit a cigarette while his pint was being poured. He looked round in surprise when a hand descended on his shoulder.

'All alone?' Walter Zwicke asked.

Son of a bitch, Julius inwardly cursed. Running into Zwicke was the last thing he wanted. 'Yeah.'

'Come on over then. I got a table all to myself.'

The guy was drunk, Julius observed. 'I'm not stayin' long.'

'Don't matter,' Zwicke slurred. 'Join me anyway. You and I should have socialised before now, sharing an office as we do. So come on over, good buddy.'

Julius winced, loathing being called that by Zwicke. 'OK, sure. Only for a couple of minutes though.'

'I'll have a large scotch to go with the pint,' he informed the barmaid when she placed his Bass in front of him. He'd need that to put up with Zwicke.

'Sorry, sir. There's none left.'

He stared at her. 'Brandy?'

She shook her head. 'We're all out of spirits and don't know when we'll have more in. That's how it is. Sorry.'

The war of course, Julius thought. At least he wouldn't

go short, there always being plenty available at the Embassy. He paid for his Bass and then reluctantly made his way across to Zwicke.

'Sure love these English pubs,' Zwicke declared as Julius sat. 'They beat the hell out of the taverns we have back home.'

Julius nodded his agreement.

'Boring party I thought,' Zwicke went on. 'I made my escape right after meeting Winant. Came in here instead.'

Julius didn't know what to say to Zwicke, doubting they had anything in common. Apart from the job that is. And he certainly didn't want to talk about that.

'So how you doing?' Zwicke demanded.

'OK.'

'I saw Marybeth at the party. She sure is some broad that woman. Yes sir.'

'As you keep mentionin',' Julius replied evenly.

'Lovely ass.'

Julius fought back the impulse to hit Zwicke. The guy really was a chromium-plated, one-hundred-per-cent creep.

Zwicke winked salaciously. 'But then I'm not telling you anything you don't already know. Isn't that right, good buddy?'

Again Julius didn't reply, instead taking several deep swallows of his pint, desperate to get out of there as soon as he could.

Zwicke sat back and sighed. 'She was missed when she left Toronto, though not by some of the wives. No sir.'

That jolted Julius. 'What do you mean?'

Zwicke was suddenly having trouble focusing his eyes. 'What does what mean?' he hiccuped.

'Marybeth wasn't missed by some of the wives.'

'You know?'

'No, I don't.'

Zwicke shook his head. 'Shouldn't say any more. It's the liquor talking.'

Julius smiled disarmingly. 'You can tell me, in confidence of course. I'm your good buddy, remember?'

'Yeah.'

'So?' Julius pressed.

Zwicke had a mouthful from his pint. 'Sure is strong this English beer. Far stronger than back home.'

'It sure is,' Julius agreed. And Zwicke clearly hadn't gotten used to it yet. 'Marybeth?' he prompted quietly.

'Real popular she was. And friendly too. Hell, half the guys must have had a piece of her tail. More than half. Young and old.'

Julius, still smiling disarmingly, went cold all over. 'That popular, eh?'

'A floozie through and through. High-class I have to admit, but a born floozie nonetheless.'

'Married guys as well?'

'She wasn't particular about whether or not the guy was married. If she was of a mind, he got laid.'

Julius swallowed hard. 'You too?'

'Nah! I tried, Jesus I tried. But she just never took a shine to me. Couldn't understand it. Still don't. I mean, what's wrong with me? I'm no different to some of those guys.'

Julius was in a daze. He'd realised Marybeth wasn't a virgin the first time he'd slept with her, but this! It made him feel sick to his stomach.

'Even the Ambassador himself had her,' Zwicke went on. 'It was after that she got posted here. He probably wanted her out of the way. Know what I mean?'

'Yes,' Julius replied in a voice that was little more than a whisper.

'I heard she was real good too. Quite a performer. Gives one helluva blowjob.'

Julius couldn't take any more. He had to get out of there, and fast, before he lost control and beat the living shit out of Zwicke. Without uttering another word he rose and strode from the pub.

'Hey, Julius, where you going? Where you going, good buddy? You've left your beer.'

Julius didn't go to Marybeth's as they'd arranged, instead he drove straight home.

What was it Ellie had said during their conversation in The Florence? Don't make a mistake you might regret for the rest of your life.

Jesus!

It wasn't fair, it just wasn't fair at all, Paul thought bitterly as he started putting on his pyjamas. His pal Eddy Ackworth now not only had the Jerry cannon shells but a piece of Perspex, given to Eddy by his father, from the cockpit of a downed Jerry plane as well. And he didn't have one, not one, souvenir to boast about and show off.

This resentment was still churning in his mind long

after Jess had kissed him goodnight and switched off the light.

It was three days now since the Ambassador's party during which Julius had succeeded in avoiding Marybeth, having lied on the telephone that feeling sick was his reason for not going to her apartment that night. Now he was there, determined to break it off for good between them.

Marybeth's face crumpled when he finished speaking, and she turned away from him. Her shoulders began to heave.

'It's all lies,' she finally croaked.

'No it isn't,' he replied patiently. 'I checked. I sent a wire to a guy I know in the Toronto Embassy and he confirmed all that Zwicke said.'

'Who was that?'

'Orin Bates. Remember him?'

She did, only too well.

'So I guess that's it.'

Marybeth crossed to a decanter of scotch and poured herself one, her hands shaking violently. When she drank some of the liquor ran down her chin.

'Don't go, please, Julius?' she pleaded.

He shook his head. 'Zwicke called you a floozie, and you've certainly acted like one. Hell, I don't want to sound self-righteous here, I'm not exactly as pure as the driven myself. I certainly have no objections to a girl havin' had a bit of experience in her past, that's only to be expected, but I'm not datin' what amounts to a goddamn amateur whore.'

Marybeth's expression was stricken, her entire body now starting to shake. 'It wasn't like that, Julius. I swear.'

'Then what was it like?'

She had another gulp of scotch. 'I was young, wild. None of it mattered, not to me anyhow. I was simply havin' a good time, enjoyin' myself.'

'Enjoyin' yourself?' He laughed cynically. 'More than that, Marybeth, far more. Half the guys in the Embassy I'm told, young and old, includin' the Ambassador. That's not enjoyin' yourself, that's bein' the easiest lay around. A piece of goodtime meat for whoever happens along.'

He paused to draw breath, his emotions a combination of anger and total contempt. 'And I want none of you.'

The tears were now freely flowing down Marybeth's face, her body continuing to shake. 'I love you, Julius. I swear to God I do. I want to marry you, settle down and have your children.'

He'd always thought Marybeth beautiful, but at that moment she was as ugly as sin. Loathing rose up inside him as he thought, pictured, what she'd been up to before they'd met. That was something he'd never, could never, forget. 'Goodbye,' he stated abruptly.

She gasped when he said that, then flew across the room to grab his arm. 'Please don't go. Forgive me. Please forgive me!'

He tried to push her off but she clung tenaciously on, all the while making gobbling sounds similar to those made by turkeys. It was horrible.

Marybeth slid down him to latch onto a leg, wrapping

her arms tightly round it. 'Please, please,' she whimpered.

'Let go, Marybeth. Let go.'

'I love you, Julius. I love you so.'

'Well, I don't love you. Now let go, for Christsake! Keep a little dignity.'

He somehow reached the door, although she continued to cling fiercely onto him. He hadn't known what to expect on coming to her apartment, but certainly not this.

He managed to open the door then attempted yet again to prise himself free. In the end there was nothing else for it. Using the palm of his hand he smacked her hard across the face.

Taken by surprise, and reeling from the force of the blow, Marybeth tumbled backwards to measure her length on the floor. Seizing his chance Julius fled, slamming the door shut behind him.

A great agonised wail went up from her apartment as he hurried for the stairs, not daring to wait for the lift.

Only when he was back in the street did he stop and take a deep breath. That had been awful, simply awful. Pitiful too.

He had just reached his car when the air-raid sirens, silent for the past few weeks, began to howl. Moments later the first of hundreds of German planes roared overhead, ack-ack guns simultaneously bursting into action, their fiery tracers lancing skywards.

The Blitz had resumed.

Chapter 19

'Is that you, Julius?'

He looked round the kitchen, wondering where his mother's voice was coming from. 'Where are you?'

'Under the table.'

He smothered a laugh to see Beulah's large and rotund posterior protruding upwards, she on all fours with her hands over her head. 'What are you doin'?' he demanded.

'What does it look like, stupid? There are bombs fallin' out there.'

'Then why not go to the shelter if you're so worried?'

'Don't give me none of your sass now. I ain't goin' to no shelter, and that's the end of it.'

The house shook as a bomb fell relatively nearby. 'Holy shit!' Beulah exclaimed. 'That son of a bitch was real close.'

A grim-faced Julius sat in a chair from where he could see Beulah's face. From outside came the crackle of ack-ack fire.

'You go to the shelter,' Beulah said.

He didn't reply to that, having no intention of doing so. Nor was he prepared to argue about it. Leaning backwards he lit a cigarette. He wasn't being particularly brave, it was simply that he believed if your number was up then that was it no matter what.

'You drive home through the bombin'?' Beulah demanded.

'Sure did.'

'You're crazy, real crazy. Why didn't you stop somewhere and get under cover?'

'I'm under cover now,' he pointed out.

Beulah pulled a face. 'There you go, sassin' me again. You know what I mean.'

He sighed. 'I wasn't in the mood to spend the night with strangers, Mom. Not in the mood at all.'

'Why's that?'

He drew in a deep lungful of smoke, then slowly exhaled. 'I broke up with Marybeth tonight, permanently, that's why.'

Beulah studied him. 'You did, huh?'

He nodded.

'Why you do that, boy? She's a good woman, that Marybeth. Good-lookin' too. I like her.'

Julius took his time in replying. 'I've mentioned the guy I share an office with, Walter Zwicke?'

'A few times. You don't care for him, do you?'

'He's a creep. A total slimeball. But that's not the point. He told me somethin' the other night, all about Marybeth's past, when she was in Toronto.'

'I take it from the tone of your voice it wasn't good?'

He closed his eyes for a moment, wondering how much longer this raid would go on for. 'No, it wasn't,' he confirmed.

Beulah waited and waited. 'Well, are you goin' to tell me?' she finally queried.

'It'll disillusion you about her.'

'That bad, eh?'

'That bad, Mom.'

'Holy sheeet!' Beulah exclaimed as another bomb exploded, this time even closer. The lights flickered, then went out, leaving them in darkness apart from the glow off the fire.

'I nearly wet my pants there,' Beulah confessed.

That made him smile, despite the danger they were in. Slowly, he began to repeat his conversation with Zwicke followed by what had taken place in Marybeth's apartment.

Ellie pulled the Buick alongside the kerb when they came across the burning wreckage of one of their station's own vehicles. 'Christ!' Ellie exclaimed. 'That's Molly Davis and Pat Halfpenny's car.'

Ellie and Josie Farnham scrambled out of the Buick and cautiously approached the wreckage. To their horror, Molly and Pat were clearly visible in the front seats, both dead, their bodies flaming torches.

'Oh!' Josie choked, and turned away, wondering if her colleagues had died instantly, or had been trapped alive to be burned to death. She prayed it was the former.

'We'd better get back in case it explodes,' Ellie advised sensibly.

'There's nothing we can do anyway.'

'No,' Ellie agreed, thinking, poor bloody cows.

'Pat owed me ten bob,' Ellie said huskily as they drove off down the street. 'That's one debt she won't be repaying.'

Behind them the makeshift ambulance that was now a funeral pyre continued to burn.

The Chicory House was jam-packed, mostly with uniforms. Nor were they all British. Numbered amongst them were Free French, Polish, Czech and Belgian service men and women, all thoroughly enjoying themselves, spellbound by the music Pee Wee and the band were playing.

They were in the middle of 'I'm A Ding Dong Daddy' when suddenly the scream of a descending bomb could be heard, seemingly right above them. Fear clutched at Pee Wee's heart, and his fingers momentarily faltered.

Several members of the audience rose and dashed for the exits, others sat as though paralysed, looking upwards.

This was it, Pee Wee thought. His time had come.

It was only a few seconds, but it seemed an eternity, before the bomb exploded not far away. Dust rained down from the ceiling while glasses and tables were knocked over, some of the glasses tinkling to the floor.

'I think I'll get my ass out of here,' John Parlour whispered to Pee Wee, the band having stopped playing.

'Yeah,' agreed Muggsy Young, the other member of the trio.

Pee Wee took a deep breath. 'Hell no,' he stated firmly. Holding up a hand he addressed the audience. 'Listen, folks, I ain't lettin' no Germans spoil my session, and we doin' real good too. So if you'll just stay right where you

315

are me and the boys here will get on with it. God bless Winston Churchill and the President of the United States!'

A great cheer greeted that, followed by tumultuous applause. One or two of those who'd dashed for the exits returned, rather shame-faced, to their seats.

'How about a jazzed-up version of "Rule Britannia"?' Pee Wee suggested.

John Parlour laughed. 'You're crazy, man. But I love it.'

Dust was still floating down from the ceiling as they swung into the new number.

Despite the bombardment Jess had managed to fall asleep, albeit a fitful one. She now came awake feeling something was wrong.

Reaching out she groped for Paul who should have been sleeping beside her, only he wasn't there. With a muffled oath she threw off her blankets and came onto her knees.

Paul glanced round from the side of the entrance to the shelter where he'd been sitting watching the raid. 'It's all right, Mum, I'm here,' he called to her.

'Get back inside this instant,' she commanded.

'Aw, Mum!'

'Get in!'

The moment he obeyed she clapped him round the ear. 'What do you think you're doing?' she scolded, voice shrill with fright. 'Do you want to get yourself killed?'

Paul clapped a hand over his ear, taken aback, for it

was rare that either Jess or Albert hit him. 'That's sore,' he complained.

'Your backside will be a lot more so if I tell your dad what you did. You stupid child.'

'I wasn't in any harm, Mum. And you should see it out there. The sky's all lit up.'

Her fury began to subside. He was safe again, that was all that mattered. 'I don't care what the sky looks like. All I know is it's full of German planes and you were in danger.'

Paul was upset because he'd upset Jess. 'I'm sorry,' he mumbled, genuinely contrite.

'And so you should be.'

Suddenly she swept him into her arms and hugged him tight. 'Oh darling,' she whispered, eyes filling with tears. 'I couldn't bear to lose you. It would break my heart.'

He didn't reply to that. He didn't think he'd been in danger, but wisely didn't push the point. He was deeply touched by this show of affection from Jess, the love he felt for her swelling within him.

Jess released Paul and wiped her eyes. 'Now you get back into bed and never do that again. Understand?'

'Yes, Mum.'

'Good.'

She fussed with his blankets, making sure he was nicely tucked in. Bending, she pecked him on the forehead.

Jess didn't get another wink of sleep for the rest of that night, her anxiety staying with her and keeping her awake.

For the first time in a long while she thought about the baby she'd lost, which had caused her so much pain.

'If this blows we've all had it,' Danny McGiver said to Albert through gritted teeth, the pair of them in charge of a hosepipe pumping water into a small distillery situated in the City Road, a distillery containing huge amounts of alcohol. It had been hit by several incendiaries and was burning fiercely.

In a loud clamour of noise more fire engines appeared to assist, their personnel quickly swinging into action. Elsewhere the police and ARP wardens were busily evacuating the surrounding streets.

There was a great whoof of flame from the top of the building that shot a good thirty feet into the air, sparks flying in every direction.

Albert winced as a falling red-hot cinder neatly sliced his cheek, blood immediately starting to flow.

'You all right?' Danny asked, having seen what had happened.

Albert nodded.

'Want to go off and get it attended to?'

'Don't be daft, Danny. It's only a scratch.'

Danny grinned wolfishly, that having been a joke. He knew Albert far better than that.

The heat was pummelling Albert, his skin glowing with sweat underneath his tunic and protective gear, his eyes gritty and sore from continued staring into the inferno. He, like Danny and the others from their station, had been on duty for almost eighteen hours. To say they were totally exhausted would have been an understatement.

Henry Leway came hurrying over. 'Water supplies are getting low. We're trying to tap into another source but having difficulty as the main access points are buried beneath rubble.'

'Christ,' Albert muttered. If they ran out of water now the building and contents would surely go up, causing utter devastation over God knew how large an area. The chances were they would also go up with it.

'Who wants to live for ever anyway?' Henry Leway said, and burst out laughing. He was known for his black sense of humour.

Albert thought of Jess, Paul and Ellie, then put them quickly out of his mind. He mustn't worry about what-ifs, but continue concentrating on the job in hand.

Julius stood at his office window staring out over London, or what was left of it anyway. Miraculously the Embassy hadn't been hit so far, though many of the buildings round about had.

Smoke from a great many smouldering fires was rising skywards, the result of the previous night's raid, the heaviest of the war to date according to what was being said. He couldn't help but wonder if there would be anything left at all of London when this was finally over.

Down below people were hurrying to and fro, going about their business as if nothing had happened. You had to admire them, he thought, you just had to. What indomitable spirit.

Turning he glanced at the neighbouring empty desk,

and smiled. A word in the right place, he'd been in this particular Embassy far longer than Zwicke after all, and Zwicke had been transferred to another office, without a murmur of complaint or resistance, Zwicke correctly guessing the reason why. On reflection it had probably suited Zwicke just as much as him.

As for Marybeth, several times she'd attempted to accost him, re-plead her case, but in each instance he'd cut her short. Hopefully she'd now give up and leave him alone.

Half the guys, and more, in the Toronto Embassy! He shook his head in disbelief. And to think he'd actually considered marrying her, a born floozie of the first water. That had been one very narrow escape for which he was most grateful.

As he'd said to her, he'd expected a bit of 'history' in a woman's past, that was only natural, at least to his mind it was, but what she'd been up to was just out-and-out promiscuity. And he didn't believe leopards ever changed their spots, no matter what promises and assurances were made.

His thoughts were interrupted by the telephone ringing.

Jess, Beulah and others were gathered outside the house of old Ma Jenkins who, it appeared, had suffered a heart attack during the raid. As chance would have it, it was Ellie's ambulance that had been despatched to take her to hospital.

'How is she?' Jess inquired anxiously when Ellie and Josie appeared carrying Ma on a stretcher. Ma's eyes were closed, her skin a muddy green colour.

'Not too clever I'm afraid,' Ellie replied, manoeuvring the stretcher round the back of the ambulance. Moments later the stretcher had been slid aboard and Josie had gone in with it.

Ellie closed the rear doors, then wiped hair that had come astray off her face. She was dead beat.

'Dad back yet?'

Jess shook her head. 'What about you, when can I expect you home?'

Ellie shrugged wearily. 'When I appear I suppose. That's all I can say.'

Jess understood.

Jess's heart sank when she saw Albert's face which was grey, sunk in on itself, and haggard. Almost stumbling to his chair he collapsed into it.

'I heard you were round at the station asking after me,' he said.

'I was worried, Albert.'

He attempted a smile. 'In case I was hurt?'

Or worse, she thought, giving a shrug. 'Your cheek has been cut.'

He explained what had happened, and then told her about the distillery which they'd managed eventually to bring under control without it blowing up.

'I'll put something on that cut,' she declared.

'Don't fuss, woman. I'm fine.'

'But it might get infected. Just let me wash it with antiseptic.'

He sighed. 'On you go then, if it'll keep you happy.'

She crossed over to the cupboard where the antiseptic and cotton wool were kept, both usually employed on Paul's various scrapes and bruises. Albert grimaced a little when she dabbed his wound.

'Are you hungry?'

'No, we ate from the mobile canteens. All I want is a wash, change of clothes, and then over to The Florence for a few pints. After that it's bed for a couple of hours, I'm on again later.'

'You'd better have a shave as well,' she advised him. 'You're as bristly as an old broom.'

Somehow he managed to laugh. 'I'd forgotten about that.'

She threw the used cotton wool onto the fire. 'Just how bad was it?'

He thought about that. 'As bad as it's been, maybe worse. But we didn't lose anyone, nor was anyone injured. Thank God.'

'I saw Ellie earlier on, old Ma Jenkins has been taken into hospital with a suspected heart attack. They sent Ellie's ambulance for her.'

'Sorry to hear that about Ma,' he sympathised. 'Ellie all right?'

'Tired, same as you.'

Albert rubbed his forehead – tired wasn't the word for it. 'And Paul?'

'Out somewhere. Well, with the school shut I can hardly keep him indoors all day. He'll be enjoying himself with his pals, probably playing a game of some sort.

They're safe enough during the day when there aren't any planes about, or bombs going off.'

'Fair enough,' Albert murmured.

Jess eyed him anxiously. 'Are you sure you don't want to go straight to bed?'

He took a deep breath, then hauled himself aloft. 'Nope. I want those couple of pints. Would you like to come with me?'

Jess considered his invitation. 'I'd better not. I should be here when Ellie gets in. And for Paul when he turns up.'

Going to Albert she kissed his unscathed cheek. 'You've earned your drink. Get yourself ready and on over there.'

Fifteen minutes later he was propping up the bar at The Florence exchanging banter with Hazel.

'You *must* return to the States, Mom, it's far too dangerous for you here.'

A look of defiance came over Beulah's face. 'Are you goin'?'

'You know I can't,' Julius protested. 'My job's in London.'

'Then I stays put, you hear? Me and Pee Wee ain't goin' nowhere if it means leavin' you behind.' She crossed her arms stubbornly across her massive bosom.

'But the air raids, Mom, the bombin'?'

'Hell, I ain't worried none about those. Sheet no! It takes more than a mess of German planes to scare Beulah Poston.'

Julius had to smile. 'Is that why you hide under the table when an attack's takin' place?'

323

She disregarded that jibe. 'I ain't goin', Julius. And that's that.'

He'd known before speaking to her this would be the case, but had felt compelled to try to talk some sense into her. 'There's a boat leavin' for Boston in three days, first-class accommodation. I can even arrange for you to sit at the Captain's table?'

Beulah snorted. 'Ain't tempted. Not even a little bit. Where you is, I is. OK?'

He went to her and took her into his arms. 'You're incorrigible, Mom.'

'I is?'

'Yes you are.'

She thought about that. 'Is you joshin' me in some way because I don't know what that means?'

What a star, he smiled, as he explained it to her.

'Thanks,' Ellie said, accepting a cup of tea from Josie. 'I'm ready for this.'

'Me too.'

Ellie glanced at the clock as it chimed, and frowned. Ten o'clock and no raid so far. 'They're late,' she commented.

'Who?'

'Who do you think? The Jerries, of course.'

Josie, who'd developed pronounced dark bags under her eyes, also glanced at the clock. Before joining the auxiliaries she'd been a shop assistant in the Co-op. 'Maybe they're not coming tonight?'

Ellie sincerely hoped that to be the case. It had been

five nights on the trot now since the last time they'd failed to appear due to awful weather conditions over the Channel.

Josie yawned. 'I'd love to get my head down.'

'Then why don't you?'

There were a number of camp beds laid out at one end of the room where the girls sometimes kipped. They weren't in the least bit comfortable but no one cared a jot about that. The alternative was to doze in one of the available chairs.

'I think I will when I finish my tea.'

Two new girls had joined them as replacements for Molly Davis and Pat Halfpenny, taking their predecessors' places in the nightly card game that went on when they weren't out on call. There hadn't been many games played of late.

Ellie lit a cigarette, thinking she too might have a turn on one of the camp beds later on. She was about to say so to Josie when outside the sirens began to wail.

'Oh well,' Josie sighed resignedly. 'No rest for the wicked.'

'Chance would be a fine thing,' Ellie retorted, and they both grinned.

Quarter of an hour later the phone rang, the first request that shift for an ambulance.

'It's only bread and dripping I'm afraid,' Jess apologised to Paul waiting expectantly at the table.

His face fell in disappointment. 'But I'm starving, Mum!'

'I'm hungry too so you're not alone,' she snapped in reply, ashamed that was all she could give the boy for his tea. Between rationing, and the price of food going through the roof, she was at her wits' end.

'My stomach's rumbling,' he complained.

She was beginning to get angry now, as much with herself as him. She could always have gone next door to see if she could scrounge something from Beulah, but her pride wouldn't let her do that. If it was offered, well that was one thing, but to ask quite another. She was enough in the black woman's debt as it was. Thank God Albert and Ellie were able to get something from the mobile canteens when they were on call.

She placed two slices of bread and dripping in front of Paul. 'There you are.'

He eyed it with distaste, not really liking bread and dripping as his mother knew only too well. 'Are you sure there's nothing else?' he asked in a small voice.

She fixed him with a beady glare. 'No, there isn't. And just be thankful there's that, me lad.'

He bowed his head. 'Yes, Mum.'

What Jess didn't tell Paul was that those were the last two slices of bread in the house. She was having to do without.

Jess, clad only in her underwear, stared at herself in the wardrobe mirror. If she'd ever moaned on about carrying too much weight, then she certainly wasn't now. She was skinny as a rake, her ribs protruding in places. Her breasts, which Albert loved so much, were reduced to half the size they'd been. It filled her with despair.

'What are you doing?' Albert queried groggily from the bed, having just woken.

She picked up and slipped on her dressing gown. 'Nothing.'

'You were gawping at yourself in the mirror. That's most unlike you.'

She went over and sat beside him on the bed. 'I really shouldn't say anything, you and Ellie are the ones at the sharp end of all this, but I've been awfully down recently, Albert. It just seems to be getting on top of me. The bombing, the food situation, the incessant worry.'

'Oh Jess,' he whispered, reaching out and taking her hand.

'I see so little of you nowadays. You're nearly always on duty, and when you are home you're invariably asleep.'

She attempted a brave smile at seeing the concern on his face. 'I'm sorry, I shouldn't have said that. You've got enough on your plate as it is.'

He pulled himself into a sitting position and drew her to him. 'This can't last for ever, Jess, it must end one day. And when that happens we'll get back to normal, things will be just as they were. I promise you.'

How safe she felt in his arms, she thought. A warm sense of peace started to steal over her.

Albert began to gently rock her to and fro, wishing with all his heart he didn't have to shortly return to work. But he had to, there was a war on and he was needed.

'This is nice,' she whispered.

He stroked her hair, she closing her eyes in appreciation. 'I'm glad I married you, Albert Sykes. They don't come any better.'

'And I'm glad I married you. We've both been lucky.'

She couldn't have agreed more.

'Why don't you come under the sheets and we'll cuddle up?' he suggested.

She didn't need any urging, and moments later they were wrapped around one another. Just like Hansel and Gretel, she thought dreamily, lost in the woods, but having each other.

They remained like that until it was time for Albert to get up and go back to the station.

Paul couldn't believe his eyes. What had been a warehouse was now in ruins, but there, right in the middle of what remained of the building, clearly visible, was part of the fuselage from a downed German plane. And on the remnant of fuselage, small enough for him to pick up and carry, were Luftwaffe markings.

Wait till he showed this to Eddy and the others, they'd be green with envy. Spitting with it. He laughed aloud as he hurriedly made for what would be a prize souvenir, far better than anything any of the other lads possessed.

There were clumps of smouldering debris everywhere, and in places small fires that had started up again after the initial blaze had been put out. Paul paid no attention to any of this as he made straight for the coveted section of fuselage.

Reaching the fuselage he attempted to pick it up,

having to struggle as it was heavier than he'd anticipated. He was still struggling with it when live cannon shells from the stricken plane, lying buried in the smouldering and burning debris, went off.

Three of the exploding shells hit Paul squarely in the back.

Chapter 20

'That's the last one gone,' Albert declared, rejoining Jess and Ellie in their kitchen. Paul had been buried several hours earlier in Highgate Cemetery, many friends, neighbours and school chums of Paul's there to pay their respects. Afterwards quite a few of them had come back to the house.

Albert now poured himself the last of the scotch, two bottles of which had been donated by Julius. Everyone had rallied round in this time of shortages; margarine, meat and cakes, not to mention bread, donated so that the wake could be done properly. The Postons' contribution was the largest of all thanks to their Embassy connection.

Jess was sitting staring blankly into space, her face red raw from crying, Ellie in another chair, curled up in a foetal ball.

Albert bit his lip, unsure of what to do or say next. He was in just as much shock as Jess and Ellie, but was handling it better.

It had been PC McKechnie who'd broken the news, assuring Jess, in that kindly way of his, that Paul had been killed outright and wouldn't have felt a thing. That had been some consolation at least.

Jess shook her head. 'I still can't really take it on board,' she husked, her voice cracked and shredded from the outpourings of grief. 'I keep expecting him to walk through that door asking what's to eat as he's starving. He was always that.'

Ellie sobbed and buried a clenched fist in her mouth.

'I got angry with him the day before because all I had for his tea was bread and dripping and he complained, but it was all we had. I'll never forgive myself for that. Never. His last full day on earth and I got angry with him.'

'Stop it, Jess,' Albert said, a choke now in his own voice.

Jess looked at him, her eyes terrible to see. 'He was a lovely lad, wasn't he, Albert?'

Albert nodded.

'I was so proud of him. A little scamp at times, but so proud of him. Since it happened I keep wondering what he would have been if he'd grown up?'

Albert swallowed the contents of his glass, shuddering as it went down.

'He wanted to be an engine driver,' Ellie suddenly stated. 'He told me that once.'

Albert smiled wryly. 'Most boys his age want to be that. It's one of those things.'

'I also keep wondering what his wife and children would have been like?' Jess said dully. 'Now I'll never know.'

Ellie stood up, she couldn't bear any more of this. 'I'm going to my room,' she declared.

'Are you all right?' Albert queried.

Of course she wasn't. She kept remembering all the times she'd been horrible to her brother. Downright nasty on occasion. Though, she reminded herself, caring and loving on others. He'd been such an irritating little sod sometimes, especially where food was concerned. No angel either, considering some of the things he'd done to her.

'I just want to be on my own for a while, Dad. Today's been . . .' She groped for a suitable word. 'Draining.'

'On you go then.'

'Don't call me for anything. I'll come back down when I'm ready.'

He wished there was more scotch, gallons of the stuff. 'Right, we won't.'

Jess took out a handkerchief that was already sodden and wiped her nose. She'd never been so mentally battered and bruised in her entire life, not even after losing the baby. She hadn't known the baby, whereas she'd given birth to Paul, brought him up, been through all the trials and tribulations of childhood with him. Loved him as you can only love your own flesh and blood.

'Would you like a cup of tea?' Albert asked. 'There's bound to be some left in the pot.'

Jess shook her head. 'I'm awash with tea as it is.'

'Can I get you anything else then?'

She looked at him, the tears having returned. 'Can you bring my son back to me?'

Albert had no answer to that. None at all.

* * *

'What was it like?' Hazel asked Julius as he came up to the bar.

His brown eyes were soulful. 'Awful, Hazel. Simply awful.'

'How are Jess and Albert?'

He shrugged. 'As you'd expect, I guess. The pair of them must be going through absolute hell.'

She made a sympathetic face. 'Pint?'

'Any Bass?'

'Sorry, we're out.'

'Then a pint of whatever.'

Hazel picked up a glass and began to pour. 'Was it a good turn-out at the service?'

'Certainly lots of people there.'

'I would have imagined there would be,' Hazel replied. 'Albert and Jess are very popular round here, highly thought of. The sort who'd always be there for you if you needed them. The salt of the earth. No offence meant, but real locals too. Both born and bred Islingtonians.'

Julius thought of Ellie, what a state she'd been in. There had been times when he'd wanted to put his arm round her, reassure her. Though what he could reassure her about he didn't know. Just be a friend, he supposed.

'Are you going back to work?' Hazel inquired, making conversation.

'No, I've taken the day off. Thought that best.'

'There you are,' Hazel declared, placing his drink in front of him. 'The way things are going there might not be any beer left come the end of the week. It's that bad.'

At which point they were interrupted by PC

McKechnie coming into the pub. 'Hello, Haze, how are you?'

'Tiptop, Dougal, and yourself?'

'Looking for someone. Taffy Roberts hasn't been in, has he?'

Hazel shook her head. ''Fraid not. Why?'

McKechnie laid his helmet on the bar and ran fingers through his sandy-coloured hair. 'He's done a runner from the Army. Gone AWOL.'

Hazel laughed. 'Well, there's a surprise! I was amazed he joined in the first place.'

'He didn't join,' McKechnie corrected her. 'He was conscripted. And then only after I had a word with him and threatened jail if he didn't report in.'

'Lying bastard,' Hazel said contemptuously. 'Not you, Dougal, Taffy. He told everyone here he'd joined up. Made a big thing about it too. Was strutting all round the bar in his uniform.'

McKechnie nodded to Julius. 'How are you?'

'Fine, officer, thank you.'

'At the funeral?'

'Yes, I was.'

'How did it go?'

'As funerals do. A lot of sadness, a lot of cryin'. A lot of pain and grief.'

McKechnie sighed. 'Rotten business. It was me who broke the news to Jess.' He paused for a brief second. 'You know, no matter how long I'm in this job that sort of thing never gets any easier, especially when you know the people involved. It's even worse when it's a child.'

Julius could well imagine.

'So much death about nowadays,' McKechnie went on. 'It's everywhere, round every corner. Did you know old Ma Jenkins has gone? Passed away yesterday.'

'I heard,' Hazel nodded. 'Grand old woman. She's another who'll be missed.'

'Aye,' McKechnie agreed softly. 'I used to call in on her from time to time to see she was all right. Never left without having had a cup of tea and piece of cake. Made lovely Dundee cake too, my favourite.'

He cleared his throat. 'There's a new family moving into her house from up Canonbury way. They've been bombed out so the Council has given them Ma's place.'

'That wasn't empty long,' Hazel commented cynically.

'It's the times we live in, Haze. The times we live in.'

Hazel looked at Julius, then back at McKechnie. 'Will you have a dram while you're here, Dougal?'

That surprised Julius, spirits hadn't been available in the pub for weeks now.

'How kind of you, Haze. I will.'

'You just wait there then.' And with that she hurried away.

'Had any more trouble recently?' McKechnie inquired of Julius, referring to the incident when Julius had been attacked by the three squaddies.

'None at all, I'm happy to say.'

McKechnie grunted. 'That's good. You and your family are a bit of a rarity round here, you understand. Though it wasn't the locals who gave you bother. If any do, or try to, they'll hear from me quickly enough. I'm a foreigner

335

here myself don't forget, I understand these things.'

Julius was impressed to hear that. 'Thank you, officer.'

Hazel reappeared carrying a huge glass of scotch. 'Get that down you, Dougal, it'll warm the cockles.'

He eyed the drink appreciatively. 'It will indeed, Haze. God bless you. *Slàinte!*'

They made small talk for a while longer, McKechnie finally leaving with the promise that either Hazel or Harry would be in touch if Taffy was spotted in the neighbourhood or came into the pub.

'You never saw that,' Hazel stated emphatically when McKechnie had gone.

Julius feigned innocence. 'Saw what? I've no idea what you're talkin' about.'

Hazel smiled. 'That's the idea. It's best to keep the police sweet, a good rule for any landlord and landlady. And in case you're wondering, we do have a few bottles of spirits on the premises. But for private consumption only. Not to be sold. Understand?'

'Perfectly.'

'Right then, another pint?'

He drained his glass. 'I'd better before you run out of beer too.'

'Let's pray it doesn't come to that.'

'Amen,' Julius concurred.

While Julius was in the pub Beulah and Pee Wee were discussing the situation with the Sykeses. 'I think I'll go round and see Jess later,' Beulah said. 'Maybe I can be of further help.'

'I wouldn't do that, hon,' Pee Wee counselled. 'Let them be, for today anyway. I'm sure they don't want no outsiders, no matter how well-meanin', buttin' in right now. They'll want to be by themselves.'

'Reckon?'

He nodded. 'We done everythin' we can for now. If they wants somethin' more they'll come knockin'. At least that's how I sees it.'

Beulah thought that was probably good advice. She'd call round next morning and find out what was what. 'He was such a nice kid too,' she mused. 'Damn shame.'

Pee Wee recalled Albert and Jess's faces at the graveside, two broken people if ever there were. He'd later spoken briefly to Albert, but what could you really say? Nothing. Words were empty at a time like that, but better spoken nonetheless.

'I keep thinkin' . . .' Beulah trailed off, her expression stricken.

'What, hon?'

'Julius and Diane and baby Bradley. What I'd be like if anythin' ever happened to one of them.' Diane was Julius's elder sister, Bradley her son.

'Yeah,' Pee Wee agreed softly. It didn't bear thinking about.

When Julius returned from the pub he couldn't understand why Beulah made such a fuss of him, and continued doing so for the rest of that day.

Jess's visits to the graveside had become a daily ritual. Every morning she caught the bus to Highgate, returning usually just before noon.

She was there now, staring at Paul's grave, the flowers adorning it withered and dead as he was. She knew she should remove the flowers and put them in the bin provided, but couldn't bring herself to do so.

Albert didn't approve of these visits, saying she was only torturing herself. And maybe she was, but come she had to.

She blamed herself for Paul's death. If only she'd left him in Devon with the Sellys he'd still be alive. But no, she'd had to go and bring him home.

It was no use reminding herself how unhappy he'd been at High Barton, that was hardly relevant now. An unhappy Paul far better than a dead one.

Jess groped for her handkerchief, and wiped her eyes. She'd already been standing there half an hour during which it had rained twice, but that didn't matter. It could have been a thunder or snow storm for all she cared. What was important was that she was with her son, her beloved boy, whom she missed so much it was mentally crucifying her.

Not only had she brought him back from Devon but had been against it when the authorities had wished to re-evacuate him, wanting to keep him with her.

Selfish, that's what she'd been, utterly selfish. And this was the result. A dead child and she with her heart broken.

If only she could turn the clock back. If only she'd never gone to Devon. If only she'd insisted he be re-evacuated.

For her, the two most painful and agonising words in the world right then.

If only . . .

* * *

Jess got wearily out of her chair when the sirens sounded, the ninth night in a row they'd wailed their warning that yet another raid was about to take place. Would it never end?

Crossing to the fireplace she picked up the small, framed photograph of Paul, the only one she possessed. For a moment she held it to her bosom and closed her eyes, then gathered up the rest of the things she'd be taking to the shelter.

'Ellie?'

'Hello, Julius.'

'I thought that was you.'

He got out of the car and closed his door. 'It's so difficult to see anything, or anyone, in this black-out. People are just shapes moving in the darkness.'

She laughed. 'Spooky, isn't it?'

He turned up the collar of his coat, for it was wild and blustery. 'Shouldn't you be on duty at this time?' he queried with a frown.

'I'm on days for the next fortnight. I think they thought I needed a bit of a rest after . . .' She trailed off and bit her lip.

'Paul?'

She nodded.

'How are your mom and dad? I haven't seen either of them for a while.'

Ellie shrugged. 'Trying to cope. Getting on with it. It isn't easy for them.'

'Or you,' he added softly.

'No,' she agreed. 'But it's worse for them, particularly Mum. She really took it badly.'

Julius glanced at the sky. 'I hope this weather keeps up. It's been over a week now since the last raid.'

'A welcome respite,' she smiled. 'The forecast is awful I'm happy to say.'

He had a sudden thought. 'Listen, what are you doin' after you've eaten?'

She wondered why he'd asked that. 'Nothing much. Listen to the wireless I suppose. Do some ironing for Mum.'

'Well, I've got a better idea. Why don't we go to The Florence for a drink? Far more excitin', don't you think?'

She couldn't disagree. It would be good to get out and enjoy herself for a bit, have a break. 'All right.'

'Fine then. It's a date.'

For some reason those words sent a thrill through her. Of course it wasn't a date in that sense, she knew that. It was only his way of saying meeting up. 'What time?'

Then he remembered the state of affairs at The Florence, no spirits. 'I've had a better thought,' he declared. 'Instead of the pub why don't you come to our house? At least there I can offer you some gin.'

She couldn't see why not. It was better than drinking beer which she didn't really like. 'As I said, what time?'

He thought about that. 'Eight?'

'Suits me.'

'That gives you time to eat and get sorted out. Me too.'

'Eight then.'

Julius found himself whistling as he went inside. He was looking forward to this.

'I'm afraid Mom's out,' he declared, ushering Ellie into the lounge. 'She decided to take advantage of the raids being stopped and go into the club with Dad. I hope you don't mind that there's only the two of us.'

'Not in the least.' She nearly said, I presume I will be safe? But decided not to. It would only have been a tease anyway. Of course she was safe. Julius had no interest in her that way.

'By the by, there's somethin' for you on that chair there,' he said, pointing.

Ellie went to the chair and picked up the carton of cigarettes lying on it. 'You really are terribly good to me, Julius. Thank you.'

'Only bein' neighbourly.'

She'd been a little tense before knocking on the door, but somehow he'd almost instantly put her at her ease. She now felt completely relaxed.

Julius waggled a glass in her direction. 'I've already started so you've got some catchin' up to do. Now make yourself comfortable while I pour you a drink.'

She sank into the chair the cigarettes had been on and gazed around. She hadn't been in this room since the Postons had arrived and invited the family in for a meal. That seemed a lifetime ago considering all that had happened since.

'Tonic water as well!' she laughed. 'You are organised. All mod cons, I must say.'

'As usual, compliments of the Embassy. Uncle Sam looks after his own.'

'Hmmh!' she grunted in appreciation on tasting the G&T he handed her. 'This is strong.'

'Complainin'?'

She shook her head. 'Don't be daft. It's wonderful.'

Julius went to the sofa, kicked off his loafers and sat with his legs along the cushions. 'So, how'ya been?'

'If you mean work, not too hectic. It'll liven up once the bombing starts again as it's bound to.'

He indicated. 'There's an ashtray there if you want to smoke.'

'What about you?'

'In a minute or two.'

What large feet he had, she noticed. Then flushed, remembering something she'd heard about men with large feet.

'What's wrong?'

'Nothing.'

'Sure? You went kind of pink all of a sudden.'

She couldn't meet his gaze. 'There's no reason,' she lied. It had been Connie Fox who'd told her about men with large feet. Connie whom she hadn't seen since joining the auxiliaries. She made a mental note to try to get in touch.

'What's the latest between you and your girlfriend?' Ellie asked. 'The last time we spoke properly she was trying to get you to marry her.'

The smile vanished from Julius's face. 'We broke up. I don't take her out any more.'

'Oh?'

He wondered if he should tell Ellie the reason why he'd broken with Marybeth, then thought the better of it. That was a bit too personal.

'I just decided to call it quits while I was ahead,' he said instead.

That pleased Ellie, though she couldn't think why. It was none of her business. 'Do you miss her?'

He considered his answer before replying. 'Some aspects of our relationship. But generally speakin', no.'

Ellie understood what he meant by that. He missed going to bed with Marybeth. How like a man, she thought a trifle prudishly. 'So is there anyone new?'

'What is this, Ellie, the Spanish Inquisition?'

This time she went bright red. 'Sorry. I wasn't being nosey. I'm genuinely interested. As a friend.'

He had a long, satisfying gulp of bourbon. 'Well, there isn't. I'm a free agent again. What about you?'

She laughed. 'When do I have a chance to meet anyone? I'm either at work or home, with nothing in-between.'

'There must be guys in the ambulance station?'

That amused her. 'Two of them, both retired. Somewhere in their late sixties I should imagine. We're auxiliaries, don't forget.'

He could understand her amusement. 'A little old for you, eh?'

'Just a little,' she agreed.

'Too bad,' he said. 'A good-lookin' doll like you shouldn't be without a gentleman caller.'

Doll! She'd never been called that before. As for

'gentleman caller', how quaint. It gave her a warm glow to think he considered her good-looking. Unless he was merely being polite of course. She couldn't tell from his expression whether or not that was the case.

She recrossed her legs, feeling one of them catch something on the chair as she did. 'Damn!' she swore when a quick examination revealed she'd snagged a stocking causing a ladder.

'What's wrong?'

She explained. 'And it's the last pair I've got too. They're not to be had in the shops for love nor money.'

Julius came over and had a look at the offending chair, a small nail that had partially worked loose being the culprit. 'I'll fix that right away,' he declared, and hurried from the room, returning almost immediately with a hammer. A couple of taps did the trick.

'Sorry about that,' he apologised.

Ellie made a face. 'Hardly your fault. It was an accident.'

'Caused by our chair,' he pointed out. 'At least let me make amends. A dozen or so pairs of nylons should be adequate compensation, wouldn't you say?'

Ellie gasped. 'Nylons! A dozen pairs!' Her eyes were shining. 'Can you really manage that?'

'Sure. It's not a problem. I'll have them for you as soon as I can.'

'Oh Julius!' she breathed. 'That would be fantastic. I'm not exaggerating when I told you they're like gold dust round here. And nylons are absolutely impossible to get hold of. If you do get lucky the stockings are lisle like I'm wearing. Horrid things really.'

It pleased him to see how delighted she was; he made a mental note to sort out the nylons first thing in the morning on arrival at the Embassy. 'Let me freshen your glass, it's empty,' he declared.

'Not too much. I don't want to get tiddly.'

When he'd refilled her glass, and his own, he produced a cigar, one of a new batch recently arrived from Cuba, clipped it and lit up. 'Would you like to hear some music?' he asked. 'We have a Victrola and a great many records. Some of them featuring my dad.'

'That would be lovely,' she exclaimed, realising that a Victrola was what she knew as a gramophone.

Julius replaced the needle before winding up the machine and putting on the first record. 'Let's try this for size, eh? It's one of my dad's called "Moonlit Eyes".'

The alcohol was beginning to take effect, she thought, as the music, a ballad, wafted dreamily over her.

'What do you think, Ellie?'

'I like it, very much.'

He beamed approval.

How much better than the music played at the Poxy Roxy, she reflected. No comparison at all.

'Care to dance?'

She'd closed her eyes for a few moments in appreciation, now she opened them again. 'I'm not very good,' she confessed, suddenly all shy and coy.

'Neither am I, so that makes us even.'

He lifted the arm of the Victrola and placed it back at the beginning of the record. 'Shall we?'

It didn't take her long to realise he'd been lying to be

kind, he could dance all right, beautifully so. He reminded her of a big black panther, she thought, as they moved round the carpet, she drinking in the smell of the cologne he was wearing, unused to men who used such a thing.

When the record was finished she asked if it could be played again, she liked it so much.

A smiling Julius complied.

Ellie found Jess asleep in the kitchen with a blanket draped over her lap. She was holding the photograph of Paul clutched in both hands.

Ellie stared at her mother who looked so settled and comfortable. Wake her or leave her as she was? In the end Ellie decided to leave her.

Going upstairs she thought about what a wonderful evening she'd had with Julius, it couldn't have gone better. They'd talked about all sorts, her life, his life, experiences they'd had, a whole range of topics.

They'd also drunk a lot – too much really, she hoped she wouldn't regret it in the morning – laughed, danced and told jokes. The time had simply flown past.

'Moonlit Eyes,' she murmured as she undressed, and smiled. None of the other records he'd played had been a patch on that. Somehow its haunting melody was special.

Just like the evening itself.

Chapter 21

Albert laid aside the book he'd been reading, and yawned. So far the shift had been uneventful and he hoped it continued that way. The recent air raids had been sporadic, sometimes the Luftwaffe came, sometimes not. There was no distinguishable pattern to it.

'I've been meaning to ask,' Danny McGiver, sitting opposite, said. 'How's Jess?'

Albert stared at his friend and colleague, thinking about his answer. 'Not so good I'm afraid,' he eventually replied.

Danny nodded. 'Understandable I suppose. It must be a terrible thing to lose a child.' Adding when he saw the look that came over Albert's face, 'For both of you.'

'Yes,' Albert agreed softly. 'At least I have my work to keep me busy, take my mind off it. Jess just sits at home and constantly broods. I know she tries to hide the fact, but she cries a lot when Ellie and I aren't there. And every morning it's the same, a trip to the cemetery to visit the grave.'

'Poor cow,' Danny whispered.

'The trouble is she blames herself for Paul's death. I've told her that's nonsense but she'll have none of it. She's convinced she's at fault and that's that.'

'Can't the doctor do something? Give her pills or what-ever?'

'He might if she'd go and see him, but she won't. She says the doctor can't help what's wrong with her.'

Albert sighed. 'If it wasn't for the war I'd take her away on holiday. A week in Brighton perhaps, that might buck her up somewhat.' He smiled cynically. 'There again, if it wasn't for the war Paul would still be alive and the holi-day wouldn't be necessary.'

Danny shook his head. 'I sometimes think this is going to go on for ever, that it'll never end. But of course it will, one way or the other, eventually. Has to.'

'She's also losing weight,' Albert went on. 'Well we all are, what with rationing and shortages, but Jess more than others. She's skin and bone, which breaks my heart.'

'She had a lovely figure too,' Danny sympathised. 'I always admired her for that. A real bobby dazzler.'

Albert smiled in memory. 'You should have seen her when I married her, Danny, a stunner if ever there was. I was the envy of nearly every bloke I knew. Now she's more like a scarecrow than anything else.'

'Christ, I'm sorry,' Danny murmured.

'Her face has gone quite haggard and lined, pasty with it. I swear she looks ten or fifteen years older than she did.'

Danny was lost for words, he simply didn't know what to reply to that.

Albert thought of his own grief, the hurt almost unbearable at times. Again and again pictures of Paul would flash through his mind. Paul playing, laughing,

Paul as a baby with Jess changing his nappies, having him at the breast. He loved Ellie of course, but Paul had been different in that Paul had been his son. Nor would there ever be another boy child to replace Paul.

'How about a cup of tea?' Danny queried, and winked. 'I've got a couple of digestives in my box, so we can have one each.'

'Grand,' Albert tried to enthuse. A biscuit was a treat nowadays.

'Shan't be long,' Danny declared, rising from his chair.

Albert watched Danny's retreating back, but in his mind he was still thinking about, and remembering, Paul.

His son.

The fire had been extensive, but was now under control. This was the sixth trip Ellie and Josie Farnham had made to the scene, currently waiting to ensure the last of the casualties had been removed, at which point they'd return to the station to be in readiness for any further call-outs.

Ellie had spotted the mobile canteen earlier during one of her previous visits, and now decided to avail herself of it while she had the time.

'I'll catch up with you in a few moments,' Josie replied when Ellie told her what she intended. 'I have to find somewhere for a crafty pee. I'm bursting.'

Ellie smiled. 'You do that.'

The canteen was manned by the WVS, the Women's Voluntary Service, a solitary member now serving. When she arrived Ellie found herself to be the only one waiting.

'A cup of tea and something to eat please,' she asked the woman who had her back to her.

Ellie had a shock when the woman turned round. Dear God, she thought.

'Hello, Miss Sykes, how are you?' Miss Oates asked, the face as stern as ever.

Ellie was further taken aback that Miss Oates had recognised her so easily as she was in full protective gear with her face filthy and dirt-streaked.

As though reading her mind Miss Oates said, 'Your voice, Miss Sykes, I never forget a voice.'

Ellie swallowed hard, quite thrown to suddenly find herself in the company of her old boss and enemy. 'I'm fine, thank you.'

Miss Oates regarded her keenly. 'Well, you don't look fine. I'd say you were totally knackered.'

Ellie's jaw literally fell open to hear Miss Oates use such language. It was beyond belief. 'I suppose I am,' she eventually mumbled.

'Not surprised in that job. I admire you for doing it, Miss Sykes. Yes indeed.'

Was there no end of surprises? Ellie watched as Miss Oates poured her a cuppa and then placed a sandwich and bun on a plate. 'These buns are fresh baked this morning. They're nice and tasty, couldn't have made better myself,' Miss Oates declared, placing the tea and plate on the canteen counter.

'Thank you.'

Ellie blew on the tea which was scalding hot, then started on the sandwich, wolfing it down as she was ravenously hungry.

'I ran into a friend of yours the other day,' Miss Oates informed her.

'Oh?'

'Miss Fox. She left the office shortly after you, but you probably know that.'

Ellie shook her head. 'I didn't.'

'There's hardly anyone there now,' Miss Oates stated. 'Reduced to a skeleton staff. Just enough to keep business ticking over. The others are all off doing war work. In Miss Fox's case she's taken over a milk round she said.'

'A milk round?' Ellie found that incredible, unable to imagine Connie driving a horse and cart.

'Releases a man for the Forces you see. Told me she was enjoying it. Loves being out in the fresh air.'

'So how is she?' Ellie asked.

'Happy as a pig in the proverbial. Took up with a new chap just before she left and, according to her, the pair of them are getting along famously. A seaman, I believe. Well, good luck to them I say. I hope it works out.'

Ellie vaguely remembered something about Connie possibly having a new boyfriend just before she herself had left the office, but as she recalled Connie had denied it at the time. She guessed Connie had done so because she and this seaman had only recently met up and she hadn't wanted to look foolish if it hadn't lasted, been a flash in the pan so to speak. She could well understand that.

Ellie tried her tea again which was now drinkable, and then had a bite of her bun. As Miss Oates had said, it was delicious.

A middle-aged ARP warden came strolling over. 'Evening, Beryl, how are tricks?'

The stern expression vanished to be replaced by a broad smile. 'Hello, Stanley. Wondered if you'd be around.'

'Here I am, in all me glory.'

Beryl? Ellie had never known what Miss Oates' Christian name was, and would certainly never have guessed something as common as Beryl. In other circumstances she would have laughed.

'Tea and two sugars is it?' Miss Oates queried winsomely.

Bloody hell! Ellie thought. Miss Oates was actually flirting with this Stanley. She simply couldn't believe it.

'That's right, ducks. Two sugars it is. If you can spare that amount.'

Miss Oates winked. 'Anything for you, Stanley. You know that.'

Stanley laughed, then turned to Ellie. 'Do you belong to that vehicle over there?' he inquired, pointing.

A stunned Ellie nodded.

'Well, you've got the all clear. No more casualties, that's been confirmed now.'

'Thank you.'

Ellie finished her bun and tea while Miss Oates and Stanley chatted, then, having said goodbye, went in search of Josie who she presumed was having difficulty finding a secluded spot.

Talk about a turn-up for the book! *Beryl*, she thought, and this time did laugh.

'Ah, there you are. Please sit down,' Station Officer Titmuss said, indicating the chair in front of her desk.

Ellie, who'd been summoned to see the SO, was wondering what this was all about. For the life of her she couldn't think of anything she'd done wrong. 'Thank you.'

SO Titmuss regarded Ellie kindly. 'What would you say to a spot of promotion, Ellie? I'd like to make you up to DSO.' That meant Deputy Station Officer.

Ellie was flabbergasted, she'd never imagined this to be on the cards. 'Why me?' she queried.

'Because you're a born leader and all the other girls look up to you. You're a natural choice for the job.'

Ellie tried to digest that, having been completely unaware she was held in such esteem by the others. 'What about DSO Winterbottom?' she asked. Alice Winterbottom was the current DSO.

'Alice is also in for promotion. She's taking over a new station being opened in the Ball's Pond Road. So her post is falling vacant as from the first of the month, and I'd like you to assume her duties. It means a little extra money of course, which always comes in handy.'

Ellie thought about that. It would mean she wouldn't be out in the ambulances as often as before, paperwork being the new priority. And lots of it.

'Well?' SO Titmuss prompted.

Ellie made a decision. Why not? Anyway, she rather fancied the idea of wearing two stripes on her arm. And as the SO said, extra money would be useful, her mother would certainly welcome it. 'Thank you, I accept.'

SO Titmuss beamed. 'Good girl. Well done. Congratulations.' Rising, she came round her desk and shook Ellie warmly by the hand, Ellie having also risen.

Josie Farnham wasn't best pleased when told the news as it meant she'd have a new partner, she and Ellie having become close during their time together. More importantly, they both got on terribly well.

Ellie found herself looking forward to her new duties, even if they wouldn't be quite as exciting as what she now did.

Maybe less exciting, but also less dangerous she reminded herself. Which, if she was honest, was something of a relief.

The date was May 10, 1941, and if Londoners thought they'd been through the worst of the Blitz, that it couldn't possibly get worse than it had been, then that night proved them horribly wrong. Later it would be called the night that nearly took the heart out of London.

The news slowly filtering through to the battling firemen was one of terrible carnage. The Chamber of the House of Commons had been reduced to rubble, the Lords' Chamber having also been hit, as had Big Ben, though that was still standing. The roof of Westminster Hall was ablaze, while the square tower at Westminster Abbey had fallen in. Miraculously, although surrounded by fires, St Paul's remained intact. The number of dead, dying and casualties didn't bear thinking about. All the services, including the Fire Brigade, were stretched to the limit, and beyond.

Henry Leway staggered up to Albert, having to shout to be heard above the roar of flames and crackle of burning buildings. 'We haven't a hope in hell of controlling this lot,' he gasped.

'We'll just have to,' Albert snapped in reply.

Henry shook his head. 'It's impossible, I tell you.'

Albert paused to stare at his colleague. Henry was on the point of breaking he realised. 'Get a grip of yourself, Henry, for Christsake!' he shouted.

To Albert's amazement Henry started to cry, tears rolling down his soot-blackened face. 'I've had enough. Can't take any more. Too much. Too much.'

Albert let go of the hosepipe he was holding and slapped Henry hard causing him to cry out. 'Stop snivelling like a child and get on with it,' Albert bellowed. 'We need every man we've got and you're one of the best. Don't let us down now. Don't let the public down, they're relying on us. All of London is relying on us tonight.' By that he meant the entire Fire Brigade.

Henry blinked several times, then ran a hand across his face. Taking a deep breath he straightened himself. 'Sorry, Albert,' he apologised. 'I don't know what came over me.'

'Are you all right now?'

Henry nodded.

Albert gripped and squeezed his arm. 'Good chap. Let's just forget this, eh?'

'Thanks.'

Turning, Henry hurried away.

'Gas!' someone yelled a little later. 'Gas escape!'

Oh my God! Albert thought. He couldn't smell anything, but that was hardly likely in the smoke-laden atmosphere that was also heavily polluted by the many combined odours from all manner of burning things.

Seconds later the gas ignited sending a searing ball of flame billowing in all directions. Albert was lifted off his feet and thrown backwards to land with a jarring thump which knocked the breath out of him, leaving him dizzy and dazed.

He slowly became aware of Henry Leway by his side. 'Are you hurt, Albert?'

He gingerly felt himself all over. 'Don't think so.'

'Then try and sit up.'

Albert hesitantly brought himself into an upright position to stare at the roaring gas escape. From the size and intensity of it he guessed a main had been breached. 'That has to be turned off,' he croaked.

'I know.'

'Then get to it. I'll be with you in a moment.'

'Right,' Henry declared, and dashed away.

Albert pulled himself to his feet where he swayed slightly. He had to hold a hand across his face to ward off the intense heat which was already blistering his skin.

'Over here!' someone shouted. 'Unconscious fireman!'

People were milling everywhere, like ants in a heap, all trying to do something specific connected with their job. Albert wondered who the fireman was. One of theirs or from another station?

He made his way over as an ambulance crew appeared carrying a stretcher between them. Albert's heart sank when he reached the prostrate figure to see it was Danny McGiver.

Instantly he was kneeling alongside Danny feeling for a neck pulse, swearing beneath his breath when he couldn't find one. Before he could try another point the ambulance chaps, regular service and not auxiliaries like Ellie's lot, were also there doing a quick examination.

'Can't tell if he's dead or not,' the older of the two shouted to Albert. 'He a friend of yours?'

Albert nodded.

'We'll get him straight to hospital where he can be dealt with.'

Albert watched numbly as Danny, one arm trailing over the side, was stretchered away.

Not Danny, he thought in despair. Please God, not Danny. Then he turned his attention again to what had to be done.

It was another half an hour before the gas main had been turned off and that particular fire extinguished.

Jess came out of the cemetery gates and crossed over to the bus stop where no one else was waiting. Twenty minutes later a bus still hadn't appeared, which didn't surprise her after the previous night's terrible raid. The buses could hardly be expected to run to schedule after that. She'd been lucky on the way there having caught one almost immediately.

Then the idea came to her. Why not walk home? It was an awful long way, miles, and would take her ages, but the more she thought about it the more determined she became that's what she'd do.

A sort of punishment, she told herself grimly. A small penance for Paul's death which had been all her fault.

She started off knowing it would probably take her a while. But no matter what, no matter how many buses passed her, it was a journey she was going to complete.

A small penance, she thought again.

Albert knocked on Danny's door. He was done in, almost dropping from exhaustion, having just come off his longest shift ever. On returning to the station it was to be told that Danny wasn't seriously hurt and was now home.

'How is he?' Albert asked Danny's wife Vera when she answered his knock.

'Come in and see for yourself. He's in bed.'

Albert followed Vera through to where Danny was. 'Hello, mate,' Danny whispered by way of greeting.

The upper part of Danny's head was swathed in bandages which ended just above his ears. There was no sign of blood on them, a relieved Albert noted.

'Some people will do anything to skive off,' Albert joked.

Danny attempted a smile, and winced. That hadn't been a good idea. 'As if.'

'He discharged himself, you know,' Vera stated disapprovingly. 'They wanted to keep him in for forty-eight hours for observation.'

'Now don't start again,' Danny chided. 'I explained,

they needed the bed for someone worse off than me. Best I was home anyway, you're a far better nurse than any they have at the hospital.'

Vera wagged a finger at him. 'Don't you try and soft-soap me, Danny McGiver. It won't work, you hear?'

'Yes, dear,' he replied meekly, knowing full well, despite what she'd said, Vera would have been delighted to be told that. Anyway, in a way it was true.

'Cup of tea, Albert?' Vera asked.

'Please. Good and strong. The sort you can stand a spoon up in.'

'Coming right away.'

'Hey, what about me?' Danny protested.

'You've already had four since you woke. We are on rationing, don't forget.'

'If you're making a pot for Albert then it'll stretch to me,' Danny pointed out.

'Well all right.' Vera pretended to concede, having been going to give him a cup anyway, and disappeared out of the room.

'She's a gem. Don't know what I'd do without her,' Danny declared, having enjoyed that little bit of banter.

Albert smiled and sat on the edge of the bed. 'You gave me a hell of a fright last night, mate,' he said softly. 'I thought we'd lost you. What's the damage?'

'Concussion, that's all. And a few abrasions. I was lucky.'

'What happened exactly?'

'Don't know, Albert. One moment someone was shouting gas, the next thing I knew I was in an ambulance. I must have been hit on the head by flying debris of some sort. Thank God for my helmet. It might have been curtains if it hadn't been for that.'

Albert was noting how pale and wan Danny was. 'Head sore?'

'More than I'm letting on to Vera. She thinks I'm a mug for discharging myself, but it was the right thing to do. There were casualties everywhere, most in a far worse state than myself.'

Danny closed his eyes for a few seconds, and grimaced. 'Christ!' he swore quietly. 'Sometimes there's a stabbing pain that goes right through my brain like a red-hot poker. Not pleasant, I can tell you. Not pleasant at all.'

Albert could well imagine. 'Well, that'll be you off work for a couple of weeks, jammy blighter.'

'Don't you believe it,' Danny retorted quickly. 'A couple of days more like. There's a war on, me old son, or have you forgotten?'

Albert laughed. 'How could I after last night. That was sheer bloody murder and no mistake. But listen, I think you should reconsider this couple of days bit. Heroics are all very well, but we need you to be fit when you get back, up to the job. You'll only be a liability to the rest of us if you're still crocked.'

Danny hadn't thought of that. Much as he hated to admit it, Albert had a point. 'All right then,' he replied reluctantly.

'Good.'

Danny was beginning to feel tired again, but didn't want to say in case Albert went. He was enjoying the company. 'How about the rest of the chaps, they safe and sound?'

'Our lads are, but a bloke from Clerkenwell got killed. Name of Nick Hastings, ring any bells?'

Danny was about to shake his head, but stopped himself in time. In his present condition that wouldn't have been wise. 'No, it doesn't. How did he get it?'

'The gas explosion. He was close by when it ignited.'

The two men stared at one another, both thinking that might well have been Danny.

'Poor bastard,' Danny whispered.

'Can I come in?' Beulah asked, popping her head round the kitchen door having found the main one ajar.

Jess was sitting with her feet in a basin of hot water. 'Do,' she replied dully.

'Sweet Jesus!' Beulah exclaimed when she got closer. The water in the basin was tinged pink from blood. 'What happened to you?'

'Nothing really.'

'Don't give me that bullshit, Jess Sykes. You's bleedin'.'

Jess spoke slowly and emphatically, explaining her reason for walking back from Highgate, Beulah gazing at her in fear – for Jess – and disbelief.

'How bad are they?' she queried, indicating Jess's feet.

'Bruising mainly, plus a few minor cuts. Nothing to worry about. Honestly.'

Beulah pulled over a chair and sat beside Jess. 'You must stop torturin' yourself like this, girl. It's no good. No good at all.'

Jess hung her head and didn't reply.

'It ain't your fault Paul died . . .'

'It was,' Jess interrupted in a whisper.

Beulah stared at her friend in consternation. 'You did what you thought best and that was bring him home again. I'd have done exactly the same thing in your situation. I swear I would.'

Again Jess didn't reply.

'If you keeps this up you're goin' to have some kind of breakdown, girl, and what good is that to anybody? None at all. You have Albert and Ellie still to think about, you must remember that. If you goes all to pieces you's lettin' them down, and they need you, probably more than they's ever done in their entire lives before. You's the rock in this here family, Jess, the one they all rely on. Besides, what would your Paul say to see you like this?'

Jess's chest heaved as she fought back tears. 'I miss him so much,' she said in a cracked voice.

'Of course you do, hon. You was his momma, that's only natural. But now he's gone you must make him proud of you, and don't think he don't know what you's goin' through. He's up there watchin' you grievin', and I'll bet my sweet ass wishin' you'd stop all this and get on with things. I'm sure that would make him happy.'

Jess blinked back a tear. 'Do you really think so?'

'I'm as certain of that as any mortal person can be. You gotta let go, Jess, for his sake as well as your own. You havin' no breakdown ain't goin' to help anythin'.'

Jess swallowed hard. Let go? That was impossible. How could she?

'You hear me, girl?'

'I can't,' she whispered.

'Oh yes you can, and will. All the grievin' in the world ain't goin' to change things, and that's a fact. Shit, he might have died of all kinds of ailments, kids do. Would you have blamed yourself for that too?'

'No,' Jess confessed.

'Well, there you are then. Grievin' is right and proper, but there comes a time when you have to stop and let go. Get on with life.'

'That's easier said than done,' Jess chided softly.

'I knows that. But done it's gotta be. And stop punishin' yourself, for Christsake! You didn't make no mistake, you did your best and no one, I repeat, no one, can do better than that.'

Beulah took a deep breath. 'I'll stop preachin' now. I've had my say. The rest is up to you.'

Jess somehow managed to smile. 'Why don't you put the kettle on while I dry my feet.'

'That's my girl.'

Jess appreciated Beulah's concern, knowing her to be well-meaning. But it wasn't her Julius lying buried up in Highgate, it was Paul.

And the fault *was* hers, despite what Beulah said.

Chapter 22

'I look like a total frump!' Josie Farnham complained, emerging from the ladies wearing one of the new uniforms they'd just been issued. Her navy blue slacks were baggy, while the matching tunic, rather similar to those worn by the RAF, though nowhere near as neatly tailored, hung loosely from her shoulders. The belt at her waist had the effect of making her hips appear twice their normal size. The ensemble was set off with a forage cap plus shirt and tie.

Ellie choked back a smile. Josie was right, she did look terrible. Frump wasn't the word for it.

Josie stared at Ellie in dismay. 'Do we have to wear this?'

Ellie nodded. ''Fraid so.'

Several of the other girls had come crowding round, their combined reaction one of consternation. They'd all been hoping for something smart and attractive that would show off their figures, but this was a disaster.

'I've seen better-dressed scarecrows,' Babette Meadows commented, and laughed.

'It doesn't even begin to fit,' Josie further complained.

Ellie dreaded to think what she was going to look like

in her new uniform which she hadn't yet tried on. It remained in her office draped over a chair.

'Don't they have different sizes?' Chris Pannell queried with an anxious frown.

'They have but . . . well, they're simply small, medium and large,' Ellie explained.

Chris groaned.

'Maybe we can do something with them, fiddle around a bit if you know what I mean. A tuck here, a little taken in there,' Babette suggested hopefully.

'Can you dressmake?' Ellie queried.

'I wouldn't go that far. But I do have a sewing machine that I have been known to run up things on.'

Ellie had to admit, the overall impression of the new uniform was pretty ghastly. It made her think enviously of a Wren she'd seen recently. Now *that* uniform had been the bee's knees. A world apart from the monstrosity Josie had on.

'And to think we've been moaning all this time waiting for these to arrive!' Josie said in disgust, shaking her head.

'They are disappointing, I have to admit,' Ellie declared. 'But these are what we've been given so I suppose we'd better make the best of them.'

A little later she tried on her own uniform which was just as badly fitting as Josie's.

'Bloody hell!' was her reaction when she saw herself in a mirror.

Albert stared in distaste at the plate Jess had set in front of him. Spam fritters yet again.

'Before you say anything that's all I could get,' Jess said defensively.

He nodded. 'I understand.' Then, with a heartfelt sigh, 'What I wouldn't give for a nice chop, or steak and kidney pie.'

'There's mock banana trifle to follow,' Jess stated.

Albert eyed her dyspeptically. 'And what exactly is that? I mean, what's mock about the banana?' Bananas hadn't been seen in Britain since the outbreak of war.

'It's really parsnip.'

'Parsnip!'

'A new recipe I'm trying. One put out by the Ministry. It's supposed to taste delicious.'

Albert barked out a cynical laugh. 'I'll bet!'

'Let me put it this way,' Jess said quietly. 'It's better than starving.'

Albert had no reply to that, so started in on his fritters, the first mouthful making him pull a face.

Jess placed her own plate on the table and sat facing him. Ellie would get hers when she came off shift.

It was three weeks now since the last air raid and things had returned to some sense of normality. No one expected this lull in the raids to go on indefinitely, but they were enjoying the respite while they could. The best part for Jess, and no doubt countless others, was that she was once more able to get a good night's uninterrupted sleep in her own bed. Sheer bliss after the discomfort of the shelter.

'I had a letter today,' she announced casually.

'Oh?'

'From the authorities. I've to report for work next Monday morning.'

Albert paused in eating to frown. 'Doing what?'

'The letter didn't say. It just gave me the address of a factory off the City Road and stated attendance was compulsory.'

Albert thought about that, his emotions mixed. It wasn't actually a surprise, more and more married women were being allocated war work, so why should Jess be any different. 'What about the hours?' he queried.

'Didn't tell me those either, so I won't find out until I get there.'

He continued eating his fritters, forcing himself to chew and swallow the horrible things. He had to keep his strength up after all, necessary in his job.

'So there we are,' Jess said, thinking it would be strange working again after all these years. She hadn't done since marrying Albert.

'How do you feel about it?'

Jess shrugged.

'I just hope it isn't too hard. Some women are expected to graft like men these days. I can understand why, but it still isn't right.'

Jess hadn't been sure what to expect from Albert when she told him, he could be extremely protective. There again, he no doubt realised there was no option in the matter. Not to report would have meant a visit from PC McKechnie and the possible threat of jail. She certainly didn't want either.

After a while Albert came to the conclusion he was

pleased Jess had to work, it would occupy her mind and hopefully stop her brooding about Paul.

Yes, all in all, it was a good thing. He approved.

Jess tensed as Albert's hand crept over her breast. His breathing had changed during the past few minutes so she knew what was coming next.

'Jess?'

'What?'

'Are you awake?'

'You know I am.'

The hand slid inside her nightdress. 'It's been a long time, Jess. Too long.'

He'd been more than patient, she told herself. Since Paul's death he hadn't made any demands, appreciating that lovemaking was the last thing she wanted. Anyway, during the air raids it had been almost impossible with him on constant night duty, coming home worn out and only wanting to sleep. But that had changed now the raids had temporarily stopped. The old patterns had had time to reassert themselves.

'I love you, Jess,' he whispered.

She smiled to hear the tenderness in his voice. 'And I love you.'

He began caressing her. 'We don't have to,' he further whispered.

A man like Albert had needs, she reminded herself. It would be cruel for her to deny him, she simply couldn't. Not after these many, long months during which he'd shown such consideration and understanding.

Taking the hand from her breast she kissed it, then drew him to her.

It was going to be another warm day, Ellie thought as she let herself out of the house, leaving to go on duty. Somewhere a bird, she had no idea what sort, was singing joyously. An uplifting sound to hear in the middle of war.

As she turned into Upper Street a milk cart was approaching her, a woman driver holding the reins. She recognised Connie Fox immediately.

Connie saw, and recognised, Ellie at the same time, her expression instantly changing. Biting her lower lip she reined in.

'Hello, Connie!' Ellie exclaimed in delight.

'Hello.'

'It's been a long time. How are you?'

Connie regarded Ellie nervously. 'Fine. And you?'

'Mustn't grumble I suppose. I came across Miss Oates some while back, running a mobile canteen for the WVS would you believe. She told me you were doing a milk round nowadays.'

'Really?' Connie replied unenthusiastically. 'Imagine that.'

Ellie frowned. 'I've never seen you on this particular round before?'

'That's because I'm new to it,' Connie explained. 'I was doing another one up in Barnsbury, but they transferred me.'

Something was wrong, Ellie realised, though she couldn't think what. Was it her imagination or was Connie trying to avoid her eyes? 'I must say you're looking well.'

Connie shrugged. 'The outdoor life agrees with me. It's certainly an improvement from being cooped up in a stuffy office all day long.'

'I don't miss that at all. Do you?'

'Not in the least,' Connie agreed.

'When the war's over I shan't be going back to office work. I've had that.'

Connie fiddled with the reins.

'Miss Oates said you were going out with a seaman and that it's all hunky-dory between you,' Ellie prompted, wanting to hear all about it.

'Yes,' Connie rather vaguely replied.

'So?'

'So what?'

Ellie sighed in exasperation. 'Who is he? What's he like? Where did you meet? Come on, I want to hear.'

Connie gave Ellie a rather sickly smile. 'I simply haven't got time to chat right now, Ellie. I wish I did but haven't. I must get on. You know how it is?'

Ellie didn't. Surely Connie could spare a few minutes. Before she could utter, or protest, further, Connie flicked the reins. 'I'll see you again no doubt. Take care.'

'And you!' Ellie called after Connie, the horse and cart having moved forward in the meantime so that now she was addressing Connie's back.

How odd, Ellie reflected as she continued on her way. How extremely strange. Why had Connie been so put out at seeing her? For Connie clearly had. Had something been said in the past that she'd forgotten about, or had she offended Connie in some way?

If it was either she certainly couldn't remember.

It was a new experience for Albert to arrive home after his shift and Jess not be there to greet him. This was going to take a bit of getting used to.

Trouble was, being her first day he had no idea when she would get in. The best thing, he decided, was just to settle down until she appeared which happened three quarters of an hour later.

Albert was instantly on his feet. 'So how did it go?' he demanded.

Jess kissed him briefly on the mouth. God she was tired, not being used to standing all day long. 'A piece of cake,' she declared. 'Couldn't have been easier. The work that is.'

He crossed over and put the kettle on, it having been standing at the ready. 'What kind of firm is it and what exactly are you doing there?'

'It's a small engineering works producing aircraft parts. I run a machine that stamps out some of the bits that then go on to be finished and assembled on to something else. As I said, couldn't be easier. Boring mind you, the same procedure over and over. But the other women are a jolly lot and we all have a good laugh together.'

He could see how tired she was, but there was an excitement in her eyes, an interest perhaps, that hadn't been there since Paul's death. That pleased him enormously.

Jess slumped into a chair. 'I'll have that cup of tea and then get going with the meal.'

Albert couldn't bring himself to ask what that meal was, dreading the answer.

'So, you'll manage all right?' he queried.

'Oh yes. If I have one complaint however, it's the noise. Some of those machines make a terrible racket. I was quite deafened for the first couple of hours. But no other moans apart from that.'

'Good.'

Jess smiled at Albert, trying to remember the last time he'd put the kettle on and made a cup of tea.

She couldn't, which made her appreciate this one all the more.

'I just can't get used to not havin' you round durin' the day, Jess. I feel so goddamn lonely all the time now,' Beulah complained.

Jess regarded her friend with sympathy. 'You have Pee Wee?'

'Ain't the same, hon. I'm talkin' female company here, good old girlie stuff. You know what I mean?'

Jess knew only too well. There was nothing like a proper chinwag with another woman.

'Anyway,' Beulah went on. 'I must say being at work has done wonders for you. I sure is delighted at that.'

Jess smiled. 'It does have its drawbacks though.'

'And what are those?'

Jess dropped her gaze to stare into her coffee, a far superior drink than the ersatz rubbish they now sold in the shops. Brought in by Julius from the Embassy of course. A cup of Beulah's coffee was a real treat.

'The main one is I don't get to the cemetery every morning any more. I miss that dreadfully.'

Now it was Beulah's turn to be sympathetic. 'Maybe that's a good thing,' she replied softly.

Jess didn't answer.

'At least I believe so. You was mopin' and grievin' too much, girl. As I've told you before, you has to get on with your life and leave the past in the past.'

'Maybe,' Jess reluctantly agreed.

'Well, that's how I sees it. And I'm sure I'm right.'

Jess pictured Paul in her mind and a lump rose into her throat. She'd have given anything, anything at all, to have him back.

'It don't mean you forget him, Jess, it don't mean that at all. Sure I know it's hard, but it's happened and that's all there is to it.'

Beulah decided to change the conversation, to try to snap Jess out of the black mood she'd suddenly fallen into. 'How would you like a piece of chocolate cake I baked this morning?' she queried.

Jess's face lit up. 'Have you really got one?'

'You bet your ass I do, hon. As chocolatey as chocolate can be.' Beulah laughed. 'Let's make pigs of ourselves and eat the whole damn thing, eh?'

'Oh I couldn't possibly!' Jess protested. 'I'd be sick.'

'No you won't. And afterwards you'll sure as hell feel a whole lot better, or my name ain't Beulah Poston.'

'It's gorgeous!' Jess declared after the first bite of the gigantic slice Beulah had placed in front of her, her eyes now shining where only minutes before they'd been dull and melancholic.

Beulah laughed again, a deep rumbling sound that came from the very bottom of her huge belly.

As she'd prophesied they did eat the entire cake and neither was sick. Full to the gills with chocolate perhaps, but certainly not sick.

Albert looked across at Ellie who'd just finished helping her mother wash and dry the dishes from their evening meal. He and Ellie were both currently on day shift. Ellie was doing the crossword puzzle that appeared daily in the newspaper they took.

'Stuck?' he queried because she was frowning.

Ellie nodded.

'What's the clue?'

'He cometh on stage. Six letters, the first is I, and the third E.'

'He cometh on stage?' Albert mused. 'Sounds Shakespearean to me.'

'That's what I think.'

Albert thought about it for a few minutes, then shook his head. 'Beats me.'

'Me too,' Ellie sighed in exasperation. Crossword puzzles were a relatively new thing she'd taken up, having found she was usually pretty good at them. That night's was particularly difficult. At least she found it so.

'Ah!' Ellie suddenly exclaimed. 'Iceman.'

'Iceman?' Albert repeated, wondering how that fitted in with Shakespeare.

'It's a play by Eugene O'Neill. *The Iceman Cometh*. Cometh on stage, see?'

'How on earth did you know that?' Jess demanded.

'We did it at school. One of a number of plays we had to study. I thought it terribly depressing.'

Albert watched her write that down. 'It's just dawned on me, tonight's Friday night,' he said slowly.

Ellie glanced across at him. 'So?'

'When was the last time you went out and enjoyed yourself? Since you joined the auxiliaries, and the Blitz started, you haven't been out of the house. At least not that I'm aware of.'

'I agree,' Jess chipped in. 'It's not right that you're home night after night as you've been.'

Ellie stared from one parent to the other, thinking what Albert said was true enough. Since George, apart from The Florence which didn't really count, she hadn't been anywhere.

'High time you had another chap,' Jess declared. 'Do you the world of good.'

Albert nodded his agreement.

'You know what it's been like,' Ellie reminded them. 'There hasn't been time for anything apart from work and sleep.'

'Well, there is now,' Albert retorted.

'But I don't want to go on my own.'

'Then hook up with a pal. One of the girls from the station, say.'

Ellie immediately thought of Josie Farnham who was also single and on the loose. Maybe Josie would fancy the idea? 'I'll think about it,' she prevaricated.

'Take the chance while it's there,' Albert urged. 'Who knows when the raids will start again and then it'll be impossible for who knows how long.'

'You could go to the Roxy,' Jess suggested.

Ellie pulled a face. 'That dump!'

'It's local and it would be best, should you meet someone nice, that he's local too. Easier that way.'

What her mother said made sense, Ellie reflected. A local chap would indeed be easier. If she went up West the chaps there would come from all over London, miles away, which would be a problem at the best of times, far more in the middle of a war when so much was disrupted and out of joint, not least the transport systems.

'Do you have a pal at the station?' Albert asked.

Ellie told them about Josie whom she'd been teamed with and the fact they got on so well together.

'Well, there you are then,' Jess declared. Rounding on Albert she then went on, 'And I'd like a night out at the pictures, Albert Sykes. Ellie isn't the only one who hasn't been anywhere in ages.'

He smiled at her. 'Tomorrow night too soon?'

'Tomorrow night would be absolutely right,' she enthused, delighted with this turn of events.

Albert was delighted too. What a change in Jess since she'd started work, she was a new woman. More like her old self. 'I'm looking forward to it,' he said, voice ringing with sincerity.

'Me too.'

If Ellie hadn't been present she'd have given Albert a kiss.

* * *

'Go on tour!' Beulah exclaimed.

'Only for a short spell, hon. Four weeks, hardly anythin'.'

Beulah wasn't pleased at all by this news that had come right out the blue. 'You wanna go?'

Pee Wee shrugged. 'Ain't got much choice in the matter. Besides, it's for a good cause. Playin' the military camps will cheer those guys up. Good for morale was how Lord Fitzaran put it.'

'And what about The Chicory House?'

'Another band will take our place while we're away so it won't shut down or anythin'.' He put on what he hoped was a winning smile. 'Look at it this way, hon, it's a great opportunity for us to see somethin' of England. We'll be goin' all over.'

'Us!' she exploded. 'I ain't goin' nowhere. I toured with you before, man, and it's a pain in the butt. I's too old for that kind of nonsense nowadays. Livin' out of a suitcase, spendin' nights travellin' in an old beat-up bus, always uncomfortable, never a hot tub available when you needs one.' She shook her head. 'You tour if you must, Pee Wee, but count this here chicken out. I'm stayin' right where I am and nothin', or nobody, will make me change my mind.'

'It's only for a month,' he repeated. 'Ain't the end of the world.'

Beulah sighed. 'I suppose if it's to help military morale. But I don't like it none, Pee Wee. I don't like it at all.'

He went to her and took her into his arms. 'I'll be back before you know it, sweetpea.'

She hated being parted from him, absolutely loathed it which was why she'd toured with him in the past. 'Yeah, a month ain't too bad I reckon,' she reluctantly replied. 'Just you see it ain't no more than that.'

'I promise. A month is the deal and that's what it'll be. I swear.'

That mollified her a little. 'When do you leave?'

'Sunday after next. We're to meet up at The Chicory House and go from there.'

'I'll fix you somethin' to eat,' she said, breaking away, still unhappy at all this.

Pee Wee wisely dropped the subject, nor did Beulah refer to it again for the rest of that day.

'Why the long face?'

Ellie came out of her reverie to find Julius standing beside her, she having popped into The Florence for a quick one. 'Sorry, I was thinking,' she explained, indicating the chair beside her. The pub was quiet as it was still early.

'Problem?' he queried, having sat.

'No, not really.'

He pulled out a packet of cigarettes and offered her one, the pair of them then lighting up.

'Want to talk about it?' he asked.

She was pleased to see him, but then always was. 'Mum and Dad think I should get out more. Socialise, that sort of thing.'

'And don't you?'

Ellie shook her head. 'As I reminded them, there's a

war on. There just hasn't been the time lately, what with one thing and another.'

'Well, you know what they say, all work and no play makes Jill a dull broad.'

She laughed. Dull broad indeed!

'That's better,' he approved. 'Hot damn if it isn't.' He suddenly became all confidential. 'Shall I tell you a secret?' he whispered.

'What's that?'

He leant closer and whispered again. 'You don't laugh enough. It suits you.'

'Idiot!'

He winked. 'It's called black humour.'

Ellie found that very funny. 'I don't know how you do it, Julius, but you always buck me up. You're a constant tonic.'

'You mean like that stuff they put in gin?'

She wagged a finger at him. 'Now you're just being plain silly.'

'Am I?'

'You know you are.'

He beamed broadly. 'But it's fun. Isn't it?'

She nodded. 'And it's bucked me up. Thank you.'

'My pleasure, Ellie.'

She could smell his cologne which seemed even stronger than usual, a smell she now associated with him. She'd come to like it.

Staring into her face Julius had a sudden idea. One he decided he'd have to give thought to.

Ellie's intended quick drink turned into three before

she and Julius finally left the pub. Afterwards it dawned on her it had been as though neither wanted to go, wanting to prolong their time together.

Subconsciously, it had certainly been so in her case.

Chapter 23

'Let's hope there are some decent-looking blokes here and we get asked up to dance,' Josie Farnham said to Ellie as they crowded into the Roxy dancehall. There were certainly plenty of people present, many of the men in uniform.

Ellie was already enjoying herself. She and Josie had stopped off for a couple of drinks on the way there which had set the mood; now they would see what was what.

Ellie didn't recognise the band, a new one since the days when she'd been a regular attender. They were currently playing a waltz, the dance floor jammed with couples dancing to it.

'Do I look all right?' Josie asked anxiously, waving a stray wisp of hair away from her eyes.

'Stop fretting, you look fine.'

Josie dusted imaginary specks of whatever off the front of her dress which had a halter neck and sleeves that ended just above her elbows. Its deep blue colour suited her dark complexion.

Ellie nudged her friend and nodded towards a chap moving in their direction. 'He's gorgeous,' she whispered.

The chap in question had pale blond hair and wore

381

the uniform of an RAF pilot. Ellie wondered if he'd fought in what was now known as the Battle of Britain.

To Ellie's disappointment the pilot brushed past them without giving either a second glance. No luck there, she thought.

The number came to an end and the dancers applauded. Some came off the floor while others remained where they were.

'God, it's hot in here,' Josie commented, for it was stifling. She hoped her carefully applied make-up didn't start to run.

Ten minutes went by and still no one approached them. Then a chap in a lounge suit came over and smiled at Josie. 'Would you care to dance?'

'I'd love to. Thank you.'

The chap, in his late twenties Ellie judged, took Josie by the arm and led her away.

He'd seemed nice enough, Ellie thought, though nowhere near as handsome as the pilot whom she now spotted with a flaming redhead much younger than himself.

Ellie glanced around, wondering idly if she'd bump into anyone she knew. It was entirely possible being the local dancehall.

'Excuse me?'

She turned to find a truly ugly young man staring at her. 'Hello.' Christ, it's Quasimodo without the hump, she thought.

'Dance?'

She couldn't refuse, that wasn't the done thing. Not

without a good excuse anyway which she didn't have. She smiled assent and they headed for the floor.

'My name's Richard by the way,' he said as she went into his arms.

'I'm Ellie.'

'Pleased to meet you.'

When he said that she got a whiff of his breath which nearly knocked her sideways. It stank!

'I haven't seen you here before?' he probed.

Ellie answered, keeping her face turned slightly away from him. Then he asked her what she did, which she explained.

'Interesting,' he commented. 'I'm a dock worker myself. Exempt, which is why I'm not in uniform.'

She didn't reply to that, wishing the number would hurry up and be over with. It was manners to accept one dance, but there was no tradition dictated she had to accept two.

Not only did his breath stink, but his personal hygiene wasn't too clever either, she realised. A good bath would have done him the world of good.

When the number finished they politely applauded. 'Will you have another?' he asked eagerly.

'I'm sorry, but I have to get back to my friend,' she lied, at which his face fell.

'Are you sure?'

'Positive,' she stated firmly. 'Thank you.' And with that she walked away leaving him standing there staring after her.

Fortunately she saw a girl she'd been to school with

and stopped beside her for a brief chat. When she looked out of the corner of her eye Richard had also left the floor and was talking to some other female which let her off the hook.

What a horrible man, she thought on leaving her school chum who was with a cousin. Josie had remained on the floor making Ellie wonder if she had clicked.

She decided to nip into the Ladies' for a cigarette and was just about to head in that direction when a couple dancing caught her attention. She couldn't believe it, she simply couldn't, for the couple were none other than George and Connie, Connie with her eyes closed and cheek pressed against George's chest.

'Bitch!' she muttered furiously. 'Bitch!' No wonder Connie had been so strange that morning in Upper Street, making excuses about having to get on so she didn't have to answer her questions about the boyfriend. A boyfriend who now turned out to be bloody George!

Suddenly Ellie felt sick to the very pit of her stomach.

Ellie had waited almost an hour, watching while George and Connie danced together. Her opportunity came when they came off the floor and Connie left George to make for the Ladies'.

Ellie caught up with her halfway down the corridor, coming up behind her and tapping her on the shoulder. 'Hello, Connie.'

Connie blanched. 'Hello, Ellie,' she stuttered.

'Let's go outside. I want a word.'

Connie's eyes flicked first one way, then the other, but

she could hardly make a run for it. What would have been the point? 'All right.'

Ellie, still fuming, continued on behind Connie and out of the main door into a balmy July night. 'So tell me about you and George?' she demanded when they'd halted and faced one another.

'What do you want to know?'

Ellie's eyes narrowed. 'You were going out with him when we were still at the office, weren't you? He was the new boyfriend you didn't want to talk about.'

Connie swallowed hard, and nodded.

'What I don't understand is how the pair of you got together when George was supposed to be at sea?'

'Have you got a cigarette?'

'Bugger a cigarette, you've mooched the last one off of me, Connie Fox. Explain,' Ellie hissed.

'George wrote to you from Liverpool, right?'

'Right. He was supposed to sail the next day.'

'Well, he did, only the ship broke down shortly after leaving harbour and had to be towed back in again. It turned out the engines were in need of extensive repair, so the majority of the crew were transferred to other vessels. In George's case it was a small ship doing coastal trips only which meant he could, and still can, get home every week to ten days. We met by chance, here actually, and have been going out together ever since.

'Honestly, Ellie, I didn't pinch him from you, he'd already broken it off before that night when we both turned up here. As God is my witness, that's the truth.'

Despite what Connie had just said, Ellie still felt

betrayed, and somehow humiliated. And still bloody angry.

Connie hung her head. 'I'm sorry, Ellie. I couldn't tell you the truth because I knew it would hurt. We were best mates after all, and you'd been so good to me, going with me to that abortionist woman when I needed a friend by my side.'

'Do you love him?'

When Connie glanced up there were tears in her eyes. 'Yes.'

'And I presume he loves you?'

Connie nodded.

Ellie couldn't resist it. 'Funny how he fell in love with you so quickly after being in love with me, don't you think?'

Connie didn't answer that.

'Are you shagging him?'

'Oh, Ellie,' Connie whispered. 'Don't ask that.'

Ellie's expression became grim. 'Which means you are. There again, you always were a tart. He's hardly the first man you've opened your legs to.'

'I'm not a tart,' Connie sobbed.

'Then what would you call yourself? I say tart, or perhaps you'd prefer slut? Whichever, you're as common as dirt.'

Ellie fought back the urge to slap Connie. It wouldn't have been so bad if Connie had taken up with George some time after she and he had broken up, but to do so almost instantly! That made her blood boil. And to think she'd considered Connie a friend. She should have known better.

'Well, you're welcome to him,' Ellie hissed. 'Good luck to the pair of you.'

And having said that she whirled round and re-entered the Roxy to find Josie and tell her she was going home.

'I see,' Jess mused after Ellie had explained what had happened. 'And I always thought George such a nice lad too.'

'But he didn't double-cross you, Ellie. You've admitted he'd broken it off before taking up with this other girl,' Albert reminded her.

Ellie glared at him. 'That's not the point.'

'Of course it isn't,' Jess chipped in.

Albert was confused. 'Then what is?'

'Connie was my friend, Dad.'

'So?'

'She might have waited a while before taking up with him.'

Albert didn't quite understand the reasoning behind that. 'But she was free and so was he. True, the timing might have been a bit unfortunate but they could hardly help that.'

'Waiting would have been the decent thing to do,' Ellie insisted.

'Quite right,' Jess nodded.

This was beyond him, Albert decided, and went back to reading his paper. He would never comprehend the female mind, not in a million years.

'I'll put the kettle on,' Jess declared brightly, as though that would sort everything.

'She might have waited, the cow,' Ellie repeated.

Albert said nothing.

Ellie had gone to bed early, still upset after the dance, and Albert had gone up a few minutes previously. Now Jess was on her own having promised Albert she'd join him soon.

Trouble was, she wasn't in the least bit tired, her worry and concern for Ellie keeping her wide awake. She hated seeing her daughter so miserable and had said everything she'd thought might help to soothe matters.

Children, she thought. What a worry they were. And it never stopped. From the moment they were born they were just one worry after another, an endless parade of troubles and anxieties.

Jess's eyes strayed to the mantelpiece and the framed picture of Paul standing on it. Well, she didn't have to worry about him any more, she thought bitterly. The poor little sod was dead.

'Dead,' she whispered aloud. Gone. For ever.

Rising, she crossed to the photo and picked it up to stare at it. Her Paul. Her darling son. And she'd . . . Jess swallowed. She'd brought him back from Devon for which she would never forgive herself. Not ever.

She carefully replaced the photograph and smiled at it. So many memories, so many good ones.

And at the end, so much heartache.

The following day Jess and Ellie were preparing lunch, a vegetable stew and boiled potatoes, when there was a knock on the outside door. Albert was over in The Florence having his customary Sunday lunchtime drink when not on duty.

'I'll get it,' Jess announced, wiping her hands on her apron, while Ellie continued peeling potatoes.

'It's Julius for you,' Jess declared on returning to the kitchen with him in tow.

'Hi!' he smiled. 'How are you?'

A mess, she thought, for she was still in her nightie and dressing gown having not yet washed or dressed which was unusual for her on a day off.

'Well, as you can see, you've caught me in my glad rags,' she retorted, matching his smile.

Julius laughed. 'Do you want me to come back later?'

She shook her head. 'What can I do for you?'

Ellie left the sink and Jess took over the potato peeling, as curious as Ellie as to why Julius was here.

'We're having a cocktail party at the Embassy next week for some Russians and I wondered if you'd like to come with me?'

'A cocktail party?' Ellie repeated in wonder. She'd never been to one of those, far less one at an Embassy.

'That's right. Friday evening at seven o'clock. There should be about thirty or forty present, including the Ambassador himself. It's a goodwill thing as we're, the White House that is, trying to keep in with the Russkies. Are you free?'

A wide-eyed Jess stared at her daughter, as taken aback as Ellie was.

'I'm free,' Ellie replied.

'Then would you like to go?' He winked. 'There will be some nice food, if that'll tempt you. Nothing serious though, mainly canapés and the like.'

Ellie had no idea what canapés were, never before having heard the word. Tasty bits and pieces, she correctly guessed. 'Sounds wonderful. I'd love to go.'

He nodded. 'That's settled then. I'll pick you up just after six. OK?'

'OK,' she agreed, repeating the Americanism.

'I'll leave you to it then.'

'I'll see you out,' Ellie offered.

'Not in your dressing gown, Ellie. People might get the wrong idea,' he teased.

Ellie blushed bright red as he, laughing, exited the kitchen.

'Well, how about that then?' Jess said after he'd gone. 'Excited?'

'Of course I am. It's something to look forward to.' A look of total panic suddenly came across her face. 'But what am I going to wear?'

After lunch when the dishes had been done and Albert had settled into his chair for a snooze, Jess went up to Ellie's bedroom where she had been busily rummaging through her wardrobe and drawers.

'Find anything?' Jess queried.

Ellie shook her head. 'None of my stuff is right, or classy enough. This will be a posh do remember.'

Jess glanced at the clothes laid out on Ellie's bed, all of them predating the war. 'If we had enough coupons we could try up West,' she said slowly. 'But I'm afraid we don't. Nowhere near enough.'

Ellie looked at the same clothes in despair. 'What am I going to do, Mum? I should have thought of this before accepting.'

'Hmmh,' Jess mused, mentally going through her own wardrobe. But she owned nothing remotely suitable either.

'Damn!' Ellie muttered. She couldn't possibly go in any of these dresses, she'd show herself up, not to mention Julius.

'I have an idea,' Jess said slowly.

'What's that?'

'Put all this away again and don't worry. I think I can sort this out again tomorrow, with a bit of luck that is.'

Despite Ellie pressing her Jess wouldn't say what her idea was, only repeating that Ellie wasn't to worry.

The following evening Ellie arrived home from work to find Albert fretting because Jess wasn't there.

'She was due in half an hour ago and still no sign of her,' a worried Albert declared, glancing yet again at the clock on the mantelpiece. 'I hope nothing's happened.'

'I shouldn't think so, Dad. She's probably had to do a bit of overtime, that's all.'

'Well, it would be a first. She hasn't had to do that up until now,' he frowned.

'There's a war on, Dad, don't forget. Nothing's set in stone.'

Ellie wondered if she should start getting the meal ready, but had no idea what Jess had planned. A look in the cupboard and larder didn't reveal what it might be.

Ellie lit up, and slumped into a·chair. Rumour round the station was that the Germans were massing across the Channel for more massive air raids, which might or might not be true. You just never knew where rumours were concerned.

The chap Josie had met at the dance had taken a shine to her and had arranged to meet her to go to the pictures on Wednesday night. His name was Harold and he was a policeman of all things. Josie had pronounced him lovely and was looking forward to seeing him again. Ellie was pleased for her.

'Why don't you make a cup of tea?' Albert suggested. 'That at least would be something.'

'Let me finish my ciggy first, then I'll do it.'

'You're smoking far too many of those things,' Albert admonished. 'You've taken to coughing first thing in the morning.'

'Have I?' Ellie answered innocently, well aware that she had.

Albert glanced again at the clock. Where was Jess? He was starving, his stomach beginning to think his throat had been cut.

It was over an hour later before Jess appeared carrying a cylindrical-shaped object wrapped in brown paper. 'Sorry I'm late,' she apologised. 'But I had a few things to do after work.'

She placed the object on the table. 'That's for you,' she informed Ellie.

'Me?' Ellie couldn't imagine what it was.

'It's part of the idea I told you about yesterday.'

Ellie gasped at what was revealed when she unwrapped the object, a bolt of magnificent black material. 'It's silk,' she croaked, running a hand over it

'Pure silk I'm assured,' Jess qualified. 'Like it?'

'Of course I do. It's beautiful. But what's it for?'

'Your cocktail dress naturally,' Jess replied. 'I nipped round yesterday afternoon and spoke to Mrs Silverman who's agreed to make it for you.' Mrs Silverman was an old Jewish woman Jess had found to alter Ellie's uniform which now fitted perfectly.

'Oh, Mum!' Ellie breathed, eyes shining.

'I can't have a daughter of mine not up to the mark, now can I?' Jess smiled.

Albert was staring in consternation at the material. 'Where did you get it from?' he asked slowly.

'Someone I know,' she replied evasively.

He took a deep breath. 'In other words, the black market. If you don't have enough coupons to buy the dress then you don't have enough for that. True?'

Jess didn't reply.

'You know how much I disapprove of the black market, Jess. And now you've done this behind my back.'

'It's not behind your back,' she prevaricated. 'The material's there for you to see.'

'You *bought* it behind my back, Jess. Don't quibble words with me.'

Jess's expression was one of defiance. 'Rules are made to be broken, Albert, and this is one such time. I have no intention of dealing on the black market ever again, so there!'

393

Albert, knowing he was beaten, sighed and turned away. 'It is lovely material,' he conceded. 'It should look good on you, Ellie.'

Ellie went to him and pecked his cheek. 'Thanks, Dad.'

'I still don't approve,' he grumbled. 'But the deed's done and that's all there is to it, I suppose. Now what about something to eat around here, I'm starving!'

Jess smiled. 'What would you say if I told you I had three pounds of sausages in my coat pocket?'

'Three pounds, woman, my God, how did you manage that!' His face clouded over. 'Not the black market again I hope?'

'No,' she lied. 'I just got lucky with the butcher.'

The sausages had come from the same source as the silk, but she wasn't admitting that to Albert. She'd snapped them up when offered them.

They were absolutely delicious.

Mrs Silverman was in her early seventies. A tailoress all her working life she was now retired but still did whatever came her way to help make ends meet.

'Very nice,' she nodded approvingly, running a hand over the bolt as Ellie had done. 'You were lucky to get it.'

'It wasn't cheap, I can tell you. But worth every penny I thought,' Jess replied. Neither Ellie nor Albert knew she'd had to pawn a brooch that had belonged to her mother to pay for the material and Mrs Silverman's services. She hoped one day, if the precious brooch hadn't been sold, to have saved up enough to redeem it. However, that was a chance she'd had to take.

Mrs Silverman didn't inquire into the material's origins, considering it to be none of her business. But she had a shrewd idea.

'Can you do it for this Friday?' Ellie asked anxiously.

'I can do it,' Mrs Silverman smiled. 'Don't you worry your pretty little head about that. But first, we have to choose a pattern.'

She turned away and crossed over to where her sewing machine stood. 'I've looked out a few that might suit, so shall we see if we can find one you like?'

Mrs Silverman eyed Ellie from top to toe. 'Something fairly simple, I would suggest. That would be best for you in my opinion.'

In the end a pattern was finally decided on, after which Mrs Silverman began measuring Ellie, a procedure, having had years of experience, she did fairly quickly.

'Ellie won't be a moment,' Jess informed Julius who was dressed in a smart charcoal grey suit with pale blue shirt and subdued tie. His topcoat, as he referred to it, was neatly fitting, black and three-quarter length.

'There's no hurry,' Julius replied. 'As long as we're there at a reasonable time.'

Mrs Silverman, good as her word, had finished the dress the previous evening, she and Ellie collecting it and she paying Mrs Silverman. Both she and, more importantly, Ellie were highly delighted with the result. It had been well worth the money.

'Have you heard from your dad?' Albert inquired, Pee Wee still off on tour.

'Yeah, Mom got a call only last night. Dad's fine and enjoyin' himself, havin' a ball as he put it. But missin' Mom.'

'Did he say where he was?'

'A place called Huddersfield, which he's not all that impressed with. But the audiences are good accordin' to him. Real appreciative, and all military. He's lookin' forward to coming back though, he's also missin' Mom's cookin'.'

Jess laughed. 'I can understand that. I only wish I could cook as well as Beulah. She's a whizz in that department.'

Albert frowned at Jess. 'I'd hate it if you went away somewhere. I wouldn't know what to do with myself.'

'You'd be in the pub every night more like,' she teased.

'Not me!' Albert protested. 'Besides, I couldn't afford to be in there every night. That's well beyond my means.'

'Da ra!' Ellie cried, coming into the kitchen.

Julius's large eyes almost popped at the vision before him. He'd never seen Ellie look anything like this, or imagined she could.

'What do you think?' Ellie, suddenly coy, asked him.

He swallowed. 'Holy Toledo. You're an absolute knock-out!'

Ellie flushed with pleasure, that being exactly what she'd wanted to hear. 'Like the dress?'

'Sure do. It could have come straight from Paris, France.'

The dress had a softly draped surplice bodice and gently flared skirt with unpressed pleats across the front. There was a self belt and buckle plus a Crown zip placket. The sleeves came to just below the elbow while the skirt ended at the knee.

Ellie had done her hair in a chignon, well pinned into place. She was wearing a pair of nylons from a number Julius had given her, her shoes soft black leather and plain, these brightly polished for the occasion. She wasn't wearing any jewellery as she didn't own any she considered appropriate.

Albert stared in admiration at his daughter. As they'd have said when he was young, she was a dish. He couldn't have been more proud.

Jess picked up the maroon-coloured velvet shoulder cape that Mrs Silverman had insisted Ellie borrow which perfectly complemented the dress. 'Don't forget this.'

Ellie took the cape and put it on. 'Ready when you are, Julius,' she smiled.

Julius shook his head in amazement. 'A knockout,' he repeated. 'When we get there I'm going to have to fight the other guys off.'

Ellie laughed.

'And I mean that. They'll be round you like bears round a honey pot.'

'I'm glad you approve.'

'Hell, yeah.'

'Then shall we?'

'OK, Cinderella, let's go to the ball.'

Cinderella! That was exactly how Ellie felt. Only in her case there were no ugly sisters.

Chapter 24

'They should be there by now,' Albert commented, having noted the time on the mantelpiece clock.

Jess paused in her darning, mending a pair of his socks. 'What's wrong with you tonight? You're ever so restless.'

He shrugged, but didn't reply.

'Why don't you nip over to The Florence and have a couple of pints? That might settle you a bit.'

'Do you want to go?'

Jess shook her head. 'I don't feel like it. But don't let that stop you. Being a Friday night there might be a sing-song later. You always enjoy those.'

True, he thought. He did. 'Nah, I won't bother either. I'll stay home with you.'

Albert fell into a brooding, introspective silence during which he stared at the empty grate. Every so often his eyes flicked back to the clock.

'Albert,' Jess finally said in exasperation. 'I know you. What's wrong? Something obviously is.'

'Nothing's wrong,' he lied.

'Yes there is,' she persisted. 'Now out with it.'

He sighed. 'It's nothing really. At least I don't think it is.'

'What?' she almost screamed.

'Ellie and Julius.'

Jess couldn't see what he was driving at. 'What about them?'

He shifted in embarrassment. 'You don't think tonight is the start of anything do you?'

That had never crossed Jess's mind. Now she considered it. 'To be honest, I've no idea.'

'It just sort of . . . worries me, that's all,' he confessed.

'Why should it do that?' a puzzled Jess queried. 'He's a nice chap, well-mannered with a terrific job. I don't know what he earns but probably a lot more than we realise. American wages, don't forget. So what's to worry about?'

Albert forced himself to say the next bit. 'He's also black, Jess.'

Now she understood, and was appalled. 'Do you hold that against him?'

'Not in the least,' Albert hurriedly replied. 'As you say, he's a nice chap, they don't come nicer. What I don't like is the notion of them getting together. I mean, what if it became serious. What then?'

'Oh, for God's sake, Albert,' Jess snapped in reply. 'He's only taken her to a cocktail party, it's not as if they're about to climb into bed together.'

Albert went puce. 'I should bloody well hope not!'

She couldn't help teasing him. 'Why, because he's black?'

'Ellie wouldn't climb into bed with any man, black, brown, white or tartan. She's been brought up properly, at least I hope she has.'

'I know she has,' Jess stated firmly. 'And you're reading far too much into this. It's only a harmless night out, nothing more. So stop worrying.'

Albert sort of snorted. 'I don't believe in mixed marriages, you see. A recipe for disaster in my book. Each kind should stick to its own. That's the way it should be. How God intended.'

Jess almost burst out laughing. 'You're on intimate terms with the good Lord now, eh? You know his mind on such matters? Honestly, I've never heard anything so ridiculously pompous in my entire life.'

'I am not being pompous,' Albert replied sharply. 'Merely saying what I think and believe. Have you considered children, eh? What about them? What kind of treatment could they expect to get being neither one thing nor the other, neither white nor black? The poor little sods would be outcasts, that's what. Probably shunned by both sides. Shunned and mistrusted.'

This was a new side to Albert that Jess had never realised existed. Even after all these years he could still surprise her, and she'd thought she knew him inside out. 'I'm ashamed of you,' she said quietly.

He opened his mouth, then shut it again.

'Thoroughly ashamed,' she qualified.

That shook him. 'I'm only thinking about Ellie, what's best for her. I don't want her to make some terrible mistake.'

'We all have to make our own mistakes, Albert,' Jess stated wisely. 'And whoever listened to advice, especially from their parents? Not many people. And I would remind you Ellie has a mind and will of her own. She'll do what she thinks fit.'

Albert, reluctantly, knew both these points to be so. 'Maybe,' he prevaricated.

'Anyway,' Jess went on, a tone of finality in her voice, 'all this is about absolutely nothing, I'm sure of it. And don't forget, you were the one said Ellie should get out and about more which is precisely what she's doing.' Jess regarded him shrewdly. 'This isn't the jealous father and daughter bit, is it?'

'No it's not,' he replied, thoroughly rattled.

'Are you sure?'

'I wasn't when George was around, was I?'

She had to admit that was true. 'So it's simply about Julius being black?'

Albert nodded.

Jess stood up, she'd had enough of this bigotry. She hadn't forgotten her own wariness and suspicions when the Postons had moved in next door, and that too had been entirely because they were black. But now she'd come to know them she couldn't have asked for nicer or kinder neighbours. As far as she was concerned they were no different to anyone else, apart from the colour of their skins that is.

'I'm going upstairs,' she announced. 'I've listened to enough nonsense for one night.'

'But it's early!' he protested.

'Thoroughly ashamed,' she repeated, and left him to it.

It upset Albert deeply that Jess felt that way about him.

He was only looking out for Ellie's best interests after all, that was a caring father's job.

'Damn!' he muttered. He should have kept his big mouth shut, not spoken up. Kept stumm.

He decided he would go to The Florence, he needed a drink after that. For the life of him he couldn't remember the last time he and Jess had argued, it being a rare occasion when it happened.

Without realising what he was doing he slammed the front door shut behind him.

Ellie had never seen such an abundance of rich goodies on one table. Smoked salmon, baked salmon, prime sliced roast beef, other meats – a whole medley of them – exquisitely cut tiny sandwiches, wondrous salads, fruit, cheeses. And all this in wartime when the general populace was on rationing. But then that didn't apply to the American Embassy. It was mind-boggling.

'What are those things?' she whispered to Julius, indicating with a slight jab of a finger.

'Quiches. Egg dishes. They're delicious.'

Quiche was a new one on her. 'And that?'

'Caviar.'

Her eyes widened. She'd heard of caviar but never thought she'd have the opportunity to taste some. She'd read somewhere that it was horrendously expensive.

'And those are spare ribs, a great American favourite – very tasty,' Julius informed her. 'I suggest you try a few.'

'I will, don't worry,' she replied earnestly, which made him laugh.

'Can I make a suggestion?'

'What's that, Julius?'

'I don't wish to sound rude, but we can come back to the table here as often as we like, so don't pile your plate too high to start with, wouldn't look good.'

She nodded that she understood.

'Other than that, the world's your oyster, which are down there by the way.' His little joke amused him.

'What are?'

'Oysters, Ellie.' He pointed, and sure enough there was a huge silver salver covered in opened oysters resting on a bed of chipped ice.

'Ever had any?' he queried, thoroughly enjoying himself.

'No.'

'Well, they're a bit of an acquired taste, rather like caviar. I love both myself.'

'Here goes,' Ellie declared, picking up a plate.

When they'd temporarily finished with the table they moved away, Ellie fascinated as she gazed round the room. The Russians were easily recognisable due to the ill-fitting suits they were wearing and the seriousness of their expressions.

'Which one is the Ambassador?' she asked, before biting into half a stuffed egg, the first egg she'd had in months.

'Second pillar to the left, got it?'

She looked in that direction. 'Got it.'

'He's the guy in the blue suit, the woman standing beside him is his wife.' They were talking to a bald Russian who was gesticulating a great deal.

'That's the head of the Russian delegation he's with,' Julius explained. 'A personal friend of Stalin I believe, and a very important man.'

Ellie was impressed, very much so. There again, the whole occasion was impressing her enormously. She felt indeed that she was Cinderella at the Ball.

'Hi there, ole buddy, how ya doin'?'

Julius hadn't been aware that he was an ole buddy of Mike Stevenson, they hardly knew one another. 'Hello, Mike.'

Mike beamed at Ellie. 'Well, come on, introduce me to this gorgeous lady,' he requested.

Julius now realised why the 'ole buddy' routine. 'Mike Stevenson, I'd like you to meet Ellie Sykes.'

'Well, hi!' Mike gushed and, taking hold of Ellie's hand, shook it.

'She's English,' Julius said.

'Really?'

'Pleased to meet you, Mr Stevenson,' Ellie nodded in return.

'Mike! Call me Mike. No need to be formal. You know this bozo long?'

She presumed he meant Julius. 'Quite a while now.'

'Uh-huh.'

Julius remained silent, and attentive, while Mike did his best to ingratiate himself with Ellie, who was having none of it.

'I think we'd better circulate,' Julius declared after a few minutes. 'See you around.'

Mike was clearly disappointed as Julius and Ellie moved

off. 'You appear to have an admirer there,' Julius commented.

'He seemed pleasant enough. Though somewhat gushy for me.'

Julius laughed. 'A lot of Americans are. They believe that's how to behave.'

'You're not.'

'Thank you. I'll take that as a compliment.'

What a wonderful smile he had, she thought. 'I suppose it was meant as one.'

Julius stopped a passing waiter and helped himself to two glasses of champagne, one of which he handed to Ellie who'd got rid of her now empty plate in the meantime. 'Bottoms up!' he toasted. 'Isn't that what you English say?'

'Some of us.'

The champagne was cold and bursting with bubbles that shot up her nose. Luckily she didn't cough or splutter.

'Like?' Julius queried.

'It's lovely.'

'I can take or leave it. I'd rather have a good shot of bourbon any day.'

Ellie's jaw literally dropped open when she saw who had just entered the room. 'Bloody Nora!' she muttered, for it was no less than the Prime Minister, Winston Churchill himself. He was smaller than she'd imagined.

'What is it?'

She swallowed. 'Over there, heading for your Ambassador.'

Julius followed her gaze. 'I knew he'd been invited, but no one was sure whether or not he could come.' Then, by way of explanation, 'The Russians are even more important to you British than us Yanks at the moment, so it's no wonder he's put himself out.'

Wait till she told Albert, Ellie thought gleefully. He'd have a fit, being an enormous admirer of Churchill's. Come to that, so was she.

'You never said he might be here,' she accused Julius, who shrugged.

'Wasn't certain he would be, so I thought I'd leave it as a surprise if he did show.'

Ellie stared at Churchill now deep in conversation with Ambassador Winant and the bald Russian, unable to believe she was actually in the same room as the great man. This would be a story to tell her children in later years. Providing she had some that was.

'Hi, Julius! Who's your ladyfriend?'

Julius went very still on hearing that. Slowly he turned to face Marybeth who he instantly knew from the glazed look in her eyes was drunk. Or, if not drunk, well on the way to being so. His heart sank, this could be trouble.

He reminded Marybeth that she and Ellie had already met, Marybeth giving Ellie a long and measured once-over as he did. When Ellie extended a hand she let it hang there.

There was a brief pause, then Marybeth pursed her lips. 'No tits,' she pronounced.

Ellie froze, incredulous that had been said, and at a loss as to what to reply, if indeed she should.

Julius was furious, and about to make a sharp retort when Marybeth burst out laughing and walked, rather unsteadily, away.

'I am sorry,' Julius apologised quietly. 'Goddammit, I am.'

The party was spoilt for Ellie, the entire evening ruined by those two words. 'What a cow,' she muttered. 'What an absolute cow.'

Julius could see how deeply upset Ellie was, and rightly so. What Marybeth had done was unforgivable. 'It isn't true,' he assured Ellie.

She stared at him, the beginnings of tears in her eyes, feeling totally humiliated. 'What isn't?'

'What Marybeth said, it isn't true. You've got a lovely figure.'

No tits, she thought in despair, having always considered herself slightly short in that department. That and a bum that was too big.

'I think I'd better go to the Ladies' if you don't mind.'

'I'll show you the way.'

Taking her by the arm he led her from the room, glimpsing Marybeth enroute with a smirk of satisfaction on her face.

'Do you want to leave?' he asked Ellie when she finally emerged from the restroom.

That was precisely what she did want. 'Would it be all right?'

'Yeah, sure. I've been seen to be here so that's all that matters. We'll blow.'

'I would rather, Julius. I just don't want to go back in there. Sorry.'

'Hey! I'm the one who's sorry, you've no need to apologise. So let's grab our things and be on our way.'

Once outside the Embassy he made a suggestion. 'There's a little pub nearby that I sometimes use. How about we have a drink?'

'That would be nice.'

'Good,' he approved.

Ellie liked The King's Head, it had a warm and friendly atmosphere. She watched Julius up at the bar ordering, and thought what a pity his evening had also been spoilt. They'd both been enjoying themselves so much too. But at least she'd seen Winston Churchill, had been in the same room as the great man, an unforgettable experience.

'Here we are,' Julius declared on rejoining her. 'No gin I'm afraid but I did manage to get you scotch.'

'Thank you,' she smiled. 'Can I have some water to go with it?'

'Sure thing.'

He hurriedly returned to the bar, coming back again with a small jug. 'Say when?'

'When.'

He put the jug down and sat facing her. 'How do you feel now?'

'Pretty rotten to tell the truth.'

He nodded his sympathy. 'I wish I hadn't taken you now, but how could I have foreseen that?'

She attempted a smile. 'You couldn't possibly, and I

wouldn't have missed it for the world. Well, most of the evening anyway.'

He reached across the table and laid a hand over hers. 'I truly am sorry, Ellie. Believe me.'

'Let's forget it, eh?'

'All right. But before we do let me just repeat that what she said was a load of hooey. Bullshit.'

How sweet he was, she thought, as upset about what had happened as she was.

As she'd requested the incident wasn't mentioned again that night.

'You're early!' Albert exclaimed in surprise when Ellie came into the kitchen, waking him up from a doze in his chair.

'It was only a cocktail party, Dad, not a full-blown knees-up.'

He smiled. 'Pardon my ignorance I'm sure. Enjoy yourself?'

'I had a wonderful time.' She certainly wasn't going to tell Albert about Marybeth. And she had had a wonderful time, for the most part. 'And you'll never guess who was there.'

'Who?'

'Someone you admire enormously.'

He was intrigued. 'Well come on, give.'

'Winston Churchill.'

The look of sheer incredulity that came across his face was a delight to see. 'You're taking the mickey?'

'No, God's honest truth. He was there.'

'The *Prime Minister*!'

'The very same.'

Albert didn't reply, being lost for words.

'Well?'

'And you actually saw him?'

'Uh-huh.'

'Did you speak?'

Ellie shook her head. 'He was with the American Ambassador and some high-ranking Russian official, all three with their heads together.'

'Wait till I tell my mates at the station about this,' Albert said in awe. 'My daughter at a cocktail party with Winston Churchill!'

'Another thing, Julius got it wrong about the canapés. There was all sorts there to be had. Smoked salmon, turkey, oysters, caviar . . .'

Albert was suddenly ravenously hungry as Ellie reeled off the list of goodies that had been on offer.

Jess glanced across at Albert as the siren sounded for the first time in weeks. Ellie, who was back on nights, was already at work.

Albert's expression became grim. This wasn't unexpected, but a nasty surprise that the Luftwaffe had returned all the same. Jess was thinking she'd have to forego the luxury of her bed yet again for the makeshift, and uncomfortable, one in the shelter.

Albert came to his feet. 'They'll need me at the station,' he declared.

'But you've already done a full shift today,' Jess protested.

'Doesn't matter, you know that. It's all hands to the pumps when those damn things go off.'

Jess also rose. 'I'll get out to the shelter then.'

They both paused to listen when there was the sound of a far-off explosion followed by the unmistakable drone of aircraft overhead. More explosions followed the first.

'Right then,' Albert said abruptly. 'I'm off.' He went to Jess and kissed her on the cheek. 'On you go now, no hanging about.'

'Don't worry, I won't.'

'You'll see me when you see me.'

'Take care, love.'

Albert strode purposefully from the kitchen leaving an anxious Jess staring after him, the lull in the raids having given her, and probably an awful lot of other people, a false sense of security. Now the nightly terror had started all over again.

She quickly gathered a few things together, not forgetting Paul's framed photograph, her most prized possession.

Outside searchlights were criss-crossing a sky also lit up by streams of tracer bullets fired by the many ground batteries. Meanwhile the sirens continued to wail.

Once in the shelter Jess settled down for what she knew from bitter experience would be a long, and harrowing, night. As usual she offered up a silent prayer for Albert and Ellie's safety.

'Hi, hon. I'm home!'

'And ain't you the sight for sore eyes,' Beulah beamed,

going to Pee Wee and encompassing him in a meaty embrace.

'Somethin' sure smells good,' he mumbled, face pressed hard against her ample bosom.

'It's tuna casserole. One of your favourites.'

Pee Wee managed to pull himself back a little and gazed into his wife's dark and soulful eyes. 'Miss me?'

'Damn right I did. And you?'

'Every moment.'

'Or was it just ma cookin'?' she teased.

'Well . . .' He played along, teasing also. 'Kinda fifty-fifty, I guess.'

Beulah laughed. She'd been terribly lonely while Pee Wee was away, but that was over now. Her man had returned and God was in His Heaven.

'I could use a cup of coffee,' he smiled.

'Comin' right up.'

While she busied herself with that Pee Wee gazed about him, absolutely delighted to be home again. 'How's things?' he asked.

Beulah shrugged. 'Just like I said when you called. Nothin's changed much. A more or less peaceful day followed by bombin' at night. You get used to it.'

'And Julius?'

'Oh, he's OK. Puttin' in long hours at work, but he says it can't be helped. Says he's gotta do it.'

Pee Wee nodded that he understood. 'I'm tired, hon, we been on the road since early.'

'Then it's straight up to bed for you after you eat.'

He raised an eyebrow. 'Alone?'

'Hell no, I'll be right there alongside.' Another tease. 'Unless you'd prefer otherwise?'

'What do you think?'

Beulah laughed. 'Here's your coffee. The pie's ready whenever you want.'

'I want right now.'

They gazed at one another, she knowing exactly what he meant by that. She felt skittish, almost like a young girl again as she hurried to the cooker.

Julius had waited to get Marybeth alone, and now his chance had come as she emerged from an office into a corridor empty apart from him.

Marybeth came up short and stared defiantly at him. 'You got something to say, say it,' she challenged.

He had something to say all right. By the time he was finished with her she too was on the verge of tears, just as Ellie had been the night of the cocktail party.

She was shaking all over when he finally walked away. Ellie had been avenged.

Ellie sighed, the paperwork she had to deal with as DSO was seemingly interminable. She no sooner got a load off her desk than it was duly replaced by another stack. Everything had to be accounted for, every call-out reported in detail, requisitions, materials. On and on and on.

And tonight two of the girls hadn't reported in which meant she personally would have to go out if a raid started, which it undoubtedly would.

She bent again to her task, stopping half an hour later when the sirens sounded. At least going out on call was a break from the paperwork, she told herself. A welcome break at that.

Jess grimaced when the same sirens went off, the damn Luftwaffe were late that night, the fourteenth in a row during which they'd pounded London. Another night in the shelter, she thought miserably, wishing there would be a change in the weather which would keep the Luftwaffe away for a couple of peaceful nights at least. Nights she could blissfully sleep all the way through.

She jumped when there was a nearby explosion. Christ, that was close she thought. Better get a move on. And with that she flew to gather up the things she always took with her.

Jess had just got into the shelter when she realised she'd left Paul's photograph behind. 'Stupid bitch,' she muttered. She'd quickly nip back for it.

High overhead the ack-ack had scored a direct hit on a Junkers bomber, blowing it to bits. The engine detached itself from its housing in what remained of the fuselage and plummeted earthwards.

Jess was just lifting Paul's photo from the mantelpiece when the plane's engine tore through the roof and then the bedroom floor.

She was directly underneath when it landed in the kitchen.

Chapter 25

Julius was lightly dozing having been running through work matters in his mind when the force of the impact threw him out of bed onto the floor where he ended up in a tangle of sheets and blankets.

'Christ!' he swore, as particles of dust and plaster swirled in a maelstrom round his room. The house had been hit.

His next thought was for his mother. Hastily he tossed the bedclothes aside and came groggily to his feet, having banged his head on the floor. Staggering, he left his room and made his way across the corridor to where Beulah slept.

He opened the door to find a thoroughly frightened Beulah sitting up in bed, her bedside light still on and working.

'What happened?' she gasped, her room also filled with swirling dust and plaster. Having asked that she immediately burst into a coughing fit.

'Dunno, Mom. I think we've been bombed.'

He went over to her, grabbed her dressing gown and whirled it round her shoulders. 'We've gotta get out of here. Are you hurt?'

Still coughing, she shook her head.

'Then come on in case this whole place collapses.'

Beulah reached out for the glass of water she habitually kept by her bedside, and gulped down several swallows which successfully cleared her throat. 'You OK?'

'I guess so.' He glanced over his pyjamas – no sign of blood while all his limbs were able to move and were apparently intact.

'Oh Julius,' she sobbed, as the realisation of what had occurred began to sink in.

'Let's go, Mom.'

They stumbled out into the corridor, he leaving her for a few brief seconds while he found his own dressing gown and slippers, then it was down the stairs and out into the street.

Their house was still in one piece, at least as far as he could make out, but next door was a wreck having partially caved in on itself. Several small fires were burning downstairs amidst piles of debris.

'Jess ain't in there,' a wide-eyed Beulah declared. 'She'll be out back in their shelter.'

Neighbours were beginning to foregather, all anxious and horror-struck. 'If it was a bomb it never went off,' someone said. 'I was already out here having just left the drinker.'

'I heard a loud noise, but not an explosion,' someone else, a woman this time, commented. 'Though there was one nearby just before.'

Harry, the pub landlord, appeared. 'I've rung the emergency services,' he informed the still swelling crowd.

'They'll be along when they can.'

Beulah clutched at Julius's arm. 'You can get to Jess through our yard,' she stated. 'Go and see she's OK.'

'Right, I'm on my way.'

Julius dashed back into their own house and moments later was out at the rear where a wooden fence separated the gardens. It wasn't easy, but after a couple of attempts he managed to get over it and drop down the other side.

Trouble was, because of the black-out, he couldn't see all that well. However, he soon found the shelter and stuck his head inside. 'Jess, are you there?'

He frowned when there was no reply. 'Jess?'

When there was still no reply he went into the shelter and flicked on his lighter.

The shelter was empty.

'Albert.'

He glanced round to find it was Danny McGiver who'd spoken. The fire they were desperately trying to bring under control was a large one involving several shops. 'What is it?'

Danny's face might have been carved from stone. 'We've just had word from the station. It's bad news, I'm afraid.'

Fear clutched at Albert's heart. 'Jess, Ellie?'

'Your house has been bombed, though they seem vague about that. Whatever, it's been hit.'

Albert felt as though he'd been punched hard in the stomach. 'Jess?'

'Nothing on her so far. All we know is that your house

has been badly damaged. The report says a couple of small fires and the roof in. That's it.'

Jess would be safe, Albert assured himself. She'd have been in the shelter. 'I must get back there right away,' he croaked, his mind both numb and whirling at the same time.

'Of course. On you go, mate.'

Albert handed Danny the hosepipe he was directing and took to his heels. The fire he'd been attending was half a mile away from Florence Street. He ran the whole way without stopping once.

Beulah took it on herself to tell Albert when he arrived at what had been his home. 'Jess ain't in the shelter,' Beulah informed him. 'Had she gone out somewhere?'

Albert shook his head. 'Not that I'm aware. As far as I know she was staying put. At least that's what she said when I left her to go on duty.'

He stared at the remains of his house, he too thinking that if it had been hit by a bomb then the bomb hadn't exploded. 'I'm going in,' he stated.

'I'll come with you,' Julius offered.

'It could be dangerous, son. There might be a UXB in there.' That meant an unexploded bomb.

'Let's go,' Julius replied.

Albert gave him a grateful nod, he might need the help. Harry Clifford and Mike Pratt now stepped forward. 'I'm with you, Albert,' Harry declared.

'Me too,' added Mike Pratt.

A lump rose in Albert's throat. 'Thanks, chaps.'

'You lead the way. You're the expert,' Julius said.

The front door was off its hinges and lying just inside the hall. Albert clambered over it and switched on his torch to light the way.

Julius tried the hall switch, without any result. Odd, he thought, remembering Beulah's bedside lamp had been working.

'Jess!' Albert called out. 'Can you hear me?'

The only sound was that of dripping water as Albert briefly closed his eyes, desperate to go on, and yet reluctant to do so for fear of what he might find. Maybe, just maybe, Jess *had* gone out. He prayed to God that was so.

A little later Beulah clutched herself when a terrible, anguished cry rent the air. The voice was plainly distinguishable as Albert's.

Ellie turned into Florence Street, and immediately halted in her tracks when she saw the cluster of people outside her house, instantly knowing something was terribly wrong. She started to walk again, and then began to run.

The cluster of people, mainly neighbours, parted to let her through, their looks pitying ones.

Workmen were already busy inside shoring up the walls with stout lengths of wood. 'Watch out!' someone in the crowd yelled, and next second a section of slates from what had been the roof clattered onto the pavement and street.

Ellie knew she was in shock having seen the same thing

in so many of those she'd been called out to. She could feel hysteria rising up inside her.

Suddenly Julius was by her side. 'Your dad's in our house,' he said quietly.

'And Mum?'

There was no easy way of doing this. He shook his head. 'She was in there when it happened. I'm sorry.'

Tears welled in her eyes. 'Dead?' she asked unnecessarily.

'I'm afraid so, Ellie. If it's any consolation she wouldn't have suffered. It must have been all over in an instant.'

She was dimly aware of Julius taking her arm and guiding her into his house where they found Albert sitting in the Postons' kitchen. The first thing that struck her was how much he'd aged. Within the space of a few short hours he'd become an old man.

'Dad!' she exclaimed, and rushed into his arms where her entire body started violently to shake.

'Sssh, girl, sssh!' Albert crooned. 'There's nothing we can do. Your mum's gone.'

Pee Wee, back hours earlier from The Chicory House, poured a large gin and added a splash of tonic. He waited patiently till he could hand it to Ellie.

Beulah's face had been ravaged by tears, the marks left by them streaked down her cheeks. Her normally huge body appeared somehow deflated, as though air had been let out of it.

'Where's Mum now?' Ellie at last asked.

Albert took a deep breath. Jesus, but this was difficult, the pain inside him excruciating, as if every last nerve in his being had been exposed. 'Still in there. We're waiting for a crane to . . .' He broke off and shook his head, unable to go on.

Julius decided he would have to explain. Going to Ellie he knelt beside her and Albert and did just that, not going into any of the gory details of what he, Albert and the others had discovered. Most of Jess was still underneath the German plane's engine.

Ellie's eyes were bulging as she listened, part of her wanting to open her mouth and scream this wasn't true. And then just scream and scream.

When she looked again at Albert through tear-filled eyes he seemed to have aged even more.

Julius sank onto the barstool and waited for Hazel to come over and serve him. He needed a few drinks before going across the road to see what was what.

'Usual?'

He nodded.

'They took the body away late this afternoon,' Hazel informed him as she poured.

Julius, who'd been at the Embassy all day, digested that.

'On the house,' Hazel said, placing a pint in front of him.

'Thanks.'

'Harry told me you were one of those who went in with Albert.'

'Yeah,' Julius whispered, knowing he'd never forget that sight until his own dying day.

'Harry said it was awful.'

Julius couldn't help but smile. 'That's an English under-statement if ever there was.'

'Poor Albert,' Hazel said softly. 'First his son, and now Jess. Poor bloody man.'

'Have you got any spirits, Haze?'

She glanced around. 'Not officially, but hang on.' And with that she disappeared out the back.

When she returned she handed Julius a teacup and saucer. 'So the other customers don't think I'm playing favourites,' she explained.

Julius sipped the scotch the cup contained, shudder-ing as it hit his empty stomach. He hadn't eaten a thing all day, nor had he wanted to. He still wasn't in the least hungry.

He thought of Ellie and what she must be going through. He'd been thinking about her on and off all day, trying to imagine how he'd have felt if it had been Beulah who'd been killed, particularly in such a gruesome manner. At least, as he'd said to Ellie, it had been instantaneous. That was something to be grateful for.

'What we need are you Yanks in this war,' Hazel declared to Julius while wiping up. 'Just like the last lot. That's what we need all right. Between us we'd soon sort Jerry out.'

Julius glanced at her. 'It's not impossible, Haze.'

She regarded him shrewdly, well aware of where he worked if not exactly what he did there. 'Do you know something?'

'I didn't say that.'

'But your tone implied it.'

422

He had to be more careful, he told himself. It was unlike him to give anything away. There again, he supposed he could make allowances, excuse himself a little, after the previous night. 'Didn't mean to, Hazel. I simply said it wasn't impossible.'

'Hmmh.' She didn't believe a word of that. 'Well, I only hope you do, and soon.'

Julius hoped so too. In a way this war had now become personal with the death of Jess Sykes.

Julius glanced round the kitchen. 'Where's Ellie?' he queried.

'Upstairs sleepin', the doc gave her a sedative. She's goin' to be stayin' here with us for a while as she can't be next door.'

Julius nodded his understanding and approval. 'What about Albert?'

'He went off some hours ago with a colleague of his called Danny McGiver. He had to fill out some official forms and then he was goin' to McGiver's as we don't have room here for two extra. Anyway, McGiver was insistent Albert beds down at his place.'

Julius ran a hand over his face. He was desperately tired having had virtually no sleep the night before. 'I'm pooped,' he declared wearily.

'Want to eat?'

He shook his head.

'What you had today then?'

'Nothin'. I couldn't face food.'

Beulah wasn't having that. 'Don't matter none, you're

gonna have somethin'. I don't want you goin' sick on me, you hear, Julius Poston?'

'I hear, Mom.' He resolved to force himself. 'They got the body out I hear.'

Beulah's face sort of crumpled in on itself. 'Yeah. That was the bit where Ellie kinda went bananas and had to be given a sedative.'

'And Albert?'

'He just cried, son. I hope never to see a grown man cry like that again.'

Julius pulled out a pack of cigarettes and lit up. The smoke he drew deep into his lungs tasted of absolutely nothing at all.

'Can I help you?'

Harry smiled. 'I believe this is where Mr McGiver lives?'

Vera nodded. 'That's so.'

'And Albert Sykes is with you?'

'Are you a friend of his?'

'Landlord of his local.'

'I see,' Vera said, now also smiling. 'Please come in.'

'I won't if you don't mind. How is Albert?'

Vera pulled a face. 'As you'd expect.'

Harry sighed, and took from his overcoat pocket a bottle wrapped in brown paper. 'Give that to him. Say it's from Harry and Hazel at The Florence.'

'Are you sure you won't come in?' Vera queried, accepting the bottle.

'No, I don't want to intrude.'

Vera didn't press further, Harry's mind clearly made

up. 'Goodbye then. And thank you on his behalf.'

'Goodbye, Mrs McGiver.'

With that Harry strode off into the night. The bottle he'd given Albert was the last one he currently possessed, and should have been for his own private consumption.

In the circumstances, he hadn't minded parting with it one little bit. It might just bring some comfort to Albert, even if it was of the liquid, and temporary, kind.

As chance would have it, the night following Jess's death was a wild and stormy one which prevented the Luftwaffe from coming. All of London gave a collective sigh of relief at this brief respite.

Julius, who'd gone to bed early, now woke when he heard a floorboard creak out in the corridor. He frowned, wondering who was up and moving about? A glance at the luminous hands on his wristwatch told him it was too early for Pee Wee to have returned, which meant it was either Beulah or Ellie. Now he was awake he decided to find out which.

Ellie was putting the kettle on when he entered the kitchen. She was wearing a shirt of his that Beulah had given her to sleep in, all her own things still being next door.

'Hi!' Julius smiled.

Ellie blushed, realising she was only half dressed, knickers the only other item of clothing she had on. 'I came down for a cup of tea,' she explained, then vaguely gestured to herself. 'Sorry, I don't have a dressing gown here.'

'Don't worry about it. Can I join you in that tea?'

'Of course.'

He sat and studied her. She looked a wreck, not in the least attractive. That was totally understandable considering. He noted she had particularly lovely legs, the first time he'd seen them so exposed.

'Couldn't sleep, uh?'

Ellie glanced over at him. 'I suppose the sedative wore off. Just as well as I was having horrible nightmares.' She shivered.

'Cold?'

'No. Remembering the nightmares.'

Julius pulled out his cigarettes. 'Like one?'

She shook her head. 'Maybe in a minute.'

He lit up. 'Want to talk about them? The nightmares that is.'

She considered that. 'I don't think so.'

'OK. Maybe you'd prefer I leave you alone?'

'No, please don't,' she replied quickly. 'I could use the company.'

He watched her as she laid out cups and saucers, then checked the sugar bowl. 'Milk's in the fridge,' he said. 'If there's any left that is.'

There was. 'Thank goodness for that,' she declared. 'I can't bear tea without.'

She poured water into the pot, swirled it round, then dumped it down the sink. 'I'll never get used to the idea of teabags,' she said, attempting a smile. 'Tea should be loose, not in paper bags.'

'We Americans are weird,' he joked. 'And we usually drink our tea iced.'

'I remember you told me that once. Iced tea, how disgusting.'

He could see she was beginning to relax, which was good. He couldn't imagine what her nightmares had consisted of. She'd called them horrible, probably another example of English understatement. 'As I said, we're weird.'

When the tea was ready she handed him his cup and saucer and holding hers made to sit opposite, stopping abruptly on remembering what she was wearing.

'That's OK,' he smiled, reading her mind. 'I promise not to look.'

Still she hesitated. 'Even so . . .'

He laid his cup and saucer on the floor and then rose, vanishing out of the room. When he returned he was carrying a large towel. 'Drape this over yourself and that'll spare your modesty.'

'Thank you.' How kind and thoughtful he was, she reflected. Always the perfect gentleman.

'Would you like that cigarette now?'

'Please.'

'Is there anythin' you would care to talk about?' he asked when he'd sat again.

'Not really.'

He didn't reply, not pushing it.

'It's Dad I'm really worried about,' she said after a while. 'He and Mum were terribly close.'

'I think you all were.'

'Yes,' she agreed softly. 'As are your family.'

'Very.'

427

Ellie sighed. 'I still can't believe that Mum's gone. It's as if I'm trapped in one of those nightmares I mentioned, and will soon wake up to find it was exactly that, a nightmare, that Mum's still alive and . . .' She broke off and took a deep breath. 'Only it's no nightmare, is it?'

'I'm afraid not,' he murmured sympathetically.

'It's all too fucking real.'

Her using that word jolted Julius who stared at her in surprise. Judging from her expression Ellie didn't seem to be aware she'd uttered it. Or perhaps she just didn't care.

'Julius . . .' She trailed off.

'What, Ellie?'

She shook her head. 'Nothing. Forget it.'

'What, Ellie?' he persisted.

'Will you do something for me?'

'If I can.'

Her pleading eyes bored into his. 'Will you hold me? Give me a cuddle?'

Again he was surprised. For a second time he laid his cup and saucer aside and stood up, she doing likewise.

She was trembling when he put his arms around her, she nestling a cheek against his chest.

After a few moments he began to gently stroke her hair.

'Ellie! Ellie, wake up, child!'

Ellie blinked open her eyes to see Beulah staring down at her. 'What time is it?' she said huskily.

'Past noon. I brought you a cup of coffee.'

It all came back now. She and Julius downstairs in the

kitchen talking for ages. Not speaking about anything in particular, just this and that. At one point he'd even made her laugh. When they'd finally returned to their respective bedrooms he'd kissed her on the forehead before saying goodnight. She'd liked that.

Ellie struggled into a sitting position and gratefully accepted the steaming mug of coffee Beulah gave her.

'What do you plan for today?' Beulah asked.

Ellie thought about that. 'I'll have to go next door and try to salvage some clothes. That's the first thing.'

Beulah frowned. 'Are you sure you want to do that, honey? Why don't I go instead?'

'Because you won't know what's what. Besides . . .' Ellie dropped her gaze. 'I just have to, that's all.'

Beulah understood. Or at least thought she did. 'I got breakfast waiting for you. Would you like a hot tub before or after that?'

Ellie had heard Beulah use the expression before and knew what it meant. 'Afterwards, if breakfast is ready.'

'OK.'

Ellie wondered if she was doing the right thing. But do it she must. For the clothes if nothing else.

Ellie stared in horror at the blood-stained walls and floor of what remained of their kitchen. For a few moments she thought she was going to be sick, but somehow fought it back.

Glancing up she saw the sky through a huge hole where the plane engine had penetrated the roof, the timbers remaining broken and jagged-edged.

All about her were the contents of her parents' bedroom, the floor of which the engine had also demolished. On her left the smashed chest of drawers and alongside it their wardrobe, its contents spilled out to lie scattered around. Their bed was on its side and jammed against the cooker, the nightie Jess had last worn dangling from exposed springs.

Breath hissed out of Ellie's mouth while her heart was frantically pounding. Why had Jess been in the kitchen instead of the shelter? They'd never know. But if she had gone to the shelter, as she was supposed to have done, then she'd be alive today. So what if the house was in ruins and most of the furniture shattered. Houses, and what went in them, could be replaced. Jess, like Paul before her, couldn't.

Ellie found her eyes drawn back to the floor where the engine had obviously come to rest, and where her mother had died. The large, dark bloodstain bore witness to that.

Ellie sobbed as fresh tears overwhelmed her. Crossing to a chair she sank onto it and bent over to hold her head in her hands.

'Oh, Mum,' she choked. 'Oh, Mum.'

Ellie had never felt so lost or lonely in her entire life.

It was a good turn-out considering so many people had to be at vital war work. Those from Florence Street who could come, had. A tight group of friends and neighbours united in grief with Albert and Ellie.

Julius stared at Ellie who was supporting her father, he clearly on the verge of collapse. A broken man if ever there was. Julius could only guess at the strength of the bond that had been between Albert and Jess. A bond now broken by death.

How strangely radiant Ellie looked, he thought. A light seemed to shine from her as if she'd been touched by the Divine. He found himself wishing he could take her in his arms as he had that night in the kitchen.

With a shock he realised he'd come to care for Ellie. Not just as a friend, but more than that. Much more.

Chapter 26

'I'm putting you on permanent days,' Station Officer Titmuss announced. 'At least for the foreseeable future.'

It was Ellie's first time back at work having been told the moment she arrived to report to the SO.

Ellie frowned. 'Can I ask why?'

SO Titmuss fiddled with a paper clip; should she tell Ellie precisely what was on her mind? She decided not. 'The raids have lessened off again which means you're not needed on the night shift as badly as you were. I think you would accomplish more during days, be more useful.'

'I see,' Ellie murmured, not really seeing at all.

'Besides, we're taking on more personnel, expanding the station, which means I'll now require two DSOs. I was hoping you might recommend someone for promotion?'

Ellie thought about that. 'I would suggest Josie Farnham. Not simply because we're friends, but because, in my opinion, she has all the right qualities for the job. She's a natural.'

The SO nodded her approval. 'Then that's who it'll be. I'll speak to her shortly. Now why don't you go home again and report tomorrow morning sharp at the changeover.'

'Right.'

SO Titmuss cleared her throat. 'I'm sorry I couldn't come to your mother's funeral, it was just impossible for me to get away.'

'I understand.'

'It went well, I believe?'

Ellie shrugged. 'As well as these things can.'

'How's your father?'

Ellie dropped her gaze to stare at the floor. 'Still taking it very badly. They were . . . very much a couple.'

'And yourself, Ellie,' the SO asked softly. 'How are you?'

How the hell do you think! Ellie nearly blurted out. But didn't, that would have been rude. The SO was only showing concern. 'I'm coping. Though it's not easy.'

Titmuss stared at Ellie's tight and drawn face, noting the dark bags under her eyes and the sallowness of her skin. She had a daughter, roughly Ellie's age, who was a nurse at the Charing Cross Hospital. More than once it had crossed her mind how alike, in many ways, Ellie and Charlotte were. Her own husband had died several years previously, after a long drawn-out illness, from cancer of the bowel, so she knew all about loss and grief.

Again the SO nodded her approval. 'Good. Now off you toddle and report back in the morning. The paperwork has got a bit behind while you were off so there's a lot to do.'

'Thank you.'

'And tell someone out there I could use a cup of tea. My throat's as dry as the Sahara.'

Ellie smiled, the SO was a great tea drinker, consuming God knows how many cups a day. It was something of a joke around the station. 'I'll do that.'

SO Titmuss sighed after Ellie had gone. The real reason she wanted Ellie on days was because it was far safer then than working nights when the majority of raids took place. Ellie's father had lost a son and wife within a relatively short space of time, so the best she could do was try to ensure nothing happened to his daughter as well.

Yes, working days was far safer.

'I've been thinking, wondering,' Danny McGiver said slowly. 'Maybe you should have a sort of holiday.'

Albert stared blankly at his friend. 'What are you talking about?'

'Get away for a while. Have a break. A change of scenery.' Danny guessed he was making a hash of this, but then tact or word usage had never been strong points of his.

'Danny has a point,' Vera chipped in. She and Danny had already discussed this at length.

'But I'll have to return to duty soon,' Albert mildly protested.

Danny took a deep breath. He was going to have to be blunt, no two ways about it. 'Albert, you're not fit enough. It's as simple as that.'

'How do you mean?'

'Jess's death has taken a lot out of you, more than you realise. Mentally as well as physically.'

Albert didn't argue, suspecting that to be true.

'Half the time your hands are shaking,' Danny went on. 'And your concentration's gone to buggery. To be honest, I wouldn't want to be on shift with you. I don't think you're safe for the time being.'

Vera glanced away when she saw the hurt expression on Albert's face.

'You know how much we rely on one another,' Danny continued. 'For our very lives at times.'

Albert swallowed hard. 'Is it that bad?'

Danny nodded.

'I wouldn't want to let anyone down.'

Christ this was painful, Danny thought. But it had to be done, for Albert's good as well as his mates. 'I've had an idea,' he declared.

'What's that?'

'Why don't I have a word with the Union and see if they'll give you some time at Huntington Hall?'

Albert knew all about Huntington Hall which was owned and run by the Union. It was where firemen went to recuperate after they'd been injured or seriously ill. He couldn't remember exactly where it was but had always heard good things about it.

'So what do you say?' Danny pressed.

'Vera?'

'I think Danny's right. A couple of weeks there, maybe longer, would be just the ticket. Hopefully set you up again.'

435

Albert ran a hand over his face. 'Are you trying to tell me you've had enough of my being here?'

'Not in the least!' Vera exclaimed. 'You're welcome to stay with us as long as you like. I said that when you arrived, and meant it.'

Albert managed a smile. 'Thanks, Vera. I appreciate that.'

'Of course it's only a suggestion,' Danny declared. 'If the idea doesn't appeal, then fine. But I do mean it when I say I wouldn't be happy working with you at the present. And that's coming from a pal, which you know I am.'

Albert bowed his head, a vision of a laughing, joking Jess in his mind. How he missed her, unbelievably so. It was as if a part of himself had been cut off. 'All right,' he whispered. 'Have a word.'

Danny shot Vera a look of relief, thankful that Albert had listened to sense. 'I'll do that, Albert. First thing.'

'Excuse me,' Albert said and left the room.

'I feel like Judas bloody Iscariot for some reason,' Danny muttered after Albert had gone.

'Judas betrayed his friend,' Vera stated quietly. 'That's not what you're doing at all. Quite the contrary.'

'Well, it feels like it.'

They both looked round when they heard the outside door click shut.

Albert had gone out.

'What!' Beulah exploded, absolutely furious.

'You heard me,' a sheepish Pee Wee replied. 'We's goin'

436

out on tour for another month. Maybe six weeks.' He shrugged. 'I can't help it none. The first one was such a huge success Lord Fitzaran has been asked to do it again.'

Beulah swore.

'I'm sorry, hon, but I ain't got no option in the matter. It's already all been agreed.'

'Were you asked?'

Pee Wee knew better than to lie to his wife, she always found out, or just plain knew, if he did. 'Yeah.'

Beulah folded her arms across her massive bosom. 'And what did you say?'

'Hell, Beulah, the other guys wanted to go and I didn't want to let them down. Or Fitzaran, he's been just great since we got here. You know that.'

Beulah had to admit to herself that was true. 'And you'd be playin' for the military?'

'That's it. To help the war effort, as Fitzaran put it.' He reached out and tried to lay a hand on Beulah's crossed arms, she shrugging the hand away.

'Don't be mad, hon,' he pleaded.

'Well, I is.'

'Please?'

Beulah snorted and moved off a few steps, turning her back on him in the process while she thought about this. It had been awful, and desperately lonely, when he'd been away before. And then she'd at least had Jess for occasional company. Now she had to go through it all again, this time without Jess.

'I'll make it up to you, Beulah. I promise.'

'And how will you do that?' she demanded sharply.

'I don't know. But I will. I swears I will.'

She took a deep breath, the beginnings of an idea coming to her. Why not? she thought after a few moments. She'd done it before. Many times. Though, she had to admit, not for a long while now. Nor was she getting any younger, there was that to be taken into account. 'When do you plan leavin'?' she queried, facing him again.

'Week after next.'

'And where you goin'?'

'All over I guess. Includin' Scotland. You know, where the guys wear skirts.'

Despite herself, Beulah almost laughed, finding the idea of men in skirts hilarious. 'No shit?'

'God's honest, Beulah. Skirts made out of plaid I'm told.'

She made a decision. She wasn't going to be left alone a second time. 'Well, OK, but I'm taggin' along this trip. And don't try to argue me out of it none.'

His face broke into a broad smile. 'You mean that, hon?'

'Sure do. It'll be as uncomfortable as hell, always is. But at least we'll be together, and that's what counts.'

'Thanks, hon.'

'Hmmh!'

He went to her and this time she didn't brush his hand away.

Albert sat back in his chair, having just broken the news about Huntington Hall to Ellie. Beulah and Pee Wee were also present.

Ellie wasn't sure what to reply, this being so unexpected. She had to admit her father didn't look at all well, a shadow of his former self. There again, what did she expect? He'd only recently lost his wife.

'I'm looking forward to it,' Albert lied. 'The countryside and all that fresh air. Just what the doctor ordered.'

'And it was Danny McGiver's suggestion?'

Albert nodded. 'To be honest, he doesn't think I'm up to work just yet and that a holiday will do me the world of good.'

'We're takin' a trip as well,' Pee Wee told him. And then explained about the forthcoming tour and that Beulah would be going along with him.

'Sounds smashing!' Albert enthused.

'It certainly won't do you any harm getting out of London for a bit,' Ellie said to Albert, thinking out of London and Islington in particular which held so many memories for him.

'I hope so,' he replied, attempting a smile which was most unconvincing.

Albert stayed another half hour before taking his leave, Ellie accompanying him to the doorway where they had a few private words together. She felt totally wretched as she watched her father disappear off into the blackout, he walking with a stoop that was new since Jess's death.

'Oh Dad,' she whispered.

'Why the long face?' Julius asked when he arrived home. Pee Wee had already left for The Chicory House and

439

Beulah was upstairs. He wasn't eating that night as he'd told Beulah at breakfast he'd be late and therefore would eat at the Embassy.

Ellie explained about her father's visit and Huntington Hall, mentioning how ill her father had looked and the fact his hands had shaken during his entire stay.

Julius listened to this in silence, occasionally nodding his head in sympathy. 'I'd say a drink is what you need, Ellie. How about we go across to The Florence?' he suggested, hoping that might cheer her up.

Ellie couldn't think of anything nicer. 'All right. If you'll just give me a few minutes to get ready.'

He pretended to groan.

'Only a few minutes, honestly.'

'Yeah yeah. OK, on you go.'

A now smiling Ellie hurried from the room.

'Hey, it must be Christmas. They got gin in,' Julius announced, setting a glass in front of Ellie. His was a pint of best.

She tasted the gin and murmured approvingly as it slipped down her throat. 'I needed that,' she declared.

Julius glanced around. The pub was quiet, Hazel behind the bar. 'Your dad was in here either before or after he called on my folks,' he stated.

'Must have been before as I watched him walk up the street when he left.'

'Before then. But he was here according to Hazel.'

Ellie stared into her drink. 'I'm so worried about him, Julius. It's as if . . . as if he's given up the will to live. It

440

frightened me tonight when I saw and spoke to him. It wasn't my dad at all, not really.'

Julius remained silent, desperately sorry for Ellie, wishing he could comfort her in some way other than merely buying her a drink. He had to stop himself from reaching out and taking hold of her hand.

'He'll be OK, you'll see,' Julius replied eventually, thinking how pathetic that sounded. 'Probably love it at this Huntington Hall.'

'God I hope so. I truly do.'

'And he'll be well away from the raids, so there won't be any worry there.'

Ellie smiled at Julius, thinking what a wonderful human being he was. 'I shall see him off at the station. He wasn't keen on that, but I insisted. I can easily arrange an hour or so away from my duties.'

'Even if he isn't keen, as you put it, he'll appreciate that. Especially on the day.' Julius coughed. 'There's something I have to ask. A little delicate perhaps.'

She frowned. 'What?'

'When my folks go that'll leave just the two of us in the house. Does that bother you?'

The same thought had already crossed her mind. 'Not in the least.'

'You sure?'

'Positive. I can't imagine you being anything other than the perfect gentleman. Besides, I trust you.'

That praise pleased him. 'I felt I had to mention it as it obviously never occurred to my folks. There again, they know what I'm like.'

It would be funny, and strange, with only Julius around, Ellie thought, her skin prickling slightly. Not that she'd see much of him as he wasn't home a great deal, often working late. 'As long as you appreciate I can't cook anywhere near as well as your mother,' she warned him. 'I don't exactly shine in that department.'

He laughed. 'Tell you what, we'll cook together. How's that?'

She was amazed. 'You can cook?'

'Yeah, enjoy it too. A lot of it Mom taught me over the years. Easy really, when you know how.'

Ellie simply couldn't imagine Albert cooking. Why, it needed a bomb under his bum for him to even make a cup of tea. Her face immediately dropped realising that had been quite the wrong analogy to make.

'What gives? Did I say somethin'?'

Ellie shook her head, then related what had gone through her mind about a bomb and bum.

'Oh!' he murmured.

Ellie had a long swig of gin, then briefly closed her eyes. 'I often wonder how all this will end. The war I mean. Do you?'

'Yeah.'

'One thing's for certain, nothing will ever be the same again. Can't be.'

'No,' he agreed.

Ellie sniffed. 'Sorry. I'm being foolish now. Letting my emotions get the better of me.'

'Very un-English,' he teased.

'Very.'

'Hey!' he suddenly exclaimed. 'I just remembered. I've brought some cigarettes home. Left them in the car so we'll pick them up when we leave here. OK?'

'OK,' she smiled, thinking how infectious his good humour could be. A right tonic, Jess would have said.

'Another thing, I have a proposition for you.'

She opened her eyes wide, they twinkling. Her turn to tease. 'I thought we agreed you'd be a gentleman, Julius Poston?'

'Oh, nothin' improper,' he grinned. 'Nothin' like that. Are you workin' this weekend?'

She nodded. ''Fraid so.'

'How about the weekend after?'

'I have that off. Or I'm supposed to anyway. It depends on the raids. There's always the possibility I might have to go in after all.'

'Well let's say you don't,' he said. 'How about we go on a picnic? Just the two of us. While the weather's still reasonable and before the Fall sets in.'

'A picnic!'

'You know, where you take food and things, spread a blanket on the grass; eat, drink and generally enjoy yourself?'

Now he was taking the mickey. 'Sounds lovely.'

'I'll get all sorts from the Embassy so we can make a proper day of it. Should be fun.'

'Should be,' she agreed. 'But what if it rains?'

'It won't. I give you my word on that. It wouldn't dare.'

Ellie laughed at the absurdity of that. 'Well, if it does we'll simply sit in the car and gorge ourselves there.'

'Hot dog!' he enthused. 'That's exactly what we'll do. But it won't rain. I won't allow it.'

Her mood changed, the laughter going out of her voice to be replaced by sincerity. 'You know something, Julius? You truly are a wonderful person. I mean that.'

He was embarrassed, and delighted at the same time. 'Thank you. You're kinda wonderful yourself.'

Now it was her turn to be embarrassed. Picking up her glass she drained the remainder of her gin. 'The next round's on me,' she declared.

'No it isn't,' he protested.

'Oh yes it is,' she stated firmly, rising to her feet. 'So you just be quiet.'

It took all his self-control not to touch her as she went past. At the funeral he'd realised how much he cared for her. He didn't know how it had happened, certainly not overnight, but somehow he'd fallen in love with Ellie Sykes.

'Platform One is over there,' Ellie declared, pointing. Euston Station was abustle with people, many of them in uniform. The smell was a combination of smoke and soot.

'I still wish you hadn't come,' Albert complained as they headed in that direction. 'I'm quite capable of putting myself on a train.'

'Oh, stop moaning,' Ellie chided him. 'You sound like an old grouch.'

Albert's suitcase contained clothes that had been donated to him by his mates, he never having gone back to retrieve what he could from the house.

'Do you want to buy a paper?' Ellie asked, glancing at the station clock to check the time.

'I already have one in my inside pocket,' Albert replied.

'Is there anything else you might need?'

'Don't think so.'

Ellie was hating this, even if it was in her father's best interests to go away for a while. With her at the Postons', and him at the McGivers', he'd been close, easily accessible. Now she'd have to keep in touch by writing which wasn't the same thing at all.

They stopped while she bought a platform ticket, and then they were moving along the length of the train looking for a suitable carriage.

'This'll do,' Albert announced on finding an empty one, hoping it would stay empty, apart from himself, as he didn't really want company during his journey.

He opened the door and heaved his case inside, following it to put it on the overhead rack. When he'd done that he rejoined Ellie.

'Now you take care of yourself, you hear?' she declared in a no-nonsense tone of voice.

Albert suddenly smiled. 'You sound just like your mother when you speak like that.'

She smiled also. 'Do I?'

'Oh yes,' he replied quietly. He took a deep breath. 'Don't hang about. I can't bear goodbyes, far less long ones.'

'All right, Dad.'

He took her into his arms and hugged her tight. 'Please don't worry about me. I'll be just fine.'

'Promise?'

'Promise.'

Before releasing her he pecked her on the cheek. 'On you go then.'

'Dad . . .?'

'What, Ellie?'

A choke came into her throat. 'Nothing.'

He knew what she'd been about to say, and it was the same with him about her.

'Don't forget to write,' she said, her voice unsteady.

'I won't. Now be off with you.'

The carriage door slammed shut behind her as she began walking away, feeling as though she'd now lost her entire family. Although, of course, that wasn't true.

Her dad had only gone on holiday, she reminded herself.

'I'm stuffed. Absolutely stuffed!' Ellie declared, flopping back onto the blanket they'd brought. As Julius had predicted it was a beautiful day, the sun shining and the temperature high considering it was the end of September.

Julius laid aside what remained of a chicken leg and wiped his lips with a napkin. 'I reckon I am too. More wine?'

'Not for the moment.'

He pulled out a packet of cigarettes, put two in his mouth, lit them and offered her one. She accepted and took a long, deep drag. She sighed, 'You brought along enough food to feed an army.'

He smiled, but didn't reply.

446

After a few moments Ellie rolled onto an elbow to stare at him. 'What are you thinking? You're looking very introspective.'

'About you actually,' he replied softly.

She frowned. 'What about me?'

'I was wonderin' what you really thought about black people, and black men in particular?'

'What a strange question,' she mused.

'Is it?' He paused, then said lightly, 'Take me for example. What do you think about me? In the context of being black that is.'

'Well, you certainly are, that can't be denied.' She took another drag on her cigarette and considered what he'd asked. 'I found it disturbing to begin with, not having had any experience of black people before. But now . . . I don't notice it any more I suppose. You're just Julius, the question of colour doesn't enter into it.'

'Are you sure about that?' he further probed.

'Yes I am. I don't think of you as being black at all now, it never crosses my mind. But why do you ask?'

He shrugged.

'Julius?'

Not yet, he thought. The time wasn't ripe. Or was he just being cowardly? He didn't know.

'Curious, that's all,' he replied, and changed the subject.

Albert crossed over to his bedroom window and stared out over the grounds. To his surprise he'd found he liked Huntington Hall, liked it a lot in fact. It was peaceful here, serene almost. And the staff, without exception, couldn't have been nicer. He'd settled in remarkably quickly.

He was also getting on well with the other patients, all firemen like himself. If anything he felt a bit of a fraud being there as some of them were recovering from horrific injuries suffered during the German raids. One poor chap from Coventry had lost both legs and an arm as well as sustaining damage to his sight.

Albert spotted a few of them now, sitting on a bench chatting, having a right old laugh by the looks of things. He decided to go and join them, he too could use a laugh.

He started humming as he left his room, and there was a spring in his step that hadn't been there when he'd arrived at Huntington Hall.

If Ellie had seen him at that moment she'd have been much relieved.

Chapter 27

Ellie arrived back to find Julius already there pottering round the kitchen. 'You're early!' she exclaimed in surprise.

'Yeah, it was an easy day.' That wasn't true, he'd purposefully hurried through his afternoon's work so he could spend more time with her, but wasn't about to tell Ellie that.

'What was your day like?' he asked.

'So-so. Mounds of paperwork to get through, but thankfully no call-outs.' There hadn't been a raid in over a week, the Germans currently concentrating their bombing further north.

'Coffee?'

'Please.'

Ellie sank onto a chair and lit up. 'I'll be washing my hair tonight, if that's all right with you?'

'Sure.'

'You going out?'

'Hadn't planned to. I might go over the road after a while for a couple. But we'll see.' He had no intentions of doing that unless Ellie came with him.

She watched him as he 'fixed' their coffee, as he called

it, admiring the litheness of his movement, and the graceful way he did things. It struck her that he was one of the most handsome men she'd ever known. But more important than that was his attitude to women; he wasn't only unfailingly courteous to them but treated them as equals, a refreshing change to what she'd been used to and brought up with. Not that her father hadn't treated Jess properly, he had. But Albert was a man of his time, and background, where the woman was always second fiddle and whose duty was to be attendant to his needs at all times.

'I thought we'd cook together tonight,' Julius announced.

'Oh?' That pleased her, he'd promised they'd be doing this. 'What do you have in mind?'

'Yankee fried rice.'

Ellie smiled. 'Sounds very exotic.'

'Not really, but it's simple. It'll be another recipe to add to your repertoire.'

'Which, as I warned you, is strictly limited. Cauliflower cheese, stew, bubble and squeak . . .'

'What the hell is that?' he queried with a laugh.

She explained.

'You English sure eat some weird stuff!' he exclaimed, shaking his head in amazement.

'No weirder than some of the things you Americans eat,' she retorted.

'Like what?'

She had frantically to think. 'Meat loaf, your favourite.'

'What's weird about meat loaf? It's mainly minced beef which you English are so fond of.'

He had her there.

'Well? Go on, name somethin'.'

She could hear the triumph in his voice. 'Oh, I don't know offhand,' she said grudgingly, hating to admit defeat.

'Ah ha!' he exclaimed, and beamed at her. 'Gotcha.'

Ellie couldn't have said how it happened, but suddenly they were both roaring with laughter.

He regarded her steadily when he eventually stopped. 'You're fun, Ellie Sykes. Real fun. Great to be with.'

'And so are you,' she replied just as sincerely.

For the space of a few moments they were absolutely still, staring into one another's eyes. Then Julius broke the spell by turning away. 'If you'll get off your butt I'll start showin' you how to make the rice.'

Ellie took her coffee with her to where he'd begun assembling the ingredients. She was skin-prickly aware when up close of the cologne he was wearing.

Albert entered the day room to find Nurse Cross, a pretty young lady about Ellie's age, busy with a screwdriver. 'What are you doing?' he queried with a frown.

'Trying to fix this shelf before it falls off the wall. It's come loose.'

'Here, let me help you.'

Albert went over and took the screwdriver from her. A quick examination of the offending shelf revealed it was going to need more than a screwdriver to put it right.

'I've no idea how it's happened but the holes the screws go into have widened. To do this properly I'll have to drill new ones. I don't suppose you have a drill handy by any chance?'

Nurse Cross was delighted at Albert's offer of help, not to mention relieved. 'There's bound to be one in the maintenance room. If you'll follow me I'll take you there.'

Albert left the screwdriver on the shelf, as he'd need it later, and followed Nurse Cross out into the corridor. 'I'm a bit puzzled,' he said. 'Why are you doing something like that? Surely there's a man does the odd jobs round here?'

'There was, two of them in fact, but they're both in the Forces now and Matron hasn't been able to replace them. As a result we nurses have to do what we can if anything goes wrong.'

The maintenance room was in the basement, where Albert hadn't been before. Nurse Cross opened the door and flicked on the light. 'Here we are.'

The first thing Albert saw were stacks and stacks of paint cans, a veritable mountain of them. 'Good God,' he murmured. 'Are those empty or full?'

'Full. The whole place was scheduled to be repainted and then the war broke out. They've been lying there ever since.'

'This lot would fetch a pretty penny on the black market,' Albert commented, paint being so difficult to come by since the advent of hostilities.

'I suppose so,' Nurse Cross mused. Then, reprovingly, 'I hope you're not getting any funny ideas, Mr Sykes?'

Albert laughed. 'Not me. I'm dead against the black market, have been all along. No, it was just an observation, that's all.'

Nurse Cross pointed to a couple of old, dilapidated chests of drawers. 'You should find a drill in there somewhere.'

Albert quickly established that the drawers were filled with all manner of tools, and soon found what he was after. 'Just the dab,' he smiled. He then selected a few other items that he'd require and they left the room.

'I'll return this lot when I'm finished,' he assured her.

'Thank you. It'll certainly save me the job, particularly as I'm useless at that sort of thing.'

'My pleasure. I was bored anyway, so this gives me something to do.'

Nurse Cross switched off the light and they made their way back upstairs where she left Albert to get on with it.

Ellie picked up the letter that had just been delivered by the morning post as she was about to set off for work. In the background was the rattle of dishes as Julius washed the breakfast things. She smiled to see the writing was her father's laboured script. Quickly she tore open the envelope and started to read.

Albert, in his own words, was having a whale of a time at Huntington Hall, everyone was friendly, lovely surroundings, etc. etc. He was also feeling a lot better and even putting on a little weight. He finished by hoping she was well and said he was looking forward to hearing from her soon.

'You almost ready?' Julius queried, appearing behind her.

'I just have to put my coat and hat on.' She held up

the letter. 'From Dad. Everything's fine and he's enjoying himself.'

'Good,' Julius replied, nodding his approval. It pleased him to see the obvious relief on Ellie's face. 'Now shall we go?'

Ellie tucked the letter into a pocket; she'd re-read it later when she had a free moment.

Julius helped her into her coat, then slipped on his own. After he'd locked the door they made their way to his car and got in.

As had become their custom Julius drove Ellie to the station before going on to the Embassy. 'I was wonderin',' he said as they turned out of Florence Street.

'What?'

'How about we take in a movie tonight?'

She glanced sideways at him. 'There is one on locally I'd like to see. *David Copperfield* with W.C. Fields. He always makes me laugh.'

'*David Copperfield*? Well why not! That's settled then, eh?'

'It's a date.'

For the life of her she couldn't think why she'd used that particular word knowing what it meant to Americans. When she glanced again at Julius he was smiling.

'Oh shit!' Julius muttered as the sirens sounded. The movie had only just started.

'I'll have to go home,' Ellie said. 'You know the arrangement.' The arrangement she was referring to was that the station would phone her should she be required. 'You do understand?'

'Of course.'

Quite a few of the audience were now on their feet and moving towards the exits. Some enroute to their shelters, others to the Angel tube, which was close by, to take refuge there.

Once outside they both glanced up to see the usual searchlights criss-crossing the night sky. So far the ack-ack guns hadn't opened up.

They'd almost reached Florence Street when, the sirens having stopped wailing, the All Clear went, bringing both Ellie and Julius up short.

They smiled at one another in the darkness. 'False alarm,' Julius said, thinking of the inconvenience they'd had in leaving the cinema.

'Better that than the real thing,' Ellie replied, turning her collar up against the cold.

'Shall we go back?'

'What do you want to do?'

He hesitated for a few moments. 'Honestly?'

'Honestly.'

'We don't know why the All Clear was sounded, but it is possible the sirens could go again. It's happened in the past.'

Ellie nodded. That was true.

'Let's forget the movie then and go to The Florence instead. That way if they do go again you only have to cross the road.'

Which made sense, Ellie thought. Anyway, the picture

was spoilt for her now. If they did return she'd just be sitting there waiting for the bloody sirens to go off a second time. 'All right.'

'Why don't you take my arm? It's treacherous in the black-out and I don't want anythin' happenin' to you.'

She appreciated his concern; twisted ankles and the like had become commonplace since the black-out was imposed. She slipped an arm round his and they proceeded on their way, she wishing he'd made the suggestion earlier. Not for safety's sake, but because she liked the idea of them being arm in arm. It was almost as if they were a couple.

'I'll get tipsy if I have any more,' Ellie declared. They'd been in the pub for nearly an hour and a half during which the sirens had remained silent.

'Oh go on, I'm goin' to have one,' he urged.

Ellie was thoroughly enjoying herself, Julius, as always, great company. They were both drinking shorts, Harry and Hazel, for once, having a seemingly plentiful supply.

'I shouldn't,' she demurred.

'But you will.'

'Oh go on then,' she conceded, and giggled.

Julius went up to the bar and ordered refills, looking back at Ellie whose face was ever so slightly flushed. Adorable, simply adorable, he thought, as she gave him a tiny wave.

'Isn't this far better than the movies?' Julius asked when he rejoined her.

'Much.'

'I think so too.'

'Maybe we can go out again another night?' It was the alcohol making her so forward, she realised. She'd never have asked that when sober.

'Of course. Whenever you wish.'

'OK,' she giggled again, thinking it funny she was using his American expression.

Before they knew it another hour, during which they'd had several more drinks, had flown past and it was approaching closing time.

Ellie finished her G&T and placed the glass firmly on the table. 'That's it. No more otherwise I might fall down.'

'A last cigarette?'

'Is that a ruse to stay on?'

'No.'

'Swear?'

'I swear, Ellie. Only a cigarette, that's all.' The truth was he was loath to break this up, thinking he could have sat there with Ellie all night long.

Cigarettes were duly lit and smoked, after which they both stood, Julius helping Ellie into her coat but deciding to carry his as it was only across the road.

'I'm glad it's you doing that,' Ellie slurred as he put the key in the door.

'Why?'

'Because I don't think I'd manage it.'

'You're not that bad,' he lied as the door swung open and they went inside.

Ellie hung up her coat. 'Well that's me. I'm off to bed where I'll no doubt sleep like the proverbial log.'

'Goodnight, Ellie.'

'Goodnight, Julius. Thanks for a wonderful evening. It was terrific.'

'For me too.'

They were both staring at one another, the mood between them having somehow changed.

'Can I kiss you?'

The breath caught in Ellie's throat to hear that, and her stomach sort of flipped over. She nodded.

It was only a peck, the briefest touching of lips, and then it was all over. Reaching out she laid the tips of her fingers lightly on his cheek, then whirled about and went running up the stairs.

Julius watched her every step of the way, her perfume lingering in his nostrils.

'Come in!' Matron Hapgood, a tallish, angular thin woman, who wore glasses, called out when there was a tap on her office door.

It was Albert. 'Are you free?'

'If you wish to see me.'

'Thank you, Matron.'

She indicated a chair in front of her desk. As he sat she removed her glasses and wiped her eyes. 'Now what can I do for you, Mr Sykes? No complaints I trust?'

He smiled. 'None at all. I've come with a request, that's all.'

The glasses were put back on and she studied him intently. 'Oh?'

'The overflow from the guttering outside my window

is very irritating, and I wondered if you'd give me permission to do something about it. I suspect it's only blocked with debris, which happens with gutters, and I'd like to not only clear that but go round the entire guttering and give it a general clean.'

That took Matron by surprise. 'I heard about you fixing the shelf in the day room. Thank you for that.'

Albert nodded. 'My pleasure. Gave me something to do, occupy my mind for a bit.'

'Uh-huh.' Matron was thinking about Albert's proposal. 'Won't it be dangerous up there on a ladder? I mean, I wouldn't want you to hurt yourself.'

Albert laughed. 'I'm a fireman, Matron, I've spent half my life up ladders. I won't fall off, I assure you.'

Matron blushed. 'Yes, of course. How stupid of me.'

'I'm bored you see. Thoroughly enjoying myself here, but bored. I'm a working man, used to doing just that. I'll be far happier being busy.'

Albert wasn't like the rest of her patients, Matron reflected. They were either recovering from injury or illness, whereas in his case he was here to get over the death of his wife. The more she thought about Albert's proposal, the more she approved. It would be good therapy for him. Ideal in fact.

'I've already been in the maintenance room,' Albert went on. 'Everything I might need is there, including overalls which looked more or less my size.'

Matron made a decision. 'All right, Mr Sykes, you carry on.' She wagged a finger at him. 'Just be careful, that's all. I've never lost a patient yet, and don't wish to start now.'

'You won't, Matron, so you can rest easy.' He rubbed his hands together. 'Well, there's no time like the present to get to it. With your permission that is?'

'Granted.'

'Thank you.'

And with that he left Matron Hapgood, heading straight for the maintenance room to sort out what was required.

Ellie arrived in her office to take over from Josie Farnham at the early morning changeover of staff. 'How was last night?' she asked brightly.

'Fine. No raid, no call-outs. I even managed to snatch a few hours sleep.'

'The SO about?'

Josie shook her head. 'But she'll probably be in later knowing her.'

'Anything to report?'

'Not really. With the exception of Annie Croxton who's been taken ill apparently, and admitted to the Royal Free.'

Ellie frowned. 'What's wrong with her?'

'The note her mother sent round didn't say. But, as she's in hospital, I presume it's serious.'

Annie worked on Ellie's day shift and was therefore her responsibility. 'I'll go and see her this evening,' she declared. 'And find out exactly what's what.'

Josie yawned. 'Home to bed for me.'

'I've been meaning to ask,' Ellie went on. 'How are you and Harold getting along? Still going strong?' Harold was the policeman Josie had met at the Poxy Roxy.

'As ever,' Josie smiled. 'He's got himself on nights as well so we see each other during the day. A bit odd perhaps, but you get used to it.'

'Might there be an engagement in the wind?'

Josie winked. 'Possibly. Too soon really to tell, but he seems keen enough. And I certainly am.'

Ellie crossed two fingers and held them up.

'Thanks. Now I'm off. Ta ra!'

'Ta ra!'

Ellie checked her appearance in the mirror, tucking away a few loose hairs, before going out to address the other girls as she did every morning.

Albert came down the ladder to find Matron standing there, where she'd been watching him for the past few minutes. 'That's it done,' he announced. 'All finished.'

'Was it bad?'

He shook his head. 'Not really. But guttering, like lots of other things, does need looking after. What I've done should be done every year. That lot up there hadn't been looked at for quite some time, which was evident. There won't be any overflows now when it rains, I'm delighted to say. And I can stop being irritated.'

Matron smiled. 'If you're willing there are some other jobs that require attending to.'

'Oh?'

'Small ones. General maintenance work, that sort of thing.'

'Well, I'll be happy to see what I can do.'

'This is very kind of you, Mr Sykes. We all appreciate it.'

'Think nothing of it,' Albert acknowledged. 'It's my pleasure.' He hesitated, then said, 'There's something else.'

'What's that?'

'How long am I due to stay here? I got the impression I had another couple of weeks. The Union was rather vague about the actual time allotted.'

'It was left to my discretion,' Matron replied. 'As far as I'm concerned it's up to you.'

Albert nodded that he understood. 'That being the case, why don't I start doing some painting for you? The inside of the building desperately needs it, and there's all that paint just lying there in the maintenance room crying out to be used.'

Matron's face lit up. 'That would be wonderful, Mr Sykes.'

'Then leave it to me. I'll organise everything.'

A treasure, Matron thought gleefully. That's what Albert was. A treasure.

Annie's bed, when Ellie located it, was surrounded by screens. She popped her head round one and smiled.

'Hello, Ellie. Come and sit down.'

Annie looked positively ghastly, Ellie thought as she sat. 'Why the screens?'

'The doctor was doing some more tests. He's finished now, but the screens still haven't been taken away.'

Ellie stared at Annie in concern. 'What's wrong?'

'They don't know yet, I started feeling unwell at home, then began vomiting. Next thing I'd passed out. When our GP was called he insisted I be brought in here.'

'I see.'

'They've already done a number of tests before these latest, but so far they're as baffled as my GP.'

'Well, all I can say is I hope you get better soon.'

Annie gave Ellie a twisted smile. 'I'm glad you've come. Mum was here earlier but had to go home for a while. It's good to have the company.'

Annie was normally a beautiful blonde with gorgeous green eyes and a figure to die for. The hair was now dull and straggly, the eyes as if the light in them had been turned out, and the figure, from what Ellie could see, seemed sort of shrunken. 'I'll stay as long as you like, or they'll let me,' Ellie said.

'Thanks.'

The following afternoon news came to the station that Annie Croxton had passed away the previous night. A post-mortem revealed the cause of death to be a tumour on the brain.

Chapter 28

'Ah, there you are, Mr Sykes,' Matron declared, breezing into the bedroom Albert was painting. 'I was told I'd find you here.'

'Hello, Matron.'

Matron gazed about, nodding her approval. 'You're doing an excellent job.'

Albert continued working. 'Thank you. I enjoy painting. Find it very relaxing. In fact, if I hadn't been a fireman I've sometimes thought I'd have become a painter and decorator.'

Matron shivered. 'It's chilly in here.'

'That's because it's November and the window's wide open. It has to be that otherwise the smell would be unbearable.'

'It's Friday afternoon, Mr Sykes.'

Albert paused to stare at her, wondering why she was stating the obvious. 'I believe it is.'

'Payday in fact.'

What on earth was she talking about?

Matron reached into a side pocket of her uniform to produce two pound notes. 'These are for you.'

Albert was taken aback to say the least. 'I'm not due

any wages, Matron. I volunteered, remember?'

'You did indeed, Mr Sykes, for which I'm most appreciative. Nonetheless, I want you to accept this, you've earned every penny of it during the past week.'

Albert laid his brush aside, telling himself not to look a gift horse in the mouth. 'It seems a bit unnecessary to me as there's nowhere to spend money,' he pointed out.

The hint of a smile curled Matron's lips fractionally upwards. 'I presume you came through Loxton on your way here?' That was the name of the nearest village situated about a mile and a half from Huntington Hall.

Albert nodded. 'I did.'

'Well there's a very nice pub there, called The Lamb Inn, which serves excellent ale I understand.'

He could really use a pint, or two, Albert thought. 'Really?'

'And there's a bicycle in the passage leading from the kitchen to the back door, the tradesmen's entrance we refer to it as. Can you ride a bike, Mr Sykes?'

'I can,' Albert mused. 'Though haven't done so in years.'

'I'm sure you'll quickly get the hang of it again. After dinner would be the best time, don't you think?'

'Sounds good to me.'

'Fine then.'

Albert regarded her with amusement. 'You seem to know a lot about men, Matron, no offence meant.' As she didn't wear a wedding ring he presumed she was unmarried.

'I should do, I was brought up with four brothers.

Ruffians all. But kindly with it. Not one of them would ever turn down the chance of a pint. Mind you, I haven't seen them in years, but I doubt they've changed their ways.'

Albert accepted the money from her. 'All I can say is thank you.'

'Think nothing of it. And, Mr Sykes, you won't be the first one to use the bicycle for that purpose. It hasn't been unheard of in the past.'

She took a deep breath. 'Now, I'd better get on, lots to do.'

And with that Matron swept from the room leaving a bemused Albert to resume painting.

Ellie was sitting in front of the fire with her eyes closed, having thought she'd have a doze, but unable to because she was acutely aware of Julius, sitting opposite, staring at her. She didn't have to look to know that was the case, she could feel his gaze. Nor was this the first time she'd been aware of his staring when he thought she wasn't watching.

'Julius?'

'What, Ellie?'

'Why are you staring?'

She opened her eyes just as he was glancing away.

'Was I?' he queried innocently.

'You know you were.'

'Sorry, I didn't mean to.'

Ellie produced her cigarettes. 'Want one?'

'Yeah.'

He came over and helped her to a light before returning to his chair. 'It's cold out there tonight,' he commented.

'Don't change the subject, Julius. Why were you staring at me? You've been doing a lot of that lately, thinking I didn't know, but I did.'

He shifted uncomfortably in his chair, unsure of what to reply.

'Well?' she demanded.

'I'm sorry,' he apologised. 'It won't happen again.' He came suddenly to his feet. 'I'm off over to The Florence for a while. See you later.'

'Julius, don't you dare!' she called out sharply as he made for the door. 'I want an answer.'

He stopped, but kept his back to her. 'Drop it, Ellie. Please.'

'No, I will not.'

'I said please.'

'And I said I want an explanation, Julius Poston. Why do you keep staring at me as if I was some kind of exotic animal or other?'

He was ages in replying. When he did his back remained firmly to her. 'I didn't intend speakin' out, Ellie. Certainly not while you're a guest in our house.'

There was another long pause. 'I'm waiting,' she reminded him, as if she had to.

'It's because I've fallen for you,' he stated quietly.

Ellie went rigid with shock. 'Fallen for me?' she croaked.

'Big-time. No lie.'

Ellie swallowed, then swallowed again. 'Are you saying you love me?'

'I guess.'

'What sort of answer is that. Yes or no?'

'Yes.'

Bloody hell, she thought, still in shock.

'Now can I go?'

Her emotions were in turmoil. This was so unexpected. Or was it? She wasn't sure. 'Turn round,' she further croaked. 'I want to find something out.'

He came about to face her. 'What?'

'Why did I have to force you into telling me that?'

He shrugged. 'All kinds of reasons.'

'Such as?'

'I didn't want to take advantage of us bein' alone in the house while my folks are away.'

'And?' she probed.

'I remember when you said that day when we went on a picnic about not seein' me as a black man any more, but simply as a man. Well that's one thing, us havin' a relationship quite another. Don't you agree? I mean, there are still parts of the States where I'd be lynched for being interested in a white girl far less takin' it further.'

He loved her – those words had burned deeply into her brain and sent her pulse racing. She'd never believed she had a chance with him, not really. Fantasised about it on occasion, but never believed it would come about.

'Ellie?'

He frowned as she got up and came across to him.

'I want you to kiss me, properly this time. As though you meant it.'

'Are you sure?'

She nodded.

He hesitated for a few moments, then took her into his arms.

Ellie felt light-headed when he finally released her, almost staggering on the spot. She'd never known a kiss like it, certainly not with George. His kisses paled by comparison.

'Well?' Julius smiled.

'You can go to the pub now. I want to think about this.'

'OK.'

When he was gone she slumped back into her chair, her mind whirling. What had started as a dull and dreary night had suddenly turned into something very, very different.

While Julius was in The Florence, Albert was standing at the bar of The Lamb Inn. He'd liked the pub the moment he'd walked through the door, its atmosphere cosy, friendly and instantly welcoming. Matron had been right about the beer, a local brew, it was good. Far better than he was used to.

'Passing through?' the barman inquired, polishing a glass.

Albert explained that he'd come from Huntington Hall.

'We occasionally get some of the nurses in here,' the barman said. 'A lively bunch, all out for a laugh.'

Before long Albert found himself chatting to a group of the villagers, feeling completely at ease as if he'd been a regular there for years.

Ellie lay in bed staring at the ceiling, the room in darkness. Julius had returned a short while ago and gone almost immediately to his room.

She couldn't get out of her mind the conversation she'd had with Annie Croxton the night Annie had died. Enjoy your life while you can, Annie had said. For you never knew what tomorrow would bring, especially with a war on.

Well, the latter was certainly true where Annie had been concerned. One moment vibrant and alive, the next ill, the next dead. Albeit in Annie's case it had nothing to do with the war.

Death – she seemed surrounded by it nowadays. Her mother, Paul, old Ma Jenkins from across the road, her two colleagues, Molly Davis and Pat Halfpenny, who'd been burned alive in their vehicle. The countless incidents she'd been called out to where the dead and dying had been all around. The injured who'd died in her vehicle while being taken to hospital, the others – so very many – who'd died after reaching there.

Ellie shivered, which had nothing to do with the temperature. She herself could be next, there was always that possibility. Every time there was a raid, and thank God they'd stopped for a while, her turn could come.

And now Julius said he loved her, which she believed after that kiss downstairs. It was as if her insides had melted, turned to mush, which had never ever happened with George or any other man she'd previously kissed.

It had just seemed so right with Julius. As if, well, as if during the kiss they'd been one person. And if that could happen with a kiss what would it be like should they make love? Her skin prickled all over at the thought.

War changed everything, she told herself. The entire world was turned on its head. She'd been brought up to be a good girl, as Annie had put it. Having sex was something that happened with your husband on your wedding night, and not before. A few liberties perhaps, but not the actual act itself. That was strictly forbidden in the fear of acquiring a reputation, or worse still, being caught out and getting pregnant. The shame of that, for her and her family, would be devastating.

But the world had turned on its head, and who knew what tomorrow would bring? Shouldn't she grab what she could, while she could? Common sense said yes. Screamed it in fact. Loud and clear.

Did she love Julius? She'd never consciously admitted she did, having considered him unobtainable. Only now he wasn't, and he loved her.

That kiss was the key which told her they were right for one another. Indisputably so. Feelings she'd kept locked away had been released, come bubbling to the surface.

She *did* love him, she realised with a jolt. And had never loved George. She'd thought she had at the time, but it hadn't been so, she'd been deluding herself. Julius was the one for her, there was no question about it. None whatsoever. And tomorrow, or the next day, she, or Julius, could be dead, just like all the others.

Her mind made up, Ellie got out of bed and shrugged into her dressing gown. Taking a deep breath she made her way to Julius's door.

Another deep breath and she knocked. 'Julius, are you awake?'

'Yeah,' came the surprised reply.

Ellie opened the door and went inside.

Ellie came awake with a smile on her face, the memories of the previous night instantly flooding back. Beside her Julius was still fast asleep.

She hadn't really known what to expect of lovemaking, but whatever, the reality had far surpassed any preconceptions she might have had.

She felt languid, her body utterly relaxed, a sense of joyous fulfilment encompassing her entire being.

She couldn't have asked for a man to be more tender or gentle with her, he only too well aware it was her first time and wanting her initiation to be a good and rewarding one. And so it had been. It couldn't have been more so.

Reaching out under the covers she ran a hand over his naked buttock, then slid it down between his legs. Hussy, brazen hussy, she thought, her smile widening and becoming knowing.

There had been no embarrassment between them, albeit she'd thought there would be, at least initially. But no. Nothing could have been more natural than their being naked together.

'You know what'll happen if you keep doin' that?' he murmured.

'What?' she replied innocently.

He laughed, a deep rumble that reverberated in the cavern of his chest. 'Well, you'd better stop it, we both have work to go to.'

A glance at the bedside clock told her there was just over half an hour before she normally got up. 'Cuddle me, Julius,' she whispered, releasing him.

He did, savouring the rich scent of her hair. 'Shall I tell you somethin'?'

'What?' she queried dreamily.

'That jibe about your breasts being small. Well they're not, they're absolutely perfect.'

'Oh,' she breathed. 'And what about my bottom?'

'Just the right size, and cute as hell.'

'Thank you.'

'Why? I'm only tellin' the truth.'

The mush was back in her stomach. 'There's still plenty of time, Julius.'

They both made good use of it.

Josie Farnham was sitting perched on the edge of their shared desk when Ellie entered the office. 'You're late,' she frowned. That was most unlike Ellie.

Ellie blushed. 'Sorry. Something came up.' She almost burst out laughing when she realised what she'd said.

'Are you all right?'

'Never more so.'

Josie studied her friend. 'You seem different somehow.'

'Do I?'

'I can't say how, but yes.'

Did it really show? It must for Josie to notice. 'Perhaps it's because I'm happy,' she prevaricated. The truth, if not the whole truth. She wasn't only happy but in love and not a virgin any more.

'Any particular reason?'

Ellie toyed with the idea of telling Josie about her and Julius, then decided not to. It wasn't that she didn't trust Josie, she did, but that was something best kept to herself. 'Just one of those days I suppose,' she replied airily.

Josie didn't believe a word of that, but didn't inquire any further. Ellie's business was her own. Instead she launched into their normal changeover procedure, and was soon on her way home leaving Ellie to it.

Albert took a sip of the tea one of the nurses had just brought him, and wandered over to the open window to stare out.

Being a born and bred townie, and an inner city one at that, his previous experience of the countryside had been extremely limited. But now he was living right in the middle of it he'd come to appreciate the sheer splendour of the land.

How quiet it could be, and peaceful, an ever-changing vista given to many moods. He found it wondrously beautiful.

The animals fascinated him, cows, sheep, and the wild ones he occasionally glimpsed. Why, only the other day he'd actually seen a badger!

And the air, so clean and fresh, often filled with nose-pleasing odours. He smiled – sometimes not so pleasing!

Yes, Albert thought, he could actually live here and not miss London, or Islington, even though the latter had always been his home.

Life moved at a different pace in the country, slower, lacking the hustle and bustle he was used to. Days somehow merged with one another, each seemingly the same, yet at the same time different. And how friendly the people were. He'd thought they might view him, an outsider amongst them, with suspicion, but so far that simply hadn't been the case. They'd accepted him without question.

It would be a sad day when he finally left, he thought ruefully. Back to where he belonged and his job as a fireman. But where to stay? That was the question. He couldn't continue imposing on Danny and Vera, no matter what they said. The alternative was a hostel, many of which had been opened up to accommodate people, like himself, made homeless from the bombing.

Christ, that would be awful. Eating and sleeping with strangers, maybe even having to put up with screaming children night after night. The thought made him shudder.

But he wouldn't be leaving Huntington Hall yet. Matron had said it was up to him when he went, so unless she changed her mind, or circumstances altered, he was staying put for at least a few more weeks. Maybe even longer.

He liked country life. He liked it a lot.

* * *

'We can't sleep in your parents' bed!' Ellie protested.

'Whyever not? They aren't usin' it.'

'That's hardly the point. It just wouldn't be right.'

'But it would be more comfortable,' he argued. 'And of course bigger being a double, and a large double at that.'

Ellie had to admit it was difficult the two of them sharing a single bed; this would be far more satisfactory.

'I'll tell you what,' Julius said, a glint in his eye. Going to Ellie he began undoing the buttons of her blouse. 'Why don't we try it out and see?'

'But it isn't even eight o'clock yet.'

'So?'

Her resistance crumbled, she wanted him so badly. In fact she couldn't get enough of him, or he her. She giggled.

'I take it that means yes?'

He removed her blouse and started on her bra. When that too was off he lowered his head and began nuzzling her.

'Oh, Julius,' she whispered. Closing her eyes she gave a soft moan.

Heaven. There was no other word for what followed, sheer heaven.

Ellie was returning from work when she spotted Connie Fox and George, arm in arm, on the other side of the road. George was speaking and Connie was avidly listening.

Ellie knew if she'd seen them a few weeks back she'd have been jealous. But now? Not one whit of it. On the contrary, she wished them well and every happiness. One thing was certain, they couldn't be any happier than she and Julius. No one could.

She briefly considered going over and saying hello, then decided against it as it would only cause them embarrassment. No, let them be.

Ellie hurried on her way, desperate to be in Julius's arms again. Just to be with him.

'Do you play darts, Albert?'

Albert looked up at the speaker, a chap called Tom whom he'd chatted to on several occasions now. 'As a matter of fact I do.' There was a board at the station which was often used while waiting for a call-out. Tom, like many of the men who came to the pub, worked on a farm which was why he wasn't in the Forces.

'Then can you help us out? One of our regulars can't make it tonight and we have a match against The Bell from Framley. We'd be obliged.' Framley was another village in the area.

'I'd be delighted to play, Tom. Thanks for asking.'

'Good chap. Come on over and have a practice with the rest of us. The Bell team should be arriving shortly.'

'One thing, Tom. I don't have any darts with me.'

'Don't you worry about that. We've got a box of spares. There's bound to be a set that suits.'

Albert was considered the best player at the station, which was something considering the standard of his colleagues. By the end of the evening he'd won his singles game plus his doubles, though they lost the match overall.

He was asked to play again the following week, to which he readily agreed. Before leaving to go back to Huntington Hall he got the distinct impression he was now fully accepted as 'one of the lads'.

That pleased him enormously.

Julius ran a hand over his face, then lit a cigarette. This really wasn't good enough, he chided himself. He had a whole stack of work to get through, but was unable to concentrate on any of it.

The trouble was Ellie, he couldn't get her out of his mind. Whenever he tried to focus on the papers before him his thoughts kept drifting back to her, wondering what she was doing right then, recalling incidents from times they'd been together, she smiling, laughing, clinging to him.

Julius sighed and decided to have a coffee break. 'Ellie.' He said her name aloud, and smiled.

He couldn't wait to see her later.

Matron stood at her window watching Albert cycle off, to The Lamb no doubt which had become a firm favourite of his. Not that that gave her any cause for worry. He never returned drunk, or belligerent in any way. A little merry perhaps, but there was no harm in that. None at all.

He was progressing quickly with the painting, and that morning had started on the day room where he'd made a good beginning.

As she was turning away from the window an idea came to her. One that made her stop and think.

* * *

'I've got a couple of complimentary tickets for a show tomorrow night,' Julius announced. 'Want to go?'

'What, do you mean a play?' Ellie queried.

He shook his head. 'A revue. It's called "Sweet and Low" starring Hermione Baddeley and Hermione Gingold. I'm told it's great.'

'Sounds wonderful,' Ellie enthused, already planning what she'd wear. 'Which theatre?'

'The Ambassador's.'

'It'll be fun,' Ellie declared. 'I'm looking forward to it already.'

Julius came over and took her into his arms. 'Me too. But then goin' anywhere with you is fun. As is just bein' with you.'

Her eyes were shining as he bent and kissed her lightly on the lips. 'Love ya, doll.'

'And I love you.'

'For ever and ever.'

'And a day,' she added, thinking with pleasure how romantic Julius could be. There were so many little things he did for her, gestures of appreciation and affection. Why, only the night before she'd gone up to bed to discover a box of chocolates, candy he called it, on her pillow. She hoped he'd never change. Please God.

'Typical woman, always having to have the last word,' he smiled. Then, suddenly all businesslike. 'Right, I'm hungry. Let's eat. I'm goin' to teach you how to cook spaghetti bolognaise.'

'Whatever's that!' she exclaimed.

'Italian. And haven't I had trouble getting the proper ingredients. Luckily one of the chefs at the Embassy owed me a favour and was eventually able to rustle up what I wanted.'

Taking her by the hand he crossed over to the large, brown paper bag he'd brought home. 'OK, let's get started.'

Later Ellie talked him out of putting garlic in it, declaring vehemently that garlic was disgusting and made your breath stink. Only Frenchies and the like used garlic.

Julius thought that was very funny.

Ellie came groggily awake as the bedroom light clicked on. Seconds later she was staring in horror at an open-mouthed Beulah and a clearly amused Pee Wee.

'Holy shit!' Julius exclaimed softly, he too having been woken.

A thoroughly embarrassed Ellie, wishing she could disappear, was only too horribly aware she was stark naked underneath the bedclothes. As was Julius.

'Hi, Mom, hi, Dad!' Julius said, attempting a smile. 'We weren't expectin' you.'

Beulah's glare would have sunk a battleship.

Chapter 29

'What in the name of Sam Hill's goin' on here?' Beulah thundered the moment Julius and Ellie, now both suitably attired, appeared in the kitchen. Pee Wee was standing leaning on the mantelpiece, a glass of scotch in one hand.

'It wasn't what it looked like, Mom,' Julius immediately protested.

Ellie, still acutely embarrassed, face flushed, was staring at the floor. What had happened was a nightmare come true, the only redeeming factor being they hadn't actually been making love when surprised.

Beulah's expression became one of incredulity. 'Well, you sure as hell weren't in bed to discuss the weather, for Christsake!'

'Why don't you sit down, Ellie,' Pee Wee suggested softly.

Ellie did, at the other end of the table to Beulah whose gaze she couldn't meet.

'Anyway, why didn't you call to tell us you were gettin' back?' Julius accused.

'Because the phone's out of order. It's been out all day.'

'Oh!' Julius exclaimed. 'I didn't know that.'

'Well, you do now.' Beulah folded her arms across her massive chest. 'And to think I trusted you, Julius. I should've known, men are all alike.'

Julius went over to an opened bottle of scotch, found a glass and poured himself one. 'Ellie?'

She shook her head. If she'd tried to drink scotch in her present state she'd have thrown up.

'As for you, Ellie Sykes,' Beulah bulldozed on, fixing her with a beady stare. 'Your mother would have been downright ashamed of you.'

Ellie's flush deepened to become bright red.

'Hold on, Mom, that isn't fair!' Julius retorted.

'It's fair, OK. Jess was my friend and we talked about all sorts of matters. Now I can't pretend we agreed on everythin', but I sure knew what her views on morality were. What possessed you, girl, eh? Did Julius sweet-talk you into it?'

'No,' Ellie managed to whisper.

'Then what?'

'We're in love, Mom.'

That momentarily deflated Beulah. 'Since when?'

Julius shrugged. 'It just sort of built up I guess. Then it all came out, and that was that.'

'Huh!' Beulah snorted. 'Love, my ass. The pair of you, bein' alone, probably just got the hots for one another.'

'No!' Ellie exclaimed, suddenly finding her voice. 'You're wrong. We do love each other. And it's my fault started sleeping together. Up until then Julius had the perfect gentleman.'

Beulah's eyes narrowed. 'Go on?'

Ellie spoke slowly, telling them about Annie Croxton, what Annie had said the night she'd died, and how it had come to her after that she too, because of the war, could die and miss out on so many things she'd always taken for granted would be hers one day.

Beulah's expression softened during this account. 'I see,' she nodded when Ellie was finally finished.

'I believe every word of that,' Pee Wee stated. 'And what's more I agree with it.'

Beulah glanced at him. 'You do?'

'As Ellie put it, war changes everythin'. Hell yeah!'

Julius came across to stand directly behind Ellie, laying his free hand on her shoulder. 'So what happens now?'

'I'll go and live elsewhere,' Ellie offered. 'That's the decent thing to do.'

'No matter what, you two can't go on sharin' a bed here. Irregardless of the rights and wrongs of this, that's final. Jess would turn in her grave if I allowed it.'

'Your father would go apeshit if he found out,' Pee Wee said to Ellie. 'And the poor guy's suffered enough as it is.'

Ellie, recognising the truth of that, nodded her agreement.

'Can she stay and share my bed if we get married?' Julius asked. 'Providin' she'll have me that is.'

Ellie sucked in a breath; this was the first time marriage had been mentioned. She couldn't think of anything she wanted more.

'What do you say to that, Ellie?' Beulah queried.

'I'd like to be asked properly by Julius if you don't mind.'

Pee Wee chuckled. He liked that.

Beulah held up a hand. 'Just one thing before any proposin' goes on. You absolutely certain, Julius? It's a huge step. And I have to say, no mixed marriage I ever heard of has gone easy. You is coloured after all, an' she's a white woman.'

'I'm certain, Mom. As certain as can be.'

'Then you'd better get on with it. Want Pee Wee and I to leave the room?'

Julius shook his head. 'That isn't necessary.'

Ellie closed her eyes for a brief second as Julius placed his glass on the table.

'Ellie?'

She looked up at him, thinking how handsome he was, and how very much she loved him.

'Will you marry me?'

'Yes.'

'Amen,' Pee Wee commented.

Julius raised Ellie to her feet and kissed her, not too passionately, mindful that his parents were present.

A tear appeared in Beulah's eye which she dashed away. 'Shit, I could sure use a drink,' she declared, and laughed.

'Well, if that don't beat all,' Pee Wee said softly, shaking his head.

When Beulah had been given her drink she and Pee Wee toasted the bride and groom-to-be.

Ellie was positively bursting with happiness. It would

be a good marriage, she knew that beyond any shadow of a doubt.

'Engaged!' Josie Farnham squealed. 'You sly old thing!'

It was the following morning and Ellie had just turned up for work to announce her news.

'And who's the lucky man? I didn't even know there was anyone.'

Ellie explained about her and Julius, though she didn't mention they'd been sleeping together.

'Well, congratulations,' Josie enthused. 'I'm ever so pleased.'

'Maybe you'll be doing the same yourself before long?'

Josie winked. 'Maybe. It's a distinct possibility I'd say. But come on, tell me what your plans are?'

'We don't have any yet,' Ellie replied. 'He only proposed last night. All I can say is it'll be soon.' She was back in her own bedroom, at Beulah's insistence, Julius in his. Torture for the pair of them now used to the same bed.

'And where, church?'

'I haven't had time to think about that. But probably not.'

'Oh?'

Ellie lit a cigarette, her first of the day, and inhaled deeply. 'This might sound silly, but I don't believe it's right with a war on. I know lots of other women disagree, but a Register Office seems more appropriate in my opinion. Also, don't forget I only recently lost my mum, and brother shortly before that.'

Josie nodded her sympathy. 'I understand.'

Ellie pictured Jess and Paul in her mind's eye, a wave of sadness sweeping over her. Yes, it was far too soon for the fripperies of a white wedding.

At least that's what she thought.

'How much!' Ellie exclaimed, shocked.

The jeweller repeated the price he'd quoted.

'It's far too expensive,' she declared to a smiling Julius.

'But you do like it?'

'Of course. It's gorgeous.'

'And it fits without havin' to be resized.'

True, Ellie reflected, turning her left hand first one way and then the other, the large single diamond shooting off sparks of blue and yellow fire. It was the sort of engagement ring she could only ever have dreamt of.

'Let me worry about the cost,' Julius said. Then, to the jeweller, 'We'll have it.'

The jeweller almost purred with satisfaction. 'A wise choice, sir, if I may say so.'

'Thank you.'

She'd be the envy of every woman she knew, Ellie thought. The girls at the station would be pea green with it. She turned to Julius, her eyes ablaze with excitement. 'You're spoiling me.'

The jeweller discreetly looked away.

'And why not? You deserve to be spoilt.'

Ellie kissed him briefly on the lips, her throat tight with emotion.

'And while we're here we'd better get a couple of gold

486

bands,' Julius said. 'It'll save makin' another trip.'

The jeweller reached into the showcase counter to extract several trays of wedding rings, one gentlemen's, the other ladies'. 'Now is there anything here that's suitable,' he smiled, laying the trays before Julius and a somewhat dazed Ellie. Every few seconds she kept glancing at the ring still on her finger, unable to believe it was actually going to be hers. She was absolutely ecstatic.

When that selection had been made the jeweller put each band into a box. When he asked Ellie about her engagement ring she replied she'd continue wearing it, thank you very much, and take its box with her. After which Julius settled the bill in cash.

'Pleased?' he queried unnecessarily when they were outside again.

'What do you think?'

Julius laughed, Ellie slipping an arm round his as they headed for home.

She hadn't told Julius that was the same shop where George had bought his ring for her. If the jeweller had recognised her he certainly hadn't betrayed the fact by so much as even a flicker.

Ellie glanced yet again at her engagement ring. One thing was certain, this one she wouldn't be throwing away.

Not in a million, trillion years.

'I believe congratulations are in order,' Hazel said to Ellie who'd just come up to the bar. Julius had telephoned to say he was going to be late from work and suggested he meet Ellie in The Florence round about eight o'clock. It was now five to. 'Oh, I say, what a corker of a ring!' Hazel oohed and aahed as she examined it. 'Have you set a date?'

'In three weeks' time at the Caxton Hall in Petty France.'

'Good for you,' Hazel beamed. She took Ellie's order, gin and tonic, and made it a large one.

'That's on the house,' Hazel declared, placing it in front of Ellie. 'All the best.'

Ellie thanked her. 'I'm meeting Julius, he should be in any minute now.'

'Smashing bloke. We all like him. You'll make a lovely couple.' She was still amazed at the news of Ellie marrying a black man, no matter how nice he was. She'd been quite shocked when she'd heard.

Ellie had a sip of her drink.

'So, where are you planning to live?'

'Where we are now, with his mum and dad.'

Hazel pulled a face. 'That'll be a bit cramped, won't it?'

'Yes,' Ellie sighed. 'But we'll just have to manage somehow. We're going to put my bed in Julius's room and place them together. It'll be a bit of a squash, I can tell you.'

It would too, Hazel thought, knowing the houses in the street well. 'Why aren't you trying for a place of your own?'

'We'd love to, but how? Anything that comes available in the area goes straight to those who've been bombed out, and rightly. So there's no hope there.'

'What about other areas?'

'Most of them are as bad, people who've been bombed out are given top priority. Besides, if we moved away it would be difficult for me to get to and from work. I could change stations I suppose, but don't want to do that. The girls I'm with are a terrific lot, and if I did transfer stations I'd probably lose my rank.' She paused, then said, 'Mum was proud I'd been promoted. Very proud.'

'We miss her,' Hazel sympathised softly. 'She was one of the best. Salt of the earth.'

A customer further down the bar gestured to Hazel. 'Excuse me,' she said, and moved away.

At which point Julius arrived and the conversation about where they'd be living was forgotten.

'What am I going to wear?' Ellie said to Beulah in despair, the pair of them of course discussing the forthcoming wedding. 'I've just nothing that's suitable. Nothing at all.'

'Then you're goin' to have to buy new,' Beulah declared.

Ellie laughed. 'How am I to do that? I would need clothes coupons don't forget, damn the rationing, and I've nowhere near enough for a dress.'

Beulah's mind was busily ticking over. 'Shouldn't be too much of a problem, hon.'

'How do you make that out?'

'Julius. Speak to him and he'll get what's necessary. OK, he ain't never got no clothes coupons before, at least not that I know, but he should be able to manage the required number. Uncle Sam, Ellie, don't forget he works for Uncle Sam. There ain't nothin' he can't lay his hands on through that Embassy. At least that's how it seems to me.'

Ellie hadn't thought of that. 'What a wonderful idea. If he can get them, will you come shopping with me?'

Beulah's eyes gleamed. 'You just try and stop me. I'll be there with bells on. Hell yeah!'

Later it dawned on Beulah that she was taking Jess's place in all this, doing things for, and with, Ellie that Jess would have done had she still been alive.

She took it as a compliment. Very much so.

Albert laid the letter from Ellie aside and leant back in his chair to think.

He'd had no idea, not an inkling, that something was going on between Ellie and Julius and now this bombshell. For that's exactly what it was.

And why were they getting married in such a hurry? Could Ellie be pregnant? He'd be furious, not to mention bitterly disappointed, if she was. The main thing of course was that Julius was a black man.

He recalled a conversation he'd once had with Jess when he'd been worried Julius was showing an interest in Ellie, a notion Jess had pooh-poohed. It appeared Jess had been wrong.

He thought about Julius and the Postons. A decent, upright family, that couldn't be denied. And damn fine neighbours, none better. Kindness itself. None of which took away from the fact they were black.

What would Jess have said? he wondered, already knowing the answer. She'd have said that if Ellie and Julius

490

loved one another then that was enough and the colour of his skin didn't matter.

Well, maybe it didn't. Ellie was grown up after all, surely she must know her own mind and what she was doing. Anyway, there was nothing he could do about it except disapprove, which would upset Ellie enormously. And that he didn't want.

Albert sighed. He'd put a brave face on it and go to the wedding, Ellie was his daughter after all. If she was happy then that was all that counted. His own misgivings and prejudices didn't come into it. Or wouldn't, as he wouldn't allow them to. Let them make a go of it with him wishing them well.

A black son-in-law! Who'd have dreamt it.

Julius returned to the kitchen after having gone to answer the phone. 'That was Hazel from across the road,' he said. 'She's asked Ellie and me to go over for a few minutes.'

Ellie frowned. 'What for?'

'She didn't say. Just asked us to go over.'

Ellie looked at Beulah, who shrugged. 'I've no idea, honey.'

'Shall we go then?' Julius said to Ellie.

'Just give me a few minutes to get ready.' She came to her feet. 'I won't be long.'

At least half an hour, Julius reflected wryly, and smiled.

'A flat?' Ellie repeated.

Hazel nodded. 'Upstairs. Small, mind you, a bedroom and sitting room and you'd have to share the bathroom with us. That won't bother Harry and me if it doesn't bother you.'

This had taken both Ellie and Julius completely by surprise, the pair of them bowled over by Hazel's offer.

'We had it done out for our daughter you see,' Hazel went on to explain. 'The idea was she'd still be with us but have a section of the accommodation on her own, more than a mere bedroom. Well, as you know, Ellie, she moved out and so it's free. If you're interested that is?'

'We most certainly are,' Julius replied, thinking this was wonderful and solved all sorts of problems. 'How much are you askin' for rent?'

'You'd better see it first. Wait here a moment.'

Hazel vanished out back to return almost instantly with Harry who declared he'd tend to the bar while Hazel showed them round.

Ellie and Julius followed Hazel up a flight of stairs, along a corridor and then into what Hazel announced was the sitting room.

Ellie glanced around, delighted at what she saw. Comfy chairs, sideboard, standard lamp plus other bits and pieces usually found in a sitting room. 'Very nice,' Ellie commented.

'Now the kitchen,' Hazel said. 'I forgot to mention that. There's not much to it but it's adequate enough.'

That contained a cooker, old but serviceable, sink and a food cupboard. As Hazel had said, it was small, a galley type, but adequate.

'You'll have to eat your meals in the sitting room I'm afraid,' Hazel went on. 'We have a spare drop leaf table and chairs we'll move in if you take it. And by the way, don't worry about linen and the like, there's masses of that.'

The bedroom proved to be almost as big as the sitting room, its main feature being a double bed. 'Well away from our bedroom,' Hazel commented with a twinkle in her eye.

Ellie coloured slightly when she realised what Hazel was getting at. She and Julius could indulge themselves without fear of being overheard.

'The one drawback is you hear the noise from the bar below, but you'd soon get used to that.'

'What about comin' and goin'?' Julius queried.

'There's a back door which can be used at anytime. You'd both have a key for it.'

Julius had a sudden thought. 'One thing is I do require a phone so that I can contact the Embassy, or more importantly, they me.'

'That isn't a problem,' Hazel smiled. 'There's the phone downstairs and an extension in our sitting room. You can use either whenever. And if the Embassy ring and either Harry or I answer then we'll just give you a shout.'

Julius turned to Ellie. 'Well?'

'It's ideal.'

'Then we'll take it, Hazel, and can't thank you enough. Consider the apartment let as from this moment.'

'Right, we'll go back downstairs and hammer out the details.'

Hazel was pleased she'd been able to help. Years before Jess had done her an enormous favour, this was her way of repaying it.

'Sir down, Mr Sykes. What can I do for you?'

Albert explained about Ellie's letter and that he intended returning to London for the wedding.

Matron stared at Albert in concern. 'Does that mean you'll be leaving us then?'

'Oh no,' he hastily replied. 'I'll only be gone a few days. There's still a lot of painting to be done.'

A relieved Matron glanced at her watch. 'I usually have a glass of sherry round about now. Would you care to join me?'

'I don't like sherry I'm afraid,' Albert apologised.

'There's scotch as well?'

'Now that I do like.'

Matron smiled as she came round from behind her desk. 'Neat or with water?'

'Neat please.'

'Do you know the young man in question?' she queried as she did the honours.

'Yes, in fact he and his parents are neighbours. They very kindly took my daughter in after . . .' He trailed off, a stricken look coming across his face, and had a sip of scotch.

'I know what happened. I'm sorry,' Matron said softly.

Albert nodded.

'It must still be very painful for you.'

'Yes,' Albert whispered, and had a larger sip.

'Has being here helped?'

He looked into Matron's warm and sympathetic eyes. 'A lot actually. It's been good to get away from . . . well where it happened. It's so peaceful at Huntington Hall, and quiet. And so very different. To be honest, I'm not sure I'm ready to return to Islington yet, but I'll have to for the wedding. I couldn't miss that.'

'No,' Matron agreed.

'But it's going to be hard. I know that.'

Matron could well imagine. 'I'm glad you've come to see me, Mr Sykes. I wanted a word.'

'Oh?'

'I wonder if you'd consider working here as an employee? Doing more or less what you're doing now, including the usual maintenance jobs that are forever springing up. I'd be willing to pay three pounds a week, plus your board and lodging. You would certainly be doing me, and the nurses, a favour if you accepted.'

This was a surprise, Albert thought. 'Do you mean work here permanently?'

'Long term, short term, that would be entirely up to you. I'd be extremely grateful for either.'

'There is an awful lot of painting still to be done,' Albert mused.

'And the outside after the inside is completed, should that come about.'

Matron was studying Albert intently. 'I've been told that you've made friends in the village. Nurse Isaac mentioned that you've become a member of the pub darts team.'

Albert nodded. 'They're a good bunch in the pub. Enjoyable company. We have great fun on the darts nights.'

'So you wouldn't have to worry about the social side of things if you stayed on, that's already taken care of.'

True enough, Albert thought, severely tempted. 'The only trouble is, Matron, I already have a job. I should really go back to that.'

She'd already foreseen this objection, and expected it to be brought up. 'I can easily arrange the necessary medical papers to relieve you of that duty,' she replied.

'You can?'

'Oh indeed.'

Albert was thinking of his mates at the station, still shorthanded with his being away. To duck out entirely wouldn't be fair on them. And what if the heavy bombing started again? Every man jack would be needed.

Albert drained his glass. 'Can I think about it?'

'Of course. Take as long as you wish.'

He placed his now empty glass on her desk. 'I'd better get back to what I was doing.'

'When are you going to London?'

Albert told her.

'I'll arrange transport to take you to the station.'

'Thank you.'

'My pleasure, Mr Sykes. My pleasure.'

Beulah wasn't a fool, they were engaged and had set the date for the wedding after all. Not to mention the fact they'd been sleeping together while she and Pee Wee had been on tour. She'd been young herself once and knew what it was like to be newly in love.

'I'll be goin' to The Chicory House with Pee Wee

tonight,' she announced over breakfast. Then, to under-line the point, 'So don't expect us back till the wee hours.'

Ellie's heart skipped a beat. She wanted to glance at Julius, but didn't in case Beulah noticed and interpreted it.

'Yeah, OK, Mom,' Julius replied.

Beulah smiled inwardly. 'Now you two better hurry up or you'll be late for work.'

Ellie had been going to have another cup of coffee, but now decided there wasn't time. She couldn't wait for the evening to come round; she and Julius would make good use of it.

Albert had knocked off for a bit to go for a walk, one of his favourite pastimes since coming to Huntington Hall. It still amazed him that he, an out-and-out townie, had come to love, and appreciate, the countryside so much.

He was heading for a nearby river, where he often went, to stroll along its banks. Sometimes, if he was lucky, he'd see fish in the water, trout he'd been told. And only the other week he'd spotted an otter, a rare occurrence in these parts one of the chaps in the darts team had informed him.

It was a cold day so he'd wrapped up warm. Snow had been forecast, but so far none had fallen. Snow in a city was a miserable affair, soon turning to slush. But out here it would just lie, a white blanket stretching for miles in every direction. He knew it would be beautiful when it happened.

He began thinking about his conversation with Matron

which he'd been doing on and off since it had taken place. My God, but he was tempted. He'd never felt so physically well in his life since arriving at Huntington Hall, the fresh air like a daily tonic. So different from the fogs and soot-laden atmosphere he was used to at this time of year.

One thing was certain, he didn't have to worry about Ellie any more. She'd be married shortly and starting a new life of her own with Julius, no longer reliant on him, and Jess, as she'd been in the past while growing up. So there was no tie there.

But there was with the station and his mates. He would be letting them down if he was to leave when there was a war on. And what if the raids did resume, as they so easily could? How would he feel, safe and secure in Huntington Hall, while they were out risking their lives? Pretty rotten, that's how.

The main thing he had to do was speak to Danny, find out how things were. He'd already written to Danny and Vera asking to be put up for several nights so they would be expecting him. He'd have the chance to talk then. Find out what was what.

Albert stopped and glanced around. It would be a terrible wrench if he did go back to London to live. He'd miss all this like billy-o.

Ellie lay wrapped in Julius's arms, one hand slowly stroking his flank, the pair of them utterly exhausted after a frantic and frenetic bout of lovemaking.

Julius laughed softly.

'What is it?'

498

'You.'

Ellie frowned. 'What about me?'

'You've certainly become enthusiastic for someone who was still a virgin only a short while ago.'

That made her smile. 'Are you complaining?'

'Not in the least,' he replied hurriedly. 'If anythin', I approve.'

'Good.'

Ellie snuggled up even closer to him. 'If I'm enthusiastic it's because I love you, and can't get enough of you. You make me so very, very happy.'

'And you me, Ellie.'

She sighed with contentment, thinking how lucky they were to have found one another.

They continued to lie like that, neither wanting to move and break the spell of total completeness that had descended on them.

Albert came out of the Angel tube station and stopped to stare around. Here he was, home.

Familiarity was everywhere, buildings, signs, the faces of passers-by. It was like putting on an old and much cherished suit or set of clothes.

No new damage since he'd left, he noted as he walked along Upper Street. That was good. He stopped briefly at a bombed-out run of shops where he and his mates had worked feverishly to put out a raging fire. Memories from that terrible night, one of the heaviest raids, flickered through his mind. Fortunately, he recalled quite clearly, there hadn't been any casualties.

He halted again outside a baker's that Jess had often used, almost seeing her go inside as she went about her daily shopping.

'Jess,' he muttered softly.

Her ghost was also going to be everywhere.

As chance would have it Danny was on the night shift and had already been to bed when Albert knocked on their door. Vera answered, giving him a warm welcome, and hug, before ushering him inside.

'My God, but you're looking well!' Danny beamed as he pumped Albert's hand.

'And I feel it. Huntington Hall has done me the world of good.'

'I'll put the kettle on,' Vera declared. 'You must be tired after your journey.'

'It was a long one,' Albert admitted. 'Though what else can you expect in wartime.'

'Take a seat,' Danny said, and did so himself. 'Now I want to hear all about it.'

Albert spoke at length about Huntington Hall and how much he'd come to love the surrounding countryside. He also mentioned the pub and the fact he played for the darts team.

'And the Matron has offered you a full-time job there,' Danny repeated when Albert had finally finished.

'Can't take it, of course. Have to get back to the station as you're short-handed.'

'Not any more,' Danny replied. 'A couple of blokes have been drafted in from outlying stations to help plus we've been assigned half a dozen auxiliaries, older retired chaps in the main who've come back into the service. So we've got a full complement again, plus some.'

'I see,' Albert mused.

Danny leant forward in his chair. 'Can I say something?'

'Go ahead.'

'You've paid your price for this war, mate. Jess and Paul, a bloody heavy price too. If you want that job at Huntington Hall I'd grab it with both hands if I was you. You've earned it in my book.'

This revelation about numbers at the station changed matters, Albert thought. If he wished he could go back to Huntington Hall with a clear conscience.

'Well?' Danny prompted.

'I'll have to explain to Jess, talk to her, before I make a final decision.'

Danny wasn't sure what to make of that. He glanced at Vera, busy with cups and saucers, who shrugged.

'Go to the cemetery,' Albert clarified.

Albert waited till Beulah had left the room before asking the question that had been worrying him. 'Are you pregnant, Ellie?'

'No, Dad, I'm not.'

Relief washed through him. 'You're not lying I hope?'

'I'm not pregnant, Dad. I swear.'

He sort of sagged where he sat. It had been important to him that she wasn't. To him, and Jess's memory. 'So why the rush to get married?'

'Because we want to. It's as simple as that. There's a war on after all, why waste time?'

Yes, Albert thought. He could understand that. 'I take it you do love Julius, and he you?'

Ellie smiled. 'As much as any two people can love one another. As much as you loved Mum, and Mum you.'

Albert glanced away so she didn't see the expression on his face. 'That's all right then,' he mumbled.

Ellie crossed over and kissed him on the cheek. 'It's going to be a good marriage, Dad, you'll see.'

He believed her.

'Well that's it, Jess. What I want to do.'

A wind was blowing, stirring the flowers he'd laid on the grave. This was the first time he'd been back since her funeral.

He waited patiently, hoping something would happen, that she'd manage to speak to him in some way.

All of a sudden he knew she understood, and approved. He couldn't have explained how he knew, he just did.

'Thanks, girl,' he whispered. 'I miss you terribly.'

And with that he turned and walked away, never looking back.

The ceremony, by special licence, was short and sweet, the appropriate words said, vows taken, rings exchanged. At the conclusion of which they were pronounced man and wife.

Ellie was dressed in a smart navy blue suit that Beulah had helped her choose, her shoes a matching colour. The blouse she had on was cream-coloured with pretty, rounded, lace-edged cuffs and collar. Everyone agreed she looked absolutely smashing.

A surprise awaited Ellie when they emerged into the street in the shape of Pee Wee's trio, who immediately struck up with 'Moonlit Eyes', Julius having told Pee Wee how fond she was of that particular number and that they'd often played it when Pee Wee and Beulah were on tour.

The trio continued to play, much to the delight of passers-by, while photographs were taken, and then the chauffeur-driven Cadillac, loaned to them for the day by the Embassy, purred into view.

Confetti in abundance was thrown as Ellie and Julius got into the car, she radiant with pleasure and happiness, after which the Caddy moved off, the tin cans that had been tied to its rear clattering noisily.

A watching Albert couldn't have been more proud.

It didn't take long for the reception at The Florence to turn into a knees-up. All the old favourites were being belted out on the piano: 'Roll Out The Barrel', 'Maybe It's Because I'm A Londoner', 'The Lambeth Walk', 'I'm Looking Over A Four-Leaf Clover', 'The White Cliffs Of Dover' . . .

There was no shortage of beer, Harry having managed to lay in a substantial supply, while Julius had arranged for several cases of spirits to be delivered from the Embassy.

Josie Farnham, having re-jigged her duty with the SO,

was there, plus other girls from the station. A number of Albert's firemen mates had turned up, though, sadly, not Danny who was on duty. Lots of the neighbours, no invitations required, had come along to join in the fun and wish Ellie and Julius all the very best.

It was in the middle of all this that Hazel appeared at Julius's elbow. 'There's a phone call for you from the Embassy,' she said, having to shout to be heard above the racket.

'Thanks, Haze. I'll be right there.' Julius turned to Ellie. 'It's probably someone calling to congratulate us. I won't be long.'

She kissed him lightly on the lips. 'Don't be.'

'How do you feel?' Albert asked, coming over to stand beside her.

'Terrific. Top of the world.'

He glanced around. 'It reminds me of our reception, your mum's and mine that is. Long time ago now.' For a moment there was a tinge of sadness in his voice when he said that, then it was gone.

When Julius returned to Ellie there was the strangest expression on his face.

'What's wrong?' she instantly demanded.

Instead of replying he held up a hand. 'Ladies and gentlemen, can I have your attention please! I have an important announcement to make.'

Gradually the room fell silent, all eyes on Julius. 'Thank you,' he said at last.

Julius took a deep breath. 'I've just received news that the Japanese have bombed Pearl Harbor, a large American

504

naval base in Hawaii. As from now, the United States is at war on the side of the Allies.'

Eyes popped, mouths dropped open in surprise. This wasn't at all what they'd been expecting to hear. Then, suddenly, pandemonium broke loose as people cheered, clapped and whooped in delight.

'We'll definitely kick Jerry's arse now!' someone shouted.

'God bless the bloody Yanks!' another voice, this one female, cried.

Julius turned to Ellie who was staring at him in astonishment. 'It's true,' he said. 'Thousands have been killed and wounded apparently, many ships sunk. But the important thing is, at long last, we're in the war alongside you British.'

Ellie was sorry for the dead and wounded, but all she could think was that she couldn't have wished for a better wedding present. It was a day to remember. In more ways than one.

Much later, having said his goodbyes, Albert slipped out into Florence Street to stand staring at what remained of the family home. The house where Jess had died, and which held so many memories for him.

Tears were glistening in his eyes when he eventually walked away. He'd be back to visit from time to time, but only to visit. He'd never live in Islington again.

In the morning he'd be catching the train back to Huntington Hall where he'd be telling Matron he was accepting her offer of a job.

505

He smiled when he remembered there was a darts match on the following night. He was looking forward to that.

Little White Lies

To Tam and Angus
my sons
of whom I am extremely proud

Chapter 1

'Sweet Jesus,' Ethne McDougall muttered on her first sighting of Thistle Street. It was a dump, an absolute, and appalling, rubbish-strewn slum. A lump rose in her throat and threatened to choke her.

Ethne's daughter Lizzie, sitting alongside, regarded the street with horror. 'Oh, Ma,' she whispered.

Damn you, Dougal, Ethne inwardly raged. It was because of him they'd been forced to come and live in this hell-hole. She vowed there and then she'd never forgive her husband as long as she lived. Never.

'What's the number?' asked Mr Walker, the haulier who'd brought them and their belongings all the way down from the Highlands to the great ugly urban sprawl that was Glasgow.

'Thirty-four,' Ethne croaked.

Mr Walker flicked the reins and the horse continued on its way, the well-laden cart rattling over the cobbles.

'It's maybe not as bad as it looks,' Lizzie said hopefully to Ethne, trying to kid herself.

Ethne shot Lizzie a glance which said she didn't believe

1

a word of it. If anything, Ethne reflected, it was probably worse.

Two middle-aged women with scarves tied round their heads, even though it was the height of summer, paused in their gossiping to stare curiously at them as they went past.

Lizzie wrinkled her nose in disgust. Thistle Street, like many they'd gone along since entering Glasgow, positively stank, reeking of chimney smoke, body odour, stale kitchen smells, human waste, and God knows what else.

'Here we are,' Mr Walker eventually announced, drawing up in front of number 34. This was his first visit to Glasgow and would certainly be the last, since he thought it was as awful as Ethne and Lizzie did. He couldn't wait to get turned round and out of the place. In truth, apart from loathing the city, he sensed a menacing air about it that frightened him.

A few moments later a smiling Dougal appeared from the mouth of the close which was the entrance to their tenement. 'There you are.' He beamed. 'I spotted you from the window. I was watching out for your arrival.'

Ethne remained silent as he helped her down on to the pavement; nor did she respond to the quick peck he gave her on the cheek.

'It's grand to see you again, lass,' he went on. 'I've missed you somewhat chronic.'

Ethne glanced into his face, and saw the sincerity there. She'd missed him too, but wasn't about to say so.

'So how was the journey down?' he asked.

'Long.'

'Aye, well it was bound to be that. Tomintoul is a long way away.'

2

Mr Walker lit up a cigarette while this exchange was taking place, and sniffed disapproval of his surroundings. The sooner he was out of here the better.

Dougal turned his attention to the hovering Lizzie. 'And how are you, my girl? You look in the pink.'

'Starving, Dad.'

He pulled a face. 'Well, you'll have to wait a wee while longer before we can attend to that. Mr Walker and I have to unload this cart first and get everything upstairs.'

'It wasn't part of my fee to unload as well as load,' Mr Walker protested. 'There was never any mention of that.'

'Oh, see sense, man. I can't do it all by myself. You must have realised.'

'I did nothing of the sort. I was contracted to load the cart and bring it here. Nothing more.'

'If Doogie has to do it by himself with the help of me and Lizzie here then it's going to take a lot longer than if you get stuck in,' Ethne pointed out shrewdly. Mr Walker saw the sense in that, not wanting to stick around Thistle Street for a second longer than he had to.

'For an extra half-crown perhaps?' he tried to bargain.

'Not a brass farthing more, Mr Walker,' Ethne retorted sharply. 'Your so-called fee is daylight robbery as it is.'

Mr Walker gazed up at the towering, to him anyway, soot-encrusted building. 'What floor?' he queried.

'Top.'

Mr Walker groaned. Just his bloody luck! It would have to be that. 'Then let's get started,' he grumbled.

'You and Lizzie go on up. The door's open,' Doogie told his wife. 'Top right hand side.'

'Take something with you,' Ethne said to Lizzie, grabbing hold of a rolled-up rug that was one of her prize

3

possessions. Then she led the way into the dark maw that was the close.

The stairs she and Lizzie climbed were made of grey slate and concave in the middle from years of use. The walls were half tiled, in a cream and brown design that wasn't wholly unattractive. Ethne was convinced she could smell damp.

Sure enough, the door to their apartment was open as Doogie had said, a cheap plate on the front proclaiming the previous occupants had been named Bell. Ethne would soon find out that Glaswegians always referred to such apartments as houses, albeit they were nothing of the sort. This one consisted of a bedroom and a kitchen, the kitchen doubling as a second bedroom. Lizzie stared in fascination at the recessed bed cut into one of the kitchen walls, thinking it looked like a small cave. She didn't have to be told that was where she'd be sleeping. For some reason, maybe because she was fifteen, the idea appealed.

'Filthy,' Ethne declared, stony-faced. And she wasn't exaggerating. God knows how long it had been since the kitchen was given a good clean. She was sure the bedroom wouldn't be much better, and when she went into it she found that to be the case.

Meanwhile Lizzie had crossed to the kitchen window, wondering what the view was like. Her heart sank at the sight of a debris-strewn back court with overflowing bins at the end. What a contrast to the view from their kitchen window in Tomintoul. That had been glorious Highland countryside with the glimpse of a loch in the distance. During winter deer would come down off the hills, often almost right up to the cottage itself. Well,

4

there wouldn't be many deer here – mangy old cats, more like.

Gingerly Lizzie tried the pump at the sink and, to her relief, found it to be working, water gushing forth as she worked the handle.

'What do you think?' Ethne asked unnecessarily, coming back into the kitchen.

Lizzie shrugged, and didn't reply.

Ethne closed her eyes for a few moments, fresh anger bubbling up inside her. If only Doogie hadn't opened his big trap and insulted the laird's wife this need never have come about. But Doogie, drunk as the proverbial skunk, had. And, worse, had done so in front of other gentry, friends of the laird. Perhaps, just perhaps, if witnesses hadn't been present, Doogie might not have been given the sack and told he would never work in that area again, but the friends had been there and the inevitable retribution had swiftly followed. And the laird would not change his mind. It was well known he never did once having taken a decision.

'Are you all right, Ma?' Lizzie anxiously inquired, observing the expression on her mother's face.

'Of course I'm not,' Ethne snapped back. 'And surely it's obvious why. Just look at this place. Just look at it!' She shook her head in disbelief, and for the second time since they'd arrived in Thistle Street tears almost overwhelmed her. She felt such despair as she'd never before felt in her entire life.

'We'll just have to make the best of it,' Lizzie commented sagely. 'That's all we can do, I suppose.'

Ethne took a deep breath and nodded her agreement. The lass was right. There was nothing else for it.

5

At which point a red-faced Doogie and a grumbling Mr Walker struggled into the apartment carrying the kitchen table.

'Thank God that's over,' Doogie wheezed, and sank into a comfy fireside chair. 'I'm whacked.'

Mr Walker, having been paid, had only just left them, having the graciousness to wish them luck before going.

Ethne eyed the kitchen range, thinking there was nothing she could do with that right now as there wasn't any coal or kindling. 'What time do the shops shut round here?' she asked Doogie.

He shook his head. 'Ages ago.'

Lizzie's stomach rumbled loudly and complainingly from lack of food.

'We're going to have to eat something,' Ethne declared. 'I don't know about you, but Lizzie and I haven't had a bite since breakfast. And heaven knows that was only a couple of slices of buttered bread and tea from a dixie.'

Doogie yawned. It had been a hard day at work, on top of which he'd brought up all their stuff, some of it really heavy, from the street. He was well and truly knackered and could easily have fallen asleep there and then.

'There's a chippie just down the street,' he announced. 'I'll give Lizzie money and she can run and get three fish suppers. How's that?'

Ethne couldn't see any alternative. 'That's fine then. Will the lass be all right?'

Doogie blinked. 'How do you mean?'

'She won't be attacked or anything?'

That amused Doogie no end. 'It's Glasgow you're in,

6

not the Wild West. There aren't any Indians lurking about outside waiting to scalp her. She'll be right as rain.'

Ethne still wasn't convinced. 'Are you certain about that? Anybody with half an eye in their head can see how rough it is round here.'

Doogie sighed. 'Take my word for it. It is rough, I grant you, but a lassie, even a single one on her own, is safe enough. A single chap maybe not so much, particularly if he isn't known, but no one will harm a female. They'd probably be bloody murdered if they did.'

'I'm not scared,' Lizzie announced bravely, motivated by hunger more than anything else.

'Good girl.' Doogie fumbled in a trouser pocket to produce a florin which he passed over. 'Now be off with you.'

'You said down the street, Da. Is that to the left?'

'Has to be as you didn't pass it on the way here. Right?'

'No, left,' Lizzie teased, and hurriedly left them.

Ethne stared grimly at her husband as the outside door snicked shut. 'Is this the best you could do?'

Doogie frowned. 'How do you mean?'

'This place. Couldn't you find anything better? I mean, I wouldn't expect pigs to live here.'

He shifted uneasily in his chair, knowing a row was about to happen. A row he'd been fully expecting. 'It was difficult for me to look around, lass, what with being at work all day and everything. Can you understand that?'

Ethne continued staring grimly, and didn't reply.

'It's handy for my job. I've only got about a five-minute walk and I'm there. It's very convenient.'

'Convenient, is it?' she murmured scornfully, resisting the urge to cross over and slap his face.

7

'And the rent's cheap. There was that to take into consideration. I'm not exactly earning a fortune at the steelworks. More or less the same as Tomintoul except there the cottage came with the job.'

He did have a point, Ethne conceded to herself. But even so . . .

'And please don't start on about the laird again,' Doogie begged wearily. 'We've been all through that a thousand times. What happened happened, and there's nothing I can do to change it. I know it was my own stupid fault, which I bitterly regret. If I could turn back the clock I would, only that's not possible. You know how sorry I am.'

Ethne didn't reply, just turned her head away so he couldn't see her expression. She doubted he was half as sorry as she was.

'Now tell me something about the journey down?' Doogie asked quietly, hoping to change the subject. 'All you've said is it was long.'

Ethne took her time in answering. 'It wasn't the most pleasant of experiences, as you can imagine. Camping out at nights under an open sky. Having to go behind a bush or tree to attend to the call of nature. And having to spend all that time in the company of Mr Walker, who's the most miserable bugger you'll ever come across. I'm convinced he kept trying to spy on Lizzie and me when we went to the toilet, especially Lizzie. He's just the kind of sleazy sort to do so.'

'Did you ever catch him at it?'

Ethne shook her head. 'But I'm still certain that was what he was trying to do. Or may even have succeeded for all I know.' She took a deep breath. 'At least it never rained during any of our nights on the road. We were spared that.'

'Well, you're here now, safe and sound, which is all that matters,' Doogie declared, attempting a smile.

Now it was Ethne's turn to change the subject. She was genuinely curious. 'You said in your letters that the hostel you've been staying in wasn't bad. Is that true?'

Doogie decided to be honest. 'No, it isn't. It was terrible. Worse than that. Every night I was surrounded by drunks, homeless and the like.' Despite himself he shuddered. 'I was never more pleased than when I left this morning for good. And that's a fact.'

There was a brief silence between them, then Ethne said in a quiet, somewhat strangulated voice, 'It broke my heart to leave the cottage. To close the door behind me for the last time. We'd lived there all our married life. Brought up three children there. Been happy there. And now . . .' She broke off. 'And now this dump.'

Doogie literally squirmed with guilt, a guilt that had been steadily eating at his insides since he lost his job on the estate, further compounded when he'd arrived in Glasgow and discovered the reality of Scotland's premier city.

'I can't disagree with you there,' he said miserably. 'For that's exactly what it is.'

Ethne bit back an angry retort. 'I'll start to unpack a few of our things before Lizzie returns,' she declared.

And swept from the kitchen.

'Excuse me, didn't you move into number thirty-four earlier?'

Lizzie looked at the girl directly ahead of her in the queue who'd turned and spoken. She nodded.

9

'I saw you arrive. I'm your neighbour, by the way. We live just below you.'

'Really?'

'Aye, that's right. I'm Pearl Baxter.'

Lizzie shook the offered hand, a bit taken aback. 'And I'm Lizzie McDougall.'

'Pleased to meet you, Lizzie.'

'And you, Pearl.'

About her own age, Lizzie judged. Maybe a year or two older.

'You're not from Glasgow, are you?'

Lizzie shook her head. 'How do you know?'

'The accent. A dead giveaway.'

'We're from the Highlands, actually. Banffshire. A place called Tomintoul.'

'Never heard of it. Is it nice there?'

Lizzie's smile was almost beatific. 'Wonderful.'

'So why did you leave?' Pearl queried.

'My father got laid off and there wasn't any other work to be had. He was told there was in Glasgow though, which is why we're here.' That might not be the whole truth, Lizzie reflected, but it was close enough. She had no intention of telling a complete stranger that her da had been sacked. Nor why that had happened.

'That's too bad – your da being laid off, I mean. So I suppose he'll be looking for work now?'

'He came down a while ago on his own and has found a job at Bailey's steelworks. It's me who'll be looking for something next.'

Pearl eyed her speculatively. 'What did you do up there?'

'I milked cows, actually.'

Pearl burst out laughing. 'You did what!'

'Milked cows and helped out with the chickens.'

Pearl was still laughing as they shuffled nearer the counter. 'You won't find many cows round here. At least not the four-legged kind. And the only chickens you'll come across are in the butcher's shop. All nicely plucked and ready for the pot. If you can afford one, that is.'

'What about yourself, Pearl?'

'I'm a machinist. You know, sewing machines? We make clothes. Male, female, children's. You name it. I've been there since leaving school.'

'Sounds interesting.'

'Bloody hard graft, I can tell you,' Pearl replied, serious again. 'But they're a good bunch of women and we have a right laugh at times. As jobs go there are worse.' She suddenly frowned. 'Here, I've just had an idea.'

'What's that?'

Pearl told her.

'You took your time,' Ethne admonished Lizzie when she got back from the chippie.

'There was a long queue, Ma. I had to wait my turn.'

'And you didn't have any trouble there and back?'

'None at all. In fact I came home with someone I met in the queue. Her name's Pearl Baxter and she lives directly below here with her parents.'

Ethne had already laid out plates on the table on which the fish suppers were now deposited. Without further ado they opened the newspaper wrappings and began to eat. Lizzie fell to with a will as she was ravenous. Starving hungry, as a Glaswegian might have said.

11

'This is good,' Doogie commented, half his fish already gone.

'So you've met a friend already,' Ethne said after a while.

Lizzie nodded. 'Who's come up with a suggestion about me getting work.'

'Oh?'

'She's a machinist in a local factory . . .'

'What sort of machinist?' Ethne cut in.

'Sewing machines. They make clothes.'

'I see.'

'Well, Pearl has suggested I go along this Friday and apply for a position as trainee. Apparently they're advertising for a couple.'

'Did she now,' Ethne mused.

'What sort of money do they pay?' Doogie asked.

Lizzie shrugged. 'Pearl didn't mention.'

'And how long does this training take?'

'Until you learn what you have to. Not long, according to Pearl.'

'What do you think, Ethne?' Doogie queried, knowing it was his wife's opinion that counted more than his own. She wore, and always had, the trousers in their family.

Ethne pursed her lips. 'I'm not sure.'

'It would be a bit different to milking cows and looking after chickens,' Lizzie commented, and smiled. 'Pearl thought it a right hoot I used to do that. Said the only cows I'd run into round here didn't have four legs.'

Ethne also smiled, warming to the notion of Lizzie's training to be a sewing machinist. A stroke of luck, really, if it worked out. 'Why Friday in particular?' she asked.

'According to Pearl that's the best day as everyone's in

a good mood with the weekend coming up. She says my chances, and anyone else's, are higher than any other day when things can be a bit fraught. Particularly if they have a big order to complete.'

That made sense to Ethne. 'Would you enjoy that sort of work, lass?'

Lizzie considered that. 'I don't know. What I do know is I must get something soon to bring money into the house.'

'True.' Ethne nodded. They could get by on what Doogie earned, but Lizzie's pay packet had been of enormous help in the past.

'There's no harm in going along to see what's what,' Lizzie pointed out.

Ethne could only agree with that.

'If I'm going I've to meet Pearl outside her house at quarter to eight. The people at the factory start at eight prompt.'

'So this factory isn't far away, then?'

'Only two streets.'

'I think you might have fallen on your feet, lass.' Doogie beamed. 'Lucky for you that you ran into this Pearl. What's her surname again?'

'Baxter.'

'And they live directly below us?'

'That's right.'

Ethne sat back to let her food digest. She was dying for a cup of tea but couldn't make one because the range was out.

Suddenly she was desperately tired. It had been a long, long day.

*   *   *

Doogie rubbed his hands together enthusiastically. 'It's going to be grand sleeping in my own bed again. The ones at the hostel were terrible – hard as bloody nails.' None too clean either, he reflected, but didn't say so in case it put Ethne off. She might imagine he'd caught fleas or something, which he hadn't, he'd checked.

'It will that,' Ethne agreed. Sleeping on the ground hadn't been much fun either.

Doogie went to her and took her into his arms. 'You've no idea how much I've missed you, girl. It's been a trial right enough.'

A trial that need never have come about if he'd only kept his big yap shut, she thought bitterly.

'Have you missed me at all, Ethne?'

'A little bit,' she conceded.

'Only that? A little bit?'

'I'm dead beat,' she prevaricated.

'Don't change the subject, woman. Only a *little* bit?'

There was that tone in his voice which she recognised of old, telling her what this was leading up to. Well, she was having none of it. He could go fly a kite as far as she was concerned. With a practised movement she squirmed free.

'Ethne?'

'What?'

'I thought . . .'

'Yes, I know what you thought,' she interrupted, her tone steely. 'And you're wrong.'

'Please, Eth?'

'No. You can forget about that.'

'But it's been so long,' he pleaded. 'I'm absolutely rampant.'

'I wouldn't care if you were the bloody Lion Rampant itself. There'll be none of that this night.' Nor the next or the next, she vowed. Not the way she felt about him.

'You're being cruel,' he accused.

'Am I?'

'You know you are.'

'I know nothing of the sort, Dougal McDougall. All I do know is I want to sleep.'

'It won't take long, lass.'

She almost laughed to hear that. Of course it wouldn't; it never did. 'I said no, and meant it. All right?'

Doogie sighed deeply, and his shoulders slumped. 'If that's what you want.'

'I do.'

Suffer, Doogie, she thought as she began undressing. And judging from his expression he was.

Lizzie lay tucked up in her 'little cave' as she'd already begun to think of the kitchen's recessed bed. It was certainly comfortable, she reflected. And somehow comforting, too, being enclosed on three sides. Fortunately for her she wasn't in the least claustrophobic.

Through the dividing wall she'd heard her parents arguing, or so it had sounded. But it had fallen silent now and she presumed they'd gone to bed.

What was life going to be like in Glasgow? she wondered. She shivered a little at the prospect, the great unknown that lay in front of her.

How she wished she was back in Tomintoul, working and living in the peace of the estate. She missed her older brothers Gordon and Stuart, whom they'd left behind, who also worked for the laird. Most of all she missed wee Mhairi, Gordon's six-year-old daughter. Mhairi had been a great favourite of hers.

She just had to put the past out of her mind, she told herself. Remembering would only bring misery and discontent. For better or worse she lived in Glasgow now, horrible place that it was. She simply had to accept that and get on with it, though it was hard.

Hard indeed.

The next day Ethne answered the door to find a smiling woman roughly her own age standing there, a bucket at her feet.

'Hello. I'm Mrs Baxter from below. I've brought you this pail of coal to tide you over till the man comes tomorrow.'

How very kind, Ethne thought. And the coal a right blessing.

She introduced herself and then invited Mrs Baxter in, apologising for the state of the house.

'Why don't you come down to me instead and have a nice cup of tea?' Mrs Baxter suggested. 'And I've just baked a sponge cake you might like to try.'

It was the beginning of an enduring friendship that would last through the years.

Chapter 2

'If you sit here I'll get you started. I'll send someone over in a moment to explain things,' Mrs Lang, the supervisor, said. She smiled encouragingly. 'Don't be put off by the din and clatter. You'll soon get used to it.'

'Thank you, Mrs Lang,' a nervous Lizzie replied, thinking she'd never heard such a racket. There were at least a hundred sewing machines on the go at the same time, plus other machines whose functions she had no idea of.

A few minutes later Pearl joined her. 'Surprise. They've picked me to teach you as we're pals. Isn't that a stroke of luck?'

Lizzie nodded, thankful for a friendly face amongst a sea of unknown ones of all ages.

Pearl sat down next to Lizzie. 'I know it looks complicated, but it isn't really. I'm sure you'll soon get the hang of it. At least the simpler stuff, anyway.'

Lizzie wasn't certain about that at all.

'The main thing is not to be afraid of the machine,' Pearl counselled. 'I know I was, which was stupid really. Got that?'

Lizzie nodded again.

'Right, pay attention. And don't be afraid to ask questions about anything you don't understand.'

Lizzie's brow furrowed in concentration as Pearl began explaining what was what.

'So, how did you get on?' Ethne demanded anxiously when Lizzie arrived home that dinner time.

'All right, I suppose.'

Ethne didn't like the sound of that. 'What do you mean, you suppose?'

'Exactly that, Ma. I've only been there a few hours, don't forget. There's a lot to take in.'

Ethne began doling out a plate of mince and potatoes. 'How long do you have, an hour?'

'That's right.'

Ethne placed the plate in front of Lizzie. 'Then get that down you. There's also bread and butter, as you can see.'

Lizzie started to eat, although she wasn't all that hungry thanks to the butterflies still fluttering in her tummy.

'One good thing is I've got Pearl to teach me,' she declared between mouthfuls.

'Whose idea was that?'

'The supervisor's. A Mrs Lang. She's rather nice, actually, and well respected there. So Pearl told me.'

'Uh-huh. And what about the factory itself?'

'Huge. And very noisy.' Lizzie suddenly laughed. 'A lot different to Tomintoul, and that's a fact.'

'But you'll be able to cope?'

'I think so, Ma. It'll just take a bit of getting used to, that's all.'

'Have you found out what the pay is yet?'

Lizzie told her.

'Well, that's fair, I should say. More than you earned on the estate.'

'They sometimes go on what they call piece work,' Lizzie explained. 'That's when instead of a weekly wage you get paid by each piece of work you do. It only happens occasionally, though, when they've got an extra large order they wish to rush through. Pearl says the machinists go like the absolute clappers when that happens as they can make extra money to what they normally earn.'

Just then Doogie arrived in from the steelworks. 'It's only me!' he announced.

'I can see that,' Ethne replied sarcastically, dishing out a second plate as Doogie plonked himself on to a chair.

'So how's it going, Lizzie?' he inquired, giving his daughter a beaming smile.

'Fine, Da.'

'Don't you go bothering the lass. She's just been through all that with me. She's managing well enough.' Ethne let out an exclamation as she set the plate in front of Doogie. 'That looks painful,' she declared, indicating a small but nasty-looking burn on his hand.

'My own fault. I got careless and that's what happened,' he replied cheerily enough.

'Is it sore?'

'A bit.'

'Do you want me to put a bandage on it?'

Doogie laughed. 'Course not. I wouldn't be able to work if you did that. No, just leave it. It'll heal soon enough.'

'Hark at the hero!' Ethne retorted scathingly, making a

19

mental note to get something from the chemist's that afternoon to put on the burn later. She could see his point about the bandage but she was damned if she was going to let the burn turn septic on him. He wouldn't be able to work then either.

At the end of the hour Lizzie was back at her machine with Pearl continuing the instruction. Gradually what Pearl was explaining to her was beginning to sink in.

'And this is Mrs Wylie who lives across the landing from me,' Dot Baxter declared, introducing Ethne to a small, white-haired woman.

There were five of them in Dot's kitchen for tea. Dot and Ethne, of course, Mrs Wylie, Mrs Millar and Mrs Carmichael. The introductions now complete, Ethne took a seat while Dot busied herself at the range.

'We get together like this every week for tea and a good old natter,' Babs Millar informed Ethne. 'I hope you'll be joining us on a regular basis.'

'That would be lovely. I'd be delighted to.' What a friendly lot, Ethne thought. Having neighbours like these was going to make life a great deal easier.

'Mind you, we all try but none of us can bake like Dot here,' Jean Carmichael confided. 'I certainly can't come anywhere near what she so effortlessly turns out.'

'Hush, you lot,' Dot admonished. 'You're embarrassing me.' She had indeed gone slightly pink, and everyone laughed.

'You're down from the Highlands, I believe,' Babs Millar said, turning back to Ethne. 'It must be quite a change for you here.'

'A total change, in fact. I've never lived in a city before.'

'I've never lived anywhere else,' Jean Carmichael declared. 'I certainly couldn't imagine staying in the country. All that peace and quiet would drive me mad.'

'Oh, it's lovely,' Ethne enthused. 'But then, it's what I was brought up to.'

'Ethne's daughter Lizzie is working with my Pearl,' Dot chipped in. 'Doing well, too, from what I understand.'

'I worked at the same factory for a while, some years back,' Chrissie Wylie informed Ethne. 'But I had to give it up on account of my hands.' She held them out and Ethne saw they were twisted and bent, the joints swollen. 'Arthritis,' Chrissie said sadly, staring at them.

Ethne pulled a sympathetic face. 'How awful for you.'

'The doctor says they'll never get better. That I'm stuck like this for the rest of my life.'

'She's a martyr to them,' Jean Carmichael stated softly. 'Aren't you, Chrissie?'

Chrissie nodded.

'We all take turns helping her on washday,' said Babs Millar. 'Trying to be good neighbours, like.'

There was something in Babs's voice which told Ethne she was supposed to volunteer to help as well, so she did.

'That's kind of you,' Chrissie beamed. 'I can't thank you enough.'

The looks of approval on the other women's faces informed Ethne she'd not only done the right thing but had been accepted into their circle. That pleased her enormously.

'Do you know the latest about Helen McQuillan two closes down?' Dot queried, pouring boiling water into her teapot.

21

'She's in the family way again,' Jean Carmichael piped up. 'I heard yesterday.'

'And her already with eight weans,' Dot commiserated.

'She's worn down to the bone as it is,' Chrissie commented, shaking her head. 'God knows how she'll cope with another.'

'Catholics, you see,' Dot explained to Ethne. 'Well, that says it all.'

'Someone should have a word with that Billy,' Babs sniffed. 'Tell him to leave the poor soul alone. He'll have her in her grave if he's not careful.'

Dot and Chrissie nodded their agreement.

'Or more than a word,' Jean declared, making a slicing motion.

Everyone present, with the exception of Ethne who thought it an horrendous idea, burst out laughing.

As the tea progressed, so did the local gossip. By the time she left Ethne had gained a deal of information about the street she'd come to live in.

Doogie decided to take a few moments' breather and stopped what he was doing to lean on his shovel. How he hated this place, he reflected as he gazed about him. The great furnaces belching flame every time they were opened, the rivers of slow-moving molten steel, the terrifying guillotines that could still make him jump when they banged home. Sweat was literally dripping off him as it did throughout his working day, having to be continually replaced with never-ending cups of water.

He couldn't help but think back to Tomintoul and

what his life had been like on the estate. Idyllic, in retrospect. He'd have given virtually anything to be back there doing his old job.

He wished with all his heart he'd never gone to those bloody Highland Games, or got as pissed as he had. Seconds, that's all it had taken: seconds for his life to be for ever transformed.

'You stupid fucking fat cow!' he'd yelled in pain when the foot had crunched down on his. The words out before he'd realised who the culprit was. The laird's wife.

He'd apologised instantly, and profusely, of course. Grovelling, almost. But the damage had been done, and was irreparable. You simply didn't call the laird's wife a stupid fucking fat cow, no matter what the circumstances, and get away with it.

The sack had followed next day, along with the rider from a still furious laird that he'd never work in the area again. The laird's word being law in those parts, he hadn't even bothered trying to find another job. After talking it over with Ethne and friends, he'd decided that Glasgow seemed the best bet and they'd ended up in Thistle Street, and where he was now.

Doogie sighed and ran a hand across his sopping brow, feeling extremely sorry for himself. One mistake, that's all it had taken, for his whole world to be overturned in the most calamitous way.

Out of the corner of his eye he caught sight of the gaffer watching him, and immediately resumed shovelling. Back-breaking work that he wasn't used to even yet.

One thing, though. He smiled. The laird's wife's face had been a picture. Poncy, stuck-up bitch that she was.

Oh aye, a picture right enough. Just remembering her outrage made him want to laugh.

Except the aftermath was no laughing matter.

'Where the hell have you been!' Ethne exploded the moment Doogie arrived in from work. It was gone nine o'clock and he should have been back hours ago. The nice tea she'd made him was ruined and long since in the bin.

'I've been to the pub with the lads,' he slurred.

'I can smell that.'

Lizzie dropped her eyes, intending to get out of there as soon as possible. She had no wish to witness yet another row between her parents. There had been too many over the years.

Doogie slowly shook his head. 'You don't understand, darling.'

'Don't *darling* me!'

Lizzie stood up. 'I'm just going downstairs to see Pearl. I won't be long.' She hurried from the kitchen and out of the door.

Doogie hiccuped.

'Look at you, pissed as a lord. A disgrace. That's what you are, Dougal McDougall, a disgrace. And I'm thoroughly ashamed of you.'

Doogie crossed over and slumped into his favourite chair. 'Can I explain?'

'What's to explain? It's pay night so you've gone off to the pub and spent God only knows how much of your wages.' She had murder in her heart as she glared at him.

'They asked me,' Doogie further slurred.

'So? You've got a tongue in your head, haven't you? You could easily have said no.'

24

'The point is, they asked me, Ethne. They've never done that before.'

She hesitated, beginning to sense there was more to this than perhaps met the eye. 'I'm listening,' she said in a softer voice.

Doogie took a deep breath, trying to clear his head. He shouldn't have had that last dram, he told himself. Most unwise, as he'd known at the time. But it would have been hard to refuse without being insulting.

'Ever since I started at Bailey's, I've been an outsider,' he stated slowly, trying to choose his words with care. 'They're all Glaswegians there, you see, and I'm not. I'm not one of them.'

Realisation was beginning to dawn. 'Go on,' she urged, voice even softer now.

'They call me the teuchter, the Highlander. And not in a complimentary way either, but as if they see me as some sort of inferior. Some sort of slow-witted idiot.'

Ethne pursed her lips, her anger towards Doogie fast disappearing. 'Do they indeed,' she almost hissed.

'It's teuchter this, and teuchter that. Mostly taking the piss. And they're always making fun of my accent.' Doogie closed his eyes for a moment, recalling the many jeers and taunts that had come his way over the past weeks, simply because he was different. Not like them.

'Bastards,' Ethne muttered between closed teeth, wishing those men were here right now. By God, she'd have given them a piece of her mind. A slow-witted idiot! Her Doogie might be many things, but he was never that.

'So why did they ask you to the pub?' she queried.

'I don't know. Honestly I don't.'

'Were they nasty?'

He shook his head. 'Not to my face, anyway.'

'So why?'

'Maybe they've begun to accept me. One or two of them were even quite friendly. There again, it might have been out of pity.'

'Pity!' That made her furious. The last thing Doogie needed was pity.

'Or it might have been their conscience. Perhaps they were trying to make amends.' He sighed. 'At least they got to know me better, and that's something, hopefully.'

Ethne had had no idea what had been going on at the steelworks, since this was the first time Doogie had spoken about it. It enraged her he was being picked on.

'It's the typical Lowlander's conception of the Highlander,' Doogie muttered. 'Not quite the full shilling.'

Ethne snorted. How wrong they were. The Highlander was just as sharp as anyone else; simply had a more relaxed way of going about things. A different philosophy from that of the average Lowlander.

'You see now why I had to go, Ethne? I thought it for the best. That it might ease things at work.'

'What you did was right, Doogie,' she conceded.

'And you're not angry with me any more?'

She had to smile. His expression was that of a little boy pleading for forgiveness. 'Not any more,' she assured him.

His relief was almost palpable. 'Thank God for that.'

Her smile widened, her forgiveness complete now that she understood. Tenderness crept into her, that and the love she had for him, stormy though the relationship might have been down through the years. 'Are you hungry?' she asked.

He nodded. 'I could eat a bite or two.'

'Well, I'm afraid your tea's in the bin.'

His face fell. 'Oh!'

'But I have some nice fresh eggs. Do you fancy an omelette?'

'An onion one?' he queried hopefully.

She laughed. 'If you wish.'

'That would be just the dab, Ethne.'

'Then I'll make it for you. Just you don't go to sleep in the meantime. Hear me?'

Doogie, smiling also, nodded. 'I hear you, woman.'

Teuchter, Ethne thought as she busied herself. An expression of contempt. She swore in Gaelic, of which she was a speaker. The men at Bailey's might well have blushed if they'd known what she'd called them.

Something a lot worse than teuchter.

Lizzie was amazed, and overawed, as she and Pearl walked along Sauchiehall Street, one of Glasgow's main arteries. 'The shops are just incredible,' she declared.

'Enjoying yourself?'

'Not half. I just wish I had money to spend in some of these places.' She gazed about her, marvelling at the crowds of people to-ing and fro-ing. Thousands of them, it seemed. What a busy, bustling city Glasgow was. So different from what she was used to.

They stopped in front of a dress shop to stare at what was on display. All manner of fabrics, cuts and styles. To Lizzie's eyes the window was dazzling. The last thing in chic.

'Hello, Pearl. Out to treat yourself?'

The speaker laughed, thinking that amusing.

'Oh, hello, Jack. What are you doing in town?'

Jack winked. 'That would be telling, eh?'

Pearl indicated her companion. 'This is Lizzie McDougall, our new neighbour. Lizzie, this is my cousin Jack White, commonly known as Whitey. He also works at the factory.'

Lizzie was taken aback. 'As a machinist?' Surely that was women's work.

'No, daftie, Jack's a mechanic. If your machine goes wrong then he comes along and fixes it. That right, Jack?'

'That's right.'

'I've never noticed you there,' Lizzie said, thinking him possibly the handsomest young man she'd ever seen. He certainly knocked spots off any of the lads in Tomintoul. By a long chalk.

'I'm around,' he replied, with a smile that made her stomach flip over and turn to jelly.

'So, who are you winching nowadays?' Pearl queried, using the Glasgow expression for courting.

Jack tapped his nose. 'Wouldn't you like to know?'

'A secret, huh?'

'Could be.'

'In other words you're seeing more than one lassie at the same time and don't want them to find out about each other?'

'As if I'd do such a thing!' Jack exclaimed, pretending innocence.

'It's me you're talking to, Jack. I know what you're like. You'll do anything if you think you can get away with it.'

'All lies,' Jack countered, continuing to pretend innocence.

'My arse,' Pearl riposted.

'And a lovely one it is too, dear cousin. I've always thought so.'

Pearl blushed bright red. 'Get on with you!'

'I'm very misunderstood. Particularly by Pearl here,' Jack protested to Lizzie.

'Understood, more like,' Pearl admonished him. 'But anyway, where are you off to?'

'A pub for a drink. Want to come?'

'You know we can't, Jack. We're both under age.'

'Ah, so you are!' His eyes were twinkling. 'No matter. There's a little pub not far from here with a snug which isn't totally overseen by the bar. If you sit there and I order the drinks, who's to know what's what?'

Lizzie was alarmed. She'd never been in a pub, far less drunk much alcohol. Pearl turned to her. 'What do you think?'

'I haven't got much money on me. About one and three is all.'

'No need to worry about that,' Jack enthused. 'I'm in the chair.'

Lizzie presumed that meant he was paying.

'Well?' Pearl pressed.

'Do you want to go?'

Pearl shrugged, affecting indifference. 'Why not?'

It would be something of an adventure, Lizzie thought, suddenly keen. One thing was certain: her mother had better not find out or there would be all hell to pay.

'Let's have a bash then.' She smiled.

29

'That's my girl.' Jack laughed and, taking each by an arm, guided them on their way.

The snug when they entered it was dark and gloomy. The smell that hit Lizzie's nostrils was an overpoweringly male one, a combination of beer, spirits and unwashed bodies.

Sure enough, as Jack had promised, there was a dog leg, containing table and chairs, not overlooked by the bar, and there Lizzie and Pearl sat.

'So, what's it to be?' Jack queried.

Lizzie looked to Pearl for help, not having a clue what to order.

'A gin and orange, please,' Pearl replied, adding quickly, 'If you can afford it, that is.'

Jack was amused. 'Of course I can. And what about you, Lizzie?'

'The same, please.'

'Coming right up.' He headed for the bar.

'Well.' Pearl smiled. 'This is a turn up for the book.'

It certainly was, Lizzie reflected. 'Have you been in a pub before?' she asked quietly.

'A couple of times. You?'

Lizzie shook her head.

'What do you think?'

'I'm not sure yet.'

Pearl gazed about her. 'It's not all that impressive, I have to admit. But exciting, eh?'

Lizzie had to admit it was.

'So tell me, what do you make of Jack?'

'He's gorgeous. Absolutely gorgeous.'

A look of concern came over Pearl's face. 'Don't you

go falling for him now. He's a real heartbreaker, that one. And, I'll say it even if he is my cousin, callous as they come where women are concerned. Anyway, he's far too old for the likes of you.'

That flustered Lizzie. 'I just mentioned he was gorgeous, that's all. You can't deny it.'

'Oh, he's that all right. And oozes charm into the bargain. He could charm the knickers off a nun if he had a mind to. And you'd better believe that.'

Lizzie regarded her friend quizzically. 'I take it you don't like him very much, then?'

'Quite the opposite. I adore Jack. But that doesn't mean I'm not aware of what he is.'

'How old is he, anyway?'

'Twenty, twenty-one coming up, I think. He started at the factory straight from school and has been there ever since.'

Lizzie smiled. 'He's got lovely eyes. I've never seen ones such a pale blue before.'

'He's got the eyes of the devil . . .' Pearl broke off when Jack appeared at the table carrying their drinks.

'Here we are then,' he declared, placing a glass in front of each of them. He disappeared again to the bar, coming back a few moments later holding a pint.

'Slainte!' he toasted, raising his glass.

Lizzie responded in further Gaelic, which astonished him.

'She's Highland,' Pearl explained. 'All the way down from Tommy something or other.'

'Tomintoul,' Lizzie elaborated.

'Well well,' he murmured. 'Are they all as pretty as you up there?'

'Jack!' Pearl warned him.

'What?'

'Don't start your nonsense.'

'What nonsense? I only said she was pretty. That's hardly a crime.'

Pretty? Lizzie had never really thought of herself as that. She certainly wasn't plain or ugly. But pretty? A warm glow filled her to think it might be true.

Jack produced a packet of twenty cigarettes. 'Lizzie?' he queried, offering it to her.

'No thank you. I don't smoke.'

'Pearl?'

'Please.'

'I didn't know you smoked,' Lizzie commented as Pearl lit up.

'Only occasionally. Sometimes I buy a single in the newsagent's, other times a packet of five. Can't afford more on my wages.'

Jack turned his pale blue eyes on Lizzie. 'Why don't you tell me about this Tomintoul you've come from? I'd love to hear.'

They spent half an hour in the pub during which Jack heard all about life in Tomintoul and the Highlands in general. He appeared fascinated.

On the way home Lizzie bought some peppermints so Ethne wouldn't smell alcohol on her breath. She couldn't remember the last time she'd enjoyed herself so much.

Chapter 3

Ethne arrived back at the close mouth, having been out going the messages, as Glaswegians called it, to find a huddle of women there. 'What's going on?' she asked Dot Baxter.

'It's Chrissie Wylie. She's fallen over and hurt herself. Broken something, they think. We're waiting for the ambulance to arrive.'

'Dear me,' Ethne breathed.

'She managed to crawl to the door and shout for help. It was Babs Millar who heard her and sent for the police. Chrissie was in a right state, apparently.'

This was shocking news. 'Is she still upstairs?'

'Oh aye. Babs is with her, and a policeman. They've done all they can to make her comfortable.'

Just then a bell could be heard ringing, and moments later an ambulance drew up. Two grim-faced men, one carrying a stretcher, emerged and went hurrying inside.

'I hope she's going to be all right,' a concerned Ethne muttered.

'We'll just have to wait and see.'

Jean Carmichael, with Mrs Edgar who also lived up the close, came over. 'Terrible business, eh?'

'How did it happen?' Ethne asked.

'God knows.'

'Someone said she was pulling herself up out of a chair when her hands gave way and she pitched over. At least that's what I was told,' Mrs Edgar informed them.

Ethne knew that Chrissie lived alone, but no more than that. She wondered what had happened to the husband, or if he was dead. She must ask Dot.

'Excuse me, ladies!' an ambulance man called out, and the gathered women immediately parted to make way for him and the stretcher he and his colleague were carrying.

Chrissie, her face milky white and screwed up with pain, glanced at them as she went past. 'Look after Sandy for me, Dot,' she pleaded.

'Don't worry about him, Chrissie. I'll see he's all right.'

'Who's Sandy?' Ethne queried as Chrissie was being taken aboard the ambulance.

'Her cat. A big ginger tom. You must have seen him about.'

Ethne had, and thought it a most unfriendly animal. It had hissed at her on the one occasion she had attempted to stroke it. 'I've seen it,' she acknowledged, her voice betraying she wasn't overly enamoured. Dot glanced at her.

Bell ringing again, the ambulance pulled away. The women watched until it had vanished from sight.

'If it isn't one thing it's another,' Mrs Edgar commented sagely, shaking her head.

'Aye, it's never quiet for long round here,' Jean Carmichael agreed.

The crowd began to disperse, some returning up the stairs, others up and down the street.

'I'm going to have a cup of tea. Would you like one?' Dot asked Ethne when they reached her door.

Ethne didn't have to be asked twice. 'That would be lovely.'

They went into the kitchen where a grateful Ethne placed her heavy shopping bag on the floor. 'Can I help?'

'No, just take a chair. I won't be a tick.'

Ethne's legs were killing her, though she couldn't think why. She hadn't been out very long, or walked that far. 'Can I ask a question, Dot?'

'Of course.'

'What happened to Mr Wylie?'

'Was in the army and got killed during the Zulu wars.' Nearly thirty years ago, Ethne thought, the current date being 1906. 'And a sod of a man he was too.'

'Oh?'

Dot glanced over at Ethne from the sink where she was filling the kettle. 'Didn't treat her at all well. Drunk and stone cold sober. Chrissie hinted once that he was funny where his rights were concerned.'

That was a new one on Ethne. 'His rights?'

'You know, in the bedroom.'

'I see.' She frowned. 'How do you mean, funny?'

'Well, he got up to all sorts that most normal men wouldn't, if you get my meaning. But don't ask me to be specific, for I can't. Chrissie only hinted, that's all. And it was a long time ago.'

Ethne wasn't shocked to hear that. She knew such things went on, though thankfully not with her Dougal.

35

He was as straightforward as could be. Boringly so at times if she was honest.

'Are there any children?'

'They were never blessed. Chrissie lives on her army pension now. It isn't much, but she manages to scrape by like most of us. Though making ends meet on that pittance must be hard.'

'It's not a lot, then?'

'She told me once. And it's not a lot. Still, she's only got herself to look after. Herself and Sandy, that is. She adores that cat, which is understandable I suppose. It's the only company she's got, apart from us up and down the close, that is.'

Ethne thought how awful it must be not to have children. What an emptiness inside Chrissie must feel. She'd been lucky with three, two strapping lads and Lizzie, all as healthy as could be. And feckless as Doogie might be at times he was a good man at heart. Yes, she had a great deal to be thankful for.

To her delight Dot produced a chocolate cake which turned out to be as scrumptious as it looked.

Mrs Lang laid down the garment she'd been inspecting while an anxious Lizzie looked on. 'Very good, Miss McDougall. I'll say this for you, you're a quick learner.'

Lizzie blushed at the praise. 'Thank you, Mrs Lang.'

'Do you feel confident in what you're doing now?'

'More or less. There are still a few things I have to stop for a few moments and think about. But more or less.'

Mrs Lang liked that honest reply. 'Right. That being the case you can start as a qualified machinist Monday morning.'

'Oh, Mrs Lang, thank you.' Lizzie beamed.

'Full wages as from that time, of course. I'll notify the pay clerk this afternoon.'

Full wages! Lizzie was ecstatic. She'd now be able to make a full contribution to the running of the house. Needless to say Ma would be pleased.

'Carry on then,' Mrs Lang instructed, and moved away.

Lizzie glanced over at Pearl and caught her friend's eye. She gave Pearl the thumbs up, and Pearl's face broke into a broad smile when she realised what Lizzie was telling her. She gave Lizzie a thumbs up in return.

A qualified machinist as from Monday, Lizzie reflected happily as she continued with her work. She felt like jumping to her feet, punching the air and giving a loud yell of triumph.

'We're going out,' Ethne declared to Doogie on Saturday afternoon. 'So get yourself ready.'

'Out?'

'That's what I said. Out. We're off to the shops.'

Doogie groaned. Shopping was anything but his cup of tea. In fact he downright loathed it. 'Do I have to come, Eth?' he pleaded.

'You most certainly do. I need you to carry the tins of distemper we're going to buy.'

He didn't like the sound of that at all. 'Distemper?'

'What are you, a parrot who repeats everything I say? Yes, distemper. You're going to do our bedroom tomorrow. Heaven knows it could use a couple of coats. It must be years since it was last done.'

Doogie knew she was right. The bedroom screamed out to be tarted up. He glanced down at the gleaming

lino that covered the kitchen floor, completely transformed since they'd taken over. You could have eaten
your breakfast off it now. And the lino wasn't the only
thing to have benefited from Ethne's housekeeping skills.
The whole kitchen sparkled and shone, bright as a new
penny.

'What colour did you have in mind, then?' he asked.

'Yellow. Any objections?'

He shook his head.

'Well, get a move on then. We haven't got all day.'

He shuffled his feet, wondering if this was a good time
to broach the subject. 'Ethne?'

'What now?' she snapped, expecting an excuse for not
being able to go with her. Well, one thing was certain:
she was damned if she was going to carry heavy cans of
distemper. That was a man's job.

Doogie cleared his throat. 'Don't you think it's high
time we called a truce?'

'Truce?'

She was his wife, and they had had three children
together, but that didn't stop him being embarrassed.
'About you know what.'

Ethne smiled inwardly. 'What?' she replied, feigning
ignorance.

He shuffled his feet some more. 'Are you going to
make me say it?'

'I assure you, Doogie, I haven't the faintest idea what
you're on about,' she lied.

In common with his kind, Doogie hated having this
sort of conversation with a woman, even his wife. It just
wasn't done. Ribald banter with other men was fine, but
intimate discussions with women were taboo.

'The ban you've put on things, Eth.'

She was enjoying watching him squirm. It was a treat. 'And what things are these?'

He cleared his throat. 'You know?'

She didn't reply to that, merely looked puzzled.

'Since you arrived here.'

She felt like laughing, but didn't.

'Oh, come on, Eth,' he suddenly blurted out. 'Stop acting daft.'

'Am I?' she teased.

'You must be. You understand what I mean all right.'

'Do I?'

'Of course you damn well do.'

He was totally discomfited now, she noted. 'I must be thick then. Why don't you spell it out?'

'Bed, woman,' he muttered, breaking eye contact. 'What we do in bed.'

She couldn't resist it. 'Sleep?'

'No, dammit! The other things.'

She pretended the penny had just dropped. 'Oh, that!'

'Yes, that,' he retorted angrily.

'Are you saying you want your rights again?'

He was flummoxed. 'Rights?'

'It's a Glasgow expression I've picked up. It means sex between man and wife.'

'Bloody hell!' he muttered.

'Is that what this is all about?'

Doogie nodded.

Ethne studied him. Truth was, she was missing it as much as he, though she'd never have admitted it in a million years.

'Well?' he demanded.

39

'I'll think about it.'

'Ethne?' he begged.

'I said I'll think about it. Now are you going to get ready for the shops?'

That night she relented, and it was a happy Doogie who shortly afterwards fell asleep.

Ethne was smiling when she too dropped off.

Lizzie stopped what she was doing and looked up when Jack came to stand beside her machine, those mesmerising pale blue eyes boring into hers.

'I hear congratulations are in order.' He smiled.

Her stomach turned over and then melted into jelly. 'Thank you.'

'I understand you learned more quickly than most. I overheard Mrs Lang saying how impressed she was.'

Lizzie didn't know what to reply to that, so kept her mouth shut.

'We must have another drink some time. Would you like that?'

Lizzie nodded.

'Then we'll arrange it. All right?'

'Pearl too, of course,' she stuttered, completely fazed by his suggestion.

Jack's smile widened. 'She doesn't have to come along. Only if you insist.'

'I think it best she does.'

Jack glanced around. 'I'd better get back to work. They don't like me talking to the girls. Unless I'm fixing their machines, that is.'

There was another smile, and then he was strolling away.

It was a good five minutes before Lizzie could again concentrate on what she was doing.

'I'm warning you, don't get involved with him,' Pearl cautioned on the way home from work. 'He's a heart-breaker through and through.'

'But I did say I wanted you along,' Lizzie protested.

'Hold on a minute.' Pearl stopped and lit a cigarette from the packet of five she'd bought the previous day. She drew the smoke deep into her lungs, and sighed. 'That's better,' she declared after exhaling.

'He caught me off guard,' Lizzie explained. 'Asking me to go for a drink came straight out the blue.'

Pearl eyed her friend as they continued walking. 'Have you had much experience of chaps? I mean real experience.'

Lizzie frowned. 'How do you mean?'

'Have you ever had one feel your tits, for example?'

Shocked, Lizzie went bright red. 'No, I have not. Have you?'

'Oh, a few times,' Pearl admitted vaguely.

Lizzie digested this. 'Was it nice?'

'Of course it was nice. Why wouldn't it be?'

That confused Lizzie, who'd never have allowed a lad to do that to her. If he'd tried he'd have got a good slap for his trouble. That was how she'd been brought up.

'You're not going to get all holier than thou on me, I hope?' Pearl queried, eyes glinting with amusement.

Lizzie shook her head.

'Good, because it's perfectly natural. The lads expect something out of you other than just a kiss. At least round here they do. What about Tommy what's it called?'

'If it does happen I've never heard of it. But don't forget, they're very religious up there, Pearl. The ministers preach real fire and brimstone stuff. Put a foot wrong, even the slightest bit, and you're damned to everlasting hell. Or perdition as they call it.'

'Really?'

'Really,' Lizzie confirmed.

Pearl thought about it. 'It probably does go on, it's just that nobody talks about it, or admits anything,' she said at last. 'I don't believe they're any different to Glasgow folk. People are people wherever they are, hell-threatening ministers or not.'

Lizzie wondered what it would be like to have a lad feel her breast. She'd never thought about it before.

'I'll tell you something if you keep it to yourself.' Pearl winked.

'I will.'

'Promise?'

'I promise, Pearl.'

'I let a lad inside my knickers once. And a right old grope he had too. It was lovely.'

Lizzie wasn't just shocked, she was stunned by this admission. She'd have been even more so if Pearl had further confided that the lad had been her cousin Jack.

'Well?' Pearl demanded, her tone daring Lizzie to be critical or condemnatory.

'Where did you do that?' Lizzie asked instead.

'The back close, late at night when it was dark. That's where a lot of courting takes place round here.' The back close was the enclosed area leading from the close itself into the back green, or yard, where the bins were. There was never any lighting there, hence its popularity with courting couples.

It sounded most uncomfortable to Lizzie. And not only sleazy, but degrading too. There again, she reminded herself, she'd had a completely different upbringing from the likes of Pearl, who was a typical Glasgow 'slummie'.

'The one thing you must remember,' Pearl went on, 'is that what people say in public and then do in private can be two entirely different things. People, especially women in my opinion, are born hypocrites. Never forget that.'

Lizzie couldn't imagine that applied to her mother. Ethne was as straightforward as could be. Wasn't she?

'Anyway, getting back to Jack,' Pearl continued. 'Take my advice and stay well clear. He's one who certainly wouldn't be content with a simple kiss.' She suddenly laughed. 'By God and he wouldn't!'

'How's Sandy?' Chrissie Wylie demanded when Dot and Ethne came to stand by her bedside on their first visit to the hospital.

'He's absolutely fine, Chrissie. Though missing you, that's obvious. I think he's wondering what's going on.'

Chrissie sighed with relief. 'I knew I could rely on you, Dot. You're a good neighbour.'

Chrissie looked dreadful, Ethne thought. She seemed to have lost weight, and dark rings had developed under her eyes.

'He's eating all right, I take it?' Chrissie went on.

'Every scrap I put down. There's nothing wrong in that direction,' Dot assured her.

'So, how are you feeling in yourself?' Ethne asked.

'Terrible. It's no fun having a broken hip, I can tell you. The pain's awful.'

'Are they giving you anything for it?'

'Oh aye. And a heavier dose in the evening to get me through the night. Even then it doesn't always work and I lie here hour after hour, counting the minutes. Waiting for dawn to come up and my first cup of tea.'

'Any idea when they'll let you home?' Dot inquired.

'None at all. But it will be some while; they've warned me of that.'

'We've taken it in turns to go in and clean the house,' Dot informed her. 'Though there's not a lot needs doing when it's empty. Dusting mainly.'

'That's kind of you all.' Chrissie smiled. 'I can't thank you enough.'

'That's what friends are for,' Dot declared. 'You'd do the same if it was one of us lying here.'

Chrissie knew that to be true.

Ethne and Dot stayed for nearly half an hour, until a nurse rang the handbell to indicate that visiting time was over and they had to leave.

'You will come again?' Chrissie asked anxiously. 'Although there are plenty of folk around I get lonely for a familiar face.'

'We'll be back, that's a promise,' Dot replied, squeezing Chrissie's hand.

Chrissie's eyes were glistening with tears when Dot and Ethne took their leave. She only wished they could bring Sandy with them next time, but of course that was impossible.

* * *

Lizzie couldn't help herself. She kept glancing over at Jack, who was mending a nearby machine which had broken down earlier.

How impossibly good-looking he was, she thought dreamily. Quite the most gorgeous man she'd ever seen. She couldn't help but wonder what it would be like to be kissed by him. Kissed and other things.

Suddenly he was staring straight at her, his face breaking into the now familiar smile. He gave her a wink before returning to the task in hand.

Lizzie swallowed hard and got on with her own work.

'Is that another burn!' Ethne exclaimed as Doogie washed his hands at the sink.

She went over to him and had a look at his arm. This burn was far larger than the previous one.

'Before you ask, yes, it hurts like buggery,' Doogie declared.

'Were you careless again?'

He nodded. 'You just have to be so careful in that place. Lose your concentration for a moment and this sort of thing can happen.'

'Do the other men get hurt as well?' she queried with a frown.

'All the time. It goes with the job.'

This was worrying her. 'Badly?'

He thought about that. 'Not since I've been there.'

Ethne examined the burn again, noting it wasn't only larger than the last, but deeper, and as a consequence would take longer to heal. She'd put something on it after they'd had their tea.

* * *

45

Lizzie was coming out of the toilet cubicle when suddenly she was pounced on by another girl. Her eyes started in surprise and fright as she was slammed against a wall.

'I want a word with you, bitch,' her assailant snarled, face contorted with hate.

'About what?' Lizzie managed to gasp.

'My fella Whitey. You keep your big mitts off him. Hear?'

It took a few seconds for Lizzie to remember that Whitey was Jack's nickname. She opened her mouth, but couldn't think what to say.

'You hear, bitch?'

'I haven't tried to get my mitts on him.'

'Lying cow. I've seen the way you look at him. Giving him the big come on. Well he's mine, understand. And when something's mine I'll fight to keep it.'

Lizzie had been unaware that Jack had a special girl-friend. Pearl couldn't have known or she'd have surely mentioned it. One thing was certain: whatever the situation, she didn't like being manhandled like this. 'Let me go,' she ordered.

'Or what?' the other girl sneered.

'So we can talk about this. There's obviously some sort of misunderstanding.'

'Misunderstanding my fucking arse. You leave off, missy, or take the consequences.'

Lizzie suddenly pushed the girl who, taken off guard, stumbled backwards.

'Why, you . . .'

Lizzie hadn't been brought up with two older brothers for nothing. She'd long since learned to give as good as she got, and she was also far stronger than she looked.

She swayed sideways when a punch was thrown at her face, and retaliated with a punch of her own which caught her antagonist on the cheek.

The girl howled, her expression one of incredulity. 'I'll get you for that,' she hissed and launched herself at Lizzie.

Lizzie knew that if the larger girl got her in a bear hug she'd probably come off worst, so she managed to dance out of the way, punching her assailant again, this time on the nose, in the process.

The girl came up short as blood spilled down her front, staining her overall. Clutching her nose she stared malevolently at Lizzie, for the first time thinking Lizzie might not be the pushover she'd expected. What she saw in Lizzie's eyes convinced her that to continue the fight was a bad idea. The strength of character, resolve, and determination there unnerved her somewhat.

'Just you keep away from Whitey. That's all,' she spat.

Lizzie didn't reply, but backed away till she was at the toilet door.

It was with relief that she walked back on to the factory floor. Only then did she allow herself to relax, and found she was trembling slightly.

That had been a nightmare, she thought. A complete nightmare. She prayed Mrs Lang didn't find out she'd been fighting, even though she hadn't been the instigator, in case she got the sack.

'I know who that is,' Pearl declared after Lizzie had described her attacker. 'She's called Scary Mary. A right nutcase.'

'Is she Jack's girlfriend?'

47

'I shouldn't think so. Jack wouldn't have anything to do with the likes of her. I'd put money on it. Unless of course he's scraping the bottom of the barrel.'

'Why Scary Mary?'

'Because she's just that, scary. A complete bampot. A fruitcake. The stories about her are terrible.'

'In what way?'

'Some of the things she's supposed to have done. And just the way she is.' Pearl regarded her friend in admiration. 'And you actually bloodied her nose?'

Lizzie nodded.

'Good for you. I'd never have thought you had it in you.'

'I'll tell you something.'

'What?'

'Neither did she.'

Pearl found that hysterically funny, and they both fell about laughing. At the same time, Pearl acknowledged a new-found respect for Lizzie. Anyone who could take on Scary Mary and walk away the victor was someone to be reckoned with.

Chapter 4

'Going out with Scary Mary! Don't be ridiculous,' Jack exclaimed, completely bemused.

'Well, she seems to think you're her boyfriend,' Pearl informed him.

'And you believed her?'

'It wasn't me she told. It was Lizzie.' And with that Pearl recounted what had occurred in the ladies' toilet.

Jack let out a long, slow whistle of admiration. 'Lizzie did that?'

'She did.'

'Well well well,' he mused. There was more to Lizzie McDougall than met the eye. A lot more.

'Have you ever taken Mary out?'

'Never. But I have to say she's been after me for quite a while now. It's there on a plate if I wanted it.'

Him and every other man, Pearl thought cynically. From all accounts Mary wasn't exactly choosy. Though in Jack's case she was at least showing some taste.

Jack shook his head in amazement. 'And Lizzie actually bloodied her nose?'

'It was all round the factory afterwards. You must have heard something?'

'Not me. Not a word.'

'Mary claimed it was an accident, but I put the record straight after Lizzie told me. She's quite the little heroine now, Mary being such a bully and all. There were many delighted to hear she'd been given her comeuppance.'

Jack smiled at the thought. He tried to visualise the fight in his mind, and simply couldn't. At least not with Lizzie coming off the better.

'What's this about you asking Lizzie out, anyway? She says you did and then never came back on it.'

'I didn't bring it up again because of you,' Jack explained. 'She wanted you to tag along. And where would the fun be in that?'

Pearl regarded her cousin thoughtfully. Truth was, she fancied him dreadfully, but he was her cousin. She also knew only too well what he was like: a philanderer through and through. A womaniser of the first degree.

'You stay away from her, Jack. She's a decent girl. Not for the likes of you.'

'Is she indeed?' he teased.

'Yes, she is. Besides, she's far too young for you. You'd be robbing the cradle.'

He couldn't resist it. 'The way you put it makes her sound almost irresistible.'

Alarm flared in Pearl. That was the last thing she'd intended. My God, how men's minds worked at times!

He saw the anxiety on her face, and laughed. 'By the by, who are you seeing at the moment?'

'No one,' she admitted.

'Dear me. No offers then?'

50

Pearl sniffed. 'Oh, I get those all right. But not from anyone I particularly want to go out with at present,' she lied.

'Pity. They don't know what they're missing. Do they, Pearl?'

She blushed furiously, knowing exactly to what he was referring. The time she'd let him inside her knickers. 'That's a rotten thing to say, Jack White.'

'Oh, don't worry. I've never told anyone, nor will I. I'm very discreet.'

'I should hope so.'

He could see how discomfited she was, which amused him. 'Your reputation's safe with me. You can count on it.'

They stopped outside Pearl's close. 'I'll be going on up then,' she declared.

'Aye, you do that.'

Despite herself, she was still blushing. Lizzie was right, she reflected. He was such an incredibly handsome bugger. Too handsome for his own good.

'Give my regards to Lizzie.' He smiled. 'Tell her I was impressed by what she did.' He paused, then added softly, 'You can also tell her there's absolutely no truth in what Scary said about being my girlfriend. None at all.'

Pearl glared at him. 'Just remember what I said about Lizzie, that's all.'

Jack was laughing as he continued on his way.

Ethne answered a knock on the front door to find Dot standing there. Judging from Dot's expression something was wrong.

'Have you seen Sandy?' she asked anxiously.

51

Ethne shook her head. 'Not for days.'

'Damn,' Dot muttered. 'He's usually there waiting for me when it's time to feed him, but there's no sign.'

'Have you called for him out the back court?'

'Twice now, and he hasn't turned up.'

Ethne thought for a moment. 'Perhaps we should both go and have a look together? Go through all the back courts. He's bound to be around somewhere.'

'That's a good idea, Ethne. It's kind of you to help.'

'Don't mention it. I'll just get a coat and then I'll be right with you.'

'I hope nothing's happened to him,' Dot said as they hurried down the stairs.

'I'm sure it hasn't. He'll turn up soon enough. You wait and see.'

They searched for nearly twenty minutes, but Sandy was nowhere to be found. Eventually they gave up and returned to their close.

'I don't know what else we can do,' Dot declared, shaking her head.

Neither did Ethne. Chrissie's reaction didn't bear thinking about if something untoward had happened to her beloved cat.

'I'll knock your door after tea and if he still hasn't appeared then we'll go round the back courts again,' Ethne proposed.

'You're a pal,' Dot replied, giving Ethne's arm a squeeze.

In the event their further tour of the back courts was as futile as the first. It seemed Sandy might be missing.

Later that night, when Lizzie was already in bed and asleep, though Doogie was still up, Ethne sat at the kitchen table and reread the letter from Stuart that had arrived in the morning post. She read it slowly, drinking in every word.

When she had finished she momentarily closed her eyes, picturing Stuart as she'd last seen him, and whom she missed dreadfully. She missed Gordon and his family, too.

'You all right, Eth?'

She glanced over at Doogie, whose fault all this was. Because of him she'd been wrenched away from all she knew and loved to be dumped down in a totally alien environment. Because of him her whole life had been turned topsy turvy, and not for the better either.

'Eth?'

'I'm just missing Stuart, that's all,' she said quietly.

Guilt flashed across Doogie's face. 'I know. Me too.'

'And Gordon. Everyone up there. Sometimes when I think about them, and Tomintoul, it physically hurts.'

Doogie dropped his gaze to stare at the floor. 'If I could turn back the clock, I would, Eth. I'd give my right arm to be able to do so. It hurts me too, you know. Perhaps even more knowing it was my doing that landed us here.'

Tears filled Ethne's eyes and she began to silently weep, a great wave of misery and sadness engulfing her. If only they *could* turn the clock back. If only they could.

Doogie wondered if he should go to her and take her into his arms, but decided not to in case he was rebuffed. 'I think we should go to bed,' he suggested instead.

'Aye.'

'A decent night's sleep will do you the world of good. Things will look brighter in the morning.'

53

Would they? She doubted it. But by the morning she'd have control of herself again.

'If you go on I'll turn out the mantles,' Doogie said, coming to his feet.

Ethne stared at him through a curtain of tears. He was basically a good man, she reminded herself. Even if he did have his faults. But then so too did she. More than enough.

'And don't expect . . . not tonight,' she said huskily.

He nodded that he understood.

'I simply couldn't . . .'

'It's all right, Ethne,' he interjected. 'I'll leave you alone.'

'Thank you.'

She stood up, and sniffed. A glance at the bed recess told her Lizzie remained fast asleep. At least she still had her daughter with her, she reflected. That was something.

'Do you think we could go back for a visit sometime?' she asked in a cracked voice.

'It wouldn't be easy. But maybe we can manage it.'

'Sometime soon?'

He knew there was very little likelihood of that. Not because of the laird, but all the other factors. The money, and lost income, it would cost. Getting there and back again. All sorts of things. 'We can try,' he prevaricated.

Ethne gave him a grateful smile, and then walked slowly, shoulders drooping, from the kitchen.

When she was gone Doogie tended to the gas mantles, plunging the room into darkness. Then, with a heavy heart, he went through to join his wife.

*　　*　　*

54

Lizzie shivered. She and Pearl were on their way to work, and the weather had turned cold and windy. 'It's bitter out,' she declared, and shivered again.

'You should be used to the cold coming from where you do,' Pearl commented.

'I am. But it's a different kind of cold. Drier somehow.'

'That's the Clyde for you. It puts moisture in the air.'

Girls and women were coming from all directions, congregating on the main factory doors. Some of them were laughing and joking, others giving off a resigned air at the prospect of another day at their machines.

Lizzie was suddenly aware of one of them glaring in her direction. Scary Mary, who else? Lizzie decided to simply ignore her.

'Morning, ladies!' a cheery voice rang out.

A beaming Jack fell into step beside them. 'And how are we this morning, eh? All bright-eyed and bushy-tailed, no doubt?'

Lizzie caught him glancing in Scary's direction, and guessed he'd already been aware of Scary's glaring at her before he joined them. Well, if it had been his intention to upset Scary, he'd certainly succeeded. Her look now was one of sheer hatred.

'You're such a charmer, Jack.' Lizzie smiled at him.

'Why, thank you.'

'I didn't mean it as a compliment.'

'No?'

By now Pearl had also spotted Scary and realised what Lizzie was thinking.

'No, I didn't.'

'Why don't you just move on ahead, Jack, before you cause further trouble,' Pearl suggested.

'Trouble? What sort of trouble?'

'The scary kind.'

But Jack didn't move on ahead. He was enjoying himself too much. And so the three of them went into the factory together with Mary following on behind.

'That man would cause uproar in a mortuary,' Pearl commented to Lizzie as they hung up their coats.

If that incident was anything to go by then Lizzie could only agree.

'You'll have to go to the doctor with that,' Ethne declared. Despite her ministrations Doogie's burn simply wasn't healing. On the contrary, it had started to suppurate.

'No fears,' Doogie replied, jerking his arm away from her. 'It'll be all right.'

What was it with men and doctors? Ethne wondered. You almost had to drag them there.

'Besides, think of the cost,' Doogie added in a bad-tempered mutter.

Ethne knew how to handle this. She'd frighten him into it. 'Suit yourself,' she replied airily. 'Don't go.'

'Don't worry, I won't.'

'Fine.'

She waited a few seconds before going on in the same airy tone: 'As long as you realise you could lose that arm. And then where would you be?'

Doogie paled. 'Lose the arm?'

'Well, it's suppurating, and if that's not attended to it could easily lead to blood poisoning. And if you got that, losing an arm would be the least of your problems. You could end up dead.'

He swallowed hard. 'You're having me on?' he queried hopefully.

'I'm nothing of the sort. Blood poisoning can be deadly. And I'm told it's a horrible way to die. Extremely painful, from all accounts.'

Doogie swallowed again. This put an entirely different complexion on matters. 'Are you sure it won't heal by itself?'

'Not when it's started to suppurate it won't. It'll just go from bad to worse with you eventually having to see the doctor, by which time it might be too late.'

'I'll go tomorrow night then,' Doogie reluctantly agreed.

Ethne glanced at the clock. 'You'll go tonight. There's still time. So get your jacket and skedaddle.'

Doogie was about to argue, then thought better of it. Ethne had fair put the wind up him. Lose an arm – end up dead! She was right, as usual. The sooner he saw the doctor the better.

'I'm on my way, lass.'

Ethne was sitting waiting for him when he returned. Lizzie was downstairs with Pearl. 'Well?' she demanded.

Doogie held up a bandaged arm. 'The doctor said I did the correct thing in going. Left a bit longer and it could have turned very nasty indeed.'

Ethne gave a small grunt of satisfaction.

'I've to take a week off work, which he's given me a sick note for. I've also got a jar of ointment to be applied twice a day with a change of bandage. He wants to see me again on Friday.'

Doogie handed Ethne the jar of ointment. She removed the lid and smelled the contents, pulling a face when she did.

'Horrible, isn't it?' Doogie smiled.

'It doesn't matter what it smells like as long as it does the trick. Now, would you like a cup of tea?'

'I'd love one.'

'So sit yourself down and put your feet up while I stick on the kettle.'

A week off work without wages, he reflected. Still, it couldn't be helped. They'd manage somehow. Ethne would see to that. And at least they'd have Lizzie's money coming in.

That night he woke up in a cold sweat, having been dreaming that a surgeon was cutting his arm off with a huge, evil-looking saw.

Ethne heard a commotion down in the back court and, glancing out of the kitchen window, saw some of the neighbours, including Dot, gathered there. Wondering what was going on she decided to join them and find out.

'Oh, Ethne, it's terrible,' Dot greeted her. 'The binmen found Sandy when they were here just now. He'd been battered to death.'

A sick feeling gripped Ethne's stomach. 'But who on earth would do such a thing?'

'The youngsters round here are quite capable of that,' Babs Millar said with a sad shake of the head.

'Aye, it was probably some of them,' Dot stated grimly. 'They've got up to a lot worse in the past.'

Ethne was appalled, and not for the first time wondered about this place where she and her family had come to live.

'Little swines, so they are,' Jean Carmichael muttered.

58

'They cut the tail off a dog once. Remember, Dot?'

Dot nodded that she did.

'The problem is,' Mrs Edgar, whose first name was Edwina, said slowly, 'who's going to tell Chrissie?'

They all looked at one another, none of them wanting to volunteer for the task.

'It'll break her heart,' Babs Millar prophesied.

Dot took a deep breath. 'It had better be me. She asked me to take care of Sandy, after all.'

'At least she can't blame you for the cat's death,' Edwina pointed out. 'It had nothing to do with you.'

'Nothing at all,' Jean agreed.

'If you like I'll come with you to the hospital,' Ethne said to Dot. 'I think you'll need a bit of support.'

Dot's relief was obvious. 'Oh, thanks, Ethne. It's awfully good of you.'

'What happened to the body?' Ethne queried.

'The binmen took it away in their cart,' Babs Millar informed her.

Ethne grimaced. 'I don't think we should tell Chrissie that. It would only make matters worse. I suggest we dig a hole before she comes home and pretend it's a grave. We could even put a little wooden cross with Sandy's name on it. That would please her.'

'I'll get my hubby Ron to do that,' Dot declared. Ron worked in a local coalyard.

'So when will we go?' Ethne asked Dot.

Dot considered. 'How about tomorrow? The sooner we get it over and done with the better.'

'Tomorrow then,' Ethne agreed.

Doogie, who'd always had a great fondness for animals, was outraged when she told him. Battering a poor cat to death for no other reason than the sport and enjoyment of it was beyond his understanding. It was lucky for them he hadn't been around to catch them in the act.

Bloody lucky for them.

'I never want to go through anything like that ever again,' Dot declared as she and Ethne emerged from the hospital. 'The poor woman was beside herself.'

'At least we spared her the truth about Sandy's death,' Ethne replied. They had decided to lie and say Sandy died a natural death. The others in the close would uphold the story for Chrissie's sake.

'What a state she was in,' Dot went on. 'At one point I thought she was going to have a heart attack.' She stopped and turned to Ethne. 'I'm in such a state myself I could use a drink. Do you fancy one?'

Ethne was taken aback. A drink at this time of day! She wasn't against alcohol, far from it. But so early! 'I don't know,' she demurred.

'Oh come on, keep me company. I need something after that.'

Ethne had heard how rough Glasgow pubs were, and that decent women on their own rarely went into them. It just wasn't done.

As though reading Ethne's mind, Dot said, 'There's a wee hotel not far from here with a nice bar. I've been before, and it's very pleasant and relaxing.'

'Just the one then,' Ethne agreed, not wanting to disappoint her friend.

'And I'm paying, so don't worry about that.'

Just as well, Ethne thought. Money was tight that week with Doogie off work.

The hotel bar was everything Dot had promised. Ethne sat herself on a comfy chair while Dot went up to the bar to place their order.

Ethne glanced about her, noting the heavy flock wallpaper and thick pile carpet. She smiled to herself, thinking what a contrast it must be to the Argyle Arms which Doogie frequented. His description of it wasn't at all attractive or complimentary.

'Here we are,' Dot declared, setting a whisky and lemonade in front of Ethne. 'Just what the doctor ordered.'

'I had an idea on the way here,' Ethne announced after she'd had a sip.

'And what's that?'

'Why don't we find a kitten to give Chrissie when she gets home? It wouldn't replace Sandy, of course, at least not to begin with. But maybe eventually it would.'

'I think that's a grand idea,' Dot enthused. 'It shouldn't be too hard to find a kitten. I'll put the word round and see what comes up.'

'Another ginger tom perhaps, if we can find one. But if we can't it'll just have to be whatever.'

Ethne enjoyed her drink, but refused another when Dot offered it. Perhaps it was her Calvinistic background, but alcohol at that time of day just didn't seem right.

Though she had to admit, the whisky did ease the pain of their visit to Chrissie a little.

Ethne peeled away the last of the bandage to reveal Doogie's burn. It was Thursday, and he was due to see the doctor again next morning.

'Well?' he asked anxiously.

61

'It's definitely on the mend. Not nearly as angry as it originally was.'

Doogie sighed with relief. 'Do you think I'll be signed off tomorrow?'

Ethne knew how desperate he was to get back to work and start earning again. 'To be honest with you, Doogie, I doubt it. I'd imagine he'll want you off another week at least.'

Doogie's face fell. 'Do you really think so?'

'I do. It's on the mend but far from healed. Is it still painful?'

Doogie thought about lying, then decided not to. Ethne always saw right through any lie he tried to tell her. 'A bit. But not as sore as it was.'

Ethne reached for the jar of ointment and began applying its contents. The ointment was clearly far stronger, and more effective, than the one she normally used.

'You're as good as any nurse.' Doogie smiled at her.

'Get on with you!'

'No, no, I mean it, woman. You have a tender touch.'

That pleased Ethne enormously, especially coming from Doogie who wasn't known to be lavish with his praise. 'Then thank you.'

His expression suddenly became serious. 'Can I say something?'

'Depends what it is.'

'I'm glad I married you.'

The simple statement left her staring at him in astonishment.

'Are you glad you married me, Ethne?'

Her astonishment turned to confusion, and she quickly averted her eyes. What a question to ask!

He was frowning now. 'Well?'

'Of course I am,' she replied hastily.

'You don't sound too sure about it?'

She continued bandaging, her mind racing. Truth was, she didn't really know the answer. Was she glad?

'Ethne?'

'I don't see things as black and white as you do, Doogie. Women are far more complicated creatures. You certainly exasperate me at times. Make me angry too. But you're a good man at heart, I'll not deny it.'

'That doesn't answer the question,' he pointed out. Then, in an abrupt change of mood, 'Well, even if you aren't, I'm glad about you.'

She could tell she'd hurt him deeply, and felt ashamed. It was just that he'd caught her on the hop.

'I am glad, Doogie,' she said in a tiny voice. 'Please believe me.'

He immediately brightened. 'No regrets then?'

'I wouldn't go that far. Not after what you said to the laird's wife which meant we had to leave Tomintoul and come here. But basically, yes I'm glad.'

With that she tied off the bandage and stood up feeling quite shaken inside.

He smiled contentedly at her back as she began washing up some dirty dishes at the sink.

Lizzie came awake wondering what had disturbed her. Then she heard it, a soft moaning overlaid by the creak of bed springs.

Her face flamed in the darkness when she realised what she was listening to. Her mother and father were 'at it'.

This was the first time she'd ever heard them, her room in Tomintoul not being in such proximity to theirs. What surprised her most was that they still did such a thing. She'd have thought them far too old for that.

She couldn't help herself, but lay listening for a few more minutes until, eventually, the moaning and bed springs fell into silence.

Well well, she thought, beginning to feel drowsy again. Well well well.

When sleep reclaimed her she dreamed that Jack was in bed with her, whispering lovely things in her ear.

And not only that, either.

Chapter 5

Christmas wasn't all that far away, Ethne reflected as she busied herself preparing tea for Doogie and Lizzie, who were due home shortly. She'd have to start thinking about that.

She paused in what she was doing as it struck her that this would be their first Christmas in Thistle Street, and the first without her sons. Stuart had still been living with them the previous year, and Gordon, with his wife Sheena and wee Mhairi, never let Christmas go by without at least calling in. She bit her lip as sadness washed through her.

The outside door clicked shut, and when she turned it was to confront a pale-faced Doogie clutching a bottle of whisky. She frowned on seeing the latter, but then noticed that Doogie's expression was strange in some way. She watched as, without greeting her, he walked over to where the glasses were kept, selected one, opened the bottle, poured himself a hefty measure, and downed it in a single gulp.

'What's wrong, Doogie?' she asked quietly, for something clearly was.

65

Without answering he poured himself another large measure, and saw off half of that.

It suddenly struck her he might have been sacked, and this his reaction to it. 'Doogie?'

'There was an accident at work this afternoon, Eth. A man got killed.'

Her hand went involuntarily to her mouth. 'Dear God,' she whispered.

'And I saw it happen.' His shoulders slumped, and then began to shake. 'It was terrible, Eth. He was . . . he was . . .' He broke off and drank what remained in his glass.

'Why don't you sit down?' she suggested.

'Aye, I'll do that.'

He took the bottle and glass with him when he crossed to the table already set for the meal, and poured himself another dram.

'Do you want to talk about it?'

Doogie took a deep breath, then another. 'I'd just stopped for a breather when one of the chains carrying an overhead bucket snapped and tipped the bucket over. The chap was standing directly below and never had a chance. He looked up just in time to see the molten metal heading straight for him. You've never heard such an agonised scream as when it hit.'

Ethne, eyes starting from her head, was listening in absolute horror.

'He went up in flames, like a match that's been struck. Whoof! Just like that. Then he sort of dissolved as the metal ate through his body. There was nothing recognisable left of him in the end.'

Ethne swallowed hard. 'Did you know him?'

'Oh aye. He was one of those call me teuchter. John something or other.'

Tea was forgotten now as Ethne came to sit facing her husband. No wonder he'd brought back a bottle of whisky, she thought. She wouldn't say a word if he drank the lot.

'He was married, I understand,' Doogie went on. 'Two children, someone said. Both young.'

'How far away were you?' Ethne asked quietly.

'Far enough not to be hit when the metal sprayed on contact with the floor. I was lucky.'

'Were other men hurt?'

'A few. They're in the hospital now being attended to. One of them got it in the chest and is in a bad way, apparently. He could die as well.'

Ethne closed her eyes and prayed he wouldn't.

'The one who got hit in the chest is an older chap due up for retirement soon. He's worked at Bailey's man and boy.'

When Doogie tried to pour himself more whisky his hand was shaking so much he spilt it over the table. 'Look at me. Look at the bloody state I'm in,' he croaked.

'It's understandable after what you've been through.' Ethne rose, wiped the table clean, then topped up his glass a little, replacing what he'd spilt.

'You know the worst thing, Eth?'

'What's that?'

'I've got to go back there tomorrow.'

She had no answer to that. None at all.

'Are you awake, Doogie?'

There was no reply.

'I know you are. I can tell.'

'I'm awake.'

'I thought you were.' She paused, then said sympathetically, 'Is it the accident?'

'I keep seeing it in my mind again and again. The chain snapping, the metal falling, that awful, blood-curdling scream, then him going up in flames.'

'Oh, Doogie,' she whispered, and pulled herself closer in order to clasp his hand.

'It could have been me, Eth. It could have been. It could have been any one of us. John was just unfortunate to be where he was at the wrong time.'

Ethne thought of John's wife and children. What were they going through, particularly the wife? It didn't bear thinking about.

'You try and get some sleep, girl. There's no use the pair of us lying here staring at the ceiling.'

She knew that to be true, but how could she when he was feeling like this?

'Eth?'

'What, darling?'

'Would you be ashamed of me if I cried? Would you think me less of a man?'

'Of course not.'

'Because I think I'm going to.'

She placed an arm round his neck and drew him down to her breasts. 'You go ahead, Doogie. Just let it come.'

'Oh, Eth,' he whispered, voice cracked and riven.

She held him like that for the rest of a long, long night.

Ethne went to the door with him, which she didn't normally do. Lizzie had already left for work. 'Will you be all right?' she asked.

Doogie nodded. 'I'll just have to be, I suppose.'

'I'll be thinking about you.'

He tried to give her a smile which didn't quite come off. 'I'll be fine, I promise.'

She kissed him on the cheek. 'Ta-ra then.'

She watched him as he walked down the stairs. He didn't glance back as he turned the corner and was lost from view.

It was a sombre Ethne who closed the door again.

'I'm only surprised there haven't been more fatal accidents at Bailey's,' Dot declared. 'The machinery and equipment is positively antediluvian, straight out of the Ark.'

'So there have been fatal accidents in the past?' Ethne queried.

'Oh, yes, though not for a few years now.'

Ethne digested that.

'And lots of minor accidents,' Dot went on. 'Plenty of them. It's a dangerous place to work and no mistake.'

Ethne chewed a nail. She had a lot to think about. She simply hadn't realised how dangerous Bailey's was.

'More coffee?'

Ethne shook her head.

'Another scone?'

'No thanks, Dot. Any more and I'll burst.'

Dot laughed. 'I doubt that.'

'Well, I feel as though I would.'

Dot studied her friend. 'How was Doogie when he went off this morning?'

'Not a very happy man.'

'I can certainly understand that. I wouldn't be either.'

In fact Doogie, although he hadn't said – he didn't have to – had been downright scared. Petrified even. But he'd gone none the less. Wages had to be brought into the house.

'There is other work around,' Dot mentioned casually. 'Perhaps he should think about that.'

'What sort of work?'

Dot shrugged. 'It depends what's going. For a start he could try the evening paper, that's always good. Another thing is to ask about. That's how my Ron got fixed up at the coalyard. A pal of his put him on to that.'

'The trouble is, being new here, Doogie doesn't have any pals in the area. There hasn't been time, or opportunity, for that yet.'

'Maybe so,' Dot mused. 'But that doesn't stop you and me doing the asking. Especially me, as I know a lot of folk. All sorts.'

Ethne smiled at her. 'I'd be ever so obliged if you do.'

'Anything specific?'

Ethne thought about that. 'Not really. General labouring like he's doing now, I suppose. He's not qualified for anything else. Not in a big city anyway. Now, if we were still in the country that would be different. There's not a lot he doesn't know about the land, and beasts of course.'

'Labouring it probably is then.' Dot nodded.

Ethne went back to chewing a nail.

'There's a dance on Saturday evening,' Pearl announced to Lizzie. 'Want to go?'

'What sort of dance?'

'The sort where two people, one of either sex, get up

and shuffle round the floor together,' Pearl replied sarcastically.

'Get away!' Lizzie exclaimed, equally sarcastically.

'So what do you think?'

'I'm not sure,' Lizzie demurred. 'I'll have to ask.'

'Fair enough. It should be a good do, mind, with lots of talent there.'

Lizzie wondered if Jack would be present, but didn't like to ask. Pearl could be funny where her cousin was concerned, and would certainly lecture her again about Jack's being the wrong sort for her, and too old as well. 'Where's it being held?'

'The hall in Brunton Street. It's only a five-minute walk away, if that.'

Lizzie liked the idea of a dance. As Pearl said, it could be fun. And who knew who she might meet?

'I'll ask Ma and Da later,' Lizzie declared, 'and let you know their decision tomorrow morning.'

'Fine, then.'

'A dance!' Ethne exclaimed later that evening when Lizzie broached the subject.

'It's local, Ma. Not up the town or anything. Only five minutes' walk away.'

'Doogie?'

'I'm not so sure,' Doogie replied eventually, having considered the matter.

'I am sixteen now, don't forget,' Lizzie reminded them. 'I'm not a child any more.'

'That's what worries me,' Doogie muttered, not at all happy with the idea.

'And you'd be going with Pearl?' Ethne queried.

'That's right, Ma. Just the two of us. We won't get into harm, I promise.'

The more Doogie thought about it, the less he liked it. His little girl at a grown-up dance! Why, it seemed only yesterday she'd still been in nappies. Besides, he knew only too well what young chaps got up to, what they tried on. He'd done it himself when he was that age. Well, his Lizzie was different; she was a decent lass. Well brought up. He and Ethne had seen to that.

'You can't expect me to stay home night after night all my life,' Lizzie argued. 'I've got to get out and about some time.'

She had a point there, Ethne reflected. 'Only five minutes' walk away, you say?'

'That's right, Ma. The hall in Brunton Street.'

'You know what Saturday nights round here can be like,' Doogie said. 'Particularly when the pubs come out. Anything can happen, and often does.'

Lizzie sighed in exasperation. 'You yourself said when we arrived here the females are safe enough. Remember, Da?'

He could, but didn't want to admit it.

'So either that's true or it isn't?'

Ethne hid a smile. Lizzie had him there.

'Even though,' Doogie prevaricated.

'Even though what, Da? It's either true or it isn't.'

Doogie shrugged. 'Ach well, suit yourself. But don't say I didn't warn you.' And with that he returned to his evening newspaper where he'd been studying the situations vacant columns.

'Ma?' Half the battle had been won. Now she had to face the possibly harder half of getting Ethne to agree, for it was her mother's decision that would be the final one.

'You really want to go?'

'Yes, I do.'

'And what time would we expect you home?'

'When the dance finishes, whatever time that is. I shouldn't imagine it would be too late.'

Ethne could see how keen Lizzie was about this and, for the life of her, couldn't really think of any valid objection. Lizzie was sixteen after all and, as she had pointed out, not a child any more.

'What do you intend wearing?' Ethne queried with a smile.

Lizzie let out a small squeal of excitement on hearing that, for it meant her mother had agreed that she could go.

Mother and daughter fell to discussing the matter of suitable dresses. Not that there was a lot to choose from. Lizzie's wardrobe was somewhat limited to say the least.

'I want a word with you, Ron,' Dot declared.

Her husband looked at her in alarm. 'Have I done something wrong?'

Dot shook her head. 'No no, nothing like that.'

Ron, a shortish plump man, sighed with relief. Thank God for that! 'So what is it then?'

'It's about Doogie McDougall upstairs. You two know each other, don't you?'

'Only to say hello to in passing. I've never actually had a conversation with him, so to speak.'

Dot paused in her knitting, a new cardy for Ron that was to be his Christmas present. She'd chosen a blue wool, and now wasn't at all sure about the colour, thinking it might clash with his usually florid complexion. But the wool was bought so he'd just have to put up with it whether it clashed or not. 'I was talking to Ethne the other day and it seems he hasn't really made any friends yet.'

Ron frowned. 'Oh aye?'

'He's a decent enough chap, but lost at the moment. Out of his element, if you get my meaning. The accident at Bailey's took him very hard, sort of knocked the stuffing out of him.'

'Bad business, that,' Ron commented. 'It would put the wind up any chap.'

'So I want you to do something for me.'

He listened intently to what she proposed.

'Ron! Come in, come in, this is a pleasure,' a surprised Ethne declared to Ron who'd just knocked their door. She had already met him on several occasions, but he had never come to their house before.

'I'm not interrupting anything, I hope?'

'Not at all. Come in.'

Doogie came to his feet when Ron entered the kitchen, wondering what this was all about. Lizzie, who was also present, was wondering the same thing.

'Would you like a cup of tea, Ron?' Ethne asked, thinking she had a sponge cake she could offer, but didn't really want to as it was nowhere near the standard Dot turned out.

'No thanks. I've just had one.' He focused on Doogie. 'We haven't been properly introduced. I'm Ron, Dot's husband, as you probably know.'

'And I'm Doogie.'

The two men shook hands.

'Hello, Lizzie. How are you?' Ron inquired.

'Fine, thank you, Mr Baxter.'

'Off to the jigging with Pearl on Saturday, I understand?'

'That's right. I'm looking forward to it.'

'Oh, what it is to be young.' Ron smiled. 'Brings back memories of my courting days with Dot.' He shook his head. 'Sadly a long time ago now.'

'Isn't it just? Courting days, I mean,' Doogie agreed, trying to be affable.

'Anyway, talking of Saturday, me and a few of the lads from round about are off to the big match and I thought you might care to come with us. We usually have a couple of pints afterwards – a wee bevvy, that's all. What do you say?'

Ethne immediately guessed Dot had put him up to this, and thought how kind and considerate it was of her.

'Eth?'

'It's entirely up to you. I certainly don't have any objections. It'll get you out from under my feet if nothing else.'

Doogie and Ron both laughed. 'Dot says the same about me,' Ron declared.

'I'd love to come,' Doogie enthused. 'Mind you, I don't know too much about football as there wasn't much of it played where we come from. Seeing a big match will be a new experience for me, and one I'm sure I'll enjoy.'

'That's a date then.' Ron nodded. He mentioned a time for Doogie to call in, said his goodbyes and left.

'Wasn't that nice.' Ethne beamed.

Doogie's expression said he agreed.

'It'll do you the world of good to get out and about with some other men,' Ethne declared, delighted by this turn of events. She heartily approved. 'Just you don't go overboard in the pub afterwards.'

He pretended to be scandalised. 'Who, me?'

'Yes you, Dougal McDougall.'

'As if I would do such a thing.'

'As if,' she retorted, and suddenly smiled. 'As if.'

It was the day Chrissie was due back from hospital, and the women up and down the close had been busy getting things ready for her.

The basics had been bought in – milk, bread, and butter, plus some tins that would come in handy. The inside of the apartment literally shone, brass gleaming, lino highly polished, every ornament and piece of glass dusted and cleaned.

They were all foregathered, with the exception of Dot who'd gone off to get the kitten they'd been promised, a surprise coming home present from them all. Ethne only hoped Chrissie took to the animal and didn't reject it in Sandy's memory.

They were all in agreement to uphold the story that Dot and Ethne had told Chrissie after Sandy's demise, that the cat had died a natural death in its sleep and was now buried out in the back court with a wooden cross, bearing Sandy's name, marking the grave.

Babs Millar came hurrying through from the bedroom where she'd been keeping watch. 'Chrissie's here,' she announced. 'The ambulance just drew up.'

A few minutes later Chrissie was helped into the apartment, and on to a chair, her expression showing how happy she was to be home again. 'Oh my, this is grand,' she murmured, the hint of a tear in her eye. She hadn't expected this at all.

Tea was made and they all chatted away nineteen to the dozen. At one point Ethne noticed Chrissie glancing forlornly at Sandy's empty basket, clearly holding herself in check because he too wasn't there to greet her.

'Where's Dot?' Chrissie asked, suddenly realising Dot wasn't present.

'She'll be along in a minute,' Jean Carmichael informed her. 'She's just gone out to get something.'

At which point Dot arrived, holding a ginger kitten cradled in her arms. 'I've brought a little friend to meet you, Chrissie,' she announced.

They all watched Chrissie's face as she realised what Dot was holding. A face that lit up in a broad smile.

'Would you like to hold him?'

'Can I?'

'Of course.' Dot passed the kitten over and then backed off a few steps.

'He's lovely,' Chrissie crooned, knowing it had to be a male as virtually all ginger cats are. Still smiling, she tickled the kitten's stomach, the little creature mewing its appreciation.

'What's he called?'

'Hasn't been named yet,' Dot informed her. 'We thought you might like to do that.'

Chrissie frowned. 'Me? Why me?'

'Because the kitten's yours. If you want him, that is.'

'Mine!' She was completely taken aback.

'We know he can't replace Sandy. Certainly not in your affections. But when we heard this little chap was in need of a good home we immediately thought of you.'

'It's either you or the canal,' Edwina Edgar declared, which wasn't true at all.

'The canal!' Chrissie repeated in a shocked whisper.

'That's right,' Ethne agreed. 'The present owner doesn't want him.'

'Oh, we can't have that,' Chrissie declared, tickling the kitten again. 'Isn't he sweet? Simply adorable.'

'Does that mean you'll keep him?' Dot queried hopefully.

'I don't see why not. I can't let the little mite be drowned, now can I?'

Dot flashed a triumphant look at Ethne whose original idea this had been.

'Is he weaned?' Chrissie asked.

'About a week ago,' Dot replied.

'Then he'd better stay here with me. I'll look after him.'

That was that then, Ethne thought, pleased with herself. Chrissie had found another companion to share the lonely nights with.

'I think I'll call him Leo,' Chrissie mused.

'Why that?' Babs asked.

'Leo the lion. I think he has a lionish look about him. Something Sandy never had.'

'Success,' Dot whispered to Ethne, who nodded her agreement.

By the time they all left Leo had been fed and firmly ensconced in Sandy's old basket.

*　*　*

'So how did it go?' Ethne demanded when Doogie returned, slightly flushed from the match.

'Terrific. We won three-two.'

'That's not what I meant. How did you get on with the others?'

Doogie flopped on to a chair. 'Like a house on fire. We all hit it off right away. Couldn't have been better.'

He certainly looked like a man who'd been out enjoying himself, Ethne reflected. Reeked like one too. Even at this distance she could smell the alcohol.

'So tell me about them.'

'Nothing to tell really. Just ordinary blokes.'

Ethne sighed in exasperation. A typical male reply! 'Well, what do they do, for a start? And how many of you were there?'

'Six, including me. There was Dave, who's in the building trade, Sammy who's a milkman, Ted who works alongside Ron in the coalyard, and Fraser who drives a tramcar. They all live round here, as Ron said.'

'The match was good, then?'

'Oh, great.'

'And the pub afterwards?'

'Aye, we went.'

'I mean, what did you talk about?'

'This and that. Football mainly. Going over the match. That sort of thing.'

'Are they all married?'

Doogie blinked at her. 'What is this, the Spanish Inquisition?'

'I'm just interested, that's all.'

'Well, I believe they are.'

'And what about next week?'

'That's an away match, so we won't be going. But we will again the Saturday after that.'

'Were you asked to join them?'

'Oh aye. As I said, we all got on well together.'

Enough for now, Ethne thought, coming to her feet. She'd get more out of him later. 'How about a cup of tea?'

'Fine. Stick the kettle on.'

Ethne was filling the kettle when Doogie suddenly started to snore. When she turned round she found him fast asleep, mouth open catching flies.

More than a couple of pints, she thought. But what the hell! He'd enjoyed himself, which was the main thing.

That and the fact he'd made some new friends.

Chapter 6

Lizzie glanced round the dance floor but there was no sign of Jack. Still, it was early; he might yet turn up. She sincerely hoped so. He fascinated her.

'So what do you think?' Pearl asked. They were sitting in chairs by the wall waiting to be asked up.

'I don't know. I'm hardly an expert on dances.' Truth was, she wasn't all that impressed so far. It seemed an awfully tame affair. The small band was adequate, and that was about all that could be said for it.

'I think I might nip out to the Ladies' for a fag in a moment,' Pearl declared.

'I'll come with you,' Lizzie said, not wanting to be left on her own.

Pearl suddenly giggled. 'Look at that idiot over there,' she whispered and surreptitiously pointed. 'He's got two left feet and no mistake.'

Lizzie smiled to herself when the chap in question tripped and nearly went tumbling over, much to the consternation of his partner.

'Is it always as quiet as this?' she queried. There couldn't have been more than a few dozen people present, most of them female.

'Oh, it'll liven up shortly. A lot of the blokes will still be in the pub fuelling themselves with Dutch courage. They'll be along, you'll see.'

'Why Dutch courage?'

'To ask someone up to dance. Despite their bravado a lot of them need the drink before coming. Where women are concerned, despite what they might say at times, many are cowards at heart.'

Lizzie hadn't realised that. But when she thought about it, it was true enough. It had been the same in Tomintoul.

'Excuse me, are you dancing?'

Pearl looked at the presentable young man who'd come over and addressed her. 'Are you asking?'

'I'm asking.'

'Then I'm dancing.' Pearl stood up and took the young man's arm. 'Don't I know you?'

'You should. We were at school together. I was the year ahead of you, mind.'

Recognition dawned. 'Willie Henderson?'

'That's me.'

'You've changed.'

'Have I?'

'For the better, I'm happy to say.'

Willie laughed. 'You've changed a bit yourself, Pearl. There's more of you than there was.'

She immediately bridled. 'That's an insult!'

'No it's not. I meant more of you in the right places. If you get my meaning?'

Pearl did. 'You're being rude.'

'It wasn't meant to be. I was being complimentary.'

She eyed him suspiciously. 'Are you sure?'

He made a sign over his chest. 'Cross my heart and hope to die if I'm lying. A compliment it was supposed to be.'

Lizzie was watching and listening to this exchange with rapt attention, thinking Glaswegians had an easy way about them when it came to banter, or patter as they called it.

'I won't be long,' Pearl declared airily to Lizzie, intending to put Willie in his place by implying she'd only be staying up for the one dance.

Half an hour later they were still on the floor. Just as Pearl had prophesied, the hall was rapidly filling as closing time approached. Lizzie had been asked up twice, enjoying both occasions, but not particularly fancying either partner. A smile and a thank you had been the end of each of them.

She was dancing with her third partner, a very small chap with a bad hygiene problem, when she suddenly spotted Jack watching her through glittering eyes, forehead furrowed.

He was here. He'd come at last! Lizzie thought with elation. She wondered if she should smile at him, then decided not to, considering that too forward. At the end of the number she excused herself, declined to stay up, and returned to her chair. She pretended not to notice when Jack came sauntering over.

'Hello, Lizzie.'

She glanced up as if in surprise. 'Oh, hello, Jack. How are you?'

'All the better for running into you.'

'I'll bet you say that to all the girls,' she riposted teasingly.

He gave her a wink. 'Possibly. I thought we might have a little fandango together?'

'What do you mean?' she further teased.

'A birl round the floor, hen.'

'Are you asking?'

'I'm asking.'

'Then I'm birling.'

Jack threw back his head and laughed. 'It hasn't taken you long to learn the Glasgow chitchat.'

'I pick things up quickly. At least, so I'm told.'

'Clever wee thing, aren't you?'

'I do my best.'

He took her by the hand. 'Come on then, let's trip the light fantastic, you and I.'

She couldn't help but notice the strong smell of alcohol wafting from him as he clutched her by the waist. A little too tightly, she thought. Any tighter and it would hurt.

'So how are you, wee Lizzie?' he slurred as they moved off into a slow waltz.

'All right. And yourself?'

'Pished as a rat. Steamboats.'

She hadn't realised he was that bad.

'Had any more run-ins with Scary Mary?'

'No.'

'Pity. I'd like to see the pair of you squaring up to one another. And you giving her another doing. But be careful of that one, she's a vicious bitch. Vicious through and through.'

Jack belched, and Lizzie jerked her head away as sour breath hit her face.

'Sorry about that,' he muttered.

How terribly disappointing, Lizzie thought. She'd been hoping against hope that he'd appear and ask her to dance, and now he had he was thoroughly drunk. She didn't like him at all this way.

When the number ended he asked her to stay up for another. She was about to refuse, then, for some inexplicable reason, agreed to do so. She must be mad, she told herself.

Jack belched again, then stopped dancing to slowly shake his head. 'Don't feel so well,' he mumbled.

Nor did he look it. His face had gone a very pale green colour.

'Are you all right?'

'I'm going to be sick.'

Not over me! she thought in alarm, and hastily moved away a few paces.

'Sorry, Lizzie.' And with that Jack turned on his heel and fled the hall.

'Charming,' Lizzie commented to herself. 'Absolutely charming!'

Lizzie was fed up. She wanted to go home, but didn't feel she could until Pearl and Willie came off the floor.

Pearl's face was flushed, her eyes bright with excitement, when she and Willie eventually rejoined Lizzie after the last dance. 'Willie's going to walk me home,' she announced.

'And what about me?'

'Oh, you too, of course. We'll all go together. Is that all right?'

It would have to be, Lizzie thought angrily, wishing she'd left long since.

'You two get your coats and I'll meet you outside,' Willie declared.

'See you there then,' Pearl replied with a huge smile on her face. 'We clicked,' she confided to Lizzie after he'd left them.

'I should hope so, considering the amount of time you spent dancing together,' Lizzie answered slightly sarcastically.

'He's ever so nice. Got a good job, too. One with prospects.'

They started towards the ladies' cloakroom where the inevitable queue was forming. 'What sort of job?' Lizzie inquired.

'In an insurance broker's office. Goes to work in a collar and tie every day. Very posh.'

'Are you seeing him again?'

'I don't know. He hasn't asked me yet. But if he does I'll certainly say yes. I'll jump at the chance.'

Lizzie was pleased for her friend, especially when she saw how animated and excited Pearl was. 'Well, he did seem pleasant enough,' she commented. 'Though obviously I haven't talked to him the way you have.'

'He took a right shine to me during the first dance, I could tell. And so easy to be with.'

'Was he like that at school?'

'To be honest, I didn't know him that well, he being in the year ahead and that. I doubt we exchanged a dozen words all the time we were there. I do recall he was shorter than he is now, and not quite so rugged in the face.' She sighed. 'He is nice, though, isn't he?'

Lizzie could only agree.

* * *

'You go on up, Lizzie. Willie and I will stay down here for a while.'

Lizzie knew what that meant. Into the back close for kissing, cuddling and whatever.

'Pleased to have met you, Lizzie.' Willie smiled.

'And you. See you again, no doubt.'

'No doubt.'

Lizzie said goodnight to Pearl, and then began trudging up the stairs. What a dreary walk home that had been for her. Talk about playing gooseberry! Willie and Pearl had been entwined the whole way, whispering to one another, laughing, while she'd walked slightly ahead feeling a right fool.

What if Jack had walked her home? Lizzie wondered. Would she have gone into the back close with him? Certainly not in the state he'd been in, drunk as a lord and then running outside to be sick. She hoped he'd have the hangover of all hangovers in the morning. Serve the bugger right.

As she'd expected, her mother and father were waiting up for her, wanting to know how the evening had gone. And, in her father's case, whether there had been any trouble.

Later, as she climbed into bed, she wondered how Jack was, and hoped he hadn't passed out in a gutter somewhere.

Why should she worry about him! she thought. Why should she?

Except she was.

The following morning, bright and early, Pearl knocked the door asking if Lizzie would like to go for a walk. Lizzie, eager to hear what Pearl had to say about the previous night, was quick to agree.

They decided to catch a tramcar to the Queen's Park, which wasn't all that far away.

'So?' Lizzie prompted as they arrived at the tram stop. No one else was there.

'He's asked me out next Saturday night.'

'Are you going?'

'Darned tooting I am. I'll be there with bells on.'

Lizzie smiled at the picture that conjured up in her mind. 'Where's he taking you?'

'Didn't say, and I don't care. As long as he takes me somewhere is all that matters.'

'You are keen.' Lizzie smiled, stating the obvious.

'I am. I've never met a chap I got on with so well. We talked and talked last night in the back close, about all sorts of things. It was magic.'

'Just talk?' Lizzie teased, still smiling.

'Don't be daft. There was lots of kissing as well.'

'And?'

'And what?'

'You know?'

'Mind your own business, Lizzie McDougall. That's strictly private.'

'I was just curious, that's all.'

'Be as curious as you like, my lips are sealed.'

Lizzie glanced up the street, but there was still no sign of a tramcar. Then she recalled it was Sunday, so they might have to wait a bit. She didn't mind that at all. It was good being out in the fresh air having been cooped up in the factory all week.

'Didn't I see you with Jack last night?' Pearl asked. 'One minute he was there, the next gone.'

Lizzie sighed, and related the story.

'Jack all over,' Pearl said when Lizzie had finished. 'It doesn't surprise me in the least.'

The one good thing was he hadn't been sick all over her, Lizzie thought grimly. She'd have sloshed him if he had.

Silly sod.

'There's someone here to see you, Doogie,' Ethne declared, ushering the visitor into the kitchen.

'Sammy!' Doogie exclaimed in delight. 'How are you?'

'Hope I'm not butting in here?'

'Not at all. Ethne, this is Sammy, a pal of Ron's, one of those who go to the football matches.'

'Pleased to meet you, Mrs McDougall.'

'And to meet you, Sammy.'

'So, what can I do for you, Sammy?' Doogie inquired.

'It's not what you can do for me, but maybe what I can do for you.'

Doogie frowned, not understanding.

Sammy went on to explain. 'Ron mentioned that not only were you looking for another job but you're good with animals. Is that so?'

'On both counts.'

'Have you found anything yet? Jobwise, I mean?'

'No, I haven't. And haven't even applied for anything as there hasn't been anything suitable in the area.'

Ethne wanted to ask Sammy if he'd care for a cup of tea, but didn't want to interrupt.

'There's a chap leaving at the dairy where I work, which means his job is coming available.'

'As a milkman, same as yourself?'

Sammy shook his head. 'He's the stableman, looks after all the horses. When I heard this morning that he was going I immediately thought of you.'

Excitement gripped Doogie. This would be ideal, and get him away from the hell-hole that was Bailey's. He still had recurring nightmares about John being burned to death.

'Are you interested?'

'Not half,' Doogie enthused.

'Then I haven't wasted my time coming here. It's an early start, mind. Can you manage that?'

'It's not a problem,' Doogie assured him.

'Right then. The boss, and owner, is called Mr Cathcart. I suggest you see him tomorrow morning at the dairy. Four to half past would be about right. Go and speak to him then.'

'I will, Sammy. I will. And I can't thank you enough.'

Sammy shrugged. 'You've got to get the job first. Do you know much about horses?'

'Oh aye. I've looked after them in the past. All sorts. From Clydesdales to hunters.'

'Right then. See you the morn's morn.'

'Where is the dairy exactly?' Ethne queried, thinking Sammy might go off without mentioning that.

Sammy told her. 'Do you know the street?'

Ethne looked at Doogie, who nodded. 'I do.'

'See you there then.'

Doogie escorted Sammy to the door, thanked him again, then returned to Ethne. 'It would be perfect,' he stated simply.

Her reply to that was to hold up two crossed fingers.

*   *   *

'Of course he might not get it,' Ethne said to Dot the following morning, at the 'steamie' where they were doing their washing.

Doogie had left just before 4 a.m. to go to the dairy. He was going straight from there to Bailey's, so Ethne wouldn't know the outcome of his interview until he got home at dinner time.

'Let's just hope he does,' Dot replied, face bright red from her exertions, delighted this chance had come up for Doogie.

'I'll have you to thank if it does. Sammy being Ron's pal and all. It wouldn't have happened if you hadn't suggested to Ron he invite Doogie to the football matches.'

Dot shrugged. 'That's what neighbours are for. We all help one another, that's how we get by.'

Ethne paused for a moment at the large mangle where she was squeezing the water out of a pair of sheets. 'It would be such a relief if he left Bailey's, I can't tell you. My heart's in my mouth every time he goes off in the morning, not knowing what could happen to him during the day.'

Dot nodded her sympathy.

'Pray God he gets it,' Ethne muttered.

About half an hour later, when they were almost ready to leave the washhouse, Dot nudged Ethne. 'See that woman over there in the blue pinny?' she whispered, indicating with a jerk of her head.

Ethne spotted the woman in question. 'Aye, what about her?'

'Her daughter Heather's up the duff and no chap to marry. The dirty dog did a bunk when she told him, and now she'll be left on her own with the wean. Everyone's talking about it.'

'Poor girl,' Ethne exclaimed. 'How old is she?'

'Nineteen, I believe. Hadn't known the lad long, either – a few months only, I hear. Stupid cow for giving in to him. Now look where it's landed her. It's one thing being a bit pregnant when you get wed; it happens and no one says a dicky bird. But to bring a bastard into the world heaps shame on her and the family. Her parents must be mortified.'

It was the same in Tomintoul, Ethne reflected. The girl's life was ruined, for who'd marry her now? No one was the answer. She was damaged goods, called all kinds of harsh names behind her back.

'You say the chap did a bunk? Where to?' Ethne asked.

'Heaven knows. He comes from over Partick way, so he isn't local. It was mentioned that he'd joined the army, though whether or not that's true I've no idea. Whatever, the lass has been left on her own to pay for her mistake.'

'I feel sorry for the girl, though,' Ethne mused. 'She's been badly let down.'

'Oh aye, but a fat lot of good that'll do her now. She's been branded a tart, and worse, and that's how it'll stay.'

They both glanced away when the woman in the blue pinny looked across at them as if knowing what they were discussing.

'Well?' Ethne demanded the moment Doogie arrived home.

'I start a week on Monday.'

'Oh, Doogie!' she exclaimed and, rushing over, threw her arms round him. This was wonderful news.

'Congratulations, Da,' chimed in Lizzie, who was already getting stuck in to her dinner.

'Thanks, pet.'

'Come on, then, tell me all about it,' Ethne urged, releasing him.

'Not much to tell, really. I spoke to Mr Cathcart, explained about my previous experience with horses, and that was more or less that. We went round the stables, and I met the horses – they're lovely animals – I also met the chap who's leaving, and that was it.'

'What about the money?' Ethne inquired eagerly.

'More than I'm earning now. So that's another plus point.'

'A lot more?'

'Ten bob a week. It's a skilled job, you see; that's why the additional cash. Things are looking up, eh?'

They certainly were, she thought. 'Why don't you nip down and tell Ron and Dot? He should be home at the moment. They'll be ever so pleased for you. You owe them that.'

'All right. I won't be long.'

The relief Ethne felt was palpable. No more worry about Bailey's and what might happen to Doogie there. And more money at the end of the week into the bargain.

Wonderful.

'Lizzie, wait up!'

Lizzie, deep in conversation with Pearl, stopped and turned to see Jack hurrying towards them.

'This is the first chance I've had to apologise for the other night,' he declared, slightly out of breath, on joining them. 'I am sorry.'

'And so you should be,' Lizzie retorted. 'I thought you were going to be sick all over me.'

Jack had the grace to look embarrassed. 'I was rather pissed.'

'Rather!' She laughed. 'That's the understatement of the year.'

'Did you get home all right?' Pearl asked.

'I must have done because I woke up in my own bed next morning. Though, to be honest, I can't remember a thing about how I got there.'

'Hmm!' Pearl snorted disapprovingly.

Well, at least she now knew what had become of him, Lizzie thought, recalling how worried she'd been. 'But you obviously remember asking me to dance, otherwise you wouldn't be apologising.'

'I remember that all right. It's afterwards that's a blank.'

Lizzie and Pearl started walking again. Jack fell into step beside Lizzie. 'So am I forgiven?'

'There's nothing to forgive. You're the one made a fool of himself.'

He winced. 'Ouch!'

'At least you didn't throw up in the hall. That would have been ten times worse.'

'I had a terrible hangover the following day,' he confessed.

'Good. It serves you right. I hope it hurt like hell.'

'It did. I didn't get out of bed till early afternoon, it was that bad.'

'Were you sick again?'

He shook his head. 'Just outside the hall.'

'Well, maybe next time you'll think twice before getting so drunk,' she admonished.

'I did want to dance with you. So I was the one who lost out.'

And she'd wanted to dance with him, had been hoping against hope he'd turn up and ask her. But she wasn't about to tell him that.

'Were you angry with me?'

Lizzie looked him straight in the eye. 'Not angry, Jack, just disappointed in you.'

For some reason those words hurt him. They wouldn't have done coming from any other lassie, but from Lizzie they did. Quite deeply, too, he realised with a shock.

He couldn't help but wonder what it was about Lizzie McDougall that made her different from the other girls.

Ethne jerked awake as the alarm went off at the ungodly hour of half past three. It was Dougie's first day in his new job.

'Doogie?'

There was no reply.

Reaching over, she switched off the alarm, not wishing to wake Lizzie as well.

'Doogie?'

This time she got a grunt.

The grunt turned to a mutter of protest when she shook him. Ethne sighed, knowing this was going to be the pattern for every working day from here on in.

One eye blinked open to stare at her. 'What is it?' he asked, voice thick with sleep.

'What do you think it is? It's time to get up.'

'Already?'

'Already. Now move your backside. You don't want to be late on your first day, do you?'

Now it was Doogie's turn to sigh. He'd assured Sammy getting up this early wouldn't be a problem, but the reality was somewhat different. It was simply something he was going to have to get used to. But he didn't like it, not one little bit.

Ethne slipped from the bed and shrugged on her candlewick dressing gown. Crossing to the window she twitched back the curtains and gazed out. Rain was teeming down.

'What's the weather like?'

He groaned when she told him, then swore.

'Come on then,' she urged, thinking that as soon as he was out of the door she'd be straight back into bed again.

'I could murder a cup of tea,' he declared, swinging his feet on to the floor.

'You know there's no chance of that until I light the range.' Even if she'd lit it there and then there wouldn't have been time to boil a kettle.

Shivering from cold, Doogie began to dress.

Chapter 7

'I'll say this for you, Doogie, you certainly know your stuff when it comes to horses.' Mr Cathcart was pleased. Doogie had been a month in the job now, and loved every minute of it. He was finding it an absolute joy being at work, though getting up in the mornings was still difficult for him, and would have been a real problem if it hadn't been for Ethne.

'Thank you, sir.'

'Yes, indeed. I've never seen the horses looking so good, or in better condition.'

Doogie ran a hand over the flank of a Clydesdale called Hercules. 'I'll need the farrier in shortly, Mr Cathcart. This week would be best.'

Cathcart nodded. 'I'll arrange that. Anything else?'

'Not really.'

The horses were just back from their morning rounds and it was now Doogie's task to put their tack away and groom them. They'd already been fed and watered earlier.

Cathcart gazed round the stables, noting how neat and tidy everything was, far neater and tidier than Bob, the previous stablehand, had kept it. He approved.

'Right then, I'll leave you to it.' Cathcart declared. 'You've a lot to do.'

Doogie watched the back of his departing employer, thinking what a smashing boss Cathcart was. The man couldn't have been nicer or more obliging. He'd certainly fallen on his feet here.

It was about ten minutes later that Daisy, who worked in the dairy, appeared carrying a cup of tea. She was a buxom female in her early thirties with a cheery face and lots of corn-coloured hair. A large, plump woman, she wouldn't have been every man's taste, but Doogie found her attractive, one of the main reasons being that she was completely down to earth and oozed sex appeal. In many ways she reminded him of a country lass albeit she was Glasgow through and through.

'There you are.' She smiled, setting the tea down beside where Doogie was working.

'Thanks, Daisy.'

'Was that Mr Cathcart I saw in here?'

Doogie stopped what he was doing and lifted the cup. He enjoyed these little chats with Daisy, finding her good company and easy to be with.

'That's right. He dropped by to see how I was getting on.'

'And?'

'Oh, everything's fine. He's pleased with me. Said so right to my face.'

Daisy beamed. 'That's good.'

Doogie had a sip from his cup. Daisy made tea just the way he liked it, strong enough to stand a spoon in. 'So what are you up to this weekend, then?'

'Going out with my boyfriend.'

'Oh aye.' He knew from previous conversations she'd been seeing this particular beau for about six months now. 'Where are you off to?'

'No idea yet. Maybe we'll go to an hotel and have a drink. He likes a drink, does Charlie.'

Doogie smiled. 'Don't we all?'

'And what about yourself?'

'A football match on Saturday and the pub afterwards. Apart from that nothing special.'

'Don't you ever take your wife out?'

'Not really. She's not one for gallivanting, more of a homebody really. I suppose that's what happens when you've had three children; you get used to staying in.'

Daisy wondered if that's how she'd become when she got married, which she hoped to one day. Get married and have lots of babies. The more the merrier as far as she was concerned.

One of the horses whinnied and began pawing the ground. Doogie immediately went to it and began calming it down. 'What's wrong, Queenie? What's upset you?'

Queenie nuzzled Doogie, then shook herself. All she wanted was some attention, which Doogie was only too willing to give to any of the horses who needed it.

'Well, I'd better get back,' Daisy declared, wishing she could stay longer as it was always a pleasure being with Doogie. She thought him a lovely man, admiring the care and loving he gave to his charges. 'I'll collect the cup later.'

'All right, Daisy. See you, then.'

He couldn't help but stare at her voluptuous backside

as she sauntered off. What went through his mind next made him smile as his imagination ran riot.

Ethne could see how distressed Dot was the moment she opened the door to her. 'Come in, come in,' she urged anxiously.

'Oh, Ethne, I've just heard some awful news,' Dot declared as they went into the kitchen.

'And what's that?'

Dot wrung her hands. 'Remember that day in the steamie when I told you about Heather Fallon being pregnant and her chap doing a bunk?'

Ethne nodded. 'I remember.'

'Well, she's gone and hung herself.'

'Dear God!' Ethne exclaimed softly.

'Couldn't bear the shame of bringing a bastard into the world, I suppose. But what a thing to do. Not only killing herself but an unborn child as well.'

'How . . .'

'Got up in the middle of the night apparently and hung herself with a piece of flex from the kitchen pulley. Or one of the rings holding up the pulley, anyway. Stood on a chair and then kicked the chair away. It was her mother found her in the morning.'

Ethne thought back to the woman in the blue pinny. What a terrible discovery to make. 'How is Mrs Fallon?'

'As you'd expect. The doctor had to be called in to give her a strong sedative. She's in a state of shock, as is her husband.'

'Dear me,' Ethne muttered. 'When did it happen?'

'Two nights ago. I've only just heard.'

God knows what state of mind the girl must have

100

been in when she killed herself, Ethne thought. She couldn't even begin to imagine.

'People can be so cruel at times,' Dot sighed.

'How do you mean?'

'All the talk that's been going on about Heather. The comments. The condemnation. The finger pointing. The sniggering. Folk are so judgemental. So bloody two-faced.' Dot took a deep breath. 'And that includes me too, I suppose. I'm just as guilty as the rest.'

Ethne didn't know what to say to that. Had she been guilty, like Dot? Possibly.

'Such a shame,' Dot said, shaking her head. 'She was a pretty lassie too. No one had a word to say against her until she got up the duff. Then they had plenty. All of it vicious and nasty.'

For want of something better to do, or say, Ethne put the kettle on, and they discussed the matter further over a cup of tea.

It was Saturday night and Lizzie was bored rigid. Pearl was still seeing Willie Henderson, and the pair of them had gone out for the evening, leaving Lizzie sitting at home with nowhere to go.

It was becoming quite a love match between Pearl and Willie, Lizzie reflected. Pearl had already announced to her that Willie was 'her fate', and the man she'd marry one day. Lizzie was convinced it was far too early in the relationship for Pearl to have made that sort of pronouncement. But there again, maybe Pearl was right. Who could tell?

'Why the long face?' Ethne inquired casually, busy darning a pair of Doogie's socks.

Lizzie shrugged, and didn't reply, wishing she too had a boyfriend to go out with.

'It's probably her age,' Doogie commented sagely from behind the evening newspaper.

'Age has nothing to do with it. Honestly, Da, you talk such tripe at times,' Lizzie said waspishly.

She fell silent again. Before long she started to think of Jack, wondering where he was that evening, and who with. The thought of him with someone else made her scowl. He was nothing to her, she reminded herself. Nothing at all.

But it would have been nice if he was.

'No, Doogie. Not tonight.'

'Oh, come on, Ethne,' he pleaded.

'I said no, and I mean it. So keep your hands to yourself.'

Doogie sighed. 'It's been a week now. Longer.'

'Well, I can't help that.'

'Please, Eth?'

'I'm not in the mood. Not even vaguely in the mood. So just roll over and go to sleep.'

Doogie knew of old there was no point in further discussion. When Ethne's mind was made up that was the end of it.

Damn!

'Hello, Daisy. Have a good weekend?'

She laid the cup of tea beside Doogie as he sat polishing tack. 'Not really. Charlie and I had an argument.'

'I'm sorry to hear that.' He frowned. 'Was it serious?'

'Oh aye. We had a right head to head.'

She was clearly agitated about what had happened. 'Want to sit down and talk about it for a few minutes?'

She could easily get away with being absent for such a short time, Daisy thought. And she did want to talk to someone, so she perched on a bale of straw alongside Doogie.

'How did it happen?' he asked gently.

'That's the funny thing, I don't know. There was no one reason, it just sort of blew up out of nowhere. And once it started it simply got worse and worse.' Her voice trembled as she spoke.

'It can do that sometimes.' Doogie nodded. Well, it certainly had between him and Ethne. On more occasions than he cared to remember. 'How did it end?'

'He said goodnight, and that was that. No kiss or anything. Just walked away leaving me standing there. It was awful.'

Doogie laid aside the piece of harness he'd just polished and picked up another. 'Are you seeing him again?'

'Nothing was arranged. So that might be it.'

'Maybe it's for the best,' Doogie said, trying to console her. 'It might be you two just weren't made for one another.'

'That's the trouble,' Daisy suddenly wailed. 'I don't seem to be made for anyone. No one really wants me. Not for long, anyway. I should be married and settled at my age, and yet here I am still a spinster, probably heading to be an old maid. Maybe it's because I'm fat and ugly.'

Doogie stared hard at her. 'You're certainly not ugly, Daisy – far from it. I think you've got a lovely face.'

'Do you?'

'I do indeed. As for being fat, I admit you've got a bit of meat on your bones, but there's lots of men like that. They want a good handful in a woman, not a skinny-malinks.'

'I hadn't thought of it that way,' she replied in a small voice.

'It's true, believe me.'

She stared at him. 'Do you like meat on bones, Doogie? Is your wife big?'

Doogie laughed. 'She's not exactly big, but bigger than she used to be when we got married. Only to be expected after three children.' He recalled Ethne on their wedding day: a handsomer woman you'd have gone a long way to find. Time had taken its toll, but there again it was the same with him. His hair was thinner than it once was, and his waist was larger. But, in his opinion, he was still a fine figure of a man. Just as Ethne was still a fine figure of a woman.

'She's very lucky to have you,' Daisy said quietly.

'Who?'

'Your wife, of course. I'll bet you're a wonderful husband.'

Not after what he'd said to the laird's wife, and the consequences of that, he ruefully reflected. 'I'm sure there are worse,' he temporised. 'I do my best.'

Daisy came to her feet. 'Thanks for cheering me up, Doogie. I appreciate it.'

'My pleasure.'

Reaching out she touched him briefly on the cheek, smiled at him, then left.

If Charlie was gone for good she'd soon get over him, Doogie thought, continuing with his polishing.

When Daisy returned later to collect his cup that particular conversation wasn't resumed.

Lizzie's heart sank when she went into the toilet to find Scary Mary alone there washing her hands. Had she walked into trouble without realising it?

Scary Mary shot Lizzie a filthy look. 'So it's you,' she snarled.

The sensible thing to do would have been to turn round and leave, but Lizzie wasn't about to do that. Why give Mary the satisfaction of thinking she was scared of her? Lizzie decided to take the bull by the horns.

'Look, you've got it all wrong about me and Jack. There is absolutely nothing between us. I swear.'

'No?'

Lizzie shook her head. 'My word on it. He's Pearl Baxter's cousin, and Pearl and I are pals, that's how I got to know him. Pearl and I are neighbours. We live up the same close.'

Mary's mood suddenly changed, and her expression softened. 'Not that I care about Jack any more. I've met someone else and we're going out together. He's a real bobby-dazzler.'

That was a relief, Lizzie thought. She was off the hook. 'Congratulations. I'm pleased for you, honestly I am.'

'In fact we're going out tonight, so there. To hell with bloody Whitey. He can crawl up his own arse and disappear for all I care.'

And having said that Mary swept from the toilet.

'Will it take much longer?' Lizzie's machine had broken down, and Jack was fixing it.

'A couple of minutes, that's all.' He grinned at her. 'Why? Are you desperate to get back to work or something?'

As always Lizzie's insides turned to jelly on gazing into those pale blue eyes of his. 'Not really. I was just asking, that's all.'

Jack reached down to his tool kit and selected a smaller spanner than the one he'd been using. 'Have you heard about the new Italian café that opened last week?'

'No.'

'Apparently they serve wonderful coffee and ice cream. At least that's what I'm told.'

Lizzie wondered why he was mentioning it. 'I wouldn't have thought coffee and ice cream would have interested you. Whisky and beer more like,' she jibed.

'I was thinking about you actually,' he grunted, putting pressure on the spanner.

'Me?'

'Aye, you.'

She regarded him quizzically. 'That's kind.'

Jack suddenly laughed. 'Though why Italians should come all the way to Glasgow to open a café beats me. They must hate the weather for a start after what they've been used to.'

'I suppose they have their reasons.'

'Aye, I suppose so. Anyway, you haven't answered my question.'

That confused her. 'What question?'

'Would you like to try it out with me on Saturday?'

She stared at him, not certain she properly understood. 'What do you mean, try it out?'

'Oh, don't be thick, Lizzie. Exactly that. Go to this

106

café for coffee and ice cream. You and me. The pair of us?'

She was stunned, unable to believe her ears. Dear God in heaven!

'Well?' he demanded.

'You and I?'

He laughed. 'That's what I said.'

Everything that Pearl had said about Jack, all the warnings, came crowding into her mind. He was no good, a womaniser and philanderer. Someone to be avoided at all costs. 'That would be lovely,' she heard herself saying.

'Good. It's settled then.'

They arranged a time and place to meet before Jack finished repairing her machine and went about his business.

Lizzie didn't tell Pearl on the walk home from work that night, knowing exactly what Pearl would have said if she had.

It was now Wednesday. Saturday afternoon seemed an eternity away.

'Of course I don't expect to stay in this dump for ever. I've got plans,' Jack declared to her over the ice cream, which Lizzie thought absolutely delicious. She'd never tasted ice cream like it.

'What sort of plans?' she queried. To begin with she'd been shy, felt ill at ease. But by now she was relaxed and thoroughly enjoying herself.

'To see something of the world. The Far East perhaps, or America. Mexico is another place I'd love to go to. Don't ask me why, it just appeals, that's all.'

She tried to hide her disappointment at the thought

of Jack's leaving Glasgow and going abroad. A strange sort of sadness settled over her.

'What do you think?' he demanded eagerly.

'I don't know what to think, Jack. It's . . . well, it's certainly ambitious of you.'

'You have to be ambitious in this life, Lizzie, otherwise you don't get on, or achieve anything. I couldn't bear the idea of working in that rotten factory for the next forty years. Or meeting a lassie and settling down to bring up a bunch of weans, and all that that entails. Being trapped. I want the freedom to go where I choose and do as I wish.'

Lizzie noted his eyes were blazing with enthusiasm, and that his face had lit up in a sort of evangelical glow. She had no doubt he'd carry out his plans. No doubt at all.

'When do you expect to leave?' she asked.

Jack shrugged. 'I don't know. I haven't decided yet. But in the not too distant future, that's for sure.'

Her ice cream suddenly didn't taste so good any more. The flavour had somehow gone out of it. 'And how are you going to get to these faraway places?'

'Again, I don't know. I'll possibly go down the docks and try to sign on a ship. Work my passage, so to speak. That could be fun.' He finished his ice cream and lit up a cigarette. 'You don't mind, do you?'

She shook her head.

'One day,' Jack murmured dreamily. 'One day.'

'Then all I can do is wish you well when that day comes.'

'Thanks, Lizzie. I appreciate that.'

If he offers to send me postcards I'll scream, she thought. But he didn't.

When Lizzie returned home she felt totally and utterly miserable, and would have gone to bed if she'd had a room of her own. But she didn't.

Lizzie shivered under her coat, for it was bitter out. The grey, leaden sky held the promise of snow, which might well come if the temperature eased.

'I'm going to Willie's house this Sunday for afternoon tea,' an excited Pearl informed her friend. 'It'll give me the chance to meet his parents and get my feet under the table.'

'You really are keen, aren't you?'

'I told you, I'm going to be Mrs Willie Henderson. You can bet your virginity on it.'

Lizzie blushed. What a thing to say! 'Your heart is set on it, then?'

'Absolutely. Engagement first, and then the wedding about a year later. You can be a bridesmaid if you want?'

Lizzie thought about that. Being a bridesmaid would be nice. In fact, she'd rather enjoy it. 'All right,' she agreed. 'You're on.'

'He makes me so happy, Lizzie. I can't tell you how much. And he says it's the same for him. Every moment together is simply wonderful.'

Lizzie couldn't help the jealousy she felt on hearing that. She was positively green with it.

'For God's sake, Doogie, why do you always have to make such a mess around you?' Ethne snapped. 'Just look. Sweetie papers on the floor, pages of newspaper, a cup of tea, half of which you've spilt into the saucer. I don't know!'

Doogie inwardly groaned. Ethne was clearly in one of

her moods again. And, as usual, he was bearing the brunt of it. 'I'm sorry, lass,' he murmured contritely. 'I'll clear it all up later.'

'What's wrong with now? Tell me that?'

'I've just got comfy.'

'Then get bloody well uncomfy. Come on, let's see you clear that lot away.'

Doogie sighed, this time out loud. He hated it when she was like this. Nag nag nag. A glance at the clock confirmed he had to get a move on anyway.

Ethne, hands on hips, watched as he began picking up the various bits and pieces. 'That's better,' she said at last when he was finally finished.

'Sorry,' he repeated. 'I'll try to be more careful in future.'

'You do that.'

'I'll be off to the stables then,' he declared, which he did every night in order to attend to the horses and see that everything was generally all right. It had turned out that being a stableman was a seven days a week job. Not that he minded; quite the contrary.

As he left the house he decided to nip into the pub and buy a half-bottle of whisky. He'd drink some of it at the stables and then hide what was left over there. He smiled to himself as he headed down the street. He had some peppermints in his pocket which would disguise the smell of alcohol on his return. It was a ploy he'd already used several times and Ethne had never guessed he'd been drinking.

He wasn't as green as he was cabbage looking, he thought, as he hurried on his way.

Not him.

* * *

Doogie sat morosely drinking the whisky, reflecting on what had occurred earlier, and many other things besides.

He felt at peace in the stables with the horses for company, listening to them shifting about in their stalls. It may have been his imagination but he was certain they looked forward to these evening sessions, enjoying his presence just as much as he enjoyed theirs.

He had another sip of whisky and gazed about him, loving the horsey smell which pervaded every last corner of the stables, combined with the scent of polish, liniment, hay and straw. It brought back memories of Tomintoul and the estate.

How he missed that place! He would have given anything to be back there. Fat chance, he mused. That would never happen; he and Ethne were in Glasgow for good.

Was it moving that had caused her to change, become cold, more strident, a nag? His forehead wrinkled as he thought about it. Sadly, the answer was no. She'd been slowly changing for years, bit by bit so that you hardly noticed it at the time, until she'd become as she was now.

It wasn't as though he didn't still love her. He did, and he knew she loved him. It was just . . . well, time had taken its toll, he supposed, time during which they'd become used to each other and only too well aware of one another's faults.

Doogie sighed, recalling how eager she'd once been about lovemaking, never saying no when he approached her. How different it was nowadays. Any advance by him was more likely to be rebuffed than welcomed. And even when they did make love the joy didn't seem to be in it for her any more. It was more dumb acceptance, and putting up with it, than anything else.

'Oh, Ethne,' he whispered, a clog coming into his throat. 'What's happened to us, lass? What's happened?'

Take tonight, for example. There had been no need for her to go on as she had. No need at all. A pleasant word would have been enough, a gentle reprimand. But no, she'd had to make an issue out of it. Lambast him as she had.

Doogie shook his head in bewilderment and sorrow. He'd have to get back shortly or she'd want to know why he'd been so long, and that would no doubt lead to another row.

He drank more whisky and reminded himself not to forget the peppermints.

Chapter 8

Lizzie popped her head round the kitchen door to find Chrissie in her favourite armchair. 'Ma sent me down to ask if you want any messages run for?'

Chrissie smiled at her, then shook her head. 'I don't need any shopping done today, Lizzie, but thank you very much for dropping by.'

'Is there anything else I can do for you?'

'As a matter of fact there is.' Chrissie pointed. 'There's a bottle of sherry in that cupboard. Could you get it and take the cork out? I can never manage to open it with my hands.'

'Of course, Mrs Wylie.'

Lizzie crossed over to the cupboard in question. 'You'll want a glass as well?'

'If you don't mind.'

'Shall I pour?'

'Please.'

Chrissie accepted the duly filled glass with both hands. 'If you've got time, sit for a moment. It's always nice to have a wee chat with whoever calls in.'

113

Lizzie felt for Chrissie, seeing the loneliness in the old woman's face. 'Are you in pain today?' she inquired.

'Only a little, and mainly in my hands. They seem to be getting worse. The doctor's tried all sorts, but nothing really works. They're just a cross I have to bear.' Chrissie had a sudden thought. 'Why don't you have a glass of sherry yourself?'

Lizzie shook her head. 'I'm not old enough.'

'Ach, to hell with that. It's not as if it's that strong anyway. You have a glass if you want.' She winked. 'I won't be letting on to anyone. It'll be our secret.'

Lizzie didn't really want to, but thought she'd better if it would please Chrissie. 'All right, then.'

'Good girl.'

When the drink was poured Lizzie sat down opposite Chrissie.

'Cheers!' Chrissie toasted.

'Cheers.'

'Now then,' Chrissie said after she'd had a sip. 'I haven't spoken to you for a long time. How are things?'

'Fine.'

'The factory?'

'Same as usual. We've been on boys' shorts all week. Not very exciting.'

Chrissie nodded that she understood, having once worked at the factory herself. 'And talking of boys, have you got a boyfriend yet?'

Lizzie coloured. 'No,' she said quietly.

'I must say I'm surprised, a good-looking lassie like you. I'd have thought they'd be buzzing like bees round a honeypot.'

'I'm afraid not. My own fault in a way. I don't get out

114

and about all that much. I'd started to with Pearl before she met her chap, but now there's no one to go with. I mean, I can hardly go by myself, can I?'

'Indeed not,' Chrissie agreed. 'That's not the done thing. At least it certainly wasn't in my day.'

'And it's the same today.'

Chrissie's eyes misted in memory. 'I remember . . . so long ago. A lifetime away. But I had quite a few beaux when I was young and before I was married. I was quite a pretty thing, if I say so myself. A right old time I had too.'

Lizzie couldn't imagine Chrissie as young. It was simply beyond her.

Chrissie's eyes twinkled. 'There was one chap called Bobby Barr. Long dead now, I understand. He was very keen, and I was keen on him too. But somehow it just didn't work out.' She paused for a few seconds, then added, 'I've often wondered what it would have been like if I'd married him instead of my husband. My whole life might have been completely different.'

Lizzie thought of Jack, who hadn't asked to see her again since their visit to the Italian café. Not that it really mattered, as there wouldn't have been any future in it. But if she was honest, there was a part of her which wished he had.

'Aye, Bobby Barr,' Chrissie murmured softly. 'I still think fondly of him from time to time, God rest his soul.'

'Do you wish . . .' Lizzie wasn't sure she should ask something so personal, 'you had married him now?'

Chrissie's lips thinned into a gentle smile. 'There's no use regretting anything, Lizzie. As I said, it just didn't work out between us, and that's that.' She finished her sherry, and sighed. 'That's the difference between you and me, lass. In my case it's all behind me, in yours it's all to come.' Her smile widened. 'I envy you that, I truly do. I only hope and pray you're luckier than I was.'

Lizzie wasn't quite sure what Chrissie meant by that, only that Chrissie was wishing her well.

'Now I think I'll spoil myself and have another glass. Will you pour it for me?'

Lizzie came to her feet. 'Certainly. And then I'll have to scoot.'

All before her, Lizzie reflected as she returned upstairs. The thought made her shiver in anticipation.

Doogie was tidying up, waiting for the horses to return from their rounds, when an excited Daisy burst into the stables. He glanced up at her in astonishment, for she wasn't due to make an appearance with his customary cup of tea for a while yet.

'Oh, Doogie,' she gushed. 'I just had to come and tell you. I had a letter from Charlie this morning asking me to meet him Saturday night.'

'That's wonderful news.' He beamed.

'Isn't it? I thought I'd heard the last of him, and then the letter. He apologised for our row, saying it was all his fault, and could we meet up?'

'Have you replied yet?'

'Don't need to. All I have to do is be there.'

'Which of course you will.'

'I'll be there all right. Early, too, if I have anything to do with it.'

'Well well.' Doogie smiled, pleased for Daisy. 'You'll have to let me know how you get on.'

'I will. Don't you worry.' On a sudden impulse, she went to Doogie and kissed him on the cheek.

'What's that for?' he exclaimed in surprise.

'For being a good friend and listening when I need someone to talk to.'

'Any time, Daisy. Any time.'

'Now I must get back before I'm missed. Toodle-oo!'

'Toodle-oo!'

He drew in the scent of her that still hung in the air. She smelled nice, he thought. Very nice indeed.

He began humming as he returned to his tidying up.

'I don't know what's wrong with me lately,' Ethne confided in Dot. 'I'm always so irritable. Bad-tempered, even.'

Dot stared at her in sympathy. 'Do you mean all the time?'

Ethne nodded. 'More or less.'

'Hmm,' Dot mused, considering.

'I had a real go at Doogie the other day, which was really uncalled for. I felt terrible afterwards.'

'More cake?'

'I've already had two slices!' Ethne protested.

'But surely you can manage a third?'

Ethne was tempted, but wouldn't succumb, delicious as the cake was. But then when wasn't Dot's baking? 'No, honestly, I can't.'

'I'll put it away, then.'

Ethne watched as Dot placed the remains of the cake in a tin. 'How old are you?' Dot asked.

Ethne told her.

'Do you think . . .' Dot hesitated. 'Well, might it be the change?'

Ethne hadn't thought of that possibility.

'Any irregularities in your monthlies?'

'No. None at all. They're the same as they've always been. Regular as clockwork.'

'I'm no expert, mind, but it could be this constant irritability is leading up to that. Though I can't say I was either irritable or bad-tempered when it happened to me.'

Was that what was happening? Ethne wondered. It would certainly explain things.

'Perhaps you should see the doctor and ask him?' Dot suggested.

'Would he know if I was on the change?'

'I imagine so. They are supposed to understand these matters, after all. I'd go if I were you.'

Ethne thought it good advice. Yes, it's what she'd do, see the doctor.

'How are things between you and Doogie?' Dot queried. 'Apart from your bad temper and so on.'

'Fine. At least I think they are. No problem there.'

'So it's nothing to do with him?'

Ethne shook her head. 'No. It's me that's at fault, no doubt about it.'

'Then I'd definitely pay the doctor a wee visit, just to set your mind at rest if nothing else.'

'I'll do that,' Ethne agreed. 'I'll make an appointment as soon as I can.'

The change? Ethne mused. It would make sense.

Doogie had his first swallow of whisky of the night, smiling to himself as the fiery liquid coursed down his throat and hit his stomach. 'That's better,' he sighed.

He gazed about him, at peace with the world as he always was during his night-time trips to the stables. For a brief moment he thought back to Bailey's, then put it straight out of his mind. He still suffered the occasional nightmare about John, but thankfully they were becoming less and less frequent. He fervently hoped they'd stop altogether before long.

What a difference in jobs, he reflected, having another swallow. He was as happy in this one as he'd been unhappy in the other.

Doogie suddenly frowned when he heard a noise that sounded suspiciously like the outside door being opened and then shut again. Next moment a distraught Daisy flew into view.

'Daisy, what are you doing here?' he queried in alarm, coming to his feet.

She rushed towards him and before he knew what was happening was in his arms. 'Oh, Doogie, Doogie,' she wailed. 'I just had to come and see you. I just had to.' And with that she burst into tears.

'Dear me,' he muttered. What on earth was this all about? Then he remembered. It was Saturday night and she was supposed to have been meeting Charlie.

Daisy held a tear-stained face up to his. 'He gave me a dissy, Doogie. The bastard gave me a dissy. I stood there for over an hour waiting for him and he never turned up.' Her entire body began to shake.

Doogie understood immediately. Not turning up at an agreed romantic rendezvous was giving a disappointment indeed. He was at a loss for what to do or say. 'He didn't, did he?'

'He did.'

'You didn't mistake the time and place?'

'Of course not. It was written down in his letter. There was no mistake.'

'Swine,' Doogie muttered, distressed that Daisy was so upset. He'd become genuinely fond of her over the past months.

'What I don't understand is why write that letter and then dissy me? It doesn't make sense,' she choked.

All Doogie could think was that Charlie must have changed his mind after sending off the letter, but he didn't say so. He held Daisy tightly as she continued to shake, trying hard not to be too aware of the large breasts crushing into him.

'Here, I've got a half-bottle. Would a wee drop of that help?' he asked.

Daisy gulped, broke away from him and wiped her face. 'I could use a drink right now. By Christ and I could.'

He retrieved the bottle and handed it to her. 'Have some of that. It'll do you good.'

Daisy had a large swallow, followed by several deep breaths, and gradually began to stop shaking. 'You don't mind me barging in like this, do you?'

'Not in the least.'

'It's just I was passing on my way home, saw the light and knew it had to be you.'

'Aye, as I said, that's fine. Now why don't you sit down and try to calm yourself?'

Daisy shook her head as she sat. 'That hurt tonight, Doogie. It really did. It made me feel so small, and unwanted.'

His heart went out to her. Being stood up must be a terrible thing, particularly for a lassie. So humiliating. He watched as Daisy had another swallow.

'Charlie must be mad,' he declared, trying to be gallant. 'I think you look a picture tonight. A real cracker.'

She stared at him, and tried to smile. 'Do you really?' she asked hopefully.

'I do indeed.'

'Even though I'm fat?'

'Meat on your bones,' he reminded her. 'And a lot of men like that. I told you.'

He went and sat beside her, took the bottle and had a swig himself. 'Sorry it's cheap stuff, but it's all I can afford.'

'It tastes all right to me, Doogie. Though normally I'd have a splash of lemonade with it.'

'I'm afraid I can't offer you that. I'm fresh out of lemonade.' It was meant as a joke, but she didn't get it. She sighed.

'Has my make-up run?'

'Just a teensy bit,' he lied. It was all over her face.

'Can I have some more of that whisky?'

'Help yourself,' he replied, giving her the bottle.

Daisy had a large swallow, and then burped. 'Oh, excuse me,' she apologised. 'How rude.'

That made him smile. She really did have a pretty face, he thought. Quite angelic in a way. The sort of face that belongs in church.

'You're terribly good to me, Doogie,' she said softly. 'I appreciate it.'

'That's what friends are for.'

121

She stared at him. 'Are we friends?'

'I should hope so,' he assured her. 'At least that's how I think of you.'

Her eyes positively shone with gratitude. 'I'm feeling better now,' she declared. 'Thank you.'

'Don't mention it.'

Something in her gaze made him look away. 'It's time I was heading back,' he said. It was true enough.

'Do you have to?'

He was about to say his wife would wonder where he'd got to if he didn't, then thought better of it. It seemed wrong somehow to mention Ethne in the circumstances. 'Another five minutes then. How's that?'

'It'll have to do.'

It was actually another ten before they said goodnight to one another outside the stables and headed off in their different directions.

Doogie felt strangely elated as he walked along the gaslit street, so much so that he almost forgot to pop a peppermint into his mouth to disguise the smell of alcohol. He remembered just in time.

'You're chipper tonight,' Ethne commented when he got in.

He affected surprise. 'Am I? No reason.'

As Ethne didn't pursue the subject he sat down and began reading the evening newspaper. At least, he pretended to read it. He was actually thinking about Daisy and her visit to the stables.

He smiled when he remembered how she'd crushed into him. He'd enjoyed that.

A lot.

*　　*　　*

'I'm really looking forward to the Christmas party,' Pearl declared. 'It's always a good laugh.'

This was the first Lizzie had heard of it. 'What Christmas party?'

'At the factory. They have one every year. Always on the same day, the last Friday before Christmas. The management lay on a bit of booze and some food – sausage rolls and the like. It's great fun.'

Lizzie liked the sound of it. 'Where's it held?'

'In the factory, on the machine floor. Trestle tables are set up, and you just sort of mill around talking to people. There's no music, or anything like that.'

Jack was bound to be there, Lizzie thought. She hadn't had a chance to speak to him of late, the opportunity never having arisen. She wondered if he'd made any headway with his plans yet. 'Are you supposed to get dressed up for this party?'

'No, no. It's held directly after work so there's no chance of that. Those wearing overalls take them off, and that's about it. Something to look forward to, eh?'

Lizzie could only agree.

Ethne came out of the doctor's surgery feeling a lot better than when she'd gone in. The doctor was certain she hadn't reached the change yet, but was worried about her none the less. He'd prescribed an iron tonic to help buck her up a bit, and told her to come back in a fortnight's time to give him a progress report.

Run down was how he'd described her, hence the tonic. And she was to get more sleep if she could. Well, she always returned to bed after she'd seen Doogie out of the door, though she never remained there for long.

From here on in she'd force herself to stay there longer.

Lizzie would just have to get her own breakfast, which she was entirely capable of doing. She'd explain matters to Lizzie so she understood. There wouldn't be any trouble from her.

Ethne couldn't wait to tell Dot it wasn't the change after all, but she was still glad Dot had talked her into seeing the doctor. As Dot had said, it had taken a load off her mind.

The following Saturday night Daisy turned up again at the stables, this time earlier and carrying a full bottle of whisky which she immediately gave to Doogie.

'What's this for?' he asked.

'To replace what I drank last week.'

He began to protest, but she quickly hushed him, smiling broadly as he opened the bottle.

'I hope you can afford this,' he said, wishing he had a couple of glasses. It didn't seem right, a woman drinking straight from the bottle when it wasn't an emergency. Ethne would certainly never have done so no matter what.

'I wouldn't have bought it if I couldn't.'

'Ladies first,' he declared, handing the bottle back to her.

Daisy laughed. 'I may be many things but I'm hardly that. Female, yes, but never a lady.'

'That's your opinion, not mine.'

She fluttered her eyelashes at him. 'Flattery will get you everywhere,' she teased.

He nearly replied, will it by God? But he didn't. 'You should be out dancing or something tonight,' he chided her. 'Not wasting your time with the likes of me.'

'I don't think it a waste of time. So there. I enjoy being with you, and talking to you.'

Truth was, he enjoyed being with her and talking to her as well. He had a swallow from the bottle when she returned it to him, and they sat alongside one another on a bale of straw. 'That's a nice dress,' he said, smiling. The dress in question was a deep shade of blue with a scoop neckline which showed off her ample breasts. It buttoned down to the waist, the buttons a matching colour.

'Thank you.'

Christ but she smelled gorgeous, he thought. Why could Ethne never smell like that?

'How are the horses tonight?' she asked.

'Oh, they're tip-top.'

'You love them, don't you?'

Doogie nodded. 'I love all animals. With the exception of foxes, that is. There aren't many country folk like them.'

She frowned. 'Why's that? I think they look adorable. Mind you, I've never seen a live one, only pictures.'

'Don't be taken in by their appearance. They're murdering bastards, each and every last one.'

'Oh?'

'I'll give you an example. If a fox manages to get into a chicken run it'll kill every single bird. Not to eat, but just for sport in a fit of blood lust. That's why country people hate and detest them. If I used to see one, and had a gun with me, which I often had, I'd shoot it on sight.'

Daisy's eyes opened wide. 'Did you really?'

'Every time. With the full approval of the laird, my boss. He detested them as much as everyone else. My sons do the same.'

'You have sons?'

'Two, Gordon and Stuart, both grown up now and working on the same estate that employed me.'

Daisy shook her head. 'You don't look old enough to have grown-up children.'

He almost preened with pleasure. 'Don't I?'

'Not in the least. I must say you're wearing well.'

'I also have a daughter, Lizzie. She's the youngest.'

'And what age is she?'

'Sixteen.'

'I'm amazed.'

Was Daisy telling the truth or simply buttering him up? Doogie wondered. Probably the latter. Still, it was nice to pretend she actually meant what she said.

'Tell me about life in the country,' Daisy prompted. 'I'd adore to hear.'

'Would you?'

'Very much so. It must be completely different to here.'

Doogie laughed. 'You can say that again.'

Daisy listened intently as he warmed to his theme.

'You're late,' Ethne commented when he arrived home.

Doogie inwardly cursed himself for not watching the time. He was almost an hour later than he would have normally been. He just hadn't been aware of the minutes flying by, so engrossed had he been with Daisy.

'I had extra to do,' he lied.

'And what sort of extra was that?' Ethne inquired casually.

Doogie's mind was working overtime as he tried to think of an explanation. 'Well if you must know, this pretty young woman turned up at the stables and threw herself at me. We got up to all sorts, and that's the real reason I'm late.'

Ethne stopped cleaning the brasses to stare at him in astonishment, while Doogie somehow managed to keep a straight face. Then she suddenly cackled. It wasn't a laugh, but a genuine cackle, the sound of which outraged Doogie.

'You stupid old fool,' she said at last. 'What other woman would look at you, far less a young one? The very thought!' And with that she burst out cackling again.

Doogie's outrage turned ice cold. How dare she say that? How bloody dare she! At that moment he hated his wife for what she thought of him. 'I don't see why you find it so funny?' he said in a voice as cold as he felt.

That set Ethne off again. 'You've given me a few laughs in your time, Dougal McDougall, but that takes the biscuit.' Using the back of her hand she wiped tears from her eyes.

'I'm glad you appreciate it.'

'Oh, I do. I do. Just wait till I tell Lizzie. She'll have a right hoot.'

'Will she now?'

'Oh aye. She will that. The idea of you and . . .' Ethne broke off. 'You're unbelievable at times, Doogie, you truly are.'

He sat down, and did not speak again until it was time for bed. Once in bed he turned his back on her.

* * *

'No, Willie,' Pearl declared firmly, pushing his hand away.

'Please, Pearl. Just a feel.'

'No, and that's final.'

Willie groaned, but kept the hand he'd had under her skirt to himself.

'Maybe after we're engaged I'll let you take some liberties. But not before. Understand?'

Willie's breath was coming in short, sharp gasps. 'All right,' he mumbled.

'And don't start complaining it's unfair. You're the one got yourself all worked up, not me.'

That wasn't quite true, but he wasn't about to argue.

She had him right where she wanted him, Pearl thought with satisfaction. There would be no hanky-panky until she had an engagement ring on her finger, and even then it would be limited till their wedding night.

She fully intended marrying Willie and wasn't about to jeopardise her chances by being too easy.

'When shall I see you again?' she asked, leading him out from the darkness of the back close.

Putty in her hands, she mused a few minutes later, going upstairs.

Putty in her hands, as long as she continued playing her cards right.

Chapter 9

'Dear God!' Ethne exclaimed, seeing Doogie's face on his return from the football match. 'What on earth's happened to you?'

'We were in the pub having a few quiet pints when suddenly Sammy fell foul of this bloke and his pals. Next thing I knew all hell had broken loose.'

He was going to have a black eye in the morning, Ethne noted. There were also cuts and abrasions plus caked blood on one cheek. He looked a right old mess.

'And of course you being you had to get involved,' she accused him.

'Not just me, all of us. We had to go to Sammy's rescue, otherwise who knows what might have happened to him.'

'Is he all right now?'

'Aye, we managed to get him out of there. And if you think I look bad, you should see the bloke and his pals who started it. They got a proper doing – which they thoroughly deserved.'

'Hmm!' Ethne snorted, and hurried to put on the kettle.

Doogie was quite proud of how he'd handled himself. It was he who'd finally dragged a nearly unconscious Sammy free and bundled him out of the door.

'You're lucky you weren't killed,' Ethne berated him. 'You know what Glasgow's like. That could easily have happened.'

'Well it didn't,' Doogie replied defiantly.

'What if they'd been carrying razors, eh? Or knives even. What then?' Ethne began rummaging in a drawer for the iodine bottle.

It had all taken place so fast, Doogie hadn't had time to think about that. Now that he did it made him go cold inside.

'Or what if you'd been glassed?' a furious Ethne went on. 'A bottle in your face and you could easily have lost an eye, if not both.'

Doogie stared at the floor. Now she'd mentioned it he knew just how lucky he had been. How lucky they'd all been.

'Is Ron hurt?' Ethne demanded, finding the iodine.

'He's worse than me and might have to have stitches. He gashed his forehead when he was knocked over and hit a table. His entire front was covered in blood after that.'

Ethne shuddered, and wondered what Dot was making of all this. She'd find out later. Suddenly, she burst into tears. It had given her a terrible fright to see Doogie in such a state.

'There's no need to be like that,' Doogie said kindly enough. 'It's all over now.'

Ethne fought to get control of herself, but still she wept.

'Ethne?'

'What?'

He went to her and tried to take her into his arms but she shrugged him away. Doogie stood staring at her, not knowing what to do next.

'Sit down,' she ordered, 'and I'll see what's what.'

He chose one of the kitchen chairs, thinking that would be easier for her.

'What you did was out and out selfishness,' she snapped.

He regarded her blankly. 'How so?'

'You went charging in there without a thought in the world for either me or Lizzie. What would we have done if you'd ended up dead? Answer me that.'

He couldn't.

'Or blinded. What good's a blind man to me? How would I manage with only Lizzie's money coming in?'

She had a point, he thought miserably. How would she have coped in either event?

Ethne picked up the singing kettle and splashed water into a bowl, then hunted out a clean rag to use. Her crying had ceased.

Doogie eyed the iodine bottle in trepidation. 'Is this going to be painful?'

'Oh aye,' she replied with grim satisfaction. 'It's going to sting like buggery, and serve you right.'

He winced when the hot rag touched his skin.

'Stay still,' she admonished, attempting to wipe off the caked blood.

'You're not very sympathetic,' he mumbled.

'Sympathetic! That's the last thing I am. Sympathetic indeed. I'll give you sympathetic.'

When it came to the application of iodine Ethne took

131

great pleasure in lashing it on, using far more than she need have. It was only with the utmost reluctance that she finally stopped.

'There,' she announced. 'All done. You'll live.'

Doogie was thinking of the whisky he had secreted in the stables. At that moment he'd have given his eye teeth for a glassful.

Two glassfuls. In fact, all that remained in the bottle.

The factory Christmas party was in full swing, and from the looks of things everyone was thoroughly enjoying themselves – with the exception of Lizzie, that was. She'd been there a full hour and not once had Jack come over to say hello.

She glanced across to where he was deep in conversation with a young woman Lizzie only knew as Isa. Isa was laughing at whatever Jack had just said, then touched him on the arm as though in approval.

Lizzie scowled with jealousy. Jack and Isa seemed quite chummy, and she could only wonder if something was going on between the pair of them.

Pearl, who had been up at the makeshift bar, rejoined her. 'Here, take this,' she said, handing Lizzie a glass. Lizzie accepted the drink, knowing she shouldn't.

'Don't worry about your age,' Pearl advised her. 'No one here gives a toss that you're only sixteen. So get it down you.'

Lizzie had a sip. She'd make it last, she told herself. Ethne would have a blue fit if she went home the worse for wear.

'Excuse me, you're Lizzie McDougall, aren't you?'

She turned to face the speaker, a young man whom

132

she guessed to be a few years older than herself. He had neatly slicked back auburn hair, a trimmed moustache, and a number of spots. 'That's right.' She smiled.

He held out a hand. 'My name's Malcolm Harvey, Malkie to my friends. I work in Despatch.'

Lizzie shook hands with him. His position in Despatch would account for why she'd never seen him before. Pearl was watching in amusement, and Lizzie quickly introduced her, but it was clear that it was Lizzie herself this Malcolm was interested in.

'If you'll excuse me for a moment there's someone I want to have a word with,' Pearl declared, having sized up the situation. She then beat a diplomatic retreat, leaving the two alone.

'I've been wanting to talk to you for ages,' Malkie confessed, 'but I've never had the opportunity until now.' Or the courage, he thought to himself.

'I see.'

'I've often spotted you coming in on the mornings, you and your pal Pearl. Being in Despatch I use a different entrance, as you probably know.'

Lizzie nodded.

'Anyway, so how are you?'

'Fine.'

'Enjoying yourself?'

'It's all right.'

'This is the third party I've been to here.' He laughed nervously. 'Being a bloke I always feel somewhat outnumbered. There must be about twenty women to every man.'

Lizzie laughed too. 'I suppose so.'

Malkie shifted his feet, obviously finding this difficult.

'I hope you don't mind me coming over and speaking like this? It's a bit forward of me.'

'I don't mind in the least.'

'Good. Good.' He shifted his feet again.

'What do you do in Despatch, Malkie?'

'I'm a packer. Not the most exciting job in the world, but it suits me. For now anyway.'

'Oh?'

'Well, one day I hope to be head packer. That would be an achievement, eh?'

Hardly much of one, Lizzie thought. But at least he had some aspirations, if not in the same league as Jack's. Out of the corner of her eye she could see Jack still talking to Isa, the pair of them appearing chummier than ever. The jealousy she'd felt earlier returned with a vengeance. Why wasn't it Jack here with her and not Malkie? Because it just wasn't, that's why.

At that moment Jack glanced over, and their eyes met. If she was expecting a wave of acknowledgement, she was disappointed. Jack almost immediately returned his attention to Isa.

'I was wondering . . .' Malkie started, then broke off in embarrassment.

'Wondering what?'

'I know it's a cheek, us only just having met. But would you care to go out with me one night?'

That rather took her aback, as she hadn't been expecting it. 'Out?'

'As I said, I know it's a cheek, but I've been wanting to ask you for months now.'

A secret admirer, she mused. How wonderful! Not to mention flattering.

'I won't take offence if you refuse,' Malkie went on rather pathetically. 'I'd fully understand.' Absent-mindedly, he scratched one of his spots.

Lizzie looked again at Jack, jealousy still burning inside her. 'That's very kind, Malkie. I'd love to go out with you.'

His face lit up, reminding Lizzie of a puppy who'd just been given an unexpected treat. 'How about next week, then? I thought we might go to the bioscope.'

Lizzie had heard of moving pictures, but never been to see one. The prospect was exciting. 'Where shall we meet, and when?'

Malkie clung to her side like a limpet till the party began to break up and it was time to go home.

They said goodnight outside the factory, and he reminded her of the details of their arrangement, before they went their separate ways. Lizzie had to put up with Pearl's teasing all the way home.

'So what is this lad's name and what does he do?' Doogie demanded when Lizzie told them about the bioscope.

'His name's Malcolm Harvey and he works in Despatch,' Lizzie informed her father, while a concerned Ethne looked on.

'And you only met him tonight?'

'That's right, Da.'

'What about his parents? Does he come from a decent family?'

Lizzie sighed in exasperation. 'I honestly have no idea. He seems nice enough, otherwise I wouldn't have accepted.'

'You can never be too careful,' Ethne chipped in.

'How do you mean, Ma?' She knew full well what her mother was getting at.

'You know.'

'No I don't. That's why I'm asking,' Lizzie replied, tongue firmly in cheek.

'She means exactly what she says,' Doogie snapped. 'Anyway, I'm against this. You're far too young to be going out with lads.'

That annoyed her. 'Am I?'

'Yes you are.'

'But not too young to hold down a full time job and contribute to the running of the house,' she reminded him.

Doogie looked away. 'That's different.'

'How do you make that out, Da?'

'It just is. That's all.'

'We're only thinking of what's best for you,' a frowning Ethne said.

Lizzie knew that to be true. But none the less . . . ! 'You have to let me grow up sometime, Ma. Other girls my age go out with chaps.'

'But they're not my daughter,' Doogie stated harshly.

Lizzie gazed from one to the other. 'I've already agreed to meet Malcolm. You wouldn't have me stand him up, would you?'

Doogie immediately thought of Daisy when she said that, remembering how terribly upset Daisy had been when it had happened to her. 'Of course not. Surely you can have a word with him at work? Tell him you can't make it after all.'

'And what reason would I give? That my parents think I'm too young and precious to go out with him, or any other lad? That would be humiliating.'

Ethne sighed. 'Perhaps we are being a bit harsh, Doogie. Lizzie's a sensible girl who knows right from wrong. I'm sure she won't come to any harm. Besides, she's right. Much as you and I might not like it we have to let her grow up some time.'

'But it's too soon, Eth,' he protested.

'Maybe not. Let's just trust her, eh?'

Doogie glared at his wife. Lizzie was his baby, his darling daughter. The thought of her with a man, any man, made his skin crawl. It would be a violation, that's what. A violation.

'Please, Da?' Lizzie begged. 'It's only a trip to the bioscope, nothing more. And I so want to go. Please?'

Her entreaties softened him, for the truth was he'd never been able to refuse her anything. He tried to blank out the images conjured up in his mind of her and this Malcolm together.

'All right then,' he reluctantly agreed. 'But it's straight home afterwards and no hanky-panky. Have you got that?'

'I've got that, Da. You have my word.'

'It's against my better judgement, mind. And we'll be waiting up for you when you get in.'

Lizzie looked at her mother who gave her a fly wink. At least Ethne had come round to her way of thinking.

Doogie buried himself in his newspaper and the subject wasn't mentioned again that night. At least, not in front of Lizzie. When Ethne and Doogie went to bed Ethne did her best to allay her husband's fears.

'I've got something for you,' Sammy declared conspiratorially when he returned from his round. He and Doogie were the only ones in the stables.

Doogie, busy undoing the traces of Sammy's horse Joxer, glanced over at him. 'Oh aye, and what's that?'

From a compartment in the cart Sammy produced two bottles which he handed to Doogie. 'Hide these quickly before anyone else comes in.'

The bottles contained clear liquid, and their labels were in a foreign language. 'What are they?'

'Vodka. Now put them away.'

Doogie did as he was told, hiding the bottles where he normally hid his whisky. 'What's vodka?' he queried on rejoining Sammy.

'Russian spirit. Packs a helluva punch.'

'Spirit? You mean like whisky?'

'That's right. I happened to come by a case from a friend of mine who works on the docks. It came off a Russian ship currently tied up there.'

Doogie was bemused. He'd never heard of vodka and wondered what it tasted like. 'Packs a punch, you say?'

'Oh, it does that. A hundred and twenty per cent proof. Remember that when you drink it.'

'Well, thanks, Sammy, it's kind of you.'

'It's not so much kind as a thank you for hauling me out of that pub the other Saturday. If you hadn't the bastards could have done me real damage before they were finished.' He touched the marks still visible on his face, as were those on Doogie's. 'Some rammy, eh?'

'You can say that again.'

'You should see my chest. I'm still black and blue from the kicking they gave me. I'm only surprised they never broke a rib or two.'

'You were lucky, then.'

'I think we all were to get out in one piece.'

Doogie nodded his agreement. Further conversation was cut short by the arrival of another milkman who'd also finished his round, but Doogie found a moment to whisper, 'Anyway, thanks again. I appreciate that.'

'You're welcome.'

Sammy exchanged a few words with the other milkman before strolling away, and Doogie began to unbridle Joxer.

'I thought that was terrific,' Lizzie enthused as she and Malkie left the bioscope. She'd been totally entranced by the film, fascinated by the moving pictures flashing before her eyes. As experiences went it had been a completely new one.

'I'm glad you enjoyed it.' Malkie smiled.

'Oh, I did that.'

Malkie congratulated himself on coming up with the idea. Several times during the performance he'd thought about holding Lizzie's hand, but hadn't been able to summon up the courage to do so, his natural shyness preventing him. He wondered now if he should ask her to take his arm, but the same hesitation prevented that as well. If she wanted to link him she would, he reasoned.

They fell into step, heading back to Thistle Street, and he desperately tried to think of something to say.

'Wasn't the heroine gorgeous?' Lizzie sighed, wishing she looked as beautiful.

'Oh aye,' Malkie agreed.

'And the hero . . . well, a real dreamboat if ever there was one.'

Malkie's heart sank as he compared himself to the actor playing the part. Never in a million years could he ever be described as a dreamboat. Suddenly he became horribly aware of his spots, a new crop of which had appeared in the last few days. Acne was the bane of his life.

Lizzie glanced at the soot-encrusted tenements surrounding her, the street lit palely by gas light. What a contrast to the scenes in the film, she thought. Those had been every bit as gorgeous, and exciting, as the leading man and lady. How dreary Glasgow was by comparison, she reflected. Dreary beyond belief. Especially at night with drizzle coming down.

By the time they arrived at her close, Malkie was inwardly cursing himself for an idiot. Try as he had he just hadn't been able to make much conversation with Lizzie during their walk. Most of what had passed between them had come from her.

Lizzie wondered if he'd ask her into the back close, having already decided, despite the promise she'd given her parents, that she'd go. If she was honest with herself it was the film that had put her in the mood, and not Malkie's company. She looked expectantly at him.

Malkie dropped his gaze to study his feet. 'Would you like to do it again sometime?'

'You mean go to the bioscope?'

'Or dancing. I don't mind which.'

He hardly sounded enthusiastic, she thought. Not like the night of the party. 'When do you have in mind?'

'Next week?'

'All right.'

Her answer surprised him, and perked him up a little. 'A week tonight, same time, same place?'

'Fine.'

140

There were so many things he wanted to say, but for the life of him he couldn't come out with them. He felt his face redden slightly in the darkness. 'Right then, I'll be there waiting for you.' He hesitated. 'Goodnight, Lizzie.'

'Goodnight, Malkie.'

She was waiting for at least a peck on the cheek, but even that wasn't forthcoming.

He abruptly turned on his heel and, stuffing his hands into his pockets, strode quickly away.

A somewhat confused Lizzie stared at his fast retreating back.

Lizzie sighed and removed her hand, wondering what the real thing was like. If only Pearl would tell her, for she was convinced Pearl was having it off with Willie. But when she'd asked, which she had on several occasions, she'd been told to mind her own bloody business. That was a laugh coming from the girl who'd once confided in her that she'd allowed Jack to get his hand inside her knickers.

Did Willie do it to Pearl in the back close, or if not, where? There were few places in their world where they could get up to such a thing, particularly during winter when it was so cold. She supposed in summer one of the many parks was a possibility, but apart from there, and the back close during the hours of darkness, there was virtually nowhere.

It had to be the back close, she decided, chilly as it would undoubtedly be. Mind you, at the time they probably didn't feel the chill. Not even on a bare bum.

Lizzie giggled quietly to herself. Her ma would have

141

been scandalised to know she had such thoughts. As for her da . . . he'd possibly have had a heart attack. Certainly have gone through the roof!

She was still dwelling on the subject when she finally fell asleep.

Daisy handed Doogie his morning cup of tea. 'Is it all right if I come and see you tonight?'

Why not? Doogie thought. Her company was always a welcome diversion. 'If you want.'

'Good. I'll be here early so we can have a bit of time together.' She made to leave, then hesitated. 'I've got a surprise for you, by the way.'

'What sort of surprise?'

'If I told you it wouldn't be a surprise, now would it?'

'I suppose not.' He was intrigued, his mind working overtime trying to guess what the surprise might be.

'Ta-ra for now, then.'

'Ta-ra, Daisy.'

For the rest of the day he kept speculating about the surprise, finally coming to the conclusion it might be absolutely anything.

Doogie unwrapped the gaily decorated parcel to discover a heavy, dark-coloured scarf inside.

'I just wanted to give you a wee something for Christmas,' Daisy beamed. 'Do you like it?'

Doogie shook out the scarf and draped it round his neck. 'Very much so. It's terrific. Thank you, Daisy.'

'You're welcome.'

'The trouble is, I've nothing for you. Sorry. I just never thought.'

142

'Don't worry about it. I wasn't expecting anything.'

All Doogie could think of was how to explain this to Ethne. He was hardly likely to have gone out and bought a scarf off his own bat. And having been given it he'd have to wear it. Not to would be bound to upset Daisy. 'I think we should have a wee drink to celebrate, though. What do you say?'

Her eyes twinkled. 'I've never been known to refuse one.'

'Ever heard of vodka?'

Daisy shook her head.

'Wait till you try it. It'll knock your head off. It tastes foul, which is why I've laid in some lemonade, and glasses. You just sit down and I'll do the honours.'

Daisy viewed the contents of the glass he gave her with suspicion. A quick sniff told her nothing.

'Here's to a happy Christmas, Daisy,' he toasted.

'And you.'

When she tasted the mixture it met with her approval. A refill quickly followed.

'I really am pleased with the scarf.' Doogie smiled. 'It was very thoughtful of you.'

'Not at all.' Daisy took a deep breath. 'You weren't joking when you said this would knock my head off. It's spinning already.'

A second refill followed, and after that a third, by which time they were both extremely tipsy. Doogie had been pouring generous measures.

'I really like you, Doogie, truly I do,' Daisy said, face flushed. 'It's just a pity you're married.'

'I like you too, Daisy,' he confessed, eyes riveted on the large breasts bulging beneath her dress. God, he'd

143

have given anything to get hold of those, he thought, his imagination running riot.

'Can I have another?' Daisy slurred.

'Of course. Have as much as you want. I've got plenty.'

Doogie didn't know how it happened, but a few minutes later she was in his arms, being passionately kissed.

'Wait a minute,' Daisy whispered huskily, and broke away. To Doogie's astonishment and delight, she began to strip.

His heart, and not only that, was pounding when she finally stood naked before him. 'You're not going to turn me down, I hope?' she queried with a smile as he sat transfixed.

That was enough for Doogie. Coming to his feet he attacked his shirt buttons.

Like floating on a great white cloud, he thought dreamily as he moved inside her. Like floating on a great white cloud.

Daisy closed her eyes and moaned in pleasure.

Chapter 10

'You're drunk!' Ethne accused when Doogie got home. He stared blearily at her. 'Damn right, woman. Pished as the proverbial fart!'

A stabbing finger indicated the scarf he was wearing. 'And where did you get that?'

Doogie had already prepared a story to explain it away. 'From Mr Cathcart the boss himself. Came into the stables and gave it to me as a Christmas present and a thank you for my hard work since starting there.' He hiccuped. 'So what do you make of that?'

Ethne regarded him stonily. 'Did any of the other men get a present?

'Oh aye. All of them, in fact. He does the same thing every year, apparently, good chap that he is.'

'Hmm!' Ethne snorted, buying the story. 'That's still no reason to get drunk.'

Lizzie was watching in amusement, thinking it was a long time since she'd seen her da so pie-eyed. He was actually swaying on the spot.

'Ach, get off my back. It's Christmas in a couple of

days and I just fancied a dram, that's all.'

'A dram is one thing, getting drunk quite another.'

Vodka, Doogie reflected. By Christ it was strong. Luckily it hadn't affected him when it mattered most. He closed his eyes for a moment, picturing Daisy in all her naked glory.

'You're not going to be sick, are you?' Ethne asked anxiously.

'No, I'm not.'

'Which pub did you go to?'

'What is this, the bloody Spanish Inquisition? Does it matter which pub I went to? If you must know, it was the Argyle. So there.'

Ethne glanced at the clock. 'I think you should go to bed. You've still got an early start in the morning, don't forget.'

Doogie drew himself up to his full height. 'Don't you tell me what to do. If I want to stay up then I will.'

Ethne sighed in exasperation. She hated it when he was like this. She could never accuse him of being a bad drunk, but he did get wilful and argumentative. 'How about a cup of tea, then? I brewed a fresh pot only a couple of minutes ago.'

He regarded her as if she was some sort of simpleton or idiot. 'Why would I want a cup of bloody tea?'

'Don't swear at me, Dougal McDougall. And the answer is to sober you up.'

He shook his head. 'But I don't want to sober up. I'm enjoying being pissed. It would be a waste of good money to sober up.'

Lizzie tried to hide a smile. This was her father at his cantankerous best. It always drove Ethne wild.

'Suit yourself then,' Ethne snapped.

'Don't worry, I will. I damn well will.'

'Right.'

'Right.'

Ethne turned away, pulled a face at Lizzie who she presumed was on her side, and got back to the ironing.

'I'm going to bed,' Doogie declared.

Ethne sucked in a deep breath. Was he taking the Michael, or what? She didn't reply.

A foolish grin lit up Doogie's face. He thought he'd got the better of her. 'So goodnight.'

'Goodnight, Da!'

Ethne remained silent.

Chuckling to himself, Doogie left the kitchen.

Wasn't that Daisy something else! Doogie reflected once he'd managed to get his pyjamas on and fall into bed. Who'd have thought she'd strip off as she had, or that she'd almost beg him to make love to her?

What a difference to Ethne, he drunkenly thought. Talk about chalk and cheese! Daisy was warm, responsive, wanting it, all the things Ethne wasn't. With Ethne it was as if she was doing it out of a sense of duty, whereas with Daisy it was the complete opposite.

All right, Daisy was fat as a pig, but somehow that hadn't mattered. On the contrary, it had simply added to her natural sexiness.

What a ride, he thought, and smiled. He'd never known anything like it. There again, the only other woman he'd ever slept with was Ethne. There had been no one else until now.

Ethne hadn't always been cold, certainly not in the

early days of their marriage. She'd been only too eager then, demanding even. But all that changed after the birth of their elder son Gordon. She'd just never been the same after that.

Daisy, he mused, thinking of her breasts, which were surprisingly firm and uplifted, despite their size. What a joy those had been, and would be again when they had their next session.

Christ, he could hardly wait.

'Are you coming downstairs to the Baxters' after the bells?' Ethne asked Lizzie. It was Hogmanay and Doogie had promised to be Dot and Ron's first foot. Doogie had just left for his nightly visit to the stables.

Lizzie shook her head. 'I don't think I will, Ma.'

Ethne frowned. 'Are you sure? It is Hogmanay after all.' It was the biggest night of the year in Scotland, far bigger than Christmas which was considered mainly for children.

'I might have done if Pearl was going to be there. But she's going out with Willie, so I'd probably be the only one my age there, which wouldn't be much fun.'

'What about this chap Malcolm you've been seeing? Hasn't he asked you out anywhere?'

This was a sore point with Lizzie, and part of the reason she was sitting there brooding. He hadn't. 'He wants to spend it with his family.'

'I see.'

That was a lie. Malkie hadn't mentioned his family. He simply hadn't asked her out.

Lizzie glanced over at the kitchen table, which Ethne had already prepared for anyone who might call in before

148

the bells or next day. Whisky, bottles of beer, shortcake, black bun and slices of Dundee cake: all the traditional things expected to be on offer in a Scottish household on that night of nights. Anyone could knock the door, even a complete stranger, and they would be made welcome.

Jealousy gnawed at Lizzie as she thought of Pearl. She and Willie were still getting on like a house on fire, their relationship going from strength to strength, whereas she and Malkie were . . . well, were what? She just wasn't sure. Three times they'd met up and not once had he asked her into the back close or even attempted to kiss her. That couldn't be right, it simply couldn't. Something had to be wrong, but what? She was damned if she knew.

Lizzie shifted restlessly in her chair, jealousy still eating into her. Maybe she should go down to the Baxters' after all. There again, as she'd said to her ma, what fun would there be in being with a lot of older people talking about things that were of absolutely no interest to her? None. None at all.

No, she would stay right where she was. Her mind was made up.

Doogie hurried on down the street, heading for the stables and another visit from Daisy. This time he mustn't go back drunk, he told himself. Besides, apart from what Ethne would have to say about that, it was going to be a long night. Hogmanay always was. It was bound to be the early hours of the morning before they returned upstairs.

The amazing thing was, he wasn't feeling any guilt

whatsoever about Daisy, and that surprised him. He'd have thought he would.

He'd been married a long time to Ethne, and they had three children together, and yet no guilt. Well, it was her own fault, he thought, treating him as she did. Taking him for granted, bullying him on occasion, and worst of all continually depriving him in bed. If they'd grown apart over the years then it was all down to her. He was blameless.

It wasn't that he didn't still care for Ethne; of course he did. They'd been through too much together for him not to. And yes, he did love her, though not in the way he once had.

A smile lit up his face at the prospect of what lay ahead. In his mind's eye he could see Daisy naked underneath him, her eyes gazing into his, filled with lust and passion, her body glistening with sweat and slippery to the touch. And heard the great cry she made when . . .

He broke into a trot, heart thumping wildly at the thought of the next hour or so.

Lizzie sighed and started to get ready for bed. It was quarter past twelve and her parents had left a few minutes previously to go downstairs. The three of them had seen in the new year together, having a drink and wishing each other all the best. She'd been allowed a well diluted whisky as her mother had forgotten to buy in any sherry, which she would have otherwise been offered.

At that moment the peace and calm was rudely interrupted by a pounding on the outside door. Now who in the hell was that? she wondered in alarm. Certainly neither of her parents – Doogie or Ethne would have used their key. Nor would either have pounded like that.

'Lizzie, open up. I've some wonderful news for you!'

Recognising Pearl's voice, Lizzie quickly opened the door. 'What's going on?' she demanded.

Pearl brushed past her and went straight into the kitchen. 'Guess what?' she queried, eyes bright, her face flushed.

'What?'

Pearl held out her left hand. 'Willie's proposed and given me this. We're now officially engaged.'

Lizzie's jaw dropped. 'Engaged!'

'Since this evening. Isn't it a smashing ring?'

Lizzie took Pearl's extended hand and peered at the ring in question, a modest enough affair comprising a single, small diamond. 'It's gorgeous,' she agreed, while privately thinking it was nothing of the sort.

'Isn't it just! Oh, Lizzie, I'm so happy.'

'I can see that,' Lizzie replied somewhat drolly.

'It was the last thing I was expecting. There was no clue, nothing at all. Willie simply produced this and proposed. I was flabbergasted.'

'Congratulations. I'm ever so pleased for you.'

'We went to his parents' first to make the announcement, and then back here to tell my folks. They're delighted, needless to say.'

'So when's the wedding?'

'Next year, if we can save up enough money in time, which I'll be doing my damnedest to make sure happens. The reason Willie decided we get engaged now is because he's had a substantial pay rise at work which means more cash coming in, and more going into the bank.'

Lizzie was genuinely pleased for her friend, and ashamed now of the jealousy she'd felt earlier. It had been mean-spirited of her.

'I can't wait to show the girls at the factory,' Pearl bubbled on. 'Just as I couldn't wait to show you.'

Lizzie re-examined the ring, which remained modest and unassuming. 'It really is nice. Congratulations again.'

'You'll have to come downstairs now and help us celebrate. Won't you? Please?'

Lizzie didn't see how she couldn't. Her best friend had just got engaged, after all, which put a whole new complexion on things. 'Of course I will. But I'll have to get changed first.'

'You don't need to bother. You're absolutely fine as you are. I promise.'

Lizzie was uncertain about that. 'Are you sure?'

'Och aye. Everyone's just dressed as they do normally. This is Thistle Street, don't forget. No airs and graces here.'

'You've made an effort,' Lizzie pointed out, still unsure.

'I was going out though, that's why.' Pearl took Lizzie by the arm. 'Come on now. Willie will be wondering where I've got to.'

Lizzie allowed herself to be persuaded and followed Pearl out of the door.

It seemed as if the entire close was crowded into the Baxters' kitchen. There were the Millars, the Edgars, the Carmichaels, the Shands who didn't normally socialise much, and Chrissie Wylie sitting in a comfy chair by the range. A beaming Willie was in conversation with his future father-in-law.

'Do you want a drink?' Pearl asked Lizzie.

Lizzie glanced across at her parents, wondering if she dare risk something alcoholic. 'Lemonade if you have it,' she replied, deciding not to.

Pearl understood the reason for the request. 'Leave it to me,' she whispered, and made for the table where the various drinks, hard and soft, were arrayed.

'Wonderful news, eh?' Edwina Edgar commented to Lizzie, en route to the toilet which was situated on the half-landing between floors, and shared by four families.

'It is that.'

'It'll be your turn next, I suppose?' Edwina teased.

'Hardly likely.'

'I hear you've got a chap, though?'

'Nothing serious, Mrs Edgar. Far from it, in fact.'

'Oh, well. Mr Right will happen along in time. You'll see.' And with that Edwina bustled off.

Music suddenly filled the room as someone put on a gramophone, the record scratchy from previous use, or misuse.

'Here you are, get that down you,' Pearl quietly declared on rejoining Lizzie, handing her a glass containing a fizzing, clear liquid. 'Lemonade.' She smiled, and added in a whisper, 'With a wee drop gin to spice it up a little.'

'Thanks.'

'Just tip me the wink when you want some more.'

Lizzie had a sip. It was the first time she'd ever tasted gin. Well, she couldn't really taste it because of the lemonade, but the effect was pleasant enough. She had another, larger sip.

Doogie was thinking about Daisy and the session they'd had earlier in the stables. If anything, it had been

153

even better than the previous one. He smiled at the memory. My God, that woman was something else, the sex unbelievable. He'd been startled to begin with when she'd started suggesting things, but only too eager to comply. It had crossed his mind to wonder where she'd learned these tricks, then decided it was best he didn't know.

Chrissie Wylie was having a grand time, thoroughly enjoying the occasion and the company. It was simply lovely to be amongst so many people, particularly as she spent night after night on her own with only Leo, the cat, to talk to.

'Are you all right, Chrissie?' Dot asked.

'Just dandy.'

'Can I get you anything?'

'A slice of black bun would be nice. I've always been partial to black bun.'

Dot laughed. 'Then a slice you shall have. Coming up in a tick.'

Chrissie settled further back into her chair, intending to stay as long as possible. There would be no going home early for her. No fears. She'd make the most of this.

'Congratulations, Willie,' Ethne said, speaking to him for the first time since her arrival. 'You must be pleased.'

'As punch, Mrs McDougall.' He glanced across to where Pearl was chatting to Mr Edgar. 'I've got myself a good one there, a real brammer. And don't I know it.'

Ethne nodded her approval, and continued to talk to him.

Lizzie joined Ron at the gramophone. 'Do you have any dance records, Mr Baxter?' she queried.

'A few, but . . .' He laughed. 'There's hardly room to dance here though.'

That was true enough, Lizzie reflected. A pity. A bit of a dance would have been just the ticket.

Ron put on another record, his favourite. 'The Old Rugged Cross'.

Several streets away Jack too was at a party, and not enjoying himself at all. It was always the same on Hogmanay: it depressed him. He might as well have been at a wake.

He drew on the cigarette he was smoking, and then had another swallow of beer. He dyspeptically eyed the gathering from which he had temporarily withdrawn by sitting in a corner, wondering if he should leave or hang on for a while longer. At least if he stayed he could continue to drink, which was something.

He found his mind turning to Lizzie McDougall, and dwelling on her. What was it about that girl which disturbed him so much? It was a question he'd asked himself many times, and to which he believed he knew the answer.

Lizzie was somehow different. Not like any of the other girls he was acquainted with. Not only different, but special. And a danger to him. Dangerous because she was the only girl he'd ever come across whom he'd consider settling down with.

It wasn't that she was particularly attractive, or charismatic, or anything else. There was simply a quality about her that he'd never found elsewhere, though what that quality was he couldn't say.

One thing was certain: he had no intention of letting

Lizzie McDougall upset his plans for travelling abroad and seeing the world. Lizzie was a trap from which, if he allowed himself to become enmeshed, he'd never escape.

He smiled grimly to himself. Funny he should know that about Lizzie when they were no more than acquaintances. But know it he did. As far as he was concerned she was trouble with a capital T.

He wondered where she was at that moment, and who with. That creep Malkie Harvey, no doubt, who'd been taking her out recently.

Christ, you'd have thought she could do better than that! Malkie wasn't only a creep but gutless to boot. No spine whatsoever. A joke of a man. A complete joke.

Jack had another draw on his cigarette, pretending he didn't envy Malkie, which he did. Even if he wasn't prepared to do anything about it.

Shughie Millar, Babs's husband, had produced a squeezebox from somewhere and now proceeded to play it, mainly his versions of old Scottish songs, the sort that go down well on Hogmanay. Occasionally he sang along in what transpired to be a fine, tenor voice.

Ethne glanced over to Doogie who was on the way to getting well oiled. Well, she could hardly complain on Hogmanay. Besides, most of the other men present were doing exactly the same – and a few of the women, too. Jean Carmichael looked as if she'd had more than enough.

'I want lots of children when we're married,' Willie declared to Ethne. 'The more the merrier.'

This was news to Pearl, standing beside him. He'd never before mentioned children. 'How many are you actually thinking of?' she asked with a frown.

'Oh, I don't know. Six, eight, something like that.'

Pearl gulped. Bloody hell!

'It's a thing of mine,' Willie went on. 'Probably because I come from a large family myself.'

'You don't always get what you want in that direction,' Ethne smiled in reply. 'No matter how hard you try.'

Pearl reddened slightly.

'Isn't that right, Pearl?'

'I suppose so, Mrs McDougall,' Pearl replied in a small voice.

'I like the "trying hard" bit,' Willie said, and roared with laughter.

Embarrassed, Pearl shot him a filthy look. Not that she was a shrinking violet by any means, but Ethne was of an older generation, after all.

'It's all up to the good Lord, or nature if you will,' Ethne went on. 'I was blessed with three, and believe you me that was enough of a handful.'

'Well, I'm sure we can cope with more than that. Isn't that so, Pearl? No offence meant, Mrs McDougall.'

Ethne was finding this highly amusing. Willie might have come from a large family but he clearly didn't know what he was talking about; the sheer hard graft involved with such numbers. She wondered what Mrs Henderson would have had to say on the subject.

'None taken, Willie.'

Six to eight children! Pearl quailed at the thought. The washing and ironing alone would be a nightmare, not to mention the small matter of giving birth so many times. Before she could reply, there was a sudden almighty crash followed by exclamations all round.

Chrissie lay flat on the floor, having fallen from her

chair and pulled over an occasional table with her.

My God, she's drunk and passed out, was Ethne's first reaction on seeing the prostrate figure.

'Too much sherry,' Babs Millar commented, thinking the same as Ethne.

Dot knelt beside Chrissie, puzzled. As far as she knew the old woman hadn't had that much to drink. 'Are you all right, hen?' she asked, gently shaking Chrissie by the shoulder. There was no reply.

'Shall we carry her through to her own house and put her to bed?' Ron queried, joining his wife.

There was more to this than alcohol, Dot realised. She'd dealt with too many drunks in her time not to know the difference. No, something was seriously wrong. She was certain of it. 'I think we'd better call the doctor,' she said, now extremely worried.

'The doctor, on Hogmanay!' Jean Carmichael exploded, and laughed. 'You'll have no chance.'

'Chrissie's ill,' said Dot. 'And I don't mean the sherry kind either. She's had an attack of some sort.'

'Dear God,' Edwina Edgar whispered, hand flying to her mouth.

'If we can't get a doctor then she must be taken to hospital,' Dot declared. 'And as soon as possible.'

That had the effect of sobering the company who were now, without exception, looking on in concern and sympathy.

Doogie pulled himself together. 'I'll try the doctor, see if he's home. I won't be long.' And with that he hurried from the room.

'Get a blanket, Ron,' Dot instructed. 'And will someone help me turn her over on her back?'

Mr Edgar did so.

'Check she's still breathing,' Ethne suggested.

Dot bent her ear to Chrissie's mouth, and nodded. 'Though it's awful shallow.'

There was nothing further anyone could do until Doogie returned, hopefully with the doctor.

'What a Hogmanay,' Doogie sighed when they eventually went back upstairs. 'I've never known one like it.'

He hadn't succeeded in fetching the doctor, who'd already been out on call and wasn't expected to return for hours yet, according to his wife. Luckily Doogie had been able to hail a cab, which had taken Chrissie, with Dot and Ron in attendance, to hospital to find out what was what. The gathering had broken up after that, everyone agreeing they could hardly continue in the festive spirit after what had happened.

Doogie went straight to the whisky bottle and poured himself a dram.

'Don't you think you've already had enough of that?' Ethne chided.

'Don't be daft, woman. And you'd do worse than to have one yourself considering what we've been through.'

'A cup of tea will do me fine, thank you very much.' She went to put the kettle on.

'Suit yourself.'

'Do you think Mrs Wylie might die?' Lizzie tentatively asked, wondering if such a question was in bad taste.

Doogie glanced over at her. 'There's no saying, lass. She certainly appeared in a bad way. We'll just have to wait on word from the hospital, whenever that might be.'

'Poor woman,' Ethne said quietly. 'She was enjoying herself so much, too.'

'Aye, you never know the moment till the moment after,' Doogie commented sagely.

Lizzie wanted to go to bed, but wouldn't until her parents left the kitchen. It was way past her normal bedtime and, with four gins inside her, she was extremely tired. She stifled a yawn.

Doogie saw off his whisky, and poured another, not only because he wanted one but also in defiance of Ethne. A picture of Daisy popped into his mind, but he quickly blanked it out. It was no time to be thinking of things like that.

'Do you think we should wait up till Dot and Ron get back?' Ethne queried.

Doogie considered the question. 'No, I don't believe so. They might be at the hospital the entire night for all we know. It's best to get some sleep and speak to them in the morning. Or some time tomorrow, anyway.'

Ethne nodded her agreement. 'Thank you for doing what you did, Doogie. It was kind of you.'

He stared across the room at her, and saw she was sincere. 'Forget it,' he replied off-handedly. 'I only did what any decent man would do.'

'None the less.'

They left it at that.

Chapter 11

'So how are you and Malkie getting on?' Pearl queried as they hurried to work, their first day back since the Hogmanay holiday.

Lizzie glanced sideways at her friend. Malkie had finally summoned up the courage to take her into the back close and kiss her. What a disappointment that had turned out to be. It had been like kissing a dead fish. Horrible. But she wasn't going to let Pearl know that. Pearl was too full of herself after the engagement.

'Excellently.' Lizzie smiled.

'Oh good. Has he had you in the back close yet?'

'I hope you mean asked me into the back close and not "had" me there,' Lizzie teased.

Pearl laughed. 'I didn't think of that when I said it.'

'Well, he has, actually.'

'And?'

'And what?'

'Did he kiss you?'

'Hmm.'

'What does hmm mean?'

161

'He's a beautiful kisser,' Lizzie lied convincingly, adopting a dreamy tone.

'Did he stick his tongue in your mouth? You know, the French way?'

'Maybe,' Lizzie prevaricated.

'What kind of answer is that?'

'The only one I'm going to give. Let's just say it was heavenly. I had goosebumps all over afterwards.'

'Really!' Pearl thought about that. She'd never had goosebumps after kissing Willie. Or while kissing him either. Was she missing something?

'And a sort of quiver between my legs. If you get my drift.'

Pearl's eyes opened wide. 'Like a thrill?'

'Exactly.'

'Just from kissing?'

'Just from kissing,' Lizzie confirmed.

'He wasn't touching you at the time?'

'Well of course he was. He had his arms round me.' Lizzie was enjoying this.

'That's not what I was getting at. I presumed he had his arms round you when he was kissing you. Chaps usually do.'

'I suppose so.'

Pearl was now becoming irritated. 'Lizzie, are you trying to be difficult?'

Lizzie suppressed a smile. 'Not in the least.'

'Was he touching you between the legs, then?'

'Are you asking if he had his hand in my knickers?'

'Precisely.'

'I would say that was my business,' Lizzie answered sweetly. 'Wouldn't you? After all, you never tell me anything about things like that where Willie's concerned, so why should I tell you regarding Malkie?'

There, Lizzie thought triumphantly. Got you. A taste of your own medicine.

A thoroughly miffed Pearl didn't speak again during the remainder of their walk.

Serves you right, Lizzie thought in satisfaction. Serves you bloody well right.

A kiss like a dead fish. Slimy and horrible. But there was no way she was going to let on to Pearl.

Doogie became aware of Ethne staring strangely at him. 'What's wrong?' he queried. 'Have I done something to upset you?'

'No.'

'Then why are you looking at me like that?'

Ethne took a moment or two before replying, and when she did it was somewhat hesitantly. 'I was just thinking how different you've been of late.'

'Different?' He frowned. 'In what way?'

She shrugged. 'I'm not sure. Sort of nicer I suppose.'

'Are you complaining then?' Nicer? He didn't think he'd been nicer.

'Of course not. Simply surprised, that's all. I'm certainly not complaining. Another thing is . . .' She broke off, and gave him another funny look. 'You haven't been pestering me in bed as you used to.'

Alarm flared in Doogie. The truth was, he'd been having so much fun with Daisy that he hadn't had to bother with Ethne. He now realised that might have been a mistake. He should have at least made the effort once in a while. Now, it seemed, he'd aroused her suspicions.

163

Or if not that, her curiosity. 'Haven't I?'

'You know you haven't.'

'I suppose that's pleased you?' he said sarcastically.

'I said surprised, not pleased.'

Doogie shrugged. 'If you really want to know I just haven't felt like it.'

'I'm amazed to hear that, knowing you.'

'People do change, Eth. And I'm not getting any younger. Besides, nowadays it's usually a waste of time when it comes to that. You're rarely interested. So why keep trying when often as not I'll be rebuffed? It simply isn't worth it.'

Now it was Ethne's turn to be alarmed. She'd never meant things to go this far, reach such a state. She considered herself as red-blooded as the next woman and the thought that she might never again have sex with her husband horrified her. 'I'm sorry,' she mumbled.

'Waste of time,' he repeated, delighted she'd apologised. He couldn't remember the last occasion she'd done that. 'Anyway, it doesn't matter now. As I said, I'm not getting any younger, so let's just leave it there.'

Ethne didn't know what to think as guilt consumed her. What had she done?

'Ach, I wouldn't worry about it,' Dot counselled later that day after Ethne had come to her for a chat and advice. 'There are months on end when my Ron's like a randy rabbit, and other months when all he cares about in bed is sleep.'

'It's never happened between us before. Doogie's always been up for it at the drop of a hat. He'd wear me out given half a chance.'

Dot smiled.

'It's nothing to smile about. You say don't worry, but I am.' Ethne shook her head. 'I suppose it's all my fault. I've never quite forgiven him for us having to leave Tomintoul, and denying him was one way of paying him back.'

Dot didn't comment on that.

'So what do you think I should do?'

'Being a bit more amenable in bed might help. For example, do you ever make the first move?'

Ethne was shocked. 'Certainly not! That's a man's job.'

'I wouldn't necessarily agree with that.'

'Are you saying you do?'

'If I'm in the mood, yes.'

Ethne was intrigued. 'How do you go about it? Do you just tell him, or what?'

Dot had suddenly become all coy. 'I sometimes whisper something suggestive in his ear. Other times . . .' She broke off, and laughed. 'This is embarrassing. I jiggle his willy and ask him if he thinks it's just for pissing out of. That never fails to get him going.'

Ethne could never imagine herself doing that in a thousand years. Jiggle his willy! The very idea was anathema to her. 'Anything else?' she croaked.

'Well . . . let me see.' Dot's forehead furrowed in thought. 'When was the last time you bought a new nightdress?'

Ethne thought about it. 'You know, I can't remember. Quite a while ago.'

'Then why not buy one? Possibly something a little provocative.'

'How do you mean, provocative?'

165

'Different to what you wear normally. Low cut at the front, maybe.'

'I'd freeze!' Ethne protested.

'I don't. I simply pull the bedclothes up higher when I want to sleep.'

This was all new to Ethne, who would never normally have considered such a thing. Dot was certainly giving her food for thought.

'And choose a nice material,' Dot went on. 'Light and shimmery is good. Men like shimmery. At least my Ron does.'

Ethne thought of the flannelette nightdress she was currently wearing. There was nothing light and shimmery about that – quite the opposite, in fact.

'Well?' Dot demanded.

'Can you suggest a shop that would have what I need?'

Dot's face lit up in a smile. 'I'll do better than that. I'll take you to a few if you like.'

'You're on.'

They agreed to meet up and go into town the following day.

'What's the verdict?' Doogie asked. He had found Hercules, the old Clydesdale, on its knees and wheezing badly when he'd arrived at the stables that morning, and had lost no time in summoning the vet. Now he and Mr Cathcart waited anxiously while Mr McLeish finished his examination.

McLeish stood up, and sighed heavily. 'It's the worst kind of news, I'm afraid. I recommend he be destroyed.'

Doogie was horrified. The old horse was a favourite of his. 'Is there no alternative?' he stammered.

McLeish shook his head. 'Not really. He's got respiratory problems, and fluid in the lungs. To try to keep him going would be cruel, in my opinion, not to mention expensive. No, he should be put down.'

A grim-faced Cathcart had been listening to this. 'If that's the case, Mr McLeish, you'd better get on and do it.'

'Right then. I'll be back in a tick.'

Doogie knelt beside his beloved Hercules and stroked his nose, the thought of losing him breaking his heart. And so unexpectedly too. Why, only the previous day Hercules had seemed right as rain, and now this.

'There there, fella, there there,' he crooned, fighting back tears.

Hercules snickered in reply, then rolled his great eyes upwards as though in pain.

'Can't be helped, Doogie,' Cathcart stated brusquely, already wondering where he could get a replacement. He would need one as soon as possible.

Hercules' tongue flickered to lick Doogie's palm. Doogie felt a traitor, though there was absolutely nothing he could do. He was going to miss the old chap dreadfully.

All too soon McLeish returned, carrying a wooden case. Placing the case on top of a straw bale he opened it and took out a revolver. When Doogie saw it he couldn't control the tears any longer. They began to trickle down his face.

McLeish loaded the revolver, then glanced sympathetically at Doogie. 'You'll have to move aside now, I'm afraid.'

Doogie reluctantly did so, giving Hercules a final,

reassuring pat before walking away. Unable to watch what was going to happen next, he turned his back on the proceedings. Seconds later a shot rang out, followed by a thump as Hercules keeled over.

'Well, that's that. Thank you, Mr McLeish,' Cathcart declared in a matter-of-fact tone. 'You'll send me a bill, of course.'

'At the end of the week.'

'That's fine. I'll settle promptly, as usual.'

'You always do, Mr Cathcart. I only wish I had more clients like that.'

Doogie was staring at the body, telling himself death had been instantaneous and Hercules wouldn't have felt a thing.

'I can leave you to dispose of the remains, I take it?' McLeish said to Cathcart.

'That's right. I'll make a telephone call after you've gone.'

Cathcart gazed at the grieving Doogie as McLeish repacked his revolver. He'd never before seen a grown man reduced to tears over a horse and found it fascinating, and a little disturbing. A horse was just a horse after all, nothing more or less. At least it proved he'd picked the right person to be his stableman.

'How do you intend disposing of the remains?' a choked Doogie asked after McLeish had taken his leave of them.

'There's a local pie factory that'll come and take the carcass away. They don't pay anything but it does save me the expense of disposing of it myself.'

Doogie couldn't believe his ears. A pie factory! 'But surely that's against the law?' he protested.

Cathcart shrugged. 'It's supposed to be, but the pie people use all sorts in their stuff. You'd be surprised.'

Dear God in heaven! Doogie thought. That was appalling. And what a terrible end for a beautiful animal like Hercules. Chopped up for pie filling. It was obscene.

'Now you'd better get on with your work,' Cathcart instructed. 'I've got that telephone call to make.'

'Bastard,' Doogie quietly hissed when Cathcart was out of earshot. 'Lousy fucking bastard.'

The tears continued to trickle down his cheeks.

Ethne let herself into Chrissie Wylie's house, intending to ask Chrissie if she needed anything from the shops. She had been home now for several days, having suffered a heart attack on New Year's Eve and been hospitalised ever since.

Ethne came up short when she found Chrissie sitting staring blankly into space, her face devoid of all emotion and expression.

'Chrissie?'

Chrissie roused herself to look at Ethne. 'Sorry, I was miles away.'

'I could see that. What on earth were you thinking about?'

'Death.'

The reply startled Ethne. 'Death!' she exclaimed. 'Why so?'

Chrissie shook her head in despair. 'Because I'm no use to anyone any more. I may as well be dead. In fact it would be a welcome relief.'

Ethne opened her mouth, then shut it again, her mind whirling as she tried to come up with a suitable answer.

'Just look at me,' Chrissie went on. 'Hands so arthritic

I can hardly pick up a cup nowadays. Legs that are rapidly becoming as bad. A broken hip not that long ago, which although it's healed is still giving me gyp. And now a heart attack to cap it all.'

'Oh, Chrissie,' Ethne said sympathetically, sitting down opposite her. 'Is there anything I can do?'

Chrissie shot her a mirthless smile. 'No. Unless you can somehow take forty years off my life, return me to the young and healthy woman I used to be.'

'I'm afraid that's beyond me. But if I could, I would. You know that.'

'It's a terrible thing, getting old,' Chrissie mused. 'Far worse than I ever imagined. My mind is still lively enough, but the body is falling apart.'

'You have us neighbours for company. Surely that's at least something?'

'True enough. And I appreciate what you all do for me. I'd be completely lost without you. All of you.'

Ethne made a mental note to speak to Dot. They must call in more often. 'How are your hands today?' she asked.

Chrissie held them out and, to Ethne's eyes anyway, they seemed more gnarled and twisted than ever. 'See for yourself.'

'Are they sore?'

'Excuse my French, but they hurt like bloody hell. My hands and other parts of me that the arthritis has affected. It's a major job just getting out of bed in the morning, let alone getting dressed. They both take a lot longer than they did only a year ago.'

It was a pity Chrissie didn't have family to take care of her, Ethne reflected. The old biddy was all alone in the world. No children or living relatives, and husband long dead. Not that he would have been much good from what Dot had told her.

'Do you know what I hope?' Chrissie gave another mirthless smile.

'What?'

'That one of these days, and the sooner the better, I simply nod off in this chair and that's that.'

Ethne was appalled. 'Don't say such a thing, Chrissie!'

'Why not? I mean it. If I could have a wish come true that would be it.'

'You're tempting fate, you know.'

'Good,' Chrissie replied stoutly. For a brief moment she closed her eyes, then opened them again. 'But enough of this. It's only upsetting you. Why don't you put the kettle on and we'll have a cup of tea. While you're doing that, look in the jar I use. I'm sure there are some chocolate biscuits left. If there are we'll have one each.'

Ethne came to her feet, only too happy to oblige. Anything to cheer up the old woman.

'Now what's the gossip?' Chrissie queried. 'I haven't heard any good gossip in ages.'

Ethne couldn't think of a single thing to tell her.

'What's wrong with you?' Ethne asked Doogie when he got home from work that evening. His face was a picture.

'Nothing.'

'Of course there is. It's obvious.'

Doogie threw himself on to a chair beside the table. 'Bad day at the stables, that's all. Nor do I wish to talk about it. All right?'

'If you wish.'

'I damn well do wish.'

171

Ethne busied herself at the range where she was preparing the meal.

Doogie would never forget the sight of Hercules being taken away, four men from the pie factory hauling the body off in chains to be loaded on to a waiting wagon. There had been no respect from any of the four: as far as they were concerned Hercules was just another piece of dead meat to be transported. It had angered him, though it shouldn't have done, reason told him that. They hadn't known Hercules, after all.

'There you are,' Ethne declared, placing a plate in front of him. 'Pie, mashed tats and peas.'

Doogie stared at the pie in horror. Jumping to his feet, he only just made it to the sink before throwing up.

Later that night Ethne slipped on one of the two new nighties she'd bought. It was a paisley pattern, low at the front and held up by ribbon straps, the satinised material giving it a shimmery look. The other nightie was predominantly blue; this one was pink.

A thoughtful Doogie was getting out of his long johns. 'I'll be late in tomorrow night,' he announced. 'Mr Cathcart wants me to go with him to select a new horse for the stables. I've no idea when I'll be home, only that I'll be late.'

Ethne said nothing, waiting for the new nightie to be noticed and commented on.

Doogie slung his long johns aside and stepped into his pyjama bottoms. 'Christ, I'm tired.' He yawned.

Ethne smoothed down the sides of the nightie, hoping to draw his attention.

Buttoning his pyjama top, Doogie crossed to the gas

mantle and turned it off, plunging the room into darkness. 'What are you waiting for?' he queried as he passed her and crawled into bed.

A crestfallen Ethne went to the other side of the bed and got in beside him as he turned his back to her.

'Goodnight,' he mumbled.

'Goodnight, Doogie.'

So much for Dot's suggestion, Ethne thought bitterly, already regretting the good money she'd spent on the nighties. Wasted, that's what it had been, completely wasted. There had been no reaction from Doogie whatsoever. She might as well have kept on her old flannelette thing.

There was an alternative. She thought of Dot, jiggling Ron's willy. No, she couldn't do that. No matter what, it just wasn't in her to do such a thing. Even considering it made her squirm inside.

A few seconds later Doogie began to snore.

Doogie felt himself relax the moment the last houses were left behind. It was the first time since arriving in Glasgow that he hadn't been surrounded by buildings. He sucked in a lungful of clean, fresh air, relishing the experience. Such a contrast to what he'd become used to in Glasgow, where the air was permanently tainted with soot and various foul smells, some of which didn't bear thinking about.

Doogie studied the land with interest. It was quite different from that of his native Banffshire. Here it was almost lush, a complete contrast to the ruggedness and grandeur of the estate where he'd worked.

'You're being quiet,' Mr Cathcart commented. They were in his motor car, heading for Croftfoot.

'Sorry. I was just enjoying being out of Glasgow. Away from the big city for a change.'

'Of course.' Mr Cathcart nodded. 'I'd forgotten you're a countryman. Glasgow must have been a bit of a shock to the system.'

Doogie laughed. 'You can say that again. I'm still not used to it, if I'm honest.'

'No jobs where you were, wasn't that it?'

'That's right, Mr Cathcart,' Doogie lied. 'I came to Glasgow to find employment.'

They passed a herd of Jerseys, which made Doogie think of the highland cattle they had on the estate, not much good for milk or meat, but spectacular in appearance. Doogie had always thought they looked as if they'd trotted straight out of the stone age.

'Will you ever go back?' Mr Cathcart inquired, making conversation.

If only, Doogie reflected. If only. Given half a chance he'd return like a shot. 'Highly unlikely,' he replied. 'I doubt it would ever be possible.'

Cathcart turned the car off the road and headed up a dirt track. Ten minutes later they were there.

'So what do you think?' Cathcart asked when Doogie had finished examining the five horses on offer.

'What about the prices?'

'Leave that to me. You just choose the most suitable beast.'

Doogie pointed at a dun-coloured mare. 'That's the one you want. Strong, sturdy, and a placid temperament. Ideal for pulling a milk cart.'

'Hmm,' Cathcart mused. 'I rather thought the black myself?'

174

Doogie shook his head. 'Bad teeth. Never buy a horse with bad teeth. It's indicative of all sorts of trouble to come. Believe me.'

Cathcart took a deep breath. 'The dun it is, then. Now, you just hang on here while I have a word with the farmer. There's bound to be a bit of haggling before we settle the matter.'

Doogie watched Cathcart walk away in the direction of the farmhouse, then turned again to gaze at the land surrounding him, his mind back in Tomintoul, remembering.

He spotted a flock of sheep in the distance, though he couldn't make out what breed they were. A large flock too, he noted. With grazing like this there should be good profit in them.

He thought of his sons, Gordon and Stuart, still working on the estate. God, how he envied them that. What a fool he'd been to say what he had to the laird's wife. What a bloody, drunken fool. For the umpteenth time he wished with all his heart he could turn back the clock and relive that fateful day.

High overhead a crow cawed. No, not a crow, a jackdaw. He followed it as it wheeled and then dived to finally disappear into a stand of trees.

A chill wind had sprung up, making him shiver. He wasn't used to being outdoors like this any more, he realised. Living and working in Glasgow had made him soft.

Doogie sighed deeply, suddenly feeling totally wretched. He'd become the original round peg in a square hole. And he only had himself to blame.

*   *   *

Lizzie was in a quandary. She wanted to stop seeing Malkie, but how could she do that having praised him to the skies to Pearl? She pulled a face at the memory of the last kiss he'd given her. Still horrible, still like kissing a dead fish. One thing was certain: that was never going to improve, no matter what.

There had to be a way, she thought. She just had to avoid arousing Pearl's suspicions that she'd been told a pack of lies. Lizzie smiled, recalling how she'd boasted that kissing Malkie had given her a thrill. Pearl had swallowed that fib hook, line and sinker. Not only swallowed it but been as jealous as anything, too.

So how to stop seeing Malkie? That was the question to which she so far didn't have an answer.

But she'd come up with one. All she had to do was keep on thinking about it till the answer came. There was a solution for every problem; at least so her da had once said. Given time she'd come up with it.

And soon, she fervently hoped. Soon.

Chapter 12

'Wouldn't it be wonderful if we could meet somewhere other than here?' Daisy sighed, her huge bosom rising and falling after their recent exertions.

'How do you mean?' Doogie frowned.

'Exactly that. Perhaps go for a drink occasionally. It wouldn't have to be a pub – a nice hotel, say.'

Doogie felt absolutely shattered. God, but Daisy was wonderful at it! And so inventive, too. Being with her was an education in itself. She regularly suggested things he'd never have thought of in a thousand years. 'It's a lovely idea,' he replied slowly. 'But quite out of the question.'

'Because you're married?'

'Uh-huh. We could easily be seen, and then what? If Ethne was ever to find out about us there would be all hell to pay. She'd probably murder me. And I'm not joking, either.'

But Daisy wasn't to be put off. 'We could go somewhere there's very little likelihood of that happening. A posh hotel in the West End, for example. Nobody from round here ever goes in one of those.'

177

'What about Mr Cathcart?'

'Doesn't drink.'

'But his wife might.'

Daisy had no information whatsoever on Mrs Cathcart. The only thing either of them knew about her was that she existed.

'Besides,' Doogie went on, 'I'd have to get dressed up for a posh West End hotel, and how would I explain that to Ethne? She'd want to know why.'

'But surely you could come up with some reason or other?'

It was now Doogie's turn to sigh. 'Married life just isn't like that, Daisy. At least not the married life I have. I come to work in the mornings, I go back for dinner, then come back to work again. Home at the same time every night. A visit to the stables later, and that's that. Regular as clockwork. The only break from my routine is when I go to a football match some Saturdays.'

Daisy quickly seized on that. 'Then why not say you're going to a football match and see me instead?'

'Because I go with the chap downstairs. If I went elsewhere he'd mention it to his wife, bound to, and she'd mention it to Ethne. The pair of them are great pals. It's just not as simple as you think. In fact it's downright impossible.'

Daisy's expression became downcast. 'This stables business is so limited. We meet up, do it, and then go our different ways. There's no romance in it.'

'You must have realised that when we started,' he pointed out. 'You knew I was married.'

'I didn't think about it then. I was just aware I fancied you rotten, and took it from there.'

Doogie wished he had some whisky on the premises. He could have used a drink right then.

'Now I more than fancy you,' Daisy added in a small voice.

'Meaning?'

'I think I'm falling in love with you.'

Holy Christ! he thought. Jesus bloody wept. He hadn't foreseen this possibility. 'You mustn't do that, Daisy,' he said hurriedly. 'You mustn't.'

She gazed at him through troubled, soulful eyes. 'Don't you feel anything at all for me?'

'Of course I do,' he protested. 'I'm awfully fond of you, for a start. But love! That's simply not on.'

'I'd like to have babies with you, Doogie. I'm getting on, you know. The time is ticking away.'

By now he was thoroughly alarmed. Babies as well as love! Why could the silly cow not just leave matters as they were? Typical woman, he thought bitterly. He'd been a fool not to see this coming.

'As I said, it's out the question. What would you have me do, divorce Ethne and marry you? Chaps like me don't get divorced, we simply don't. It's almost unheard of. The cost alone would be quite beyond me.'

Daisy bit her lip. 'A girl can have dreams, can't she? There's no harm in that.'

As long as they remained dreams, Doogie thought, staring at her nakedness, thinking how vulnerable she looked. And ever so slightly, he had to admit, pathetic. Despite himself, and what had been happening only minutes previously, he felt a familiar stirring. 'None at all.' He smiled.

'I was wrong to bring all this up, wasn't I?'

He could see she clearly wanted him to say no. 'Perhaps

179

we should end it here and now, Daisy. Call it a day. That might be for the best.'

'Do you want to?'

He shook his head. 'Not really. But you must understand we can't go any further than we have. I'm sorry, but that's how it is.'

A stricken expression came over her face, and she turned her head away.

Please don't cry, he thought silently. That would only make things worse.

'I think I'd better go,' Daisy said huskily.

Damn it, she was crying. 'Maybe you should.'

'But I will stay if you want.'

The stirring was becoming urgent, and obvious as he too was stark naked. He didn't miss Daisy's eyes flicking to his crotch as she noted the fact.

'Oh, Doogie,' she whispered. 'You're such a man.'

'I'll have to go myself in a minute.' He smiled weakly. 'If I don't Ethne will want to know why I'm late home. She always does if I am.'

'Would you like me to give you a jolly before you do?' Daisy suggested, wiping away her tears.

It was a code word they used. He should refuse, Doogie told himself. Certainly after the conversation they'd just had. But he didn't have the willpower to do so.

Taking his silence as agreement Daisy rose, waddled across to him and sank to her knees.

'Just be quick,' he urged.

And she was.

It was already the talk of the factory when Lizzie and Pearl arrived in that Monday morning. Scary Mary had

180

been in a fight on Saturday night and spent the rest of the weekend in police custody as a result. She was due up before the beak later that morning.

According to rumour Mary had been in a dance hall when the fight had broken out between her and another girl. It had only ended when the law had appeared to drag the assailants apart, and then haul both of them off to the cells.

'Heard the latest?' Jack queried, appearing beside Lizzie and Pearl.

'You mean about Scary Mary?' said Pearl.

Jack nodded. 'I just hope, for her sake, she didn't stab the other woman.'

Lizzie's eyes opened wide. 'Stab?'

'That's right. She often carries a knife on her when she goes out on the town. I warned you she was trouble. She's not called Scary Mary for nothing, you know.'

'Nobody's said anything about a stabbing,' said Pearl.

Lizzie had gone pale, thinking back to the incident with Mary in the toilets. She might not have done what she had if she'd known that Mary sometimes carried a knife. Though, on reflection, Mary would hardly bring one to work. Even though, it was still a shock.

'Are you all right, Lizzie?' Jack asked in concern, having noticed her change of colour.

'I'm fine.'

'Sure?' His light blue eyes twinkled in amusement. 'I think I can guess what's just gone through your mind.'

She didn't answer, knowing he probably could.

'Time to get busy,' Pearl declared. 'Otherwise we'll have Mrs Lang after us.'

Both girls took their leave of Jack and hurried to their

machines. Soon they were going at it hammer and tongs, all thoughts about Mary quite forgotten.

Mary arrived in the factory after the dinner hour, but before she could take her coat off Mrs Lang homed in on her to have a word. A few moments later they were heading for management.

Mary was gone for about fifteen minutes. When she returned her face was like thunder as she marched straight for the door. 'The fucking sack!' she yelled en route. 'The bastards have given me the fucking sack!'

Lizzie glanced up from her machine to watch Mary's progress, wincing when Mary stopped to kick the door before slamming through it and going off down the street. She had to admit to herself she was relieved that Mary wouldn't be working there any more. In fact it was quite a weight off her mind, for who knew if Mary might not have turned on her again in an act of retribution? 'Good riddance to bad rubbish,' she muttered, and concentrated again on the task in hand.

'What's this?' Ethne demanded.

Doogie went cold all over when he saw what was in her hand. A sheath. Obviously one of his. 'Have you been going through my pockets?' he said angrily.

'Just as well, wouldn't you say?'

Doogie was desperately trying to think of an explanation she'd accept. He inwardly cursed himself for leaving the sheath in his jacket. His normal practice was to secrete them at the stables directly after purchase.

'I'm listening,' Ethne hissed, eyes blazing.

Doogie laughed. 'I found it on one of the carts when

I was unhitching the horse and stuck the damn thing in my pocket, meaning to chuck it in the bin later on. As you can see, I forgot.'

'Hmm!' Ethne snorted.

'That's a fact. Like it or not.' Then, sarcastically: 'I'm sorry to disappoint you, woman. Anyway, as you know, I've already told you I've gone off that sort of thing. Not interested any more. Don't feel the need.'

Something crumpled inside Ethne. That was certainly true as far as she was concerned. He hadn't laid a hand on her in God knows how long.

'Now, if you've finished with this silliness can I have my tea? I'm starving,' Doogie declared.

Ethne opened the door to the range and threw the sheath on to the fire.

'I've never used one of those articles in my life,' Doogie lied, delighted to have got off the hook. 'What's to eat, anyway?'

'Sausages.'

'And?'

'And what I give you,' Ethne replied waspishly.

'Charming,' Doogie sneered. 'Just like yourself.'

The conversation was cut short by the arrival in of Lizzie, home from the factory.

He'd have to be more careful in future, Doogie warned himself. He might get away with that once, but never twice.

How could he have been so bloody stupid!

Jack had gone down to the docks to stare at the ships tied up there. So many ships of different sizes and flags, their home ports painted on their sterns. Not long to go

183

now, he thought. He had decided to leave Glasgow that coming summer, for by then he should have enough saved up to buy a ticket, with some left over, if he couldn't secure a job for himself aboard ship.

His latest idea was Singapore, or even Hong Kong. He'd heard wonderful tales of the Far East recently in a dockside pub he occasionally frequented where he rubbed shoulders with crews off the ships. Terrific chaps, in his opinion, with stories to tell that could be both wondrous and enthralling.

This summer, he promised himself. Definitely then. And to hell with Glasgow. He'd be well rid of the filthy place.

He started for the nearest pub, more of a dive than a bar, where he intended having a couple of pints before going home again.

Which is exactly what he did.

'It's just a wee half-bottle, Doogie. But better than nothing, eh?'

'You're a gem, Daisy. An absolute gem. I'm skint myself till pay day, so this is very welcome.'

She beamed at him. 'And no more talk about us splitting up?'

He regarded her keenly. 'If there's no more talk about love and weans. I've made my position on both quite clear.'

'So you have, Doogie. I've got the message.'

'Good.'

'Things will just stay as they are for as long as we want them to.'

'That's the girl.'

'I still fancy you rotten, though. You don't mind if I say that?'

'Say it as much as you like. Now I'll just get the glasses, and the lemonade for you.'

There was nothing coy or shy about Daisy. She'd already stripped off in anticipation by the time he'd poured their drinks and handed her hers.

Lizzie and Pearl stared in astonishment at the factory windows. Every one they could see had been broken. Bricked, as they were soon to discover.

'They're going to cost a bob or two to get replaced,' Pearl commented quietly.

'But who would do such a thing? What's the point?'

'I think I can guess.'

Lizzie turned to her friend. 'Who?' But even before Pearl could answer she too had guessed.

'Scary Mary,' they both said in unison.

That was what the rest of the workers believed as well, although it was never proved.

Doogie lay in bed listening to Ethne's steady breathing. It wasn't often he didn't nod off the moment his head hit the pillow, but this was one of those nights.

He was thinking about Daisy and her wish that he would get divorced in order to marry her. Daft, of course. As he'd said, men in his position simply didn't get divorced: they just couldn't afford it. Divorce cost an arm and a leg, and then some.

But what if it hadn't been like that? Would he have considered divorcing Ethne? They'd been through a lot together, after all, including bringing up three children, not to mention all the daily trials of working-class life.

Ethne had been a good wife in many ways, he couldn't deny it. But over the past few years she'd become something of a shrew and a scold. The sweetness seemed to have gone out of her; the sheer joy he'd once found so attractive.

Truth was, there were times nowadays when he didn't even like being in her company, finding her mere presence unsettling and aggravating. He wondered if she found it the same with him? It was a possibility.

Mind you, on the other hand, what would it be like being married to Daisy? At least he felt alive with her, felt important, felt . . . well, all sorts of things that had long disappeared out of the window where Ethne was concerned.

As for sex, Daisy was in a league of her own. Ethne couldn't hold a candle to her, now or in the past. It was the difference between a cold pork pie and a sizzling steak. No contest.

Ethne versus Daisy?

Anyway, the whole business was hypothetical. He was married to Ethne and that's how he'd stay. Have to stay.

But if divorce had been possible, what then?

He simply didn't know.

'I'm sorry, Malkie, but I want to finish it.' God, she'd been dreading this moment, Lizzie reflected. Absolutely dreading it.

Malkie's face fell. 'You don't mean that, Lizzie. You can't!'

'I'm afraid I do.'

'But why?' he almost wailed.

She'd known he was going to take it badly, which was why she'd been putting it off, waiting to screw up enough courage to deliver, from his point of view, the bad news. 'I think you're a smashing chap, Malkie, I honestly do, but not right for me. We simply don't click, as they say round here.'

'I thought we were getting on so well, too,' he protested.

'We do get on,' she admitted. 'But I need more than that. A lot more.'

'Just tell me what and I'll come up with it. I promise. Only don't end it, Lizzie. Please?'

'You can't come up with these things, Malkie. They're either there or they aren't.'

'Have you met someone else?'

She shook her head. 'No.'

'Someone better-looking than me, is that it?'

'I said no, Malkie. There isn't anyone.'

That mollified him a little. 'I just don't understand. I truly don't.' He grabbed her by the arm. 'Say you'll change your mind, Lizzie. I'll do anything. Anything at all.'

She gently prised his fingers free. This was becoming downright embarrassing. Not to mention pitiful. Why couldn't he just take it like a man? 'There's nothing you can do, Malkie. Now, thank you for the evening. I'll see you round the factory sometime, no doubt.'

'Oh, Lizzie,' he whispered. 'Don't do this.'

'Goodnight, Malkie.' And with that she turned and hurried into the close mouth and up the stairs. She half expected him to call out after her but, to her relief, he didn't.

She felt rotten when she opened the door and went inside.

Absolutely rotten.

'I thought you two got on so well?' Pearl frowned when Lizzie told her about the split with Malkie.

'We did.'

'Then why give him up? I mean, you said he gave you a thrill just by kissing you.' That still irked Pearl, who'd never had the same experience with Willie. Not even come close.

Lizzie smiled inwardly. If only Pearl knew the truth about Malkie's kissing. 'He just wasn't right for me, kissing or not. It simply took a while for me to realise, that's all.'

'Well,' Pearl mused. 'He was a bit plooky when you come down to it.'

'Pimply or not, it's over,' Lizzie declared with finality. She changed the subject.

Dot started when there was a hammering at their door. 'Who on earth is that?' she wondered aloud.

'You won't find out until you answer it,' Ron drily informed her from where he was sitting.

'Maybe you should go, in case it's trouble.'

He considered that. 'Aye, perhaps you're right.' He sighed, and came to his feet. 'I'd just got comfortable, too,' he grumbled.

When he opened the door he found a distraught Jean Carmichael there. Her face was bruised and swollen.

'Oh, Ron!' Jean sobbed, and fell into his arms.

'There there. There there,' he said consolingly, patting her on the back.

'Who is it?' Dot queried anxiously from the kitchen.

'It's Jean. She's in a bit of a state.'

Dot instantly appeared, and took the still sobbing Jean away from Ron. 'Let's get you into the kitchen and you can tell us all about it,' she declared, helping Jean on through.

Jean collapsed on to a chair and tried to pull herself together. 'Look at what that bastard did to me,' she said, indicating her face. 'And all I did was burn his bloody tea.'

'You mean Walter?'

Jean nodded. 'He suddenly exploded and lashed out at me. Just for burning the tea! You'd have thought I'd done it on purpose.'

Dot clucked her sympathy. Jean's face was in a right old mess, and would be a lot worse by morning unless something was done right away. 'Where is he now?'

'Where I left him a few moments ago. The swine.'

'Ron, put the kettle on,' Dot instructed. 'I'll need hot water.' She thought for a moment. 'And I'll need something for that bruising.'

'He's hit me before, you know,' Jean choked. 'But not for a long time. I just can't think what came over him.'

Dot rummaged in a cupboard and came up with a bottle of antiseptic, the best she could do. She began applying it with a clean rag, Jean wincing as she did so.

Dot was boiling inside, absolutely furious. How could a man do this to his wife? He should be taught a lesson, a good one, so he'd never do it again. She suddenly straightened. 'Ron, I want you to go and have words with Walter. In fact more than words. Give the bastard a hiding. That might teach him.'

Ron shook his head. 'Forget it, Dot. I'm going nowhere.'

That outraged her. 'But look what he's done to poor Jean. And for what? Nothing. Go on, you sort him out.'

'I'm staying right where I am, woman. What's happened is between a man and his wife. It's not my place to interfere. Nor will I. If Jean wishes to involve the police then that's up to her. But I'm staying put, and that's an end of it.'

Dot glared at him. 'You're not scared, are you?'

'I think you know me better than that,' Ron replied softly. 'I just refuse to get mixed up between man and wife. Now leave it at that.'

It wasn't till later, when Dot had calmed down and Jean had gone home, that she realised Ron was probably right. What went on between a married couple was strictly their affair.

Lizzie and Ethne were halfway along Sauchiehall Street, looking for a new skirt for Lizzie, when Lizzie suddenly spotted Jack heading in their direction. Would he stop and chat? she wondered.

'Hello, Lizzie.' He smiled. Then, smooth as butter, the old cliché: 'I didn't know you had a sister?'

Ethne giggled. 'Mother, you mean.'

'Really!' Jack exclaimed in pretended amazement. 'I genuinely thought you were Lizzie's sister.'

Lizzie smiled inwardly, and made the introductions. Jack and Ethne shook hands, and he said how nice it was to meet her. For the next few minutes Lizzie listened to Jack giving her mother the biggest load of old flannel she'd ever heard, while Ethne lapped up every last word of it.

'What a charming young man,' she declared when they finally continued on their way. 'So polite, too.'

Lizzie glanced sideways in disgust. Her mother had been acting as though she really was the age Jack had initially pretended. The simpering tone, the preening, the subtle flirting; Lizzie had never seen that side of Ethne before. Her disgust deepened as Ethne rattled on, describing Jack in ever more glowing terms, her face flushed from the flattery and attention she'd just received.

It made Lizzie want to throw up.

Ethne came flying in the door to find Doogie already there waiting for his dinner. 'I'm so sorry,' she apologised. 'I dropped in to see Dot and just couldn't get away again. You know what she's like at times, simply can't stop talking.'

Doogie grunted, and didn't reply. Lizzie arrived to take her place at the table, and Ethne gave a sudden exclamation.

'What is it?' asked Doogie, realising something was wrong.

Ethne turned a stricken face to him. 'Damn that Dot and her yapping! I've gone and burnt the casserole.'

Doogie stared hard at her, his expression blank. 'You've done what?'

'Burnt the casserole.'

'Badly?'

Ethne bit her lip, and nodded.

Lizzie got a fright when Doogie gave a sudden roar and jumped to his feet. 'You stupid bloody woman!' he shouted, sending his chair toppling over with a crash.

Ethne recoiled in fear, her heart thumping wildly.

Doogie raised a fist and shook it at her. 'A taste of this is what you need. A bloody good smacking for being so stupid. And that's exactly what you're going to get!'

'No, Da, don't!' Lizzie screamed.

Doogie advanced on Ethne. Her eyes were riveted on his fist when, on reaching her, he drew it back.

The fist dropped to his side as Doogie burst out laughing. 'By God, you should have seen your face,' he managed to splutter at last. 'It was a picture. An absolute picture.'

'You bastard,' Ethne spat, realising he'd been having her on by re-enacting what had happened to Jean Carmichael.

'That wasn't funny, Da,' Lizzie chided.

But Doogie thought it hysterical, and continued laughing throughout their dinner of potatoes and veg.

For two peas Ethne could have sloshed him.

Chapter 13

'Come on, Doogie.' Ethne yawned. 'It's time for you to get up.' It was the same every morning, she thought, when there was no reply or movement. He was terrible at getting out of bed.

Reaching across, she shook him by the shoulder. 'You're just making it worse for yourself. Now come on.'

Doogie groaned.

Ethne slipped into her dressing gown, tying the cord round her waist. At least it wasn't so cold with spring almost upon them. Some of the winter mornings had been arctic.

'Ethne?' he said piteously.

'What?'

'I don't feel well.'

She frowned. That was unlike him. If it was some sort of dodge it was a new one. 'In what way?'

'Hot. Awfully hot. And my throat feels like sandpaper. Honestly.'

Maybe he was ill, she thought. Going round to his side of the bed she sat beside him. Her eyebrows shot up in surprise when she felt his forehead. It was like a furnace.

She pulled back the bedclothes a little to discover his pyjama top was sodden with sweat. Something was definitely wrong.

'Bad headache,' he mumbled. 'It's kept me awake most of the night.'

He had been particularly restless, she now recalled. Hot, too: on several occasions she'd had to move away from him in order to cool down.

'Can you get me some water?' he rasped.

Ethne first lit the gas mantle then crossed to the sink where she filled a glass. She had to help him struggle on to an elbow to get the water down.

His face looked ghastly, a definite shade of grey, while his eyes were red-rimmed and sunken. This was certainly no act: he was genuinely out of sorts.

'Just lie there, Doogie, and I'll send for the doctor later. All right?'

'Thanks, Eth.'

Well, there was no going back to bed now, that was certain. She didn't want to catch whatever it was he had, if she hadn't already.

'Somebody will have to let the dairy know,' he croaked.

'Don't worry. I'll see to it.'

She went to light the range and put the kettle on.

'Wake up, Lizzie! I need you.'

Lizzie came groggily awake. 'Is it that time already?'

'No, it's earlier than usual. Your da's ill and I want you to run to the dairy and tell them he won't be in today. I'd go myself but I don't think I should leave him.'

Lizzie stared at her mother in the darkness. 'What's wrong with Da?'

'I don't know, but he's in a right old state. I'll have to have the doctor in later. Run to the dairy and I'll have your breakfast waiting for you when you get back.'

'Can you do me a favour, Dot?'

'Aye, sure. What is it?'

Ethne explained about Doogie. 'Will you sit with him for a wee while so I can go and get the doctor?'

'Of course. I'll be right up.'

'Thanks. You're a pal.'

Dot hesitated. 'Would it be better if I went for the doctor and you stayed with him? I'd be only too happy to do so.'

Ethne quickly agreed.

'The surgery won't be open yet, but I'll be down there just as soon as it is.'

'I'd better get back to him, then.'

Dot watched in concern as her friend hurried off. It was clear Ethne was worried.

'Influenza, no doubt about it,' Dr Gilmour pronounced. 'I've had quite a few cases over the past week.'

Ethne knew that having the flu was no joke. People had been known to die of it. 'So what's to be done?'

'Not a lot, I'm afraid. Keep Mr McDougall warm and give him lots of liquids, and light food from time to time if he can keep it down. I would suggest some broth to begin with. Or poached fish, that sort of thing.'

Ethne nodded that she understood.

'Don't you have any pills, doctor?' Doogie pleaded. 'At least something for this headache? It's murder.'

195

'A couple of aspirins should help that. Do you have any in the house?'

'We do,' Ethne confirmed.

'Then try those. But remember not to exceed the stated dose no matter what.'

'I won't, doctor,' Ethne assured him.

'And you appreciate you might be in for the long haul? Influenza doesn't just last a day or two – a few weeks, more like. Possibly three. Certainly that before Mr McDougall can return to work. He'll be weak as a kitten when he finally does start to recover.'

'I'm with you,' Ethne replied grimly.

'Right then. There's nothing more I can do for the moment. I'll call in again tomorrow to see how things are.'

'Thank you, doctor.'

Gilmour turned his attention back to Doogie. 'And no trying to get out of bed until I say so. All that would do is make matters worse.'

'I won't, doctor. I promise,' Doogie replied, giving him a strained smile.

'I'll see you to the door,' Ethne offered.

'Thank you.'

When she returned to Doogie, he gave her a weak smile. 'Sorry about this, lass.'

'It's not your fault.'

Doogie closed his eyes. 'I just hope I don't lose my job over this. I mean, they'll need someone to take care of the horses in the meantime. What if Mr Cathcart replaces me?'

'We'll worry about that when the time comes. For now, getting you better is all that counts.'

Ethne went off to fetch the aspirin, then used a towel to wipe away some of the sweat Doogie was covered in. Soon, to her relief, he fell into a deep and untroubled sleep.

'How's Da?' was the first thing Lizzie asked on returning home for dinner.

'He's got the flu.'

Lizzie digested that.

'So things are going to be topsy-turvy round here for a while. With him to look after full time you're going to have to help me more than usual.'

'Of course, Ma.'

'You can start by boiling an egg for yourself. I'm sorry there's nothing more substantial for you but I just haven't had the time to cook. Or go to the shops, come to that.'

'Can I go in and see him?'

'Aye, but keep your distance. I don't want you coming down with it as well.'

Lizzie found her father awake, his eyes swivelling to her when she entered the room. 'It's only me. How are you feeling?'

'Bloody awful, if I was telling the truth. Steaming hot one minute, freezing cold the next.'

Lizzie noticed that the quilt off her bed was lying on the floor, no doubt brought through by her ma to use when he was having the freezing bit.

'Is there anything I can get you?' she asked, shocked at how haggard he looked.

'No, lass. But thanks for the offer.'

'I'll leave you to it, then. I'd better go on through and have my dinner.'

'Aye, fine.'

She was shaken. Her father was ill all right, if appearances were anything to go by.

'Hold my hand, Eth. Hold my hand?' Doogie pleaded on the fourth day of his illness.

His hand, when she took it, was cold as ice. She stood by helplessly as he began to shake, Lizzie's quilt already on the bed.

Ach, to hell with it. If she was going to catch it herself then she was going to catch it.

'What are you doing?' he chittered when she kicked off her shoes and started to climb in beside him. She had spent the last three nights with Lizzie in the kitchen bed.

'Getting you warm. What do you think?'

'Oh, Ethne,' he whispered, touched to the core.

'Now cuddle up.'

'Chrissie's down with it now,' Dot announced to Ethne the following day.

'Oh dear.' This was dreadful news.

'The women in the close are taking it in turn to look after her. Except you, of course. You've got your hands full with Doogie.'

Ethne ran a weary hand over her forehead. 'Is Chrissie bad?'

'You can imagine, a woman her age.'

They looked grimly at each other, both thinking the same thing. Chrissie's age and her already enfeebled state of health were the big worries.

'I'm surprised the doctor didn't suggest she go into hospital,' Ethne commented. 'Surely that would be the best place for her?'

'He did suggest it, but Chrissie refused point blank to go. She said she's had enough of hospitals lately. She was quite adamant about it.'

'Even though.' Ethne frowned.

'It might reach the stage where the doctor forcibly makes her go. But it hasn't come to that yet.'

'Would you like a cup of tea?' Ethne offered. 'I could certainly use one myself.'

'I'll tell you what. Sit down and I'll make it. What's more, I've got a lovely cake I baked this morning which I'll fetch. How does that sound?'

'Sheer heaven.'

Dot laughed. 'It's chocolate, too.'

Ethne smiled for the first time in days.

'Oh, God, Eth, I'm sorry. I couldn't help myself.'

Ethne didn't have to ask him what he was apologising for; the smell gave the game away.

Tears crept into Doogie's eyes. 'I feel so ashamed and embarrassed. So humiliated.'

Ethne shrugged. 'We're man and wife, Doogie. In sickness and in health, remember?'

She set about doing what had to be done, thanking God it was a Thursday, late night at the steamie. Lizzie could go when she got in from work.

Ethne opened the door in answer to a knock to find a well-dressed stranger standing there. 'Yes?'

The man removed his bowler hat. 'I'm Mr Cathcart, owner of the dairy. I've dropped by to see how Doogie is.'

Ethne immediately wiped her hands on her pinny. 'Come in, Mr Cathcart. Come in. This is kind of you.'

She ushered him into the kitchen, and his eyes flicked briefly round the room before settling again on Ethne. 'Flu, I was told.'

'That's right. He's confined to bed on doctor's orders until he gets better.'

'And how is he?'

Ethne pulled a face. 'Not good, I'm afraid.'

'I'm sorry to hear that.'

'Would you care to speak to him? He's awake – at least, he was five minutes ago.'

'That's one of the reasons I'm here. I wanted a word.'

Was it her imagination, or did that sound ominous? 'If you'll just follow me.'

The moment Doogie saw Cathcart he tried to struggle upright. 'Mr Cathcart,' he stammered in surprise.

'No, no, just stay as you are, Doogie. No need to stand on ceremony.'

Doogie gratefully sank back on to his pillows. 'How are the horses? Who's looking after them?' he asked in a shaky voice.

'You've not to worry, Doogie. Everyone has pitched in and the horses are just fine. Though missing you, I dare say.'

'Pitched in?'

'All the milkmen and myself. I doubt we're taking as good care of them as you do, but they're being fed and watered, and appear content enough.'

Doogie gave a sigh of relief. He'd been genuinely concerned about the horses and their welfare. 'I'll be with them again just as soon as I'm able,' he assured Cathcart.

'Any idea when that might be?'

'The doctor said it could be as long as three weeks,'

Ethne informed him. 'So it could still be another fort-night.'

'I won't lose my job, I hope?' Doogie was worried.

'Of course not.' Cathcart smiled. 'I'm not about to get rid of the best stableman I've ever had.'

The relief Doogie felt was reflected on his face.

'As I said to you, we're getting by. The one thing is, I hadn't realised just how much work is involved since I expanded the rounds several years back, so I've taken on a lad to help you. A sort of apprentice, if you will. I hope you approve?'

'Of course, Mr Cathcart. Whatever you think's best.'

'That'll be a bit of a burden off your shoulders when you return – which I don't expect until you're fully fit. Understand?'

'I understand,' Doogie acknowledged gratefully.

'Now, I'd better make a move. Lots to do.'

'Thank you for coming, Mr Cathcart. I appreciate it.'

'That's all right. So, if you'll show me out, Mrs McDougall?'

Cathcart stopped at the outside door and laid a restraining hand on Ethne's shoulder before she could open it. 'How are you coping for money, by the way?'

Ethne decided to be honest. 'Not too well, I'm afraid. We have a daughter who works, but she doesn't earn a lot. So it's a struggle.'

'I thought as much.' Cathcart produced his wallet and took out two five pound notes. 'This should help.'

Like most people of her background and class, Ethne had an aversion to even the idea of charity, far less accepting any. 'Oh, no, sir. I couldn't possibly.'

'Yes you can, Mrs McDougall. In fact I insist on it.

And I am Doogie's boss, don't forget – used to having my own way where employees are concerned.'

Ethne reluctantly took the notes, which were indeed a godsend. 'We'll pay you back, of course.'

'There's no need,' Cathcart said kindly, waving the offer aside. 'Just get that man of yours well again. He's sorely missed. I wasn't exaggerating when I said he's the best stableman I've ever had. He is by a mile.'

Ethne felt proud. 'Thank you, sir,' she said in a quiet voice, eyes shining.

When Cathcart had gone Ethne hung her head for a few moments, wanting to cry but not allowing herself to. Then she went through to Doogie and showed him the money. They both agreed that Cathcart was a boss in a million.

A real gem.

Ethne woke, and wondered what had disturbed her. Beside her Lizzie slept on.

Then she heard it again. Doogie was talking, though she couldn't make out what he was saying. Swinging her legs out of bed she reached for her dressing gown. Then she padded through to the bedroom, where she found Doogie, fast asleep, tossing and turning and spouting absolute gibberish. She crossed to the gas mantle and lit it, filling the room with soft, yellow light.

She winced on feeling his forehead, which was not only covered in sweat but red hot. He was clearly delirious.

What to do? She bit her lip as she thought about that. A glance at the bedside clock told her it was twenty past two in the morning. Should she get Lizzie up and ask her to go and fetch the doctor?

Ethne shivered from cold. Returning to the kitchen she picked up one of the wooden chairs at the table and carried it back through to the bedroom where she placed it beside the bed. She then went for her coat and put it on over her dressing gown.

She'd sit with him, she decided. See how things went. If he got any worse she'd wake Lizzie.

'Ma?'

Ethne came quickly awake to find Lizzie gazing at her in concern. 'I must have dozed off,' she muttered.

'Have you been there all night?'

'Most of it, lass. Your da was delirious.'

'Well, he looks all right to me now.'

Ethne glanced at Doogie, who was sleeping peacefully as a baby. Relief surged through her at the sight of him. 'Thank God,' she whispered, coming to her feet.

Bending over Doogie she kissed him lightly on the forehead. She'd change the bedclothes later, she decided. They'd need changing after the previous night.

'I'll get you some breakfast,' she yawned, addressing Lizzie.

'I'll do that myself, Ma. You should go back to bed.'

Ethne shook her head. 'I'm fine. Don't worry about me.'

The pair of them returned to the kitchen where Lizzie began to dress, and Ethne fired up the range to make tea.

'How's Chrissie?' Ethne asked when Dot called in later that day to see if she needed anything.

'More or less the same. How about Doogie?'

203

Ethne explained how worried she'd been.

'He's all right now, though?' Dot queried.

'The best he's been since falling ill. He's well on the mend, I'm sure of it. Last night was a turning point.'

Dot smiled. 'You must be relieved.'

'You can say that again. I can't wait for all this to be over and him back at the dairy again. For things to be normal, in other words.'

'I can imagine. It's been quite an ordeal for you.'

'And him, don't forget.'

Dot shook her head. 'Men! They can be a pain in the backside, but it's at times like this you appreciate them and wonder what you'd do without the sods.'

Ethne couldn't have agreed more.

Doogie improved rapidly after that, gaining strength with every passing day, impatient to be told by the doctor he could get up. He was heartily sick of being in bed.

He'd been lost for words on learning that Ethne had stayed up all night at his bedside when he was delirious, something he had no recollection of. Finally he'd shyly thanked her, but Ethne had dismissed the whole business as if it had been nothing.

His illness, and Ethne's care, had given Doogie a lot to think about.

Dot was coming out of the lav when a scream rang out. Jesus Christ! she thought in alarm. What was going on?

Babs Millar burst on to the landing from Chrissie's house, eyes wide with shock.

'What is it, Babs? What's the matter?' Dot demanded, hurrying down the stairs to join her.

Babs took a deep breath, then another. 'It's Chrissie,' she managed to gasp at last. 'She's dead.'

Dot stared at her neighbour, who was obviously in a state of shock. 'Are you sure?'

'I didn't touch her or anything, but she's dead. There was no mistaking it.'

Ethne, who'd also heard the scream, appeared. 'What's up?'

'It's Chrissie. Babs says she's dead,' Dot replied.

Ethne's hand went to her mouth. This was awful, though not entirely unexpected considering Chrissie's age and frailty. 'Oh dear,' was all she could think of to say.

'Let's go and check,' Dot declared. 'And if she is we'll have to get the doctor.'

Chrissie, who'd been sitting up in bed, had slumped sideways. Her eyes were closed and there was a waxy pallor to her face. Bracing herself, Dot felt for a pulse, but couldn't find one.

'She's dead all right,' she said quietly. 'God rest her soul.'

'Amen,' Babs added, starting to get over her scare.

'Well, it's what she wanted,' said Ethne.

'How do you mean?' asked Babs.

Ethne shrugged. 'I had a conversation with her some while back and she told me she wanted to go. Said she was useless nowadays, no good to anyone, and that it would be for the best if she simply nodded off in her chair.' Ethne paused for a moment. 'Well, she got her wish, only she nodded off in her bed not the chair.'

Dot sighed. 'Poor soul.'

'I'll go for the doctor,' Babs volunteered. 'It was me who found her, after all.'

When she returned half an hour later Dr Gilmour was with her.

'According to the post mortem it was a heart attack, brought on by the flu, that killed Chrissie,' Ethne informed Doogie, having just learnt this from Dot.

'She was a nice old biddy,' Doogie commented, though in truth he'd only ever spoken to her a few times.

'She'll be missed, at least by those in the close.'

'Aye,' Doogie agreed. 'When's the funeral?'

'As soon as Dot can get it organised. Luckily Chrissie left a policy that'll take care of the funeral expenses, otherwise I don't know what we'd have done. And we're going to take it in turns to feed Leo until we can find him a new home.'

'So, we'll be having new neighbours,' Doogie mused.

Ethne hadn't thought of that. Doogie was right, and it would be soon, too. The factor who handled the rental of the tenement wouldn't leave it empty for long.

'Ma?'

'Yes? What is it, Pearl?'

'I've been thinking.'

'Uh-huh?'

'About Mrs Wylie's house.'

Dot frowned. 'What about it?'

'Would it be in bad taste if Willie and I went after the place?'

Dot stared at her daughter in astonishment. 'You and Willie? But you won't be getting married for ages yet.'

'We can easily change that. Instead of a church wedding we could go to the register office and have it done there.

It would save a lot of money, apart from anything else. And when you think about it, living in Mrs Wylie's house would be perfect for us. I mean, we'd be in the same close as you and Da.'

'Would you want that?'

'Oh aye.'

Dot continued to frown. 'Have you spoken to Willie about this?'

'Not yet, but I could go round to his house now and have a word. The thing is, if he agrees we'll have to move quickly before someone else gets it.' Pearl hesitated, then went on. 'There's something else, Ma.'

'Which is?'

'Wasn't Mrs Wylie all alone in the world, no relatives or anything?'

Dot nodded.

'So that means there's no one to claim her furniture and other belongings, in which case Willie and I could just take them over should we move in. Think of the money that would save.'

Pearl had a point, Dot thought grimly. And a very practical one too. Would Chrissie have approved? she wondered. And the answer was yes. She most certainly would have done if it gave a young couple a good start to their marriage.

As it transpired Willie was all for the idea, so Pearl and Dot went to see the factor at the earliest opportunity. Pearl paid the first week's rent there and then.

Chapter 14

'I still can't believe this is Willie's and mine!' Pearl exclaimed excitedly, gazing round. She and Lizzie were standing in what had been Mrs Wylie's kitchen. 'I mean, we have absolutely everything laid on. We don't have to buy a knife, a fork or anything. It's all here.'

Lizzie didn't think she'd like to take over a dead person's house. It didn't seem right to her, somehow, though it obviously wasn't bothering Pearl.

'There is one thing I am going to buy, though,' Pearl went on.

'What's that?'

'New sheets for the bed. I don't mind the blankets or the quilt, but not the sheets. She died in those, for God's sake.'

Lizzie suppressed an inward shudder. 'I don't blame you there,' she replied.

'Oh, Lizzie, I'm so happy! Just think, two weeks on Saturday and I'll be Mrs Willie Henderson. I can't wait!'

'Have you found a dress yet?'

Pearl shook her head. 'Not so far. But I will. Have no

doubt about that.' Her expression became one of reflection. 'It would have been nice to be married in a church wearing a bridal gown, mind you, I'm not saying it wouldn't. But I'll settle for the register office and what goes with that as it means getting married more quickly. And think of the money we're saving. An awful lot, I can tell you.'

She crossed to a cupboard and opened it. 'Fancy a sherry?' she asked, taking out a bottle, then laughed when she saw the look on Lizzie's face. 'Oh, it's all right. Mrs Wylie won't be needing it any more, will she? Anyway, the sherry's mine now, like everything else in the house.'

'I don't know,' Lizzie demurred, still uncertain.

'Well, I'm having one, so there. Last chance?' Pearl offered when she'd filled a glass for herself.

'Oh, all right,' Lizzie agreed, thinking, what the hell!

'Why don't we have a toast?' Pearl suggested when she'd given Lizzie her drink. 'You make it.'

Lizzie had a quick think. 'To you and Willie and a wonderful life together.'

'And a wean before long. Willie's desperate to have one of those.' She paused for a second. 'Actually, a lot more than one,' she added, laughing again.

The sherry turned out to be so nice they finished the bottle.

It was Doogie's first day back at the stables and he was nervous as could be, knowing he was going to have to speak to Daisy at some point and tell her what he'd decided. He wasn't looking forward to that at all.

He'd already met John, the lad Mr Cathcart had hired

as an apprentice, who'd turned out to be a likeable, lively young man, eager to please and quick on the uptake. He knew he wasn't going to have any trouble working with the boy.

Doogie had been delightfully surprised at how well the horses, and the stables themselves, had been looked after in his absence. Even so, there was still an awful lot of catching up to do.

His heart sank when Daisy eventually appeared with the morning tea, a cup for him and another for John.

'Fully recovered, eh?' She smiled.

'Still a bit weak, I have to admit. But fit enough for a return to duty.' He was having to force himself to look her in the eye.

'You've lost weight,' she commented good-humouredly.

'Aye, I have that. But I'll put it on again before long.'

Daisy's gaze flicked to John, then back again to Doogie, the smile never leaving her face. 'Can I have a private word, Doogie?'

'Of course.'

She moved away and he went with her. 'Can I come tonight, usual time?' she whispered. 'Or is John going to be here?'

'Leave him to me. I'll be expecting you.'

'Right.'

'I'll see that gets attended to,' Doogie declared in his usual voice, though John, drinking his tea, didn't appear to be paying them any particular attention.

'Thanks, Doogie,' Daisy replied, and walked off.

A little later Doogie explained to John that, after being away from the horses for so long, he wanted to spend time alone with them that night to re-establish his relationship with each and every one. A lie, of course. But John was delighted to have the night off.

Tears, Doogie thought, there were bound to be lots of those. And undoubtedly a scene. But, as far as he was concerned, his argument was flawless. With the advent of John it was going to be impossible to meet up in the stables in future. And there was nowhere else they could go.

He started when he heard a noise. Turning, he saw that Daisy had arrived, carrying what looked like a bottle of whisky. She came straight up to him and kissed him full on the lips, and he did his best to respond as if he was enjoying it.

'I brought a bottle of whisky as I presumed you'd be skint after weeks off work,' she said, smiling at him.

'You presumed right.'

She handed him the bottle. 'Make mine a large one.'

His hands were trembling as he poured, though she didn't seem to notice when he gave her her glass.

'Slainte!' she said, still smiling.

'Slainte.' He downed his in a single swallow. 'That's better,' he breathed.

'First for a while?'

He nodded.

'Then you'd best have a refill.'

He did, and had another, though smaller, swallow from that. He was hating this, absolutely hating it. But his mind was made up. From here on in he was going to be faithful to Ethne.

'I've missed you,' Daisy said. 'Quite a lot, actually.'

Doogie inwardly groaned.

'But I'm afraid that doesn't change matters.'

He blinked. What was she on about?

'I've got some bad news, I'm afraid, Doogie.' She indicated a nearby bale. 'Let's sit and talk.'

Christ, she was bloody pregnant! he suddenly thought. But she couldn't be. He'd always been careful. Used a sheath every time, except the first.

He glanced at her waist, but couldn't tell if she was up the duff or not due to the roll of fat already bulging there. 'So what's this bad news?' he croaked when they were both sitting down.

Daisy reached over and stroked his hand. 'You really are a smashing bloke, Doogie. And we've had a terrific time together, right?'

He nodded.

'I know this is going to upset you, but the fact is I've met someone else.'

He couldn't believe his ears. 'You've what?'

'Met someone else while you were off ill. He's single, and madly keen on me. Daft on me, you could say. Thinks the sun shines out of my backside.'

Doogie stared blankly at her. If this meant what he thought it did then his luck was well and truly in. He wasn't going to have to break it off with her after all – she was breaking off with him. 'I see,' he murmured, trying to look crestfallen.

'So I think . . . well, I just can't come here any more. I'm sorry, but it wouldn't be fair on Percy.'

Percy! What sort of name was that? Doogie frowned. 'Is he English?'

'No. Why do you ask?'

'His name. I just wondered.'

'He's from Maryhill.'

Doogie drank more of his whisky, trying not to show his relief. 'So, that's that then.'

'I really am sorry. But this is a chance for me, Doogie, you must see that. I'm not getting any younger and this could lead to marriage, which is what I want.'

'I understand, Daisy. I just hope he's good enough for you. You deserve the best.'

She positively beamed. 'Do you really think so?'

'Oh aye,' he lied. 'In a way I'm pleased. For you, that is. And I wish the pair of you every happiness.'

Daisy laughed. 'Hold on there. Percy hasn't proposed yet. But I'm sure he will, given time. I'm almost certain it's on the cards.'

Doogie tore his gaze away from the voluptuous swell of her bosom. There would be no more of that. Or the other. 'It would have been difficult to go on anyway,' he said sorrowfully. 'Because of John, you realise.'

'Aye,' she agreed. 'It would have been.'

He couldn't help asking, curiosity getting the better of him. 'Have you and Percy . . . you know?'

'No. I didn't think it was fair until after I'd had this wee chat with you.'

For some reason he was touched. 'Thank you. I appreciate that.'

She waggled her now empty glass. 'I could use some more whisky, Doogie.'

He immediately jumped to his feet and took the glass from her. 'Coming right up.'

She watched him as he refilled both glasses, her eyes shining in memory. If only he hadn't been married, or had agreed to leave his wife. But he was and he wouldn't.

213

More's the pity on both counts. Doogie would have suited her down to the ground. There again, Percy wasn't such a bad catch – if and when she landed him, that was.

'Will you miss me?' she asked wistfully when he handed her the refill.

'Of course.' At least that was true. He would.

'And I'll certainly miss you.'

He took a deep breath. 'I'd better get on in a minute. I still have plenty to do here before I go home.'

'Doogie?'

'What?'

'How about one last time? I'm willing if you are.'

His initial reaction was to refuse. He had promised himself to be faithful from here on in to Ethne, after all. Again his eyes were drawn to her bosom, and his resistance, not to mention his good intentions, began to fail. He suddenly realised his mouth had gone dry, and he'd begun to twitch in the trouser department. Oh, but he was tempted.

'I don't think I have a sheath,' he croaked.

'Go and check.'

He went to their special hidey-hole, which fortunately no one had discovered while he was off ill, to find there was one left.

'Well?' she demanded.

He picked it up and showed it to her.

'So what do you say?'

Where was the harm? he asked himself. As she said, it would be the last time. He'd be a mug to pass it up.

'All right, Daisy.'

She laid her drink aside and, standing, began to strip.

*　　*　　*

214

Doogie shook his head in awe as he made his way home. As of yet this Percy bloke had no idea what lay in store for him. What a truly amazing lover Daisy was.

Lucky, lucky bastard.

The Baxters' house was jam-packed with people celebrating Pearl and Willie's wedding. There were so many present they'd spilled out on to the landing and up and down the stairs. Shughie Millar was in the kitchen playing on his squeezebox.

'Hello, gorgeous.'

Lizzie started, not having seen Jack making his way towards her through the crowd. 'Oh, it's you.'

'Some sort of greeting that,' he replied, trying to make out he'd taken offence at the coolness of it.

He'd had a few, Lizzie noted. There again, so had most of the folk. There was alcohol everywhere. Some supplied by the Baxters, other bottles brought along by the guests themselves. She raised an eyebrow.

'I mean it, you know. You are gorgeous.'

'Don't try your flannel on me, Jack White. It won't work.'

'I wasn't flannelling you. I was telling the truth.'

'There you go again,' she admonished. 'More of the guff.'

Jack's pale blue eyes, which she still found mesmerising, bored into hers. 'You're dangerous, Lizzie, do you know that?'

She laughed. 'How so?'

'You just are. You're the sort of lassie a chap falls for. Even the likes of me.'

'Is that a fact?'

'That's a fact. I assure you.'

She was finding this amusing. 'I think you're the one who's dangerous, Jack. Very much so.'

'Me?'

'Oh yes,' she said softly. 'You.'

'Is that because you're as attracted to me as I am to you?'

He really was laying it on thick, she told herself. With a bloody trowel in fact. 'I'm not attracted to you in the least,' she lied.

'No?'

'Not in the least.'

He gave her a wolflike smile which reduced her knees to jelly.

'Now why don't I believe that?'

'Because you're bigheaded, that's why. With far too big a tip for yourself.'

The wolflike smile widened even further. 'What would you do if I kissed you here and now?'

It was a game, she thought. Though she'd have loved him to kiss her, but certainly not in full view of everyone. 'Slap your face for you, that's what.'

'Would you indeed?'

'Yes I would. So there.'

'I'd better not, then.'

'No, you'd better not.'

He leaned close and whispered in her ear, 'What if I felt your arse? I could do it so no one would see.'

She flamed scarlet. 'Don't you dare, Jack White! Don't you bloody well dare.'

'It's a beautiful arse too,' he further whispered. 'I've often admired it.'

'Excuse me,' she declared, and pushed her way into the crowd.

She was sure she could hear Jack laughing behind her.

'Do you remember our wedding?' Doogie said.

'Of course I remember our wedding. How could I forget it? I mean, you don't, do you?'

'We had a wonderful time. It went on for three days, as I recall.'

Ethne smiled, thinking back. It had indeed gone on for three days, but then Highland weddings were like that. A few snatched hours' sleep here and there and then back into the fray again. 'Aye, it did,' she agreed.

'And you were not only the bride, but the bonniest lass there. I was proud to be your husband.'

Ethne blinked at him in astonishment, unable to remember the last time Doogie had paid her a compliment. 'Were you?'

'I was. Proud as punch. The envy of every other man present.'

He hadn't been so bad-looking himself in those days, she reflected. Not that he'd changed all that much. He was carrying a bit more weight than he had, and his hair was thinner, the face a little lined where it hadn't been before. But all in all the years had been kind to him.

Doogie slipped an arm round her waist and drew her closer. 'You were aye the one for me, you know. Aye the one. I fell for you the first time I clapped eyes on you.'

A warm feeling that had nothing to do with the heat of the room spread through her. She suddenly giggled. 'You're embarrassing me now.'

'Am I?' he teased.

'Yes you are, Dougal McDougall.'

'And you're still the bonniest lass as far as I'm concerned. And always will be.'

She looked into his face and saw he meant it. 'Oh, Doogie,' she whispered, not sure what to make of this declaration of affection.

Doogie smiled, then pecked her on the cheek. 'And before you ask what that's for, it's just for being you.'

Ethne quickly brushed away the tear that glistened briefly in her eye.

'So what do you think of Willie, Jack?' Pearl asked. Her cousin had only met Willie for the first time that day.

'Seems a nice enough chap.'

'Is that the best you can do?'

Jack shrugged. 'In the circumstances.'

'Don't you think he's terribly handsome?'

'Oh, terribly,' Jack replied sarcastically. 'I always notice that about other men.'

Pearl playfully punched him on the arm. 'Be serious.'

'I am. Anyway, being beautiful, or handsome, is in the eye of the beholder. Isn't that what they say?'

Pearl wasn't quite sure whether that was some sort of jibe or not. 'Thanks for coming today, Jack. I appreciate it.'

'Of course I came. You're my cousin, aren't you?' He lowered his voice. 'Even if we have got up to a few shenanigans in the past.'

'Don't you dare ever mention that to anyone,' she hissed.

'As if I would,' he teased.

'You just better not.'

He made a sign over his chest. 'Cross my heart I won't. Satisfied now?'

'I suppose I'll have to be.'

'And very pleasurable it was too. Indeed it was.'

'Jack!'

'Only joking.'

She frowned. 'You mean it wasn't pleasurable?'

'Of course it was. And I'd love to do it again given half the chance.'

'You really are a rogue,' she admonished, but secretly delighted. She'd always fancied Jack, and still did even though she'd just got married. He was simply that sort of man.

'A rogue through and through,' he agreed. 'Through and through.'

'And wicked with it.'

'Oh, I wouldn't say that. I've certainly never considered myself wicked.'

'Well you are. Believe me. Anyone who's said what you just have has to be.'

'You mean about . . .'

'Jack!' She laughed, cutting him off. 'Enough.'

'Then enough it is. Let's change the subject. I thought you looked very fetching during the ceremony.'

'Do you like my suit?'

The suit she was wearing was grey, nipped at the waist, the skirt full length. Her white blouse was tied at the neck with a black choker.

'Very nice.'

'There's that word again!' she exclaimed. 'Willie's nice, my suit's nice. Can't you say anything else?'

'I think it's lovely. As are you. How's that?'

Pearl sighed in exasperation, knowing she wouldn't get anything sensible out of him now.

Dressed up or not, she wasn't a patch on Lizzie, Jack reflected after Pearl had left him to mingle some more. Not a patch.

He went in search of another drink.

'So how does it feel to be an old married woman?' Lizzie teased Pearl that Monday morning as they met up for work. Honeymoons were strictly for the better off and idle rich.

'Just fine, thank you very much.'

Lizzie looked expectantly at Pearl, waiting for her to elaborate. 'And?'

'And what?'

'You know?'

Pearl decided to confide in Lizzie, who was her best friend after all. 'Well, Saturday night was a waste of time, if you get my meaning. Willie was far too pissed to do anything. But Sunday morning . . .' She broke off to smile knowingly. 'It was fabulous. Far better than I imagined it would be. Simply terrific.'

'Better than before?'

Pearl frowned. 'How do you mean?'

'Was it better because you were in bed and not out the back close?'

Pearl sniffed. 'I'll have you realise I was a virgin up until then. I don't know what gave you the idea I wasn't.'

Lizzie stared incredulously at her friend. Who was she trying to kid? Of course she'd had sex with Willie prior to the wedding. She'd almost admitted as much on several occasions. 'Oh aye,' she said sarcastically.

220

'It's true, I tell you.'

'And I'm a four foot black pygmy. Pull the other one, Pearl Baxter.'

'It's true,' Pearl insisted indignantly. 'I was a virgin until yesterday morning.'

Lizzie didn't believe a word of it.

The nights were lengthening out nicely, Doogie reflected as he trudged back to the stables for his evening stint. Summer wasn't all that far away.

He was thinking about that when he suddenly saw Daisy walking towards him in the company of a man. Percy? Yes – the couple were arm in arm.

Should he stop and say hello, or just go on by? Just go on by, he decided. Unless Daisy halted and talked, that was. And why shouldn't she? To Percy he'd simply be someone she knew from work.

They were close enough for him to get a good look at Percy now, and he wasn't impressed by what he saw. The man was tall and gangly, skinny as the proverbial rake. As a couple they appeared quite incongruous. A tall skinny man with a far shorter, fat woman. They looked ridiculous together.

Closer still, Doogie could now make out that Percy had a beak of a nose and one funny in-turned eye. He wondered if he had shagged her yet, feeling a pang of jealousy despite himself.

'Evening, Doogie,' Daisy said as they passed one another.

'Evening, Daisy,' he replied politely, continuing on his way as she'd given no sign of stopping and initiating a conversation.

He waited till he'd turned a corner before bursting out laughing. The pair of them had looked a right pair of misfits. A right couple of clowns.

For some reason that made him feel better about the situation. Percy was a joke as far as he was concerned.

'Why are you so fidgety tonight?' Ethne demanded from the chair facing Doogie. Lizzie was downstairs visiting Pearl and Willie.

'Am I?'

'You have been ever since you got back from the stables. Fidget, fidget, fidget. It's getting on my nerves.'

Doogie was only too aware he'd been fidgeting, having decided this was to be the night. He couldn't understand why he was so nervous. He'd shagged Ethne a thousand times and more. But not for some while, he reminded himself. And there had been Daisy in between – something he now felt rather ashamed about.

'I think I might nip to the Argyle and have a dram?' he said tentatively, certain she'd put her foot down.

Ethne glanced at the clock. 'Aye, well, you'd better hurry, then. It's almost closing.'

'You don't mind?'

'Not if it'll stop you fidgeting. Now get on with you.'

Doogie didn't need a second telling.

'Ethne?'

'What?'

'I thought we might . . .' He ran a hand lightly over her backside.

So that was it, Ethne thought, her libido firing up. How she'd missed this, though she would never have

222

admitted it to anyone. Least of all to Doogie.

She giggled as his hand moved up to find a breast, then slowly turned towards him. 'It's taken you long enough,' she chided gently.

Doogie took that for consent. He musn't initiate any of the many tricks Daisy had taught him, he reminded himself. He didn't want to arouse any suspicions.

'I explained, I'm not getting any younger. I haven't felt the need,' he lied.

'And you do now?'

He could feel himself hardening. 'I do now,' he said huskily.

Ethne smiled in the darkness. Perhaps from here on in things would go back to how they'd once been.

'Then come here,' she crooned, putting her arms round him.

It was only after they'd finished that Doogie realised he hadn't once thought of Daisy. Not once.

It pleased him.

Chapter 15

'You seem a lot happier of late,' Dot commented to Ethne over a cup of tea in Ethne's kitchen.

'Do I?'

'It appears to me you are. You're smiling more, and there's a difference about you. Any particular reason?'

Ethne took her time in replying. 'It's Doogie.'

'Oh aye?'

'Remember that conversation we had when I told you he'd gone off "it"? That he wasn't interested any more?'

Dot's eyes twinkled with amusement. 'And I told you that my Ron went through spells of either being like a randy rabbit or else not wanting to know?'

'Well . . . how shall I put this? Doogie has rediscovered his enthusiasm, shall we say.'

'I see.'

'Very much so. Not that I'm complaining or anything like that,' she added hastily. 'I'm not. But he's gone from one end of the scale to the other. Now he can't keep his hands off me.'

'Men are such funny creatures,' Dot mused, shaking

her head. 'So simple to read in many ways, so difficult in others.'

Ethne couldn't have agreed more. 'Mind you, I blame myself for what happened. I was far too hard on him after we'd had to leave Tomintoul. In hindsight that was a mistake.' She'd long since confided in Dot the real reason why they'd come to Glasgow.

'We all make those.' Dot smiled. 'It's human nature.'

'In a way I was cutting off my nose to spite my face.' Ethne blushed. 'Well I can't help it if I enjoy it as much as he does.'

Dot reflected on that. She couldn't have said the same, but on the other hand it pleased her to keep Ron happy when required. If nothing else it made for an easier life.

'So, it's back to normal then,' Dot declared.

'With a little more enthusiasm than before. But that'll probably wear off in time and then we'll be back to normal.' Ethne hesitated. 'I shouldn't really ask – it's rude, I suppose – but how are Pearl and Willie getting on where that's concerned? Everything as it should be?'

'As far as I know,' Dot replied. 'She hasn't exactly said anything, which is understandable as I'm her mother, but yes, I believe it is.'

'That's good. These things don't always work between a couple. Or so I've been led to understand.'

Dot nodded. 'Which must be terrible for those involved, if you think about it. At least that's never been the case between Ron and me, I'm delighted to say.'

Or herself and Doogie, Ethne thought.

There was a knock on the door and the conversation came to an end as they were joined by Babs Millar, and a little later by Jean Carmichael, who had also been invited to tea.

'Lizzie! Lizzie!'

Lizzie stopped in her tracks and, having recognised the voice, inwardly groaned.

'Wait up, Lizzie!'

She turned to Pearl. 'You go on ahead and I'll catch up if I can.'

Pearl glanced in the direction of Malkie, who was hurrying towards them. 'Are you sure?'

'Well I can't just ignore him, can I?'

'I suppose not.'

'See you shortly, then.'

Malkie came up as Pearl continued on her way home.

'Hello, Lizzie. How are you?' he asked.

'Just fine. And you?'

'Terrible, actually.'

'Oh?'

He cleared his throat, then lowered his voice. 'I miss you, Lizzie. Something chronic. I'm desperate for us to get back together again.' *

She remembered his kissing while noting he had a fresh crop of pimples on his face and neck. 'I'm sorry, Malkie. But I meant what I said. It simply doesn't work between us.'

'It does, Lizzie, it does! Why can't you see that?'

He was pitiful, she thought. Then she chided herself for being too harsh. She should be flattered he was so keen. She was about to reply when, out of the corner of her eye, she spotted a grinning Jack watching them. She felt uncomfortable. If only it was Jack pleading to be with her and not

Malkie. She'd have given anything for that to be the case.

She looked into Malkie's earnest features, and for the first time felt herself actually repelled by him. A weak man, she suddenly realised. The last thing she needed, or wanted. 'Malkie, just accept my decision, and leave it at that. Please?'

'But . . .'

'I said accept it!' she interjected sternly, and walked swiftly away after Pearl.

She hoped that was the end of it, and Malkie wouldn't bother her again.

He never did.

'So what's wrong with it?' Pearl demanded.

Willie moved his spoon around the bowl in front of him. 'It's not the same as my ma used to make.'

'Rice pudding is rice pudding, for Christ's sake!' Pearl retorted angrily.

'No it's not,' he countered. 'Ma always made milky rice whereas this is . . . well, not milky. It just doesn't taste right.'

Pearl glared at him. 'Well it's the best I can do. So there.'

Willie stared into his bowl, and didn't answer.

'Is there anything else you wish to criticise?'

Willie knew he shouldn't go on, but did anyway. 'Your mince is different as well.'

'My mince!'

'Ma's mince is . . .'

Pearl lost her temper. 'Damn your ma's mince! I'm sick to death hearing about your ma's this and your ma's that. It's me you're living with now and not your bloody ma. If my cooking is so horrible then why don't you go back to her, Mrs Perfect Henderson? My arse!'

Willie was shocked. He had never meant things to go this far. Pearl was being completely unreasonable. 'You don't mean that?'

'I damn well do. I didn't marry you to compete with your mother. I married you because I love you and thought you loved me.'

'But I do!' he protested.

'Then accept me for what I am. There's nothing wrong with either my rice pudding or my mince. It's obviously just different to what you're used to. Either come to terms with that or crawl on back to your ma like the good little mummy's boy you're turning out to be.'

Willie was appalled to be called that. 'I'm nothing of the sort,' he snapped.

'Aren't you?'

'No, I'm not.'

'Then stop damn well acting like one.'

Flouncing from the room, Pearl picked up her coat with the intention of going for a long walk to cool down. Willie finished his pudding vowing to keep his mouth shut in future. At least where Pearl's cooking was concerned.

He thought wistfully of the rice pudding his mother served up. There was no comparison.

'You've got to get a certificate of seamanship to work on a ship,' the Irishman told Jack. They were in one of the dockside bars Jack frequented.

Jack sighed. 'I know that. And I've tried. They won't entertain me, though, the excuse being there are more than enough deckhands already.'

Paddy eyed Jack shrewdly. 'Where there's a will there's a way, pal. If you know what I mean.'

228

Jack frowned. 'No, I don't.'

'In a word, cash. You come up with the right amount of that and I can get a certificate for you. In someone else's name mind, but a certificate just the same.'

Jack considered. 'How much?'

'Let me see now,' Paddy mused, his eyes never leaving Jack's. 'How about thirty quid?'

'And a berth to go with the certificate?'

Paddy sucked in a breath. 'Possible. But 'twould cost more.'

'How much more?'

'Another tenner.'

If his plans were going to work he needed that certificate, Jack thought. But could he trust the Irishman? He had no choice. 'It's a deal,' he agreed.

'Something in advance. A fiver maybe?'

Jack smiled thinly. 'Nope. Thirty quid when you deliver the certificate, and the tenner when I'm aboard ship and know the berth is mine.'

Paddy nodded slowly. 'All right. Meet me here, at this time, ten days from now. And bring your gear with you, for we'll be shipping out next morning.'

Excitement raced through Jack at the prospect. At long last he was finally on his way. 'I'll be here,' he promised.

'Now why don't you buy me a drink as I've solved all your problems for you? It's a large Irish, by the way.'

'One and only one. Understand?'

Paddy didn't reply. Simply gave a curt nod of his head, struck a match and began lighting his pipe.

Jack went up to order the Irish.

*   *   *

'Here's your tea, Mr McDougall,' said the girl, handing it to Doogie.

'And what's your name?'

'Sandra.'

'Well, thank you, Sandra. Daisy off ill, is she?'

'No. She's decided not to bring the tea through any more and told me to do it instead.'

The boy John came over and took his cup from her. 'No chocolate biscuits to go with it?' he joked.

'Get away with you. Daisy never brought you biscuits, chocolate or otherwise. You're pulling my leg.'

John laughed and moved away.

'So we'll be seeing you from now on,' Doogie mused thoughtfully.

'Aye, that's right. I hope you've no objections?'

'None whatsoever.'

'I'd better get back then. Ta-ra!'

'Ta-ra!' Doogie responded, while John kept silent.

Daisy was obviously trying to completely cut off any contact between them, Doogie reflected. Maybe it was just as well. It made the break between them a clean one.

He assumed things must be going well between her and Percy. Just as they were between him and Ethne, who'd stopped nagging as she had been.

He began humming in between sips of tea.

'They're desperate to have a baby,' Dot announced, referring to Pearl and Willie. She shook her head. 'Thank God those days are over for me. I'd hate to have to deal with that lot again.'

Ethne thought of the teething she'd had to go through with all three of hers, the awful croup Stuart had had when he was about eighteen months old, the childhood diseases, the accidents. And last, but not least, the ever ongoing worry about them as they grew up. 'Me too,' she agreed. It would be a nightmare.

'You love them dearly,' Dot went on, 'but, apart from anything else, they're so tiring. Especially when they're babies. I used to be completely drained at the end of the day.'

'Was Pearl a difficult child?'

'Not particularly. Though she could be a right cheeky monkey at times.' Dot paused, then smiled. 'Still is on occasion.'

They both laughed.

'What about yours?' Dot inquired.

'Nothing out the usual. My elder son Gordon did go through a problem stage for a couple of years, but it passed eventually.'

'I've always thought the lovely thing about grand-children is that you can hand them back. You have one, haven't you?'

Ethne nodded. 'Wee Mhairi, Gordon's lassie. I miss her dreadfully being down here. She's probably grown quite a bit since I last saw her.'

'It must be hard being separated from your two sons as you are?'

'Aye,' Ethne agreed wistfully. 'It is that. Even though they're both adults now, and Gordon married, it often brings a tear to my eye just thinking about them.'

'Well at least you've still got Lizzie,' Dot consoled. 'And a fine young woman she is too. A credit to you and Doogie. You must be proud of her.'

'We are. Very much so.'

231

'It's a pity you can't go back to Tomintoul.'

'I only wish we could,' Ethne sighed. 'Doogie's promised we will for a visit sometime, but it's going to be difficult. There's his job, for a start; he can't take time off from that until the apprentice is fully trained. And then there's the cost – we only scrape by as it is. Some weeks I can put a few bob by, but mostly I can't. It's usually a case of just making ends meet.'

'Same with us. Although I have to admit it's easier now that Pearl's out of the house, God bless her.'

Babies, Ethne thought, going back to the beginning of their conversation. Lovely really, but not for her.

Aye, for someone else.

'These are for you,' Doogie declared to an astounded Ethne, thrusting a bunch of flowers at her.

For a few moments she was completely lost for words. 'Me?' she eventually managed to say.

'That's right.'

She accepted the flowers and looked from them to his beaming face. 'But you've never bought me flowers before.'

'Well, there's always a first time.'

They were nice flowers too, she observed. Carnations mixed with pinks. 'What have you been up to, then?' she suddenly queried with a frown.

That took him aback. 'Nothing!' he protested.

'Oh, come on, Dougal McDougall. You wouldn't buy me flowers unless you had a reason.'

Doogie fought down his rising panic. It had never crossed his mind they would make her suspicious. 'I haven't been up to anything,' he insisted. 'I simply bought them to show my appreciation. And because I thought it would be a nice thing to do.'

'Appreciation for what?'

'How you looked after me when I was ill. And how you've been since then.'

Ethne's suspicions vanished and a lump came into her throat. 'You're nothing but a big soft nellie.' She smiled.

'Do you like them, then?'

'I think they're wonderful. Thank you.'

Going to him, she kissed his cheek. 'Thank you,' she repeated quietly.

'You'd better get them in water, then. And don't think I'll be making a habit of this. I won't.'

Ethne held the flowers to her nose, and smelled them. They were gorgeous.

She couldn't have been more delighted.

Should he hand in his notice, or simply disappear? Jack wondered. Disappear, he decided. That way if the Irishman let him down he would still have a job to go to. No point in burning bridges unnecessarily, after all.

And then there were his parents. He'd have to tell them, explain what he intended. If he disappeared without rhyme or reason they'd think God knows what, while his mother for one would be heartbroken, imagining all sorts.

He'd speak to them later that night, though he wasn't looking forward to it one little bit.

Pearl sighed. This marriage lark wasn't all it was cracked up to be. On top of working at the factory she had cooking and cleaning, not to mention the washing and ironing, to contend with.

At least she'd be able to give up the factory when a baby came along; it would be impossible to do otherwise. She fervently hoped she fell pregnant soon.

The other thing was Willie himself. Oh, they were getting on well enough, but she hadn't realised what a pernickety man he was. Thoroughly spoilt by his ma, of course. And now she was expected to spoil him the same way. Well, to hell with that.

'How's the stew?' she inquired politely, smiling at him across the table.

'Fine.'

'Are you sure?'

'Sure I'm sure.'

'Is it as good as your mother makes?'

Alarm bells rang in his head. 'Oh aye,' he lied.

'That's good then.'

'And the dumplings are great.'

'As good as your ma's?'

Oh Christ, he thought. She did go on. 'Even better, I'd say.'

Pearl expressed surprise, unsure whether or not he was fibbing. 'Really?'

'I promise you.'

'There's no pudding, I'm afraid. Just haven't had the time to make one.'

His mother always served a pudding, he reflected ruefully. Her roly poly was out of this world. 'That's all right. Doesn't do us any harm to go without.'

'No it doesn't. I am working full time, don't forget. While your ma doesn't at all.'

He elected not to answer that.

Pearl ate some of her stew, thinking it tasted excellent

234

to her. A recipe of Dot's. 'I'll be doing some ironing after the dishes,' she declared.

Willie wanted to ask her to take more care with his shirts. The last one he'd put on had been creased at the front, which he hadn't dared mention at the time.

The thing was, it was important to look neat and smart at the office. It mattered enormously if he was to get ahead. He'd never had any trouble before, when his mother had been ironing for him. Each and every shirt had been perfect when she'd finished with it.

But no, it wouldn't be a good idea to bring up the subject. It would only cause another row.

And as for the stew!

'I'll be working late all next week, Ma,' Lizzie announced.

'Why's that?'

'There's a big order coming in which we have to deal with as soon as possible. Mrs Lang, the supervisor, asked for people to work overtime and I volunteered.'

'More money, I hope?'

Lizzie laughed. 'Well, I'm not doing it for nothing, and that's a fact. They're paying one and a half times our normal hourly rate.'

Ethne nodded her approval. You could say what you liked about Lizzie, but she was certainly a grafter. 'Any idea when you'll be coming home?'

'About ten, I should think. At least at the beginning of the week. Maybe later towards the end depending on how we get on.'

'I'll keep something by for you,' Ethne assured her. 'You won't go without.'

'Thanks, Ma.'

'Is Pearl doing overtime as well?'

'She turned it down. Says she's got far too much to do at home. What with Willie's tea and the like. Between you and me, I think she's finding it all a bit much.'

'Aye, she'll be busy right enough,' Ethne agreed. 'Running a house is a full-time occupation by itself. As I'm sure she's now found out.'

Lizzie crossed over to the sink and washed her hands in preparation for having her meal. A hard week lay ahead, she reflected. But the extra money would come in handy. It always did.

'Lizzie, wait up!'

She stopped, and turned, to find Jack only a few feet behind her. He fell into step alongside.

'It's late for you to be out by yourself, isn't it?' he said.

'I've been doing overtime.'

He'd forgotten some of the girls had stayed on for that. 'I'll walk you to your close.' He smiled. 'Safer for you that way. You never know what could happen round here.'

Lizzie was glad of the company, especially Jack's. She caught a whiff of alcohol and realised he'd been drinking. 'How was the pub?'

'You can tell, eh?'

'The smell, Jack.'

'Aye well, I only had a few pints.' The truth was, he'd been celebrating, for the next night was when he was due to meet the Irishman. What he didn't mention was that a number of whiskies had accompanied the pints. He wasn't exactly drunk, but not far off it.

'Hold on a sec,' he said and, taking out a packet of cigarettes, lit one.

'So how are things?' he inquired politely.

'So so. And you?'

'Never better.'

'Oh?'

He declined to elaborate. 'You must be tired after such a long day?'

'Dead beat,' she confessed.

It was a lovely night, warm and sultry. Millions of stars twinkled down from above. An easy night, the sort to make a person feel relaxed.

They chatted all the way, Jack being very agreeable and funny with it, making her laugh more than once.

'Well, here we are,' she said when they arrived at her close mouth.

'Here we are indeed,' he agreed.

He glanced up and down the street, which was deserted. A sudden idea had come to him. 'Do you remember at Pearl's wedding I offered to kiss you?' he asked.

Lizzie nodded.

'Well, why not now? We can go into the back close and I'll kiss you there. We'll be quite alone this time.'

Lizzie's knees immediately turned to jelly at the prospect. Kiss Jack! There was nothing in the world she wanted more.

'Well?'

She made up her mind. 'All right,' she said quietly, unable to believe her luck. This was something she'd dreamed of.

'You lead the way.'

She shivered when his arms went round her and he leaned her against a wall. 'I've wanted to do this for a long, long time,' he whispered.

Then his lips were on hers, his eager tongue probing her mouth, her tongue responding.

'My God, you are a dangerous female,' he said when the kiss was over.

'Why dangerous?'

'You just are. At least as far as I'm concerned.'

Before she could reply he was kissing her again. She tensed slightly when his hands began to explore, then relaxed. She didn't care. It felt too good for that.

Her senses were swimming as the kissing went on, and his hands continued to move with even more urgency.

What had she done? an appalled Lizzie asked herself later, when she got into bed. What had she done!

Closing her eyes, she prayed that everything would be all right.

Jack stood at the ship's rail and watched Glasgow fall away behind him. Not only had the Irishman been able to get him a certificate of seamanship, but he had procured a berth aboard the SS *Clanranald* as well. The *Clanranald* – bound for Rangoon carrying a cargo of whisky and machine parts.

The great adventure had finally begun. He was off to see the world at last and have, hopefully, the time of his life.

For a brief moment he thought of Lizzie and the night before, and smiled. Then he put her out of his mind. She was in the past now, just as Glasgow was.

Chapter 16

E thne watched Doogie puzzling over the crossword in the evening newspaper. It still intrigued her that he'd taken up doing such a thing, albeit the crossword was a particularly simple one. Doogie just wasn't the type.

Doogie grunted, then scratched his chin with the end of the pencil he was holding, brow furrowed in concentration.

'How's John getting on?' Ethne inquired, making conversation.

'Fine,' Doogie replied without glancing up.

'He must be a big help to you?'

'He is.' Doogie's gaze remained riveted to the newspaper.

'He gets on well enough with the horses, then?'

Another grunt.

'I will say one thing, Doogie – I'm glad you've given up drinking at nights when you're out at the stables.'

The penny didn't drop for a moment or two, then he looked at her with an expression of astonishment. He

239

reminded Ethne for all the world of a little boy who'd been caught out doing something naughty.

'What's that?'

'You heard me. I'm glad you've given up drinking at nights. Apart from anything else we really can't afford for you to be spending money like that.'

Doogie swallowed hard. 'I wasn't drinking at nights.'

'Don't lie to me, Dougal McDougall. Of course you were. Do you think I'm daft or something?'

'I don't know where you got that idea from,' he blustered.

'Peppermints.'

'Eh?'

'I presume they were supposed to disguise the smell.' She laughed. 'Some hope! If anything they were a dead giveaway. I mean, why should a man like you suddenly take up peppermints, and always at the same time, unless he was trying to hide something? Stands to reason.'

Doogie didn't know what to say. He'd thought he was being crafty, getting away with it. But she'd known all along.

Ethne's eyes glittered with amusement. 'Still want to deny it?'

'Maybe I had the odd dram or two on the way home,' he finally conceded.

'The odd dram or two?' she repeated, voice laced with a combination of sarcasm and disbelief.

Lizzie, who was listening to this, had no wish to become involved. It was none of her business. Strictly between her parents.

Doogie glanced away, unable to hold Ethne's accusing stare. 'That's what I said, woman. One or two.'

'I hate it when you lie, Doogie. I truly do. Most times you had considerably more than that. I could tell by the way you spoke and carried yourself. I'm not stupid, you know.'

Doogie began to get angry, his anger fuelled by guilt. 'May I remind you that you're my wife, not my bloody keeper. You'd do well to remember that.' Throwing the newspaper to the floor, the crossword forgotten, he came to his feet. 'I'm going out,' he declared belligerently.

'Suit yourself.'

'To the Argyle. So there.'

Ethne didn't reply to the taunt.

'For a pint and a couple of drams,' he almost snarled.

Again Ethne didn't reply.

It wasn't until he was outside and striding towards the pub that Doogie remembered he was skint, without even a brass farthing to his name. He came up short, wondering what to do. He could hardly go back straight away; he'd look a right fool.

The only answer he could come up with, for the Argyle didn't do tick, was to walk the streets until closing time.

'Have you seen Jack recently?' Lizzie asked casually.

Pearl thought about that, and frowned. 'Now you mention it, I haven't. Strange that. Why do you ask?'

Lizzie shrugged, pretending indifference. 'No reason really. I just haven't seen him and wondered if he was ill or something.'

'That could well be it. There again, maybe he's been around and we simply haven't noticed.'

Lizzie knew fine well he hadn't been on the factory

floor all week. She'd been keeping an eye out for him.

'He'll turn up again soon enough,' Pearl went on. 'Bad pennies always do.'

Lizzie hoped her friend was right.

'Can I come in, Ma?'

'Of course, lass.' Dot saw immediately that Pearl was looking terrible. 'What's wrong?'

'I just wanted to talk, that's all.'

'Then I'll put the kettle on. I was about to anyway.'

Pearl glanced around the kitchen. 'Where's Dad?'

'He developed a headache so he's taken a powder and gone to bed early. Was it him you wanted to speak to?'

Pearl shook her head. 'No, you actually.'

'Well here I am, and all ears.'

Pearl collapsed into a chair. 'I'm so unhappy, Ma. I can't tell you how much.'

Dot stared at her daughter in consternation. 'What's making you that?'

'Everything, just about. But mainly the house, and Willie.'

Oh dear, Dot thought. This sounded ominous. 'Is he downstairs?'

'No, he's gone to the Masons. He does every week.'

'The Masons!' Dot exclaimed. 'I didn't know he was one of those?'

'Neither did I until after we were married. He hardly ever mentions it, says he's not supposed to. It's all sort of secret stuff apparently.'

'Well well,' Dot mused.

'According to Willie he joined them because it'll help him get on at the office. And that's about all he's told me.'

Dot laughed, having heard the stories of Masons rolling up their trouser legs at certain ceremonies, and identifying one another by funny handshakes. The whole business seemed rather childish to her.

Pearl ran a weary hand over her face. 'It's getting me down, Ma. I never seem to stop. Up in the morning to go to the factory, then home at night to make Willie's tea. He makes do with sandwiches at dinner time, as do I, though I still come back to eat them. Then after tea there's the never ending housework to be getting on with. Honestly, at the moment I've got a pile of ironing a mile high.'

Dot clucked her sympathy. 'That bad, eh?'

'Worse, Ma. And on top of that there's Willie himself.' She stopped for a moment, wondering how to go on.

'He's not hitting you or anything like that?' an anxious Dot queried before she could do so.

'No no,' Pearl quickly assured her. 'He's never laid a finger on me.' She hesitated. This was embarrassing. 'It's the sex, Ma,' she eventually said in a quiet voice.

Dot frowned. 'Is something wrong in that department?'

Pearl couldn't help but laugh. 'Far from it. And that's the trouble. He wants it every single night and morning. The only time he'll leave me alone is when I'm having my monthlies. But as soon as that's over he's at it again.'

'Well, he is young and virile, I suppose,' Dot commented slowly. 'And don't forget you're not long married so it'll still be something of a novelty for him.'

'But every night and morning, Ma! Without fail! I mean, where's the enjoyment in that? On top of which it's downright knackering.'

Dot could understand Pearl's complaint. You could have too much of a good thing, after all.

'I swear if he could he'd come home at dinner time and do it to me then as well.'

'As I said, his demands are bound to ease off in time. I promise you.'

'Not until I get pregnant they won't. He's obsessed about us having children, absolutely obsessed. I never knew men could be that way.'

'Have you spoken to him about it?'

'I've tried to, but he doesn't pay any heed. We're hardly in bed at night before he's on me. And in the morning it's not unusual for me to wake up and find him already pounding away.' Pearl shook her head. 'And often it's sore, as he . . . well, he doesn't wait for me to get ready, if you take my meaning. That can damn well hurt.'

Selfish, insensitive bugger, Dot thought. At least her Ron knew enough to hang on until she was moist. 'Have you explained that to him?'

'Oh aye, for all the good it's done me. Once he's up he just can't wait. And believe me he's up almost instantly.'

Dot didn't know what to say to that. Bloody men! she inwardly raged. Some of them had simply no thought for their wives, none at all. Their needs came first and foremost.

Pearl sighed. 'I'm sorry to talk to you about this, Ma, but who else could I turn to for advice? Certainly not Lizzie – she knows nothing about these things.'

That was true, Dot mused.

'So can you suggest anything?'

'Not really, short of having an all out row about it. If the man won't listen then he won't. But if I were you I'd try again, see if you somehow can't make him take heed.

Particularly about the pain he's causing you. That's unforgiveable.'

'I doubt it'll make any difference, Ma. But I'll try.'

'But there is something you can do when you finally fall pregnant. And from the sound of things the sooner the better.'

'What's that?'

'Play on this obsession of his about having children. Convince him he mustn't do it too often as it might damage the unborn baby, or cause you to miscarry. He might well fall for that.'

Pearl's face lit up. 'What a brilliant idea!'

'And lie, tell him he must wait until you're ready, or the same things could happen, miscarriage and what have you. Surely to God he'll listen then if he wants a wean so much.'

Pearl felt better than she had done in ages. Her ma's suggestion at least offered some hope for the future.

'It's been done before,' Dot went on. 'So it's not as if it's something new.'

The more Pearl considered the idea the more it appealed. She smiled at her mother. 'Aren't you the devious one?'

'Not really. It's just having a woman's mind, that's all. There are occasions in life when men have to be manipulated, which happens far more often than they're aware of.'

'Do you do that with Da?'

'Of course. Or I have done in the past when it was required. You see, women tend to be a mystery to men, whereas we understand them only too well. That gives us the advantage.'

The advantage, Pearl mused. Now why had she never thought of that, instead of seeing herself, as a female and a wife, in an entirely different light?

'In this case, Willie's weakness is desperately wanting children.' Dot smiled. 'That's something you can always turn against him when the time is right.'

'To my advantage,' Pearl said, matching Dot's smile.

'Exactly. Now, you'll be stopping work when the baby comes, I presume?'

Pearl nodded.

'That'll make things easier for you as well. Take a lot of the pressure off. In the meanwhile I'll do what I can to help. I can get stuck into that ironing for a start. And there's no reason, if you give me a spare key, why I can't go in and do housework for you sometimes.'

The relief Pearl suddenly felt was evident in her face. 'Oh, thanks, Ma. You're a gem.'

'I had thought of offering before, but didn't want to stick my big nose in where it might not be wanted. There's nothing worse than a mother doing that.'

Pearl got up, went to Dot and threw her arms round her. 'I really do appreciate this. Believe me I do. The advice and the help.'

'Let's look on the bright side. If he's at you as much as you say then surely it can't be long before you're expecting. Stands to reason.'

That made sense, Pearl reflected. She hadn't thought of it like that.

'Now,' Dot declared, breaking away as the kettle had begun to boil. 'I baked a lovely apple cake this afternoon. Would you like a piece?'

'Please,' Pearl enthused, eyes shining. Dot must be one

246

of the best mothers in the world. Pearl was pleased she'd had the courage to come and have a word with her.

Later that night Pearl spoke to Willie again, to no avail. He continued to insist on every morning and night. And he still wouldn't take his time before climbing aboard.

'Having trouble with the machine, Lizzie?' The speaker was Alan Duffie, who was employed at the factory doing the same job as Jack.

'That's right Alan. Can you fix it for me?'

'No doubt, lassie. But first tell me what's wrong.'

Alan was a man in his fifties, short with broad shoulders and grey, grizzled hair. He listened intently as Lizzie described the problem.

'Right, let's have a looksee,' he declared eventually.

Lizzie pulled her chair back to give him access to the machine, watching him as he went to work.

'I believe Jack is still off,' she said casually.

'He is that.'

'Is he ill or something?'

Alan shrugged. 'Search me. He just didn't turn up one day and hasn't reappeared since. There's been no word of explanation, at least none I've heard, which means he's right in the shite – pardon my French! – when he eventually does show up. It'll be the sack for him, I shouldn't wonder. The management doesn't take kindly to that sort of thing, believe me.'

'Oh!' Lizzie exclaimed softly. This was terrible news. 'You really think he might be given the sack?'

'Oh aye. Unless he's got one hell of an explanation as to why he hasn't been in touch. Serves him right, too, in my opinion. You just can't behave like that.'

It took Alan less than ten minutes to fix the fault, which had been a minor one.

It was a morose and depressed Lizzie who resumed work. From all accounts Jack was due for the high jump.

'What!' a furious Pearl exclaimed.

Willie inwardly squirmed under her accusing glare. 'I didn't think you'd mind,' he said lamely.

'Well I bloody well do.'

'There's no need to swear, Pearl. It's quite unnecessary.'

She was absolutely fuming by now. 'Let me get this straight. Starting tomorrow you'll be having tea at your mother's once a week?'

'Uh-huh.'

'But why, for Christ's sake?'

Willie shifted uncomfortably in his chair, unable to understand what all the fuss was about. 'Because she says she's not seeing enough of me recently.'

'Well isn't that surprising.' Pearl sneered. 'Has she forgotten you're now a married man?'

'What's that got to do with it?'

'It means your place is now with me and not her.'

'Of course it is. No one's arguing about that. But Mother and I have always been very close, closer probably than any other members of the family. She's simply missing me.'

'You certainly are a mummy's boy.'

'I'm nothing of the sort!' Willie snapped back. 'And I don't want to hear you say that again.'

A suspicious thought came into Pearl's mind. 'Has this got anything to do with my cooking? Have you been telling Mummy dear that I'm not very good at it? That I'm nowhere near her exalted standard?'

'Don't be ridiculous. Cooking's got nothing to do with it.'

'Are you sure?'

'Cross my heart.'

Pearl didn't believe him. If he was telling the truth then why wasn't he able to look her straight in the eye? 'You have been moaning to your mother about me, haven't you? And knowing her she's been only too happy to listen and probably run me down into the bargain.'

'That's nonsense.'

'Is it?'

'Yes it damn well is!'

'Now who's swearing, Mr Pure and Pious? Eh?' He pointed a finger at Pearl. 'It's all right for you. Your mother lives up the same close as us so you can drop in and see her any time you like. Isn't that so?'

Pearl bit her lip. It was. She couldn't deny it.

'Well?'

'That's not the point,' she prevaricated.

'Oh yes it is. Very much so.'

'But why every week?' she queried in despair. 'Isn't that a bit much?'

'Why every day if *you* want to?' he countered.

'But I don't see my mother every day.'

'But you could if you wished. So what's wrong with me seeing mine once a week?'

Pearl reached for her cigarettes and lit up. She needed something to calm her down. Willie smirked, thinking he'd won the argument. At that moment Pearl could have slapped him. He'd changed so much since their

249

marriage, she thought. He simply wasn't the same man at all.

'You know what I think?' she said eventually.

'What?'

'Your mother's jealous of me.'

Willie was incredulous. 'That is a complete load of rubbish.'

'Is it?'

'Why on earth would she be jealous of you?'

'Because I've taken her precious son away from her. I'm doing the things she used to, and more. Because I've got you and she hasn't.'

'You're being ridiculous.'

She studied him through a haze of smoke. 'I don't think so. I truly don't.'

Willie snorted.

'She's never liked me. I knew that the first time I met her. And you know something? I'll bet she was the same with your previous girlfriends. I'd put money on it.'

'Would you indeed?'

'Yes I would. Am I right?'

'Not in the least.' In fact, she was, but he was hardly going to admit it. His mother had always found fault with his previous girlfriends, every single one. He'd realised that long ago.

'While we're at it, there's another thing I want to talk to you about.'

'Oh aye?'

'We never go out any more. You haven't taken me for a drink, or to the dancing, since we got married. All I do nowadays is go to the factory, and then come home again to slave my guts out here.'

'But staying in is what married life's all about. Or didn't you realise that?'

She glared at him. 'No, quite honestly I didn't.'

'Painting the town red is for when you're younger and single, or when you're winching. We should be past all that now.'

'I wasn't talking about painting the town red, Willie. I was talking about going out for a quiet drink sometime. Or why not an evening dancing? We used to enjoy that.'

He shrugged. 'I just don't feel like doing those things any more.'

'You go to your Masonic meetings,' she pointed out.

'That's different.'

'How so?'

'It's sort of business. I need to go if I want to get on, which I do.'

'And you've been known to go to the pub on a Friday after the office.'

'With colleagues. And again, that's business. Some of the bosses go too, don't forget.'

'And what about me, Willie? When do I get to go to a meeting, or slip out for a bevvy, eh? Answer me that.'

He didn't reply.

'You can't, because I don't. I'm here, stuck at home. Always stuck at home. I might as well be one of the fixtures and fittings.'

'Now you're exaggerating,' he said scathingly.

'Where's the exaggeration?'

'In comparing yourself to a fixture and fitting. Really!'

She could feel that tears weren't that far away. He'd somehow turned into a monster. Where was the happy-go-lucky, great-to-be-with chap she used to know? Gone, it seemed. Or was this the real Willie all along, the person who'd courted her merely an act? Black despair filled her to think she was going to have to live the rest of her life with him.

'Besides,' Willie went on, 'we'll have to stay in when the first baby comes along. We can't go gallivanting then, so we may as well get used to it.'

'You mean I may as well get used to it. But don't you see, it doesn't have to be that way. My mother would look after the baby for a few hours to give us a break. That wouldn't be a problem. Not unless you make it one.' She stubbed out the remains of her cigarette and immediately lit another while he looked on disapprovingly. 'Something wrong?' she snapped.

'Those things cost money.'

'So they do,' she replied sarcastically.

'I thought you were going to give up?'

'I have to have some pleasure in life. Surely you wouldn't grudge me a fag?'

'It just seems such a waste of cash to me.'

'That's because you don't smoke. I enjoy them. So there.'

Now it was his turn to glare at her.

'You still haven't replied to the suggestion about my mother,' she reminded him.

'Why can't it be my mother who looks after the baby?'

Oh God, Pearl thought. Back to his bloody mother again. 'No reason. It's simply mine lives upstairs so would be right on hand. Using my mother would be easier, that's all.'

Willie knew that to be true. 'It's something we can discuss after the baby comes,' he prevaricated.

'And in the meantime?'

'In the meantime what?'

'Are we going out at some point? Just the two of us?'

'If you want.'

'I insist,' she said steelily.

'Do you indeed?'

'Yes, I damn well do.'

'Well, not Friday night as I'll be with the lads from work.'

'Saturday then?'

'You know what Glasgow pubs are like on a Saturday, Pearl. Mayhem. No place for a woman.'

'It never stopped us before,' she said, eyes glinting.

'That was different.'

'How so?'

He was lost for an answer to that one. 'It just was.'

Pearl shook her head in disbelief. He was talking absolute tripe, and knew it. The answer was that before he'd wanted to take her out, now he didn't. 'Well, if that's the case we can go to a nice hotel bar. Shouldn't be any trouble there.'

'Hotel bars are expensive,' he muttered.

'We can afford it once in a while. It won't cost that much.'

Still he was reluctant. 'All right then,' he grudgingly agreed at last.

'Don't seem so happy about it,' she jibed.

He certainly wasn't, but wasn't about to say so. 'I'm looking forward to it,' he lied.

So too was she. It would be paradise just to get out socially again. She couldn't wait.

There was a knock on the outside door. 'Who the hell

is that at this hour!' Willie exclaimed. 'I'll get it.' Whoever, the person had at least interrupted the conversation, which pleased him.

Pearl frowned when she heard an exclamation of delight overlaid by the sound of another man's voice.

'You'll never guess what?' A beaming Willie re-entered the kitchen with a chap Pearl had never seen before. 'This is Pete Milroy, whom I went to school with. We go way back.'

The newcomer was a good-looking man about the same age as Willie, same build and height.

'Pete, this is the wife, Pearl.'

Pete came over and shook Pearl by the hand. 'Pleased to meet you.'

'And you.'

'This is just fantastic,' Willie enthused. 'Are you visiting from Edinburgh, or what?'

'I've got a new job back in Glasgow. A promotion, I'm delighted to say. So I'm living here again.'

'That's terrific news. Staying with your parents?'

Pete nodded.

'I wish I had something in to offer you,' Willie apologised. 'But I haven't.'

Pete produced a half-bottle of whisky from his pocket. 'Not to worry. I've brought this.'

They didn't stop talking for the rest of the evening.

'Oh, by the way – I've found out what's happened to Jack,' Pearl announced to Lizzie next morning as they hurried to work. 'My ma bumped into Auntie Agnes yesterday. It seems he's signed on board some ship or other and gone to sea.'

Lizzie's heart sank. Her fears had proved correct. Jack had finally embarked on his big adventure just as he'd always said he'd do.

'Lizzie?'

'Good for him,' Lizzie replied in a strangulated voice. 'Though he might have taken the trouble to say goodbye.'

'Well, you know Jack.'

Lizzie did. Only too well. And not in the way Pearl meant, either.

Chapter 17

Pearl was still cross that Willie had invited Pete to join them on their first night out together since getting married. But there had been absolutely nothing she could do about it as the invitation had been extended the night Pete had turned up at their door.

'I must say I approve of Willie's taste in a wife.' Pete was smiling at her. Willie was up at the bar ordering a round.

She flushed slightly at this unexpected compliment. 'Why, thank you.'

His smile widened.

'So tell me, are you missing Edinburgh at all?' She already knew Pete had been living there for the past five years.

Pete considered. 'Yes and no. It's a lovely city, and I got on well with the people. And of course I miss my friends. But I have to say it's good to be home again. And by that I mean Glasgow. I shan't be staying with my parents for long.'

'Oh?'

'I had a small apartment in Edinburgh, so I'm used to my freedom. Being able to come and go as I wish without being accountable to anyone. I shall be looking for one here before long.'

'Your own apartment,' she murmured, highly impressed.

'Somewhere in the West End, probably. Or in the Byers Road area. I've always liked it round there.'

'So what's it like working in the civil service?' Pearl queried, thinking that whatever else it was, it must be well paid for him to get his own bachelor place.

Pete laughed. 'Not very exciting, I'm afraid. What it boils down to is being a glorified pen pusher. But I enjoy it, and it's a good, secure job. There's a lot to be said for that.'

Pearl took out her cigarettes.

'Here, have one of mine,' Pete offered before she could extract one from the packet.

An expensive brand, Pearl noted when he produced his. Which only confirmed he must be making good money.

Pete lit her cigarette, then his own.

'Willie doesn't approve of my smoking,' Pearl said.

'And why's that?'

'Says it's a waste of cash.'

Pete laughed. 'The old bugger always was a bit tight. I wouldn't worry if I were you. Just keep on puffing away and eventually he'll get fed up and stop moaning. You work, don't you?'

Pearl nodded, and mentioned the name of the factory.

'Then the cost is coming out of your pay packet and not his. You're entitled.'

Pearl was rapidly warming to Pete, who was proving a very personable companion. 'So tell me, did you leave a girlfriend behind?'

That amused Pete, who considered it a very feminine question. 'I didn't, as a matter of fact. At least, no one I was serious about.'

'Which means you're footloose and fancy-free?'

That further amused him. 'I suppose you could say that.'

Pearl was wondering if it would be worthwhile introducing him to Lizzie. Who knew, the pair of them might click? She'd have a word with Lizzie about it. Pete was something of a catch, after all.

'This job of yours,' Pearl went on. 'What is it precisely that you do?'

'I push a pen.'

'You've already said that. But where exactly?'

'I'm in Naval Requisitions and Supply.'

'Sounds fascinating.'

Pete laughed. 'I wish it was. But I like it, boring as it might be at times.'

'You mentioned the other night that you were sent back to Glasgow because of a promotion?'

'Transferred, actually. I'm now in charge of a small department.'

Pearl was even more impressed. Pete struck her as someone who was going places. Then she had a sudden thought. Lowering her voice, she asked, 'Are you a Mason, same as Willie?'

Pete stared at her. 'Has he gone and joined that lot?'

Pearl nodded. 'Which, I take it, means you haven't?'

'I have thought about it,' Pete replied slowly. 'But in

the end I decided I wasn't interested. I don't know why, maybe it's all the mumbo jumbo, but it just doesn't appeal.'

They were interrupted by Willie, returning with a small tray of drinks. 'Bloody expensive in here,' Willie complained, and couldn't understand why Pearl and Pete both burst out laughing.

Lizzie sat worrying a nail. She mustn't jump to conclusions, she told herself. Her period had been late before. Not often, but it had happened. Only those times she hadn't been with Jack.

'Are you all right, Lizzie?' Ethne inquired. 'You're looking a bit tired and drawn. What do you think, Doogie?'

He glanced over at his daughter. 'Aye, she's peely wally right enough.'

Panic flared in Lizzie. Was pallor another sign? She hadn't noticed she was looking any different.

'Lizzie?' That was Ethne.

'I haven't been sleeping very well recently,' Lizzie lied. 'Just a phase, I suppose.'

'There's usually a reason for not sleeping well,' Doogie commented. 'Have you got anything on your mind that's worrying you?'

'Nothing.' It was another lie: she certainly had, though it hadn't so far interfered in any way with her sleeping.

'How about work? Any particular problems there?' Ethne probed.

'Work's fine, Ma.'

'Well, you're eating properly. I can vouch for that.'

'So too can I.' Doogie smiled. 'We all are.'

259

Ethne was pleased with the compliment. 'Maybe you should call in and see the doctor?' she suggested to Lizzie.

'I tell you, there's no need. I'm right as rain.'

'Well you don't look it, and that's a fact.'

'Stop worrying, Ma. I'm not.'

Ethne changed the subject.

'I suppose you're going to your mother's for tea tomorrow night,' Pearl said, ever so slightly sarcastically, to Willie.

'Tomorrow's Wednesday, so I'll be going.'

'That'll be nice for you.'

He ignored the jibe.

'Tell me something,' Pearl said after a few moments.

'What's that?'

'Does she ever mention me when you're there?'

'What sort of question is that?' Willie queried in astonishment.

'A straightforward one I would say.'

He was baffled. 'Well of course she mentions you. You're my wife, after all. It would be funny if she didn't.'

'I was just wondering. No other reason.'

'Fine then.'

'What does she say?' Pearl persisted.

Willie inwardly groaned. 'I don't know. All sorts. How are you doing, are you well. That sort of thing.'

'Nothing else?'

Willie stared at Pearl. 'Like what?'

Pearl shrugged. 'I've no idea.'

'Well if you've no idea then I haven't either.'

'All right, then. Does she criticise me, for example?'

This was beginning to thoroughly cheese him off. 'We're not back to cooking, are we?'

'Amongst other things.'

'No, she doesn't,' he lied. 'Now can we please leave it at that.'

'You can't blame a girl for wondering, though, can you?'

He didn't reply.

'Can you, Willie?'

She'd have a fit if he told her some of the things his mother had said, Willie reflected. His mother was not exactly a fan of hers. 'I said leave it,' he growled.

Pearl felt she had no other option.

Sandra handed Doogie and John their morning tea.

'Thank you,' they both said almost in unison.

'I'm also here to collect for Daisy's present. If you'll contribute, that is,' Sandra announced.

Doogie stared blankly at her. 'Present?'

'Haven't you heard? She's getting married and I've been asked to organise a whip-round to give her something.'

Well well, Doogie mused. She'd landed Percy. And it hadn't taken her that long either. He wasn't sure whether he was relieved or disappointed. A dozen memories of them in the stables together came flooding back, and made him smile.

John laid down his tea and fumbled in his trouser pockets. 'I'm afraid I can only offer a tanner,' he apologised. 'It's all I can afford. I don't exactly get paid a fortune in this job, you know.'

'Christ, even I'm giving more than that,' Sandra chided him.

John shrugged. 'Take it or leave it.'

Sandra turned her attention again to Doogie. 'And you, Mr McDougall?'

'When's the wedding?' he asked amiably.

'Saturday after next.'

'In church?'

'No, register office.'

Doogie smiled again at the idea of Daisy's being married in white. A virgin Daisy most certainly wasn't, as he could well testify. No, a register office was the right and proper place for her wedding.

He took out his change and selected two half-crowns, feeling he owed Daisy a decent contribution. 'Here you are,' he declared, handing over the coins.

'Five bob! That's kind of you,' Sandra enthused.

'Aye well, I'm known for my generosity,' he joked. 'Mr Moneybags, that's me. All heart.'

He was laughing as Sandra left.

Lizzie stopped machining, sat back in her chair and closed her eyes. She'd never known such indigestion as she'd recently been suffering. It was chronic.

'Something wrong, Lizzie?'

She opened her eyes again to find Mrs Lang, the supervisor, standing beside her. 'A bit of indigestion,' she explained. 'It'll soon go away.'

Mrs Lang stared at her in concern. 'Do you want to take a few minutes' break?'

Lizzie didn't see what good that would do, and shook her head.

'Are you sure? Have you anything to take for it?'

'I'm sure, Mrs Lang. And no, I haven't. As I said, it'll soon pass.'

'Right then.'

Lizzie sucked in a deep breath, and then another. 'Damn!' she muttered to herself. This attack was the worst yet.

Trying to ignore the discomfort, she got on with the job.

'I was thinking this morning about Leo, Chrissie Wylie's cat,' Ethne said.

Doogie frowned. 'What about it?'

'I was just wondering what became of the poor thing, that's all. Remember how it disappeared shortly after Chrissie's death? Just went out one day and never came back?'

'Cats are strange animals,' Doogie declared, shaking his head. 'They've got a mind of their own.'

'Chrissie was devoted to that cat. Spoilt it rotten.'

'Maybe somebody kidnapped it and turned it into a pair of gloves,' Doogie joked.

Ethne shot him a withering look. 'That isn't even remotely funny.'

'Sorry.' He wasn't sorry at all. He had thought it very amusing.

'Well, I just hope it's found a good home,' Ethne mused.

'I'm sure it has.'

Ethne would like to think so.

'I wish you'd reconsider and meet Pete,' said Pearl.

'Will you stop harping on about him? I've told you I'm not interested,' Lizzie snapped in reply. She had dropped by as it was Willie's night at the Masons.

'He's not bad-looking and ever such a good catch,' Pearl went on.

Lizzie sighed. 'I'm not interested in any man at the moment, good catch or not. Meeting someone is the furthest thing from my mind.'

'That's a bit sad, at your age.'

Lizzie was becoming irritated by the conversation. If Pearl kept on she'd go back upstairs. 'Let's just drop the subject, eh?'

Pearl studied her friend, who was beginning to worry her. Lizzie had not been herself of late. Pearl couldn't put her finger on it, but there was definitely something wrong somewhere.

'Willie told me this morning that he was surprised I wasn't already up the duff,' she declared. 'I'm surprised too, considering the amount of sex he demands.'

Lizzie went cold all over. Now why had Pearl suddenly mentioned that?

'As I explained to him,' Pearl continued, 'these things don't always happen overnight. They can take time.'

Or not, as the case may be, Lizzie reflected ruefully. Her period still hadn't arrived and she was beginning to think she was going to miss it altogether. Now that had never happened before.

Oh God, she begged. Please let it not be that. Please please please! It would be so unfair in the circumstances.

'Hello. Long time no see.'

Doogie had gone to collect his pay packet and run into Daisy who was doing the same.

'Why, hello, Doogie.'

'I believe congratulations are in order. Tomorrow, isn't it?'

Daisy nodded.

'Well all I can do is wish you the very best. Percy is a lucky man and no mistake.'

Daisy caught the nuance in his tone and knew to what he was referring. 'I'll take that as a compliment.'

'It was certainly meant as one.'

He couldn't help but drop his gaze to those ample breasts he remembered so well, the memory of which made his mouth go dry.

'It was good while it lasted, eh?' Daisy smiled, lowering her voice so only he could hear.

'I won't dispute that.'

'We had quite a laugh, eh?'

More than a laugh, he thought. Far more than that. 'As long as you're happy, that's the main thing.'

'I am. Percy and I get on like a house on fire. It's as if we were meant for one another.'

He could see she was telling the truth, and was delighted for her. She deserved it, in his opinion.

The conversation ended there as it was Daisy's turn to go forward and pick up her wages. Doogie watched her waddle away as he collected his, memories again flitting through his mind.

She'd been a revelation, he thought. Truly a revelation. God bless her.

'Pete!' Willie exclaimed. This was an unexpected visit. 'Come on through.'

'Hello, Pearl,' Pete said as he entered the kitchen.

She hurriedly patted her hair into place, thinking that

if she'd known he was coming she'd have made a bit of an effort to be more presentable. 'Hello, Pete.'

'I'm here to ask you to celebrate with me,' he declared, placing a bottle of whisky on the table.

'So what's the celebration in order of?' Willie queried, signalling Pearl to get some glasses.

'I've found an apartment.'

'Oh, that's wonderful!' Willie enthused. 'When do you move in?'

'The first of next month.'

'Where is it?' Pearl inquired.

'Just off the Byers Road. A one-bedroom apartment with inside toilet.'

'Lucky sod.' Willie smiled. He'd have given anything to have an inside toilet.

'Is it furnished?' Pearl asked.

'Oh aye. It's got everything. All I have to do is move in.'

Willie whipped the top off the whisky bottle as Pearl laid out the glasses. 'We've no lemonade, I'm afraid,' he apologised to Pete. 'But there is water.'

'That's fine for me.'

'On the other hand,' Willie suggested, 'why don't you run down to the chippie and get some, Pearl? It'll only take you a minute.'

The truth was she much preferred lemonade to water. 'All right.'

'No, that's unfair. I'll go,' Pete volunteered. 'I should have thought to bring some with me anyway.'

'You'll do no such thing,' Willie told him. 'That's what wives are for. Isn't that right, Pearl?'

He might have made it sound like a joke, but Pearl

knew he meant every word. Apart from bed, women were mere skivvies to him, to be there at the man's beck and call. His mother had acted like that.

'I won't be long,' she said, hurrying from the room. Was it her imagination or had she caught a disapproving glint in Pete's eyes?

It heartened her to think she had.

Ethne came awake as Doogie began violently thrashing about, his arms flailing left and right.

'No!' he suddenly screamed, and sat bolt upright in bed, eyes open and bulging.

'Doogie, Doogie,' Ethne said urgently, putting her arms round him. 'Wake up, you're having a nightmare.'

He shuddered, and then went limp, his breathing long and laboured. 'Sorry, lass,' he whispered eventually.

'Was it the same one?'

He nodded in the darkness. 'I was back at Bailey's seeing John go up in flames. It was terrible.'

This was the first time in a long while that he'd had the nightmare, Ethne thought. She'd been hoping it had gone for good.

He was covered in sweat, Ethne realised, which was about par for the course. She pulled him even closer to her.

'Sorry for waking you, Eth.'

'Don't you worry about that.'

'Oh Christ,' he muttered, and ran a hand over his forehead.

'Are you all right now?'

'Just about.'

'Can I get you anything?'

'No thanks. Just keep hugging me, that's all.'

Reaching up she stroked his sweat-slicked hair, wishing there was some way of ridding him of these nightmares. But there wasn't. There simply wasn't.

They stayed like that in silence for a few minutes until Doogie had calmed down and his breathing was back to normal. 'I should be fine now,' he said at last. She released him, and they both lay down again. 'Thank God I don't work in that hell-hole any more.'

Ethne thanked God as well.

'I could actually smell the burning flesh,' Doogie murmured. 'Horrible.'

Ethne could well imagine. The very thought made her stomach turn.

Doogie twisted round and this time it was he who put his arms round her. 'Safe here,' he whispered. 'Safe with you.'

There was a lump in Ethne's throat. 'Of course you are, Doogie.'

He buried his face in her breasts, enjoying the warmth of them. This was where he was safest of all.

'So, what do you think?'

It was Pearl and Willie's first visit to Pete's new apartment, as he insisted on calling it.

Pearl gazed around her. 'It's nice. Very nice.'

'Willie?'

'It looks comfy, all right. I like that couch. It's big enough to sleep on.' The couch in question was well upholstered in brown leather.

'There's only a small kitchenette, I'm afraid. But that suits me as I won't be cooking very often. There's a canteen

268

at work where I can get most of my meals.'

The apartment consisted of sitting room, bedroom, kitchenette and toilet. There was patterned carpet on the sitting room floor, and the curtains were made of heavy brocade.

'The wallpaper isn't exactly my taste,' Pete declared. 'But it doesn't offend me too much so I suppose I'll just put up with it.'

'I think the wallpaper's rather lovely,' Pearl said, peering at it. 'It's certainly better than ours.' She made a mental note to try to cajole Willie into repapering their bedroom.

'You've really landed on your feet here.' Willie was nodding his approval. 'Christ, how I envy you.'

Pete frowned. 'How so?'

Willie glanced sideways at Pearl, wondering whether or not to answer truthfully. 'Being away from your parents, I mean, while still a bachelor. Opens up all sorts of possibilities.'

'Are you talking women here?' Pete queried drily.

'What else? Pearl and I had to do our courting in the back close, hardly the best of places to be romantic.'

'Enough of that,' Pearl stated firmly.

Pete took the point. 'Now, who's for a drink?'

They all were.

'You're what!' Doogie exploded, his face rapidly turning puce.

'Expecting a baby,' Lizzie repeated, shaking all over.

Ethne's mouth had fallen open on hearing the news. Now she regained something of her composure. 'Are you absolutely certain about that?'

'I'm three months gone, Ma. Yes, I'm certain.'

Doogie leaped to his feet and advanced on Lizzie, pulling his arm back as he got near.

'No, Doogie!' Ethne shouted. 'Don't hit her!'

Doogie came to a halt, and slowly lowered his arm. 'Whoever the father is he'll have to marry you. And right away. If he tries to get out of it I'll kill the bastard,' Doogie hissed at Lizzie, his expression frightening.

'Who is the father anyway?' Ethne demanded, shaken to the core.

'Jack White, Pearl's cousin. You met him once in Sauchiehall Street.'

Ethne remembered only too clearly. 'That nice young man!' she exclaimed in surprise. 'I thought he was ever so pleasant.'

'Where does he live?' Doogie queried in a strangulated voice. 'You and I are going straight round there to confront him about this.'

'We can't, Da,' Lizzie stammered. 'Jack isn't there any more. He's gone to sea as a sailor.' This was proving as terrible as she'd imagined it would be.

'Gone to sea,' Doogie repeated in a hoarse whisper.

'Shortly after he and I . . .' Lizzie broke off, and gulped.

Ethne staggered to the nearest chair and slumped into it. In the last few minutes her entire world had come crashing down around her. The shame and humiliation this was going to bring on them didn't bear thinking about.

'It was only once, Ma,' Lizzie said quietly, her voice quavering.

Ethne looked up at her. 'And before?'

Lizzie shook her head. 'I swear. There's only been Jack.'

'But why . . . why let him?' Ethne was bewildered.

Lizzie had always been such a good, respectable girl.

'He was persistent, Ma. Wouldn't take no for an answer.'

'Are you saying he forced you?' Doogie thundered, he too starting to shake.

Lizzie took her time in replying. 'He didn't exactly force me, not in the way you mean. I suppose I could have stopped him, but I didn't. It . . . it just seemed right at the time.'

'Do you love him?' Ethne asked softly.

Lizzie shrugged. 'I think it could have come to that, if the circumstances had been different. I knew he was going away, you see, but not when. He told me ages ago. It was his big dream.' She started crying. 'It's so unfair, so unfair. It was only the once, after all.'

'That's all it takes, you little idiot,' Doogie declared harshly.

Ethne put a hand to her forehead. She had to think about this. There had to be something they could do to avoid the terrible consequences of Lizzie's having a child out of wedlock. There just had to be. But what?

'I'm so sorry,' Lizzie whispered.

'You're lucky your mother was here to stop me or I'd have given you the thrashing of your life,' Doogie told her, and meant it.

Lizzie burst into hysterical sobbing.

Chapter 18

'She'll never get wed now,' Doogie said later that night as he and Ethne were getting into bed.' Who'd take a lassie who's had another man's bastard?'

Ethne knew that was probably true. Lizzie's reputation would go straight down the plughole once it became known she was pregnant, and she'd be the talk of the street, if not the entire area. Ethne could almost hear the wagging tongues at work, not only about Lizzie but about herself and Doogie as well. She inwardly cringed.

'What possessed her?' Doogie queried in despair. 'What in God's name made her do such a thing?'

Ethne pictured Jack in her mind. Certainly an attractive chap, with winning ways about him. She could easily understand Lizzie's being attracted, but to take it that far when she knew there was no future in it was sheer madness.

'Ethne?'

'I met him, Doogie, and a very nice lad he was too. Struck me as a fine upstanding young man.'

Doogie snorted. 'Oh aye, he was upstanding all right. But not in the way you mean.'

272

Any other time Ethne might have laughed at that. But not now.

'You know what this means for us as well, don't you?' Doogie went on.

'Of course I do.' Ethne was thinking of Mrs Fallon whose daughter Heather had hanged herself when her boyfriend had refused to marry her after making her pregnant. Run off and joined the army by all accounts. Only the other week Babs Millar had bumped into Mrs Fallon, who, according to Babs, had become something of a pariah in the area. Despite her daughter's suicide, her neighbours had turned against her, most of them not even speaking to her any more. And, again according to Babs, those who did were patronising and condescending. Babs said Mrs Fallon had lost a lot of weight and had looked, even after all this time, absolutely dreadful.

'I just hope Mr Cathcart doesn't find out.' Doogie sighed. 'I could lose my job over this.'

'Don't be daft!' Ethne chided him.

'I'm being nothing of the sort. It's a possibility. He might think it reflected badly on him and his business.'

Fear clutched at Ethne. Pray God that never happened. For if Doogie did lose his job because of it who knew how long it would be before he got another, if indeed he ever did.

'What a bloody awful mess Lizzie has got us into.' There was anger in Doogie's voice.

Ethne had to agree: Lizzie had. Yet part of her was sympathetic. Lizzie had said she and Jack had only done it once. The outcome was a rotten stroke of luck.

'I must think of something,' she said quietly. 'I have to, there's no two ways about it.'

273

'Are you suggesting what I think you are?'

She turned to face him in the darkness. 'It's a possibility. Except I wouldn't know where to find such a person without asking someone like Dot. And if I did that then the cat would be well and truly out of the bag.'

Doogie's hopes, which had flickered briefly, died away again. 'Aye, you're right,' he acknowledged. 'None of these women, including Dot, would be able to keep their big traps shut.'

Ethne wasn't so certain about that. Dot might. They were good friends, after all. But it would be an enormous risk all the same.

'Try and get some sleep,' she said. 'I know it'll be hard with this on your mind, but you've still got an early rise.'

'I'll try.'

As it turned out neither of them slept a wink all night. Nor did Lizzie.

'What's wrong?' Ethne asked a few mornings later as Lizzie struggled with her skirt.

The look Lizzie gave her mother was filled with anguish. 'It's so tight I'm having trouble doing it up.'

Oh God, Ethne thought. Lizzie had started putting on weight. How long till it became obvious, and how would they be able to explain it away?

'What about your other skirt?'

'It's the same size, Ma. It'll be tight as well.'

'Here, let me help you.'

Ethne hurried over and between the pair of them they managed to get it fastened.

'It's killing me, Ma. I can hardly breathe.'

'Well you'll just have to put up with it, for today

274

anyway. I'll see what I can do with the other one.'

'Thanks, Ma.'

Ethne stared into her daughter's troubled face. 'Now don't you start crying again. It upsets me something dreadful.'

Lizzie sniffed, and wiped her nose with the back of her hand. 'Sorry, Ma. I just seem to dissolve into tears at the slightest thing.'

'It was the same with me when I was expecting. Particularly with you. I was forever bawling my eyes out.'

Lizzie hesitated. 'There's something I want to say.'

'Go on.'

'You know you and Da mentioned about having the baby done away with?'

Ethne nodded. They'd also explained the difficulties involved.

'I've been thinking, and I don't believe I could go through with that.'

Relief washed through Ethne when Lizzie said that. 'Why not?' she queried softly, curious.

'Women have died having that done to them, haven't they?'

'Aye, they have,' Ethne agreed. 'And afterwards. It's a dangerous thing to do, especially if the person doing the abortion makes a muck of it, as can happen.'

'The other thing is . . .' Lizzie broke off and bit her lip. 'Wouldn't it be murder?'

Ethne blanched. She gazed with new respect at her daughter. 'And you're not sure you could live with that on your conscience?'

'I don't think I could, Ma. It would haunt me for the rest of my days.'

Ethne knew she'd have felt exactly the same way. Once you thought of abortion as murder there was no getting away from the fact that that was exactly what it was. 'I agree with you, lass. The only question is, what would be worse? Having the baby and suffering the consequences, or getting rid of it and suffering the consequences of that.'

Lizzie swallowed hard. 'It's a decision I won't have to make, Ma, unless you do come up with someone who can do it. Only then will there be a choice.'

'You're right.' Ethne smiled slowly. 'But it might be wise to think about it just the same, in case the decision does have to be made.'

Lizzie glanced at the clock. 'I'll have to go or I'll be late for work. Pearl must be wondering what's keeping me.'

Ethne put the kettle back on after Lizzie had left. There was lots of housework to be done – the range wanted blackleading for a start – and she should be getting on. But she couldn't. She needed time to sit quietly and try to come up with some sort of solution to the problem.

She sat for hours, desperately trying to think of something. Anything.

But nothing came.

'You look troubled, Ethne,' commented Babs Millar, who had dropped by for a cup of tea and a natter.

Ethne immediately feigned innocence. 'Do I?'

'Not your usual cheery self.'

Ethne shrugged. 'There's nothing particularly bothering me,' she lied. 'At least not that I'm aware of.'

'So have you heard any juicy gossip lately?' Babs asked eagerly.

'None.'

Babs pulled a face. 'Nor me, I'm afraid. Not a thing.'

Ethne had a sip of tea, thinking to herself that she could have given Babs something to talk about all right. Oh aye, she certainly could have done that. But so far Lizzie's secret was safe. Though for how long? That was the question.

For how long?

Ethne was out shopping when the germ of an idea came to her. An idea that quickly began to develop and take shape.

An incredulous Doogie sat staring at his wife.

'Well?' Ethne demanded.

Lizzie, who was also present, was dumbstruck by what her mother had just proposed.

Doogie roused himself. 'Let me get this straight,' he said slowly. 'You want to pass the baby off as your own. As ours?'

Ethne nodded. 'That's right.'

'Lizzie is to say that she's returning to Tomintoul because Stuart is ill and needs someone to look after him?'

'Uh-huh.'

Doogie ploughed on. 'When she arrives there Lizzie declares she's now married to Jack White, which makes her Mrs White. Her husband's a seaman off on a voyage to the Far East, with Australia and New Zealand after that, which means he'll be gone for a long time, thereby freeing up Lizzie to go back to Tomintoul.'

Ethne nodded.

'Meanwhile, you've let it be known that you're pregnant. Correct?'

'I'll use padding to gradually make it appear as if I am. Luckily I always had a small bump in my previous pregnancies so I don't have to end up seeming to be the size of a house. It'll be authentic enough, I promise you.'

If this hadn't been so serious Doogie would have found it hilarious. He had to give full marks to Ethne for her ingenuity and imagination, though, preposterous as her story might be.

'The next bit,' Doogie continued, 'is that when you're close to your so-called "time" you too return to Tomintoul, saying you want the doctor who delivered you previously to do so again.'

'That's it.'

'Now, at this point both you and Lizzie are in Tomintoul. Right?'

'Right.'

'Lizzie then has her baby, and when you both return here you'll pass it off as ours.'

'Simple, isn't it?'

'Hardly,' Doogie commented drily.

'The beauty of it is that Lizzie retains her good name and reputation as there won't be any scandal. There's simply a new addition to the family, only I'll be the mother and not Lizzie. That's if Lizzie agrees, of course.' She glanced over at her daughter.

Lizzie didn't know what to think. This was a bombshell right enough.

'No scandal and chinwagging,' Doogie mused. That certainly appealed.

'Do you honestly think it'll work?' Lizzie queried.

'I don't see why not. Who in Tomintoul, apart from your brothers, is to know you're not married? And who in Thistle Street is to know the baby isn't mine? No one.'

Doogie was rapidly warming to the idea, daft as it might have seemed at first.

'So, Lizzie, do you agree?' Ethne asked.

'It means me giving up the baby,' Lizzie murmured, not sure she wanted to do that.

'But keeping your good character and marital prospects,' Ethne reminded her. 'Besides, you wouldn't really be giving up the baby as it will be living right here in the house with us. Only now you'll be the baby's sister and not its mother.'

What were the alternatives? Lizzie thought. Have an abortion or suffer horribly from the clacking tongues of the neighbours, neither a prospect she relished. 'I agree,' she said, hoping she was doing the right thing.

'What about Gordon and Stuart? They'll have to be in on this,' Doogie pointed out.

'And Sheena too. But only those three. No one else must ever know. I'll write to Gordon tonight, since he's the eldest, and put it to him. He can discuss it with Stuart.'

'What if they won't go along with it?' Lizzie queried.

A glint came into Ethne's eyes. 'They won't want to see the family name tarnished. Oh, they'll go along all right. Just leave that to me.'

'My God, you're a devious woman.' Doogie smiled reluctantly. 'Only you would have come up with a plan like that.'

Ethne was pleased with herself. There again, she'd just had to come up with something!

Doogie felt relief for the first time since this thing had started. 'I think I'll drop into the Argyle and have a couple,' he announced.

Ethne wagged a finger at him. 'Not a word to anyone, mind. Not a single soul. Have you got that?'

He was still smiling when he came to his feet. 'Don't you worry about me, Ethne. My lips are sealed on the subject where anyone outside this room is concerned. Pulling this off is to my advantage as well, don't forget.'

'Just you remember that when the whisky starts going down your throat, that's all.'

'I will. I promise.'

Ethne also stood up. 'I think I'll write to the boys straight away rather than leave it for later. The sooner the letter goes off the sooner we'll get a reply.'

Lizzie couldn't help herself. She burst out crying.

Mrs Jack White, Lizzie mused in bed that night. Oh, if only it were true and she and Jack genuinely were married. She'd have given anything for that to be the case. Not just because of the expected baby, but because of Jack himself.

She wondered how he was getting on in his big adventure. Was he on the high seas at that moment, or in some exotic port having a right old time? If it was the latter he might well be chatting up some foreign beauty, hoping to have his way with her just as he'd had with Lizzie herself in the back close.

Whatever, she wished him well. And she missed him terribly, more than she'd have thought possible.

How would he have reacted to being told she was pregnant? Would he have done the decent thing and married her? He certainly would've if her da had had anything to do with it. Her da would've threatened bloody murder if he hadn't.

Funny, she reflected. They'd never really gone out together, and now she was going to have his child.

She smiled, remembering their encounter in the back close. She'd tried to resist, to begin with anyway. Really put up a bit of a struggle. But Jack had been persistent, and then they'd reached the point where she had wanted him every bit as much as he wanted her.

'Oh, Jack,' she murmured dreamily, images of the two of them together going through her mind.

Images that melted her insides.

Ethne recognised Gordon's handwriting. At long last the reply to her letter had arrived.

Hastily she tore open the letter and began to read.

'As you can see from the letter, they aren't exactly over-enthusiastic about the plan, Gordon in particular, but they've both agreed to play their part.'

'If Gordon appears unenthusiastic it's because of Sheena,' Doogie commented. 'You know what she's like. A right Holy Mary if ever there was one.'

'But a good woman none the less,' Ethne responded, well aware that what he said was true enough.

Doogie sniffed. 'I've never understood what Gordon saw in her. Oh, I grant you she's not bad-looking, but inside she's a proper little psalm-singing bitch.'

'Doogie!' Ethne chided him. 'She's your daughter-in-law, don't forget.'

'What's that got to do with it? She is what she is,

daughter-in-law or not.' He shook his head. 'I do believe she gives Gordon a dog's life. Poor bugger.'

Ethne had never been madly keen on Sheena either. But she was Gordon's choice and that's all there was to it as far as she was concerned. She decided to change the subject.

'Right,' she declared, focusing on Lizzie. 'First things first. You'll hand in your notice this Friday. All right?'

Lizzie nodded.

'And on Saturday you and I are paying a visit to the pawn shop to buy a ring. You'll need to be wearing a gold band when you reach Tomintoul. That's an absolute must.'

'I understand, Ma.'

'We'll see if we can get some sort of engagement ring to go with it. But it depends on the price. We haven't got all that much money to play around with.'

'Why don't you just lend her yours?' Doogie suggested. 'I'm sure nobody up there will remember it. And if anyone does comment Lizzie can just say it's similar, but not quite the same. How about that?'

'Good idea.' Ethne nodded. 'If it fits, that is. Here, try it on, lass.'

The ring proved slightly loose on Lizzie's finger, but nothing to worry about. It wouldn't fall off.

'That's one problem solved then,' Ethne declared, slipping the ring back on her own finger. 'Now I'm going to see what I can find for padding. Want to help me, Lizzie?'

Lizzie took up the offer, and for the next hour she and Ethne had a right old laugh rummaging through all sorts before finally settling on various pieces of material that Ethne would use to give the impression of pregnancy.

'I'm handing in my notice today,' Lizzie announced to Pearl that Friday morning as they hurried to work.

Pearl came up short. 'You're what?'

'Handing in my notice.'

'But why? Have you found a better job?'

'No, I'm returning to Tomintoul for a while,' Lizzie informed her as they continued on their way. 'My brother Stuart is ill and needs someone to look after him until he gets better again. And I've been elected.'

'What's the matter with him?' Pearl queried with a frown.

'The doctor isn't certain yet. But it's quite bad whatever it is,' Lizzie lied smoothly, remembering the story she and Ethne had agreed on.

'I'm sorry to hear that,' Pearl said sympathetically.

'He's a bachelor, you see; lives on his own. Usually he's quite capable, but since taking ill he just can't look after himself. Ma's very worried about him.'

Pearl shook her head. 'I'm going to miss you.'

'As I said, it'll only be for a while. I'll be back, you'll see.'

'So when are you going?'

'As soon as I've served my notice.'

'I'd have thought your ma would have gone instead of you,' Pearl commented.

'We talked it over and decided it had better be me.' Lizzie laughed. 'Da hated the notion of him and Ma being parted. Kicked up quite a rumpus about it. He was quite unreasonable, in fact, which is why I'm going and not Ma.'

Pearl didn't find that strange, knowing how selfish and self-centred some men could be, even when it came to matters regarding their own family. She had no doubt her Willie would have been just the same. Wouldn't want to miss out on his twice-daily sex if nothing else.

The more Lizzie thought about Tomintoul the more excited she was becoming at the prospect of returning there.

Fact was, she couldn't wait.

'I really am sorry to hear this,' Mrs Lang said to Lizzie who'd just told her she was leaving, and why. 'But I fully understand.'

'Thank you, Mrs Lang.'

'You'll be missed, of course. Particularly by me as I consider you to be one of our finest machinists. You've certainly come on by leaps and bounds since joining us.'

High praise indeed, Lizzie thought.

'And I want you to know there will always be a job here for you when you return.'

That delighted Lizzie even further. 'Thank you again.'

Mrs Lang gave Lizzie a warm smile before walking away.

'Expecting!' Edwina Edgar exclaimed. 'That's certainly a turn-up for the book.'

'Took me by surprise, I have to admit,' Ethne said.

The women of the close were gathered in Jean Carmichael's house for tea and scones, and Ethne had taken this opportunity to make a general announcement rather than do it piecemeal.

'Congratulations!' Babs Millar enthused. 'Fancy that.'

'Well well,' Dot mused, remembering how Ethne had thought she might be starting the change not all that long ago. Now she was pregnant.

'How far gone are you?' Jean asked.

'A little over three months.'

Babs peered at her waistline. 'No sign of it yet.'

Ethne laughed. 'There is a bit. But hopefully, if my last three pregnancies are anything to go by, I won't get too large.'

'Lucky you,' Dot sighed. 'I was like an elephant towards the end when I was carrying Pearl. Bloody huge.'

'Me too,' Babs added. 'Absolutely enormous. It was like carrying a sack of coal around under my jumper.'

They all laughed.

'So what are you hoping for?' Jean inquired.

Ethne shrugged. 'I don't really have a preference. As long as the baby is healthy with all its bits and pieces in the right places then I'll be happy enough.'

Dot and Edwina nodded their agreement.

'And what's Doogie got to say about it?' Babs asked.

'Not much he can say, considering it was him put it there.'

Again everyone laughed.

'Mind you,' Jean said a few moments later, 'if I was being honest I wouldn't want to go through all that palaver again. I'm far too long in the tooth.'

'Aye,' Babs agreed, nodding. 'The interrupted sleep, the nappies, the colic, the teething, the whole business. You'll have your work cut out for you, Ethne, and no mistake.'

True enough, Ethne thought grimly. All that lay ahead. But it wasn't as if she'd be on her own. Lizzie would be on hand to help. And help Lizzie would, Ethne'd make sure of it.

'Don't take offence, Eth, but I still have some baby clothes put away, kept them over the years in case they came in handy at some future date . . .'

'If you got up the spout again,' Babs interjected with a smile.

'Exactly. Anyway, that never happened and now it won't. So you're welcome if you want them, Ethne.'

If one thing was worrying Ethne it was the added expense the child was going to cost. But they'd manage somehow. They'd just have to. 'I'd be delighted. Thank you.'

'I'll look them out nearer your time.'

'It'll be nice having a baby up the close again,' Jean declared. 'It's been a while since the last one.'

'Now, who's for more tea and another scone?' Jean queried, coming to her feet.

Ethne said she'd have another cup, but declined the scone, just as she had the first time one was offered. Jean kept a dirty house, in her opinion, and she never ate anything there.

You just never knew.

'What time are you off tomorrow?' Pearl asked. Lizzie had come to say goodbye.

'First thing.'

Pearl shook her head. 'I've said it before and I'll say it again. I'm going to miss you something chronic.'

'I'll be back before you know it,' Lizzie smiled, putting her arms round Pearl and squeezing her.

'Good luck to you. I hope your brother gets well soon,' Willie chipped in from where he was sitting.

'Thank you. So do I.'

'Keep in touch, will you?' Pearl implored. 'The odd letter would be welcome. Let us know how you're getting on.'

'I'll do that. It's a promise. And you write too?'

'I promise as well.'

It was with a heavy heart that Lizzie left Pearl and went back upstairs.

Tomorrow, and Tomintoul, lay ahead.

Chapter 19

'Would you like to lie down, Lizzie?' asked Stuart. 'Why should I want to do that?'

'Well, it is a long journey, so I thought you might be tired. Especially as . . .' He broke off, looking embarrassed. 'You know?'

'I'm pregnant?'

Stuart, who'd coloured slightly, nodded.

'Actually I'm not tired. At the moment anyway. It might strike me later.'

Lizzie glanced round the small sitting room she'd been ushered into. It was immaculate, everything spotless. 'I must say, for a bachelor you're very neat and tidy,' she commented.

Stuart shrugged. 'That's just the way I am. So what do you think of the cottage then?' It had been allocated to him by the estate after his parents and Lizzie had moved to Glasgow.

'Very nice, from what I've seen so far, which isn't much.'

'Would you like a cup of tea?'

'Love one, Stuart.'

'I'll put the kettle on then.'

'Do you want me to do it?'

'Good Lord no. But come on through to the kitchen and keep me company.'

The kitchen proved as immaculate as the sitting room, with everything in its place.

Lizzie sat beside the range, which was identical to theirs in Thistle Street. She didn't fail to note it had been recently blackleaded, a job her mother would have been proud of.

'I'll have to go back to work shortly. I hope you don't mind?' he apologised.

'Of course not.'

'Luckily I was able to arrange the time off to meet you, but I don't want to take advantage.'

'I understand.'

Stuart rinsed out the teapot after seeing to the kettle. 'It's grand to see you again, Lizzie.'

'And you.'

He glanced sideways at her. 'I have to admit it was a bit of a shock when Gordon showed me Ma's letter. What happened?'

At least he wasn't being condemnatory, Lizzie thought as she told him about Jack. She doubted it would be the same with Gordon and Sheena.

'Only the once?' Stuart frowned, when she had finished.

'As Da said, once is enough.'

'You were bloody unlucky, girl.'

Lizzie sighed. 'You can say that again. I couldn't believe it when I realised I was up the duff. I really couldn't. It just seemed so very cruel.'

Stuart couldn't have agreed more. 'How did Ma and Da take it?'

'How do you think? Da went through the roof and was all for rushing round to Jack's and forcing him to marry me. That's when I explained Jack had left and God knew when he'd return.'

'I must say this is a rather ingenious scheme of Ma's. She pretending to be pregnant and you to be married.' He shook his head. 'It might just work.'

'It has to, Stuart. The alternative doesn't bear thinking about.'

'Aye, that's true enough,' he agreed sombrely.

'Ma's going to use padding to give the right effect. She's got it all ready. She intends adding to it as the weeks go by.'

'And then she's coming here to have her so-called baby. That right?'

'That's right. Only it will be me having the child.'

'Which Ma will claim as hers when you go back to Glasgow?'

'To be brought up as my sister or brother, whichever the baby turns out to be.'

'Pretty desperate measures,' Stuart said grimly.

'It was a pretty desperate situation. I was at my wits' end, and thoroughly ashamed of myself to say the least, particularly when I realised what the outcome would mean for the family.'

'Would you like something to eat?'

Lizzie shook her head.

'There's rabbit stew for later. That all right?'

'Sounds wonderful. So you now cook too?'

He shrugged. 'It was either learn or starve. I've become

pretty good at it if I say so myself. Probably because I enjoy it. I find it relaxing after a day working on the estate.'

He picked up the kettle, which had begun to boil, and poured some of the contents into the teapot, swirling the water round and then sloshing it away before adding the tea.

Lizzie had never before noticed how like their ma Stuart was, facially as well as in build and mannerisms. It might have been Ethne filling the pot.

'Are you terribly disappointed in me, Stuart?' she asked in a quiet voice.

He paused in what he was doing. Looked at her, then away again. 'You want me to be honest?'

'Yes.'

'Well, I am. I just never thought of you as that kind of girl.'

'And what kind of girl is that?'

'One who would . . . well . . . before marriage.'

'You mean a tart?'

He blushed bright red. 'I don't think you're that, Lizzie.'

'Are you sure?'

'You said yourself it was only once.'

'It was. I swear.'

'It's just . . . even once.'

'Before marriage?'

'Aye, that's about it.' He hesitated, then asked, 'Would you have done it again with this Jack if he hadn't gone to sea?'

'That's impossible to answer, Stuart. If I hadn't got pregnant then who knows? It's possible. There again, to be brutal, Jack might not have tried.'

291

Stuart's hand was shaking as he poured the tea. 'Has he no feelings for you, then?'

God, Lizzie thought miserably. This was all beginning to sound horrible. 'I believe he has. Though he never actually admitted as much.'

'And how about you?'

'I've been attracted to Jack ever since we first met. There's simply something about him that makes him different to all the other chaps. Let me just say that if I hadn't been pregnant and he'd asked me to marry him I'd have jumped at the chance.'

'So you love him?'

Lizzie frowned. These questions were getting more and more difficult to answer. 'I think I could easily have done.'

'And so you gave in to him?'

Now it was Lizzie's turn to blush. 'Obviously. I simply couldn't stop myself at the time. Couldn't, and didn't want to. Don't ask me to explain further than that. I can't.'

'Still sugar and milk?'

'Please.'

Stuart handed her a cup and saucer, then sat down facing her. His eyes were brooding as he gazed at her.

'What?'

'I'm just trying to make sense of it all, Lizzie.'

She attempted a smile which didn't quite come off. 'You and me both. It's turned my whole world upside down, I can tell you.'

'And the rest of the family's. Ma's most of all. She's the one who's going to become a "mother" again at her age. It won't be easy. Or for Da.'

'I know,' Lizzie whispered in reply, feeling riven with guilt.

'Still, what's done cannot be undone, as they say. You're all going to have to make the best of it.'

Lizzie dropped her gaze to stare at the floor. 'Da suggested I have an abortion,' she mumbled. 'But we didn't know anyone who would carry it out. Besides, I wouldn't have been able to go through with it. As I said at the time, it would be murder, and I couldn't live with that on my conscience. It would destroy me.'

Stuart didn't know what to reply, so stayed silent.

When Lizzie looked again at her brother she was crying. 'Oh, Stuart,' she wailed.

Stuart laid his cup and saucer on the floor, crossed over and took her in his arms. 'Wheesht, lassie. Wheesht. Stop your bubbling. You've got me to look after you and take care of you till you go back to Glasgow. And that's exactly what I'm going to do.'

'Thanks, Stuart.'

'We all make mistakes, Lizzie. In your case it's a rather far-reaching one, but you're only human after all.'

A sense of peace crept over her at that.

'This is your room. I hope it's comfortable enough.'

They'd finished their tea and Stuart had brought her upstairs before leaving for work.

It was a lovely room, Lizzie thought. She'd be quite at home here. 'Decorate it yourself?'

'Of course.'

'You've made a smashing job of it.'

'Thank you, kind sister,' he replied, giving a mock bow.

'How about the curtains?' They were an appealing shade of powder blue, and lined.

'Made those too.'

She regarded him in astonishment. 'You did?'

'Borrowed Sheena's pedal sewing machine and went from there. It wasn't that difficult, really. Don't forget I'm a practical person. Have to be, working on the estate.'

Lizzie was very impressed. As a machinist herself she appreciated the skill involved.

'Anyway, I'd better be moving,' Stuart declared. 'One word of warning, though. Sheena said she'll probably drop by later. Just so you know.'

'Thanks.'

Stuart gave her a brotherly peck on the cheek and left her to unpack.

Later, when there was a knock on the door, Lizzie guessed who it was.

'So, you've arrived safely,' Sheena declared when Lizzie opened the door. Gordon's wife was a blonde woman in her early twenties with a scar on her face that was the result of a childhood accident. Her figure was slim and willowy, the legs long and graceful.

'As you can see. Come on in.'

Sheena swept inside and immediately went into the sitting room. 'I'm only here for a few minutes,' she explained. 'I've got to pick Mhairi up from school.'

'I was hoping she'd be with you. How is she?'

'Growing, starting to show a mind of her own. Otherwise mostly the same.'

'Can I get you anything?'

Sheena shook her head. 'As I said, I've only got a few

minutes. One of the reasons I'm here is to invite you and Stuart for Sunday dinner.'

'That's kind of you.'

Sheena's green eyes, by far her best feature, glittered. 'It's what would be expected in the circumstances, after all.'

There was a coldness in Sheena's voice which Lizzie didn't fail to note. That, and disapproval. If Sheena was trying to bait her then she wasn't going to rise to it. 'What time?' she asked instead.

'Round about one o'clock. That's when we usually have it.'

'Assuming Stuart can manage it, we'll be there.'

'Good.' Sheena hesitated, then asked sweetly, 'Is there anything you can't eat? Sometimes happens in your condition.'

Lizzie inwardly winced. The question hadn't been asked out of concern; far from it. She shook her head. 'Nothing at all. Except sprouts, but then I've never liked those.'

'Fine, then.'

'Will I be seeing Gordon before Sunday?'

'I doubt it. He's terribly busy at the moment. Busy time, you know.'

Lizzie didn't reply.

Sheena glanced at the rings Lizzie was wearing. 'And what do I now call you if asked?'

'Mrs Jack White.'

'Is he the father?'

Lizzie nodded.

'Hmm.'

'He's a seaman on a long voyage, if you're asked about that as well. Which is true enough.'

295

Sheena came to her feet. 'Well, I'd better be going. Just one other thing.'

'What's that?'

'I hope you're not intending going to church while you're here. I wouldn't approve of that at all.'

'As it happens, Sheena, I don't intend going. We've rather lapsed on church attendance since moving to Glasgow.'

'And why's that?' her sister-in-law demanded harshly.

Lizzie shrugged. 'No particular reason. We just have, that's all.'

Sheena was about to make a caustic retort, then decided not to, although she thought it was disgraceful. She never missed a Sunday, though Gordon sometimes had to because of his job.

'Right, Sunday then,' she declared, and strode from the room.

Lizzie let her find her own way out. Bitch, she thought after Sheena had gone.

Bloody bitch!

Pearl's patience snapped as Willie's eager hand reached for her. 'Can't you leave me alone for one night!' she exploded.

Willie frowned in the darkness. 'What's wrong?'

'I'm tired, Willie, that's what's wrong. I want to sleep.'

'You can sleep soon enough. I won't take long.'

'I'm still sore from this morning. You went at me like a bull in a china shop.'

'I'm sorry about that. I didn't mean to hurt you.'

Pearl sighed with exasperation, then wriggled away as his hand again groped towards her. 'Willie!'

'Oh, come on, don't be like that?' he pleaded.

'I just want to sleep,' she repeated, still bubbling inside with anger.

'Can I help it if I fancy you so much?'

'Don't try and soft-soap me, Willie Henderson. You're a randy sod, and that's all there is to it. Randy morning, noon and night.'

She jumped when his hand clamped on to her backside. 'Willie!'

'I'm your husband, Pearl. It's my right.'

'Maybe so. But not all the bloody time, for Christ's sake!'

He was damned if he was going to admit defeat: his need was too great. With a swift yank he had her on her back, a moment later her nightie round her waist. And a moment after that he was inside her.

'This is rape,' Pearl muttered through gritted teeth.

Willie paid absolutely no heed, keeping her pinned to the bed until he was finished.

'That's more like it.' He smiled in satisfaction as he rolled away.

The man was a pig, Pearl thought. A pig through and through. She wished to God she'd never married him.

'It seems strange not having Lizzie around,' Ethne mused out loud.

'Aye,' Doogie agreed. 'It does that.'

'The house is quieter somehow. Though I can't say she made much of a noise when she was home.'

'True.'

'I just hope she's all right, that's all.'

Doogie gazed at his wife, seeing the concern written

on her face. 'Of course she is, lass. She's with Stuart, don't forget, with Gordon and Sheena not that far away. She's probably thoroughly enjoying herself being back on the estate.' He was in two minds about asking the question, but did anyway. 'Do you still miss Tomintoul?'

'Of course I do. Don't you?'

Doogie thought about that. 'Not as much as I used to. I suppose I'm sort of getting settled here, though I'll always be a countryman at heart. Working with horses helps. I might feel differently if it wasn't for them.'

It surprised Ethne to realise she felt more or less the same way. She'd become used to Glasgow, and Thistle Street, nasty and smelly as they were. Also, she'd made good friends in the close, especially Dot.

'I'm still looking forward to returning,' she declared nevertheless.

'I don't blame you for that. I know I would.'

'Seeing the boys again, and wee Mhairi.'

Doogie noticed she didn't mention Sheena. 'I wish I could come with you,' he said wistfully. But that was impossible. He had to stay behind and bring money into the house: there was nothing else for it. They would need all the money they could get now they were going to be bringing up another child.

'I wonder what Lizzie's doing at the moment?'

Doogie glanced at the clock. 'Well, she won't be out gallivanting, that's for sure.' He laughed. 'Tomintoul isn't exactly the place for that.'

Ethne smiled, having to agree.

'She's probably sitting having a chat with Stuart,' Doogie speculated. 'Just like the pair of us.'

'Aye, probably,' Ethne agreed.

They were right.

Stuart glanced sideways at Lizzie, who had a face like fizz. They had just left Gordon and Sheena's after Sunday dinner. 'I didn't think it was that bad,' he said softly.

'Gordon hardly said a word to me the entire time we were there. I might not have existed as far as he was concerned.'

'He's never been one to talk much, you know that,' Stuart reminded her.

'Even though. He could have made an effort.'

Stuart thought his brother and sister-in-law had behaved disgracefully, but he wasn't about to say so. 'At least wee Mhairi was delighted to see you.'

Lizzie's face immediately softened. 'She's certainly shot up, just as Sheena said she had.'

'Made a right fuss of you. Auntie Lizzie this, and Auntie Lizzie that. And I heard her insisting on sitting beside you at the table.'

'Which Sheena was none too happy about.'

'Ach, don't worry about her. I know I wouldn't.'

'You're not the one with a bun in the oven, and not wed.'

'I should hope not!' Stuart laughed. 'It would cause a sensation if I was. I can just imagine how the newspapers would report it. The Miracle of Tomintoul!'

'I'm glad it's you I'm staying with and not them. That would have been awful, considering their attitude.'

'And I'm glad you're staying with me as well. Not only do I have my favourite sister . . .'

'What do you mean, your favourite sister?' she interjected. 'You only have the one.'

'You know what I mean.'

Lizzie was beginning to feel better after the ordeal that had been Sunday lunch. She wouldn't be going back there in a hurry. No fears. Not after the way she'd been treated. As if she was a leper or something.

'What gets me most about Sheena is that she's a Christian who's supposed to love her neighbour. There was very little love shown towards me this afternoon.'

Stuart couldn't disagree.

'And where was the charity, eh? Not much of that on show. All I got were sly innuendoes from her and silence from my brother. He didn't even ask how I was!'

'He's always been the silent type.'

'Silent is one thing, downright rude another.'

Stuart glanced up at the sky. 'I think it's going to rain,' he commented.

'Doesn't bother me. I've no intention of going out again.'

'We'll get the range fired up and make toast later. All nice and comfy. How does that sound?'

'Wonderful.'

Lizzie suddenly stopped and clutched her stomach, her expression changing into one of wonderment.

'What is it?' Stuart asked anxiously.

'I felt the baby move. I'm sure of it.'

He frowned. 'Isn't it early days for that?'

Lizzie smiled. A strange, ethereal sort of smile. 'It was lovely.'

'Have you heard the latest?' Molly O'Sullivan, at the machine next to Pearl's, was bursting with the news.

'What's that?'

'Scary Mary's been found murdered, so she has.'

Pearl's eyes widened in shock. 'No!'

'It's true, I tell you. Belle Finlay had it off her husband who's in the polis. Mary was found in an alleyway with her throat cut.'

'Jesus Christ!' Pearl swore softly. This was terrible. She'd had no liking for Scary, but no one deserved that.

'Happened late at night, apparently, after the pubs had shut. So far the polis have no idea who did it, or why.'

'Where is this alleyway?'

'Down by the docks.'

Now why would Scary be down there? Pearl wondered. Unless of course she had been selling herself. 'Poor thing,' she muttered.

'To be sure,' Molly agreed. 'Makes me shiver just to think about it.'

Scary's death was the talk of the factory for the rest of the day. No one was ever brought to book for her murder, nor was the reason behind it discovered.

It was a beautiful autumn day and Lizzie had decided to go for a walk. The best thing about being back in Tomintoul was the air, she reflected. Pure and fresh, in total contrast to what passed for air in Glasgow. She sucked in a deep lungful appreciatively.

She halted when she saw the figure of a man approaching her: an estate employee, judging from his clothes. Mid-twenties, she guessed, as he got closer. Powerfully built, with a shock of dark auburn hair. She'd thought she knew all the estate workers, but this one was new to her.

'Morning.' He smiled, coming to a stop a few feet away.

'Good morning.'

'It's a fine day.'

'Gorgeous.'

Lizzie looked into his eyes and, with a shock, saw they were a similar pale blue to Jack's. For a moment she was slightly unnerved.

'You must be Mrs White,' the young man said.

'That's right.'

'I'm Ross Colquhoun. I work alongside your brothers.'

'Pleased to meet you, Ross.'

'And you, Mrs White. Come home to have a baby, I understand, while your husband's away at sea?'

'You're well informed.'

'Stuart mentioned it a while back. Are you out for a walk?'

'I was. Now I'm about to head back again.'

Ross suddenly pointed skywards. 'Look at that! Now there's a bonny sight.'

Lizzie glanced up in the direction he was indicating, shading her eyes with a hand to get a better view. 'Golden eagle,' she declared, delighted.

'Not many of those round here.'

Lizzie, born and brought up on the estate, knew that to be true. 'Magnificent, aren't they?'

'That one certainly is.'

They both admired the bird for a few moments before again focusing on one another.

'Aren't you working?' Lizzie queried.

'Been sent on an errand. If you're returning to Stuart's do you mind if I tag along? It's on my way.'

Lizzie decided she'd like that. 'Of course.' They fell into step together. 'Are you from round here?'

'Oh aye.' He mentioned the name of a tiny hamlet on the other side of Tomintoul. 'Do you know it?'

'Of it. I've never been there.'

'When do you expect the baby?'

Lizzie told him.

'You'll be excited about that, eh?'

'Terrified, more like,' she confessed.

He didn't laugh as some men might have done, but instead nodded sympathetically. 'All I can say is I'm glad I'm not a woman having to go through that.'

He had an easy, friendly manner about him. Again like Jack, Lizzie thought.

She decided she liked Ross Colquhoun.

Chapter 20

'I was talking to Sammy at the dairy today,' Doogie said to Ethne over tea. 'Do you remember him – one of the milkmen?'

'I remember.'

'Well, he works Saturday nights at the *Sunday Chronicle* as a packer. Sorting the papers into bundles and tying them up for distribution. He tells me it's extremely well paid for a single night's work.'

'Oh aye?'

'One of the chaps is leaving in a couple of weeks and Sammy feels certain he can get me the job if I want it.'

Ethne laid down her knife and fork to stare at Doogie across the table. 'And do you?'

'Extra cash would certainly come in handy when the baby arrives, don't you think?'

'Extra cash comes in handy any time. What about the horses at the dairy, though?'

'I'll strike a deal with young John. He can do the Saturday evening shift and I'll go straight from the *Chronicle* and do the Sunday morning one. Should pan out all right.'

'So you're going to apply?'

Doogie shrugged. 'Too good an opportunity to miss. It's hard graft, mind, but that won't worry me. I've done enough of that in my time.'

What a good man he really was, Ethne thought, a warm glow filling her. Oh, he did have his bad points, but then who didn't? Overall, he wasn't such a bad stick when it came down to it.

'Do I have your approval, then?'

'Of course you do.'

Doogie suddenly smiled. 'I'm looking forward to having a baby around again.'

'Are you?'

'I am indeed.'

'And all the problems and worries that go with it?'

'We've coped three times already so I don't see a fourth being any different. Do you?'

'Not really. Except we're older now. It'll take more of a toll.'

'Older, but not yet past it,' he joked, a twinkle in his eye. 'As you can testify, woman.'

She knew what he was referring to, and smiled.

'Now if you have no objections I'm going to the Argyle for a couple of pints before heading off to the dairy.'

'I've no objection,' she replied softly.

'Good.'

She surprised him as he was leaving by giving him a kiss on the cheek. There was a broad smile plastered all over Doogie's face as he hurried down the stairs. It was rare for Ethne to do that. He must be in her good books.

*   *   *

305

'Oh, hello, Pete!' Pearl exclaimed, answering a knock on the door.

'I've come to see Willie. Is he in?'

'I'm afraid not. He goes to his ma's for tea every Wednesday night.'

Pete stared at her in amazement. '*Every* Wednesday night?'

'That's right. Pathetic, isn't it?'

Pete thought it unusual, to say the least.

'Anyway, come on through and I'll put the kettle on.'

'That's kind of you.'

'Take a pew,' Pearl said as they entered the kitchen. She was about to fill the kettle when she remembered there was whisky in the house. She doubted Willie would be best pleased if she used it, tight sod, but he'd drunk Pete's often enough. Time to repay Pete a little.

'Would you like a dram instead of tea?' she asked.

'Only if you'll have one with me.'

'Then drams it is.' She poured two generous measures. 'Lemonade?'

'Please.'

She handed him his drink then sank into the chair facing the one he was in. 'Up your kilt!' she toasted, which made him laugh.

She was delighted Pete had called by. He was such good company, she thought, and relaxing to be with.

'So how long has this been going on?' Pete inquired casually.

'You mean Willie at his mother's?'

Pete nodded.

'Quite a while now. Willie doesn't think all that much of my cooking, I'm afraid, whereas his mother's a dab hand. He won't admit it but one of the reasons he goes there is to get a decent meal.'

'You're not that bad, surely!' Pete protested.

'Willie thinks I am.'

'But he hasn't actually said so?'

'He doesn't have to say so, Pete. I know from comments he's made in the past.'

Pete was beginning to realise there were sides to Willie he hadn't been aware of when they'd been pals together in the old days. A tendency towards being careful with money, yes. But there appeared to be a lot more than that.

'Anyway, the reason I called by was to ask if you'd like to make up a foursome for this Saturday? I thought we might go to a restaurant for a meal.'

'A restaurant,' Pearl exclaimed. 'Sounds fabulous. Any one in particular?'

'I haven't decided yet. Can you recommend somewhere?'

Pearl laughed. 'You want the truth?'

Pete nodded.

'I've never been to a restaurant in my life.'

'Really!' He was flabbergasted.

'Aye, really. Not unless you call a sit-down fish and chip shop a restaurant.'

Pete laughed. 'No, I don't think so. I have seen the occasional one called a fish restaurant, but they hardly merit the title in my opinion.'

'It'll be fun,' Pearl enthused.

'So you agree, then?'

Willie would be livid, Pearl thought. If it was up to him he'd find some way of wriggling out of it, thinking it would cost far too much money. Well, to hell with him. A good night out was just what she needed. 'I agree.' She smiled.

'Excellent.'

She frowned. 'You said a foursome?'

'I'll be bringing a lady friend of mine. Her name's Elspeth.'

'Elspeth, eh? When did this start?'

'Only a couple of weeks ago.'

Pearl was intrigued. 'What's she like?'

'You can find out for yourself on Saturday.'

Pearl sipped her whisky, eyeing Pete over the rim of her glass. 'How did you meet?'

By the time Pete left they'd finished all the whisky and had a right old blether together, and enjoyed every minute of it.

Lizzie was feeding Stuart's chickens, a task she had taken over on a permanent basis. There was a nip in the air so she'd wrapped up warm in an old coat of her brother's which was miles too big for her.

'Hello again.'

She turned to find Ross smiling at her. 'Where did you come from?'

'I popped out of the ground. It's called magic.'

She laughed. 'Off on another errand?'

'That's right. Sometimes I think I'm no more than a message boy. I'm always the one they send.'

'Is that a complaint?'

He shook his head. 'Not really. It's a lot less tiring than actual work.'

Lizzie threw the last of the grain to the chickens, then dusted off her hands. 'Fancy a cup of tea?'

''Fraid I can't stop. Not that long, anyway. But thank you for asking.'

'Another time, perhaps?'

'I'll hold you to that.'

Again she was struck by the similarity of his eyes to Jack's. That particular shade of pale blue wasn't all that common. She found herself wondering where Jack was, and what he was up to.

'A penny for them?'

'Pardon?'

'You looked deep in thought there for a moment or two.'

She flushed. 'Sorry. I didn't mean to be rude.'

'You weren't. Just lost in thought. Oh well, I'd better be getting on. Duty calls.'

'Nice to see you, Ross.'

'And you, Mrs White.'

'Call me Lizzie, please. There's no need to be so formal.'

He smiled again. 'Then Lizzie it is.'

'Good.'

He was about to move away, then hesitated. 'Are you and Stuart going to the ceilidh on Saturday night?'

This was news to Lizzie. 'He hasn't mentioned anything.'

'Well, you should. I'd imagine you'd enjoy yourself. I'll certainly be there. Wouldn't miss it.'

'All those lassies, eh?' she teased.

'Hundreds and thousands. All shapes, sizes and whatever else you can think of.'

Lizzie laughed. 'I'll bet you're a great ladies' man.'

He winked at her. 'That's for me to know and you to wonder about.'

'And drinker too, no doubt?'

'I've been known to take a dram or two. Who here-abouts doesn't?'

True enough, Lizzie thought. Whisky was part of the local culture.

'I'll look for you there,' said Ross. 'And if you do turn up maybe you'll give this poor message boy a dance?'

'In my condition?'

He eyed her waist. 'You're not that far gone. It wouldn't hurt. As long as you don't get thrown all over the place. These ceilidhs can get wild, you know. Oh aye, lots of wheeching goes on.'

'Wheech yourself. Now off you go before you land yourself in trouble.'

'You're right. 'Bye then, Lizzie. I'll keep an eye out for you on Saturday night.'

'The ceilidh?' Stuart queried later that night when she mentioned the matter. 'It just never crossed my mind.'

'Why not?'

Stuart shrugged. 'To be honest with you, Lizzie, I'm not that sociable a chap. I prefer staying in to going out.'

'But you must sometimes. What about the pub?'

'On occasion I've been known to drop in. But it rather bores me, so I never stay long.'

He'd changed a lot from the Stuart she remembered, Lizzie thought. He used to be more outgoing. 'There should be lots of lassies there. You might even find your-self a girlfriend.'

Stuart shot her an odd look. 'I'm not that interested in women, actually.'

That shocked her. 'Why ever not?'

'Oh, there's nothing wrong, you understand,' he replied quickly. 'It's just . . . well, I feel uncomfortable in their company, I suppose.'

Now she was puzzled. 'Do you?'

'Aye, with some anyway. I mean, I'm all right with you.'

Lizzie laughed. 'I should hope so, you big dope. I am your sister, after all. You've known me all my life.'

He had to smile.

'So which women make you uncomfortable?' she persisted, intrigued.

'The younger, eligible ones, when I think about it. They kind of put me off.'

'But why?'

Stuart shrugged. 'They just do.'

'There must be a reason, Stuart. There has to be.'

He sighed.

'Well?'

'It's difficult to say. I really don't know the answer.'

'But surely you've been attracted to some female or other before now?'

He shook his head. 'There have been a few interested in me. But I wasn't in them.'

'Haven't you ever wanted to . . .' She broke off, remembering this was her brother she was talking to, not Pearl.

'That's enough of that,' Stuart said firmly, meaning it. 'I don't wish to discuss this any further. Let's just leave it.' He decided to change the subject. 'You said it was Ross who told you about the ceilidh?'

'He stopped by to say hello when I was feeding the chickens. That's when he mentioned it. A nice chap, don't you think?'

Stuart grunted. 'Nice enough. A good worker, I'll give him that. Knows how to graft. He's highly thought of in that respect.'

'Is he married?'

Stuart didn't catch the coy tone that had come into her voice. 'No, he's single like me.'

'Oh?'

'He's got a nickname, you know. They cry him the gypsy.'

'The gypsy! He doesn't look at all like one.'

'No, that's not the reason. It's because he lives in a genuine Romany caravan which he brought with him when he came to work on the estate.'

A genuine Romany caravan! Lizzie marvelled. How utterly romantic. Ross Colquhaun had just gone up in her estimation.

'Wasn't Elspeth a cracker?' Willie enthused as he and Pearl made their way to the tram stop.

Pearl glanced sideways at him, amazed he wasn't complaining about what the meal had cost. 'You thought so, eh?'

'Oh aye. A real smasher.'

Pearl regarded him grimly. She hadn't been impressed in the least by the beautiful Elspeth. 'I couldn't stand her. That voice of hers nearly drove me up the wall.'

Willie frowned. 'What was wrong with her voice?'

'It was so affected. As if she thought she really was something. She didn't sound natural at all.'

'Pete seems well taken with her. Lucky bastard.'

'And she's flat-chested. Didn't you notice?' Pearl retorted cattily.

Willie thought about it. 'Can't say I did.'

'And even worse than her voice was her air of superiority. It was as though she was talking down to us all the time. There was one point where I could easily have sloshed her.'

'Are you just a teensy bit jealous?' Willie teased.

'Not in the least!' Pearl exclaimed hotly. 'Who needs to be jealous of that?'

Willie didn't believe a word of it. 'We'll be seeing her again if the four of us go out another time.'

'Which you'll be keen to do, no doubt?'

'I've certainly nothing against it. I enjoyed her company even if you didn't.'

'You mean you fancied her rotten?' Pearl accused him.

A gleam came into Willie's eyes which Pearl didn't fail to notice. 'I wouldn't say that,' he lied.

'You did. It was obvious.'

'Suit yourself. I'm not arguing.'

'Because you can't. That's why.'

He shrugged and didn't reply.

'You'd love to shag her given half the chance.'

How very true, Willie thought. By God, he'd give her a right seeing to.

'Wouldn't you?' Pearl, now seething inside, persisted.

'I'll remind you I'm a happily married man.'

'That's got nothing to do with it. It's what's in your mind I'm talking about.'

'Nonsense.'

'Oh no it's not. I know you only too well, Willie Henderson.'

'Do you now?' he sneered.

'Damn right I do.'

'Huh!' he retorted scornfully.

Before the row could continue their tram clattered alongside and they got on board. As the tram was nearly full, they let the matter drop.

'Mind if I join you?'

Lizzie smiled at Ross, and indicated the vacant chair beside her. Stuart had gone off to the Gents'.

'I see you made it then,' Ross remarked.

'And to prove it I'm here.'

He laughed at that. 'Enjoying yourself?'

Lizzie glanced at the makeshift dance floor where typical Highland dancing was in full fling. 'Oh, I am that all right. It's great fun. And, I have to say, good to be out of the house for a change.'

Ross produced a bottle of whisky from his pocket. 'Care for a top-up?'

She smiled at him, dazzled by those blue eyes she remembered so well. 'Thank you. But not too much.' Although she was still under age no one would comment on Lizzie's drinking as she was now, supposedly, a married woman carrying a child. Technically that made her an adult in onlookers' eyes.

Ross poured her a small one, then refilled his own glass. 'Happy days!' he toasted.

'And the same for you.' Just then a loud wheech rang out, followed by an even louder one. 'Well, you weren't wrong about the wheeching.'

'It'll get noisier as the night goes on,' Ross prophesied. 'I must say I'm a bit surprised you got Stuart to bring you along. He's not exactly known for mixing with others. He's got a name for being something of a recluse.'

'I know. He told me. Any idea why?'

Ross shrugged. 'Not really.'

'He didn't use to be like that.'

'Well, he has been all the time I've known him. Keeps himself to himself. Perhaps he's just shy.'

Lizzie thought about that. 'Could be. Though if he is he's changed. But then people do, I suppose.'

'So I believe.'

Lizzie was enjoying being in Ross's company. Like Jack, he was relaxing to be with. 'Stuart tells me you have a genuine Romany caravan?' she said.

'Aye, I do.'

'Do you own it?'

'Bought it some years back when I was living with my parents. We have quite a large family and it got to the stage where we were getting cramped to say the least. The caravan came up for sale when its owner died, and I bought it. I parked it behind my parents' house and moved in. When I landed the job on the laird's estate I brought it with me as I'm used to living in it now.'

Lizzie was fascinated. 'Is it painted in lovely colours?'

'Indeed it is. And quite comfy inside – you'd be surprised. I love it. Home sweet home, you might say.'

'I wouldn't mind seeing it sometime.'

'Whenever. A Sunday would be best. You just name one and I'll happily come over and take you there. It'll be my pleasure.'

'How about a week tomorrow? If the weather's good, that is.'

'Morning or afternoon?'

'Morning's best for me, Ross. I tend to get tired as the day wears on nowadays.'

His face was instantly filled with concern. 'I hope coming here to the ceilidh isn't too much for you?'

She appreciated his care for her. 'I had a weel sleep earlier. Besides, I'm just sitting down as I would be at Stuart's, so it's not a problem.'

'You've still got the walk home.'

'I'll cope. Don't worry.'

'A week tomorrow it is then,' Ross confirmed as he spotted Stuart returning.

How lovely, Lizzie thought. How very lovely. She was looking forward to it and just hoped the weather behaved itself.

Ross turned up directly after breakfast and had a cup of tea with them before he and Lizzie set off. Although cold, it was a crisp, clear December day, perfect for walking.

'Now you're sure you're up to this?' Ross asked as they left the cottage.

'Don't you worry about me. I'll be fine.'

He was wearing an old sheepskin coat, she noticed, which she thought looked rather good on him. 'Is it far?'

'Not too bad. About twenty minutes. Is that all right?'

Lizzie laughed. 'Will you stop worrying! I've got a good Scots tongue in my head and will soon tell you if I'm struggling.'

'I don't know how you can live in Glasgow,' Ross said after a while. 'I went there once and thought it was an awful place.'

'What were you doing in Glasgow?'

'Just wanted to see what it looked like. Two days there was enough for me, then I couldn't wait to get back. Apart from anything else there were just so many people!

You can hardly move for them.'

Lizzie knew what he meant. She'd felt the same when she'd first arrived there. 'You get used to it after a while.' She smiled.

He shook his head. 'I never would.'

'I'm afraid we had to,' she replied quietly.

He glanced at her, then away again. 'Aye, I heard about that. The laird's wife, wasn't it?'

'It was. Stupid of my da, but he was drunk at the time and simply spoke without thinking.'

'Funny, though, in a way. I'd love to have seen the laird's wife's face when your da came out with what he did. It must have been a picture.'

'I believe so. From what I heard afterwards, that is.'

'Your da's now working in a stables, I understand?'

'And thoroughly enjoying it. He just loves horses. Most other animals too. Do you?'

'I can't honestly say I love them. They're simply around most of the time. Something I was brought up with.'

Lizzie shivered as an icy wind went right through her. 'It's turning colder.'

'We'll soon be there and I'll put the stove on. That'll quickly warm you up again.'

She flashed him a smile of appreciation, and they continued talking, getting to know one another better, as they went on their way.

A little later Lizzie halted in her tracks when the caravan came into view. It was painted green and red with splashes of other colours here and there, and was everything she'd imagined it would be.

'What do you think?' Ross asked.

'It's gorgeous. Like something out of a picture book.'

Ross laughed, never having thought of it like that before. 'Come on, have a closer look.'

The detail was magnificent, Lizzie saw when they got nearer. There were gaudy flowers, small pictorial scenes, swirls and sworls and intricate designs of all sorts. The overall effect was a riot of colour.

'Let's get that stove on,' Ross declared, leading the way inside.

The interior was compact, to put it politely, and there wasn't exactly a lot of headroom. And Ross certainly couldn't be accused of tidiness. But within minutes he had the stove blazing away and almost instantly the inside of the caravan was filled with heat.

'Sit down,' he invited.

Lizzie gazed about her, quite enthralled.

'Like it?'

'Mmm,' she murmured. 'I really do.'

He was clearly pleased. 'Now, how about some coffee? Or a dram if you prefer.'

'Coffee would be nice.'

'It won't take long.'

Lizzie stayed for half an hour before saying she should start back. They had been chatting non-stop, each thoroughly enjoying the conversation.

'I'll walk you home again,' Ross offered as she rose to leave.

'There's no need. I know the way now.'

'I won't hear of it,' he insisted. 'Besides, it'll be my pleasure.'

A gentleman, Lizzie thought as she stepped outside. A real gentleman.

She liked that.

Chapter 21

Doogie stared in admiration as Ethne began unravelling the padding round her waist. When she was finally free of it she gave a huge sigh of relief, and scratched her protesting skin.

'I have to say, girl, I'm ever so impressed by the way you're pulling off this so-called pregnancy. You're doing it a treat. If I didn't know better you'd certainly fool me.'

'It's not that difficult. Not when you know what the real thing's like.'

'You even walk as though you are.' He shook his head. 'I think you missed your vocation. You should have been an actress.'

Ethne laughed. 'Hardly.'

'No, I'm serious.'

She gazed fondly at him, thinking what a great support he'd been in all this. Not once had he ever let slip, even in drink, that her pregnancy was an illusion. 'I bumped into Babs Millar in the street the other day,' she said.

'Oh aye?'

'Hadn't seen her for a couple of weeks. No real reason,

we'd just missed one another, that's all. Anyway, she told me I was absolutely glowing and that being an expectant mother obviously suited me. Said she'd never seen me look better.'

Doogie chuckled.

'She was full of it. Even insisted my skin had improved thanks to my condition. Mentioned the fact several times.'

'I'm going to miss you terribly when you return to Tomintoul,' said Doogie suddenly.

She glanced over at him. 'Will you?'

'You know I will. It's not just the business of looking after myself, pain in the arse though that's going to be. It's you yourself. We've been together a long time, don't forget. Oh, I know we've had our ups and downs – what couple hasn't? But we've always gone to bed together, and got up the same way in the morning. Apart from that wee spell when I came to Glasgow ahead of you, that is.'

It touched her deeply to hear the tenderness in his voice.

'Coming home to an empty house is going to be awful. Rattling around by myself. No one to talk to. No one to keep me in check and tell me off when I deserve it.'

She looked into his eyes and saw the love there. 'I'll miss you too, Doogie. All I can promise is I won't stay away a day longer than I have to.'

'I know that.'

'Will you write?'

'Och, Eth, don't ask the impossible. I'm no use with paper and pen, never have been. The odd note or list is about all I can ever manage. And when I say note I'm talking a couple of lines, nothing more. But . . .' He paused. 'I will be thinking about you all the time. You can bank on that.'

'Well, I'll write to you. Especially after the baby's born. You'll want to know how everything went.'

His face clouded over. 'I just hope it all goes well with Lizzie and the baby. Childbirth can be a tricky business, as we both know.'

'I'm sure it'll be all right. Lizzie's a strong lass. She shouldn't have too much trouble if she takes after me.' Still, you never knew, Ethne reflected grimly. Childbirth was like that. You just never knew.

There again, Dr MacKay would be in attendance. The same Dr MacKay who'd delivered her three.

As doctors went they didn't come much better. Or more experienced. Lizzie would be in the best hands possible.

'I was wondering,' Lizzie said.

Stuart glanced over at her. 'What?'

'How would you feel about us inviting Ross here for a meal one evening?'

'What's brought this on?' Stuart asked quietly.

Lizzie rubbed her stomach. The baby was kicking again, which it was doing more and more frequently of late. 'It can't be very pleasant having to cook and eat by himself all the time. I just thought it might be a nice break for him. And us too, having company for a change.'

'Is that all?'

She frowned. 'How do you mean?'

'Is that the only reason?'

'What other reason could there be?'

Stuart sat back in his chair and studied her. 'It seems

to me the pair of you are getting awfully friendly.'

'And what's wrong with that?'

'Normally, nothing. But you are supposed to be a married woman, don't forget.'

Lizzie flushed as the penny dropped. 'It's nothing like that,' she protested. 'We're just friends, that's all.'

'Are you sure about that?'

'Of course I'm sure about it. As you say, I'm in no position for it to be anything else.'

'I've seen the way he looks at you, Lizzie. He fancies you all right.'

And she fancied Ross, but certainly wasn't going to admit to the fact. 'Don't be daft!' she retorted.

Stuart gave her an infuriating smile. 'Am I?'

'Totally. There's nothing between us. I swear.'

'But there could be,' Stuart went on. 'It's plain as day. To me, anyway.'

Lizzie turned her back on him so he couldn't see her face. Inside, her heart was fluttering. 'You're talking nonsense. We like each other's company, that's all. Where's the harm in that?'

Stuart didn't reply.

'Well?'

'I'm only thinking of you, Lizzie. I don't want to see you get hurt any further.'

She could feel tears welling up, and desperately fought them back. Her emotions were all over the place since falling pregnant, up one moment, down the next. 'Do I take it that means we won't be inviting him, then?'

Stuart shrugged. 'We can if you still want to.'

'I wouldn't have suggested it otherwise,' she snapped.

'Fine. When?'

'You choose the date. Whatever's the most suitable.'

'Right then. I'll have a word with him tomorrow.'

'Good.'

Oh dear, Stuart inwardly sighed. He just hoped and prayed his sister knew what she was doing.

Dr MacKay might have been a prophet who'd stepped straight out the pages of the Old Testament. His face was wizened and heavily lined and his nose a beak, while his white hair, though neatly trimmed, was unfashionably long, falling almost to his shoulders. His gaze was the keenest, and most penetrating, Lizzie had ever experienced. Now well into his seventies, he was still practising and simply adored by all his patients.

'All right, Lizzie, you can put your things back on,' he announced. 'I'll just go and wash my hands.'

'Is everything as it should be, doctor?' Lizzie queried anxiously.

'No problems that I can see.' He smiled. 'Should be a straightforward birth.'

Lizzie sighed with relief.

'Why, are you worried about something?'

'Not really. But you never know, do you?'

'True enough,' he acknowledged. 'But as far as I can ascertain everything is progressing nicely.'

'Thank you, doctor.'

He gazed at her, remembering. 'It was me brought you into this world, you know. Now it's your turn to have a child.' He shook his head. 'Time flies. It seems just yesterday that I was attending your mother.'

He glanced away as Lizzie stood up. 'I'll see you down in the kitchen before I go.'

'Fine, doctor.'

A few minutes later she joined him downstairs. 'Now, what about a cup of tea?' she asked.

'I won't if you don't mind. You wouldn't believe the amount of tea I get offered in this job. If I accepted every cup of the damn stuff it would be spouting out of my ears.'

Lizzie laughed at the mental image this conjured up. 'I suppose so.'

'And cake. If I wasn't careful I'd be fat as a pig.'

Lizzie found that hard to believe. He was reed slim to the point of gauntness.

'So, how are your mother and father doing in that wicked city to the south?'

She told him.

'Shall we sit over?' Lizzie suggested when the meal was finally finished.

'Can I help with the dishes?' Ross asked.

'Don't be ridiculous. I'll do those later.'

'I have to say you're a marvellous cook, Lizzie. That was wonderful.'

'Why, thank you.' She wondered briefly if she should explain that Stuart had done most of it, and decided not to. Let him think what he liked. But she didn't fail to catch the amused glint in Stuart's eyes when she didn't explain.

'Dram, Ross?' Stuart asked.

'That would be nice.'

Stuart crossed to the sideboard where the whisky and glasses were kept.

'I understand you had Dr MacKay in to see you the other day,' Ross said.

Lizzie glanced at him in astonishment. 'How did you know that? Did Stuart mention it?'

'No, he didn't. But word gets round. It's hard to keep anything secret in a place like Tomintoul. People talk. Nothing better to do, I suppose.'

'Aye, the doctor was here.'

'Everything fine, then?'

She heard the concern in his voice, which both pleased and touched her. 'According to the doctor it is.'

'That's excellent.'

'She'll slip the baby out no bother,' Stuart declared. 'I have a feeling about it.'

'And what would you know about childbirth?' Lizzie challenged.

'Not exactly childbirth. Sheep and cows are my speciality. God alone knows how many of those I've delivered. Hundreds, if not thousands, over the years. Ross and I both have. It's part and parcel of working on the estate.'

'I suppose so,' Lizzie murmured.

'Humans and animals, whatever. When you get down to it the procedure's more or less the same. Don't you agree, Ross?'

Ross nodded as he accepted the whisky Stuart handed him.

'Lizzie?'

'A small one.' She patted her bump. 'I have to consider my little friend in here.'

They chatted amiably for a while, mainly about the doings of the estate, which didn't bore Lizzie as it might have other women. She'd been brought up there, after all, and was used to these conversations.

'Tell me, Lizzie,' Ross said, turning his attention to her. 'Have you ever seen a play?'

The question caught her by surprise. 'You mean like in the theatre?'

'That's right.'

She shook her head. 'Can't say I have.'

'What about you, Stuart?'

'Me neither.'

'Well, that makes three of us. There's a touring troupe of actors coming to Tomintoul the week after next and I was wondering if the pair of you would like to go with me? They're putting on something called *Tartuffe* by Molière. If that's how you pronounce it. He's French.'

'French!' Lizzie exclaimed.

'Aye, but it's been translated. It could be a good night. Certainly a different one.'

Stuart was watching in amusement the chemistry flowing between Ross and his sister. He knew he'd only been asked along because it would have been deemed improper for Ross to take Lizzie on his own.

'Stuart, what do you say?' Lizzie asked excitedly. 'I think it's a brilliant idea.'

'I can see that.'

'Well, what about it?'

He could refuse, Stuart thought. But that would clearly be a terrible disappointment for Lizzie. There was no harm in it, after all, as long as the three of them went together. 'Fine by me.'

Lizzie clapped her hands in glee. 'That really will be something to look forward to.'

Ross beamed at Lizzie, who beamed back.

*   *   *

'I've decided to return to Tomintoul to have the baby,' Ethne announced to Dot and the others present in Dot's kitchen.

'But why?' Dot asked.

Ethne glanced from puzzled face to puzzled face, her explanation well prepared. 'Dr MacKay up there delivered my other three and I want him to deliver this one as well.'

'Is there something wrong with the doctors round here?' Babs Millar queried with a frown.

'Nothing at all. I'm sure they're excellent. The hospitals too. It's just that I'd be happier with Dr MacKay, more relaxed with someone I know so well. Someone I've been through it with before.'

'I can see the sense in that.' Dot nodded. 'Though it is an awfully long way to go.'

'I can't argue with you there.' Ethne replied. 'But my mind's made up. I want Dr MacKay to do the delivery.'

'So, when will you leave?' Jean Carmichael asked.

'I'm not certain yet. Probably a few weeks before my due date. It all depends how I get on,' Ethne answered smoothly.

'What about Doogie?' Edwina Edgar queried.

'Och, he'll be all right. He'll manage just fine by himself for a while. He's quite capable, you know.'

'My Shughie would have a conniption if I went off and left him on his own,' Babs declared. 'He's such a useless bugger round the house. In all the years we've been married he's never so much as made a cup of tea. I doubt the eejit knows how.'

Everyone laughed.

There, Ethne thought with satisfaction. That was that

out of the way. They'd swallowed her story hook, line and sinker.

Lizzie stared at her sister-in-law in surprise. It was only Sheena's second visit to Stuart's cottage since she'd taken up residence. 'Come in.'

Sheena swept past. 'I'm only here for a couple of minutes. I thought it was high time I dropped by again.'

Lizzie didn't comment.

'I felt I was neglecting my Christian duty in staying away, so here I am.'

Lizzie smiled, but really could have slapped her. What a pious, sanctimonious, patronising bitch, she thought.

'How are you?' Sheena queried.

'Absolutely fine. In the pink, as you can see.'

Sheena glanced around, then back at Lizzie. 'You've brought great shame on this family, you know. Gordon was mortified when your mother wrote and told him what had happened. As for me . . . well, no doubt you can guess my opinion on the matter.'

Lizzie was getting angry, and trying not to show it, not wanting to give Sheena the satisfaction. 'I envy you,' she said instead.

Sheena frowned, not understanding. 'Why would you envy me?'

'Being such a perfect specimen. Never making any mistakes in life. You're so pure and holy I bet you don't even have to shite like everyone else.'

Sheena's face flamed scarlet. 'How dare you, you little slut!' she hissed.

Lizzie smiled sweetly. 'I think you'd better go.'

And so Sheena did, banging the door behind her.

Well, she said it would be a brief visit, Lizzie thought, and promptly burst out laughing.

She'd rather enjoyed that.

Lizzie glanced sideways at Ross, who was sitting on one side of her, Stuart on the other. He was rapt, his attention riveted on the play unfolding before them. It was obvious he was thoroughly enjoying himself, as indeed was she.

Tartuffe, she thought. She was loving every minute of it.

'I'm glad you enjoyed yourself,' Ross said to Lizzie as they made their way home. Stuart had gone slightly ahead.

She flashed him a smile in the moonlight. 'I certainly did.'

'Me too. It was well worth going.'

'Oh aye, it was.'

'Tell me something,' Ross said hesitantly a few minutes later.

'What's that?'

'Why do you never speak of your husband?'

Ouch! Lizzie thought. It was true; she never mentioned Jack. 'I wasn't aware I didn't,' she lied.

'Everything's all right between the pair of you, I take it?'

Lizzie's heart sank. 'Of course. Couldn't be better.'

Ross glanced sideways at her. 'You must miss him a lot. Especially with a baby coming.'

'I knew what I was getting into when we married,' she said untruthfully. 'Being parted, sometimes for long periods of time, is what happens when your husband's a seaman. You get used to it, I suppose.'

'Hmm,' Ross murmured. 'Stuart mentioned somewhere along the line that Jack — that's your husband's name, I believe?'

Lizzie nodded.

'— is going to be away for anything up to a couple of years this trip.'

'That's right.'

Ross thought about that. 'Wouldn't do me to be separated from my wife for so long. My word and it wouldn't.'

Lizzie didn't reply, just kept walking, head slightly bowed against the bitter wind that was blowing. A wind that had brought a glisten of tears to her eyes and flushed her cheeks.

'You must love him very much to put up with his absences,' Ross went on, probing further.

'I do,' she whispered. Well, what else could she say? She could hardly tell Ross the truth.

'That's good, then.'

Happy as Larry only a few minutes previously, Lizzie was now as miserable as sin. Why oh why had Ross brought up the subject of Jack? But in her heart of hearts she knew why, and the knowledge deepened her misery.

'And what about you, Ross? I'm surprised you haven't settled down yet.'

Ross shrugged. 'I have to admit, there have been a few adventures along the way. But so far no one special. No one I'd want to marry.'

'I'm sure she'll come along one day.' Lizzie smiled, trying to inject a cheery note into her voice. 'And when it does happen it'll probably be when you least expect it.'

'You think so?'

'Probably.'

'Is that how it was with you and Jack?'

Jack again! Why couldn't he get off the subject? The last thing she wanted to talk about was Jack. 'In a way, I suppose. I met him through a pal of mine who lives up the same tenement close. He's her cousin.'

'Love at first sight, eh?'

'Not exactly.'

'So it took a while?'

'Not that either. A shortish period, you might say,' she demurred.

'And then that was it?'

How to reply to that? 'In a manner of speaking.'

'Well, all I can say is he's a lucky chap, your Jack. Very lucky indeed.'

Oh, my God! Lizzie thought. 'Thank you.'

'And I'm sure you'll make a marvellous mother into the bargain. I can see that in you.'

'Can you indeed?' She tried to laugh.

'Oh, yes.'

She wasn't paying enough attention to the ground, and her foot suddenly caught in a root. She cried out and stumbled, and would have fallen if Ross hadn't quickly caught hold of her and kept her upright.

For the space of a few seconds it was like an embrace, then Ross released her as Stuart came running back.

'What happened?' he demanded.

Lizzie explained, thanking Ross at the same time for saving her from what might have been a bad tumble.

'Can you walk on that foot?' Stuart asked in concern.

Lizzie tried it. 'It's all right. No sprain or anything. I'll manage.'

They went on their way together, Stuart's presence putting a stop to the conversation Lizzie and Ross had been having.

Lizzie was relieved.

Later, on his way to bed, Stuart heard the sound of crying from Lizzie's room.

He stopped outside her door, debating with himself whether or not to knock and try to find out why she was upset.

In the end he didn't, and she wouldn't have told him if he had.

Chapter 22

'A penny for them?' Lizzie came out of her reverie and glanced across at her brother, who'd been studying her. 'I beg your pardon?'

'I said, a penny for them?'

'My thoughts, you mean?'

'That's right. You looked sunk in absolute gloom.'

Lizzie smiled. 'Hardly that.'

'Well then?'

'Oh, I was just thinking about Glasgow, and Jack. Wondering where he is and what he's up to.'

'And Glasgow?'

'I know you'll find this strange, but I'm missing it. Quite a lot, actually.'

'Really?' That surprised him.

'I enjoyed my job there, you see. And I miss my pal Pearl who lives downstairs. We had some good laughs together.' Lizzie paused, then went on. 'She's married now, so I wasn't seeing as much of her as I had. But we used to go to the factory and come home together, so it was a right old blether there and back.'

Stuart shook his head. 'I can't understand anyone missing Glasgow. From all accounts it's a violent, nasty, smelly place.'

Lizzie laughed. 'True enough – I can't deny it. But it has its good points too. The neighbours are very friendly, for example. Anything goes wrong and they quickly rally round. I know Ma finds that a great comfort.'

'And Jack?' Stuart asked softly.

'I keep wondering what would have happened if he'd found out about the baby. Would he still have gone to sea, or stayed behind and done the decent thing?'

'What do you think?'

'To be honest, I really don't know. It could easily have been either.'

'Describe him to me.'

'You mean physically?'

Stuart nodded.

Lizzie did so, even down to the pale blue eyes which Ross's so resembled. If Stuart noticed the connection he didn't comment.

'What about his character?' he asked.

'He has a sort of mesmeric quality about him which I find fascinating. He's a bit of a lad, if you know what I mean. But underneath it all there's a very nice, caring person.'

'Did he ever say what he really thought of you?'

'He said I was dangerous.'

Stuart frowned. 'In what way?'

'He never elaborated. Just said I was, that's all.'

How curious, Stuart reflected. The last thing he'd have thought of Lizzie was that she was dangerous. Perhaps this Jack knew something he didn't. Or saw a side to his sister he was unaware of.

'Anyway, not long to go now before the baby arrives.' He smiled.

'Not long,' she agreed. 'As far as I'm concerned the sooner it's over the better.'

'At least you'll have your reputation intact if Ma's plan goes to order, as it seems to be doing so far. It was clever of her to come up with it.'

Lizzie gave a low laugh. 'It must be a funny sight seeing her waddling around all padded up.'

'Aye, it must be.'

'Shall I put the kettle on?'

'Lovely. A cup of tea would go down a treat.'

Imagine missing Glasgow, Stuart thought as she got up to fill the kettle. The concept was quite beyond him. He would live and die in Tomintoul if he had his way.

God's country as far as he was concerned.

Pearl sat watching Willie at the table rearranging his stamp collection. What a boring hobby for a chap like him, she thought. It never ceased to amaze her that he'd taken it up.

'Enjoying yourself?' she asked sarcastically.

He blinked, and glanced over at her. 'Thoroughly. Why?'

'Just wondered, that's all. You seem engrossed.'

'I am. I find it fun.'

Fun fiddling around with old stamps! For two pins Pearl would have burst out laughing at the sheer ludicrousness of it. 'Don't you think it's a bit of a pansy thing to do?' she jibed.

'No I don't,' he snapped, riled by the accusation.

'Lots of people might think it was.'

'Well let them. Doesn't bother me in the least. There's nothing pansy about me.' His eyes glittered as he stared at her. 'As you should well know.'

To annoy him even further Pearl lit a cigarette.

'How did it go?' Ethne asked anxiously as Doogie arrived home from the dairy after his Saturday night stint at the *Chronicle*.

He yawned. 'I'm knackered. Not as young as I used to be, that's the trouble.'

'Well, sit down and I'll get you breakfast. Bacon, egg and sausages. How does that sound?'

'Wonderful. I'm absolutely starving.'

'Fried bread too if you want?'

'Please.'

She poured him a cup of tea from a pot already brewed, then got on with the cooking. Although she was still in her dressing gown she had her padding on underneath in case anyone called unexpectedly, as could easily happen.

The bacon was sizzling nicely when Doogie began to snore, his mouth wide open, catching flies.

She smiled indulgently, promising herself she'd have him straight into bed and tucked up as soon as he'd eaten.

Lizzie shivered. Christ it was cold! She was in the outside privy that served the cottage; she hated using the chamber pot during the day.

She grunted in sudden pain as cramp seized her stomach, not for the first time. 'Bloody hell!' she groaned as the discomfort intensified. Suddenly she began to cry, feeling overwhelmed by it all, wishing with all her heart that Ethne was there. She wanted her ma. Desperately. To hold her and comfort her, assure her that everything was going to be all right. To take her in her arms and soothe away all the worries and anxieties.

But Ethne wouldn't be arriving for weeks yet. Almost a month.

Lizzie's tears continued to flow while the cramps got worse.

It was Saturday afternoon and Pearl had taken the opportunity to go into town and do some shopping. She'd completed her purchases and was about to catch a tram back to Thistle Street when she suddenly spotted Pete Milroy staring at a window display.

'Hello.' She laughed when Pete started.

'My God, Pearl. You gave me the fright of my life, sneaking up on me like that.'

'I didn't sneak, I walked. You just never heard me, that's all.'

He took a deep breath. 'I almost jumped out of my skin.'

'Damn!' She swore as it began to rain. She hadn't brought a headscarf with her which meant her hair was going to get wet.

'Where's Willie?' Pete asked.

'At home doing something or other. Don't ask me what.'

Pete glanced up at the heavens, whose grey was rapidly turning to black. 'It seems we're in for a downpour.'

'Aye, it does,' Pearl agreed. She looked up the street but there wasn't a tram in sight. She was going to get well and truly soaked.

'Tell you what, there's a tearoom just round the corner. Shall we go there until it passes?'

The idea appealed. 'Why not?'

'Come on then.'

True enough, the tearoom was literally round the corner. It was a new establishment that had opened only shortly before. Pearl's eyes widened when they went inside. Talk about swanky! This was the bee's knees.

They sat down and ordered a pot of tea from a waitress wearing a black dress and a white, crisply starched apron and matching cap.

'So what are you doing in town?' Pearl queried when the waitress had left them.

'I've been measured up for a new suit. The two I've got are becoming a bit shabby and need replacing. So I'll chuck one now and replace the other at a later date.'

They chatted amiably until the waitress returned with their tea and a stand filled with cakes. Pearl's mouth watered at the sight of them.

'They look scrumptious,' she exclaimed.

'Which one do you fancy?'

'The chocolate eclair.'

'Then help yourself. Have as many as you like. There's no need to hold back.'

'Can I?'

He laughed at her enthusiasm. 'Of course you can. Eat the lot if you want.'

'So how's Elspeth these days?' she asked after she'd demolished the eclair in record-breaking time.

'I've no idea. I don't see her any more.'

Pearl stared at him. 'What happened? Or shouldn't I ask?'

'No, that's all right. It was just . . .' He paused to think for a moment. 'We didn't really get on, I suppose. The more I saw her the more she irritated me. And to be fair, I don't think she was madly struck on me either. So that was that. End of story.'

Pearl helped herself to another cake, this one topped with glazed strawberries set in whipped cream. 'I have to admit, Pete, I didn't take to her. Though Willie certainly did.'

'Oh?'

'He thought her a right cracker. Went on about it afterwards. He was quite jealous of you.'

Pete frowned. 'Did he really say that?'

'He didn't have to – it was obvious. He'd have had his hand up her skirt given half a chance.'

'I see,' Pete murmured.

'He's a right randy sod.' She stopped there, not wanting to elaborate.

'And why didn't you take to her, Pearl?'

'That voice of hers drove me up the wall. She talked as if she had a mouth full of marbles. And chipped ones at that.'

Pete laughed, for that was exactly what Elspeth's voice had sounded like. 'Why chipped?'

'They'd grate together. And her voice grated.'

He laughed again, finding that extremely funny. 'Anyway, she's gone now, voice and all. And I can't say I'm sorry.'

'Is there anyone else? Someone new, I mean?'

Pete shook his head. 'Not yet.'

'Well, there will be soon enough. You mark my words. A good-looking chap like yourself won't have any trouble in that direction.'

They continued talking, getting on famously, until the rain stopped, at which point Pete paid the bill and then insisted on walking Pearl to her tram stop.

'Thanks ever so much, Pete. I thoroughly enjoyed that,' she declared as her tram clattered to a standstill in front of them.

'Me too.'

'Ta-ra then.'

''Bye, Pearl.'

What a lovely man, she thought as she took a seat. She really had thoroughly enjoyed the time they'd spent in the tearoom. Not to mention the cakes.

It was rare for Stuart and Gordon to work alone together. In fact, it almost never happened, and when Stuart leaned on his spade, intent on taking a breather, he decided to make the most of the opportunity. 'I want to have a word with you,' he declared.

Gordon straightened, and also leaned on his spade. 'What's up?'

'You are.'

'Me?'

'You and Sheena. I think it's despicable the way you're treating Lizzie. Quite disgraceful.'

A dark cloud came over Gordon's face. He was shorter than his younger brother, and extremely broad-shouldered. Apart from that the family resemblance was obvious. 'I don't want to talk about it. All right?'

'Well I do, Gordon. She is our sister, don't forget. Our own flesh and blood.'

'She's nothing more than a common tart as far as I'm concerned,' Gordon stated brutally. 'And that's all there is to it. When she leaves here I hope we never see her again.'

Stuart was genuinely shocked. 'You can't mean that, surely?'

'I do. I'm only going along with this plan of Ma's because she wants me to. I wouldn't let Ma down for the world, as you well know.'

'And what's she going to think when she finds out how you've been treating Lizzie? She's going to be hurt, that's what. And angry too, I would imagine.' Stuart shook his head as he took in Gordon's glare of defiance. 'You were never like this until you met Sheena. She's changed you from the brother I used to know and like.'

'You leave my wife out of this!' Gordon retorted angrily. 'She's got nothing to do with it.'

'Of course she has,' Stuart snapped back. 'She's the one who's poisoned you against Lizzie because of her religious mania.'

'Shut your mouth!' Gordon yelled. 'Just shut it!'

'And if I don't?'

'I'll shut it for you.'

Stuart took a deep breath. He was getting nowhere. Talking to Gordon had been a complete waste of time. Sighing, he went on with the job in hand. Gordon followed suit a few moments later.

Neither spoke again to the other for the rest of the day.

'This gammon's good,' Ron Baxter declared, nodding approval to Dot. 'Did you get it from your usual butcher?'

'Aye, McNab's.'

'Well, it's a lot better than it normally is.'

341

Dot was pleased. She'd thought the gammon expensive, but when Ron showed his appreciation as he just had it made it all worthwhile.

Dot turned her attention to Pearl, who was eating with them, it being a Wednesday night. 'How are things at the factory?'

'Fine. Same as always. It's been a bit slow these past few weeks but I hear on the grapevine that new orders are starting to come in so no doubt the work will pick up.'

'Good.'

'I was thinking . . .'

'Oh aye?'

'Shouldn't Lizzie be back by now? She's been gone absolutely ages. Surely her brother's well again after all this time? What was wrong, anyway? No one ever said.'

'Pleurisy,' Dot replied. 'A bad case of it, apparently. And then when he got over it there had to be a lengthy recuperation period. It left him as weak as a kitten.'

'Bad business, pleurisy.' Ron nodded. 'I had a pal die from it once. A long time ago now.'

'It's funny, but I was asking Ethne about Lizzie only a couple of days back,' Dot went on. 'Her brother's fine now but she's decided to stay on there until Ethne goes up to have the baby. That way all three of them can travel back together. Made sense to me.'

It made sense to Pearl as well, though she'd have preferred Lizzie to return sooner. She was really missing her.

Lizzie stared out of the window in dismay. The snowstorm which had hit Tomintoul in the early hours had

342

come out of nowhere and hadn't been forecast. All she could see was a vast expanse of white. She hoped Stuart was all right. He and Ross were out in it together.

And still the snow continued to fall, pretty as a picture.

Stuart shivered, then banged his hands against one another in an attempt to warm them. They were freezing despite the thick woollen gloves he was wearing. All that morning he and Ross had been rescuing trapped sheep and taking them to a nearby barn for shelter.

'What do you think?' Ross asked.

'What do you mean?'

'Next time we're in the barn can we stop and have some of the tea I brought in my flask? I don't know about you but I could certainly use some.'

'Aye, we'll do that. We need a break.'

Ross paused to listen when he heard a faint baa-ing sound. Another trapped animal. He pointed. 'Over there.'

Stuart had also heard the call of distress. 'Let's get to it then.'

They trudged through the snow, trying to ignore the icy wind howling all around them.

Lizzie was climbing the stairs to her bedroom when she suddenly felt a rush of liquid between her thighs. Dear God, I'm haemorrhaging! she thought in panic.

Pulling up her skirt she was relieved to find no trace of blood, just a sticky wetness that reached as far as her knees. It struck her then what had happened. Her waters had broken. The baby was on its way. And she was all alone in the cottage not knowing when Stuart would turn up to go for Dr MacKay. That's if he could struggle through to the doctor's in this weather.

Get a grip, she told herself as the panic she'd felt a few moments previously returned. Just keep your head. You'll be all right.

She decided the best thing to do would be to continue on up to her bedroom and lie down.

'This tea's going down a treat,' Stuart declared with a smile. 'Just what the doctor ordered.'

Ross produced a bar of chocolate, snapped it in two and gave Stuart half. 'Here, take that.'

Stuart gratefully accepted the offering, the only food he'd have until he got home later that night. Normally he'd have gone back for his midday meal, but that was impossible under the present conditions. They'd go on rescuing as many sheep as they could until the light failed.

Ross sat on a convenient bale of straw, alternately sipping tea and munching chocolate. 'I suppose Lizzie will be all right?' he commented between bites.

'Why shouldn't she be? She's in the cottage with the range going full blast. She'll be snug as the proverbial bug in a rug. Take my word for it.'

'I just hope you're right.'

'You and she have got quite close of late,' Stuart remarked casually, curious as to what Ross's reply would be.

Ross nodded. 'Yes, we have.'

'Become fond of her, have you?'

Ross glanced at Stuart, then away again. 'What's that supposed to mean?'

'Exactly what I said.'

'The laird's going to be very unhappy if we lose too many sheep,' Ross declared, changing the subject. 'Which we're bound to. If only we'd had some warning about this snowstorm, but we didn't. It's caught everyone by surprise.'

Stuart grunted his agreement.

'More tea?'

'If there's some left.'

'Enough for another half a cup each, I should say.'

Stuart watched as Ross poured out exactly that into the cup he'd found in the barn, and then the same amount into the top of his flask.

'About Lizzie,' Ross murmured.

Stuart said nothing, and waited for him to go on.

'If things had been different, then who knows? But the fact remains she's a married woman in love with her husband. Does that answer your question?'

Stuart nodded.

'Let's just say I admire her enormously, and leave it at that.'

Stuart smiled. 'All right.' And did.

Lizzie screamed as a fresh pain exploded inside her, feeling as if she was being ripped in two. She'd already taken off her skirt and underthings in preparation for the forthcoming birth. She wasn't sure how long it was now between contractions, but the time was certainly getting shorter.

'Oh, Stuart, come home. Please come home!' she pleaded aloud. She was terrified of having to go through this all on her own.

* * *

345

'I think you'd better stay the night with us, Ross,' an exhausted Stuart said when at last they decided to call it a day. 'It'll save you the added walk to the caravan. Besides, Lizzie's bound to have something hot waiting.'

Ross didn't need asking twice. Like Stuart, he was all but done in. 'Thanks.'

As they headed slowly for the cottage, Stuart came up short when he heard what might have been a faint scream. If it was, he couldn't tell from which direction it had come due to the howling wind buffeting his ears.

Nothing to be done, he thought, and went on.

They both stumbled into the cottage, thankful for the warmth that hit them. 'Lizzie, I'm back!' Stuart called out, starting to take off his coat. He froze when there was an almighty scream from upstairs. 'Dear God!' he muttered, and than a second scream galvanised both men into action.

They burst into the bedroom and pulled up short at the sight of Lizzie, legs wide apart and panting.

'Thank God you're here at last,' she groaned. 'The baby's decided to arrive early.'

Stuart glanced at Ross, then moved to the side of the bed. 'How long between contractions?' he asked quietly.

'They're almost directly after each other now.' And as if to prove her point she threw back her head and screamed again.

'No point in going for Dr MacKay,' Stuart said decisively. 'This will be over long before he could get here. That's if he could get here at all, the weather conditions being what they are and he the old man he is.' Rounding on Ross, he started issuing instructions, and Ross quickly left the room to carry them out.

'I won't be a mo', Lizzie, but I've got to wash my hands first,' Stuart said, preparing to follow him.

'I understand.'

In a very few minutes he was back. 'Right,' he declared. 'I'm afraid I'm going to have to have a feel to make sure everything's as it should be. Is that all right?'

She managed a weak grin, reassured by her brother's presence and the fact he knew what he was doing. 'On you go.'

She tried not to tense as his fingers explored her. In the middle of his examination she screamed again.

Stuart straightened. 'The head's in the proper place so there shouldn't be any complications.'

'Dr MacKay said there shouldn't be.'

Ross reappeared with fresh towels and a small basin of cold water. Dipping one of the towels in the basin, he proceeded to wipe away the sweat streaming down Lizzie's face.

Curiously, she realised she wasn't embarrassed by Ross's presence. If anything, she found it comforting. 'Hold my hand,' she asked, when he'd temporarily finished with her face.

He did just that, smiling down at her. 'Everything's going to be fine. We're . . .'

Lizzie screamed yet again.

'It's a girl,' Stuart announced triumphantly a little later.

'Are all her bits and pieces in the proper places?' Lizzie asked anxiously.

'Indeed they are.'

'Thank God for that,' she whispered, and closed her eyes, feeling more tired than she ever had in her life before.

347

She convulsed slightly as the afterbirth was ejected. Stuart cut the cord, ensured the baby's airway wasn't blocked by mucus, and wrapped her in a towel.

'Let me have her,' Lizzie said, smiling.

As the baby was placed in Lizzie's arms she opened her mouth and bawled lustily.

'Now there's a fine pair of lungs for you.' Stuart grinned.

'I'm going to call her Jacqueline,' Lizzie stated. 'Jacky for short.'

It was obvious to both Stuart and Ross why Lizzie had chosen that particular name.

Chapter 23

'I couldn't have done a better job myself,' Dr MacKay declared. It was three days since the start of the snow-storm and the first time he had been able to get to Stuart's cottage.

One thing had been worrying Lizzie. 'Will there be any after-effects because she was early?' she queried.

MacKay shook his head. 'She's a little underweight, but will soon catch up with regular feeding.'

Lizzie gave a sigh of relief. Thank goodness for that!

'She is taking to the breast, I presume?' MacKay asked.

'Yes. Quite a greedy little mite, too.'

'So your milk is coming through without any bother?'

Lizzie nodded. 'I'm flooded with it at times. One moment nothing, the next I'm gushing.'

'It'll regulate itself in time,' MacKay assured her. 'That should only be a temporary inconvenience.'

Lizzie moved over to a chair and sat down. She was still sore after the birth and expected to be that way for a while. 'There's something I want to ask you, doctor.'

'Which is?'

'I want to change Jacky on to a bottle as soon as possible. Will that be all right?'

MacKay frowned. 'I'm afraid I'm very old-fashioned in that respect. I believe breastfeeding is best every time – as long as the mother can produce enough milk, that is.'

'But it won't harm Jacky in any way to go on to a bottle, will it?'

MacKay studied her, his disapproval obvious. 'Do you have a reason for wishing to bottle-feed?'

Lizzie had, but could hardly explain. What she said next was the truth, if only part of it. 'When I get back to Glasgow I'll have to resume work right away – I need the money. Ma will be looking after Jacky for most of the day, which means she will have to be bottle-fed.'

'I see,' MacKay murmured.

'So you understand the problem?'

'I take it you can't nip home from work to feed the baby yourself, then?'

Lizzie shook her head. 'That's impossible. Completely out of the question.'

'Why do you have to work, Lizzie? Doesn't your husband support you?'

This was getting complicated, she thought grimly, mind racing. 'Of course he does. But we're saving up to get a place of our own, as well as having Jacky now to consider. She'll have to be fed and clothed on top of everything else.'

'Then bottle-feeding it is,' he grudgingly agreed. 'But if I were you I'd keep on breastfeeding for as long as you can. Despite what some people claim, it's my firm belief breast milk is far better for the child. Particularly in this

350

instance, where the baby's slightly premature.'

Lizzie took his point, if reluctantly. 'One other thing, doctor. Once I stop breastfeeding, how long before my milk dries up?'

'That varies, depending on the person involved. But not too long. When nature realises there isn't a need it cuts off the supply. It's as simple as that. Now, if you'll excuse me I'd better go. I have other patients to see this morning.'

He raised a hand when she started to stand. 'You stay where you are. I'll see myself out.'

'Thank you, doctor.'

Lizzie closed her eyes when she heard the outside door click shut. Christ, but she was tired. Dead beat. If she could get Jacky off to sleep then maybe she could have a little nap herself.

Which is precisely what happened.

'Bloody hell!' Ethne exclaimed on reading the letter that had just arrived in the post. Lizzie had prematurely given birth to a wee lassie, whom she had named Jacqueline. Mother and baby were thriving. What was more, Lizzie and Stuart had been snowed in at the time so Stuart had been the one to deliver the child, not Dr MacKay.

'Well well,' she murmured aloud, thoughts whirling. This altered things. The sooner she got to Tomintoul the better.

A wee girl, Ethne reflected, and smiled. She couldn't wait to tell Doogie when he got in from the dairy.

'I've brought someone to see you,' Stuart announced on arriving home from work.

'Who is it?' Lizzie called out from the kitchen where she was cooking the evening meal.

'Only me,' Ross grinned, popping his head round the door. It was the first time he'd been back to the cottage since the night of Jacky's birth.

'Come in, come in,' Lizzie enthused. 'To what do I owe the honour?'

Ross brandished a brown paper parcel. 'I've brought Jacky a present. How is she?'

'In the pink.' Lizzie indicated the crib Stuart had borrowed from Gordon. 'Go and have a look.'

Ross crossed over to the crib, knelt down and smiled at the baby staring up at him. 'Hello. How are you today, sweetness?'

Stuart came into the kitchen. 'Is there enough for Ross to join us?'

'Oh aye. It's stew so it'll stretch.' Lizzie quickly checked a bubbling pan containing potatoes to verify there was enough to go round. Luckily, there was.

'I've got something for you, sweetheart,' Ross cooed, and began unwrapping the parcel. Inside was a furry rabbit which he'd bought in Tomintoul. 'There we are. What do you think of that?' He waggled the rabbit in front of Jacky, who at least appeared to be delighted.

'That's kind of you, Ross,' Lizzie said.

'Don't mention it.'

'Would you like a dram before we eat?' Stuart asked him.

'Don't mind if I do.'

'Lizzie?'

She shook her head. 'Not for me, thanks. I'm trying to get my figure back, remember?'

'A dream won't hurt. Go on, spoil yourself.'

'Oh, all right then,' Lizzie conceded. 'But just a small one.'

Ross continued talking to Jacky while Stuart poured. He was good with children, Lizzie noted. In fact he was a good man all round in her opinion. He'd make some woman a fine husband.

When he left, several hours later, she was sorry to see him go.

'He fancies you, you know,' Stuart said out of the blue later that night.

Lizzie pretended innocence. 'Who does?'

'Ross, of course. Who else?'

Lizzie flushed slightly. 'And how do you know that?'

'He more or less told me the day you were having the baby. I happened to mention that you and he seemed to be getting very close, and his answer was that you were a happily married woman in love with her husband.'

'That doesn't mean he fancies me,' she protested.

Stuart smiled. 'You didn't hear the tone of voice he used, or see the expression on his face.'

Lizzie dropped her gaze to stare at the floor. How she wished things had been otherwise, that she wasn't entangled in the net that trapped her now.

'Well?' Stuart prompted.

'I like him, as well.'

'Just like?' Stuart teased.

Lizzie didn't reply.

Stuart got up, squatted in front of the range, opened the fire door and shovelled in more coal. Closing the door again, he resumed his seat. 'It's a pity things are the way they are,' he commented quietly.

Lizzie nodded.

'He's obviously taken a big shine to Jacky.'

Lizzie looked up at her brother. 'You know it's impossible, Stuart. What would he think of me if I was to tell him the truth? That I'm not really married and Jacky's a bastard. Eh?'

This time it was Stuart who didn't reply.

'He might not be so interested then.'

'And if he still was?'

She shook her head. 'Everyone in Tomintoul believes the story Ma concocted. Can you imagine their reaction if they found out I'd got pregnant out of wedlock? I'd be shamed and damned for ever, as you well know. Then there's Gordon, Sheena and Mhairi to consider, albeit I can't stand Sheena. Shame would fall on them also, being my relatives. Even though they haven't done anything wrong the fingers would still point.'

Stuart hated to admit it, but she was right.

Tears came into Lizzie's eyes. 'It's simply not to be, Stuart. I accepted that some while ago. Much as I might wish it otherwise.'

'It is a bit of a pickle, isn't it?' Stuart said sympathetically.

'Just a bit,' she agreed in a whisper.

'How about if . . .'

'No more, Stuart, please. I've already thought through all the possibilities and they either won't work, or are unacceptable, or too risky. Believe me. Ross respects me as he believes me to be. I can't take the chance of telling him the truth, or him finding out, and losing that respect.

Ma's plan is the best for Jacky and me, and that's what I'm going to stick to.' She came to her feet. 'Now if you don't mind I'm going upstairs to give Jacky a feed and then go to bed. Goodnight.'

'Goodnight, sis,' he said quietly, sorrow in his voice.

She had thought everything through, Lizzie reassured herself as she climbed the stairs. She only wished she'd been able to come to a different conclusion.

But she hadn't.

'Ma!' Lizzie flew across the room into Ethne's outstretched arms. 'It's so good to see you,' she gasped when the hugging was over. 'When did you arrive?'

'Not an hour since. I came straight here after dropping my things at Gordon's.'

Lizzie glanced down at Ethne's waist. 'When did you lose the padding?'

'On the way here. And good riddance. It was becoming a right pain in the backside having to wear that day in day out.' She paused for breath. 'Now, where's Jacqueline?'

'Come with me.'

Jacky was in her crib gurgling away nineteen to the dozen, having not long been fed and changed.

'My my,' Ethne breathed, staring down at her. 'Isn't she just beautiful? Can I pick her up?'

'Of course. You're going to be doing a lot of that from here on in.'

That was true enough, Ethne thought as she bent over the crib. 'There there, wee lass,' she murmured when Jacky was cradled in her arms. 'Aren't you the bonny one?'

'I'll put the kettle on and you can tell me all about

355

the goings on in Thistle Street. I've missed it, you know.'

That surprised Ethne. 'Have you?'

'Yes, I have.'

'I'd have thought you'd prefer it here?'

'In some ways I do. But . . . despite everything I just miss Glasgow, horrible dirty place that it is. Now, you get to know Jacky while I put that kettle on.'

'I must say you're looking well,' Ethne commented later, Jacky in the crib beside them.

'Fat as a pig, you mean. I've been trying to lose weight but probably won't until I stop breastfeeding.'

'Aye, there's that.' Ethne nodded. 'That's something I can't do, pretend or otherwise. Feed the baby myself, I mean.'

'I'll start Jacky on a bottle first thing tomorrow morning and see how she gets on with it.'

'That's good.'

'How long are you here for?'

'I thought a few weeks should do it. Maybe a little more.'

'And no one in Thistle Street suspects what's going on?'

'Not one. Your da says I missed my vocation and should have been an actress.'

That made Lizzie laugh. 'How is he?'

Ethne shrugged. 'Same as always.'

'Still enjoying his job at the dairy?'

'Oh aye, he loves that. And his part-time stint on the *Sunday Chronicle*.'

Lizzie gazed at her mother. 'It's wonderful to see you, Ma.'

'And you, Lizzie. Not to mention Jacky. What do Gordon and Sheena think of her?'

Lizzie's expression hardened. 'They haven't been to see her yet.'

Ethne was incredulous. 'Not once?'

'Not once,' Lizzie confirmed. 'They . . . well, don't approve of me, shall we say. They think I'm some sort of tart.'

Ethne glanced away, furious to hear that. She'd give the pair of them the sharp end of her tongue. By God and she would!

'This is very good,' Willie declared, tucking into the meal Pearl had set before him.

'Well don't sound so bloody surprised!' she retorted sharply. 'It's insulting.'

'Sorry,' he mumbled. 'I didn't intend to be.'

She glared at him. 'As it happens I've been collecting recipes from some of the girls at work, a number of whom are particularly good cooks. So there.'

'Excellent idea,' he muttered.

'So I'm doing my best.'

'I didn't mean to be critical, Pearl. Honest.'

'Then don't be.'

They ate in silence for a few moments, and then he said, 'You'll never guess who I bumped into today?'

'Who?'

'Jack White.'

That interested her. 'Really? Is he home on leave?'

'So he said.'

'How is he?'

'Fine, as far as I could make out. Life at sea certainly

357

seems to suit him. He was full of it. Where he'd been to, some of the things he'd done. According to him he's having a whale of a time.'

Pearl was pleased to hear that. 'Did he mention anything about dropping by to say hello?'

Willie shook his head.

Pity, Pearl thought. She'd have loved to see Jack again and hear some of his stories for herself.

'He asked after Lizzie, though.'

'Oh?'

'Seemed quite disappointed when I told him she was up north visiting her brother. Said he'd been looking forward to having a natter with her.'

A stab of jealousy sliced through Pearl. She had to remind herself that Jack, being her cousin, had always been forbidden territory. Then she smiled. There had been those incidents when they'd both been younger . . .

'What are you smiling at?' Willie queried with a frown, interrupting her thoughts.

She shrugged. 'Just remembering the old days. Jack and I were close pals for a while. More like brother and sister than cousins.' Brother and sister! That was a good one. 'When's he off again?'

'No idea. He never said. We only chatted for a minute or two as I had to get back to the office and he was going into a pub.'

A pub, Pearl thought. How like Jack. No change there then. Pubs and women, his two great interests in life.

Ethne waited till Mhairi was in bed and the three of them had settled down for the evening. 'Lizzie tells me you haven't been to see Jacky yet,' she stated quietly.

Gordon, who'd been thinking about estate matters, blinked rapidly, then glanced at his wife, who'd suddenly gone very still. 'That's right, Ma.'

'Can I ask why?'

'I think you can guess why,' Sheena declared.

'I'd still like you to tell me.'

'You tell her, Sheena,' said Gordon. He'd known this confrontation was bound to happen but hadn't expected it quite so soon.

'If you wish,' Sheena replied. 'We agreed to go along with your plan for your sake, Mother, but that doesn't mean we have to condone the situation. We've had Lizzie here for a meal, and I've visited her on several occasions, and that's as far as we're prepared to go.'

Ethne's eyes slitted as she stared hard at her daughter-in-law. 'I take it you did these things for appearances' sake?'

'It was our Christian duty. We felt obligated.'

'Did you indeed?' Ethne replied sarcastically.

'Yes, we did.'

Gordon shifted uncomfortably in his chair. He and Sheena had already had a couple of raging arguments about this, and he had lost both of them. Sheena had taken a stand and simply wouldn't budge.

Ethne spoke slowly and carefully. 'What Lizzie did was wrong, she's the first to admit it. But it only happened once, and hasn't she paid the price for that folly?'

'Only once?' Sheena sneered.

'That's right. I have Lizzie's solemn oath on that, so I believe her.'

Sheena's expression said she remained unconvinced.

'You don't, I take it?'

Sheena's answer was to shrug.

Ethne turned to Gordon. 'Like it or not, Jacky is your flesh and blood. Your niece whether she's born in wedlock or not. And I would remind you, Gordon, that when I return to Glasgow she will become your so-called sister.'

He bit his lip.

'Well, what do you have to say about that?'

'It doesn't alter the fact she's illegitimate, Ma.'

'No, it doesn't. But that's hardly the child's fault, is it?'

'I suppose not,' he conceded grudgingly.

'So, in other words, you're holding the child responsible for the mother's sin by not even acknowledging her existence?'

'We have acknowledged it,' Sheena stated coldly.

'To whom? Other people?'

'That's right.'

'But not to Lizzie or the child herself.' Anger flared in Ethne, which she fought to keep under control. 'By God, you're heartless, woman. And you a so-called devoted Christian. You make me sick.'

'Enough, Ma. I won't have you insulting Sheena,' Gordon declared. 'Don't forget she's my wife. I'll have nothing said against her.'

Ethne decided it was time to take the gloves off and expose Sheena for the hypocrite she was. 'How's Tod Gemmill these days?' she asked.

Sheena frowned. 'What's he got to do with this?'

Ethne sat back in her chair and gave her daughter-in-law a thin, razored smile. 'Quite a lot, actually.'

'I don't understand.'

'You were seeing him before Gordon, right?'

Sheena nodded.

'Well one night, years ago, Doogie was in the pub when he happened to overhear a conversation between Tod and a friend of his. Both were drunk at the time – legless, according to Doogie. And Tod was boasting about what he'd got up to with you.'

Sheena went white. 'It's a lie!'

'What's a lie, Sheena? I haven't yet said what Tod told his friend.'

Sheena seemed to shrink in on herself, a look of naked fear flitting across her face.

'Let's just put it this way,' Ethne went on. 'According to Tod, you weren't exactly a virgin when you married my son. But of course those were the days before you got so wrapped up in the church and became holier than thou.'

A stunned silence greeted her declaration. Gordon looked as if he'd just been hit over the head by the proverbial pikestaff while Sheena's eyes were literally bulging.

'It's a lie,' she finally croaked.

'You're repeating yourself now. Anyway, why would Tod lie?'

'I was pure when I married Gordon. I swear it.'

Ethne didn't reply, merely smiled.

Sheena focused on Gordon. 'You must believe me. You must.'

'Why did you never mention this before, Ma?' Gordon asked.

Ethne shrugged. 'It was none of my business. Up until now, that is.' She came to her feet. 'Now, even though it's early yet I'm off to bed. It's been a long hard day. Goodnight.'

*   *   *

361

Ethne lay in the darkness listening to the argument that had been raging for the best part of an hour, Gordon and Sheena going at it hammer and tongs. At one point she'd heard the sound of hysterical crying, followed shortly afterwards by sobs. Now there came the slam of the outside door.

Ethne had no regrets about what she'd done. Sheena had asked for it. By God and she had. But it was impossible to remain here now, she decided. First thing in the morning she'd repack her case and take it over to Stuart's for the rest of her stay in Tomintoul. It would mean sharing Lizzie's bed, as Stuart had only one spare room, but that didn't bother her, and she didn't think it would bother Lizzie either.

She wouldn't tell Stuart about her disclosure to Gordon, but she would tell Lizzie.

Aye, she'd tell Lizzie all right. Lizzie was owed that.

Lizzie had taken to having a long walk every day in an effort to lose weight, and it seemed to be having the desired effect. She strode on over the heather thoroughly enjoying the clean, fresh, if bitterly cold, air stinging her nostrils. So far she'd studiously avoided going in a certain direction, but that day, for whatever reason, she felt compelled to.

A little later she came in sight of the gaily decorated caravan, which looked every bit as splendid as she remembered. Was she unconsciously hoping that Ross might be around? If so, she was disappointed. There was no sign of him. Just the caravan in all its romantic glory.

Ross would be at work, she reminded herself. So of course it was highly unlikely she'd run into him. But still . . .

She stood staring at the caravan for all of five minutes before turning round and, head bowed, starting back the way she'd come.

Ethne opened the door to find a sheepish-looking Gordon standing there. 'Hello, son.'

'Can I come in, Ma?'

'Of course.'

'Is Lizzie about?'

'Aye, she's in the kitchen with Jacky.'

'Actually it was the pair of them I came to see.'

Lizzie glanced up in surprise when Gordon entered the kitchen. He spoke before she could. 'How's Jacky?'

'Fine.'

He went over and stared down at the baby fast asleep in her crib. 'She's a bonny lass,' he declared. 'Takes after her mother.'

'Does Sheena know you're here?' Ethne asked quietly.

Gordon looked at her. 'She does. She won't come herself, but I have.'

Ethne nodded her approval, pleased her son was showing some gumption at last where his wife was concerned.

Gordon dug in a pocket, pulled out a coin and handed it to Lizzie. 'That's for the bairn, to bring her luck.'

Lizzie stared at the sovereign she was holding. 'Thank you, Gordon. I'll keep it for her until she grows up.'

Bending down, he kissed Lizzie on the cheek, then, kneeling, kissed Jacky on the forehead. Ethne's eyes were shining as she watched.

They talked for a few minutes, and then Gordon said he had to be returning to work.

'I'll see you out,' Ethne declared.

At the door Gordon kissed her on the cheek. ''Bye for now, Ma.'

'That was a good thing you just did, son. I'm delighted that you're wearing your trousers again.'

He'd gone quite a distance before the penny dropped. Wearing the trousers. Aye, well, that was how it was going to be from here on in between him and Sheena.

Chapter 24

'Ah well, here we are. Home again,' Ethne declared, standing in the middle of her kitchen and gazing round.

'Dishes piled in the sink, I see,' Lizzie commented, almost laughing. What else should they have expected? Doogie was a man, after all. And, like most men, housewifely things didn't come naturally to him.

'You start on those and I'll change Jacky,' Ethne said, taking the baby from Lizzie. 'And just remember, from here on in I'm her mother, not you.'

Lizzie gazed lovingly at her daughter, whom she could never call that any more. Still, look on the bright side, she told herself. It wasn't as if they were being parted. Quite the contrary: they'd be sharing the same house, after all.

There was a knock on the outside door and Lizzie went to answer it, wondering which of the neighbours would be first to welcome them back. It was Dot.

'I saw you coming up the street from the window,' Dot declared, going straight to Ethne and the baby.

'What a little darling,' she cooed. 'Doogie told me you'd named her Jacqueline.'

'That's right. Jacky for short.'

'She's beautiful, Ethne. You must be proud.'

'Indeed I am.'

'How was the birth, then?'

'Not too bad, as births go. I'm over it now.'

There was another knock on the door. Lizzie smiled. 'I'll go.' This time it was Babs Millar.

'Hello hello, and where's the wean?' Babs said excitedly.

For a moment or so Lizzie felt quite out of it. Jealous, too, as both visitors fussed over Jacky.

'Does Doogie know you're coming home today?' Dot asked.

'No, I didn't write. Thought I'd surprise him.'

Dot glanced at the dishes in the sink, and the unlit range. 'I'm sure you'll do that all right.'

'Now if you'll excuse me, Jacky needs seeing to,' Ethne declared, and left them for the bedroom.

'Would you like a hand, Lizzie?' Dot queried.

'That would be kind of you.'

Within minutes Dot had the range lit and the kettle on, while Babs did a bit of general tidying up.

'Is she a good baby?' Dot asked as she worked.

'Good as gold. Couldn't ask for better.'

'And how does it feel having a wee sister?' Babs queried.

'Lovely,' Lizzie replied, thinking she was going to have to get used to hearing Jacky being referred to as that.

'Tell you what,' Dot said. 'As we're making tea I'll just nip downstairs and get a sponge cake I baked earlier.

How about that?'

'Oooh, yummy!' Babs enthused.

'Won't be a tick,' Dot declared, and hurried off.

The tea was ready and the cake cut when Ethne returned with Jacky. 'There's a cot in the bedroom your da must have got from somewhere,' Ethne informed Lizzie. 'Bedclothes for it too. Fine chap that he is.'

'Can I hold her?' Dot asked hopefully.

'Of course you can,' Ethne said, smiling, and passed Jacky over.

'Ethne!' Doogie exclaimed, when he came home from work.

'Sssh! You'll wake the baby.'

'Oh, sorry.' He dropped his voice to just above a whisper. 'Is she in the bedroom?'

'Aye. Come on – I'll take you through.'

'In a minute.' He went over to Lizzie and gave her a hug. 'How are you, lass?'

'All right, Da.'

'Fully recovered?'

'Physically, yes, but still a bit weepy from time to time. Though that's improving.'

He nodded that he understood. 'You're looking well.'

'I need to lose more weight to get back to what I was. But I'm getting there.'

'Good.'

'Don't I get a cuddle and kiss?' Ethne demanded.

'Of course.'

And then Ethne took him through to meet his daughter.

* * *

Pearl stared wistfully at the sleeping Jacky, having come straight upstairs on being told Lizzie was back. 'She's simply adorable,' she said quietly. 'I wish I had one just like her.'

'Still no luck in that direction, I take it?' Lizzie queried.

Pearl shook her head.

'I'm sorry.'

'Me too,' Pearl replied bitterly. 'Morning and night, morning and night, and no result. Willie's getting quite funny about it at times. As if it was my fault in some way.'

'It'll happen. You'll see.'

'But when? That's the question, when?' She straightened, having been bending over the cot. 'I have to apologise for not having written for so long. But you know what they say: the road to hell is paved with good intentions.'

Lizzie smiled. Although each had promised faithfully to write the reality was that only two letters had passed between them, and those very early on. 'Don't worry. I'm just as much at fault as you, so we're even.'

Pearl frowned. 'I don't mean to be catty, but have you put on weight?'

''Fraid so. It's all that good country living, you see. Lots of butter and cream. But I'll soon get my figure back. I'm determined about that.'

'Oh, I don't know,' Pearl mused. 'I think being that little bit heavier suits you. Especially in the bust department.'

Lizzie's milk had dried up quite quickly once she'd stopped breastfeeding, but her bosom was still fuller than it had been.

'By the way,' Pearl said suddenly, changing the subject, 'you'll never guess who was asking after you while you were away?'

Lizzie had no idea. 'Who?'

'My cousin Jack. Willie bumped into him one day when he was home on leave. Told Willie he'd been hoping to have a natter with you. According to Willie he seemed terribly disappointed to learn you were up north.'

Lizzie's stomach had given a flip on hearing Jack's name. The back close seemed an eternity away now. Something that had happened in another lifetime. 'It would have been nice to speak to him,' she said carefully.

'Willie said he's having a whale of a time at sea. Loving every minute of it.'

'I'm sure he is,' Lizzie answered, slightly sarcastically. She wouldn't have expected anything else.

Pearl looked down again at Jacky, and sighed.

If only . . .

Ethne sat on the edge of their bed feeling dead beat. It had been a long and arduous day, not to mention worrying. She hadn't said anything to Lizzie, but she'd been on tenterhooks about the reception she'd get from the women up the close. What if any of them had guessed her secret? Though why should they?

'I do believe we got away with it,' she said quietly to Doogie.

He frowned. 'Got away with what?'

'Passing Jacky off as our own.'

'Oh, that. Aye, everyone's accepted your story all right. But there again, you were brilliant during your so-called pregnancy. You certainly would have fooled me if I hadn't been in on it.'

'And you never let it slip?'

'I promised you I wouldn't, woman, and I kept my word.'

She regarded him warmly. 'You did indeed, Dougal McDougall. I'm proud of you.'

He snorted with pleasure.

'Lizzie's character and reputation have remained intact, which is the main thing. In that we appear to have succeeded. Thank God.'

'Aye, thank God right enough.'

'There'll be no stain for her to carry through life. No one to point the finger, or snigger behind her back.'

Doogie crossed over and sat beside his wife. 'You look done in, girl.'

'I am.'

He'd had plans for that night. Urgent ones as far as he was concerned. But because of her obvious tiredness he'd put them on hold. Another night's wait would hardly kill him, after all.

'Will you be feeding the baby later on?'

Ethne nodded. 'She'll let me know when she's ready. I hope we won't disturb you, what with your early rise for work.'

'It doesn't matter if you do.' He smiled, squeezing her hand. 'I'll soon get used to it.'

'Well, I know how much you like your sleep. You're a bugger to get up in the morning.'

'I'll be fine, Eth. I promise you. Now why don't you get changed for bed before you drop off where you are?'

Ethne ran a weary hand over her face, thinking if she

didn't get between the sheets straight away she could easily do that.

'Welcome home, lass. I've really missed you.'

'And I've missed you, Doogie.'

Less than five minutes later she was tucked up and fast asleep.

That night Lizzie had a dream which she remembered vividly in the morning. She was with Jack, the pair of them laughing and joking, when suddenly Jack turned into Ross and it was him she was laughing and joking with.

Jack, Ross, Jack, Ross. The transformation happened over and over, the only constant being the pale blue eyes they both shared.

Now she was kissing Jack, now Ross, though the latter had never happened in reality.

Jack was pressing her to him, whispering in her ear. Only it wasn't Jack but Ross, alone with her in his gypsy caravan.

Finally Jack was leaving her, waving as he walked off down the street. When he reached the corner round which he'd disappear he turned to wave one last time – except it was Ross who was waving, and did the disappearing.

Her final recollection was of standing, head bowed, silently weeping, with huge crystal tears splashing down her cheeks.

'At last we can have a proper natter.' Willie was out at the Masons, and Pearl had invited Lizzie down for a cup of tea. 'And I want to hear all about your time in Tommy-whatever-it's-called.'

Lizzie smiled as she sank into a chair. 'Not much to tell, really. It's very quiet there, you know. Not a lot happens.'

'What about men? Did you meet anyone nice?'

Lizzie took her time in answering. 'There was one. His name's Ross Colquhoun and he lives in a gypsy caravan.'

Pearl's eyes widened. 'A gypsy caravan!'

'All brightly painted and so on. He works on the estate alongside my brothers. That's how I met him.'

'And?' Pearl prompted.

'There is no and. We got on well and became good friends. That's all there was to it.'

Pearl's face registered her disappointment. 'Was he good-looking?'

Lizzie nodded. 'I certainly thought so.'

'Did he fancy you?'

Oh yes, Lizzie thought. She was certain of it. Just as she'd fancied him. Quite a lot, if she was honest. 'Nothing happened, so he couldn't have done,' she replied.

'And what about you? Did you fancy him?'

Lizzie shrugged. 'Not really,' she lied. 'I enjoyed his company, though. He could be a bit of a laugh.'

'That's a pity.'

'What? That he could be a bit of a laugh?'

'No. That he didn't fancy you and you didn't fancy him. It's high time you had another boyfriend, you know. There's been no one since Malkie Harvey.'

Malkie Harvey! God, she'd forgotten all about him. 'I'm in no hurry. The right one will happen along in time. I've no doubt about that.'

Pearl's eyes took on a dreamy look. 'I like the idea of

a gypsy caravan. It must be great fun living in one.'

'I suppose it is.'

'Ever so romantic.'

Lizzie smiled. She'd thought exactly the same. She remembered the last time she and Ross had spoken, when he had come over specially to say goodbye. At one point she'd thought he was going to kiss her, but of course he hadn't. He believed her to be a married woman in love with her husband.

'Here!' Pearl had suddenly remembered something. 'I haven't told you yet about Scary Mary.'

'What about her?'

'She was murdered down by the docks.'

'Murdered!' Lizzie was incredulous.

'Down by the docks. The girls at the factory all think she must have been on the game.'

'Did they catch her killer?'

Pearl shook her head. 'And I don't think they ever will. There are ships in and out of there all the time. If it was a seaman, and it probably was if she was on the game, then he could be anywhere by now. He might even have sailed before the body was found.'

How terrible, Lizzie thought. She hadn't liked Mary, but even Scary hadn't deserved that. No one did. 'How was it done?'

'She had her throat cut.'

Lizzie blanched. 'Dear God.'

'Horrible, eh?'

Lizzie could only agree. 'Why do the girls at the factory think she was on the game?'

'Why else would she be down at the docks on her own? Stands to reason.'

Again Lizzie could only agree. No single female in her right mind, at least of that age, would go near the docks unless she was selling herself.

'Looking forward to going back to work?'

Lizzie had been to see Mrs Lang the day after she'd arrived home and the supervisor had welcomed her with open arms. She was due to start on Monday morning. 'I am.'

'It'll be just like old times, eh?'

'Just like old times,' Lizzie echoed, the difference being Jacky. She stared at Pearl, wondering what her friend's reaction would have been if she'd told her the truth about why she'd gone to Tomintoul.

But she never would. Not Pearl or anyone else. She couldn't.

Ethne was bent over the sink, washing nappies. Babies, she reflected. There never seemed to be a moment's let-up.

Pausing for a breather, she pushed a stray strand of hair back into place. A glance at the clock on the mantel-piece told her it wouldn't be long before Doogie and Lizzie turned up for their dinner. She'd get that ready just as soon as she'd finished these never-ending nappies.

In the next room, Jacky began to cry. With a heavy sigh, Ethne dried her hands and went to find out what the trouble was.

Pearl opened the door to find Pete Milroy there, supporting an obviously drunk Willie.

'He needs to go straight to bed,' Pete declared.

'I can see that.' What a state Willie was in. She doubted

he could stand upright by himself. 'Bring him through.'

Pete manoeuvred Willie on to the bed and Pearl began stripping off his clothes, absolutely furious with him. 'Is this your fault?' she demanded of the watching Pete.

He held up his hands. 'Not guilty. I swear.'

'So what happened to get him like this?'

'Search me. I had to work late tonight and decided, when I finally left, to go for a drink before going back to the apartment. Willie was already there with two pals of his when I arrived, all three of them drinking pints and half gills. I was introduced to the two pals and, although it wasn't said, I got the distinct impression they were Masons, same as Willie.'

'Here, help me.'

With Pete's assistance Pearl removed Willie's trousers and then his shirt. Together they got Willie under the bedclothes, where he immediately began to snore.

'Have you eaten anything?' Pearl asked.

Pete shook his head.

'Then come and have Willie's tea if you want. That's if it's not ruined by now.'

Pete grinned, grateful for the invitation. 'It'll save me cooking when I get home.'

Once in the kitchen Pearl invited him to sit at the table while she busied herself at the range. 'Go on with the story,' she prompted.

'The other two left and it was just Willie and me. He insisted we have another drink together, and that he buy.'

Pearl raised an eyebrow. Willie insisting on paying! He *must* have been drunk.

'Well, we had that drink, and another and another. I tried to talk Willie into leaving before each one, but he'd have none of it. Finally, at long last, I managed to get him out into the street, where he nearly collapsed. The cold air did for him, I imagine. It was obvious he'd never make it here on his own so I called a cab and brought him.'

Pearl glanced over at Pete and smiled. 'That was kind of you.'

He waved a hand in dismissal. 'I'm sure he'd have done the same for me.'

'Possibly. Though I can't see you getting as drunk as that. You're just not the type.'

'Oh, I've had my moments!' Pete laughed. 'I'm no goody goody.'

Pearl smiled again, but didn't comment. 'Did he give you a reason for going into the pub?' she asked instead. 'It's quite unlike him on a weekday.'

Pete shook his head. 'Nothing was said.'

Pearl placed a plate of food in front of him. It was a pork and apple dish she was trying out for the first time. 'Get stuck into that. And I hope you like it.'

Stuck by a sudden idea, she took an enamel bowl from the sink into the bedroom and placed it on the floor where Willie could easily reach it should he decide to be sick. Then she went back through to the kitchen.

'This is delicious,' Pete announced. 'I'm thoroughly enjoying it.'

That pleased Pearl enormously. She too had enjoyed it when she'd had it earlier. 'Thank you. So, how's the girlfriend situation?' she inquired as he continued to eat.

'Nobody at the moment.'

'Oh?'

'Nobody serious, that is. There are a couple of girls I

occasionally take out, but they're nothing special. Why do you ask?'

'Just curious. Simply bringing myself up to date, as Willie and I haven't seen you for a while.'

'That's true enough,' he acknowledged. 'Been busy at work. I got promoted again, which is all very well, but it means having to put in extra hours. Not that I mind all that much. I like what I do.'

'Maybe I shouldn't ask – it's none of my business – but does the promotion mean more money?'

Pete laughed. 'Darn tootin'. Not a huge amount, but enough to make a difference.'

Pearl wondered what Pete earned. A lot more than Willie, she guessed.

He finally finished his meal and again told Pearl how much he'd enjoyed it. She revelled in the praise, little of which she got from Willie. When Pete announced he really must be going, she was disappointed.

'Do you have to?'

''Fraid so. But I will call in again soon and perhaps we can arrange another night out together?'

'That would be nice.'

She saw him to the door, where he gave her a friendly peck on the cheek before hurrying off down the stairs.

She'd give Willie hell in the morning, Pearl promised herself as she closed the door again.

Pearl came awake to the sound of Willie vomiting into the bowl she'd left out. Moments later the alarm went off.

She continued to lie there out of habit, waiting for the usual onslaught. It was several minutes before it dawned on her he might not be up to it.

'Are you all right?' she asked eventually, when the vomiting had stopped.

'Of course I'm not all right,' he snarled in reply. 'I'm bloody dying, that's what.'

'Well, it's your own fault for getting so drunk. Don't look for any sympathy from me. Why did you do it, anyway?'

Willie groaned. 'I was wetting a baby's head with a couple of pals, one of whom's wife had had a baby the night before.'

'Masonic friends?'

'Mind your own bloody business.'

She fought back her anger. Why did he have to be so rude! 'Fine, I will.' She slipped from the bed and headed towards the kitchen, intending to wash at the sink as she usually did.

Willie was sitting up with his head in his hands when she returned. So far so good, she thought. It seemed she might escape for once.

'I won't be going to work today,' he announced in a feeble voice. 'Not the way I'm feeling.'

'Suit yourself.' She hurriedly began to dress.

Willie eyed her balefully. 'You seem bloody pleased with yourself.'

'Do I?'

'Aye, you do.'

'It's your imagination, that's all.'

Willie ran a hand over his face. 'Did I bump into Pete last night?'

'You did. He brought you home in a cab as you were unable to even stand. Pitiful.'

'I told you, I was wetting a baby's head. At least

378

someone knows how to do their duty, even if you don't.'

For a moment, she didn't understand. 'How do you mean?'

'At least someone can have a baby, which you seem unable to do. Bloody useless you are in that department. Worse than useless,' he spat nastily.

Pearl's cheeks flamed. What a terrible thing to say. How dare he! How bloody dare he! 'Maybe the fault isn't mine,' she snapped back.

He was outraged. 'Are you implying it's mine?'

'It could be. There's always that possibility.'

'Like hell there is!' he yelled at her. 'The men in my family have never had any trouble producing weans.'

'That doesn't mean you're not the exception.'

He glared at Pearl, loathing her for such a suggestion. If he hadn't been so hungover he'd have got out of bed and given her a good crack across the face for her insolence. 'Bitch,' he muttered.

'I'm nothing of the sort. Far from it. As you well know.'

'If I say you're a bitch then you damn well are.'

'And you're a bastard, Willie. Through and through. I wish to God I'd never married you.'

'And I wish I'd never married you, useless as you are. Even my ma wonders what's wrong with you.'

Pearl snorted. 'I wondered when you'd bring her into it.'

'She says you should go to the doctor and get checked over. She says something has to be the matter with you.'

'Just me? Why not you as well?'

'Don't be ridiculous. My cock performs as well as any man's.'

As she was only too aware. At least she was being spared that this morning. 'It's not just how your cock performs, Willie. There's more to it than that.'

'I can come with the best of them. You've seen what I can do. Felt it.'

This was getting them nowhere, Pearl decided. Time for her to be off to work. 'I'm going.'

'And good riddance, barren bitch.'

Pearl clenched her hands in fury, tears suddenly springing to her eyes. What if he was right? What if it was her fault? What if she was barren?

'Now get the hell out of here!' he roared.

She went.

Chapter 25

'Happy birthday to you, happy birthday to you. Happy birthday dear Jacky, happy birthday to you!'

Everyone present, with the exception of the birthday girl herself, applauded, and Ethne took Jacky by the hand. 'You have to blow out the candles on the cake, darling. All three of them. Can you manage that?'

Jacky nodded, riddled with shyness at being the centre of attention.

'Good.'

Ethne lifted Jacky on to a chair at the table where the cake, made by Dot of course, was proudly displayed.

'Take a deep breath,' Ethne instructed.

Jacky did so.

'Now blow.'

There was more applause as the three candles were extinguished on the second attempt.

Lizzie stood watching, her emotions mixed. It seemed only yesterday that Jacky had been born, and now here she was three years old. Lizzie could hardly credit it.

Other children, friends of Jacky from the street, milled

around, all hoping to be the first to get a slice of cake, their eager faces shining with expectation. There had already been jelly, sweets and homemade fudge, with lemonade to wash it down. They would all have agreed it was a smashing party. A real humdinger of one.

'Doesn't she look simply gorgeous?' Pearl said to Lizzie, who could only nod in reply. 'Did your ma make the dress?' The dress in question was white and edged in pink. Jacky might have been a fairy princess come to life.

'She did.'

'Clever old her.'

'Hand stitched it too. I would have run it up myself at the factory but as you know personal work isn't allowed under any circumstances, which is a pity. I could have done it in a fraction of the time.'

'Perhaps your ma preferred making it herself. I could understand if that was the case. A sort of personal thing.'

If so, Ethne had never mentioned it, Lizzie reflected.

'At least none of them has been sick yet,' Pearl commented, thinking that was a wonder considering how much some of them had already managed to stuff down their throats.

'Aye, there is that to be thankful for,' Lizzie agreed. She had been proud to note that Jacky hadn't been as greedy as many of the others. It had pleased Ethne too, no doubt.

'After you've all had your cake we're going to play more games,' Ethne announced. 'Ring a ring a roses to start with. Then Blind man's buff.'

'I want to be the blind man,' a little red-haired boy called Duncan shouted. 'That's fun.'

'Right then, you shall be first,' Ethne promised him.

Duncan looked triumphantly around as if he'd just pulled off some great coup or other. Lizzie glanced at the clock on the mantelpiece. It was proving to be a long Saturday afternoon. And there were hours still to go.

'I'm worried about Pearl,' Dot said.

Ron lowered his newspaper and glanced across at her. 'Why?'

'Her and Willie. They just don't seem to be getting on nowadays. Haven't for quite some time, come to that.'

Ron knew that to be true. It was obvious every time you saw them together.

'Do you think there's anything we can do?'

Ron shook his head. 'We musn't interfere. What goes on between them is their business.'

'It's just . . . I hate to see her so unhappy.'

It pained him too. During the years of his daughter's marriage he'd come to actively dislike Willie. Not for anything specific, but in general.

'Do you think he hits her?' Dot asked quietly.

'If he does I've never seen any evidence of it. Have you?'

Dot shook her head. 'Never. But you do wonder.'

'Has Pearl ever said anything?'

'No, she hasn't. But then I'm not certain she would. She's a proud lass, don't forget.'

Ron sighed. 'Let's just hope they work out their differences in time.'

A child would help, Dot reflected, well aware of Willie's fixation with not only having a family but having a large one. She was almost certain that was the main bone of contention between them.

383

'Talking of men hitting women, I see Jean Carmichael has another black eye,' Ron stated grimly. 'When did that happen?'

'A couple of nights ago.'

'Do we know why?'

'Something to do with his tea that he didn't like. According to Jean he just flew off the handle and smacked her one. She said she saw stars afterwards.'

He didn't believe in interfering between husband and wife, Ron thought. But if Willie ever did anything like that to Pearl then he damn well would.

He'd flatten the sod.

Pearl and Willie had joined Pete and his new girlfriend Vera in a pub where women were welcome in the snug. It was the first time Pearl had met Vera, the latest in a long line of Pete's girlfriends, and she didn't think much of her, considering her rough and common even by Thistle Street standards. She couldn't imagine what Pete saw in her.

'I'm off to London in a couple of days,' Pete announced.

'Work?' Willie queried.

'Aye. They want me at head office for a fortnight. I'm to get some special training.'

Vera took hold of Pete's arm and proceeded to cling to him like a limpet. 'He's dead brainy, my Pete,' she declared loudly. 'Scrumptious too, aren't you, pet?'

Pete blushed, while Willie laughed. 'Are you scrumptious, son?' he mocked.

'Leave him alone,' Pearl chided.

'Oh, dry your eyes and stop nagging, woman,' Willie

instantly retorted, none too pleasantly either. 'I'm only having a laugh.'

Embarrassed, Pearl glanced away, a fact that was not lost on Pete, who felt sorry for her. He'd noticed more and more over the past few years how quick Willie was to put Pearl down, sometimes quite viciously. He didn't like it at all.

'Will you bring me back a present from London, Pete?' Vera asked in what she imagined was a sultry tone of voice.

'Of course. Anything in particular?'

Vera frowned as she thought about that. 'No, you make it a surprise,' she replied when she failed to come up with anything.

'A surprise it is then.' He finished his pint and replaced the glass on the table. 'Now, whose turn is it to get them in?'

Willie reluctantly admitted it was his, and Pearl watched in disgust as he made his unwilling way up to the bar.

Tight as a midge's arse.

'Can you keep a secret?'

Lizzie glanced at her friend. They were on their way to the factory. 'Of course I can.'

'I'm three days late with my monthlies.'

Lizzie came up short to stare at a beaming Pearl. 'Do you think you're up the duff?'

'I don't know. It's too soon to tell. But I could be.'

'Oh, Pearl, I hope you are,' Lizzie said. 'I truly do. It would be wonderful for you.'

'I'm keeping my fingers crossed.' She made Lizzie

385

smile by literally holding up two crossed fingers.

'Have you told Willie yet?'

Pearl shook her head. 'But I will in a couple of days if I still haven't come on.'

They resumed walking. 'He'll be thrilled,' Lizzie commented.

'He'll be more than that, believe me. He'll be out of his head with delight.'

Please God, let me be pregnant, Pearl silently prayed. Please please please God.

'Are you still seeing that Bobby chap?' Pearl asked that evening as they were making their way home again.

Some while back Lizzie had chummed up with another girl from the factory called Isa Hetherington, and started going to the dancing with her on Saturday nights. She had met Bobby Clark there four weeks previously and been out with him three times since. She nodded. 'We're off to the bioscope this Friday.'

Pearl frowned at Lizzie's apparent lack of enthusiasm. 'You don't seem too keen?'

Lizzie thought about that. 'He's nice enough. But . . .' She trailed off.

'But what?'

Lizzie shrugged. 'I don't know. He's pretty dull, if you know what I mean.'

'Boring?'

'You could say. He works on the railways and that's all he can talk about. I've tried to get him on to other subjects but before you know where you are we're back on the railways again.'

'Oh dear.'

'So I think this Friday is going to be the last time I see him.'

'You don't seem to have much luck with men, do you?' Pearl commiserated. 'Though I have to say I think you're at least partially at fault.'

'How so?'

'You're so bloody fussy, Lizzie. You've only been out with a couple during the past year.'

'I can't help it if I don't find anyone who interests me,' Lizzie protested. Jack had, of course. And Ross. But Jack was gone and Ross believed her married.

'Someone will happen along. You'll see.' Pearl smiled encouragingly.

The truth was, although Lizzie would never have admitted it, she really wasn't all that bothered.

'Do you think you could be a bit more gentle, Willie?'

He paused in mid-action. 'What are you moaning about this time? I am being gentle.'

Like hell he was, Pearl thought. He was giving her a right pounding. 'It's just that I think I might be expecting.'

He gaped at her. 'You what?'

'I think I might be expecting. I'm not absolutely sure yet, but my monthlies are a week overdue.'

'Holy shit!' he breathed. Pearl was up the clout at last. At long bloody last. Disengaging, he came to his feet to stare at her. 'That's brilliant. Absolutely brilliant, Pearl. I couldn't be happier.'

'I only said might be, mind,' she reminded him.

But he wasn't listening. Didn't want to know. 'Oh, my darling. My lovely darling,' he uttered, voice tight with emotion.

'Are you going to finish, or what?'

For the next couple of minutes, much to her delight, he treated her like rare porcelain.

'How long is it now?' Lizzie asked.

'Eleven days.'

'And how do you feel?'

Pearl thought about that. 'Same as usual, I suppose. Not different in any way.'

'That'll probably change before long.' Lizzie knew from first hand experience that it would, but could hardly say so.

'Willie's still in seventh heaven,' Pearl declared. 'You wouldn't believe how well he's been treating me since I broke the news. It's lovely.'

'Good for him.'

'He's a new man and no mistake.'

Lizzie couldn't have been more pleased for her friend.

'How was your tea?'

'Excellent,' Willie replied, nodding his approval. 'Couldn't have been better.'

'Would you like some more?'

'If there's any going. No, you stay where you are,' he said when she started to rise. 'I'll get it myself.'

She watched in amazement as he did just that.

Lizzie knew something was wrong the moment Pearl appeared on the landing. 'What is it?' she demanded.

'I came on last night.'

'No!'

Pearl's eyes misted over. 'It happened just before we went to bed. I absolutely flooded.'

'Oh, Pearl, I am sorry,' Lizzie said sympathetically, knowing how much this had meant to her pal. 'How's Willie taking it?'

'You can imagine. Let's just say he wasn't best pleased. I won't repeat some of the things he said, but they were hardly complimentary. To hear him you'd have thought I came on intentionally.'

Lizzie put her arms round Pearl and held her tight. 'I'm so sorry,' she repeated, thinking, what a swine. What a right bloody swine.

'Going out with Lizzie for a drink!' Willie exclaimed, clearly both put out and annoyed.

'Why not?' Pearl declared defiantly. 'You have your nights at the Masons, not to mention Wednesdays at your ma's.'

'That's different.'

Pearl laughed. 'Why is it different?'

'It just is, that's all.'

'Nonsense.'

'It's nothing of the sort!'

'Lizzie's upset because she's broken up with her latest boyfriend,' Pearl lied. 'So we're going to have a get together to talk about things.'

'Hmm!' he snorted, not liking it one little bit. As far as he was concerned a woman's place was in the home, not out gallivanting. His mother would never have dreamed of doing anything like that. 'What sort of things?'

'Women's things.'

'And why can't you do that here?'

Pearl rolled her eyes heavenwards. 'Because it's nice to get out of the house once in a while.'

'I take you out,' he protested.

'Very occasionally. Anyway, this is to help Lizzie.'

'Where will you go?' he queried suspiciously.

'I don't know. We haven't decided yet.'

'And how long will you be out for?'

'Oh, for Christ's sake, Willie, we're not going to get up to anything. Just have a quiet drink, that's all.'

He could put his foot down and forbid it, he thought, toying with the idea. There again, there would be all hell to pay if he did, and who needed that?

'All right,' he conceded.

'Thank you,' she replied tartly.

And with that they both lapsed into silence.

'Why don't you just leave him?' Lizzie suggested. She and Pearl were in the same snug bar that Pearl and Willie had come to with Pete and Vera, before Vera had been given the elbow shortly after Pete's return from London.

'Oh, don't be daft, Lizzie. People like us don't leave their husbands. It isn't the done thing. Besides, where would I go? My parents certainly wouldn't have me back, and even if they did I wouldn't want to be living up the same close as Willie. That would be terrible.'

'Isn't there anywhere else?'

Pearl shook her head.

'How about a place of your own?'

'I couldn't afford that on what I earn. It's out of the question.' Pearl's expression became grim. 'And what would people say? They've no truck with women who run out on their husbands round here. No matter what the provocation you're expected to stay put and get on with it. No, I've made my bed and now I must lie on it.'

Lizzie sighed, and had a sip of her whisky.

'I wish I'd never married him,' Pearl stated quietly. 'God, how I've regretted it.'

Lizzie's heart went out to her friend. What an awful predicament to be in. 'It's a pity you're not a member of the aristocracy,' she said.

Pearl frowned. 'I don't understand?'

'I read somewhere once that when a female aristocrat can't get pregnant by her husband she has an affair and gets pregnant that way.'

'How appalling!'

'I'm only mentioning it. Not suggesting for one moment you do it.'

'I should hope not. I'm not some loose woman, you know. It would never cross my mind to cheat on Willie. I'm married to him, don't forget.'

'I repeat, I wasn't suggesting you do it. Only telling you how the upper classes sometimes solve the problem.'

Despite her protests, Pearl was becoming more intrigued by the second. 'How do they go about it? The wives, I mean.'

Lizzie shrugged. 'I've no idea. They just do.'

'How extraordinary,' Pearl exclaimed.

'Apparently it's sometimes done to give a duke, or a lord, an heir when he can't manage one on his own. The continuation of the title, you see.' Lizzie dropped her voice till it was just above a whisper. 'Apparently there are suspicions about some of our own royal family.'

Pearl's eyes opened wide. 'No!'

'Apparently.'

Pearl suddenly giggled. 'You're not saying the King's a bastard, are you?'

'Of course not. But it is a very large family, after all. Lots of heirs required for all those titles. As for the King, he might well be a bastard – I certainly don't know – but not in the illegitimate sense.'

Pearl's mind was whirling. 'Well well well,' she murmured.

'Adultery does go on amongst us working classes as well,' Lizzie continued slowly. 'But I shouldn't imagine for one minute they do it to put the woman concerned up the duff.'

'Oh, adultery does happen,' Pearl agreed. 'I heard my mother and Mrs Millar talking about it once. His "little bit of fluff" was how they described the female in question. Needless to say both Ma and Mrs Millar were most disapproving. Outraged even.'

'Aye, they would be.' Lizzie nodded.

'Where did you read about this?' Pearl queried.

'I honestly can't remember. It was some years ago.'

Pearl lit a cigarette, her third since entering the snug. She was smoking more and more of late, a fact which annoyed the hell out of Willie, who still considered it a dreadful waste of money.

'It's good for us to get out like this,' Lizzie declared. 'We should try and do it more often.'

'We should,' Pearl agreed.

'That's if Willie doesn't mind?'

Pearl gave Lizzie a thin smile. 'Oh, he minds all right. But too bad. He can like it or lump it as far as I'm concerned. He goes out often enough by himself. What's good for the goose, eh?'

'Precisely.'

*   *   *

Pearl lay in the darkness later that night unable to sleep for thinking about what Lizzie had said earlier in the pub. The more she thought about the idea the more it intrigued and fascinated her.

It was ages before she finally dropped off.

'Stuart!' Ethne exclaimed, unable to believe her eyes.

'Hello, Ma.'

She flew into his arms and hugged him tight. 'Son! Son! It's grand to see you.'

'And it's grand to see you, Ma. Are you going to invite me in?'

She wiped away a few tears from her eyes. 'Of course. Come on through. My, but this is a surprise.'

Doogie came to his feet the moment Stuart entered the kitchen. 'By all that's holy!' he cried. A bracing handshake followed, and Stuart was slapped heartily on the back.

'Hello, sis.'

'Hello, Stuart.' She kissed him on the cheek, as delighted as her parents by his turning up so unexpectedly.

He glanced around. 'Where's Jacky?'

Ethne pointed to Lizzie's hole-in-the-wall bed. 'Fast asleep, I'm afraid. It's past her bedtime.'

Stuart peered into the recess. 'She's grown.'

'Well of course she has.' Ethne laughed. 'Children usually do.'

'Doesn't our talking keep her awake?'

'She's used to it,' Ethne explained. 'We could shout and scream and I doubt it would wake her.'

Stuart pulled a bottle of whisky from his pocket and

handed it to Doogie. 'I thought we might have a celebratory dram,' he declared.

Doogie accepted the bottle with alacrity. 'Coming right up.'

'So,' Ethne said eagerly. 'What brings you to Glasgow?'

'I'm on the laird's business,' Stuart informed them, sitting down on one of the kitchen chairs. 'I'm booked into a small hotel for the night. Then tomorrow morning I'm off to the cattle market to look over, and hopefully buy, a prize bull the laird is interested in. If I do buy it then I have to arrange for it to be transported to Tomintoul.'

'On the laird's business!' Ethne marvelled. 'He must think highly of you.'

'I suppose so,' Stuart answered somewhat sheepishly.

'Have you had your tea yet?'

'I had it at the hotel before coming here, Ma,' Stuart replied, which was a relief to Ethne, who didn't have much in. She, like everyone else in Thistle Street, shopped on a daily basis.

Stuart was appalled by what he'd seen so far. The whole area was nothing more than a slum, and a smelly one at that. He couldn't understand how his parents could bear to live in such squalor after Tomintoul. There again, he reminded himself, there probably wasn't any alternative.

Doogie handed round glasses, then raised his in a toast. 'To Stuart, whom I'm well proud of.'

'Aye, to our big son,' Ethne added, tears back in her eyes.

Moved, Stuart gazed lovingly from face to face before tasting his own drink.

'How are Gordon and Sheena and wee Mhairi?' Ethne asked.

'More or less the same.'

'Sheena still as churchy as ever?'

Stuart laughed. 'No change there, Ma. I swear she'd go every day, twice a day, if there was a service.'

'And Gordon?'

'Fit as a flea. And, if I dare say it, not quite as down-trodden as he once was.'

Ethne smiled to hear that. 'Good.'

'And how about wee Mhairi?' Doogie queried.

'Doing well at school, I understand. Otherwise the same bundle of mischief as ever.'

'Now then,' Ethne declared, taking a seat. 'Tell us all the news from Tomintoul. I want to hear everything.'

'And I'd like to hear about this bull you're looking at tomorrow, son. A prize one, you say?'

Stuart nodded.

'That'll cost the laird a pretty penny.'

'The reason he wants to buy it is to improve the herd.'

The hours fled by, and soon it was time for Stuart to leave them. 'Can I have a private word with you before I go, Lizzie?' he asked.

'Of course.'

'Use our bedroom,' Ethne said, wondering what couldn't be said in front of her and Doogie.

In the bedroom, with the door closed, Stuart looked seriously at Lizzie. 'I just wanted you to know, as you were such good friends, that Ross got married last month. She's called Meg Dalrymple, and a very nice lassie.'

Lizzie smiled. 'I'm delighted to hear that. Will you give him my congratulations?'

'I will, sis,' Stuart said softly.

'Thanks for telling me.'

She was still smiling, though there was now a rather fixed quality about it, when they rejoined their parents.

Chapter 26

'What are you staring at?' Willie demanded harshly. Pearl instantly dropped her gaze. 'Sorry. I didn't mean to.'

'Well you were.'

He glared at her, thinking how much she irritated him of late. It was getting to the stage where he was reluctant to come home at night. Sometimes he even hated having to.

'Sorry,' she repeated.

'Have I suddenly grown horns or something?' he went on, not prepared to let the matter drop.

Pearl sighed inwardly. He was obviously in one of his moods, which were becoming more and more common. 'Of course not.'

'Or a bloody great wart on the edge of my nose?'

'Don't be silly, Willie.'

His eyes narrowed meanly. 'I may be many things, but I'm not silly. Understand?'

She nodded. 'Shall I put the kettle on for a cup of tea?'

Tea was the last thing he wanted. What he did want was out of there, and out of her company. He came to his feet. 'I'm off to the Argyle for a pint.'

Pearl glanced at him in astonishment. It was most unlike Willie to drink during the week.

'You got something to say about that?'

'No,' she whispered.

'Speak up, woman. I can't hear you.'

'No, Willie, I haven't.'

'Just as well,' he growled, and left the room.

Pearl bit her lip when the outside door banged shut. It was now six months since she'd thought herself pregnant, and during that time things between them had worsened. Nothing she did was right any more.

What a difference from what he'd been like when he'd thought her to be expecting. He'd been sweet as pie then. Couldn't do enough for her. Why, he'd even been gentle and considerate in bed. Well, as gentle and considerate as he knew how to be.

There was ironing to be got on with, she reminded herself. Plenty of it, despite the fact that her mother was still helping out.

With a sigh Pearl came to her feet. She felt wretched and in despair: the failure Willie was forever cruelly calling her.

Pearl didn't know where she'd found the nerve, but somehow she had, and now she was in Pete's apartment, having turned up at his door.

Pete smiled at her. 'So, what's this all about then?'

'Do you have a drink? I really need one.'

'Things that bad, eh?' he joked.

She nodded, her stomach a riot of butterflies and other sensations.

'Willie?'

She nodded again.

'I thought that might be it. I'm afraid there's only gin. Will that do?'

'It's fine, Pete. And make it a large one, if you have it.'

'There you are,' he declared a few moments later, handing her a glass. 'I won't join you if you don't mind. It's a bit early for me.'

But not for her that day, she thought, gulping down half of the glass's contents, which made her shudder. 'I wasn't sure you'd be in,' she said. 'Though I was hoping you would be, it being Saturday afternoon.' She paused, then asked anxiously, 'I'm not stopping you from going out or anything, am I?'

'Not at all.'

'Good. Can I smoke?'

'I'll get an ashtray.'

What had Willie been up to? he wondered as he went in search of one. Well, whatever, he'd soon find out.

Pearl's hands were shaking as she lit her cigarette. She took a deep drag, exhaled, and then swallowed more gin. 'I've come to ask you a favour. A big favour,' she declared eventually.

'Oh aye?'

Christ, this was difficult. 'You must know Willie and I haven't exactly been getting on for some while now?'

'I have noticed. It's pretty obvious, actually.'

'Well, most of it's down to us not having any children. He wants loads of them and so far we haven't even managed one. For some reason he blames me for that.'

Pete wasn't quite sure how to reply. 'I presume the mechanics are all right?'

She frowned. 'How do you mean?'

'Everything's in working order?'

Pearl blushed. 'No trouble there. Either for him or me.'

'Then perhaps you should both consult a doctor. Be examined for other causes.'

Pearl laughed bitterly. 'Willie would never agree to that. He'd see it as an insult to his manhood. As for me, I've already been.'

'And?'

'According to the doctor, as far as he could make out, I'm fine. Absolutely fine.' Pearl drained her glass. 'Do you think I could have some more? I'm finding this terribly hard.'

Pete decided to change his mind and join her. The last thing he'd been expecting was this kind of chat.

'Willie's made life hell for me,' Pearl went on. 'A complete misery. I know it'll be different once I'm up the duff. But until that happens he's being rotten.'

Pete's expression was grim as he handed Pearl her refill. 'I truly am sorry to hear that. I have to admit, he's not the Willie I used to know. He's changed.'

'He's not the Willie who courted me either. The one I fell in love with.'

Pete couldn't help but ask. 'Are you still in love?'

She shook her head. 'Not really. Perhaps things will change back to how they were when children come along. I'd like to think they will.'

'And what if they don't?' Pete queried softly.

Pearl sighed. 'Christ knows. That's why I've come to you.'

'How can I help?'

Here it was, Pearl thought. The nitty gritty. 'Do you find me attractive?'

He studied her closely. 'Yes, I do. Why?'

'Would you consider . . .' She stopped and drank more gin. Come on, girl, get on with it, she urged herself. 'Would you go to bed with me?' she suddenly blurted out.

Pete stared at her in amazement. 'Did you just say what I thought you said?'

Pearl nodded. 'Will you shag me?'

Pete was stunned, to say the least. Talk about being up front! He opened his mouth, then closed it again. 'Willie's my friend,' he croaked at last.

'So am I, I hope.'

'Of course.'

Pearl's shoulders began to shake, tears not far away. This was humiliating. She'd die of shame if he turned her down.

'Let me get this straight,' Pete said slowly. 'You want me to go to bed with you. Right?'

'To try to make me pregnant, which Willie can't seem to do.'

'And that's the only reason?'

She nodded.

'I see.'

'Willie will never know he's not the father. He'll be ecstatic, and hopefully treat me better. Understand?'

Pete was bemused, still trying to take it in. 'How on earth did you come up with such an idea?'

Pearl related the conversation she'd had with Lizzie in

the pub all those months ago. 'And I finally came to the conclusion that if the women of the aristocracy can do it, then why not me?'

'So I'd not only be doing you a favour, but Willie as well?'

'That's right.'

'And what . . . well, what if I too fail to make you pregnant? What then?'

The tears had receded; she was fully in control of herself again. 'Then, despite the doctor's assurances, it must be me at fault. But I'm sure that won't happen.'

Pete suddenly realised he'd finished his drink, and badly wanted another. He noted Pearl's glass was also empty. 'Some more?' he asked, indicating the bottle.

'Please.'

His mind was working overtime as he poured their refills, acutely aware that Pearl's eyes were riveted on him.

'So this wouldn't be just a one off?' He handed her her glass again.

'A regular thing until I get pregnant. That's if you agree.' Doubt crept into her voice. 'You did say you found me attractive?'

'I do, Pearl. I wasn't lying about that. I presume you find me the same?'

'Naturally. I wouldn't be here otherwise.'

My God, handed it on a plate like this, he marvelled. He couldn't believe his luck. It was the sort of request most red-blooded men would have given their eye teeth for.

'Would you please give me an answer, Pete,' she begged. 'The suspense is killing me.'

He smiled. 'When would you like to start?'

Relief whooshed through her. He'd agreed! 'Why not

here and now? No time like the present, eh?'

'You mean in this room?' he teased.

She coloured. 'Of course not. I meant the bedroom.'

'Then drink up and we'll go on through.'

Pearl hesitated. 'Excuse me if I'm shy. Willie's the only man who's ever seen me with my clothes off.'

'Then I'll go first, shall I?'

'We'll go together.'

What a cracker, he thought, when she was finally standing naked in front of him. He'd known she had a good figure, but the reality was even better than he'd expected. 'You're beautiful,' he said softly.

'Hardly that. My bum sags.'

'It's perfect. I assure you.'

'So you still find me attractive?'

'Oh yes,' he whispered. 'Very much so.'

Pearl suddenly giggled, which had the effect of relaxing her. 'Yes, I can see you do.'

He laughed. 'I suppose it is obvious.' Going to her, he took her into his arms and kissed her. She responded in kind. Then, taking her by the hand, he led her to the bed.

Pete stood at a window watching Pearl walking off down the street. They'd agreed she'd return on Tuesday night when Willie was at a Masonic meeting which wouldn't be ending till late.

Shaking his head in disbelief he turned away, intending to pour himself another drink. He couldn't wait to see her again.

And again take her to bed.

* * *

403

That night Pearl lay in a dreamy doze going over the events of the day in her mind, Willie snoring beside her.

She couldn't help but compare how it had been with Pete to Willie's usual nocturnal performance. Not to put too fine a point on it, there hadn't been any comparison. None at all.

Her body shivered in memory.

'Do you remember that conversation about dukes and lords we had the first time we came here?' Pearl asked casually. Going out for a drink with Lizzie had become something of a regular event.

'The one about women having affairs in order to get a bun in the oven?'

'That's it.'

'Of course I remember.'

Pearl took her time in lighting a cigarette, enjoying the bombshell she was about to drop. 'Well, I went ahead and did it.'

Lizzie frowned. 'Did what?'

'Started having an affair.'

Lizzie's expression was one of sheer incredulity. 'You did what!'

'With Willie's pal Pete Milroy, whom you've still never met. I explained the situation to him, he agreed, and we toddled off to bed.'

'Jesus Christ!' Lizzie swore softly. 'Are you taking the mickey?'

'Nope.'

'You and he actually . . .'

'Have been doing it for several weeks now,' Pearl interjected. 'I just couldn't keep it to myself, which is why

I'm telling you. You and only you, understand?'

Lizzie nodded, not sure whether to be shocked or pleased for her friend.

'Promise me you'll keep this to yourself?'

Lizzie swallowed hard. 'I promise.'

'I mean that, Lizzie. You're not to breathe a word. God knows what would happen if Willie ever found out. He'd probably murder me, so he would.'

Lizzie agreed. There was a violent streak in Willie which she'd observed more than once. 'So . . . how did you put it to this Pete?' she asked, fascinated.

'I went to his apartment and, as I've already said, explained the situation. He was a bit taken aback, to say the least. Even found it funny, I think. Eventually he agreed to help, and we went to bed.'

'Just like that?'

'Just like that.'

'And up until then you hadn't even so much as kissed him?'

'Nope.'

'Bloody hell!' Lizzie swore.

'It took a lot of guts on my part, I can tell you. I mean, what if he'd refused? I'd have felt a right idiot. Humiliated through and through. Luckily, he didn't.'

Lizzie shook her head, still unable to get over this disclosure. She found it mind-boggling.

'Shall I tell you something, Lizzie?'

'What?'

'He's absolutely terrific at it. Knocks spots off Willie.'

Lizzie frowned. 'In what way?'

'Of course, you wouldn't know about shagging, would you? Well, with Willie it's bang bang bang and finish.

All he cares about is himself. Never me. But with Pete it's different. He takes his time. Before getting started, and during it. We go at it for absolutely ages, much to . . .' She broke off, and smiled. 'Let's just say I have more than one result.'

'Really?'

'Really. That's never happened with Willie. In fact with him it's rare for me to have a result at all. Whereas, so far, I've had them every time I've been to bed with Pete.' Her eyes gleamed. 'Christ but he's good. No, fantastic. Bloody fantastic!'

'When are you seeing him again?'

'Saturday afternoon. That's become a regular with us.'

'And what excuses do you make to Willie to explain your absences?'

Pearl laughed. 'To be honest, I think he's pleased to see the back of me for a while. Besides, he's got things he does himself at that time. So it isn't really a problem.'

Lizzie looked into Pearl's face. 'Maybe it's my imagination, but you do look different somehow. Happier, more . . . content.'

'Yes.' Pearl nodded slowly. 'I do feel both of those things. It's as if my life has taken on a whole new meaning.' She leaned closer to Lizzie, and lowered her voice. 'Know something?'

'What?'

'I'm hoping I don't get pregnant too quickly. That's how much I'm enjoying myself.'

'And when you do get up the duff?'

Pearl sighed. 'Then the arrangement will have to stop.'

'Until you want another child?'

Pearl's expression dissolved into the widest of smiles.

'You know, I hadn't thought of that. And Willie does want lots of children. Lots,' she repeated a few seconds later, and laughed.

'Will you kiss me goodnight, Mummy?'

'Of course, darling. Don't I always?' Wiping her hands on the pinny she was wearing, Ethne went to Jacky and kissed her on the cheek. 'There.'

'And you, Daddy?'

'Come here, my poppet, and I'll give you a big smacker.' He assisted Jacky on to his lap and did just that.

A stab of envy lanced through Lizzie. She had watched this scene a thousand times before, and she had no idea why it should upset her on this particular occasion. But it did.

'And you, Lizzie?'

Lizzie squatted down, took Jacky into her arms, and kissed her soundly on the cheek. 'Goodnight, little one.'

'Goodnight, Lizzie.'

Lizzie busied herself at the sink as Ethne put Jacky to bed, not wanting either Ethne or Doogie to see her expression.

She was attempting to swallow back the lump that had suddenly come into her throat.

'It just gets better and better,' Pearl murmured, thoroughly sated.

Pete ran a finger over her sweat-slicked thigh. 'Doesn't it just.'

She wondered where he'd learned to do the things he did to her, and who with, but she didn't ask. It was none of her business, though she'd have loved to know. Or would she? Maybe not.

'More wine?'

'Please.'

She watched lazily as he swung himself out of bed, picked up their empty glasses and padded from the room, admiring the body that had just given her so much pleasure.

'I think you're getting to like drinking wine,' he said when he returned.

'I am.'

'Not very common in Glasgow, I'm afraid. They don't know what they're missing.'

'I couldn't agree more.'

He sat on the bed beside her. 'You'll have to sit up to drink it.'

She did so, and took the glass he handed her. 'That really was quite something,' she declared softly.

'Yes, it was.'

She gazed at him in open admiration. 'I never knew trying to get pregnant could be so much fun.'

Pete laughed.

'Or deliciously wicked,' she added, a twinkle in her eye.

'Is that how you feel with me, wicked?' he teased.

'Sometimes. I am a married woman, after all.'

'But not to me.'

'No, Pete, not to you.'

He glanced away, his expression hard to read.

'It doesn't bother you, does it?'

'The fact you're married to a friend of mine?'

Pearl nodded.

'Not any more. It did to begin with, but not any more. I just wish . . .'

'What?' she prompted when he trailed off.

He shook his head. 'Nothing.'

'Are you sure?'

'Yes,' he replied, finality in his voice.

'All right then.'

He had a sip of wine. 'By the way, they want me in London again. I've to go on another fortnight's training.'

She stared at him in dismay. 'When do you leave?'

'A week on Sunday.'

Two weeks without making love! It was going to seem like an eternity. 'I'll miss you,' she said quietly.

'And I'll miss you, Pearl.'

'Will you? Or are you just saying that?'

'I will. And I'm not just saying it.'

He stroked her arm, watching the fine downy hairs on it sway to his touch. 'I'm sorry, but I have to go.'

'Of course, Pete. I understand. Work is work, after all.'

He smiled disarmingly at her, causing her insides to knot. 'And play is play.'

'Yes,' she agreed, her voice suddenly husky.

'Are you cold? I could light the fire.'

That almost made her laugh. 'Cold after what we've been doing? I'm boiling actually. Here, feel.' Taking his hand she placed it on her breast.

'It is warm.'

'Very.'

He flicked his thumb over her nipple. 'You like me doing that, don't you?'

The atmosphere between them had changed during

the past few seconds. Where before it had been one of some levity, it was now charged with raw sexuality. Pearl knew what was going to happen next. And wanted it to.

'It's nice,' she murmured.

'Would you like to try a variation on a theme?' he asked softly.

'Don't tell me what it is. Just surprise me.'

And surprised she was. Delightfully so.

'Hello, Lizzie. How are you?'

She gaped at the speaker. It was none other than Jack White. 'What are you doing here?' she stammered.

He laughed. 'I live round here. Remember?'

'But you're supposed to be at sea.'

'Given all that up now and am home for good.' He glanced down at Jacky, whose hand Lizzie was holding. 'And who's this?'

Lizzie's mind was numb from shock. 'My little sister.'

'I didn't know you had one.'

'A late addition to the family. She's called Jacqueline.'

Jack squatted in front of the child. 'Hello, young lady.'

Jacky stuck a thumb in her mouth and stared steadfastly at the pavement.

'My name's Jack.'

Panic gripped Lizzie as she saw the similarity between them. It was obvious to her, anyway, though she hoped and prayed it wouldn't be to other people.

Jack straightened again when there was still no reply from Jacky. 'Shy, I suppose.'

Lizzie nodded.

'Still at the factory?'

'Yes.'

'It's good to see you again.' He smiled.

She didn't reply.

'No wedding or engagement ring, I notice. Does that mean you're still footloose and fancy-free?'

'You could put it that way. And you?'

'The same.'

'So why are you home for good?'

He shrugged. 'Simple really. I got fed up with the sea. I've had my fill, you might say. So here I am.'

Panic was really taking hold of her now. She wanted away from there, and him. 'I doubt they'll have you back at the factory after leaving them in the lurch as you did.' And that's exactly what he'd done to her, she thought bitterly. Left her in the lurch.

'I'm not interested in the factory, Lizzie. I have plans of my own.'

'Oh?'

'I intend opening a bicycle and general repair shop. I've always been good at fixing things, as you'll recall.'

She nodded. That was true enough. 'Good luck to you, then. Now I must be off. I'm in a hurry.'

'Nice bumping into you again, Lizzie.'

'And you, Jack.'

''Bye.'

''Bye now.'

His expression was sad as he watched her walk away, so fast she was almost dragging Jacky along.

Chapter 27

Pearl sat back on her haunches with the intention of having a breather. She was waxing and polishing the linoleum on the kitchen floor, and it was hard work. Sweat was streaming down her face, back and breasts.

She glanced over at Willie dozing in a chair, his mouth wide open, and smiled, remembering the last time she'd sweated like this.

She really was missing Pete, who was still in London. Not just for the glorious sex, but for himself. She'd become very fond of Pete Milroy and, she suspected, he of her.

How different he was to Willie, she reflected, not for the first time. In almost every way you could think of. He was kind, caring, thoughtful, considerate – all the things Willie wasn't.

How she now wished she'd never married Willie. But the fact was she had, much to her regret. If she could have waved a magic wand to undo the marriage, she would. But sadly, in life, there were no magic wands. Just harsh reality.

Willie snorted, then reached up and scratched his

nose. For a moment or two it seemed he might come awake, but then he resumed snoring even more loudly than before.

Pearl wondered what Pete was doing in London, when not at work, that was. Were there any women involved? Perhaps someone from the office that he'd met?

Pearl shook her head and dismissed the speculation from her mind. It was none of her business what Pete got up to with other women, either here in Glasgow, or in London. What went on between the two of them was strictly an arrangement to help her out. Nothing more, nothing less.

She sighed, a huge one that came from the very depths of her being. With something of a shock she realised just how unhappy she was. Not with Pete, of course, but with everything else. Particularly Willie.

Still, she consoled herself, it should all change when a baby came along. Willie would surely be far more amenable, easier to get on with. Less demanding. Please God.

She bent again to her waxing and polishing, aching all over from the effort and thankful for the pad she was kneeling on to save her knees.

Lizzie arrived home from work to find a grim-faced Ethne, and an equally grim-faced Doogie, waiting for her.

'There's a parcel and a letter for you,' Ethne declared, indicating the table where she'd placed them.

'For me!'

'I just said that.' Ethne turned away.

Lizzie frowned when she saw that there was only her name on the envelope, no address or stamp.

413

'They were delivered at the door,' Ethne explained, glancing sideways at her.

Lizzie decided to open the parcel first, gasping when a blood red silk scarf with black silk tassels, one on each corner, was revealed. 'It's gorgeous!' she exclaimed, flicking it to full size, and then holding the material to her cheek. 'Real silk, too.'

Doogie and Ethne both looked sourly on.

Laying the scarf down, Lizzie tore open the envelope and quickly scanned its contents. She swallowed hard when she came to the end of it.

'Well?' Ethne demanded harshly.

'It's from Jack. You know . . .' She nodded to where Jacky was happily playing houses with two small cardboard boxes and her golliwog called Sambo.

'I didn't recognise him when he was at the door. He never said who he was, just asked me to make sure you got the parcel and the letter. It wasn't until he was gone that the penny dropped.'

'So what does he want?' Doogie asked, a tremor of anger in his voice.

'He's invited me out for a drink on Saturday night,' Lizzie replied, quite shaken by this turn of events. 'I'm to meet him at the close mouth at seven. He also says he'll fully understand if I don't turn up.'

'Which you won't,' Doogie stated. 'What a cheek. What a bloody cheek after what he did to you!'

'I've a good mind to turn up instead of you and give him a piece of my mind,' Ethne snapped. 'But of course I can't. That would let the cat out the bag.'

'Don't forget he knows nothing about . . .' Again Lizzie nodded in Jacky's direction. 'I introduced her as my little

414

sister when we bumped into him in the street.'

'And just when was this?' Ethne queried. 'You never said.'

'The other day. He told me he's given up the sea and is home for good. Apparently he intends opening a bicycle and general repair shop.'

'So why didn't you mention it?' Doogie insisted.

Lizzie shrugged. 'I just didn't. I didn't think it was important, I suppose.'

Ethne stared at her, not fully believing that. She'd always suspected her daughter still carried a torch for this Jack, though Lizzie had never actually said as much.

Lizzie laid down the letter, picked up the scarf again and carefully refolded it. It truly was beautiful, she reflected. Must have cost an absolute fortune. Well, it certainly would have done if it had been bought in Glasgow.

'You're not actually considering going out with him?' Ethne queried, eyes narrowing.

'Would it be so awful, Ma? As I said, he knows nothing about the outcome of that night. He didn't exactly swan off aware of the pickle he'd left me in.'

'I'm dead against you seeing him.' Doogie frowned. 'He'll only try it on again. His sort always do.'

'Then I can assure you he'd be in for a disappointment. I've made one mistake; I'm not about to make another.'

'I'm pleased to hear it,' said Ethne.

'You'd be a fool to go out with him,' Doogie declared. 'An absolute idiot in my opinion.'

Lizzie rubbed her forehead. She was completely confused. Confused and . . . exhilarated, too, if she was honest.

'Anyway,' Ethne said, 'if you'll sit down at the table I'll put out the tea. It's sausages, mash and cabbage. And I don't want to hear any moaning about the cabbage either. It's cheap and good for you.'

Lizzie placed the scarf and letter on the mantelpiece, then sat as instructed. The subject of Jack wasn't broached again that night.

'I've just realised we haven't seen Pete for ages,' said Willie. 'It must be months now.'

'Haven't we?'

'No, we haven't. Why don't you drop him a line suggesting we meet up at that pub we went to last time?'

'I could do.'

'It'll be good to have a pint with the old bugger and hear what he's been up to,' Willie enthused. 'So you write that letter and I'll post it in the morning.'

If only you knew, Pearl thought, smiling inwardly. If only you knew.

'More wine?'

'Do I ever say no?'

Pete laughed. 'Depends what you're referring to, I suppose.'

'Why, wine of course!' Pearl teased.

Pete gave her a playful smack on the bare bottom before getting off the bed to go for the wine bottle.

Pearl lay back and stared at the ceiling, thinking how wonderful their lovemaking had just been. But then it always was with Pete.

'Now what about that letter you sent me?' Pete queried on his return.

Pearl sat up to accept her refill. 'Willie insisted. Says we haven't seen you in ages. What do you think?'

Pete's expression became pensive. 'To be honest, I'm not exactly keen. I'll be sitting there with my friend, knowing I'm shagging the arse off his wife. Not very nice.'

'I'll be aware of that as well, don't forget. It's my arse that's being shagged off.'

He had to laugh. 'You make it sound like something it isn't.'

'I don't understand?' Pearl frowned.

Her face went beetroot when he explained. 'There'll be none of that, thank you very much. The very idea!'

'I merely said it sounded like it, that's all.'

Pearl sipped her wine while her blushing died away, thinking that one way or another it was always fun being with Pete. He had a wonderful sense of humour, outrageously so at times.

'So what about next Saturday, then?'

She shrugged. 'It's entirely up to you.'

'Would you be embarrassed? Especially if you'd been here that afternoon.'

Pearl bit her lip as she thought about that. Would she be embarrassed when the three of them were together? She didn't think so. 'I'll tell you what, why don't you write back suggesting Friday night rather than Saturday? That might make it easier for both of us.'

Pete nodded his agreement.

'Is that what we'll do, then?'

'Fine by me.'

'So Friday night it is.'

Pete wasn't very happy with the arrangement. On

417

the bright side, though, it gave him another opportunity to be with Pearl. Even if Willie was going to be present.

As for the embarrassment, he'd somehow cope.

'Made up your mind yet?' Ethne asked. Lizzie was sitting staring into space. A glance at the clock told Ethne it was almost half past four. Two and a half hours to go before Lizzie was due to meet Jack.

'I'm still thinking about it, Ma.'

Doogie looked up from his crossword. Since starting at the *Chronicle* he'd given up going to football matches. He didn't see the point when he couldn't go to the pub with the lads afterwards and have a right good bevvy. He could hardly do that when he was due at the newspaper later. If he'd appeared smelling of alcohol he'd have been sacked on the spot.

'And I'm still dead against you meeting up,' he declared. 'Do yourself a favour and give it a miss.'

Lizzie stared at her father, but didn't reply.

'Jacky's to be collected at five,' Ethne said. 'Do you want to go, Lizzie, or shall I?' Jacky had been taken round to a friend's house to play.

'Will you do it, Ma?'

Ethne nodded. 'I've plenty to be getting on with here. But if you wish.'

Lizzie again lapsed into a brooding silence.

Seven o'clock on the dot. Jack would be downstairs waiting by now. Should she go or not? Lizzie worried a nail, trying to decide.

* * *

418

'Oh, there you are. I was beginning to think you weren't going to turn up.' It was ten past the hour.

Lizzie didn't tell him how close that was to being the case. 'So where are we off to, then?'

He raised an eyebrow at the curtness of her tone, noticing she wasn't wearing the scarf he'd given her. 'I have somewhere in mind. It's a tram ride, though.'

'That's all right. Doesn't bother me.'

They headed for the nearest tram stop.

'I brought you here specially,' Jack declared, placing a port and lemon in front of Lizzie before sitting down opposite her.

'Why?'

'Didn't you notice the name of the hotel on the way in?'

She frowned, trying to remember. The journey there couldn't exactly have been described as warm and chatty. They had only exchanged a few words, although Jack had been fully prepared to talk.

'Is it the Lorne?'

'That's right.'

What was the significance of that? 'So?'

'Your surname is McDougall.'

It still didn't click.

'The McDougalls of Lorne. Isn't that where the Clan McDougall come from?'

She suddenly smiled, and fractionally thawed. How clever, and thoughtful, of him. 'I'm with you now.' She nodded. 'I'm only surprised you knew that.'

'Well I did, so there.'

She studied him, thinking his face was considerably

changed. Older somehow, more mature. Lines where there hadn't been any before. But it wasn't only that. The old piratical air he'd always affected, which she remembered so well, was nowhere in evidence, and appeared to be gone. The skin of his face and hands was weather-beaten, quite a different colour from what it had been. Years at sea, braving the elements on a daily basis, had done that, she presumed.

'Why did you do what you did?' she asked quietly, but with steel in her voice. 'Disappearing off like that without a word of explanation. Particularly after what happened that last night.'

'I can only apologise, Lizzie, which I do unreservedly. It's been on my conscience ever since.'

'Has it now?' she replied sarcastically.

'Yes, it has, Lizzie. I swear.'

There was something in his tone which made her want to believe him. Which rang of sincerity. 'Go on.'

Jack took a deep breath. 'I didn't tell anyone, other than my parents, that I was leaving because it wasn't absolutely certain.' He then went on to relate how he'd met the Irishman and what had transpired as a result.

'So you see, Lizzie, I wasn't at all sure I actually had a berth until I went aboard that ship. I swear that's the truth. God's honest.'

'You were keeping your options open, in other words?'

'Correct. If there had been no berth I would simply have turned up for work at the factory, and that would have been that. No one would have been any the wiser.'

She regarded him grimly. 'That still doesn't excuse what you did to me that night, does it?'

'No, it doesn't. All I can say in my defence is that I

was drunk, had the good fortune to run into you whom I'd always fancied rotten, and we both know what happened next. I admit it shouldn't have happened; I shouldn't have let it. But come on, I'm a bloke and blokes are like that. You know what they say about men: when their cock is up all sense flies out of the window.' He hesitated for a few moments, then added, 'Also, if you recall, you weren't exactly protesting or pushing me off, now were you?'

She'd never thought of it that way before. 'Are you saying I'm as much to blame as you?'

Jack shrugged. 'The difference was I knew I might be disappearing off in the morning, whereas you didn't.' He brightened, and smiled. 'Anyway, no harm was done, was it?'

'Oh, how tempted she was to tell him about Jacky. No harm, indeed! He'd made her pregnant and caused her, and her family, no end of grief. For two pins she'd have wiped that smile off his face. But she couldn't. Simply couldn't.

'Am I forgiven?' he asked. Reaching across the table, he took her by the hand, and squeezed. 'Please?'

'I suppose so,' she muttered. She told herself she had to see things from his point of view. He'd believed, and still did, that it was a one night stand with no consequences.

'Good.'

She stared at him, thinking him handsomer than ever. And somehow even more charismatic. 'Thank you for the scarf. It's lovely.'

'You're not wearing it?'

'It's still lovely, Jack. I will wear it, but I didn't think

421

tonight was the appropriate occasion. We had to have this talk first. Sort matters out between us.'

'I understand.' He nodded.

'Where did you get it?'

'Shanghai in China. I saw it and immediately thought of you.'

She laughed. 'Thought of me! Are you asking me to believe that?'

A look of sadness and pain swept across his face. 'Yes, Lizzie,' he said quietly. 'I am.'

That stunned her. 'I would have thought you'd have forgotten all about me.'

Jack shook his head. 'No.'

Shanghai, China! she marvelled. How exotic.

'Nor did I bring back presents for anyone else, other than my parents, that is. Just them and you.'

She was impressed. 'What was Shanghai like?'

For the next hour he regaled her with his adventures at sea, and descriptions of the places he'd been. From the Great Barrier Reef in Australia to the ports of India and South America, he recounted tales that sometimes made her laugh and at other times held her spellbound.

'So now you've given all that up?' she said when he'd finally finished.

'I'm home to settle down. Start a business of my own, and who knows what else?'

'No regrets at all?'

Jack shook his head. 'None. There will be no more itchy feet. I can assure you they're well and truly scratched. Now, how about another drink? I've been doing so much talking we've neglected that part of the evening.'

'Please.'

'Same again?'

She nodded.

He was changed, she thought as he made his way up to the bar. It was good to have him back. And to be in his company again.

She was loving every second of it.

'Well?' Ethne demanded the moment Lizzie got home. She had been waiting up for her.

'I had a great time, Ma.'

Ethne snorted. 'I'm sure.'

'No, I did. Honestly. In fact it couldn't have gone better.'

Ethne's eyes narrowed in suspicion. 'I hope you didn't go into the back close with him?'

'I didn't, as it happens. He didn't ask and I would have refused if he had. I think he guessed that.'

'Are you seeing him again?'

Lizzie slumped into a chair. 'Next Saturday night. He's taking me to a dinner dance he's heard about. Somewhere in town.'

'Your father won't be pleased,' Ethne pointed out. 'Not after him running off and leaving you the way he did.'

Lizzie told her what Jack had said about that, while Ethne listened intently. 'Hmm,' she muttered, when Lizzie had finished.

'He was most apologetic. Said it's been on his conscience ever since.'

'Oh, really?' Ethne's tone was disbelieving.

'He bought the scarf for me in Shanghai, China. He said he chose it especially for me.'

'He sounds a right smooth talker, this Jack White,'

Ethne declared. 'Too smooth for my liking.'

'Oh, go on, Ma. You're prejudiced.'

'Of course I am!' Ethne snapped. 'And so should you be in my opinion.'

'Well, I was before I met up with him tonight. But now . . . I have to admit I've changed my mind. I wouldn't be going out with him again if it was otherwise.' She glanced at the recess bed where Jacky was fast asleep. Jack's child.

'So where did you go?'

'An hotel called the Lorne. Jack chose it because of our surname. The McDougalls of Lorne. I thought it was lovely of him.'

'It's obvious he's made a big impression,' Ethne said disapprovingly.

Lizzie sat back and sighed. 'He has, actually.'

'I can see that. Tell me something?'

'What, Ma?'

'Have you carried a torch for him all these years? I want to know. Be honest now.'

'I suppose I have,' Lizzie admitted after a few seconds' thought. 'Yes, I suppose I have.'

Ethne wasn't at all pleased to have her suspicions confirmed. This Jack was a bad one as far as she was concerned. And if not bad, then feckless. She was convinced of it.

Pete knew the moment Pearl arrived at the apartment that something was wrong. 'Here, let me take your coat.'

'Thank you,' she replied, her tone icy.

'Drink?'

'That would be nice.'

'Wine? I've already opened a bottle.'

'Fine.'

He gave her a sideways glance as he poured. 'Is it my imagination or are you upset?'

Pearl glared at him. 'You're damned right I'm upset.'

He'd never seen her like this before. 'Willie?'

'No, you.'

'Me!' he exclaimed in surprise. 'What have I done?'

'Last night, to be precise.'

'What about last night? I thought it went off rather well, myself.'

'Did you now.' Her voice dripped sarcasm.

'Yes, I did.'

'Why did you bring that . . . tart along?'

So that was it, he thought. 'That tart, as you call her, was there to make up the numbers. You and Willie, me and Moira. I thought it would be easier for the pair of us that way.'

Pearl accepted the glass he handed her, although she didn't really want it. For one brief moment she was tempted to throw its contents in his face. 'You should have warned me,' she snapped. 'Instead of just turning up with her the way you did.'

'I'm sorry,' he apologised. 'I only decided to take her a couple of days ago so there was no way of giving you any advance notice.'

Pearl snorted. 'She was all over you like a fucking rash. Hands everywhere. At one point I thought she was going to undo your flies for a good old grope.'

Pete winced at her use of the f word, not liking it one little bit. It was less than ladylike, to say the least. By God she was angry.

'How long have you been going out with her, anyway?'

'I haven't been going out with her,' a shaken Pete protested. 'Last night was the first and last time.'

'I'll bet!'

He was beginning to get angry himself now. 'I'm telling the truth, Pearl. Moira is nothing to me. On my life!'

'Well, she certainly didn't behave as if it was your first time out together. Hands all over you like a bloody octopus.'

'I can't deny it. She was very touchy feely. I hadn't expected that.'

'So where did you dig her up from?'

'I've known Moira for years. We were at school together. I happened to run into her in the street last Wednesday, and while we were talking had the idea of asking her along last night to make it a foursome. I have absolutely no intention of seeing her again.'

Pearl drank off half the wine, took a deep breath, then saw off the remainder. 'Can I have some more?'

'If you wish.'

She studied him as he was pouring. Her insides were heaving and she'd suddenly gone light-headed thanks to the wine she'd just whoofed down. She knew she was behaving badly, not to mention irrationally, but she simply couldn't help herself.

Pulling out her cigarette packet, Pearl lit up.

'There,' Pete said, giving her the refill.

'It's just . . .' Pearl began, only to trail off.

'Just what?'

Pete had a perfect right to go out with anyone he chose, she reminded herself. She knew that. Theirs was only an arrangement, after all. No more than that. He was doing her a favour.

'Pearl?'

'I have to sit down.'

Her hands were shaking when she placed her glass on the mantelpiece and stubbed out her hardly smoked cigarette. Suddenly her eyes filled with tears and she was sobbing her heart out.

Frowning, Pete went to her and took her into his arms. Jealousy? he wondered, at a loss as to what else it might be.

'Oh, Pete,' she whispered between sobs. 'I'm sorry. I'm so sorry.'

'That's all right.'

'It's just . . .' She swallowed before going on. 'I'm pregnant. I'm certain of it.'

Chapter 28

As Willie was at one of his interminable Masonic meetings Pearl had decided to invite Lizzie down for a cup of tea.

'I'll get the kettle going,' she declared as Lizzie sat down. 'I also have some nice Dundee cake my ma made. Fancy a slice?'

'Oh, yes, please. Yummy.'

Lizzie settled herself back into her chair. She was tired. It had been a long, hard day. And the following week was going to be even worse as there was a special order to be finished and despatched by the end of it.

'Damn!' Pearl muttered, putting a hand to her chest.

'What's wrong?'

'Indigestion. I keep getting it of late. It's being up the duff, of course.'

'Still having the morning sickness?'

'Without fail. It has its benefits, though.'

Lizzie frowned. 'In what way?'

'It puts Willie off to see and hear me being sick into the pot. So it's a bit of a blessing in disguise.'

Lizzie smiled, finding that amusing. Being Pearl's best friend she knew all about Willie and his incessant sexual demands.

'So when are you seeing Jack again?' Pearl queried.

'Friday night. We're just going out for a drink, nothing special.'

'That's nice.'

Lizzie thought so too. She and Jack had been going out for some weeks now, and were getting closer and closer, much to her parents' dismay. Her mother and father didn't even try to hide their disapproval.

'I'd better take a powder for this indigestion,' Pearl declared, hoping she hadn't used them all. She had forgotten to buy more earlier when the shops were open.

Lizzie studied her pal, remembering what she'd felt like at that stage with Jacky. It seemed so long ago. An eternity away.

'So is it serious, then?' Pearl asked, rummaging in a drawer.

'You mean me and Jack?'

Pearl glanced over at her. 'Well, I didn't mean you and the bloody Pope.'

Lizzie thought about it. Was it serious? It certainly appeared to be heading that way. There again, it was early days yet. 'Possibly,' she demurred.

'Just possibly?'

'Aye, that's right.'

Pearl, much to her relief, found the powder she was searching for. The last one, too, so she was lucky. Crossing to the sink, she poured herself a glass of water. 'I got the impression it was more than that,' she said.

'What gave you that idea?'

'Oh, the way you talk about him. You seem dead keen. But then you always were keen on Jack.'

Lizzie didn't reply.

'Weren't you?' Pearl probed.

'I've always liked him, if that's what you mean,' Lizzie replied cautiously.

'More than like, as I remember,' Pearl went on, teasing now. 'You were forever watching him when you thought he wasn't aware of it, and asking questions about him. You were keen all right.'

Lizzie had coloured. 'Your memory must be better than mine.'

'I always felt he was fond of you too.'

'Well if he was he didn't do anything about it, did he?' Lizzie replied tartly.

'That doesn't mean he wasn't fond.'

Fond enough to give her a child, Lizzie thought grimly. 'As I just said, if so he didn't do anything about it.'

'I always wondered about that,' Pearl mused. 'Out of character for him.'

'Well, he's a changed person now, I can assure you of that. All the wildness has gone out of him, thanks to his time at sea. He's far more settled. Far more grown up, you could say.'

'I'm pleased to hear it.' Pearl eyed Lizzie shrewdly. 'He was always a decent man underneath, you know. He just needed calming down a little.' She smiled, recalling her own escapades with Jack.

'Let's change the subject,' Lizzie said, not wanting to continue talking about Jack. 'Have you heard anything from Pete?'

Pearl paused in what she was doing as a great wave of

sadness swept through her. 'No,' she replied softly. The arrangement had been that she would keep visiting Pete until she became pregnant, and then the visits would stop. Now they had stopped, much to her regret.

'Sounds as if you'd like to?'

Oh, she would, Pearl thought. But what was the point? She was married to Willie, and that was that. All the wishing in the world that it was otherwise wouldn't bring it about. She shrugged. 'It would be nice – he's great fun to be with. But he's got his own life to be getting on with, just as I've got mine.'

Lizzie could hear the longing in Pearl's voice, and felt for her friend. 'How's that tea doing?' she asked.

Pearl shook herself. 'The kettle will soon boil. I'll get that cake I promised you.'

Lizzie just hoped Pearl hadn't fallen in love with Pete Milroy. It would be a tragedy if she had. A complete and utter tragedy.

'Out with him again?' Ethne snorted, her expression one of disapproval, as it always was where Jack was concerned.

'That's right, Ma. You know that. I mentioned it the other night.'

'Well all I can say is I hope you're still keeping away from the back close.'

'I am, Ma. I promise you.'

'I just hope you are, that's all.'

'Can I come?' Jacky asked, appearing at Lizzie's side.

Lizzie squatted down. 'I'm afraid you can't, angel. It's nearly your bedtime.'

'Aw, Lizzie! Please?'

431

How like Jack she was, Lizzie reflected. Fortunately she didn't have his distinctive pale blue eyes, or the likeness would have been even more obvious.

'I'm going to a nasty smelly place called a pub. You'd hate it there. Trust me, angel, you would.'

'Dada goes to pubs. Don't you, Dada?'

'When I can afford to.' Doogie smiled at her.

'But Lizzie says they're nasty and smelly.'

'Oh, they are. She's telling the truth.'

'So why go, Dada?'

'It's called whisky and beer,' Ethne chipped in. 'That's the reason they go.'

'Not the only one,' Doogie retorted, a twinkle in his eye.

'Oh?'

'It also gets you away from the wife.'

Both he and Lizzie burst out laughing to see the expression on Ethne's face. It was a picture.

'I think I've found a shop to rent that fits the bill for what I'm looking for,' Jack announced to Lizzie later that night in the bar of the Lorne hotel.

'That's terrific, Jack. Where is it?' When he told her, she shook her head. It wasn't a part of Glasgow she was acquainted with.

'It needs quite a bit doing to it, mind,' Jack went on. 'The person who previously rented has really let it go. But nothing I can't do myself.'

Lizzie was pleased to hear the enthusiasm in his voice. 'Will it take long?'

'A couple of weeks should see it right. A month at most. Then I can open up for business.'

Reaching across, she squeezed his hand. 'I'm so pleased for you, Jack.'

'I was wondering . . . Well, I'd like you to see it before I sign the rental papers. Give it your approval, so to speak.'

She stared at him. What a lovely, touching request. 'I'd be delighted to.'

'Tomorrow afternoon?'

'Fine.'

Pete stood at the window staring down into the gaslit street below. He was thinking about Pearl, and how much he missed her. Far more than he'd ever expected.

He closed his eyes for a few moments, remembering how it had been when they were together. Not just the lovemaking, but the laughs they'd had, the conversations. The sheer pleasure he'd always felt at simply being in her company.

All over now, he reflected, desperately wishing it was otherwise. With a shock, he realised he'd fallen in love with her somewhere along the way. Head over heels.

The realisation stunned him, almost took his breath away. He was in love with Willie's wife.

'Shit,' he murmured, and shook his head. 'Holy shit.'

So what to do? Except there was nothing he could do. She was a married woman, even if it wasn't the happiest of marriages. She'd told him that many times.

They'd been together for a while, and now she was gone out of his life, leaving him bereft. One thing was certain: there would be no more meeting up with her and Willie for drinks. He couldn't face that.

Pete took a deep breath. He was wrong in thinking

433

there was nothing he could do. He could get the hell out of Glasgow and away from her, never see her again, never run the risk of bumping into her in the street, which was always a possibility in Glasgow.

He knew there was a job falling vacant in the London office sometime in the near future, and was almost certain he'd get it if he applied. He'd made a good impression during his visits to London, got on well with everyone there.

Yes, that's what he'd do. Apply for the job when it came up. Possibly even put out feelers beforehand to let them know he was interested. It was a big step to take, but surely worthwhile in the long term? And it would do his career prospects no harm. None whatsoever.

His mind was made up.

'Thanks for the drinks, Jack. I thoroughly enjoyed myself,' Lizzie declared, back at her close.

'Till tomorrow.'

'I'm looking forward to it.'

He smiled at her, then kissed her briefly on the cheek. 'Goodnight, Lizzie.'

'Goodnight, Jack.'

This was silly, she thought, as he started to walk away. Surely she could trust him by now. Trust herself. 'Jack?'

He stopped. 'What is it?'

'Let's go into the back close for a wee while.'

That surprised him. 'You mean that? I thought the back close was strictly out of bounds.'

Ma would kill her if she found out, Lizzie thought. Go absolutely bananas. But there was no reason why she should. If she asked Lizzie direct, a little white lie was all that was required.

'Only kissing and cuddling, though,' Lizzie said to Jack. 'And I mean that. There'll be no repeat of what happened before. Promise me?'

For a brief second the old piratical expression flashed across his face. Then it was gone. 'I promise, Lizzie. My word of honour.'

'See you keep your word, then.'

Taking him by the hand, she led the way.

'So what do you think?'

Lizzie gazed about her. 'You were right about it needing tarted up. It's filthy apart from anything else.'

'Cleaning isn't a problem. Lots of elbow grease and I'll soon have it spotless. After that it's painting, which again won't take long once I get stuck in.'

'Why this location in particular?'

'Oh, there is a reason. There are a couple of distilleries plus a large carpet factory nearby. The men employed there – well, a lot of them, anyway – use bikes to get to and from work. That alone should give me a fair amount of business. Then there's always the local trade, which should be substantial if I'm any judge.'

She nodded her approval. It was obvious he'd given it a great deal of thought.

'I'll take you upstairs now,' he went on.

'There's an upstairs as well?'

'Oh aye. Living accommodation. It's where I intend staying. Come on, I'll show you.'

They climbed stairs, which Lizzie hadn't noticed, to

emerge into the first of four spacious rooms. There was also a kitchen area, plus bathroom and toilet.

'This is huge!' Lizzie marvelled.

Jack escorted her from room to room, explaining in each what he meant to do with it. Lizzie thought it made the house she lived in look like a rabbit hutch. 'Is the rent expensive?'

'Not really. At least I don't think so. In fact I reckon it's very fair, considering the size of the place.'

Lizzie shook her head. 'You're never going to get all this done in under a month. I just don't see how it's possible.'

Jack smiled. 'Sorry. I misled you there. I was talking about the shop itself. That I can do in the time.' He waved a hand. 'All this will take me far longer. I could get someone in to help, I suppose, but I'd prefer to do it myself.'

'Getting someone in would cost a bit,' she pointed out. 'You'll be saving money doing it yourself.'

'Money isn't a problem, Lizzie. Within reason, that is. Now, I have another request to make,' Jack went on.

'Which is?'

He took out his cigarettes, and lit up. 'I was rather hoping you'd help me choose the carpets, curtains and furniture. I'm sure your taste is better than mine. All brand new, of course, and best quality.'

'What have you been up to?' she asked. 'Robbing banks while you were away?'

Jack laughed, finding that funny. 'Not quite.'

'So how can you afford brand new this, that and the next thing on a seaman's wage? It doesn't make sense.'

Jack stared at her, turning something over in his mind.

'If I explain can you keep quiet about it? I'd rather what I'm about to tell you didn't get around.'

Lizzie nodded.

He sucked in a deep breath. 'I used to supplement my wages with a little smuggling on the side. Gold, mainly. For example, you buy it in India where it's cheap and then sell it in a country where it's not. All strictly illegal, of course, but quite a few sailors do it.'

Smuggling! She was bemused by that disclosure.

'The trick is never to be greedy. Deal in small amounts. Be careful and discreet. It's amazing how quickly the profits add up. Especially if you're doing it over a number of years, as I was.'

Lizzie wasn't sure what to say.

'Do you disapprove?'

'I honestly don't know, Jack.'

'Small amounts, remember, and nobody ever got hurt. At least not that I ever heard of.'

Lizzie suddenly laughed. 'Trust you, Jack White! Smuggling indeed.'

'You find it amusing?'

'No, no, it's just . . . well, so like the Jack I remember, that's all. Up to all sorts.'

'As I said, Lizzie, no one got hurt, so where's the harm?'

'And what if you'd been caught?'

'I wasn't.'

'But what if?'

He shrugged. 'I'd have paid the penalty. That's the risk you take.'

She was intrigued. 'What other things did you smuggle besides gold?'

'Pearls, jade – that's a green stone from China which is extremely valuable – jewellery. And diamonds on several occasions.'

'Diamonds!'

'Very lucrative. The only trouble was I only ever docked in South African ports a few times, which is where I would pick them up.' He hesitated, then said softly, 'I've kept one of them, which I have at home. A real beauty. I'll show it to you sometime. Would you like that?'

'Oh, yes, please.'

'I kept it for a special reason,' Jack added mysteriously. 'A very special reason.'

Lizzie wondered what that could be, but when she asked Jack he wouldn't tell her. He said that was his business.

Pearl stared across the dinner table at Willie, who was still unwashed and unshaven despite the time of day. It was becoming a habit of his on Sundays.

'How's the meal?'

'Fine,' he grunted.

'Are you going out later?'

'Nope.'

Pearl winced when he broke wind. 'Willie!' she admonished him sharply.

'What?'

'We're at the table.'

'You don't say?' he replied sarcastically.

His breaking wind had put Pearl off her own dinner. She pushed it away, her stomach suddenly turning queasy. She eyed him dyspeptically, thinking what a slob he was rapidly becoming. He'd put on weight recently, and now had a distinct beer belly.

She too had put on weight, but there was a reason for that. It would've been strange if she hadn't. 'Tell me something, Willie.'

'Tell you what?'

What a rude tone of voice, she thought. She'd hoped he'd treat her differently now she was pregnant, and to begin with he had. Far better than before. But that hadn't lasted long, and now he was back to his old ways.

'I was thinking about your friend Pete Milroy the other day.'

'Oh aye?'

'Why don't you ever get promoted at work like he does?'

Willie stared at her. 'Are you getting at me, woman?'

'No,' she lied. 'I'm just curious.'

He shrugged. 'It's true. I'm overdue for promotion, and overdue for more money too.'

'Perhaps you should have a word with your boss?' she suggested.

'Naw, no point in that.'

'Why not?'

'The old bastard doesn't like me. He's forever finding fault, miserable sod that he is. There's been a few times I've come close to punching him for some of the things he's said. Criticisms he's made.'

Pearl's heart sank. She'd been curious, and now she knew. Knowing Willie as she did, she had no doubt his boss was justified in his criticisms.

'He called me lazy once,' Willie went on, sheer hatred in his voice. 'Lying bastard. He's got it in for me and no mistake.' He sat back and belched, making no apologies for doing so, just as he hadn't when breaking wind. 'That's better.'

Pearl could have wept.

'Your da and I have been talking,' Ethne announced, 'and we both agree it's time we met this Jack White you've been seeing so much of.'

That took Lizzie by surprise. 'But you have met him, Ma.'

'I meant properly,' Ethne snapped. 'Not just a few words in the street. We thought you might invite him here for Sunday tea.'

'This Sunday?'

'That's as good as any.'

Lizzie considered. 'He is awfully busy trying to get his shop ready. He's been working morning, noon and night on it.'

'Obviously not every night as he's still taking you out,' Ethne replied tartly.

Lizzie couldn't deny it.

'Or do you think he might not be willing to face us?' Ethne was certain she'd dislike Jack if he did turn up.

'That's enough, woman,' Doogie reprimanded her.

Ethne glared at him, but didn't reply.

'I'll speak to Jack,' said Lizzie. 'I'm sure he'll be more than happy to accept your invitation.'

'Hmm!' Ethne snorted.

Lizzie glanced at the clock on the mantelpiece. Only a few more minutes till Jack was due to arrive. Please God let him not be late, she silently prayed. That would be bound to get things off to a bad start.

'I'm hungry,' Jacky complained.

'Not long now, darling.' Ethne smiled at her. 'We're having a lovely joint of lamb. You'll enjoy that.' She paused, then added dramatically, 'I hope we all do, considering how much it cost.'

Lizzie knew that to be a dig, but ignored it. The joint of lamb was Ethne's choice, no one else's. If her ma had decided to lash out then that was up to her.

She came quickly to her feet when there was a knock on the outside door. Dead on time: what a relief.

'Now behave yourself,' Doogie said quietly to Ethne while Lizzie was out of the room. 'Mind your manners.'

'I don't need anyone to tell me that, Dougal McDougall,' she snapped back.

'Just reminding you, that's all.' Doogie stood up in readiness for the forthcoming introduction.

'Da, this is Jack White. Jack, this is my father.'

'Pleased to meet you, Mr McDougall,' Jack declared as the two men shook hands. 'This is for you.'

Doogie beamed as he accepted the bottle of whisky. 'That's kind, son. Thank you very much. I'll pour us all a dram before we sit down.' He bustled over to where the glasses were kept.

'And this is my mother.'

'Pleased to meet you again, Jack.' Ethne's smile was a little false.

'And you, Mrs McDougall. I hope you like these.'

Ethne stared at the bunch of flowers. This was the last thing she'd been expecting. 'Why, thank you,' she stammered, completely taken aback and wrong-footed. 'I'd better find something to put them in.'

How handsome Jack looked, Lizzie thought. He was

wearing a dark suit, crisp white shirt and red tie. Quite the gentleman.

'I brought some sweets for Jacky,' he was saying to Ethne. 'Is that all right?'

'Of course.'

Jack squatted down and offered the bag of goodies to the shy little girl trying to hide behind Ethne's skirt. 'Here you are. But I don't think you should have them till after tea.'

Jacky looked from the sweets to Jack's face and then back to the bag of sweets again, the temptation enough to overcome her shyness. Coming forward, she accepted the bag.

Ethne smiled. 'What do you say?'

'Thank you.'

'You're very welcome, Jacky.'

The resemblance between them wasn't as marked as Lizzie had claimed, Ethne noted. But there certainly was one.

'I hope you like lamb,' she said, wondering where to look for the only vase she possessed.

'Love it, Mrs McDougall.'

'Here you are,' Doogie declared, handing Jack a large dram. When Ethne and Lizzie had also been served, Doogie held up his glass in a favourite Glasgow toast. 'All the best, all the time,' he said, and drank.

'Well, what did you think?' Lizzie demanded when Jack had gone.

'I liked him.' Doogie nodded. 'He was certainly entertaining with those tales of his about abroad. Don't you agree, Ethne?'

Ethne nodded.

'Did *you* like him, Ma?'

'Of course she did. It was as plain as the nose on her face,' Doogie declared.

'I can speak for myself, thank you very much,' Ethne rebuked him.

'Well, Ma?'

'Honestly?'

'Honestly, Ma.'

'I found him perfectly charming,' Ethne admitted.

Lizzie gave a sigh of relief. Thank God for that! It had gone better than she could possibly have hoped.

Jacky, under the table tucking into her bag of sweets, thought so too.

Chapter 29

'A glass of wine?' Pete asked. He'd been surprised to find a nervous Pearl on his doorstep.

'Do you have anything stronger?'

'Gin?'

'That would be lovely.'

Pearl glanced around her. It was months since she'd last been here, but everything was just as she remembered it. 'I'm glad I caught you alone,' she said, focusing again on Pete. 'I wasn't sure you would be.'

'Tonic?'

'If you have some.'

He was smiling as he brought her drink over. 'I invariably am on Saturday afternoons. Except when you used to visit, of course.'

Her insides were fluttering, her pulses racing. It had taken all her will-power to come and see him again. She had a quick gulp of gin, then another. Pete raised an eyebrow, but didn't comment.

'So, to what do I owe this honour?'

She had another gulp of gin, working herself up to

reply. 'I simply wanted to see you again,' she confessed. 'I hope that's all right?'

'Of course it's all right, Pearl. I'm delighted to have you here. I've been wanting to see you again as well.'

That cheered her. 'You have?'

He nodded. 'Very much so.' He gestured towards her stomach. 'That's got a lot bigger. Everything fine in that direction?'

'Oh, yes. I've had some bad morning sickness, but happily that's now past.'

'Good.'

'How's life treating you then, Pete? Got a new girl-friend yet?'

He laughed. 'I haven't actually. And to be honest, I haven't really been looking.'

'Oh?'

'You're a hard act to follow, Pearl.'

That made her catch her breath. 'So are you.'

The two of them were staring at one another, hunger in both pairs of eyes.

'How's Willie?' Pete asked.

She shrugged. 'The same, more or less.'

'What does more or less mean?'

'The same, only a bit worse, I suppose.'

Pete's expression became grim. 'You're not exactly happy, I take it?'

She shook her head.

'I see.'

Pearl had more of her gin. 'I stopped work last week. It had become almost impossible to use the machine. Just couldn't get at the damn thing. My bun in the oven kept getting in the way.'

445

'Yes, it would be a problem, I suppose.'

'So, that's the end of that. We'll miss the money, naturally. But it's the price that has to be paid for starting a family.'

'More gin?'

She considered the offer. 'I shouldn't really, not in my condition. But go on. Over-indulging myself just once shouldn't hurt.'

He refilled her glass, and when he turned to face her again he saw a look in her eyes which he recalled only too well. It made him shiver inside.

'There you are.' He handed the drink to her.

Pearl tried to smile, but it came out all crooked and lopsided. Suddenly she knew what she had to do – desperately wanted to do, if she had the courage, that was.

'Pete.'

'Yes, Pearl?'

She set her drink down on the floor, rose to her feet, and went to him. 'Will you cuddle me? Please?'

He hesitated for the briefest of seconds, then laid his own drink aside and took her into his arms.

'I've missed you dreadfully,' she whispered.

'I've missed you too.'

'Have you?'

'I think about you all the time. There's hardly a waking hour goes by when you're not in my thoughts.'

'Oh, Pete,' she sighed. It was exactly what she'd wanted to hear.

He began stroking her hair, while she held on to him as tightly as her bump would allow.

'I've fallen in love with you,' Pearl said quietly. 'Being a married woman I shouldn't tell you that. But it's the truth. I never thought when we started out it would end up this way. Only it has.'

'What about Willie?'

'I fell out of love with him a long time ago. I don't even like him any more. He's an uncouth pig.'

Pete winced. 'That bad, eh?'

'Worse.'

So much for Willie, Pete thought. He too had stopped liking his old pal, who'd changed so much over the years.

'Can I start visiting again, Pete? Go back to the way it was when I was trying to get pregnant? Unless . . .' She hesitated. 'Unless you don't fancy me any more now I'm fat and horrible.'

He couldn't help laughing. 'You're neither of those things, Pearl. Well, a bit more weighty than you were, I grant you that. But that's only a temporary condition, one that'll disappear when the baby arrives. As for horrible, you're certainly not that, and never could be.'

'Oh, Pete,' she whispered.

'And I've fallen in love with you. I didn't realise it until after you'd stopped coming here. I'd been aware of being terribly fond of you, but the realisation of actually being in love came later.'

She couldn't have been more thrilled. She literally tingled. 'I only wish I'd met you first, Pete. Now look at the pickle we've landed ourselves in.'

A bigger pickle than she knew, he thought in despair. Wait till he told her his news.

'So can I start visiting again?'

He pushed her gently from him. 'I need a cigarette. How about you?'

'I've none with me.'

'Don't worry, I have.'

It was a clichéd thing to do, but somehow it felt right in the circumstances. He put two between his lips, lit them both, then passed one over. 'There's something you have to know,' he said slowly.

'What's that?'

'I applied for a job in London, and I've got it. I start down there at the beginning of next month.'

She stared at him, her expression stricken. 'Next month?'

He nodded in confirmation.

'But why?'

'Once you'd gone I didn't want the pain of seeing you again, bumping into you in the street and having to make small talk. I certainly didn't want to go out for drinks with you and Willie. That would have been too much. So I decided to get out of Glasgow, and away from you, for ever. The London job was coming up and seemed to be the solution to my problem. I duly applied and, well, there we are.'

'I have to sit down. I've come over all dizzy.' Mind numb, Pearl staggered to the nearest chair and sank into it.

'I'm sorry.' Pete felt wretched. 'But how was I to know you'd want us to start again?'

'You weren't,' Pearl somehow managed to reply, in a tone of complete anguish.

'And before you ask, now I've accepted the job I have to take it. There's no way round that, I'm afraid. Apart from anything else they've already filled my current position. My replacement starts here the same day I do in London.'

Pearl drew heavily on her cigarette, then took another gulp of gin.

'I don't know what else to say,' Pete confessed.

'But you do love me?'

'Yes. With all my heart. I swear it.'

'As I love you.'

Pregnant she might be, but Pete thought he'd never seen Pearl look so desirable. He positively ached for her.

'At least you didn't just disappear out of my life without an explanation,' Pearl mumbled. 'That would have been dreadful.'

Which is exactly what would have happened if she hadn't turned up like this, a stricken Pete reflected.

There was a few minutes' silence between them, each deep in thought, before Pete went over and squatted down beside her. 'You would still have been married, Pearl. Don't forget that.'

'I know. But at least . . .' She broke off and shook her head in despair, tears creeping into her eyes.

'Please don't cry, Pearl,' he begged.

'I'm trying not to.'

It was like a knife twisting in his belly when a solitary tear rolled down her cheek. If only he could somehow change things. If only she wasn't already married. If only he hadn't applied for the bloody London job. If only . . .

'Pete?'

'What, darling?'

'Will you make love to me one last time?'

'Won't that just make matters worse?'

'Not for me it won't.'

'Then that's what we'll do. One last time.'

'Are you sure?'

His reply was to stand up again, take her hand and lead her into the bedroom.

'That was wonderful, Pete. Simply wonderful. Thank you for being so gentle with me.'

The implication being that Willie wasn't, Pete reflected grimly, but he didn't comment. Reaching out, he caressed her bump, thinking of the child inside. Their child.

Pearl sighed with contentment, refusing to think of the time ticking by and the fact that she'd shortly have to leave.

'There is one possible solution to all this,' Pete murmured.

Pearl didn't reply.

'Did you hear me?'

She frowned. 'Sorry. I was miles away.'

'I said, there is one possible solution to our problem. If you're brave enough, that is.'

The last statement caught her full attention. Rolling on to her side, she stared at him. 'Brave enough for what?'

'It's obvious, really. You leave Willie and come to London with me.'

'Leave . . .' She broke off, her mind racing.

'We'll live together as man and wife until you can get a divorce and we can marry. Which is precisely what we'll do the moment you're free.'

'Live together as man and wife?'

'Why not? Who in London is to know otherwise?'

'But surely they would at work?'

'I wrote a letter to apply for the job – didn't have to fill out any sort of form as I'm already employed by them. What do you think?'

Pearl shook her head, trying to take this in. 'Divorces are expensive, I'm told. Very expensive.'

'Don't you worry about that. I'll take care of it. And, as a matter of interest, I understand divorces are easier to obtain in England than they are here, so you should be able to get one in a relatively short period of time.'

'But . . . women don't leave their husbands. It just isn't done.'

'For practical reasons, Pearl. They're dependent on their husbands for food, clothes and a roof over their heads and those of any family they might have. They can't leave because there's nowhere for them to go; it's as simple as that. There's also the social stigma, but that wouldn't apply in England where no one knows you.'

Was it possible? Was it really possible?

'Well, Pearl?'

'You make it sound easy.'

'It is. Believe me. You walk out of one life and into a brand new one with a new identity. An identity which becomes reality once we get wed.'

It would mean leaving her parents behind, Pearl realised. Perhaps never seeing them again, or at least not for years. That would be awful. Heartbreaking for her, and for them. And what about Willie? He was her husband, after all. He'd be devastated, not to mention humiliated. But did she care? The truth was, she didn't. Not one little bit. He could go to hell in a handcart as far as she was concerned.

'What about accommodation once we get there?' she queried tremulously.

'Leave that to me. I'll make all the necessary arrangements. So what do you say?'

451

Live amongst the English? She wasn't sure she liked the idea of that. She had never even been outside Glasgow before, far less to a foreign country.

'I'll fully understand if you feel you can't do it,' Pete said quietly. 'It's a big step. A huge one.' He waited a moment. 'Do you need time to think about it?'

She made up her mind. It was a choice between life with Pete, or life with Willie. There was no contest. 'I'll go with you.'

He stared into her eyes. 'I do love you, Pearl.'

'You'd bloody well better if I'm about to run off with you,' she joked, which made them both laugh.

'It's going to be all right. I know it,' Pete assured her.

'I know it too.'

Lizzie stared at the three piece suite she was standing in front of, trying to visualise it in Jack's place. Jack looked on in amusement while she ruminated.

'Well?' he said eventually.

'Don't rush me, Jack. I don't want to make a mistake on your behalf.'

He smiled to hear that. 'Take your time by all means. But not all day.'

She glanced at him, brow furrowed in concentration. 'Do you like this suite?'

'It's fine by me.'

'I mean, better than the others?'

'God, I don't know, Lizzie. That's why I asked you to help me choose. So choose.'

She sighed. This was so difficult with so much money at stake. 'Perhaps we should decide on the curtains first?' she suggested.

He had absolutely no idea why she'd want to do that, but wasn't about to argue. He knew enough about women to appreciate that when it came to household matters it was always best to let them have their way, do things as they saw fit. 'Whatever.'

'Well don't sound so enthusiastic,' she chided him.

'Maybe that's because I'm not. It's all a bit of a bore as far as I'm concerned.'

She placed a hand on his arm. 'I'm only trying to get things right for you, Jack. I want your place to look lovely. A real home from home.'

That touched him. 'And I'm sure you'll succeed, Lizzie. In fact I know you will. Just don't ask me to get all excited about furniture and curtains, though. I can't.'

'Do you want us to leave and come back another time?'

He shook his head. 'Now we're here let's get it over and done with.'

'Curtains first then?'

'All right.'

Lizzie was thoroughly enjoying herself, even if Jack wasn't. She made a mental note to suggest they had a drink after they'd finished shopping. That was bound to cheer him up.

As luck would have it they found the perfect curtains almost straight away, after which they returned to the furniture department and settled on the three piece suite they'd been considering. Everything was to be delivered the following week.

Enough for one day, Lizzie decided. Jack couldn't have been more relieved.

*　　*　　*

'My God, you're serious!' Lizzie exclaimed.

'Of course I am,' Pearl responded. 'That's why I'm telling you. I couldn't leave without letting you know what's what. You're my best friend, after all.'

Lizzie was dumbfounded. It was a bolt right out the blue. 'You're actually leaving Willie?'

Pearl nodded. 'And going to London with Pete. You're to keep stumm about that, mind. Not tell a soul. Promise me?'

'I promise, Pearl.'

'Not even your ma and da.'

'Cross my heart and hope to die.' Lizzie studied her friend in wonder. 'You plan to live in sin?'

'Until my divorce comes through. Pete and I will marry directly after that.'

Lizzie continued studying her friend. 'I have to say, you're brave. I'll give you that. To go and live in England, too!'

'Aye, well, that's the one part of it I'm not sure about. It's going to be strange, to say the least. I've lived in Thistle Street all my life, don't forget. Moving anywhere would be a wrench, but London! I have to admit it frightens me.'

'I can understand that. I felt the same way when we came here from Tomintoul. Very scary. But I soon settled, and now it's as if I've been here for ever.'

They were in the snug of the pub where they always came on their nights out together. They were the only ones there, which meant they could talk freely.

'Well, let's just hope that happens to me.'

'Willie's going to go berserk when you tell him,' Lizzie said in concern.

'I've thought about that and I'm not going to. Not face to face anyway. I shall leave him a letter and by the time he reads it I'll be long gone on a train travelling south.'

Lizzie frowned. 'Isn't that a bit cruel?'

Pearl paused to light a cigarette. 'It's not that I'm being a coward, but there's a violent streak in Willie. He's never yet hit me but I'm certain he's come close to it on several occasions. This could well send him over the edge and I've got to think not only of myself but of the baby as well. I'm taking no chances.'

Lizzie could see the sense in that. 'Are you going to mention Pete by name?'

Pearl shook her head. 'I want Willie to know as little as possible. Better that way – safer, too.'

'And what about your parents? Surely you're going to tell them?'

'I want to, Lizzie, I truly do. But they're going to go through the roof as well. Marriage is sacrosanct in their book. No doubt they'll think me a right little tart.'

'I still believe you should speak to them,' Lizzie advised. 'They are your parents, after all. You owe them an explanation.'

In her heart of hearts Pearl knew that was true. But it was something she was dreading.

'Get off me! Bloody well get off me!' Pearl exclaimed, pushing Willie aside.

'It's been ages,' he protested.

'I had another show of blood today,' Pearl lied. 'So we're not taking any chances. Try and get that through your thick skull, will you? No more sex until after the

455

baby's born. And don't even think of forcing me. If you did, and I lost the baby as a result, it would make you a murderer.'

Willie inwardly cringed at the thought, and moved away from her. She smiled in the darkness. She hadn't allowed Willie to shag her since making her decision, and fully intended him never to do so again. The very thought of it made her skin crawl.

'The accommodation is all settled,' Pete declared. 'A rented two-bedroom house, fully furnished, in a nice part of London which is convenient for my work.'

Pearl beamed at him. 'That's terrific.'

'I said I'd organise everything. And I will.' He took her in his arms and kissed her. 'Not long now, eh?' He smiled.

'Not long now,' she echoed. 'I can't wait.'

'Neither can I.'

It was still going to be awful leaving Thistle Street, and Glasgow. Absolutely terrible. But she had to look to the future, and that lay elsewhere.

With Pete.

'So that's it. I'm off tomorrow morning.'

Dot and Ron Baxter were staring at their daughter as if she'd sprouted wings while at the same time announcing the Second Coming.

'I'm sorry I left telling you until the last minute, but I thought it would be better that way,' Pearl added nervously.

'Let me get this straight,' Ron said eventually. 'You're ditching Willie to run off to London with another man?'

456

'That's right, Da.'

'A man we've never even met.'

Pearl nodded.

'Whose baby you're carrying,' Dot muttered, in a state of shock.

'I just explained all that, Ma.'

Ron slowly shook his head in disbelief.

'I don't expect either of you to approve. But I'm doing the right thing, try to understand that. I haven't loved Willie for a long time now, but I do love Pete. And he loves me.'

'You're quite certain he does?' Dot queried.

'Quite certain, Ma.'

'Will we . . . will we ever see you again?' Ron frowned.

'I just don't know, Da. I hope so. Perhaps I can come back and visit when it's all blown over.'

'The scandal, you mean?' Dot said grimly. 'For there's bound to be one. A scandal that'll reflect on us as well, don't forget.'

Pearl dropped her gaze to stare at the floor, and didn't reply.

'Are you certain it's this Pete's child?' Ron asked.

'It's his all right, Da.'

'But you were . . . with both of them at the same time? I mean . . .'

'I know what you mean, Da. And the answer's yes.'

'How can you be so sure?'

'I just can, that's all. The whole point of me originally sleeping with Pete was to get pregnant, as Willie was incapable of doing the job on his own.'

Ron blanched. How cold-blooded it sounded when put like that. Then he reminded himself that Pearl had only done it to help her marriage, to try to give Willie what he so desperately wanted. It wasn't her fault the whole thing had backfired.

'You say you're leaving Willie a letter?' Dot croaked, totally and utterly stunned by these revelations.

'There's a side to Willie you've never seen, Ma. I simply don't wish to take any chances.'

Both Dot and Ron understood what Pearl was insinuating. They might not have seen that side of their son-in-law but they had been aware of its possible existence.

Dot sighed, and came to her feet. 'I'll put the kettle on,' she declared. 'I'm sure we can all use a good strong cup of tea.'

'Please don't be angry with me, Ma. Or you, Da. Though you've every right to be.'

'I'm not angry,' Dot replied. 'To be truthful, I don't know what I am.'

It was a full hour later before Pearl left them after tearful goodbyes.

They'd taken it better than she'd expected, Pearl reflected. A lot better. God bless the pair of them.

Pearl threw open the door the moment it was knocked. 'I heard the taxi draw up outside.'

'Ready?'

She nodded.

'The letter written?'

'Written and on the table.'

'Good. How are you feeling?'

'Nervous as hell. You?'

'Not nervous or apprehensive. Sort of calm, really, which surprises me.'

'Kiss me before we leave, Pete?' He did so, and when it was over Pearl took a deep breath. 'We'd better go, then. Don't want to keep the taxi waiting with its meter ticking over.'

That made Pete smile. 'Where's your case?'

'In the bedroom.'

While Pete was collecting it Pearl had a last look round. Then they were out on the landing, where she locked the door and dropped the key through the letter box.

As they were driving away, Pearl turned and looked through the rear window. As she'd half expected, Dot was at her window watching their departure. A clog came into Pearl's throat that felt the size of a grapefruit. Her life in Thistle Street, where she'd been born and brought up, was over.

Next stop London.

Chapter 30

'I've never had champagne before,' Lizzie declared, excited at the prospect. The rooms above the shop were finally finished and Jack had invited her over to celebrate. He himself had moved in the previous week.

'Well it's high time you did,' he replied, wrestling with the cork. Lizzie squealed with delight when it finally popped, flying across the room to bounce off a wall. Jack quickly began filling the two flutes he'd bought for the occasion, thoroughly enjoying himself, mentally keeping his fingers crossed that it was going to turn out as he was hoping.

'There you are,' he said, handing her a glass, and picking up his own.

'Can I make a toast?'

'Of course.'

'To your new business. Long may it flourish.' They each had a sip from their respective glasses.

'And to you, Lizzie, for all the help you've given me here. Thank you.' They had another sip.

She glanced around her. 'I think we've done a rather good job. Don't you?'

'I most certainly do.'

'Even if it did cost a pretty penny. You didn't stint on anything.'

'You said you'd make it into a home from home, which is exactly how it's turned out.'

It was her turn to say thank you.

Jack gazed speculatively at her. 'Sit down, Lizzie. I've something to show you. I won't be a minute.' He laid his glass aside and left the room.

What was this all about? she wondered. He'd sounded almost mysterious there.

She had another sip of champagne, and smiled as bubbles seemed to run up the inside of her nose. How lovely the wine was. It made her want to giggle.

Jack came back into the room. 'Do you remember I promised you I'd show you the diamond I kept from the smuggling?' he asked.

Lizzie nodded.

'Well, here it is.' And with that he presented her with a small, blue, gold-edged box.

She gasped when she opened it and saw what was inside. 'It's beautiful,' she breathed, taking it from the box and holding it up to the light so that it sparkled and flashed with fire. 'But you never mentioned you'd had it made into a ring?'

'I hadn't when we spoke that time. That came afterwards.'

'It truly is beautiful, Jack. But why a ring?'

He ignored that for the moment. 'I want to tell you a story which should explain.'

Lizzie carefully returned the ring to its box and snapped the lid shut. 'Go on.'

He sat facing her, thinking how lovely she was. But then, she always had been in his eyes.

'Do you recall, a long time ago, I said you were a dangerous woman?'

She nodded. 'I never could understand what you meant by that.'

'Dangerous, but only where I was concerned. You see, I realised that only you had the power to stop me fulfilling my dream of travelling the world.'

That astonished her. 'Me!'

'Yes, you, Lizzie McDougall. I knew if I ever got involved with you then that would be it. I'd stay in Glasgow, marry you, and settle down. Well, the last thing I wanted was to settle down, so I purposely didn't get involved. That's why I never asked you out.'

Lizzie was amazed, to say the least. 'I often wondered why you never asked, and thought it was because . . . well, you didn't fancy me.'

Jack laughed. 'Quite the opposite. I fancied you rotten. But you were a temptation I managed to resist. Though, I have to admit, it was bloody hard at times.' He hesitated, then went on. 'The only reason the incident in the back close happened was because I was off the next day. At least, I was hoping to be off. I'm not quite sure what would have happened next if it had fallen through.'

He drank some of his champagne, staring at her all the while. She stared back.

'When I went to sea,' Jack continued, 'I believed I could put you out of my mind. Forget about you. Only I was wrong. Quite wrong. I never forgot you. I never stopped missing you and wondering what might have been.'

Lizzie was shaken, at a complete loss for what to reply.

'Want to comment?' Jack asked softly.

She shook her head.

'When I finally came home to stay I fully expected you'd already be married, and was surprised and delighted to find out you weren't. That you were still available. So I asked you out to see how things went between us. You might have changed, after all, or I might have without being aware of it.'

Lizzie found her voice at last. 'You thought about me all the time you were at sea?'

'Yes.'

She was dumbfounded. 'I find that hard to believe.'

'It's true, Lizzie. I swear.'

Just as she'd thought about him. Though she wasn't about to tell him that. Not yet, anyway. 'Have I changed?'

'Not really.'

'You have.'

'In what way?'

'You're not as wild as you once were. Not so much of the buccaneer.'

'If so it's because I've lived my dream, Lizzie. Been where I wanted to go, done what I wanted to do.'

'If anything, it's a change for the better, Jack. I thoroughly approve.'

'I'm glad to hear it.' He smiled.

Lizzie guessed what this was leading up to, and why Jack had had the diamond made into a ring. Her insides rippled with excitement, and she could only pray she was right.

'But you're still the essential you, Jack. The Jack I remember with so much affection.'

He raised an eyebrow. 'Just affection?'

Lizzie glanced away, and didn't reply. The hand holding the ring box was clutching it so tightly that her knuckles shone white.

'Did you ever think of me when I was away?' he asked, a tightness in his voice.

There it was, a direct question. She had to tell the truth. 'Yes,' she admitted. 'Quite often, if you must know.'

'Kind thoughts, I hope?'

'Well, they weren't bad ones,' she prevaricated. It wasn't completely true. He had left her pregnant, after all.

'The reason I wanted you to help me furnish these rooms was because I was hoping we'd be living here together.'

The breath caught in her throat. 'How do you mean?' she croaked.

'Exactly what I said.'

'In sin?'

Jack laughed, amused. 'Not at all. As man and wife.'

Her gaze was boring into his, and she could see the sincerity there. 'Are you proposing, Jack White?'

'I certainly am, Lizzie McDougall.'

Her stomach was doing flip-flops. 'Then ask me properly.'

'Would you like me to go down on one knee?' he teased.

She thought about that. 'I don't think so. You'd only succeed in looking ridiculous.'

'I quite agree.'

'So?' she prompted after a few seconds' hiatus.

'Will you marry me, Lizzie?'

'Of course I will, you idiot. But only after you've said you love me.'

'I wouldn't ask you to marry me if I didn't,' he protested.

'I still want to hear it.'

'I love you, Lizzie. And have done for a long, long time. Probably since we first met.'

'And I love you, Jack. Probably since we first met.'

'You accept, then?'

'I accept.'

He came to his feet and crossed over to her. Taking her by the hand, he raised her up. 'I'll try and be a good husband and provider. You have my word.'

'And I'll do my very best to be a good wife.'

'Oh, Lizzie,' he whispered.

'Just one thing, Jack.'

'What's that?'

'The same rules as the back close still apply. There'll be no sex until our wedding night. Understand?'

'If that's what you want.'

'It is.'

'Then that's how it'll be.'

Feeling on top of the world, throbbing with excitement, she closed her eyes as he bent to kiss her.

'Engaged!' Ethne exclaimed.

'That's right, Ma. And there's the ring to prove it.' Lizzie waggled her left hand in front of her mother's face.

'Dear God, just look at the size of that stone,' Ethne declared in wonder.

Doogie came out of his chair, smiling fit to burst. 'Congratulations, son,' he enthused, pounding a grinning Jack on the back before shaking his hand.

'Thank you, Mr McDougall.'

465

'Doogie, please, if you're going to be my son-in-law.'

Ethne hugged Lizzie, tears coming into her eyes. 'I'm so happy for you, Lizzie. So very happy.'

'Thanks, Ma.'

Ethne broke away. 'And you too, Jack.'

'Thank you, Mrs McDougall.'

'You can call me Ethne,' she sniffed, taking her lead from Doogie.

Doogie hugged his daughter, truly delighted for her. Then it was his turn to admire the ring, and comment on the size of the stone.

'Lizzie getting married?' Jacky said. Everyone had momentarily forgotten about her.

Lizzie squatted down beside her 'sister'. 'I am, poppet. And you're to be a bridesmaid. What do you think about that?'

Jacky's eyes shone. 'Will I get a new dress?'

'You certainly will. And new shoes too.'

Jacky clapped her hands in glee.

'I wish I had a drink in to celebrate the occasion,' Doogie muttered wistfully.

'I brought something,' Jack returned to where he'd left his coat and produced a bottle of whisky from an inside pocket.

'So when will the wedding be?' Ethne queried as Doogie dealt with the bottle.

'As soon as we can arrange it, Ma. There's no need for us to save up for anything as it's all already there.'

'Down to the last teaspoon,' Jack agreed, accepting a glass from Doogie.

'Church or register office?' Doogie inquired.

'Church,' said Lizzie.

Doogie frowned. As the bride's father he would be expected to pay for the wedding, which meant a substantial outlay of cash he didn't have.

'Don't worry, Doogie,' Jack said, guessing what was troubling him. 'Lizzie and I have already discussed this. I appreciate it's awfully short notice for you, so if you won't take offence I'll be picking up the bill for everything.'

Doogie's relief was obvious. 'Are you sure, son?'

'Absolutely.'

Thank Christ for that, Doogie thought. It would have taken him ages to save up the amount required, even for a small wedding.

'Why the rush anyway?' Ethne queried suspiciously.

Lizzie knew precisely what was going through her mother's mind. 'Simply because that's how we want it,' she replied. Then she smiled. 'There are no hidden motives. I promise.'

Ethne nodded. 'That's all right, then. Though folk are bound to talk.'

'Let them,' Jack answered. 'I for one don't care what they say. We just want to get married straight away, and we will because we have the means to do so. That's the long and short of it.'

Doogie had now passed glasses all round. 'Here's to the happy couple!' he toasted.

Jack beamed at Lizzie, who beamed right back, both of them thinking that's exactly what they were. A happy couple.

'So, what do you think?' Doogie asked Ethne later that night as they were getting ready for bed.

'About Lizzie and Jack?'

'What else?'

Ethne sat on the edge of the bed and began brushing her hair. 'I'm pleased.'

'For a long time there you weren't very keen on him,' Doogie reminded her.

'That's true. But I was wrong, and don't mind admitting it.'

Doogie nodded his approval. 'Looking at them tonight you could see they're right for one another. That they fitted together.'

'Aye, that's so,' Ethne agreed. They had.

'Got his own business, too, which I've no doubt he'll make a go of. He strikes me as the type.'

Again Ethne had to agree.

'We must take him up on his offer and visit the shop to have a gander at where the pair of them will be living,' Doogie went on.

'Yes, I'd like that.'

'So would I.'

'We must arrange it with Lizzie.'

Doogie shook his head. 'When you think about it it's funny how things have turned out.'

'You're referring to Jacky?'

'Aye, I was.'

'You're right.' Ethne smiled. 'It is funny how things have turned out there. And I don't mean funny hilarious either.'

'No.' Doogie nodded.

Ethne started wondering about what kind of dress to buy for the wedding as she went on brushing her hair.

* * *

'I understand congratulations are in order, Miss McDougall.'

Lizzie stopped machining and turned to face Mrs Lang, the supervisor. 'Thank you.'

'Can I see the ring? Everyone's talking about it.'

Lizzie proudly held up her left hand.

Mrs Lang's eyes widened. 'The rumour, for once, is true. It's absolutely enormous. Lovely setting, too.'

'Eighteen carat.'

'Really! That must have cost a pretty penny.'

Lizzie smiled, but didn't reply.

'Your fiancé is Jack White, I believe?'

'That's right, Mrs Lang.'

'A nice chap. I always had time for him. A pity the way he left, though. Simply not turning up for work like that. It was most regrettable.'

Lizzie had coloured slightly. 'He had his reasons, which I won't go into. But at the time it was the only thing he could do.'

'Will you be staying on with us after the wedding?'

This was something she'd already discussed with Jack. 'To begin with, anyway. It'll be a bit of a journey for me, so I'll just have to wait and see how I get on.'

'If you do decide to leave I hope you'll be giving us proper notice?' Mrs Lang said, half smiling.

'Of course,' Lizzie quickly assured her. 'I wouldn't dream of doing otherwise.'

Mrs Lang nodded her approval. 'Good.' She hesitated, then said, 'I shall be sorry if you do go, as you're one of our best machinists. You'll be sorely missed.'

'Thank you, Mrs Lang. I appreciate that.'

'Lovely ring. Congratulations again. And I wish the

469

pair of you all the very best for the future.'

And with that Mrs Lang walked away, while Lizzie got on with her work.

'I've got news for you,' Ethne announced when Lizzie arrived in for dinner.

'What's that, Ma?'

'Dot heard this morning that Pearl's had a wee boy. They're calling him Duncan.'

Lizzie couldn't have been more pleased. 'That's wonderful!'

'The baby arrived early, apparently. But according to Dot both mother and child are well.'

She'd write to Pearl that evening, Lizzie promised herself, having news of her own to tell her friend. A little boy! How fabulous. The thought made her feel quite broody.

'I wonder how Willie will take it when he hears?' Ethne mused.

'If he hears,' Lizzie qualified. 'Since he moved back in with his mother he's never seen in the street. And I can't imagine anyone going out of their way to tell him.'

'True enough,' Ethne agreed. 'Mind you, I'm not surprised he left after what Pearl did to him. The humili-ation must have been terrible. And for him to find out in a letter that the baby wasn't even his, and she'd been carrying on behind his back!'

Lizzie didn't comment. It wasn't a subject she wished to pursue.

'If I may say so, madam looks quite stunning,' the shop assistant declared.

Lizzie studied herself in the full length mirror provided. The waisted dress was made of white crêpe, and had a small train. Lace details enhanced the high collar which covered her throat, and there were seed pearls and embroidery on the bodice and sleeves. The veil was a wisp of muslin which dropped low on Lizzie's brow.

'Ma?'

Ethne's eyes were shining. 'I agree. You do.'

'How about the veil? I'm not sure about that.'

'It's perfect,' Ethne assured her. 'Everything is just perfect. I doubt you'll find better.'

Lizzie took a deep breath, and made up her mind. 'This is the one, then. I only hope Jack approves.'

'He will, believe me,' Ethne said.

And, when the big day came, Jack most certainly did.

'What's the matter? Having second thoughts?'

Lizzie roused herself out of her reverie. 'What was that, Ma?'

'I said, are you having second thoughts? You've been sitting there in a dwam, looking troubled, and staring into space for the past ten minutes.'

'It's a little late to have those when I'm getting married tomorrow.'

Alarm flared in Ethne. 'So you are having them?'

Lizzie shook her head. 'Not at all. I'm just . . . having a fit of the jitters, I suppose.'

'Well, that's natural enough. I had them myself the night before I wed your father. I can remember shaking like a leaf at the thought of what lay ahead. Daft, really. I was calm as could be the next day, and everything went smoothly as you please.' Ethne paused, then went on.

'Mind you, we have had our ups and downs over the years, not least having to leave Tomintoul and come here because of what your da said to the laird's wife. Stupid bugger. But I wouldn't change him for anyone else. We both made the right choice.'

'Oh, I have no doubt Jack's the right choice for me, Ma. No doubt at all. If anything I'm just surprised that we ended up together after his vanishing off for years like he did. I never really expected to see him again, far less marry him.'

Ethne stared hard at her daughter. 'You haven't told him about Jacky, have you?'

'No. And never will. In a way it's a pity – Jacky is his, after all. And if things had been different . . .' She broke off and shrugged. 'But they weren't. Now Jacky's your daughter, and my sister, which is how it's going to remain.'

Further conversation was interrupted by Doogie's noisy return from the Argyle, where he'd been celebrating the forthcoming nuptials.

'You're drunk!' a furious Ethne accused him.

'As a skunk,' he agreed, and hiccuped loudly.

Lizzie couldn't help but burst out laughing at the ludicrous expression on her father's face. He might have been a little boy who'd been let loose in a sweet shop.

'Don't you encourage him,' Ethne admonished her.

'Sorry, Ma.'

'Pished. And I'm off to bed.' Doogie turned and staggered away.

'If nothing else that's cheered me up no end,' Lizzie declared. 'Good old Da.'

Ethne put the kettle on.

* * *

'I now declare you man and wife,' the minister intoned. Then, smiling at Jack, he added: 'You may kiss the bride.'

They stared into one another's eyes, Lizzie's heart feeling as though it might explode from sheer happiness. And as their lips met, the church bells began to ring out all the joy in the world.